Praise for these
New York Times
bestselling authors

Linda Lael Miller

Named the "Most Outstanding
Writer of Sensual Romance."
—*Romantic Times Magazine*

"Her characters come alive and walk right off the pages
and into your heart."
—*Rendezvous*

Barbara Delinsky

"When you care to read the very best,
the name of Barbara Delinsky should come
immediately to mind."
—*Rave Reviews*

"One of this generation's most gifted writers of
contemporary women's fiction."
—*Affaire de Coeur*

Tess Gerritsen

"Tess Gerritsen brings us action, adventure
and compelling romance."
—*Romantic Times Magazine*

"Gerritsen's romances are thrillers from
beginning to end."
—*Portland Press Herald*

New York Times bestselling author **Linda Lael Miller** started writing at age ten and has made a name for herself in both contemporary and historical romance. Her bold and innovative style has made her a favorite among readers. Named by *Romantic Times Magazine* "The Most Outstanding Writer of Sensual Romance," Linda Lael Miller never disappoints.

Barbara Delinsky was born and raised in suburban Boston. She worked as a researcher, photographer and reporter before turning to writing full-time in 1980. With more than fifty novels to her credit, she is truly one of the shining stars of contemporary romance fiction! This *New York Times* bestselling author has received numerous awards and honors, and her books have appeared on many bestseller lists. With over 12 million copies of Barbara's books in print worldwide, her appeal is definitely universal.

When **Tess Gerritsen** was a third-year medical resident, one of her patients presented her with a bag of romance novels. By the second chapter of the first book she was hooked. She has been reading and writing romances ever since—and using her medical knowledge to add to her intricate and dramatic stories. A *New York Times* bestselling author, she is also writing mainstream medical thrillers with much success.

LINDA LAEL MILLER

BARBARA DELINSKY

TESS GERRITSEN

Heatwave

HARLEQUIN®

TORONTO • NEW YORK • LONDON
AMSTERDAM • PARIS • SYDNEY • HAMBURG
STOCKHOLM • ATHENS • TOKYO • MILAN • MADRID
PRAGUE • WARSAW • BUDAPEST • AUCKLAND

HARLEQUIN BOOKS
225 Duncan Mill Road, Don Mills,
Ontario, Canada M3B 3K9

ISBN 0-373-83459-4

HEATWAVE

Visit us at www.eHarlequin.com

Printed in U.S.A.

CONTENTS

PART OF THE BARGAIN

Linda Lael Miller

For Laura Mast
Thank you for believing and being proud.

CHAPTER ONE

THE LANDING GEAR made an unsettling *ka-thump* sound as it snapped back into place under the small private airplane. Libby Kincaid swallowed her misgivings and tried not to look at the stony, impassive face of the pilot. If he didn't say anything, she wouldn't have to say anything either, and they might get through the short flight to the Circle Bar B ranch without engaging in one of their world-class shouting matches.

It was a pity, Libby thought, that at the ages of thirty-one and thirty-three, respectively, she and Jess still could not communicate on an adult level.

Pondering this, Libby looked down at the ground below and was dizzied by its passing as they swept over the small airport at Kalispell, Montana, and banked eastward, toward the Flathead River. Trees so green that they had a blue cast carpeted the majestic mountains rimming the valley.

Womanhood being what it is, Libby couldn't resist watching Jess Barlow surreptitiously out of the corner of her eye. He was like a lean, powerful mountain lion waiting to pounce, even though he kept his attention strictly on the controls and the thin air traffic sharing the big Montana sky that spring morning. His eyes were hidden behind a pair of mirrored sunglasses, but Libby knew that they would be dark with the animosity that had marked their relationship for years.

She looked away again, trying to concentrate on the river, which coursed beneath them like a dusty-jade ribbon woven into the fabric of a giant tapestry. Behind those mirrored glasses, Libby knew Jess's eyes were the exact same shade of green as that untamed waterway below.

"So," he said suddenly, gruffly, "New York wasn't all the two-hour TV movies make it out to be."

Libby sighed, closed her eyes in a bid for patience and then opened them again. She wasn't going to miss one bit of that fabulous view—not when her heart had been hungering for it for several bittersweet years.

Besides, Jess had been to New York dozens of times on corporation business. Who did he think he was fooling?

"New York was all right," she said, in the most inflamatory tone she could manage. *Except that Jonathan died,* chided a tiny, ruthless voice in her mind. *Except for that nasty divorce from Aaron.* "Nothing to write home about," she added aloud, realizing her blunder too late.

"So your dad noticed," drawled Jess in an undertone that would have been savage if it hadn't been so carefully modulated. "Every day, when the mail came, he fell on it like it was manna from heaven. He never stopped hoping—I'll give him that."

"Dad knows I hate to write letters," she retorted defensively. But Jess had made his mark, all the same—Libby felt real pain, picturing her father flipping eagerly through the mail and trying to hide his disappointment when there was nothing from his only daughter.

"Funny—that's not what Stace tells me."

Libby bridled at this remark, but she kept her composure. Jess was trying to trap her into making some foolish statement about his older brother, no doubt, one that he could twist out of shape and hold over her head. She raised her chin and choked back the indignant diatribe aching in her throat.

The mirrored sunglasses glinted in the sun as Jess turned to look at her. His powerful shoulders were taut beneath the blue cotton fabric of his workshirt, and his jawline was formidably hard.

"Leave Cathy and Stace alone, Libby," he warned with blunt savagery. "They've had a lot of problems lately, and if you do anything to make the situation worse, I'll see that you regret it. Do I make myself clear?"

Libby would have done almost anything to escape his scrutiny just then, short of thrusting open the door of that small four-passenger Cessna and jumping out, but her choices were undeniably limited. Trembling just a little, she turned away and fixed her attention on the ground again.

Dear heaven, did Jess really think that she would interfere in Cathy's marriage—or any other, for that matter? Cathy was her *cousin*—they'd been raised like sisters!

With a sigh, Libby faced the fact that there was every chance that Jess and a lot of other people would believe she had been involved with Stacey Barlowe. There had, after all, been that exchange of letters, and Stace had even visited her a few times, in the thick of her traumatic divorce, though in actuality he had been in the city on business.

"Libby?" prodded Jess sharply, when the silence grew too long to suit him.

"I'm not planning to vamp your brother!" she snapped. "Could we just drop this, please?"

To her relief and surprise, Jess turned his concentration on piloting the plane. His suntanned jaw worked with suppressed annoyance, but he didn't speak again.

The timbered land below began to give way to occasional patches of prairie—cattle country. Soon they would be landing on the small airstrip serving the prosperous 150,000-acre Circle Bar B, owned by Jess's father and overseen, for the most part, by Libby's.

Libby had grown up on the Circle Bar B, just as Jess had, and her mother, like his, was buried there. Even though she couldn't call the ranch home in the legal sense of the word, it was *still* home to her, and she had every right to go there—especially now, when she needed its beauty and peace and practical routines so desperately.

The airplane began to descend, jolting Libby out of her reflective state. Beside her, Jess guided the craft skillfully toward the paved landing strip stretched out before them.

The landing gear came down with a sharp snap, and Libby drew in her breath in preparation. The wheels of the plane screeched and grabbed as they made contact with the asphalt, and then the Cessna was rolling smoothly along the ground.

When it came to a full stop, Libby wrenched at her seat belt, anxious to put as much distance as possible between herself and Jess Barlowe. But his hand closed over her left wrist in a steel-hard grasp. "Remember, Lib—these people aren't the so-phisticated if-it-feels-good-do-it types you're used to. No games."

Games. *Games?* Hot color surged into Libby's face and pounded there in rhythm with the furious beat of her heart. "Let go of me, you bastard!" she breathed.

If anything, Jess's grip tightened. "I'll be watching you," he warned, and then he flung Libby's wrist from his hand and turned away to push open the door on his side and leap nimbly to the ground.

Libby was still tugging impotently at the handle on her own door when her father strode over, climbed deftly onto the wing and opened it for her. She felt such a surge of love and relief at the sight of him that she cried out softly and flung herself into his arms, nearly sending both of them tumbling to the hard ground.

Ken Kincaid hadn't changed in the years since Libby had seen him last—he was still the same handsome, rangy cowboy that she remembered so well, though his hair, while as thick as ever, was iron-gray now, and the limp he'd acquired in a long-ago rodeo accident was more pronounced.

Once they were clear of the plane, he held his daughter at arm's length, laughed gruffly, and then pulled her close again. Over his shoulder she saw Jess drag her suitcases and portable drawing board out of the Cessna's luggage compartment and fling them unceremoniously into the back of a mud-speckled station wagon.

Nothing if not perceptive, Ken Kincaid turned slightly, as-sessed Senator Cleave Barlowe's second son, and grinned. There was mischief in his bright blue eyes when he faced Libby again. "Rough trip?"

Libby's throat tightened unaccountably, and she wished she could explain *how* rough. She was still stung by Jess's insulting opinion of her morality, but how could she tell her father that? "You know that it's always rough going where Jess and I are concerned," she said.

Her father's brows lifted speculatively as Jess got behind the wheel of the station wagon and sped away without so much as a curt nod or a halfhearted so-long. "You two'd better watch out," he mused. "If you ever stop butting heads, you might find out you like each other."

"Now, that," replied Libby with dispatch, "is a horrid thought if I've ever heard one. Tell me, Dad—how have you been?"

He draped one wiry arm over her shoulders and guided her in the direction of a late-model pickup truck. The door on the driver's side was emblazoned with the words "CIRCLE BAR B RANCH," and Yosemite Sam glared from both the mud flaps shielding the rear tires. "Never mind how I've been, dumplin'. How've *you* been?"

Libby felt some of the tension drain from her as her father opened the door on the passenger side of the truck and helped her inside. She longed to shed her expensive tailored linen suit for jeans and a T-shirt, and—oh, heaven—her sneakers would be a welcome change from the high heels she was wearing. "I'll be okay," she said in tones that were a bit too energetically cheerful.

Ken climbed behind the wheel and tossed one searching, worried look in his daughter's direction. "Cathy's waiting over at the house, to help you settle in and all that. I was hoping we could talk…"

Libby reached out and patted her father's work-worn hand, resting now on the gearshift knob. "We can talk tonight. Anyway, we've got lots of time."

Ken started the truck's powerful engine, but his wise blue eyes had not strayed from his daughter's face. "You'll stay here awhile, then?" he asked hopefully.

Libby nodded, but she suddenly found that she had to look away. "As long as you'll let me, Dad."

The truck was moving now, jolting and rattling over the rough ranch roads with a pleasantly familiar vigor. "I expected you before this," he said. "Lib…"

She turned an imploring look on him. "Later, Dad—okay? Could we please talk about the heavy stuff later?"

Ken swept off his old cowboy hat and ran a practiced arm

across his forehead. "Later it is, dumplin'." Graciously he changed the subject. "Been reading your comic strip in the funny papers, and it seems like every kid in town's wearing one of those T-shirts you designed."

Libby smiled; her career as a syndicated cartoonist was certainly safe conversational ground. And it had all started right here, on this ranch, when she'd sent away the coupon printed on a matchbook and begun taking art lessons by mail. After that, she'd won a scholarship to a prestigious college, graduated, and made her mark, not in portraits or commercial design, as some of her friends had, but in cartooning. Her character, Liberated Lizzie, a cave-girl with modern ideas, had created something of a sensation and was now featured not only in the Sunday newspapers but also on T-shirts, greeting cards, coffee mugs and calendars. There was a deal pending with a poster company, and Libby's bank balance was fat with the advance payment for a projected book.

She would have to work hard to fulfill her obligations—there was the weekly cartoon strip to do, of course, and the panels for the book had to be sketched in. She hoped that between these tasks and the endless allure of the Circle Bar B, she might be able to turn her thoughts from Jonathan and the mess she'd made of her personal life.

"Career-wise, I'm doing fine," Libby said aloud, as much to herself as to her father. "I don't suppose I could use the sunporch for a studio?"

Ken laughed. "Cathy's been working for a month to get it ready, and I had some of the boys put in a skylight. All you've got to do is set up your gear."

Impulsively Libby leaned over and kissed her father's beard-stubbled cheek. "I love you!"

"Good," he retorted. "A husband you can dump—a daddy you're pretty well stuck with."

The word "husband" jarred Libby a little, bringing an unwelcome image of Aaron into her mind as it did, and she didn't speak again until the house came into sight.

Originally the main ranch house, the structure set aside for the general foreman was an enormous, drafty place with plenty of Victorian scrollwork, gabled windows and porches. It over-looked a sizable spring-fed pond and boasted its own sheltering copse of evergreens and cottonwood trees.

The truck lurched a little as Ken brought it to a stop in the gravel driveway, and through the windshield Libby could see glimmering patches of the silver-blue sparkle that was the pond. She longed to hurry there now, kick off her shoes on the grassy bank and ruin her stockings wading in the cold, clear water.

But her father was getting out of the truck, and Cathy Bar-lowe, Libby's cousin and cherished friend, was dashing down the driveway, her pretty face alight with greeting.

Libby laughed and stood waiting beside the pickup truck, her arms out wide.

After an energetic hug had been exchanged, Cathy drew back in Libby's arms and lifted a graceful hand to sign the words: "I've missed you so much!"

"And I've missed you," Libby signed back, though she spoke the words aloud, too.

Cathy's green eyes sparkled. "You haven't forgotten how to sign!" she enthused, bringing both hands into play now. She had been deaf since childhood, but she communicated so skill-fully that Libby often forgot that they weren't conversing ver-bally. "Have you been practicing?"

She had. Signing had been a game for her and Jonathan to play during the long, difficult hours she'd spent at his hospital bedside. Libby nodded and tears of love and pride gathered in her dark blue eyes as she surveyed her cousin—physically, she and Cathy bore no resemblance to each other at all.

Cathy was petite, her eyes wide, mischievous emeralds, her hair a glistening profusion of copper and chestnut and gold that reached almost to her waist. Libby was of medium height, and her silver-blond hair fell just short of her shoulders.

"I'll be back later," Ken said quietly, signing the words as he spoke so that Cathy could understand too. "You two have plenty to say to each other, it looks like."

Cathy nodded and smiled, but there was something sad trem-bling behind the joy in her green eyes, something that made Libby want to scurry back to the truck and beg to be driven back to the airstrip. From there she could fly to Kalispell and catch a connecting flight to Denver and then New York....

Good Lord—surely Jess hadn't been so heartless as to share his ridiculous suspicions with Cathy!

The interior of the house was cool and airy, and Libby followed along behind Cathy, her thoughts and feelings in an incomprehensible tangle. She was glad to be home, no doubt about it. She'd yearned for the quiet sanity of this place almost from the moment of leaving it.

On the other hand, she wasn't certain that she'd been wise to come back. Jess obviously intended to make her feel less than welcome, and although she had certainly never been intimately involved with Stacey Barlowe, Cathy's husband, sometimes her feelings toward him weren't all that clearly defined.

Unlike his younger brother, Stace was a warm, outgoing person, and through the shattering events of the past year and a half, he had been a tender and steadfast friend. Adrift in waters of confusion and grief, Libby had told Stacey things that she had never breathed to another living soul, and it was true that, as Jess had so bitterly pointed out, she had written to the man when she couldn't bring herself to contact her own father.

But she wasn't in love with Stace, Libby told herself firmly. She had always looked up to him, that was all—like an older brother. Maybe she'd become a little too dependent on him in the bargain, but that didn't mean she cared for him in a romantic way, did it?

She sighed, and Cathy turned to look at her pensively, almost as though she had heard the sound. That was impossible, of course, but Cathy was as perceptive as anyone Libby had ever known, and she often *felt* sounds.

"Glad to be home?" the deaf woman inquired, gesturing gently.

Libby didn't miss the tremor in her cousin's hands, but she forced a weary smile to her face and nodded in answer to the question.

Suddenly Cathy's eyes were sparkling again, and she caught

Libby's hand in her own and tugged her through an archway and into the glassed-in sunporch that overlooked the pond.

Libby drew in a swift, delighted breath. There was indeed a skylight in the roof—a big one. A drawing table had been set up in the best light the room offered, along with a lamp for night work, and there were flowering plants hanging from the exposed beams in the ceiling. The old wicker furniture that had been stored in the attic for as long as Libby could remember had been painted a dazzling white and bedecked with gay floral-print cushions. Small rugs in complementary shades of pink and green had been scattered about randomly, and there was even a shelving unit built into the wall behind the art table.

"Wow!" cried Libby, overwhelmed, her arms spread out wide in a gesture of wonder. "Cathy, you missed your calling! You should have been an interior decorator."

Though Libby hadn't signed the words, her cousin had read them from her lips. Cathy's green eyes shifted quickly from Libby's face, and she lowered her head. "Instead of what?" she motioned sadly. "Instead of Stacey's wife?"

Libby felt as though she'd been slapped, but she recovered quickly enough to catch one hand under Cathy's chin and force her head up. "Exactly what do you mean by that?" she demanded, and she was never certain afterward whether she had signed the words, shouted them, or simply thought them.

Cathy shrugged in a miserable attempt at nonchalance, and one tear slid down her cheek. "He went to see you in New York," she challenged, her hands moving quickly now, almost angrily. "You wrote him letters!"

"Cathy, it wasn't what you think—"

"Wasn't it?"

Libby was furious and wounded, and she stomped one foot in frustration. "Of course it wasn't! Do you really think I would do a thing like that? Do you think Stacey would? He *loves* you!" *And so does Jess,* she lamented in silence, without knowing why that should matter.

Stubbornly Cathy averted her eyes again and shoved her hands into the pockets of her lightweight cotton jacket—a sure signal that as far as she was concerned, the conversation was over.

In desperation, Libby reached out and caught her cousin's shoulders in her hands, only to be swiftly rebuffed by an eloquent shrug. She watched, stricken to silence, as Cathy turned and hurried out of the sunporch-turned-studio and into the kitchen beyond. Just a moment later the back door slammed with a finality that made Libby ache through and through.

She ducked her head and bit her lower lip to keep the tears back. That, too, was something she had learned during Jonathan's final confinement in a children's hospital.

Just then, Jess Barlowe filled the studio doorway. Libby was aware of him in all her strained senses.

He set down her suitcases and drawing board with an unsympathetic thump. "I see you're spreading joy and good cheer as usual," he drawled in acid tones. "What, pray tell, was *that* all about?"

Libby was infuriated, and she glared at him, her hands resting on her trim rounded hips. "As if you didn't know, you heartless bastard! How could you be so mean...so thoughtless..."

The fiery green eyes raked Libby's travel-rumpled form with scorn. Ignoring her aborted question, he offered one of his own. "Did you think your affair with my brother was a secret, princess?"

Libby was fairly choking on her rage and her pain. "What affair, dammit?" she shouted. "We didn't *have* an affair!"

"That isn't what Stacey says," replied Jess with impervious savagery.

Libby felt the high color that had been pounding in her face seep away. *"What?"*

"Stace is wildly in love with you, to hear him tell it. You need him and he needs you, and to hell with minor stumbling blocks like his wife!"

Libby's knees weakened and she groped blindly for the stool at her art table and then sank onto it. "My God..."

Jess's jawline was tight with brutal annoyance. "Spare me

the theatrics, princess—I know why you came back here. Dammit, *don't you have a soul?*"

Libby's throat worked painfully, but her mind simply refused to form words for her to utter.

Jess crossed the room like a mountain panther, terrifying in his grace and prowess, and caught both her wrists in a furious, inescapable grasp. With his other hand he captured Libby's chin.

"Listen to me, you predatory little witch, and listen well," he hissed, his jade eyes hard, his flesh pale beneath his deep rancher's tan. "Cathy is good and decent and she loves my brother, though I can't for the life of me think why she condescends to do so. And I'll be *damned* if I'll stand by and watch you and Stacey turn her inside out! Do you understand me?"

Tears of helpless fury and outraged honor burned like fire in Libby's eyes, but she could neither speak nor move. She could only stare into the frightening face looming only inches from her own. It was a devil's face.

When Jess's tightening grasp on her chin made it clear that he would have an answer of some sort, no matter what, Libby managed a small, frantic nod.

Apparently satisfied, Jess released her with such suddenness that she nearly lost her balance and slipped off the stool.

Then he whirled away from her, his broad back taut, one powerful hand running through his obsidian hair in a typical gesture of frustration. "Damn you for ever coming back here," he said in a voice no less vicious for its softness.

"No problem," Libby said with great effort. "I'll leave."

Jess turned toward her again, this time with an ominous leisure, and his eyes scalded Libby's face, the hollow of her throat, the firm roundness of her high breasts. "It's too late," he said.

Still dazed, Libby sank back against the edge of the drawing table, sighed and covered her eyes with one hand. "Okay," she began with hard-won, shaky reason, "why is that?"

Jess had stalked to the windows; his back was a barrier between them again, and he was looking out at the pond. Libby longed to sprout claws and tear him to quivering shreds.

"Stacey has the bit in his teeth," he said at length, his voice low, speculative. "Wherever you went, he'd follow."

Since Libby didn't believe that Stacey had declared himself to be in love with her, she didn't believe that there was any danger of his following her away from the Circle Bar B, either. "You're crazy," she said.

Jess faced her quickly, some scathing retort brewing in his eyes, but whatever he had meant to say was lost as Ken strode into the room and demanded, "What the hell's going on in here? I just found Cathy running up the road in tears!"

"Ask your daughter!" Jess bit out. "Thanks to her, Cathy has just gotten *started* shedding tears!"

Libby could bear no more; she was like a wild creature goaded to madness, and she flung herself bodily at Jess Barlowe, just as she had in her childhood, fists flying. She would have attacked him gladly if her father hadn't caught hold of her around the waist and forcibly restrained her.

Jess raked her with one last contemptuous look and moved calmly in the direction of the door. "You ought to tame that little spitfire, Ken," he commented in passing. "One of these days she's going to hurt somebody."

Libby trembled in her father's hold, stung by his double meaning, and gave one senseless shriek of fury. This brought a mocking chuckle from a disappearing Jess and caused Ken to turn her firmly to face him.

"Good Lord, Libby, what's the *matter* with you?"

Libby drew a deep, steadying breath and tried to quiet the raging ten-year-old within her, the child that Jess had always been able to infuriate. "I hate Jess Barlow," she said flatly. "I hate him."

"Why?" Ken broke in, and he didn't look angry anymore. Just honestly puzzled.

"If you knew what he's been saying about me—"

"If it's the same as what Stacey's been mouthing off about, I reckon I do."

Libby stepped back, stunned. "What?"

Ken Kincaid sighed, and suddenly all his fifty-two years showed clearly in his face. "Stacey and Cathy have been having trouble the last year or so. Now he's telling everybody who'll listen that it's over between him and Cathy and he wants you.''

"I don't believe it! I—''

"I wanted to warn you, Lib, but you'd been through so much, between losing the boy and then falling out with your husband after that. I thought you needed to be home, but I knew you wouldn't come near the place if you had any idea what was going on.''

Libby's chin trembled, and she searched her father's honest, weathered face anxiously. "I...I haven't been fooling around with C-Cathy's husband, Dad.''

He smiled gently. "I know that, Lib—knew it all along. Just never mind Jess and all the rest of them—if you don't run away, this thing'll blow over.''

Libby swallowed, thinking of Cathy and the pain she had to be feeling. The betrayal. "I can't stay here if Cathy is going to be hurt.''

Ken touched her cheek with a work-worn finger. "Cathy doesn't really believe the rumors, Libby—think about it. Why would she work so hard to fix a studio up for you if she did? Why would she be waiting here to see you again?''

"But she was crying just now, Dad! And she as much as accused me of carrying on with her husband!''

"She's been hurt by what's been said, and Stacey's been acting like a spoiled kid. Honey, Cathy's just testing the waters, trying to find out where you stand. You can't leave her now, because except for Stace, there's nobody she needs more.''

Despite the fact that all her instincts warned her to put the Circle Bar B behind her as soon as humanly possible, Libby saw the sense in her father's words. As incredible as it seemed, Cathy would need her—if for nothing else than to lay those wretched rumors to rest once and for all.

"These things Stacey's been saying—surely he didn't unload them on Cathy?''

Ken sighed. "I don't think he'd be that low, Libby. But you know how it is with Cathy, how she always knows the score.''

Libby shook her head distractedly. "Somebody told her, Dad—and I think I know who it was."

There was disbelief in Ken's discerning blue eyes, and in his voice, too. "*Jess?* Now, wait a minute..."

Jess.

Libby couldn't remember a time when she had gotten along well with him, but she'd been sure that he cared deeply for Cathy. Hadn't he been the one to insist that Stace and Libby learn signing, as he had, so that everyone could talk to the frightened, confused little girl who couldn't hear? Hadn't he gifted Cathy with cherished bullfrogs and clumsily made valentines and even taken her to the high-school prom?

How could Jess, of all people, be the one to hurt Cathy, when he knew as well as anyone how badly she'd been hurt by her handicap and the rejection of her own parents? How?

Libby had no answer for any of these questions. She knew only that she had separate scores to settle with both the Barlowe brothers.

And settle them she would.

CHAPTER TWO

LIBBY SAT at the end of the rickety swimming dock, bare feet dangling, shoulders slumped, her gaze fixed on the shimmering waters of the pond. The lines of her long, slender legs were accentuated, rather than disguised, by the old blue jeans she wore. A white eyelet suntop sheltered shapely breasts and a trim stomach and left the rest of her upper body bare.

Jess Barlow studied her in silence, feeling things that were at wide variance with his personal opinion of the woman. He was certain that he hated Libby, but something inside him wanted, nonetheless, to touch her, to comfort her, to know the scent and texture of her skin.

A reluctant grin tilted one corner of his mouth. One tug at the top of that white eyelet and...

Jess caught his skittering thoughts, marshaled them back into stern order. As innocent and vulnerable as Libby Kincaid looked at the moment, she was a viper, willing to betray her own cousin to get what she wanted.

Jess imagined Libby naked, her glorious breasts free and welcoming. But the man in his mental scenario was not himself—it was Stacey. The thought lay sour in Jess's mind.

"Did you come to apologize, by any chance?"

The question so startled Jess that he flinched; he had not noticed that Libby had turned around and seen him, so caught up had he been in the vision of her giving herself to his brother.

He scowled, as much to recover his wits as to oppose her. It was and always had been his nature to oppose Libby Kincaid, the way electricity opposes water, and it annoyed him that, for all his travels and his education, he didn't know why.

"Why would I want to do that?" he shot back, more ruffled by her presence than he ever would have admitted.

"Maybe because you were a complete ass," she replied in tones as sunny as the big sky stretched out above them.

Jess lifted his hands to his hips and stood fast against whatever it was that was pulling him toward her. *I want to make love to you,* he thought, and the truth of that ground in his spirit as well as in his loins.

There was pain in Libby's navy-blue eyes, as well as a cautious mischief. "Well?" she prodded.

Jess found that while he could keep himself from going to her, he could not turn away. Maybe her net reached farther than he'd thought. Maybe, like Stacey and that idiot in New York, he was already caught in it.

"I'm not here to apologize," he said coldly.

"Then why?" she asked with chiming sweetness.

He wondered if she knew what that shoulderless blouse of hers was doing to him. Damn. He hadn't been this tongue-tied since the night of his fifteenth birthday, when Ginny Hillerman had announced that she would show him hers if he would show her his.

Libby's eyes were laughing at him. "Jess?"

"Is your dad here?" he threw out in gruff desperation.

One shapely, gossamer eyebrow arched. "You know perfectly well that he isn't. If Dad were home, his pickup truck would be parked in the driveway."

Against his will, Jess grinned. His taut shoulders rose in a shrug. The shadows of cottonwood leaves moved on the old wooden dock, forming a mystical path—a path that led to Libby Kincaid.

She patted the sun-warmed wood beside her. "Come and sit down."

Before Jess could stop himself, he was striding along that small wharf, sinking down to sit beside Libby and dangle his booted feet over the sparkling water. He was never entirely certain what sorcery made him ask what he did.

"What happened to your marriage, Libby?"

The pain he had glimpsed before leapt in her eyes and then faded away again, subdued. "Are you trying to start another fight?"

Jerry shook his head. "No," he answered quietly, "I really want to know."

She looked away from him, gnawing at her lower lip with her front teeth. All around them were ranch sounds—birds conferring in the trees, leaves rustling in the wind, the clear pond water lapping at the mossy pilings of the dock. But no sound came from Libby.

On an impulse, Jess touched her mouth with the tip of one index finger. Water and electricity—the analogy came back to him with a numbing jolt.

"Stop that," he barked, to cover his reactions.

Libby ceased chewing at her lip and stared at him with wide eyes. Again he saw the shadow of that nameless, shifting ache inside her. "Stop what?" she wanted to know.

Stop making me want to hold you, he thought. *Stop making me want to tuck your hair back behind your ears and tell you that everything will be all right.* "Stop biting your lip!" he snapped aloud.

"I'm sorry!" Libby snapped back, her eyes shooting indigo sparks.

Jess sighed and again spoke involuntarily. "Why did you leave your husband, Libby?"

The question jarred them both: Libby paled a little and tried to scramble to her feet; Jess caught her elbow in one hand and pulled her down again.

"Was it because of Stacey?"

She was livid. "No!"

"Someone else?"

Tears sprang up in Libby's dark lashes and made then spiky. She wrenched free of his hand but made no move to rise again and run away. "Sure!" she gasped. "'If it feels good, do it'—that's my motto! By God, I *live* by those words!"

"Shut up," Jess said in a gentle voice.

Incredibly, she fell against him, wept into the shoulder of his blue cotton workshirt. And it was not a delicate, calculating sort of weeping—it was a noisy grief.

Jess drew her close and held her, broken on the shoals of

what she was feeling even though he did not know its name. "I'm sorry," he said hoarsely.

Libby trembled beneath his arm and wailed like a wounded calf. The sound solidified into a word usually reserved for stubborn horses and income-tax audits.

Jess laughed and, for a reason he would never understand, kissed her forehead. "I love it when you flatter me," he teased.

Miraculously, Libby laughed too. But when she tilted her head back to look up at him, and he saw the tear streaks on her beautiful, defiant face, something within him, something that had always been disjointed, was wrenched painfully back into place.

He bent his head and touched his lips to hers, gently, in question. She stiffened, but then, at the cautious bidding of his tongue, her lips parted slightly and her body relaxed against his.

Jess pressed Libby backward until she lay prone on the shifting dock, the kiss unbroken. As she responded to that kiss, it seemed that the sparkling water-light of the pond danced around them both in huge, shimmering chips, that they were floating inside some cosmic prism.

His hand went to the full roundness of her left breast. Beneath his palm and the thin layer of white eyelet, he felt the nipple grow taut in that singular invitation to passion.

Through the back of his shirt, Jess was warmed by the heat of the spring sun and the tender weight of Libby's hands. He left her mouth to trail soft kisses over her chin, along the sweet, scented lines of her neck.

All the while, he expected her to stiffen again, to thrust him away with her hands and some indignant—and no doubt colorful—outburst. Instead, she was pliant and yielding beneath him.

Enthralled, he dared more and drew downward on the uppermost ruffle of her suntop. Still she did not protest.

Libby arched her back and a low, whimpering sound came from her throat as Jess bared her to the soft spring breeze and the fire of his gaze.

Her breasts were heavy golden-white globes, and their pale

rose crests stiffened as Jess perused them. When he offered a whisper-soft kiss to one, Libby moaned and the other peak pouted prettily at his choice. He went to it, soothed it to fury with his tongue.

Libby gave a soft, lusty cry, shuddered and caught her hands in his hair, drawing him closer. He needed more of her and positioned his body accordingly, careful not to let his full weight come to bear. Then, for a few dizzying moments, he took suckle at the straining fount of her breast.

Recovering himself partially, Jess pulled her hands from his hair, gripped them at the wrists, pressed them down above her head in gentle restraint.

Her succulent breasts bore his assessment proudly, rising and falling with the meter of her breathing.

Jess forced himself to meet Libby's eyes. "This is me," he reminded her gruffly. "Jess."

"I know," she whispered, making no move to free her imprisoned hands.

Jess lowered his head, tormented one delectable nipple by drawing at it with his lips. "This is real, Libby," he said, circling the morsel with just the tip of his tongue now. "It's important that you realize that."

"I do...oh, God...Jess, *Jess*."

Reluctantly he left the feast to search her face with disbelieving eyes. "Don't you want me to stop?"

A delicate shade of rose sifted over her high cheekbones. Her hands still stretched above her, her eyes closed, she shook her head.

Jess went back to the breasts that so bewitched him, nipped at their peaks with gentle teeth. "Do you...know how many... times I've wanted...to do this?"

The answer was a soft, strangled cry.

He limited himself to one nipple, worked its surrendering peak into a sweet fervor with his lips and his tongue. "So... many...times. My God, Libby...you're so beautiful..."

Her words were as halting as his had been. "What's happening to us? We h-hate each other."

Jess laughed and began kissing his way softly down over her

rib cage, her smooth, firm stomach. The snap on her jeans gave way easily—and was echoed by the sound of car doors slamming in the area of the house.

Instantly the spell was broken. Color surged into Libby's face and she bolted upright, nearly thrusting Jess off the end of the dock in her efforts to wrench on the discarded suntop and close the fastening of her jeans.

"Broad daylight..." she muttered distractedly, talking more to herself than to Jess.

"Lib!" yelled a jovial masculine voice, approaching fast. "Libby?"

Stacey. The voice belonged to Stacey.

Sudden fierce anger surged, white-hot, through Jess's aching, bedazzled system. Standing up, not caring that his thwarted passion still strained against his jeans, visible to anyone who might take the trouble to look, he glared down at Libby and rasped, "I guess reinforcements have arrived."

She gave a primitive, protesting little cry and shot to her feet, her ink-blue eyes flashing with anger and hurt. Before Jess could brace himself, her hands came to his chest like small battering rams and pushed him easily off the end of the dock.

The jolting cold of that spring-fed pond was welcome balm to Jess's passion-heated flesh, if not his pride. When he surfaced and grasped the end of the dock in both hands, he knew there would be no physical evidence that he and Libby had been doing anything other than fighting.

LIBBY ACHED WITH EMBARASSMENT as Stacey and Senator Barlowe made their way down over the slight hillside that separated the backyard from the pond.

The older man cast one mischievously baleful look at his younger son, who was lifting himself indignantly onto the dock, and chuckled, "I see things are the same as always," he said.

Libby managed a shaky smile. *Not quite,* she thought, her body remembering the delicious dance Jess's hard frame had choreographed for it. "Hello, Senator," she said, rising on tiptoe to kiss his cheek.

"Welcome home," he replied with gruff affection. Then his

wise eyes shifted past her to rest again on Jess. "It's a little cold yet for a swim, isn't it, son?"

Jess's hair hung in dripping ebony strands around his face, and his eyes were jade-green flares, avoiding his father to scald Libby's lips, her throat, her still-pulsing breasts. "We'll finish our...discussion later," he said.

Libby's blood boiled up over her stomach and her breasts to glow in her face. "I wouldn't count on that!"

"I would," Jess replied with a smile that was at once tender and evil. And then, without so much as a word to his father and brother, he walked away.

"What the hell did he mean by that?" barked Stacey, red in the face.

The look Libby gave the boyishly handsome, caramel-eyed man beside her was hardly friendly. "You've got some tall explaining to do, Stacey Barlowe," she said.

The senator, a tall, attractive man with hair as gray as Ken's, cleared his throat in the way of those who have practiced diplomacy long and well. "I believe I'll go up to the house and see if Ken's got any beer on hand," he said. A moment later he was off, following Jess's soggy path.

Libby straightened her shoulders and calmly slapped Stacey across the face. "How dare you?" she raged, her words strangled in her effort to modulate them.

Stacey reddened again, ran one hand through his fashionably cut wheat-colored hair. He turned, as if to follow his father. "I could use a beer myself," he said in distracted, evasive tones.

"Oh, no you don't!" Libby cried, grasping his arm and holding on. The rich leather of his jacket was smooth under her hand. "Don't you *dare* walk away from me, Stacey—not until you explain why you've been lying about me!"

"I haven't been lying!" he protested, his hands on his hips now, his expensively clad body blocking the base of the dock as he faced her.

"You have! You've been telling everyone that I...that we..."

"That we've been doing what you and my brother were doing a few minutes ago?"

If Stacey had shoved Libby into the water, she couldn't have been more shocked. A furious retort rose to the back of her throat but would go no further.

Stacey's tarnished-gold eyes flashed. "Jess was making love to you, wasn't he?"

"What if he was?" managed Libby after a painful struggle with her vocal cords. "It certainly wouldn't be any of your business, would it?"

"Yes, it would. I love you, Libby."

"You love *Cathy!*"

Stacey shook his head. "No. Not anymore."

"Don't say that," Libby pleaded, suddenly deflated. "Oh, Stacey, don't. Don't do this…"

His hands came to her shoulders, fierce and strong. The topaz fever in his eyes made Libby wonder if he was sane. "I love you, Libby Kincaid," he vowed softly but ferociously, "and I mean to have you."

Libby retreated a step, stunned, shaking her head. The reality of this situation was so different from what she had imagined it would be. In her thoughts, Stacey had laughed when she confronted him, ruffled her hair in that familiar brotherly way of old, and said that it was all a mistake. That he loved Cathy, wanted Cathy, and couldn't anyone around here take a joke?

But here he was declaring himself in a way that was unsettlingly serious.

Libby took another step backward. "Stacey, I need to be here, where my dad is. Where things are familiar and comfortable. Please…don't force me to leave."

Stacey smiled. "There is no point in leaving, Lib. If you do, I'll be right behind you."

She shivered. "You've lost your mind!"

But Stacey looked entirely sane as he shook his handsome head and wedged his hands into the pockets of his jacket. "Just my heart," he said. "Corny, isn't it?"

"It's worse than corny. Stacey, you're unbalanced or something. You're fantasizing. There was never anything between us—"

"No?" The word was crooned.

"No! You need help."

His face had all the innocence of an altar boy's. "If I'm insane, darlin', it's something you could cure."

Libby resisted an urge to slap him again. She wanted to race into the house, but he was still barring her way, so that she could not leave the dock without brushing against him. "Stay away from me, Stacey," she said as he advanced toward her. "I mean it—stay away from me!"

"I can't, Libby."

The sincerity in his voice was chilling; for the first time in all the years she'd known Stacey Barlowe, Libby was afraid of him. Discretion kept her from screaming, but just barely.

Stacey paled, as though he'd read her thoughts. "Don't look at me like that, Libby—I wouldn't hurt you under any circumstances. And I'm not crazy."

She lifted her chin. "Let me by, Stacey. I want to go into the house."

He tilted his head back, sighed, met her eyes again. "I've frightened you, and I'm sorry. I didn't mean to do that."

Libby couldn't speak. Despite his rational, settling words, she was sick with the knowledge that he meant to pursue her.

"You must know," he said softly, "how good it could be for us. You needed me in New York, Libby, and now I need you."

The third voice, from the base of the hillside, was to Libby as a life preserver to a drowning person. "Let her pass, Stacey."

Libby looked up quickly to see Jess, unlikely rescuer that he was. His hair was towel-rumpled and his jeans clung to muscular thighs—thighs that only minutes ago had pressed against her own in a demand as old as time. His manner was calm as he buttoned a shirt, probably borrowed from Ken, over his broad chest.

Stacey shrugged affably and walked past his brother without a word of argument.

Watching him go, Libby went weak with relief. A lump rose in her throat as she forced herself to meet Jess's gaze. "You were right," she muttered miserably. "You were *right*."

Jess was watching her much the way a mountain cat would watch a cornered rabbit. For the briefest moment there was a look of tenderness in the green eyes, but then his expression turned hard and a muscle flexed in his jaw. "I trust the welcome-home party has been scheduled for later—after Cathy has been tucked into her bed, for instance?"

Libby gaped at him, appalled. Had he interceded only to torment her himself?

Jess's eyes were contemptuous as they swept over her. "What's the matter, Lib? Couldn't you bring yourself to tell your married lover that the welcoming had already been taken care of?"

Rage went through Libby's body like an electric current surging into a wire. "You don't seriously think that I would... that I was—"

"You even managed to be alone with him. Tell me, Lib— how did you get rid of my father?"

"G-get rid..." Libby stopped, tears of shock and mortification aching in her throat and burning behind her eyes. She drew a deep, audible breath, trying to assemble herself, to think clearly.

But the whole world seemed to be tilting and swirling like some out-of-control carnival ride. When Libby closed her eyes against the sensation, she swayed dangerously and would probably have fallen if Jess hadn't reached her in a few strides and caught her shoulders in his hands.

"Libby..." he said, and there was anger in the sound, but there was a hollow quality, too—one that Libby couldn't find a name for.

Her knees were trembling. Too much, it was all too much. Jonathan's death, the ugly divorce, the trouble that Stacey had caused with his misplaced affections—all of those things weighed on her, but none were so crushing as the blatant contempt of this man. It was apparent to Libby now that the lovemaking they had almost shared, so new and beautiful to her, had been some sort of cruel joke to Jess.

"How could you?" she choked out. "Oh, Jess, how could you?"

His face was grim, seeming to float in a shimmering mist. Instead of answering, Jess lifted Libby into his arms and carried her up the little hill toward the house.

She didn't remember reaching the back door.

"WHAT THE DEVIL happened on that dock today, Jess?" Cleave Barlowe demanded, hands grasping the edge of his desk.

His younger son stood at the mahogany bar, his shoulders stiff, his attention carefully fixed on the glass of straight Scotch he meant to consume. "Why don't you ask Stacey?"

"Goddammit, I'm asking *you!*" barked Cleave. "Ken's mad as hell, and I don't blame him—that girl of his was shattered!"

Girl. The word caught in Jess's beleaguered mind. He remembered the way Libby had responded to him, meeting his passion with her own, welcoming the greed he'd shown at her breasts. Had it not been for the arrival of his father and brother, he would have possessed her completely within minutes. "She's no 'girl,'" he said, still aching to bury himself in the depths of her.

The senator swore roundly. "What did you say to her, Jess?" he pressed, once the spate of unpoliticianly profanity had passed.

Jess lowered his head. He'd meant the things he'd said to Libby, and he couldn't, in all honesty, have taken them back. But he knew some of what she'd been through in New York, her trysts with Stacey notwithstanding, and he was ashamed of the way he'd goaded her. She had come home to heal—the look in her eyes had told him that much—and instead of respecting that, he had made things more difficult for her.

Never one to be thwarted by silence, no matter how eloquent, Senator Barlowe persisted. "Dammit, Jess, I might expect this kind of thing from Stacey, but I thought you had more sense! You were harassing Libby about these blasted rumors your brother has been spreading, weren't you?"

Jess sighed, set aside the drink he had yet to take a sip from, and faced his angry father. "Yes," he said.

"Why?"

Stubbornly, Jess refused to answer. He took an interest in

the imposing oak desk where his father sat, the heavy draperies that kept out the sun, the carved ivory of the fireplace.

"All right, mulehead," Cleave muttered furiously, "don't talk! Don't explain! And don't go near Ken Kincaid's daughter again, damn you. That man's the best foreman I've ever had and if he gets riled and quits because of you, Jess, you and I are going to come to time!"

Jess almost smiled, though he didn't quite dare. Not too many years before the phrase "come to time," when used by his father, had presaged a session in the woodshed. He wondered what it meant now that he was thirty-three years old, a member of the Montana State Bar Association, and a full partner in the family corporation. "I care about Cathy," he said evenly. "What was I supposed to do—stand by and watch Libby and Stace grind her up into emotional hamburger?"

Cleave gave a heavy sigh and sank into the richly upholstered swivel chair behind his desk. "I love Cathy too," he said at length, "but Stacey's behind this whole mess, not Libby. Dammit, that woman has been through hell from what Ken says—she was married to a man who slept in every bed but his own, and she had to watch her nine-year-old stepson die by inches. Now she comes home looking for a little peace, and what does she get? Trouble!"

Jess lowered his head, turned away—ostensibly to take up his glass of Scotch. He'd known about the bad marriage—Ken had cussed the day Aaron Strand was born often enough—but he hadn't heard about the little boy. My God, he hadn't known about the boy.

"Maybe Strand couldn't sleep in his own bed," he said, urged on by some ugliness that had surfaced inside him since Libby's return. "Maybe Stacey was already in it."

"Enough!" boomed the senator in a voice that had made presidents tremble in their shoes. "I like Libby and I'm not going to listen to any more of this, either from you or from your brother! Do I make myself clear?"

"Abundantly clear," replied Jess, realizing that the Scotch was in his hand now and feeling honor-bound to take at least one gulp of the stuff. The taste was reminiscent of scorched rubber, but since the liquor seemed to quiet the raging demons in his mind, he finished the drink and poured another.

He fully intended to get drunk. It was something he hadn't done since high school, but it suddenly seemed appealing. Maybe he would stop hardening every time he thought of Libby, stop craving her.

Too, after the things he'd said to her that afternoon by the pond, he didn't want to remain sober any longer than necessary. "What did you mean," he ventured, after downing his fourth drink, "when you said Libby had to watch her stepson die?"

Papers rustled at the big desk behind him. "Stacey says the child had leukemia."

Jess poured another drink and closed his eyes. *Oh, Libby,* he thought, *I'm sorry. My God, I'm sorry.* "I guess Stacey would know," he said aloud, with bitterness.

There was a short, thunderous silence. Jess expected his father to explode into one of his famous tirades, was genuinely surprised when the man sighed instead. Still, his words dropped on Jess's mind like a bomb.

"The firewater isn't going to change the fact that you love Libby Kincaid, Jess," he said reasonably. "Making her life and your own miserable isn't going to change it either."

Love Libby Kincaid? Impossible. The strange needs possessing him now were rooted in his libido, not his heart. Once he'd had her—and have her he would, or go crazy—her hold on him would be broken. "I've never loved a woman in my life," he said.

"Fool. You've loved one woman—Libby—since you were seven years old. Exactly seven years old, in fact."

Jess turned, studying his father quizzically. "What the hell are you talking about?"

"Your seventh birthday," recalled Cleave, his eyes far away. "Your mother and I gave you a pony. First time you saw Libby Kincaid, you were out of that saddle and helping her into it."

The memory burst, full-blown, into Jess's mind. A pinto pony. The new foreman arriving. The little girl with dark blue eyes and hair the color of winter moonlight.

He'd spent the whole afternoon squiring Libby around the yard, content to walk while she rode.

"What do you suppose Ken would say if I went over there and asked to see his daughter?" Jess asked.

"I imagine he'd shoot you, after today."

"I imagine he would. But I think I'll risk it."

"You've made enough trouble for one day," argued Cleave, taking obvious note of his son's inebriated state. "Libby needs time, Jess. She needs to be close to Ken. If you're smart, you'll leave her alone until she has a chance to get her emotional bearings again."

Jess didn't want his father to be right, not in this instance, anyway, but he knew that he was. Much as he wanted to go to Libby and try to make things right, the fact was that he was the last person in the world she needed or wanted to see.

"BETTER?"

Libby smiled at Ken as she came into the kitchen, freshly showered and wrapped in the cozy, familiar chenille robe she'd found in the back of her closet. "Lots better," she answered softly.

Her father was standing at the kitchen stove stirring something in the blackened cast-iron skillet.

Libby scuffled to the table and sat down. It was good to be home, so good. Why hadn't she come sooner? "Whatever you're cooking there smells good," she said.

Ken beamed. In his jeans and his western shirt, he looked out of place at that stove. He should, Libby decided fancifully, have been crouching at some campfire on the range, stirring beans in a blue enamel pot. "This here's my world-famous red-devil sauce," he grinned, "for which I am known and respected."

Libby laughed, and tears of homecoming filled her eyes. She went to her father and hugged him, needing to be a little girl again, just for a moment.

CHAPTER THREE

LIBBY NEARLY CHOKED on her first taste of Ken's taco sauce. "Did you say you were known and respected for this stuff, or known and feared?"

Ken chuckled roguishly at her tear-polished eyes and flaming face. "My calling it 'red devil' should have been a clue, dumplin'."

Libby muttered an exclamation and perversely took another bite from her bulging taco. "From now on," she said, chewing, "I'll do the cooking around this spread."

Her father laughed again and tapped one temple with a calloused index finger, his pale blue eyes twinkling.

"You deliberately tricked me!" cried Libby.

He grinned and shrugged. "Code of the West, sweetheart. Grouse about the chow, and presto—you're the cook!"

"Actually," ventured Libby with cultivated innocence, "this sauce isn't too bad."

"Too late," laughed Ken. "You already broke the code."

Libby lowered her taco to her plate and lifted both hands in a gesture of concession. "All right, all right—but have a little pity on me, will you? I've been living among dudes!"

"That's no excuse."

Libby shrugged and took up her taco again. "I tried. Have you been doing your own cooking and cleaning all this time?"

Ken shook his head and sat back in his chair, his thumbs hooked behind his belt buckle. "Nope. The Barlowes' housekeeper sends her crew down here once in a while."

"What about the food?"

"I eat with the boys most of the time, over at the cook shack." He rose, went to fill two mugs from the coffeepot on the stove. When he turned around again, his face was serious. "Libby, what happened today? What upset you like that?"

Libby averted her eyes. "I don't know," she lied lamely.

"Dammit, you *do* know. You fainted, Libby. When Jess carried you in here, I—"

"I know," Libby broke in gently. "You were scared. I'm sorry."

Carefully, as though he feared he might drop them, Ken set the cups of steaming coffee on the table. "What happened?" he persisted as he sat down in his chair again.

Libby swallowed hard, but the lump that had risen in her throat wouldn't go down. Knowing that this conversation couldn't be avoided forever, she managed to reply, "It's complicated. Basically, it comes down to the fact that Stacey's been telling those lies."

"And?"

"And Jess believes him. He said...he said some things to me and...well, it must have created some kind of emotional overload. I just gave out."

Ken turned his mug idly between his thumb and index finger, causing the liquid to spill over and make a coffee stain on the tablecloth. "Tell me about Jonathan, Libby," he said in a low, gentle voice.

The tears that sprang into Libby's eyes were not related to the tang of her father's red-devil taco sauce. "He died," she choked miserably.

"I know that. You called me the night it happened, remember? I guess what I'm really asking you is why you didn't want me to fly back there and help you sort things out."

Libby lowered her head. Jonathan hadn't been her son, he'd been Aaron's, by a previous marriage. But the loss of the child was a raw void within her, even though months had passed. "I didn't want you to get a firsthand look at my marriage," she admitted with great difficulty—and the shame she couldn't seem to shake.

"Why not, Libby?"

The sound Libby made might have been either a laugh or a sob. "Because it was terrible," she answered.

"From the first?"

She forced herself to meet her father's steady gaze, knew

that he had guessed a lot about her marriage from her rare phone calls and even rarer letters. "Almost," she replied sadly.

"Tell me."

Libby didn't want to think about Aaron, let alone talk about him to this man who wouldn't understand so many things. "He had...he had lovers."

Ken didn't seem surprised. Had he guessed that, too? "Go on."

"I can't!"

"Yes, you can. If it's too much for you right now, I won't press you. But the sooner you talk this out, Libby, the better off you're going to be."

She realized that her hands were clenched in her lap and tried to relax them. There was still a white mark on her finger where Aaron's ostentatious wedding ring had been. "He didn't care," she mourned in a soft, distracted whisper. "He honestly didn't care..."

"About you?"

"About Jonathan. Dad, he didn't care about his own son!"

"How so, sweetheart?"

Libby dashed away tears with the back of one hand. "Th-things were bad between Aaron and me b-before we found out that Jonathan was sick. After the doctors told us, it was a lot worse."

"I don't follow you, Libby."

"Dad, Aaron wouldn't have anything to do with Jonathan from the moment we knew he was dying. He wasn't there for any of the tests and he never once came to visit at the hospital. Dad, that little boy cried for his father, and Aaron wouldn't come to him!"

"Did you talk to Aaron?"

Remembered frustration made Libby's cheeks pound with color. "I *pleaded* with him, Dad. All he'd say was, 'I can't handle this.'"

"It would be a hell of a thing to deal with, Lib. Maybe you're being too hard on the man."

"Too hard? *Too hard?* Jonathan was terrified, Dad, and he

was in pain—constant pain. All he asked was that his own father be strong for him!''

"What about the boy's mother? Did she come to the hospital?''

"Ellen died when Jonathan was a baby.''

Ken sighed, framing a question he was obviously reluctant to ask. "Did you ever love Aaron Strand, Libby?''

Libby remembered the early infatuation, the excitement that had never deepened into real love and had quickly been quelled by the realities of marriage to a man who was fundamentally self-centered. She tried, but she couldn't even recall her ex-husband's face clearly—all she could see in her mind was a pair of jade-green eyes, dark hair. Jess. "No,'' she finally said. "I thought I did when I married him, though.''

Ken stood up suddenly, took the coffeepot from its back burner on the stove, refilled both their cups. "I don't like asking you this, but—''

"No, Dad,'' Libby broke in firmly, anticipating the question all too well, "I don't love Stacey!''

"You're sure about that?''

The truth was that Libby *hadn't* been sure, not entirely. But that ill-advised episode with Jess at the end of the swimming dock had brought everything into clear perspective. Just remembering how willingly she had submitted to him made her throb with embarrassment. "I'm sure,'' she said.

Ken's strong hand came across the table to close over hers. "You're home now,'' he reminded her, "and things are going to get better, Libby. I promise you that.''

Libby sniffled inelegantly. "Know something, cowboy? I love you very much.''

"Bet you say that to all your fathers,'' Ken quipped. "You planning to work on your comic strip tomorrow?''

The change of subject was welcome. "I'm six or eight weeks ahead of schedule on that, and the mechanicals for the book aren't due till fall. I think I'll go riding instead, if I can get Cathy to go with me.''

"What's a 'mechanical'?''

Libby smiled, feeling sheltered by the love of this strong and steady man facing her. "It's the finished drawing that I turn in, along with the instructions for the colorist."

"You don't do the colors?" Ken seemed surprised at that, knowing, as he did, her love for vivid shades and subtle hues alike.

"No, I just do the panels and the lettering." It was good to talk about work, to think about work. Disdainful as he had been about her career, it was the one thing Aaron had not been able to spoil for her.

Nobody's fool, Ken drew her out on the subject as much as he could, and she found herself chattering on and on about cartooning and even her secret hope to branch out into portraits one day.

They talked, father and daughter, far into the night.

"YOU DESERVE THIS," Jess Barlowe said to his reflection in the bathroom mirror. A first-class hangover pounded in his head and roiled in his stomach, and his face looked drawn, as though he'd been hibernating like one of the bears that sometimes troubled the range stock.

Grimly he began to shave, and as he wielded his disposable razor, he wondered if Libby was awake yet. Should he stop at Ken's and talk to her before going on to the main house to spend a day with the corporation accountants?

Jess wanted to go to Libby, to tell her that he was sorry for baiting her, to try to get their complex relationship—if it *was* a relationship—onto some kind of sane ground. However, all his instincts told him that his father had been right the day before: Libby needed time.

His thoughts strayed to Libby's stepson. What would it be like to sit by a hospital bed, day after day, watching a child suffer and not being able to help?

Jess shuddered. It was hard to imagine the horror of something like that. At least Libby had had her husband to share the nightmare.

He frowned as he nicked his chin with the razor, blotted the small wound with tissue paper. If Libby had had her husband during that impossible time, why had she needed Stacey?

Stacey. Now, there was someone he could talk to. Granted, Jess had not been on the best of terms with his older brother of late, but the man had a firsthand knowledge of what was happening inside Libby Kincaid, and that was reason enough to approach him.

Feeling better for having a plan, Jess finished his ablutions and got dressed. Normally he spent his days on the range with Ken and the ranch hands, but today, because of his meeting with the accountants, he forwent his customary blue jeans and cotton workshirt for a tailored three-piece suit. He was still struggling with his tie as he made his way down the broad redwood steps that led from the loftlike second floor of his house to the living room.

Here there was a massive fireplace of white limestone, taking up the whole of one wall. The floors were polished oak and boasted a number of brightly colored Indian rugs. Two easy chairs and a deep sofa faced the hearth, and Jess's cluttered desk looked out over the ranchland and the glacial mountains beyond.

Striding toward the front door, in exasperation he gave up his efforts to get the tie right. He was glad he didn't have Stacey's job; not for him the dull task of overseeing the family's nationwide chain of steak-house franchises.

He smiled. Stacey liked playing the dude, doing television commercials, traveling all over the country.

And taking Libby Kincaid to bed.

Jess stalked across the front lawn to the carport and climbed behind the wheel of the station wagon he'd driven since law school. One of these times, he was going to have to get another car—something with a little flash, like Stacey's Ferrari.

Stacey, Stacey. He hadn't even seen his brother yet, and already he was sick of him.

The station wagon's engine made a grinding sound and then huffed to life. Jess patted the dusty dashboard affectionately and grinned. A car was a car was a car, he reflected as he backed the notorious wreck out of his driveway. The function of a car was to transport people, not impress them.

Five minutes later, Jess's station wagon chortled to an asthmatic stop beside his brother's ice-blue Ferrari. He looked up at the modernistic two-story house that had been the senator's wedding gift to Stacey and Cathy and wondered if Libby would be impressed by the place.

He scowled as he made his way up the curving white-stone walk. What the hell did he care if Libby was impressed?

Irritated, he jabbed one finger at the special doorbell that would turn on a series of blinking lights inside the house. The system had been his own idea, meant to make life easier for Cathy.

His sister-in-law came to the door and smiled at him somewhat wanly, speaking with her hands. "Good morning."

Jess nodded, smiled. The haunted look in the depths of Cathy's eyes made him angry all over again. "Is Stacey here?" he signed, stepping into the house.

Cathy caught his hand in her own and led him through the cavernous living room and the formal dining room beyond. Stacey was in the kitchen, looking more at home in a three-piece suit than Jess ever had.

"You," Stacey said tonelessly, setting down the English muffin he'd been slathering with honey.

Cathy offered coffee and left the room when it was politely declined. Distractedly Jess reflected on the fact that her life had to be boring as hell, centering on Stacey the way it did.

"I want to talk to you," Jess said, scraping back a chrome-and-plastic chair to sit down at the table.

Stacey arched one eyebrow. "I hope it's quick—I'm leaving for the airport in a few minutes. I've got some business to take care of in Kansas City."

Jess was impatient. "What kind of man is Libby's ex-husband?" he asked.

Stacey took up his coffee. "Why do you want to know?"

"I just do. Do I have to have him checked out, or are you going to tell me?"

"He's a bastard," said Stacey, not quite meeting his brother's eyes.

"Rich?"

"Oh, yes. His family is old-money."

"What does he do?"

"Do?"

"Yeah. Does he work, or does he just stand around being rich?"

"He runs the family advertising agency; I think he has a lot of control over their other financial interests too."

Jess sensed that Stacey was hedging, wondered why. "Any bad habits?"

Stacey was gazing at the toaster now, in a fixed way, as though he expected something alarming to pop out of it. "The man has his share of vices."

Annoyed now, Jess got up, helped himself to the cup of coffee he had refused earlier, sat down again. "Pulling porcupine quills out of a dog's nose would be easier than getting answers out of you. When you say he has vices, do you mean women?"

Stacey swallowed, looked away. "To put it mildly," he said.

Jess settled back in his chair. "What the hell do you mean by that?"

"I mean that he not only liked to run around with other women, he liked to flaunt the fact. The worse he could make Libby feel about herself, the happier he was."

"Jesus," Jess breathed. "What else?" he pressed, sensing, from Stacey's expression, that there was more.

"He was impotent with Libby."

"Why did she stay? Why in God's name did she stay?" Jess mused distractedly, as much to himself as to his brother.

A cautious but smug light flickered in Stacey's topaz eyes. "She had me," he said evenly. "Besides, Jonathan was sick by that time and she felt she had to stay in the marriage for his sake."

The spacious sun-filled kitchen seemed to buckle and shift around Jess. "Why didn't she tell Ken, at least?"

"What would have been the point in that, Jess? He couldn't

have made the boy well again or transformed Aaron Strand into a devoted husband.''

The things Libby must have endured—the shame, the loneliness, the humiliation and grief, washed over Jess in a dismal, crushing wave. No wonder she had reached out to Stacey the way she had. No wonder. ''Thanks,'' he said gruffly, standing up to leave.

''Jess?''

He paused in the kitchen doorway, his hands clasping the woodwork, his shoulders aching with tension. ''What?''

''Don't worry about Libby. I'll take care of her.''

Jess felt a despairing sort of anger course through him. ''What about Cathy?'' he asked, without turning around. ''Who is going to take care of her?''

''You've always—''

Jess whirled suddenly, staring at his brother, almost hating him. ''I've always *what?*''

''Cared for her.'' Stacey shrugged, looking only mildly unsettled. ''Protected her...''

''Are you suggesting that I sweep up the pieces after you shatter her?'' demanded Jess in a dangerous rasp.

Stacey only shrugged again.

Because he feared that he would do his brother lasting harm if he stayed another moment, Jess stormed out of the house. Cathy, dressed in old jeans, boots and a cotton blouse, was waiting beside the station wagon. The pallor in her face told Jess that she knew much more about the state of her marriage than he would have hoped.

Her hands trembled a little as she spoke with them. ''I'm scared, Jess.''

He drew her into his arms, held her. ''I know, baby,'' he said, even though he knew she couldn't hear him or see his lips. ''I know.''

LIBBY OPENED HER EYES, yawned and stretched. The smells of sunshine and fresh air swept into her bedroom through the open window, ruffling pink eyelet curtains and reminding her that she was home again. She tossed back the covers on the bed she had once shared with Cathy and got up, sleepily making her way into the bathroom and starting the water for a shower.

As she took off her short cotton nightshirt, she looked down at herself and remembered the raging sensations Jess Barlowe had ignited in her the day before. She had been stupid and self-indulgent to let that happen, but after several years of celibacy, she supposed it was natural that her passions had been stirred so easily—especially by a man like Jess.

As Libby showered, she felt renewed. Aaron's flagrant infidelities had been painful for her, and they had seriously damaged her self-esteem in the bargain.

Now, even though she had made a fool of herself by being wanton with a man who could barely tolerate her, many of Libby's doubts about herself as a woman had been eased, if not routed. She was not as useless and undesirable as Aaron had made her feel. She had caused Jess Barlowe to want her, hadn't she?

Big deal, she told the image in her mirror as she brushed her teeth. *How do you know Jess wasn't out to prove that his original opinion of you was on target?*

Deflated by this very real possibility, Libby combed her hair, applied the customary lip gloss and light touch of mascara and went back to her room to dress. From her suitcases she selected a short-sleeved turquoise pullover shirt and a pair of trim jeans. Remembering her intention to find Cathy and persuade her to go riding, she ferreted through her closet until she found the worn boots she'd left behind before moving to New York, pulling them on over a pair of thick socks.

Looking down at those disreputable old boots, Libby imagined the scorn they would engender in Aaron's jet-set crowd and laughed. Problems or no problems, Jess or no Jess, it was good to be home.

Not surprisingly, the kitchen was empty. Ken had probably left the house before dawn, but there was coffee on the stove and fruit in the refrigerator, so Libby helped herself to a pear and sat down to eat.

The telephone rang just as she was finishing her second cup of coffee, and Libby answered cheerfully, thinking that the caller would be Ken or the housekeeper at the main house, relaying some message for Cathy.

She was back at the table, the receiver pressed to her ear, before Aaron spoke.

"When are you coming home?"

"Home?" echoed Libby stupidly, off-balance, unable to believe that he'd actually asked such a question. "I *am* home, Aaron."

"Enough," he replied. "You've made your point, exhibited your righteous indignation. Now you've got to get back here because I need you."

Libby wanted to hang up, but it seemed a very long way from her chair to the wall, where the rest of the telephone was. "Aaron, we are divorced," she reminded him calmly, "and I am never coming back."

"You have to," he answered, without missing a beat. "It's crucial."

"Why? What happened to all your…friends?"

Aaron sighed. "You remember Betty, don't you? Miss November? Well, Betty and I had a small disagreement, as it happens, and she went to my family. I am, shall we say, exposed as something less than an ideal spouse.

"In any case, my grandmother believes that a man who cannot run his family—she was in Paris when we divorced, darling—cannot run a company, either. I have six months to bring you back into the fold and start an heir, or the whole shooting match goes to my cousin."

Libby was too stunned to speak or even move; she simply stood in the middle of her father's kitchen, trying to absorb what Aaron was saying.

"That," Aaron went on blithely, "is where you come in, sweetheart. You come back, we smile a lot and make a baby, my grandmother's ruffled feathers are smoothed. It's as simple as that."

Sickness boiled into Libby's throat. "I don't believe this!" she whispered.

"You don't believe what, darling? That I can make a baby?

May I point out that I sired Jonathan, of whom you were so cloyingly fond?''

Libby swallowed. ''Get Miss November pregnant,'' she managed to suggest. And then she added distractedly, more to herself than Aaron, ''I think I'm going to be sick.''

''Don't tell me that I've been beaten to the proverbial draw,'' Aaron remarked in that brutally smooth, caustic way of his. ''Did the steak-house king already do the deed?''

''You are disgusting!''

''Yes, but very practical. If I don't hand my grandmother an heir, whether it's mine or the issue of that softheaded cowboy, I stand to lose millions of dollars.''

Libby managed to stand up. A few steps, just a few, and she could hang up the telephone, shut out Aaron's voice and his ugly suggestions. ''Do you really think that I would turn any child of mine over to someone like you?''

''There is a child, then,'' he retorted smoothly.

''No!'' Five steps to the wall, six at most.

''Be reasonable, sweetness. We're discussing an empire here. If you don't come back and attend to your wifely duties, I'll have to visit that godforsaken ranch and try to persuade you.''

''I am not your wife!'' screamed Libby. One step. One step and a reach.

''Dear heart, I don't find the idea any more appealing than you do, but there isn't any other way, is there? My grandmother likes you—sees you as sturdy peasant stock—and she wants the baby to be yours.''

At last. The wall was close and Libby slammed the receiver into place. Then, dazed, she stumbled back to her chair and fell into it, lowering her head to her arms. She cried hard, for herself, for Jonathan.

''LIBBY?''

It was the last voice she would have wanted to hear, except for Aaron's. ''Go away, Stacey!'' she hissed.

Instead of complying, Stacey laid a gentle hand on her shoulder. "What happened, Libby?" he asked softly. "Who was that on the phone?"

Fresh horror washed over Libby at the things Aaron had requested, mixed with anger and revulsion. God, how self-centered and insensitive that man was! And what gall he had, suggesting that she return to that disaster of a marriage, like some unquestioning brood mare, to produce a baby on order!

She gave a shuddering cry and motioned Stacey away with a frantic motion of her arm.

He only drew her up out of the chair and turned her so that he could hold her. She hadn't the strength to resist the intimacy and, in her half-hysterical state, he seemed to be the old Stacey, the strong big brother.

Stacey's hand came to the back of her head, tangling in her freshly washed hair, pressing her to his shoulder. "Tell me what happened," he urged, just as he had when Libby was a child with a skinned knee or a bee sting.

From habit, she allowed herself to be comforted. For so long there had been no one to confide in except Stacey, and it seemed natural to lean on him now. "Aaron...Aaron called. He wanted me to have his...his baby!"

Before Stacey could respond to that, the door separating the kitchen from the living room swung open. Instinctively Libby drew back from the man who held her.

Jess towered in the doorway, pale, his gaze scorching Libby's flushed, tear-streaked face. "You know," he began in a voice that was no less terrible for being soft, "I almost believed you. I almost had myself convinced that you were above anything this shabby."

"Wait—you don't understand..."

Jess smiled a slow, vicious smile—a smile that took in his startled brother as well as Libby. "Don't I? Oh, princess, I wish I didn't." The searing jade gaze sliced menacingly to Stacey's face. "And it seems I'm going to be an uncle. Tell me, brother—what does that make Cathy?"

To Libby's horror, Stacey said nothing to refute what was obviously a gross misunderstanding. He simply pulled her back into his arms, and her struggle was virtually imperceptible because of his strength.

"Let me go!" she pleaded, frantic.

Stacey released her, but only grudgingly. "I've got a plane to catch," he said.

Libby was incredulous. "Tell him! Tell Jess that he's wrong," she cried, reaching out for Stacey's arm, trying to detain him.

But Stacey simply pulled free and left by the back door.

There was a long, pulsing silence, during which both Libby and Jess seemed to be frozen. He was the first to thaw.

"I know you were hurt, Libby," he said. "Badly hurt. But that didn't give you the right to do something like this to Cathy."

It infuriated Libby that this man's good opinion was so important to her, but it was, and there was no changing that. "Jess, I didn't do anything to Cathy. Please listen to me."

He folded his strong arms and rested against the door jamb with an ease that Libby knew was totally feigned. "I'm listening," he said, and the words had a flippant note.

Libby ignored fresh anger. "I am not expecting Stacey's baby, and this wasn't a romantic tryst. I don't even know why he came here. I was on the phone with Aaron and he—"

A muscle in Jess's neck corded, relaxed again. "I hope you're not going to tell me that your former husband made you pregnant, Libby. That seems unlikely."

Frustration pounded in Libby's temples and tightened the already constricted muscles in her throat. "I am not pregnant!" she choked out. "And if you are going to eavesdrop, Jess Barlowe, you could at least pay attention! Aaron wanted me to come back to New York and have his baby so that he would have an heir to present to his grandmother!"

"You didn't agree to that?"

"Of course I didn't agree! What kind of monster do you think I am?"

Jess shrugged with a nonchalance that was belied by the leaping green fire in his eyes. "I don't know, princess, but rest assured—I intend to find out."

"I have a better idea!" Libby flared. "Why don't you just leave me the hell alone?"

"In theory that's brilliant," he fired back, "but there is one problem: I want you."

Involuntarily Libby remembered the kisses and caresses exchanged by the pond the day before, relived them. Hot color poured into her face. "Am I supposed to be honored?"

"No," Jess replied flatly, "you're supposed to be kept so busy that you won't have time to screw up Cathy's life any more than you already have."

If Libby could have moved, she would have rushed across that room and slapped Jess Barlowe senseless. Since she couldn't get her muscles to respond to the orders of her mind, she was forced to watch in stricken silence as he gave her a smoldering assessment with his eyes, executed a half salute and left the house.

CHAPTER FOUR

WHEN THE TELEPHONE RANG AGAIN, immediately after Jess's exit from the kitchen, Libby was almost afraid to answer it. It would be like Aaron to persist, to use pressure to get what he wanted.

On the other hand, the call might be from someone else, and it could be important.

"Hello?" Libby dared, with resolve.

"Ms. Kincaid?" asked a cheerful feminine voice. "This is Marion Bradshaw, and I'm calling for Mrs. Barlowe. She'd like you to meet her at the main house if you can, and she says to dress for riding."

Libby looked down at her jeans and boots and smiled. In one way, at least, she and Cathy were still on the same wavelength. "Please tell her that I'll be there as soon as I can."

There was a brief pause at the other end of the line, followed by, "Mrs. Barlowe wants me to ask if you have a car down there. If not, she'll come and pick you up in a few minutes."

Though there was no car at her disposal, Libby declined the offer. The walk to the main ranch house would give her a chance to think, to prepare herself to face her cousin again.

As Libby started out, striding along the winding tree-lined road, she ached to think that she and Cathy had come to this. Fresh anger at Stacey quickened her step.

For a moment she was mad at Cathy too. How could she believe such a thing, after all they'd been through together? How?

Firmly Libby brought her ire under control. *You don't get mad at a handicapped person,* she scolded herself.

The sun was already high and hot in the domelike sky, and Libby smiled. It was warm for spring, and wasn't it nice to look up and see clouds and mountaintops instead of tall buildings and smog?

Finally the main house came into view. It was a rambling structure of red brick, and its many windows glistened in the bright sunshine. A porch with marble steps led up to the double doors, and one of them swung open even as Libby reached out to ring the bell.

Mrs. Bradshaw, the housekeeper, stepped out and enfolded Libby in a delighted hug. A slender middle-aged woman with soft brown hair, Marion Bradshaw was as much a part of the Circle Bar B as Senator Barlowe himself. "Welcome home," she said warmly.

Libby smiled and returned the hug. "Thank you, Marion," she replied. "Is Cathy ready to go riding?"

"She's gone ahead to the stables—she'd like you to join her there."

Libby turned to go back down the steps but was stopped by the housekeeper. "Libby?"

She faced Marion, again, feeling wary.

"I don't believe it of you," said Mrs. Bradshaw firmly.

Libby was embarrassed, but there was no point in trying to pretend that she didn't get the woman's meaning. Probably everyone on the ranch was speculating about her supposed involvement with Stacey Barlowe. "Thank you."

"You stay right here on this ranch, Libby Kincaid," Marion Bradshaw rushed on, her own face flushed now. "Don't let Stacey or anybody else run you off."

That morning's unfortunate scene in Ken's kitchen was an indication of how difficult it would be to take the housekeeper's advice. Life on the Circle Bar B could become untenable if both Stacey and Jess didn't back off.

"I'll try," she said softly before stepping down off the porch and making her way around the side of that imposing but gracious house.

Prudently, the stables had been built a good distance away. During the walk, Libby wondered if she shouldn't leave the ranch after all. True, she needed to be there, but Jonathan's death had taught her that sometimes a person had to put her own desires aside for the good of other people.

But would leaving help, in the final analysis? Suppose Stacey did follow her, as he'd threatened to do? What would that do to Cathy?

The stables, like the house, were constructed of red brick. As Libby approached them, she saw Cathy leading two horses out into the sun—a dancing palomino gelding and the considerably less prepossessing pinto mare that had always been Libby's to ride.

Libby hesitated; it had been a long, long time since she'd ridden a horse, and the look in Cathy's eyes was cool. Distant. It was almost as though Libby were a troublesome stranger rather than her cousin and confidante.

As if to break the spell, Cathy lifted one foot to the stirrup of the Palomino's saddle and swung onto its back. Though she gave no sign of greeting, her eyes bade Libby to follow suit.

The elderly pinto was gracious while Libby struggled into the saddle and took the reins in slightly shaky hands. A moment later they were off across the open pastureland behind the stables, Cathy confident in the lead.

Libby jostled and jolted in the now unfamiliar saddle, and she felt a fleeting annoyance with Cathy for setting the brisk pace that she did. Again she berated herself for being angry with someone who couldn't hear.

Cathy rode faster and faster, stopping only when she reached the trees that trimmed the base of a wooded hill. There she turned in the saddle and flung a look back at the disgruntled Libby.

"You're out of practice," she said clearly, though her voice had the slurred meter of those who have not heard another person speak in years.

Libby, red-faced and damp with perspiration, was not surprised that Cathy had spoken aloud. She had learned to talk before the childhood illness that had made her deaf, and when she could be certain that no one else would overhear, she often spoke. It was a secret the two women kept religiously.

"Thanks a lot!" snapped Libby.

Deftly Cathy swung one trim blue-jeaned leg over the neck of her golden gelding and slid to the ground. The fancy bridle jingled musically as the animal bent its great head to graze on the spring grass. "We've got to talk, Libby."

Libby jumped from the pinto's back and the action engendered a piercing ache in the balls of her feet. "You've got that right!" she flared, forgetting for the moment her earlier resolve to respect Cathy's affliction. "Were you trying to get me killed?"

Watching Libby's lips, Cathy grinned. "Killed?" she echoed in her slow, toneless voice. "You're my cousin. That's important, isn't it? That we're cousins, I mean?"

Libby sighed. "Of course it's important."

"It implies a certain loyalty, don't you think?"

Libby braced herself. She'd known this confrontation was coming, of course, but that didn't mean she wanted it or was ready for it. "Yes," she said somewhat lamely.

"Are you having an affair with my husband?"

"No!"

"Do you want to?"

"What the hell kind of person do you think I am, Cathy?" shouted Libby, losing all restraint, flinging her arms out wide and startling the horses, who nickered and danced and tossed their heads.

"I'm trying to find that out," said Cathy in measured and droning words. Not once since the conversation began had her eyes left Libby's mouth.

"You already know," retorted her cousin.

For the first time, Cathy looked ashamed. But there was uncertainty in her expression, too, along with a great deal of pain. "It's no secret that Stacey wants you, Libby. I've been holding my breath ever since you decided to come back, waiting for him to leave me."

"Whatever problems you and Stacey have, Cathy, I didn't start them."

"What about all his visits to New York?"

Libby's shoulders slumped, and she allowed herself to sink to the fragrant spring-scented ground, where she sat cross-legged, her head down. With her hands she said, "You knew about the divorce, and about Jonathan. Stacey was only trying to help me through—we weren't lovers."

The lush grass moved as Cathy sat down too, facing Libby. There were tears shining in her large green eyes, and her lower lip trembled. Nervously she plied a blade of grass between her fingers.

"I'm sorry about your little boy," she said aloud.

Libby reached out, calmer now, and squeezed Cathy's hands with her own. "Thanks."

A lonely, haunted look rose in Cathy's eyes. "Stacey wanted us to have a baby," she confided.

"Why didn't you?"

Sudden color stained Cathy's lovely cheeks. "I'm deaf!" she cried defensively.

Libby released her cousin's hands to sign, "So what? Lots of deaf people have babies."

"Not me!" Cathy signaled back with spirited despair. "I wouldn't know when it cried!"

Libby spoke slowly, her hands falling back to her lap. "Cathy, there are solutions for that sort of problem. There are trained dogs, electronic devices—"

"Trained dogs!" scoffed Cathy, but there was more anguish in her face than anger. "What kind of woman needs a dog to help her raise her own baby?"

"A deaf woman," Libby answered firmly. "Besides, if you don't want a dog around, you could hire a nurse."

"No!"

Libby was taken aback. "Why not?" she signed after a few moments.

Cathy clearly had no intention of answering. She bolted to her feet and was back in the palomino's saddle before Libby could even rise from the ground.

After that, they rode without communicating at all. Knowing that things were far from settled between herself and her cousin, Libby tried to concentrate on the scenery. A shadow moved across the sun, however, and a feeling of impending disaster unfolded inside her.

JESS GLARED AT THE SCREEN of the small computer his father placed so much store in and resisted a caveman urge to strike its side with his fist.

"Here," purred a soft feminine voice, and Monica Summers, the senator's curvaceous assistant, reached down to tap the keyboard in a few strategic places.

Instantly the profit-and-loss statement Jess had been trying to call up was prominently displayed on the screen.

"How did you do that?"

Monica smiled her sultry smile and pulled up a chair to sit down beside Jess. "It's a simple matter of command," she said, and somehow the words sounded wildly suggestive.

Jess's collar seemed to tighten around his throat, but he grinned, appreciating Monica's lithe, inviting body, her profusion of gleaming brown hair, her impudent mouth and soft gray eyes. Her visits to the ranch were usually brief, but the senator's term of office was almost over, and he planned to write a long book—with which Monica was slated to help. Until that project was completed, she would be around a lot.

The fact that the senior senator did not intend to campaign for reelection didn't seem to faze her—it was common knowledge that she had a campaign of her own in mind.

Monica had made it clear, time and time again, that she was available to Jess for more than an occasional dinner date and subsequent sexual skirmish. And before Libby's return, Jess had seriously considered settling down with Monica.

He didn't love her, but she was undeniably beautiful, and the promises she made with her skillfully made-up eyes were not idle ones. In addition to that, they had a lot of ordinary things in common—similar political views, a love of the outdoors, like tastes in music and books.

Now, even with Monica sitting so close to him, her perfume calling up some rather heated memories, Jess Barlowe was patently unmoved.

A shower of anger sifted through him. He *wanted* to be moved, dammit—he wanted everything to be the way it was before Libby's return. Return? It was an invasion! He thought about the little hellion day and night, whether he wanted to or not.

"What's wrong, Jess?" Monica asked softly, perceptively, her hand resting on his shoulder. "It's more than just this computer, isn't it?"

He looked away. The sensible thing to do would be to take Monica by the hand, lead her off somewhere private and make slow, ferocious love to her. Maybe that would exorcise Libby Kincaid from his mind.

He remembered passion-weighted breasts, bared to him on a swimming dock, remembered their nipples blossoming sweetly in his mouth. Libby's breasts.

"Jess?"

He forced himself to look at Monica again. "I'm sorry," he said. "Did you say something?"

Mischief danced in her charcoal eyes. "Yes. I offered you my body."

He laughed.

Instead of laughing herself, Monica gave him a gentle, discerning look. "Mrs. Bradshaw tells me that Libby Kincaid is back," she said. "Could it be that I have some competition?"

Jess cleared his throat and diplomatically fixed his attention on the computer screen. "Show me how you made this monster cough up that profit-and-loss statement," he hedged.

"Jess." The voice was cool, insistent.

He made himself meet Monica's eyes again. "I don't know what I feel for Libby," he confessed. "She makes me mad as hell, but..."

"But," said Monica with rueful amusement, "you want her very badly, don't you?"

There was no denying that, but neither could Jess bring himself to openly admit to the curious needs that had been plaguing him since the moment he'd seen Libby again at the small airport in Kalispell.

Monica's right index finger traced the outline of his jaw, tenderly. Sensuously. "We've never agreed to be faithful to each other, Jess," she said in the silky voice that had once enthralled him. "There aren't any strings tying you to me. But that doesn't mean that I'm going to step back and let Libby Kincaid have a clear field. I want you myself.''

Jess was saved from answering by the sudden appearance of his father in the study doorway.

"Oh, Monica—there you are,'' Cleave Barlowe said warmly. ''Ready to start working on that speech now? We have to have it ready before we fly back to Washington, remember.''

Gray eyes swept Jess's face in parting. ''More than ready,'' she replied, and then she was out of her chair and walking across the study to join her employer.

Jess gave the computer an unloving look and switched it off, taking perverse pleasure in the way the little green words and numbers on the screen dissolved. ''State of the art,'' he mocked, and then stood up and strode out of the room.

The accountants would be angry, once they returned from their coffee break, but he didn't give a damn. If he didn't do something physical, he was going to go crazy.

BACK AT THE STABLES, Libby surrendered her horse to a ranch hand with relief. Already the muscles in her thighs were aching dully from the ride; by morning they would be in savage little knots.

Cathy, who probably rode almost every day, looked breezy and refreshed, and from her manner no one would have suspected that she harbored any ill feelings toward Libby. ''Let's take a swim,'' she signed, ''and then we can have lunch.''

Libby would have preferred to soak in the hot tub, but her pride wouldn't allow her to say so. Unless a limp betrayed her, she wasn't going to let Cathy know how sore a simple horseback ride had left her.

''I don't have a swimming suit,'' she said, somewhat hopefully.

''That's okay,'' Cathy replied with swift hands. ''It's an indoor pool, remember?''

''I hope you're not suggesting that we swim naked,'' Libby argued aloud.

Cathy's eyes danced. ''Why not?'' she signed impishly. ''No one would see us.''

"Are you kidding?" Libby retorted, waving one arm toward the long, wide driveway. "Look at all these cars! There are *people* in that house!"

"Are you so modest?" queried Cathy, one eyebrow arched.

"Yes!" replied Libby, ignoring the subtle sarcasm.

"Then we'll go back to your house and swim in the pond, like we used to."

Libby recalled the blatant way she'd offered herself to Jess Barlowe in that place and winced inwardly. The peaceful solace of that pond had probably been altered forever, and it was going to be some time before she could go there comfortably again. "It's spring, Cathy, not summer. We'd catch pneumonia! Besides, I think it's going to rain."

Cathy shrugged. "All right, all right. I'll borrow a car and we'll drive over and get your swimming suit, then come back here."

"Fine," Libby agreed with a sigh.

She was to regret the decision almost immediately. When she and Cathy reached the house they had both grown up in, there was a florist's truck parked out front.

On the porch stood an affable young man, a long, narrow box in his hands. "Hi, Libby," he said.

Libby recognized Phil Reynolds, who had been her classmate in high school. *Go away, Phil,* she thought, even as she smiled and greeted him.

Cathy's attention was riveted on the silver box he carried, and there was a worried expression on her face.

Phil approached, beaming. "I didn't even know you were back until we got this order this morning. Aren't you coming into town at all? We got a new high school..."

Simmonsville, a dried-up little community just beyond the south border of the Circle Bar B, hadn't even entered Libby's thoughts until she'd seen Phil Reynolds. She ignored his question and stared at the box he held out to her as if it might contain something squirmy and vile.

"Wh-who sent these?" she managed, all too conscious of the suspicious way Cathy was looking at her.

"See for yourself," Phil said brightly, and then he got back into his truck and left.

Libby took the card from beneath the red ribbon that bound the box and opened it with trembling fingers. The flowers couldn't be from Stacey, please God, they couldn't!

The card was typewritten. *Don't be stubborn, sweetness,* the message read. *Regards, Aaron.*

For a moment Libby was too relieved to be angry. "Aaron," she repeated. Then she lifted the lid from the box and saw the dozen pink rosebuds inside.

For one crazy moment she was back in Jonathan's hospital room. There had been roses there, too—along with mums and violets and carnations. Aaron and his family had sent costly bouquets and elaborate toys, but not one of them had come to visit.

Libby heard the echo of Jonathan's purposefully cheerful voice. *Daddy must be busy,* he'd said.

With a cry of fury and pain, Libby flung the roses away, and they scattered over the walk in a profusion of long-stemmed delicacy. The silver box lay with them, catching the waning sunlight.

Cathy knelt and began gathering up the discarded flowers, placing them gently back in their carton. Once or twice she glanced up at Libby's livid face in bewilderment, but she asked no questions and made no comments.

Libby turned away and bounded into the house. By the time she had found a swimming suit and come back downstairs again, Cathy was arranging the rosebuds in a cut-glass vase at the kitchen sink.

She met Libby's angry gaze and held up one hand to stay the inevitable outburst. "They're beautiful, Libby," she said in a barely audible voice. "You can't throw away something that's beautiful."

"Watch me!" snapped Libby.

Cathy stepped between her cousin and the lush bouquet. "Libby, at least let me give them to Mrs. Bradshaw," she pleaded aloud. "Please?"

Glumly Libby nodded. She supposed she should be grateful

that the roses hadn't been sent by Stacey in a fit of ardor, and they *were* too lovely to waste, even if she herself couldn't bear the sight of them.

Libby remembered the words on Aaron's card as she and Cathy drove back to the main house. *Don't be stubborn.* A tremor of dread flitted up and down her spine.

Aaron hadn't been serious when he'd threatened to come to the ranch and "persuade" her to return to New York with him, had he? She shivered.

Surely even Aaron wouldn't have the gall to do that, she tried to reassure herself. After all, he had never come to the apartment she'd taken after Jonathan's death, never so much as called. Even when the divorce had been granted, he had avoided her by sending his lawyer to court alone.

No. Aaron wouldn't actually come to the Circle Bar B. He might call, he might even send more flowers, just to antagonize her, but he wouldn't come in person. Despite his dismissal of Stacey as a "softheaded cowboy," he was afraid of him.

Cathy was drawing the car to a stop in front of the main house by the time Libby was able to recover herself. To allay the concern in her cousin's eyes, she carried the vase of pink roses into the kitchen and presented them to Mrs. Bradshaw, who was puzzled but clearly pleased.

Inside the gigantic, elegantly tiled room that housed the swimming pool and the spacious hot tub, Libby eyed the latter with longing. Thus, it was a moment before she realized that the pool was already occupied.

Jess was doing a furious racing crawl from one side of the deep end to the other, his tanned, muscular arms cutting through the blue water with a force that said he was trying to work out some fierce inner conflict. Watching him admiringly from the poolside, her slender legs dangling into the water, was a pretty dark-haired woman with beautiful gray eyes.

The woman greeted Cathy with an easy gesture of her hands, though her eyes were fixed on Libby, seeming to assess her in a thorough, if offhand, fashion.

"I'm Monica Summers," she said, as Jess, apparently oblivious of everything other than the furious course he was follow-

ing through the water, executed an impressive somersault turn
at the poolside and raced back the other way.

Monica Summers. The name was familiar to Libby, and so,
vaguely, was the perfect fashion-model face.

Of course. Monica was Senator Barlowe's chief assistant.
Libby had never actually met the woman, but she had seen her
on television newscasts and Ken had mentioned her in passing,
on occasion, over long-distance telephone.

"Hello," Libby said. "I'm—"

The gray eyes sparkled. "I know," Monica broke in
smoothly. "You're Libby Kincaid. I enjoy your cartoons very
much."

Libby felt about as sophisticated, compared to this woman,
as a Girl Scout selling cookies door-to-door. And Monica's
subtle emphasis on the word "cartoons" had made her feel
defensive.

All the same, Libby thanked her and forced herself not to
watch Jess's magnificent body moving through the bright blue
water of the pool. It didn't bother her that Jess and Monica had
been alone in this strangely sensual setting. It didn't.

Cathy had moved away, anxious for her swim.

"I'm sorry if we interrupted something," Libby said, and
hated herself instantly for betraying her interest.

Monica smiled. Clearly she had not been in swimming herself, for her expensive black swimsuit was dry, and so was her
long, lush hair. Her makeup, of course, was perfect. "There
are always interruptions," she said, and then she turned away
to take up her adoring-spectator position again, her gaze following the play of the powerful muscles in Jess's naked back.

My thighs are too fat, mourned Libby, in petulant despair.
She took a seat on a lounge far removed from Jess and his
lovely friend and tried to pretend an interest in Cathy's graceful
backstroke.

Was Jess intimate with Monica Summers? It certainly
seemed so, and Libby couldn't understand, for the life of her,
why she was so brutally surprised by the knowledge. After all,
Jess was a handsome, healthy man, well beyond the age of
handholding and fantasies-from-afar. Had she really ever be-

lieved that he had just been existing on this ranch in some sort of suspended animation?

Cathy roused her from her dismal reflection by flinging a stream of water at her with both hands. Instantly Libby was drenched and stung to an annoyance out of all proportion to the offense. Surprising even herself, she stomped over to the hot tub, flipped the switch that would make the water bubble and churn, and after hurling one scorching look at her unrepenting cousin, slid into the enormous tile-lined tub.

The heat and motion of the water were welcome balm to Libby's muscles, if not to her spirit. She had no right to care who Jess Barlowe slept with, no right at all. It wasn't as though she had ever had any claim on his affections.

Settling herself on a submerged bench, Libby tilted her head back, closed her eyes, and tried to pretend that she was alone in that massive room with its sloping glass roof, lush plants and lounges.

The fact that she was sexually attracted to Jess Barlowe was undeniable, but it was just a physical phenomenon, certainly. It would pass.

All she had to do to accelerate the process was allow herself to remember how very demeaning Aaron's lovemaking had been. And remember she did.

After Libby had caught her husband with the first of his lovers, she had moved out of his bedroom permanently, remaining in his house only because Jonathan, still at home then, had needed her so much.

Before her brutal awakening, however, she had tried hard to make the rapidly failing marriage work. Even then, bedtime had been a horror.

Libby's skin prickled as she recalled the way Aaron would ignore her for long weeks and then pounce on her with a vicious and alarming sort of determination, tearing her clothes, sometimes bruising her.

In retrospect, Libby realized that Aaron must have been trying to prove something to himself concerning his identity as a man, but at the time she had known only that sex, much touted in books and movies, was something to be feared.

Not once had Libby achieved any sort of satisfaction with Aaron—she had only endured. Now, painfully conscious of the blatantly masculine, near-naked cowboy swimming in the pool nearby, Libby wondered if lovemaking would be different with Jess.

The way that her body had blossomed beneath his seemed adequate proof that it would be different indeed, but there was always the possibility that she would be disappointed in the ultimate act. Probably she had been aroused only because Jess had taken the time to offer her at least a taste of pleasure. Aaron had never done that, never shown any sensitivity at all.

Shutting out all sight and sound, Libby mentally decried her lack of experience. If only she'd been with even one man besides Aaron, she would have had some frame of reference, some inkling of whether or not the soaring releases she'd read about really existed.

The knowledge that so many people thought she had been carrying on a torrid affair with Stacey brought a wry smile to her lips. If only they knew.

"What are you smiling about?"

The voice jolted Libby back to the here and now with a thump. Jess had joined her in the hot tub at some point; indeed, he was standing only inches away.

Startled, Libby stared at him for a moment, then looked wildly around for Cathy and the elegant Ms. Summers.

"They went in to have lunch," Jess informed her, his eyes twinkling. Beads of water sparkled in the dark down that matted his muscular chest, and his hair had been towel-rubbed into an appealing disarray.

"I'll join them," said Libby in a frantic whisper, but the simple mechanics of turning away and climbing out of the hot tub eluded her.

Smelling pleasantly of chlorine, Jess came nearer. "Don't go," he said softly. "Lunch will wait."

Anger at Cathy surged through Libby. Why had she gone off and left her here?

Jess seemed to read the question in her face, and it made

him laugh. The sound was soft—sensuously, wholly male. Overhead, spring thunder crashed in a gray sky.

Libby trembled, pressing back against the edge of the hot tub with such force that her shoulder blades ached. "Stay away from me," she breathed.

"Not on your life," he answered, and then he was so near that she could feel the hard length of his thighs against her own. The soft dark hair on his chest tickled her bare shoulders and the suddenly alive flesh above her swimsuit top. "I intend to finish what we started yesterday beside the pond."

Libby gasped as his moist lips came down to taste hers, to tame and finally part them for a tender invasion. Her hands went up, of their own accord, to rest on his hips.

He was naked. The discovery rocked Libby, made her try to twist away from him, but his kiss deepened and subdued her struggles. With his hands, he lifted her legs, draped them around the rock-hard hips she had just explored.

The imposing, heated length of his desire, now pressed intimately against her, was powerful proof that he meant to take her.

CHAPTER FIVE

LIBBY FELT AS THOUGH HER BODY had dissolved, become part of the warm, bubbling water filling the hot tub. When Jess drew back from his soft conquering of her mouth, his hands rose gently to draw down the modest top of her swimsuit, revealing the pulsing fullness of her breasts to his gaze.

It was not in Libby to protest: she was transfixed, caught up in primal responses that had no relation to good sense or even sanity. She let her head fall back, saw through the transparent ceiling that gray clouds had darkened the sky, promising a storm that wouldn't begin to rival the one brewing inside Libby herself.

Jess bent his head, nipped at one exposed, aching nipple with cautious teeth.

Libby drew in a sharp breath as a shaft of searing pleasure went through her, so powerful that she was nearly convulsed by it. A soft moan escaped her, and she tilted her head even further back, so that her breasts were still more vulnerable to the plundering of his mouth.

Inside Libby's swirling mind, a steady voice chanted a litany of logic: she was behaving in a wanton way—Jess didn't really care for her, he was only trying to prove that he could conquer her whenever he desired—this place was not private, and there was a very real danger that someone would walk in at any moment and see what was happening.

Thunder reverberated in the sky, shaking heaven and earth. And none of the arguments Libby's reason was offering had any effect on her rising need to join herself with this impossible, overbearing man feasting so brazenly on her breast.

With an unerring hand, Jess found the crux of her passion, and through the fabric of her swimsuit he stroked it to a wanting Libby had never experienced before. Then, still greedy at the nipple he was attending, he deftly worked aside the bit of cloth separating Libby's womanhood from total exposure.

She gasped as he caught the hidden nubbin between his fingers and began, rhythmically, to soothe it. Or was he tormenting it? Libby didn't know, didn't care.

Jess left her breast to nibble at her earlobe, chuckled hoarsely when the tender invasion of his fingers elicited a throaty cry of welcome.

"Go with it, Libby," he whispered. "Let it carry you high... higher..."

Libby was already soaring, sightless, mindless, conscious only of the fiery marauding of his fingers and the strange force inside her that was building toward something she had only imagined before. "Oh," she gasped as he worked this new and fierce magic. "Oh, Jess..."

Mercilessly he intensified her pleasure by whispering outrageously erotic promises, by pressing her legs wide of each other with one knee, by caressing her breast with his other hand.

A savage trembling began deep within Libby, causing her breath to quicken to a soft, lusty whine.

"Meet it, Libby," Jess urged. "Rise to meet it."

Suddenly Libby's entire being buckled in some ancient, inescapable response. The thunder in the distant skies covered her final cry of release, and she convulsed again and again, helpless in the throes of her body's savage victory.

When at last the ferocious clenching and unclenching had ceased, Libby's reason gradually returned. Forcing wide eyes to Jess's face, she saw no demand there, no mockery or revulsion. Instead, he was grinning at her, as pleased as if he'd been sated himself.

Wild embarrassment surged through Libby in the wake of her passion. She tried to avert her face, but Jess caught her chin in his hand and made her look at him.

"Don't," he said gruffly. "Don't look that way. It wasn't wrong, Libby."

His ability to read her thoughts so easily was as unsettling as the knowledge that she'd just allowed this man unconscionable liberties in a hot tub. "I suppose you think...I suppose you want..."

Jess withdrew his conquering hand, tugged her swimsuit back into place. "I think you're beautiful," he supplied, "and I want you—that's true. But for now, watching you respond like that was enough."

Libby blushed again. She was still confused by the power of her release, and she had expected Jess to demand his own satisfaction. She was stunned that he could give such fierce fulfillment and ask nothing for himself.

"You've never been with any man besides your husband, have you, Libby?"

The outrageous bluntness of that question solidified Libby's jellylike muscles, and she reached furiously for one of the towels Mrs. Bradshaw had set nearby on a low shelf. "I've been with a thousand men!" she snapped in a harsh whisper. "Why, one word from any man, and I let him...I let him..."

Jess grinned again. "You've never had a climax before," he observed.

How could he guess a thing like that? It was uncanny. Libby knew that the hot color in her face belied her sharp answer. "Of course I have! I've been married—did you think I was celibate?"

The rapid-fire hysteria of her words only served to amuse Jess, it seemed. "We both know, Libby Kincaid, that you are, for all practical intents and purposes, a virgin. You may have lain beneath that ex-husband of yours and wished to God that he would leave you alone, but until a few minutes ago you had never even guessed what it means to be a woman."

Libby wouldn't have thought it possible to be as murderously angry as she was at that moment. "Why, you arrogant, *insufferable*..."

He caught her hand at the wrist before it could make the intended contact with his face. "You haven't seen anything yet, princess," he vowed with gentle force. "When I take you to bed—and I assure you that I will—I'll prove that everything I've said is true."

While Libby herself was outraged, her traitorous body

yearned to lie in his bed, bend to his will. Having reached the edges of passion, it wanted to go beyond, into the molten core. "You egotistical bastard!" Libby hissed, breaking away from him to lift herself out of the hot tub and land on its edge with an inelegant, squishy plop, "You act as if you'd invented sex!"

"As far as you're concerned, little virgin, I did. But have no fear—I intend to deflower you at the first opportunity."

Libby stood up, wrapped her shaky, nerveless form in a towel the size of a bedsheet. "Go to hell!"

Jess rose out of the water, not the least bit self-conscious of his nakedness. The magnitude of his desire for her was all too obvious.

"The next few hours will be just that," he said, reaching for a towel of his own. Naturally, the one he selected barely covered him.

Speechless, Libby imagined the thrust of his manhood, imagined her back arching to receive him, imagined a savage renewal of the passion she had felt only minutes before.

Jess gave her an amused sidelong glance, as though he knew what she was thinking, and intoned, "Don't worry, princess. I'll court you if that's what you want. But I'll have you, too. And thoroughly."

Having made this incredible vow, he calmly walked out of the room, leaving Libby alone with a clamoring flock of strange emotions and unmet needs.

The moment Jess was gone, she stumbled to the nearest lounge chair and sank onto it, her knees too weak to support her. *Well, Kincaid,* she reflected wryly, *now you know. Satisfied?*

Libby winced at the last word. Though she might have wished otherwise, given the identity of the man involved, she was just that.

With carefully maintained dignity, Jess Barlowe strode into the shower room adjoining the pool and wrenched on one spigot. As he stepped under the biting, sleetlike spray, he gritted his teeth.

Gradually his body stopped screaming and the stubborn evidence of his passion faded. With relief, Jess dived out of the shower stall and grabbed a fresh towel.

A hoarse chuckle escaped him as he dried himself with brisk motions. Good God, if he didn't have Libby Kincaid soon, he was going to die of pneumonia. A man could stand only so many plunges into icy ponds, only so many cold showers.

A spare set of clothes—jeans and a white pullover shirt—awaited Jess in a cupboard. He donned them quickly, casting one disdainful look at the three-piece suit he had shed earlier. His circulation restored, to some degree at least, he toweled his hair and then combed it with the splayed fingers of his left hand.

A sweet anguish swept through him as he remembered the magic he had glimpsed in Libby's beautiful face during that moment of full surrender. *My father was right,* Jess thought as he pulled on socks and old, comfortable boots. *I love you, Libby Kincaid. I love you.*

Jess was not surprised to find that Libby wasn't with Cathy and Monica in the kitchen—she had probably made some excuse to get out of joining them for lunch and gone off to gather her thoughts. God knew, she had to be every bit as undone and confused as he was.

Mostly to avoid the sad speculation in Monica's eyes, Jess glanced toward the kitchen windows. They were already sheeted with rain.

A crash of thunder jolted him out of the strange inertia that had possessed him. He glanced at Cathy, saw an impish light dancing in her eyes.

"You can catch her if you hurry," she signed, cocking her head to one side and grinning at him.

Did she know what had happened in the hot tub? Some of the heat lingering in Jess's loins rose to his face as he bolted out of the room and through the rest of the house.

The station wagon, an eyesore among the other cars parked in front of the house, patently refused to start. Annoyed, Jess "borrowed" Monica's sleek green Porsche without a moment's hesitation, and his aggravation grew as he left the driveway and pulled out onto the main road.

What the hell did Libby think she was doing, walking in this rain? And why had Cathy let her go?

He found Libby near the mailboxes, slogging despondently along, soaked to the skin.

"Get in!" he barked, furious in his concern.

Libby lifted her chin and kept walking. Her turquoise shirt was plastered to her chest, revealing the outlines of her bra, and her hair hung in dripping tendrils.

"*Now!*" Jess roared through the window he had rolled down halfway.

She stopped, faced him with indigo fury sparking in her eyes. "Why?" she yelled over the combined roars of the deluge and Monica's car engine. "Is it time to teach me what it means to be a woman?"

"How the hell would I know what it means to be a woman?" he shouted back. "Get in this car!"

Libby told him to do something that was anatomically impossible and then went splashing off down the road again, ignoring the driving rain.

Rasping a swearword, Jess slipped the Porsche out of gear and wrenched the emergency brake into place. Then he shoved open the door and bounded through the downpour to catch up with Libby, grasp her by the shoulders and whirl her around to face him.

"If you don't get your backside into that car *right now,*" he bellowed, "I swear to God I'll *throw* you in!"

She assessed the Porsche. "Monica's car?"

Furious, Jess nodded. Christ, it was raining so hard that his clothes were already saturated and she was standing there talking details!

An evil smile curved Libby's lips and she stalked toward the automobile, purposely stepping in every mud puddle along the way. Jess could have sworn that she enjoyed sinking, sopping wet, onto the heretofore spotless suede seat.

"Home, James," she said smugly, folding her arms and grinding her mud-caked boots into the lush carpeting on the floorboard.

Jess had no intention of taking Libby to Ken's place, but he said nothing. Envisioning her lying in some hospital bed, wasted away by a case of rain-induced pneumonia, he ground the car savagely back into gear and gunned the engine.

When they didn't take the road Libby expected, the smug look faded from her face and she stared at Jess with wide, wary eyes. "Wait a minute..."

Jess flung an impudent grin at her and saluted with one hand. "Yes?" he drawled, deliberately baiting her.

"Where are we going?"

"My place," he answered, still angry. "It's the classic situation, isn't it? I'll insist you get out of those wet clothes, then I'll toss you one of my bathrobes and pour brandy for us both. After that, lady, I'll make mad love to you."

Libby paled, though there was a defiant light in her eyes. "On a fur rug in front of your fireplace, no doubt!"

"No doubt," Jess snapped, wondering why he found it impossible to deal with this woman in a sane and reasonable way. It would be so much simpler just to tell her straight out that he loved her, that he needed her. But he couldn't quite bring himself to do that, not just yet, and he was still mad as hell that she would walk in the pouring rain like that.

"Suppose I tell you that I don't want you to 'make mad love' to me, as you so crudely put it? Suppose I tell you that I won't give in to you until the first Tuesday after doomsday, if then, brandy and fur rugs notwithstanding?"

"The way you didn't give in in the hot tub?" he gibed, scowling.

Libby blushed. "That was different!"

"How so?"

"You...you *cornered* me, that's how."

His next words were out of his mouth before he could call them back. "I know about your ex-husband, Libby."

She winced, fixed her attention on the overworked windshield wipers. "What does he have to do with anything?"

Jess shifted to a lower gear as he reached the road leading to his house and turned onto it. "Stacey told me about the women."

The high color drained from Libby's face and she would not

look at him. She appeared ready, in fact, to thrust open the door on her side of the car and leap out. "I don't want to talk about this," she said after an interval long enough to bring them to Jess's driveway.

"Why not, Libby?" he asked, and his voice was gentle, if a bit gruff.

One tear rolled over the wet sheen on her defiant rain-polished face, and Libby's chin jutted out in a way that was familiar to him, at once maddening and appealing. "Why do you want to talk about Aaron?" she countered in low, ragged tones. "So you can sit there and feel superior?"

"You know better."

She glared at him, her bruised heart in her eyes, and Jess ached for her. She'd been through so much, and he wished that he could have taken that visible, pounding pain from inside her and borne it himself.

"I don't know better, Jess," she said quietly. "We haven't exactly been kindred spirits, you and I. For all I know, you just want to torture me. To throw all my mistakes in my face and watch me squirm."

Jess's hands tightened on the steering wheel. It took great effort to reach down and shut off the Porsche's engine. "It's cold out here," he said evenly, "and we're both wet to the skin. Let's go inside."

"You won't take me home?" Her voice was small.

He sighed. "Do you want me to?"

Libby considered, lowered her head. "No," she said after a long time.

THE INSIDE OF JESS'S HOUSE was spacious and uncluttered. There were skylights in the ceiling and the second floor appeared to be a loft of some sort. Lifting her eyes to the railing above, Libby imagined that his bed was just beyond it and blushed.

Jess seemed to be ignoring her; he was busy with newspaper and kindling at the hearth. She watched the play of the muscles in his back in weary fascination, longing to feel them beneath her hands.

The knowledge that she loved Jess Barlowe, budding in her subconscious mind since her arrival in Montana, suddenly burst into full flower. But was the feeling really new?

If Libby were to be honest with herself—and she tried to be, always—she had to admit that the chances were good that she had loved Jess for a very long time.

He turned, rose from his crouching position, a small fire blazing and crackling behind him. "How do you like my house?" he asked with a half smile.

Between her newly recognized feelings for this man and the way his jade eyes seemed to see through all her reserve to the hurt and confusion hidden beneath, Libby felt very vulnerable. Trusting in an old trick that had always worked in the past, she looked around in search of something to be angry about.

The skylights, the loft, the view of the mountains from the windows beyond his desk—all of it was appealing. Masculine. Quietly romantic.

"Perfect quarters for a wealthy and irresponsible playboy," she threw out in desperation.

Jess stiffened momentarily, but then an easy grin creased his face. "I think that was a shot, but I'm not going to fire back, Libby, so you might as well relax."

Relax? Was the man insane? Half an hour before, he had blithely brought her to climax in a hot tub, for God's sake, and now they were alone, the condition of their clothes necessitating that they risk further intimacies by stripping them off, taking showers. If they couldn't fight, what *were* they going to do?

Before Libby could think of anything to say in reply, Jess gestured toward the broad redwood stairs leading up to the loft. "The bathroom is up there," he said. "Take a shower. You'll find a robe hanging on the inside of the door." With that, he turned away to crouch before the fire again and add wood.

Because she was cold and there seemed to be no other options, Libby climbed the stairs. It wasn't until she reached the loft that her teeth began to chatter.

There she saw Jess's wide unmade bed. It was banked by a line of floor-to-ceiling windows, giving the impression that the room was open to the outdoors, and the wrinkled sheets probably still bore that subtle, clean scent that was Jess's alone...

Libby took herself in hand, wrenched her attention away from the bed. There was a glass-fronted wood-burning stove in one corner of the large room, and a long bookshelf on the other side was crammed with everything from paperback mysteries to volumes on veterinary medicine.

Libby made her way into the adjoining bathroom and kicked off her muddy boots, peeled away her jeans and shirt, her sodden underwear and socks. Goosebumps leapt out all over her body, and they weren't entirely related to the chill.

The bathtub was enormous, and like the bed, it was framed by tall uncurtained windows. Bathing here would be like bathing in the high limbs of a tree, so sweeping was the view of mountains and grassland beyond the glass.

Trembling a little, Libby knelt to turn on the polished brass spigots and fill the deep tub. The water felt good against her chilled flesh, and she was submerged to her chin before she remembered that she had meant to take a quick shower, not a lingering, dreamy bath.

Libby couldn't help drawing a psychological parallel between this tub and the larger one at the main house, where she had made such a fool of herself. Was there some mysterious significance in the fact that she'd chosen the bathtub over the double-wide shower stall on the other side of the room?

Now you're really getting crazy, Kincaid, she said to herself, settling back to soak.

Somewhere in the house, a telephone rang, was swiftly answered.

Libby relaxed in the big tub and tried to still her roiling thoughts and emotions. She would not consider what might happen later. For now, she wanted to be comforted, pampered. Deliciously warm.

She heard the click of boot heels on the stairs, though, and sat bolt upright in the water. A sense of sweet alarm raced through her system. Jess wouldn't come in, actually *come in,* would he?

Of course he would! Why would a bathroom door stop a man who would make such brazen advances in a hot tub?

With frantic eyes Libby sought the towel shelf. It was entirely too far away, and so was the heavy blue-and-white velour robe hanging on the inside of the door. She sank into the bathwater until it tickled her lower lip, squeezed her eyes shut and waited.

"Lib?"

"Wh-what?" she managed. He was just beyond that heavy wooden panel, and Libby found herself hoping...

Hoping what? That Jess would walk in, or that he would stay out? She honestly didn't know.

"That was Ken on the phone," Jess answered, making no effort to open the door. "I told him you were here and that I'd bring you home after the rain lets up."

Libby reddened, there in the privacy of that unique bathroom, imagining the thoughts that were probably going through her father's mind. "Wh-what did he say?"

Jess chuckled, and the sound was low, rich. "Let me put it this way: I don't think he's going to rush over here and defend your virtue."

Libby was at once pleased and disappointed. Wasn't a father *supposed* to protect his daughter from persuasive lechers like Jess Barlowe?

"Oh," she said, her voice sounding foolish and uncertain. "D-do you want me to hurry? S-so you can take a shower, I mean?"

"Take your time," he said offhandedly. "There's another bathroom downstairs—I can shower there."

Having imparted this conversely comforting and disenchanting information, Jess began opening and closing drawers. Seconds later, Libby again heard his footsteps on the stairs.

Despite the fact that she would have preferred to lounge in that wonderful bathtub for the rest of the day, Libby shot out of the water and raced to the towel bar. This was her chance to get dried off and dressed in something before Jess could incite her to further scandalous behavior.

She was wrapped in his blue-and-white bathrobe, the belt

securely tied, and cuddled under a knitted afghan by the time Jess joined her in the living room, looking reprehensibly handsome in fresh jeans and a green turtleneck sweater. His hair, like her own, was still damp, and there was a smile in his eyes, probably inspired by the way she was trying to burrow deeper into her corner of the couch.

"There isn't any brandy after all," he said with a helpless gesture of his hands. "Will you settle for chicken soup?"

Libby would have agreed to anything that would get Jess out of that room, even for a few minutes, and he would have to go to the kitchen for soup, wouldn't he? Unable to speak, she nodded.

She tried to concentrate on the leaping flames in the fireplace, but she could hear the soft thump of cupboard doors, the running of tapwater, the singular whir of a microwave oven. The sharp *ting* of the appliance's timer bell made her flinch.

Too soon, Jess returned, carrying two mugs full of steaming soup. He extended one to Libby and, to her eternal gratitude, settled in a chair nearby instead of on the couch beside her.

Outside, the rain came down in torrents, making a musical, pelting sound on the skylights, sliding down the windows in sheets. The fire snapped and threw out sparks, as if to mock the storm that could not reach it.

Jess took a sip of the hot soup and grinned. "This doesn't exactly fit the scenario I outlined in the car," he said, lifting his cup.

"You got everything else right," Libby quipped, referring to the bath she'd taken and the fact that she was wearing his robe. Instantly she realized how badly she'd slipped, but it was too late to call back her words, and the ironic arch of Jess's brow and the smile on his lips indicated that he wasn't going to let the comment pass.

"Everything?" he teased. "There isn't any fur rug, either."

Libby's cheekbones burned. Unable to say anything, she lowered her eyes and watched the tiny noodles colliding in her mug of soup.

"I'm sorry," Jess said softly.

She swallowed hard and met his eyes. He did look contrite,

and there was nothing threatening in his manner. Because of that, Libby dared to ask, "Do you really mean to...to make love to me?"

"Only if you want me to," he replied. "You must know that I wouldn't force you, Libby."

She sensed that he meant this and relaxed a little. Sooner or later, she was going to have to accept the fact that all men didn't behave in the callous and hurtful way that Aaron had. "You believe me now—don't you? About Stacey, I mean?"

If that off-the-wall question had surprised or nettled Jess, he gave no indication of it. He simply nodded.

Some crazy bravery, carrying her forward like a reckless tide, made Libby put aside her carefully built reserve and blurt out, "Do you think I'm a fool, Jess?"

Jess gaped at her, the mug of soup forgotten in his hands. "A fool?"

Libby lowered her eyes. "I mean...well...because of Aaron."

"Why should I think anything like that?"

Thunder exploded in the world outside the small cocoonlike one that held only Libby and Jess. "He was...he..."

"He was with other women," supplied Jess quietly. Gently.

Libby nodded, managed to look up.

"And you stayed with him." He was setting down the mug, drawing nearer. Finally he crouched before her on his haunches and took the cup from her hands to set it aside. "You couldn't leave Jonathan, Libby. I understand that. Besides, why should the fact that you stuck with the marriage have any bearing on my attitude toward you?"

"I just thought..."

"What?" prodded Jess when her sentence fell away. "What did you think, Libby?"

Tears clogged her throat. "I thought that I couldn't be very desirable if my o-own husband couldn't...wouldn't..."

Jess gave a ragged sigh. "My God, Libby, you don't think that Aaron was unfaithful because of some lack in you?"

That was exactly what she'd thought, on a subliminal level at least. Another woman, a stronger, more experienced, more alluring woman, might have been able to keep her husband happy, make him want her.

Jess's hands came to Libby's shoulders, gentle and insistent. "Lib, talk to me."

"Just how terrific could I be?" she erupted suddenly, in the anguish that would be hidden no longer. "Just how desirable? My husband needed other women because he couldn't bring himself to make love to me!"

Jess drew her close, held her as the sobs she had restrained at last broke free. "That wasn't your fault, Libby," he breathed, his hand in her hair now, soothing and strong. "Oh, sweetheart, it wasn't your fault."

"Of course it was!" she wailed into the soft green knit of his sweater, the hard strength of the shoulder beneath. "If I'd been better...if I'd known how..."

"Shhh. Baby, don't. Don't do this to yourself."

Once freed, Libby's emotions seemed impossible to check. They ran as deep and wild as any river, swirling in senseless currents and eddies, causing her pride to founder.

Jess caught her trembling hands in his, squeezed them reassuringly. "Listen to me, princess," he said. "These doubts that you're having about yourself are understandable, under the circumstances, but they're not valid. You are desirable." He paused, searched her face with tender, reproving eyes. "I can swear to that."

Libby still felt broken, and she hadn't forgotten the terrible things Aaron had said to her during their marriage—that she was cold and unresponsive, that he hadn't been impotent before he'd married her. Time and time again he had held up Jonathan as proof that he had been virile with his first wife, taken cruel pleasure in pointing out that none of his many girlfriends found him wanting.

Wrenching herself back to the less traumatic present, Libby blurted out, "Make love to me, Jess. Let me prove to myself—"

"No," he said with cold, flat finality. And then he released her hands, stood up and turned away as if in disgust.

CHAPTER SIX

"I THOUGHT YOU WANTED ME," Libby said in a small, broken voice.

Jess's broad back stiffened, and he did not turn around to face her. "I do."

"Then, why...?"

He went to the fireplace, took up a poker, stoked the blazing logs within to burn faster, hotter. "When I make love to you, Libby, it won't be because either one of us wants to prove anything."

Libby lowered her head, ashamed. As if to scold her, the wind and rain lashed at the windows and the lightning flashed, filling the room with its eerie blue-gold light. She began to cry again, this time softly, wretchedly.

And Jess came to her, lifted her easily into his arms. Without a word, he carried her up the stairs, across the storm-shadowed loft room to the bed. After pulling back the covers with one hand, he lowered her to the sheets. "Rest," he said, tucking the blankets around her.

Libby gaped at him, amazed and stricken. She couldn't help thinking that he wouldn't have tucked Monica Summers into bed this way, kissed *her* forehead as though she were some overwrought child needing a nap.

"I don't want to rest," Libby said, insulted. And her hands moved to pull the covers down.

Jess stopped her by clasping her wrists. A muscle knotted in his jaw, and his jade-green eyes flashed, their light as elemental as that of the electrical storm outside. "Don't Libby. Don't tempt me."

She *had* been tempting him—if he hadn't stopped her when he did, she would have opened the robe, wantonly displayed her breasts. Now, she was mortally embarrassed. What on earth was making her act this way?

"I'm sorry," she whispered. "I don't know what's the matter with me."

Jess sat down on the edge of the bed, his magnificent face etched in shadows, his expression unreadable. "Do we have to go into that again, princess? Nothing is wrong with you."

"But—"

Jess laid one index finger to her lips to silence her. "It would be wrong if we made love now, Libby—don't you see that? Afterward, you'd be telling yourself what a creep I was for taking advantage of you when you were so vulnerable."

His logic was unassailable. To lighten the mood, Libby summoned up a shaky grin. "Some playboy you are. Chicken soup. Patience. Have you no passion?"

He laughed. "More than I know what to do with," he said, standing up, walking away from the bed. At the top of the stairs he paused. "Am I crazy?"

Libby didn't answer. Smiling, she snuggled down under the covers—she was just a bit tired—and placidly watched the natural light show beyond the windows. Maybe later there would be fireworks of another sort.

Downstairs, Jess resisted a fundamental urge to beat his head against the wall. Libby Kincaid was up there in his bed, for God's sake, warm and lush and wanting him.

He ached to go back up the stairs and finish what they'd begun that morning in the hot tub. He couldn't, of course, because Libby was in no condition, emotionally, for that kind of heavy scene. If he did the wrong thing, said the wrong thing, she could break, and the pieces might not fit together again.

In a fit of neatness, Jess gathered up the cups of cold chicken soup and carried them into the kitchen. There he dumped their contents into the sink, rinsed them, and stacked them neatly in the dishwasher.

The task was done too quickly. What could he do? He didn't like the idea of leaving Libby alone, but he didn't dare go near her again, either. The scent of her, the soft disarray of her hair, the way her breasts seemed to draw at his mouth and the palms of his hands—all those things combined to make his grasp on reason tenuous.

Jess groaned, lifted his eyes to the ceiling and wondered if he was going to have to endure another ice-cold shower. The telephone rang, startling him, and he reached for it quickly. Libby might already be asleep, and he didn't want her to be disturbed.

"Hello?"

"Jess?" Monica's voice was calm, but there was an undercurrent of cold fury. "Did you take my car?"

He sighed, leaning back against the kitchen counter. "Yeah. Sorry. I should have called you before this, but—"

"But you were busy."

Jess flinched. Exactly what could he say to that? "Monica—"

"Never mind, Jess." She sighed the words. "I didn't have any right to say that. And if you helped yourself to my car, you must have had a good reason."

Why the hell did she have to be so reasonable? Why didn't Monica yell at him or something, so that he could get mad in good conscience and stop feeling like such an idiot? "I'm afraid the seats are a little muddy," he said.

"Muddy? Oh, yes—the rain. Was Libby okay?"

Again Jess's gaze lifted to the ceiling. Libby was not okay, thanks to him and Stacey and her charming ex-husband. But then, Monica was just making polite conversation, not asking for an in-depth account of Libby's emotional state. "She was drenched."

"So you brought her there, got her out of her wet clothes, built a fire—"

The anger Jess had wished for was suddenly there. "Monica."

She drew in a sharp breath. "All right, all right—I'm sorry. I take it our dinner date is off?"

"Yeah," Jess answered, turning the phone cord between his fingers. "I guess it is."

Monica was nothing if not persistent—probably that quality

accounted for her impressive success in political circles. "Tomorrow night?"

Jess sighed. "I don't know."

There was a short, uncomfortable silence. "We'll talk later," Monica finally said brightly. "Listen, is it okay if I send somebody over there to get my car?"

"I'll bring it to you," Jess said. It was, after stealing it, the least he could do. He'd check first, to make sure that Libby really was sleeping, and with luck, he could be back before she woke up.

"Thanks," sang Monica in parting.

Jess hung up the phone and climbed the stairs, pausing at the edge of the bedroom. He dared go no further, wanting that rumple-haired little hellion the way he did. "Libby?"

When there was no answer, Jess turned and went back down the stairs again, almost grateful that he had somewhere to go, something to do.

Monica hid her annoyance well as she inspected the muddy splotches on her car's upholstery. Overhead, the incessant rain pummeled the garage roof.

"I'm sorry," Jess said. It seemed that he was always apologizing for one thing or another lately. "My station wagon wouldn't start, and I was in a hurry..."

Monica allowed a flicker of anger to show in her gray eyes. "Right. When there is a damsel to be rescued, a knight has to grab the first available charger."

Having no answer for that, Jess shrugged. "I'll have your car cleaned," he offered when the silence grew too long, and then he turned to walk back out of the garage and down the driveway to his own car, which refused to start.

He got out and slammed the door. "Damn!" he bellowed, kicking yet another dent into the fender.

"Problems?"

Jess hadn't been aware of Ken until that moment, hadn't noticed the familiar truck parked nearby. "It would take all day to list them," he replied ruefully.

Ken grinned a typical sideways grin, and his blue eyes twinkled. He seemed oblivious of the rain pouring off the brim of his ancient hat and soaking through his denim jacket and jeans. "I think maybe my daughter might be at the top of the list. Is she all right?"

"She's…" Jess faltered, suddenly feeling like a high-school kid. "She's sleeping."

Ken laughed. "Must have been real hard to say that," he observed, "me being her daddy and all."

"It isn't…I didn't…"

Again Ken laughed. "Maybe you should," he said.

Jess was shocked—so shocked that he was speechless.

"Take my truck if you need it," Ken offered calmly, his hand coming to rest on Jess's shoulder. "I'll get a ride home from somebody here. And, Jess?"

"What?"

"Don't hurt Libby. She's had enough trouble and grief as it is."

"I know that," Jess replied, as the rain plastered his hair to his neck and forehead and made his clothes cling to his flesh in sodden, clammy patches. "I swear I won't hurt her."

"That's good enough for me," replied Libby's father, and then he pried the truck keys out of his pocket and tossed them to Jess.

"Ken…"

The foreman paused, looking back, his eyes wise and patient. How the hell was Jess going to ask this man what he had to ask, for Libby's sake?

"Spit it out, son," Ken urged. "I'm getting wet."

"Clothes—she was…Libby was caught in the rain, and she needs dry clothes."

Ken chuckled and shrugged his shoulders. "Stop at our place and get some of her things then," he said indulgently.

Jess was suddenly as confused by this man as he was by his daughter. What the hell was Ken doing, standing there taking this whole thing so calmly? Didn't it bother him, knowing what might happen when Jess got back to that house?

"See ya," said Ken in parting.

Completely confused, Jess got into Ken's truck and drove away. It wasn't until he'd gotten a set of dry clothes for Libby and reached his own house again that he understood. Ken trusted him.

Jess let his forehead rest on the truck's steering wheel and groaned. He couldn't stand another cold shower, dammit. He just couldn't.

But Ken trusted him. Libby was lying upstairs in his bed, and even if she was, by some miracle, ready to handle what was destined to happen, Jess couldn't make love to her. To do so would be to betray a man who had, in so many ways, been as much a father to him as Cleave Barlowe had.

The problem was that Jess couldn't think of Libby as a sister.

JESS SAT GLUMLY at the little table in the kitchen, making patterns in his omelet with a fork. Tiring of that, he flung Libby a beleaguered look and sneezed.

She felt a surge of tenderness. "Aren't you hungry?"

He shook his head. "Libby..."

It took all of her forbearance not to stand up, round the table, and touch Jess's forehead to see if he had a fever. "What?" she prompted softly.

"I think I should take you home."

Libby was hurt, but she smiled brightly. "Well, it *has* stopped raining," she reasoned.

"And I've got your dad's truck," added Jess.

"Um-hmm. Thanks for stopping and getting my clothes, by the way."

Outside, the wind howled and the night was dark. Jess gave the jeans and loose pink sweater he had picked up for Libby a distracted look and sneezed again. "You're welcome."

"And you, my friend, are sick."

Jess shook his head, went to the counter to pour coffee from the coffeemaker there. "Want some?" he asked, lifting the glass pot.

Libby declined. "Were you taking another shower when I got up?" she ventured cautiously. The peace between them, for all its sweet glow, was still new and fragile.

Libby would have sworn that he winced, and his face was unreadable. "I'm a clean person," he said, averting his eyes.

Libby bit the inside of her lower lip, suddenly possessed by an untimely urge to laugh. Jess had been shivering when he came out of that bathroom and unexpectedly encountered his newly awakened houseguest.

"Right," she said.

Jess sneezed again, violently. Somehow, the sound unchained Libby's amusement and she shrieked with laughter.

"What is so goddamn funny?" Jess demanded, setting his coffee cup down with an irritated thump and scowling.

"N-nothing," cried Libby.

Suddenly Jess was laughing too. He pulled Libby out of her chair and into his arms, and she deliberately pressed herself close to him, delighting in the evidence of his desire, in the scent and substance and strength of him.

She almost said that she loved him.

"You wanted my body!" she accused instead, teasing.

Jess groaned and tilted his head back, ostensibly to study the ceiling. Libby saw a muscle leap beneath his chin and wanted to kiss it, but she refrained.

"You were taking a cold shower, weren't you, Jess?"

"Yes," he admitted with a martyrly sigh. "Woman, if I die of pneumonia, it will be your fault."

"On the contrary. I've done everything but throw myself at your feet, mister, and you haven't wanted any part of me."

"Wrong." Jess grinned wickedly, touching the tip of her breast with an index finger. "I want this part..." The finger trailed away, following an erotic path. "And this part..."

It took all of Libby's courage to say the words again, after his brisk rejection earlier. "Make love to me, Jess."

"My God, Libby—"

She silenced him by laying two fingers to his lips. Remembering the words he had flung at her in the Cessna the day of her arrival, she said saucily, "If it feels good, do it."

Jess gave her a mock scowl, but his arms were around her now, holding her against him. "You were a very mean little kid," he muttered, "and now you're a mean adult. Do you know what you're doing to me, Kincaid?"

Libby moved her hips slightly, delighting in the contact and the guttural groan the motion brought from Jess. "I have some vague idea, yes."

"Your father trusts me."

"My father!" Libby stared up at him, amazed. "Is that what you've been worried about? What my father will think?"

Jess shrugged, and his eyes moved away from hers. Clearly he was embarrassed. "Yes."

Libby laughed, though she was not amused. "You're not serious!"

His eyes came back to meet hers and the expression in their green depths was nothing if not serious. "Ken is my best friend," he said.

"Shall I call him up and ask for permission? Better yet, I could drive over there and get a note!"

The taunts caused Jess to draw back a little, though their thighs and hips were still touching, still piping primitive messages one to the other. "Very funny!" he snapped, and a muscle bunched in his neck, went smooth again.

Libby was quietly furious. "You're right—it isn't funny. This is my body, Jess—mine. I'm thirty-one years old and I make my own living and I *damned well* don't need my daddy's permission to go to bed with a man!"

The green eyes were twinkling with mischief. "That's a healthy attitude if I've ever heard one," he broke in. "However, before we go up those stairs, there is one more thing I want to know. Are you using me, Libby?"

"Using you?"

"Yes. Do I really mean something to you, or would any man do?"

Libby felt as though she'd just grabbed hold of a high-voltage wire; in a few spinning seconds she was hurled from pain to rage to humiliation.

Jess held her firmly. "I see the question wasn't received in the spirit in which it was intended," he said, his eyes serious now, searching her burning, defiant face. "What I meant to ask was, are we going to be making love, Libby, or just proving that you can go the whole route and respond accordingly?"

Libby met his gaze bravely, though inside she was still

shaken and angry. "Why would I go to all this trouble, Jess, if I didn't want you? After all, I could have just stopped someone on the street and said, 'Excuse me, sir, but would you mind making love to me? I'd like to find out if I'm frigid or not.'"

Jess sighed heavily, but his hands were sliding up under the back of Libby's pink sweater, gently kneading the firm flesh there. The only sign that her sarcasm had rankled him was the almost imperceptible leaping of the pulsepoint beneath his right ear.

"I guess I'm having a little trouble understanding your sudden change of heart, Libby. For years you've hated my guts. Now, after confiding that your ex-husband put you through some kind of emotional wringer and left you feeling about as attractive as a sink drain, you want to share my bed."

Libby closed her eyes. The motion of his hands on her back was hypnotic, making it hard for her to breathe, let alone think. When she felt the catch of her bra give way, she shivered.

She should tell him that she loved him, that maybe, despite outward appearances, she'd always loved him, but she didn't dare. This was a man who had thought the worst of her at every turn, who had never missed a chance to get under her skin. Allowing him inside the fortress where her innermost emotions were stored could prove disastrous.

His hands came slowly around from her back to the aching roundness of her breasts, sliding easily, brazenly under the loosened bra.

"Answer me, Libby," he drawled, his voice a sleepy rumble.

She was dazed; his fingers came to play a searing symphony at her nipples, plying them, drawing at them. "I...I want you. I'm not trying to p-prove anything."

"Let me look at you, Libby."

Libby pulled the pink sweater off over her head, stood perfectly still as Jess dispensed with her bra and then stepped back a little way to admire her.

He outlined one blushing nipple with the tip of his finger, progressed to wreak the same havoc on the other. Then, with strong hands, he lifted Libby up onto a counter, so that her breasts were on a level with his face.

She gasped as he took languid, tentative suckle at one peak, then trailed a path with the tip of his tongue to the other, conquering it with lazy ease.

She was desperate now. "Make love to me," she whispered again in broken tones.

"Make love to me, *Jess*," he prompted, nibbling now, driving her half-wild with the need of him.

Libby swallowed hard, closed her eyes. His teeth were scraping gently at her nipple now, rousing it to obedience. "Make love to me, Jess," she repeated breathlessly.

He withdrew his mouth, cupping her in his hands, letting his thumbs do the work his lips and teeth had done before. "Open your eyes," he commanded in a hoarse rumble. "Look at me, Libby."

Dazed, her very soul spinning within her, Libby obeyed.

"Tell me," he insisted raggedly, "that you're not seeing Stacey or your misguided ex-husband. Tell me that you see *me*, Libby."

"I do, Jess."

He lifted her off the counter and into his arms, and his mouth came down on hers, cautious at first, then almost harshly demanding. Libby was electrified by the kiss, by the searching fierceness of his tongue, by the moan of need that came from somewhere deep inside him. Finally he ended the kiss, and his eyes were smiling into hers.

Feeling strangely giddy, Libby laughed. "Is this the part where you make love to me?"

"This is it," he replied, and then they were moving through the house toward the stairs. Lightning crackled and flashed above the skylights, while thunder struck a booming accompaniment.

"The earth is moving already," said Libby into the Jess-scented wool of his sweater.

Jess took the stairs two at a time. "Just wait," he replied.

In the bedroom, which was lit only by the lightning that was sundering the night sky, he set Libby on her feet. For a moment they just stood still, looking at each other. Libby felt as though she had become a part of the terrible storm that was pounding at the tall windows, and she grasped Jess's arms so that she wouldn't be blown away to the mountaintops or flung beyond the angry clouds.

"Touch me, Libby," Jess said, and somehow, even over the renewed rage of the storm, she heard him.

Cautiously she slid her hands beneath his sweater, splaying her fingers so that she could feel as much of him as possible. His chest was hard and broad and softly furred, and he groaned as she found masculine nipples and explored them.

Libby moved her hands down over his rib cage to the sides of his waist, up his warm, granite-muscled back. *I love you,* she thought, and then she bit her lower lip lest she actually say the words.

At some unspoken urging from Jess, she caught his sweater in bunched fists and drew it up over his head. Silver-blue lightning scored the sky and danced on the planes of his bare chest, his magnificent face.

Libby was drawn to him, tasting one masculine nipple with a cautious tongue, suckling the other. He moaned and tangled his fingers in her hair, pressing her close, and she knew that he was experiencing the same keen pleasure she had known.

Presently he caught her shoulders in his hands and held her at arm's length, boldly admiring her bare breasts. "Beautiful," he rasped. "So beautiful."

Libby had long been ashamed of her body, thinking it inadequate. Now, in this moment of storm and fury, she was proud of every curve and hollow, every pore and freckle. She removed her jeans and panties with graceful motions.

Jess's reaction was a low, rumbling groan, followed by a gasp of admiration. He stood still, a western Adonis, as she undid his jeans, felt the hollows of his narrow hips, the firmness of his buttocks. Within seconds he was as naked as Libby.

She caught his hands in her own, drew him toward the bed. But instead of reclining with her there, he knelt at the side, positioned Libby so that her hips rested on the edge of the mattress.

His hands moved over every part of her—her breasts, her

shoulders, her flat, smooth stomach, the insides of her trembling thighs.

"Jess..."

"Shh, it's all right."

"But..." Libby's back arched and a spasm of delight racked her as he touched the curls sheltering the core of her passion, first with his fingers, then with his lips. "Oh...wait...oh, Jess, no..."

"Yes," he said, his breath warm against her. And then he parted her and took her fully into his mouth, following the instinctive rising and falling of her hips, chuckling at the soft cry she gave.

A violent shudder went through Libby's already throbbing body, and her knees moved wide of each other, shaking, made of no solid substance.

Frantic, she found his head, tangled her fingers in his hair. "Stop," she whimpered, even as she held him fast.

Jess chuckled again and then went right on consuming her, his hands catching under her knees, lifting them higher, pressing them farther apart.

Libby was writhing now, her breath harsh and burning, her vision blurred. The storm came inside the room and swept her up, up, up, beyond the splitting skies. She cried out in wonder as she collided with the moon and bounced off, to be enfolded by a waiting sun.

When she came back inside herself, Jess was beside her on the bed, soothing her with soft words, stroking away the tears that had somehow gathered on her face.

"I've never read..." she whispered stupidly. "I didn't know..."

Jess was drawing her up, so that she lay full on the bed, naked and sated at his side. "Look it up," he teased, kissing her briefly, tenderly. "I think it would be under O."

Libby laughed, and the sound was a warm, soft contrast to the tumult of the storm. "What an ego!"

With an index finger, Jess traced her lips, her chin, the moist length of her neck. Small novas flashed and flared within her as her pulsing senses began to make new demands.

When his mouth came to her breast again, Libby arched her back and whimpered. "Jess...Jess..."

He circled the straining nipple with a warm tongue. "What, babe?"

No coherent words would come to Libby's beleaguered mind. "I don't know," she managed finally. "I don't know!"

"I do," Jess answered, and then he suckled in earnest.

Powerless under the tyranny of her own body, Libby gave herself up to sensation. It seemed that no part of her was left untouched, unconquered, or unworshiped.

When at last Jess poised himself above her, strong and fully a man, his face reflected the flashing lightning that seemed to seek them both.

"I'm Jess," he warned again in a husky whisper that betrayed his own fierce need.

Libby drew him to her with quick, fevered hands. "I know," she gasped, and then she repeated his name like some crazy litany, whispering it first, sobbing it when he thrust his searing magnificence inside her.

He moved slowly at first, and the finely sculptured planes of his face showed the cost of his restraint, the conflicting force of his need. "Libby," he pleaded. "Oh, God...Libby..."

She thrust her hips upward in an instinctive, unplanned motion that shattered Jess's containment and caused his great muscular body to convulse once and then assert its dominance in a way that was at once fierce and tender. It seemed that he sought some treasure within her, so deeply did he delve, some shimmering thing that he would perish without.

His groans rose above the sound of thunder, and as his pace accelerated and his passion was unleashed, Libby moved in rhythm with him, one with him, his.

Their bodies moved faster, agile in their quest, each glistening with the sheen of sweet exertion, each straining toward the sun that, this time, would consume them both.

The tumult flung them high, tore them asunder, fused them together again. Libby sobbed in the hot glory of her release and heard an answering cry from Jess.

They clung together, struggling for breath, for a long time

after the slow, treacherous descent had been made. Twice, on the way, Libby's body had paused to greedily claim what had been denied it before.

She was flushed, reckless in her triumph. "I did it," she exalted, her hands moving on the slackened muscles in Jess's back. "I did it...I responded..."

Instantly she felt those muscles go taut, and Jess's head shot up from its resting place in the curve where her neck and shoulder met.

"*What?*"

Libby stiffened, knowing now, too late, how grave her mistake had been. "I mean, *we* did it..." she stumbled lamely.

But Jess was wrenching himself away from her, searching for his clothes, pulling them on. "Congratulations!" he yelled.

Libby sat up, confused, wildly afraid. Dear God, was he going to walk out now? Was he going to hate her for a few thoughtless words?

"Jess, wait!" she pleaded, clutching the sheet to her chest. "Please!"

"For what, Libby?" he snapped from the top of the stairs. "Exhibit B? Is there something else you want to prove?"

"Jess!"

But he was storming down the stairs, silent in his rage, bent on escaping her.

"Jess!" Libby cried out again in fear, tears pouring down her face, her hands aching where they grasped the covers.

The only answer was the slamming of the front door.

CHAPTER SEVEN

KEN KINCAID LOOKED UP from the cards in his hand as the lights flickered, went out, came on again. Damn, this was a hell of a storm—if the rain didn't let up soon, the creeks would overflow and they'd have range calves drowning right and left.

Across the table, Cleave Barlowe laid down his own hand of cards. "Quite a storm, eh?" he asked companionably. "Jess bring your truck back yet?"

"I don't need it," said Ken, still feeling uneasy.

Lightning creased the sky beyond the kitchen window, and thunder shook the old house on its sturdy foundations. Cleave grinned. "He's with Libby, then?"

"Yup," said Ken, smiling himself.

"Think they know the sky's turning itself inside out?"

There was an easing in Ken; he laughed outright. "Doubt it," he replied, looking at his cards again.

For a while the two men played the two-handed poker they had enjoyed for years, but it did seem that luck wasn't running with either one of them. Finally they gave up the effort and Cleave went home.

With his old friend gone, Ken felt apprehensive again. He went around the house making sure all the windows were closed against the rain, and wondered why one storm should bother him that way, when he'd seen a thousand and never found them anything more than a nuisance.

He was about to shut off the lamp in the front room when he saw the headlights of his own truck swing into the driveway. Seconds later, there was an anxious knock at the door.

"Jess?" Ken marveled, staring at the haggard, rain-drenched man standing on the front porch. "What the hell...?"

Jess looked as though he'd just taken a first-rate gut punch. "Could I come in?"

"That's a stupid question," retorted Ken, stepping back to admit his unexpected and obviously distraught visitor. "Is Libby okay?"

Jess's haunted eyes wouldn't quite link up with Ken's. "She's fine," he said, his hands wedged into the pockets of his jeans, his hair and sweater dripping rainwater.

Ken arched an eyebrow. "What'd you do, anyway—ride on the running board of that truck and steer from outside?"

Jess didn't answer; he didn't seem to realize that he was wet to the skin. There was a distracted look about him that made Ken ache inside.

In silence Ken led the way into the kitchen, poured a dose of straight whiskey into a mug, added strong coffee.

"You look like you've been dragged backward through a knothole," he observed when Jess was settled at the table. "What happened?"

Jess closed his hands around the mug. "I'm in love with your daughter," he said after a long time.

Ken sat down, allowed himself a cautious grin. "If you drove over here in this rain just to tell me that, friend, you got wet for nothing."

"You knew?" Jess seemed honestly surprised.

"Everybody knew. Except maybe you and Libby."

Jess downed the coffee and the potent whiskey almost in a single gulp. There was a struggle going on in his face, as though he might be fighting hard to hold himself together.

Ken rose to put more coffee into Jess's mug, along with a lot more whiskey. If ever a man needed a drink, this one did.

"Maybe you'd better put on some dry clothes," the older man ventured.

Jess only shook his head.

Ken sat back in his chair and waited. When Jess was ready to talk, he would. There was, Ken had learned, no sense in pushing before that point was reached.

"Libby's beautiful, you know," Jess remarked presently, as he started on his third drink.

Ken smiled. "Yeah. I've noticed."

Simple and ordinary though they were, the words triggered

some kind of emotional reaction in Jess, broke down the barriers he had been maintaining so carefully. His face crumbled, he lowered his head to his arms, and he cried. The sobs were deep and dry and ragged.

Hurting because Jess hurt, Ken waited.

Soon enough, his patience was rewarded. Jess began to talk, brokenly at first, and then with stone-cold reason.

Ken didn't react openly to anything he said; much of what Jess told him about Libby's marriage to Aaron Strand came as no real surprise. He was wounded, all the same, for his daughter and for the devastated young man sitting across the table from him.

The level of whiskey in Ken's bottle went down as the hour grew later. Finally, when Jess was so drunk that his words started getting all tangled up with each other, Ken half led, half carried him up the stairs to Libby's room.

In the hallway, he paused, reflecting. Life was a hell of a thing, he decided. Here was Jess, sleeping fitfully in Libby's bed, all alone. And just up the hill, chances were, Libby was tossing and turning in Jess's bed, just as lonely.

Not for the first time, Ken Kincaid felt a profound desire to get them both by the hair and knock their heads together.

LIBBY CRIED until far into the night and then, exhausted, she slept. When she awakened, shocked to find herself in Jess Barlowe's bed, she saw that the world beyond the windows had been washed to a clean sparkle.

The world inside her seemed tawdry by comparison.

Her face feeling achy and swollen, Libby got out of bed, stumbled across the room to the bathroom. Jess was nowhere in the house; she would have sensed it if he were.

As Libby filled the tub with hot water, she wondered whether she was relieved that he wasn't close by, or disappointed. A little of both, she concluded as she slid into her bath and sat there in miserable reverie.

Facing Jess now would have been quite beyond her. Why, why had she said such a foolish thing, when she might have known how Jess would react? On the other hand, why had *he* made such a big deal out of a relatively innocuous remark?

More confused than ever, Libby finished her bath and climbed out to dry herself with a towel. In short order she was dressed and her hair was combed. Because she had no tooth-brush—Jess had forgotten that when he picked up her things—she had to be content with rinsing her mouth.

Downstairs, Libby stood staring at the telephone, willing her-self to call her father and confess that she needed a ride home. Pride wouldn't allow that, however, and she had made up her mind to walk the distance when she heard a familiar engine outside, the slam of a truck door.

Jess was back, she thought wildly. Where had he been all night? With Monica? What would she say to him?

The questions were pointless, for when Libby forced herself to go to the front door and open it, she saw her father striding up the walk, not Jess.

Fresh embarrassment stained Libby's cheeks, though there was no condemnation in Ken's weathered face, no anger in his understanding eyes. "Ride home?" he said.

Unable to speak, Libby only nodded.

"Pretty bad night?" he ventured in his concise way when they were both settled in the truck and driving away.

"Dismal," replied Libby, fixing her eyes on the red Hereford cattle grazing in the green, rain-washed distance.

"Jess isn't in very good shape either," commented Ken after an interval.

Libby's eyes were instantly trained on her father's profile. "You've seen him?"

"Seen him?" Ken laughed gruffly. "I poured him into bed at three this morning."

"He was drunk?" Libby was amazed.

"He had a nip or two."

"How is he now?"

Ken glanced at her, turned his eyes back to the rutted, wind-ing country road ahead. "Jess is hurting," he said, and there was a finality in his tone that kept Libby from asking so much as one more question.

Jess is hurting. What the devil did that mean? Was he hung over? Had the night been as miserable for him as it had been for her?

Presently the truck came to a stop in front of the big Victorian house that had been "home" to Libby for as long as she could remember. Ken made no move to shut off the engine, and she got out without saying good-bye. For all her brave words of the night before, about not needing her father's approval, she felt estranged from him now, subdued.

After forcing down a glass of orange juice and a slice of toast in the kitchen, Libby went into the studio Cathy and her father had improvised for her and did her best to work. Even during the worst days in New York, she had been able to find solace in the mechanics of drawing her cartoon strip, forgetting her own troubles to create comical dilemmas for Liberated Lizzie.

Today was different.

The panels Libby sketched were awkward, requiring too many erasures, and even if she had been able to get the drawings right, she couldn't have come up with a funny thought for the life of her.

At midmorning, Libby decided that her career was over and paced from one end of the studio to the other, haunted by thoughts of the night before.

Jess had made it clear, in his kitchen, that he didn't want to make love just to let Libby prove that she was "normal." And what had she done? She'd *gloated.*

Shame ached in Libby's cheeks as she walked. *I did it,* she'd crowed, as though she were Edison and the first electric light had just been lit. God, how could she have been so stupid? So insensitive?

"You did have a little help, you know," she scolded herself out loud. And then she covered her face with both hands and cried. It had been partly Jess's fault, that scene—he had definitely overreacted, and on top of that, he had been unreasonable. He had stormed out without giving Libby a chance to make things right.

Still, it was all too easy to imagine how he'd felt. Used. And the truth was that, without intending to, Libby had used him.

Small, strong hands were suddenly pulling Libby's hands away from her face. Through the blur, she saw Cathy watching her, puzzled and sad.

"What's wrong?" her cousin asked. "Please, Libby, tell me what's wrong."

"Everything!" wailed Libby, who was beyond trying to maintain her dignity now.

Gently Cathy drew her close, hugged her. For a moment they were two motherless little girls again, clinging to each other because there were some pains that even Ken, with his gruff, unswerving devotion, couldn't ease.

The embrace was comforting, and after a minute or two Libby recovered enough to step back and offer Cathy a shaky smile. "I've missed you so much, Cathy," she said.

"Don't get sloppy," teased Cathy, using her face to give the toneless words expression.

Libby laughed. "What are you doing today, besides being one of the idle rich?"

Cathy tilted her head to one side. "Did you really stay with Jess last night?" she asked with swift hands.

"Aren't we blunt today?" Libby shot back, both speaking and signing. "I suppose the whole ranch is talking about it!"

Cathy nodded.

"Damn!"

"Then it's true!" exalted Cathy aloud, her eyes sparkling.

Some of Libby's earlier remorse drained away, pushed aside by feelings of anger and betrayal. "Has Jess been bragging?" she demanded, her hands on her hips, her indignation warm and thick in her throat.

"He isn't the type to do that," Cathy answered in slow, carefully formed words, "and you know it."

Libby wasn't so certain—Jess had been very angry, and his pride had been stung. Besides, the only other person who had known was Ken, and he was notoriously tight-lipped when it came to other people's business. "Who told you?" she persisted, narrowing her eyes.

"Nobody had to," Cathy answered aloud. "I was down at the stables, saddling Banjo, and one of the range crews was there—ten or twelve men, I guess. Anyway, there was a fight out front—Jess punched out one of the cowboys."

Libby could only gape.

Cathy gave the story a stirring finale. "I think Jess would have killed that guy if Ken hadn't hauled him off."

Libby found her voice. "Was Jess hurt? Cathy, did you see if he was hurt?"

Cathy grinned at her cousin's undisguised concern. "Not a scratch. He got into an argument with Ken and left."

Libby felt a strong need to find her father and ask him exactly what had happened, but she knew that the effort would be wasted. Even if she could find Ken, which was unlikely considering the size of the ranch and all the places he could be, he wouldn't explain.

Cathy was studying the messy piece of drawing paper affixed to the art board. "You're not going to work?" she signed.

"I gave up," Libby confessed. "I couldn't keep my mind on it."

"After a night with Jess Barlowe, who could?"

Libby suddenly felt challenged, defensive. She even thought that, perhaps, there was more to the deep closeness between Jess and Cathy than she had guessed. "What do you know about spending the night with Jess?" she snapped before she could stop herself.

Cathy rolled her beautiful green eyes. "*Nothing*. For better or worse, and mostly it's been better, I'm married to Jess's brother—remember?"

Libby swallowed, feeling foolish. "Where is Stacey, anyway?" she asked, more to make conversation than because she wanted to know.

The question brought a shadow of sadness to Cathy's face. "He's away on one of his business trips."

Libby sat down on her art stool, folded her hands. "Maybe you should have gone with him, Cathy. You used to do that a lot, didn't you? Maybe if you two could be alone...talk..."

The air suddenly crackled with Cathy's anger and hurt. "*He* talks!" she raged aloud. "I just move my hands!"

Libby spoke softly, gently. "You could talk to Stacey, Cathy—really talk, the way you do with me."

"No."

"Why not?"

"I know I sound like a record playing on the wrong speed, that's why!"

"Even if that were so, would it matter?" signed Libby, frowning. "Stacey knew you were deaf before he married you, for heaven's sake."

Cathy's head went down. "He must have felt sorry for me or something."

Instantly Libby was off her stool, gripping Cathy's shoulders in firm, angry hands. "He loves you!"

Tears misted the emerald-green eyes and Cathy's lower lip trembled. "No doubt that's why he intends to divorce me and marry you, Libby."

"No," insisted Libby, giving her cousin a slight shake. "No, that isn't true. I think Stacey is confused, Cathy. Upset. Maybe it's this thing about your not wanting to have a baby. Or maybe he feels that you don't need him, you're so independent."

"Independent? Don't look now, Libby Kincaid, but *you're* the independent one! You have a career…you can hear—"

"Will you stop feeling sorry for yourself, dammit!" Libby almost screamed. "I'm so tired of hearing how you suffer! For God's sake, stop whining and fight for the man you love!"

Cathy broke free of Libby's grasp, furious, tears pouring down her face. "It's too late!" she cried. "You're here now, and it's too late!"

Libby sighed, stepped back, stricken by her own outburst and by Cathy's, too. "You're forgetting one thing," she reasoned quietly. "I'm not in love with Stacey. And it would take two of us to start anything, wouldn't it?"

Cathy went to the windows and stared out at the pond, her chin high. Knowing that her cousin needed this interval to restore her dignity and assemble her thoughts, Libby did not approach her.

Finally Cathy sniffled and turned back to offer a shaky smile. "I didn't come over here to fight with you," she said clearly. "I'm going to Kalispell, and I wanted to know if you would like to come with me."

Libby agreed readily, and after changing her clothes and leaving a quick note for Ken, she joined Cathy in the shiny blue Ferrari.

The ride to Kalispell was a fairly long one, and by the time Cathy and Libby reached the small city, they had reestablished their old, easy relationship.

They spent the day shopping, had lunch in a rustic steak house bearing the Circle Bar B brand, and then started home again.

"Are you really going to give that to Jess?" Cathy asked, her eyes twinkling when she cast a look at the bag in Libby's lap.

"I may lose my courage." Libby frowned, wondering what had possessed her to buy a T-shirt with such an outlandish saying printed on it. She supposed she'd hoped that the gesture would penetrate the barrier between herself and Jess, enabling them to talk.

"Take my advice," said Cathy, guiding the powerful car off the highway and onto the road that led to the heart of the ranch. "Give him the shirt."

"Maybe," said Libby, looking off into the sweeping, endless blue sky. A small airplane was making a graceful descent toward the Circle Bar B landing strip.

"Who do you suppose that is?" Libby asked, catching Cathy's attention with a touch on her arm.

The question was a mistake. Cathy, who had not, of course, heard the plane's engine, scanned the sky and saw it. "Why don't we find out?"

Libby scrunched down in her seat, sorry that she had pointed out the airplane now. Suppose Stacey was aboard, returning from his business trip, and there was another uncomfortable scene at the airstrip? Suppose it was Jess, and he either yelled at Libby or, worse yet, pretended that she wasn't there?

"I'd rather go home," she muttered.

But Cathy's course was set, and the Ferrari bumped and jostled over the road to the landing strip as though it were a pickup truck.

The plane came to a smooth stop as Cathy parked at one side of the road and got out of the car, shading her eyes with one hand, watching. Libby remained in her seat.

She had, it seemed, imagined only part of the possible scenario. The pilot was Jess, and his passenger was a wan, tight-lipped Stacey.

"Oh, God," said Libby, sinking even further into the car seat. She would have kept her face hidden in her hand forever, probably, if it hadn't been for the crisp, insistent tap at her window.

Having no other choice, she rolled the glass down and squinted into Jess Barlowe's unreadable, hard-lined face. "Come with me," he said flatly.

Libby looked through the Ferrari's windshield, saw Stacey and Cathy standing nearby, a disturbing distance between them. Cathy was glaring angrily into Stacey's face, and Stacey was casting determined looks in Libby's direction.

"They need some time alone," Jess said, his eyes linking fiercely, warningly, with Libby's as he opened the car door for her.

Anxious not to make an obviously unpleasant situation any worse, Libby gathered up her bags and her purse and got out of the car, following along behind Jess's long strides. The station wagon, which she hadn't noticed before, was parked close by.

Without looking back at Stacey and Cathy, Libby slid gratefully into the dusty front seat and closed her eyes. Not until the car was moving did she open them, and even then she couldn't quite bring herself to look at the man behind the wheel.

"That was touching," he said in a vicious rasp.

Libby stiffened in the seat, staring at Jess's rock-hard profile now. "What did you say?"

The powerful shoulders moved in an annoying shrug. "Your wanting to meet Stacey on his triumphant return."

It took Libby a moment to absorb what he was implying. When she had, she slammed him with the paper bag that contained the T-shirt she'd bought for him in Kalispell and hissed, "You bastard! I didn't know Stacey was going to be on that plane, and if I had, I certainly wouldn't have been there at all!"

"Sure," he drawled, and even though he was grinning and looking straight ahead at the road, there was contempt in his tone and a muscle pulsing at the base of his jaw.

Libby felt tears of frustration rise in her eyes. "I thought you believed me," she said.

"I thought I did too," Jess retorted with acid amusement. "But that was before you showed up at the landing strip at such an opportune moment."

"It was Cathy's idea to meet the plane!"

"Right."

The paper bag crackled as Libby lifted it, prepared to swing.

"Do that again and I'll stop this car and raise blisters on your backside," Jess warned, without so much as looking in her direction.

Libby lowered the bag back to her lap, swallowed miserably, and turned her attention to the road. She did not believe Jess's threat for one moment, but she felt childish for trying to hit him with the bag. "Cathy told me there was a fight at the stables this morning," she dared after a long time. "What happened?"

Another shrug, as insolent as the first, preceded his reply. "One of Ken's men said something I didn't like."

"Like what?"

"Like didn't it bother me to sleep with my brother's mistress."

Libby winced, sorry for pressing the point. "Oh, God," she said, and she was suddenly so tired, so broken, and so frustrated that she couldn't hold back her tears anymore. She covered her face with both hands and turned her head as far away from Jess as she could, but the effort was useless.

Jess stopped the station wagon at the side of the road, turned Libby easily toward him. Through a blur, she saw the Ferrari race past.

"Let go of me!"

Jess not only didn't let go, he pulled her close. "I'm sorry," he muttered into her hair. "God, Libby, I don't know what comes over me, what makes me say things to hurt you."

"Garden-variety hatred!" sniffled Libby, who was already forgiving him even though it was against her better judgment.

He chuckled. "No. I couldn't ever hate you, Libby."

She looked up at him, confused and hopeful. Before she could think of anything to say, however, there was a loud *pop* from beneath the hood of the station wagon, followed by a sizzle and clouds of steam.

"Goddammit!" rasped Jess.

Libby laughed, drunk on the scent of him, the closeness of him, the crazy paradox of him. "This crate doesn't exactly fit your image, you know," she taunted. "Why don't you get yourself a decent car?"

He turned from glowering at the hood of the station wagon to smile down into her face. "If I do, Kincaid, will you let me make love to you in the back seat?"

She shoved at his immovable chest with both hands, laughing again. "No, no, a thousand times no!"

Jess nibbled at her jawline, at the lobe of her ear, chuckled huskily as she tensed. "How many times no?"

"Maybe," said Libby.

Just when she thought she would surely go crazy, Jess drew back from his brazen pursuits and smiled lazily. "It is time I got a new car," he conceded, with an evil light glistening in his jade eyes. "Will you come to Kalispell and help me pick it out, Libby?"

A thrill skittered through Libby's body and flamed in her face. "I was just there," she protested, clutching at straws. "It shouldn't..."—Jess bent, nipped at the side of her neck with gentle teeth—"take long. A couple of days at the most."

"A couple of days!"

"And nights." Jess's lips were scorching their way across the tender hollow of her throat. "Think about it, Lib. Just you and me. No Stacey. No Cathy. No problems."

Libby shivered as a knowledgeable hand closed over one of

her breasts, urging, reawakening. "No p-problems?" she echoed.

Jess undid the top button of her blouse.

Libby's breath caught in her throat; she felt heat billowing up inside her, foaming out, just as it was foaming out of the station wagon's radiator. "Wh-where would we s-stay?"

Another button came undone.

Jess chuckled, his mouth on Libby's collarbone now, tasting it, doing nothing to cool the heat that was pounding within her. "How about"—the third button gave way, and Libby's bra was displaced by a gentle hand—"one of those motels...with the...vibrating beds?"

"Tacky," gasped Libby, and her eyes closed languidly and her head fell back as Jess stroked the nipple he'd just found to pebble-hard response.

"My condo, then," he said, and his lips were sliding down from her collarbone, soft, soft, over the upper rounding of her bare breast.

Libby gasped and arched her back as his lips claimed the distended, hurting peak. "Jess...oh, God...this is a p-public road!"

"Umm," Jess said, lapping at her now with the tip of his tongue. "Will you go with me, Libby?"

Wild need went through her as he stroked the insides of her thighs, forcing her blue-jeaned legs apart. And all the while he plied her nipple into a panic of need. "Yes!" she gasped finally.

Jess undid the snap of her jeans, slid his hand inside, beneath the scanty lace of her panties.

"Damn you," Libby whispered hoarsely, "s-stop that! I said I'd go—"

He told her what else she was about to do. And one glorious, soul-scoring minute later, she did.

Red in the face, still breathing heavily, Libby closed her jeans, tugged her bra back into place, buttoned her blouse. God, what if someone had come along and seen her letting Jess...letting him play with her like that?

All during the ride home, she mentally rehearsed the blistering diatribe he deserved to hear. He could just go to Kalispell by *himself,* she would tell him. If he thought for one damned minute that he was going to take her to his condo and make love to her, he was sadly mistaken, she would say.

"Be ready in half an hour," Jess told her at her father's front door.

"Okay," Libby replied.

AFTER LANDING THE CESSNA in Kalispell and making arrangements to rent a car, which turned out to be a temperamental cousin to Jess's station wagon, they drove through the small city to an isolated tree-dense property beyond. There were at least a million stars in the sky, and as the modest car rattled over a narrow wooden bridge spanning a creek, Libby couldn't help giving in a little to the romance of it all.

Beyond the bridge, there were more trees—towering ponderosa pines, whispering, shiny-leaved birches. They stopped in the driveway of a condominium that stood apart from several others. Jess got out of the car, came around to open Libby's door for her.

"Let's get rid of the suitcases and go out for something to eat," he said.

Libby's stomach rumbled inelegantly, and Jess laughed as he caught her hand in his and drew her up the darkened walk to the front door of the condominium. "That shoots my plans for a little fun before dinner," he teased.

"There's always after," replied Libby, lifting her chin.

CHAPTER EIGHT

THE INSIDE OF THE CONDOMINIUM was amazingly like Jess's house on the ranch. There was a loft, for instance, this one accessible by both stairs and, of all things, a built-in ladder. Too, the general layout of the rooms was much the same.

The exceptions were that the floors were carpeted rather than bare oak, and the entire roof was made of heavy glass. *When we make love here, I'll be able to look up and see the stars,* Libby mused.

"Like it?" Jess asked, setting the suitcases down and watching her with discerning, mirthful green eyes.

Libby was uncomfortable again, doubting the wisdom of coming here now that she was faced with the realities of the situation. "Is this where you bring all your conquests?"

Jess smiled, shrugged.

"Well?" prodded Libby, annoyed because he hadn't even had the common decency to offer a denial.

He sat down on the stone ledge fronting the fireplace, wrapped his hands around one knee. "The place does happen to be something of a love nest, as a matter of fact."

Libby was stung. Dammit, how unchivalrous could one man be? "Oh," she said loftily.

"It's my father's place," Jess said, clearly delighting in her obvious curiosity and the look of relief she couldn't quite hide.

"Your father's?"

Jess grinned. "He entertains his mistress here, from time to time. In his position, he has to be discreet."

Libby was gaping now, trying to imagine the sedate, dignified Senator Barlowe cavorting with a woman beneath slanted glass roofs, climbing ladders to star-dappled lofts.

Jess's amused gaze had strayed to the ladder. "It probably

puts him in mind of the good old days—climbing into the hay-loft, and all that.''

Libby blushed. She was still quite disturbed by that ladder, among other things. ''You did ask the senator's permission to come here, didn't you?''

Jess seemed to know that she had visions of Cleave Barlowe carrying some laughing woman over the threshold and finding the place already occupied. ''Yes,'' he assured her in a teasing tone, rising and coming toward her. ''I said, 'Mind if I take Libby to your condo, dear old dad, and take her to bed?' And he said—''

''Jess!'' Libby howled, in protest.

He laughed, caught her elbows in his hands, kissed her play-fully, his lips sampling hers, tugging at them in soft entreaty. ''My father is in Washington,'' he said. ''Stop worrying.''

Libby pulled back, her face hot, her mind spinning. ''I'm hungry!''

''Umm,'' replied Jess, ''so am I.''

Why did she feel like a sixteen-year-old on the verge of big trouble? ''Please...let's go now.''

Jess sighed.

They went, but they were back, arms burdened with cartons of Chinese food, in less than half an hour.

While Jess set the boxes out on the coffee table, Libby went to the kitchen for plates and silverware. Scribbled on a black-board near the sink, she saw the surprising words: ''Thanks, Ken. See you next week. B.''

A soft chuckle simmered up into Libby's throat and emerged as a giggle. Could it be that her father, her serious, hardworking father, had a ladyfriend who visited him here in this romantic hideaway? Tilting her head to one side, she considered, grinned again. ''Naaaah!''

But Libby's grin wouldn't fade as she carried plates, forks, spoons and paper napkins back into the living room.

''What's so funny?'' Jess asked, trying to hide the hunk of sweet-and-sour chicken he had just purloined from one of the steaming cartons.

''Nothing,'' said Libby, catching his hand and raising it to his mouth. Sheepishly he popped the tidbit of chicken onto his tongue and chewed.

"You lie," Jess replied, "but I'm too hungry to press the point."

While they ate, Libby tried to envision what sort of woman her father would be drawn to—tall, short? Quiet, talkative?

"You're mulling over more than the chow mein," accused Jess presently in a good-natured voice. "Tell me, what's going on in that gifted little head?"

Libby shrugged. "Romance."

He grinned. "That's what I like to hear."

But Libby was thinking seriously, following her thoughts through new channels. In all the years since her mother's death, just before Cathy had come to live on the ranch, she had never imagined Ken Kincaid caring about another woman. "It isn't as though he's old," she muttered, "or unattractive."

Jess set down his plate with a mockingly forceful thump. "That does it. Who are you talking about, Kincaid?" he demanded archly, his wonderful mouth twitching in the effort to suppress a grin.

She perused him with lofty disdain. "Am I correct in assuming that you are jealous?"

"Jealous as hell," came the immediate and not-so-jovial response.

Libby laughed, laid a hand on his knee. "If you must know, I was thinking about my father. I've always kept him in this neat little cubicle in my mind, marked 'Dad.' If you can believe it, it has just now occurred to me that he's a man, with a life, and maybe even a love, of his own."

Mirth danced in Jess's jade eyes, but if he knew anything about Ken's personal life, he clearly wasn't going to speak of it. "Pass the eggroll," he said diplomatically.

When the meal was over, Libby's reflections began to shift to matters nearer the situation at hand.

"I don't know what I'm doing here," she said pensively as she and Jess cleared the coffee table and started toward the kitchen with the debris. "I must be out of my mind."

Jess dropped the cartons and the crumpled napkins into the

trash compactor. "Thanks a lot," he said, watching her attentively as she rinsed the plates and silverware and put them into the dishwasher.

Wearing tailored gray slacks and a lightweight teal-blue sweater, he was devastatingly attractive. Still, the look Libby gave him was a serious, questioning one. "What is it with us, Jess? What makes us behave the way we do? One minute, we're yelling at each other, or not speaking at all, and the next we're alone in a place like this."

"Chemistry?"

Libby laughed ruefully. "More like voodoo. So what kind of car are you planning to buy?"

Jess drew her to him; his fingertips were butterfly-light on the small of her back. "Car?" he echoed, as though the word were foreign.

There was a soft, quivering ache in one corner of Libby's heart. Why couldn't things always be like this between them? Why did they have to wrangle so fiercely before achieving this quiet accord? "Stop teasing me," she said softly. "We did come here to buy a car, you know."

Jess's hands pulled her blouse up and out of her slacks, made slow-moving, sensuous circles on her bare back. "Yes," he said in a throaty rumble. "A car. But there are lots of different kinds of cars, aren't there, Libby? And a decision like this can't be made in haste."

Libby closed her eyes, almost hypnotized by the slow, languid meter of his words, the depth of his voice. "N-no," she agreed.

"Definitely not," he said, his mouth almost upon hers. "It could take two—or three—days to decide."

"Ummm," agreed Libby, slipping deeper and deeper under his spell.

Jess had pressed her back against a counter, and his body formed an impassable barricade, leaning, hard and fragrant, into hers. He was tracing the length of her neck with soft, searing lips, tasting the hollow beneath her ear.

Finally he kissed her, first with tenderness, then with fervor, his tongue seeking and being granted sweet entry. This prelim-

inary joining made Libby's whole entity pulse with an awareness of the primitive differences between his body and her own.
Where she was soft and yielding, he was fiercely hard. Her
nipples pouted into tiny peaks, crying out for his attention.

Seeming to sense that, Jess unbuttoned her blouse with deft,
brazen fingers that felt warm against her skin. He opened the
front catch on her bra, admired the pink-tipped lushness that
seemed to grow richer and rounder under his gaze.

Idly he bent to kiss one peak into ferocious submission, and
Libby groaned, her head falling back. Etched against the clear
roof, she saw the long needles of ponderosa pines splintering
the spring moonlight into shards of silver.

After almost a minute of pleasure so keen that Libby was
certain she couldn't bear it, Jess turned to the other breast,
kissing, suckling, nipping softly with his teeth. And all the
while, he worked the opposite nipple skillfully with his fingers,
putting it through delicious paces.

Libby was almost mindless by the time she felt the snap and
zipper of her jeans give way, and her hands were still tangled
in his dark hair as he knelt. Down came the jeans, her panties
with them.

She could manage no more than a throaty gasp as his hands
stroked the smooth skin of her thighs, the V of curls at their
junction. She felt his breath there, warm, promising to cherish.

Libby trembled as he sought entrance with a questioning
kiss, unveiled her with fingers that would not await permission.

As his tongue first touched the tenderness that had been hidden, his hands came to Libby's hips, pressing her down onto
this fiery, inescapable glory. Only when she pleaded did he tug
her fully into his mouth and partake of her.

Jess enjoyed Libby at his leisure, demanding her essence,
showing no mercy even when she cried out and shuddered upon
him in a final, soaring triumph. When her own chants of passion had ceased, she was conscious of his.

Jess still knelt before her, his every touch saying that he was
worshiping, but there was sweet mastery in his manner, too.
After one kiss of farewell, he gently drew her jeans and panties
back into place and stood.

Libby stared at him, amazed at his power over her. He smiled at her wonder, though there was a spark of that same emotion deep in his eyes, and then lifted her off her feet and into his arms.

Say "I love you," Libby thought with prayerful fervor.

"I need you," he said instead.

And, for the moment, it was enough.

STARS PEEKED THROUGH the endlessly varied patterns the fallen pine needles made on the glass roof, as if to see and assess the glory that glowed beneath. Libby preened under their celestial jealousy and cuddled closer to Jess's hard, sheet-entangled frame.

"Why didn't you ever marry, Jess?" she asked, tracing a soft path across his chest with her fingers.

The mattress shifted as he moved to put one arm around Libby and draw her nearer still. "I don't know. It always seemed that marriage could wait."

"Didn't you even come close?"

Jess sighed, his fingers moving idly in her hair. "A couple of times I seriously considered it, yes. I guess it bothered me, subliminally, that I was looking these women over as though they were livestock or something. This one would have beautiful children, that one would like living on the ranch—that sort of thing."

"I see."

Jess stiffened slightly beneath the patterns she was making in the soft swirls of hair on his chest, and she felt the question coming long before he uttered it.

"What attracted you to Aaron Strand?"

Libby had been pondering that mystery herself, ever since her marriage to Aaron had begun to dissolve. Now, suddenly, she was certain that she understood. Weak though he might be, Aaron Strand was tall, dark-haired, broad in the shoulders. He had given the impression of strength and self-assurance, qualities that any woman would find appealing.

"I guess I thought he was strong, like Dad," she said, because she couldn't quite amend the sentence to a full truth and admit that she had probably superimposed Jess's image over Aaron's in the first place.

"Ummm," said Jess noncommittally.

"Of course, he is actually very weak."

Jess offered no comment.

"I guess my mistake," Libby went on quietly, "was in seeing myself through Aaron's eyes. He made me feel so worthless…"

"Maybe that made him feel better about himself."

"Maybe. But I still hate him, Jess—isn't that awful? I still hate him for leaving Jonathan in the lurch like that, especially."

"It isn't awful, it's human. It appears that you and Jonathan needed more than he had to give. Unconsciously, you probably measured him against Ken, and whatever else he is, your dad is a hard act to follow, Libby."

"Yes," said Libby, but she was thinking: *I didn't measure Aaron against Dad. God help me, Jess, I measured him against you.*

Jess turned over in a graceful, rolling motion, so that he was above her, his head and shoulders blocking out the light of the stars. "Enough heavy talk, woman. I came here to—"

"Buy a car?" broke in Libby, her tone teasing and full of love.

He nuzzled his face between her warm, welcoming breasts. "My God," he said, his voice muffled by her satin flesh, "what an innocent you are, Libby Kincaid!" One of his hands came down, gentle and mischievous, to squeeze her bottom. "Nice upholstery."

Libby gasped and arched her back as his mouth slid up over the rounding of her breast to claim its peak. "Not much mileage," she choked out.

Jess laughed against the nipple he was tormenting so methodically. "A definite plus." His hand moved between her thighs to assert an ancient mastery, and his breath quickened at Libby's immediate response. "Starts easily," he muttered, sipping at her nipple now, tugging it into an obedient little point.

Libby was beyond the game now, rising and falling on the

velvet swells of need he was stirring within her. "I...Oh, God, Jess...what are you...ooooh!"

Somehow, Jess managed to turn on the bedside lamp without interrupting the searing pace his right hand was setting for Libby's body. "You are a goddess," he said.

The fevered dance continued, even though Libby willed herself to lie still. Damn him, he was watching her, taking pleasure from the unbridled response she could not help giving. Her heart raced with exertion, blood boiled in every vein, and Jess's lazy smile was lost in a silver haze.

She sobbed out his name, groping for his shoulders with her hands, holding on. Then, shuddering violently, she tumbled into some chasm where there was no sound but the beat of her own heart.

"You like doing that, don't you?" she snapped when she could see again, breathe again.

"Yes," replied Jess without hesitation.

Libby scrambled into a sitting position, blue eyes shooting flames. "Bastard," she said.

He met her gaze placidly. "What's the matter with you?"

Libby wasn't quite sure of the answer to that question. "It just...it just bothers me that you were...you were looking at me," she faltered, covering her still-pulsing breasts with the bedclothes.

With a deliberate motion of his hands, Jess removed the covers again, and Libby's traitorous nipples puckered in response to his brazen perusal. "Why?" he asked.

Libby's cheeks ached with color, and she lowered her eyes. Instantly Jess caught her chin in a gentle grasp, made her look at him again.

"Sweetheart, you're not ashamed, are you?"

Libby couldn't reply, she was so confused.

His hand slid, soothing, from Libby's chin to the side of her face. "You were giving yourself to me, Libby, trusting me. Is there shame in that?"

She realized that there wasn't, not the way she loved this brazen, tender, outlandish man. If only she dared to tell him verbally what her body already had.

He kissed her softly, sensing her need for greater reassurance. "Exquisite," he said. "Even ordinarily, you are exquisite. But when you let me love you, you go beyond that. You move me on a level where I've never even been touched before."

Say it now, Libby urged silently, *say you love me.*

But she had to be satisfied with what he had already said, for it was immediately clear that there would be no poetic avowals of devotion forthcoming. He'd said she was exquisite, that she moved him, but he'd made no declaration.

For this reason, there was a measure of sadness in the lovemaking that followed.

Long after Jess slept, exhausted, beside her, Libby lay awake, aching. She wanted, needed more from Jess than his readily admitted lust. So much more.

And yet, if a commitment were offered, would Libby want to accept it? Weren't there already too many conflicts complicating their lives? Though she tried to shut out the memory, Libby couldn't forget that Jess had believed her capable of carrying on with his brother and hurting her cousin and dearest friend in the process. Nor could she forget the wedge that had been driven between them the first time they'd made love, when she'd slipped and uttered words that had made him feel as though she'd used him to prove herself as a woman.

Of course, they had come together again, despite these things, but that was of no comfort to Libby. If they were to achieve any real closeness, more than just their bodies would have to be in accord.

After several hours, Libby fell into a fitful, dream-ridden sleep. When morning came, casting bright sunlight through the expanse of glass overhead, she was alone in the tousled bed.

"Lib!"

She went to the edge of the loft, peering down over the side. "What?" she retorted, petulant in the face of Jess's freshly showered, bright-and-shiny good cheer.

He waved a cooking spatula with a flourish. "One egg or two?"

"Drop dead," she replied flatly, frowning at the ladder.

Jess laughed. "Watch it.. You'll get my hopes up with such tender words."

"What's this damned ladder for, anyway?"

"Are you this grouchy every morning?" he countered.

"Only when I've engaged in illicit sex the night before!" Libby snapped, scowling. "I believe I asked you about the ladder?"

"It's for climbing up and down." Jess shrugged.

Libby's head throbbed, and her eyes felt puffy and sore. "Given time, I probably could have figured out that much!"

Jess chuckled and shook his head, as if in sympathy.

Libby grasped the top of the peculiar ladder in question and gave it a vigorous shake. It was immovable. Her puzzlement made her feel even more irritable and, for no consciously conceived reason, she put out her tongue at Jess Barlowe and whirled away from the edge of the loft, out of his view.

His laughter rang out as she stumbled into the bathroom and turned on the water in the shower stall.

Once she had showered and brushed her teeth, Libby began to feel semihuman. With this came contrition for the snappish way she had greeted Jess minutes before. It wasn't his fault, after all, that he was so nauseatingly happy in the mornings.

Grinning a mischievous grin, Libby rummaged through the suitcase she had so hastily packed and found the T-shirt she had bought for Jess the day before, when she'd come to Kalispell with Cathy. She pulled the garment on over her head and, in a flash of daring, swung over the loft to climb down the ladder.

Her reward was a low, appreciative whistle.

"Now I know why that ladder was built," Jess said. "The view from down here is great."

Libby was embarrassed; she'd thought Jess was in the kitchen and thus unable to see her novel descent from the loft. Reaching the floor, she whirled, her face crimson, to glare at him.

Jess read the legend printed on the front of the T-shirt, which was so big that it reached almost to her knees, and laughed explosively. "'If it feels good, do it'?" he marveled.

Libby's glare simply would not stay in place, no matter how hard she tried to sustain it. Her mouth twitched and a chuckle escaped her and then she was laughing as hard as Jess was.

Given the situation, his words came as a shock.

"Libby, will you marry me?"

She stared at him, bewildered, afraid to hope. "What?"

The jade eyes were gentle now, still glistening with residual laughter. "Don't make me repeat it, princess."

"I think the eggs are burning," said Libby in tones made wooden by surprise.

"Wrong. I've already eaten mine, and yours are congealing on your plate. What's your answer, Kincaid?"

Libby's throat ached; something about the size of her heart was caught in it. "I...what..."

"I thought you only talked in broken sentences at the height of passion. Are you really as surprised as all that?"

"Yes!" croaked Libby after a struggle.

The broad shoulders, accentuated rather than hidden by a soft yellow sweater, moved in a shrug. "It seemed like a good solution to me."

"A solution? To what?"

"All our separate and combined problems," answered Jess airily. Persuasively. "Think about it, Lib. Stacey couldn't very well hassle you anymore, could he? And you could stay on the ranch."

Despite the companionable delivery, Jess's words made Libby's soul ache. "Those are solutions for me. What problems would marriage solve for you?"

"We're good in bed," he offered, shattering Libby with what he seemed to mean as a compliment.

"It takes more than that!"

"Does it?"

Libby was speechless, though a voice inside her kept screaming silly, sentimental things. *What about love? What about babies and leftover meatloaf and filing joint tax returns?*

"You dad would be happy," Jess added, and he couldn't have hurt Libby more if he'd raised his hand and slapped her.

"My dad? My *dad?*"

Jess turned away, seemingly unaware of the effect his convoluted proposal was having on Libby. He looked like exactly what he was: a trained, skillful attorney pleading a weak case. "You want children, don't you? And I know you like living on the ranch."

Libby broke in coldly. "I guess I meet all the qualifications. I do want children. I do like living on the Circle Bar B. So why don't you just hog-tie me and brand me a Barlowe?"

Every muscle in Jess's body seemed to tense, but he did not turn around to face her. "There is one other reason," he offered.

For all her fury and hurt, hope sang through Libby's system like the wind unleashed on a wide prairie. "What's that?"

He drew a deep breath, his hands clasped behind him, courtroom style. "There would be no chance, for now at least, of Cathy being hurt."

Cathy. Libby's knees weakened; she groped for the sofa behind her, fell into it. Good God, was his devotion to Cathy so deep that he would marry the woman he considered a threat to her happiness, just to protect her?

"I am so damned tired of hearing about Cathy," she said evenly, tugging the end of the T-shirt down over her knees for something to do.

Now Jess turned, looked at her with unreadable eyes.

Even though Libby felt the guilt she always did whenever she was even mildly annoyed with Cathy, she stood her ground. "A person doesn't have to be handicapped to hurt, you know," she said in a small and rather uncertain voice.

Jess folded his arms and the sunlight streaming in through the glass ceiling glittered in his dark hair. "I know that," he said softly. "And we're all handicapped in some way, aren't we?"

She couldn't tell whether he was reprimanding her or offering an olive branch. Huddling on the couch, feeling foolish in the T-shirt she had put on as a joke, Libby knotted her hands together in her lap. "I suppose that remark was intended as a barb."

Jess came to sit beside her on the couch, careful not to touch her. "Libby, it wasn't. I'm tired of exchanging verbal shots with you—that was fine when we had to ride the same school bus every day, but we're adults now. Let's try to act as such.''

Libby looked into Jess's face and was thunderstruck by how much she cared for him, needed him. And yet, even a week before, she would have said she despised Jess and meant it. All that rancor they'd borne each other—had it really been passion instead?

"I don't understand any of this."

Jess took one of her hands into both of his. "Do you want to marry me or not?"

Both fear and joy rose within Libby. In order to look inward at her own feelings, she was forced to look away from him. She did love Jess, there was absolutely no doubt of that, and she wanted, above all things, to be his wife. She wanted children and, at thirty-one, she often had the feeling that time was getting short. Dammit, why couldn't he say he loved her?

"Would you be faithful to me, Jess?"

He touched her cheek, turning her face without apparent effort, so that she was again looking into those bewitching green eyes. "I would never betray you."

Aaron had said those words too. Aaron had been so very good with words.

But this was Jess, Libby reminded herself. Jess, not Aaron. "I couldn't give up my career," she said. "It's a crazy business, Jess, and sometimes there are long stretches of time when I don't do much of anything. Other times, I have to work ten- or twelve-hour days to meet a deadline."

Jess did not seem to be dissuaded.

Libby drew a deep breath. "Of course, I'd go on being known as Libby Kincaid. I never took Aaron's name and I don't see any sense in taking yours—should I agree to marry you, that is."

He seemed amused, but she had definitely touched a sore spot. That became immediately obvious. "Wait a minute, lady. Professionally, you can be known by any name you want. Privately, however, you'll be Libby Barlowe."

Libby was secretly pleased, but because she was angry and hurt that he didn't love her, she lifted her chin and snapped,

"You have to have that Circle Bar B brand on everything you consider yours, don't you?"

"You are not a thing, Libby," he replied rationally, "but I want at least that much of a commitment. Call it male ego if you must, but I want my wife to be Mrs. Barlowe."

Libby swallowed. "Fair enough," she said.

Jess sat back on the sofa, folded his arms again. "I'm waiting," he said, and the mischievous glint was back in his eyes.

"For what?"

"An answer to my original question."

Fool, fool! Don't you ever learn, Libby Kincaid? Don't you ever learn? Libby quieted the voice in her mind and lifted her chin. Life was short, and unpredictable in the bargain. Maybe Jess would learn to love her the way she loved him. Wasn't that kind of happiness worth a risk?

"I'll marry you," she said.

Jess kissed her with an exuberance that soon turned to desire.

JESS FROWNED at the sleek showroom sports car, his tongue making one cheek protrude. "What do you think?" he asked.

Libby assessed the car again. "It isn't you."

He grinned, ignoring the salesman's quiet disappointment. "You're right."

Neither, of course, had the last ten cars they had looked at been "him." The sports cars seemed to cramp his long legs, while the big luxury vehicles were too showy.

"How about a truck?" Libby suggested.

"Do you know how many trucks there are on the ranch?" he countered. "Besides, some yokel would probably paint on the family logo when I wasn't looking."

Libby deliberately widened her eyes. "That would be truly terrible!"

He made a face at her, but when he spoke, his words were delivered in a touchingly serious way. "We could get another station wagon and fill the backseat with kids and dogs."

Libby smiled at the image. "A grungy sort of heaven," she mused.

Jess laughed. "And of course there would be lots of room to make love."

The salesman cleared his throat and discreetly walked away.

CHAPTER NINE

"I THINK YOU SHOCKED that salesman," observed Libby, snapping the seat belt into place as Jess settled behind the wheel of their rental car.

Jess shrugged. "By wanting a station wagon?" he teased.

"By wanting *me* in the station wagon," clarified Libby.

Jess turned the key in the ignition and shifted gears. "He's lucky I didn't list all the other places I'd like to have you. The hood, for instance. And then there's the roof..."

Libby colored richly as they pulled into the slow traffic. "Jess!"

He frowned speculatively. "And, of course, on the ladder at the condo."

"The ladder?"

Jess flung her a brazen grin. "Yeah. About halfway up."

"Don't you think about anything but sex?"

"I seem to have developed a fixation, Kincaid—just since you came back, of course."

She couldn't help smiling. "Of course."

Nothing more was said until they'd driven through the quiet, well-kept streets to the courthouse. Jess parked the car and turned to Libby with a comical leer. "Are you up to a blood test and a little small-town bureaucracy, Kincaid?"

Libby felt a wild, twisting thrill in the pit of her stomach. A marriage license. He wanted to get a marriage license. In three short days, she could be bound to Jess Barlowe for life. At least, she *hoped* it would be for life.

After drawing a deep breath, Libby unsnapped her seat belt and got out of the car.

Twenty minutes later, the ordeal was over. The fact that the wedding itself wouldn't take nearly as long struck Libby as an irony.

On the sidewalk, Jess caught her elbow in one hand and helped her back into the car. While he must have noticed that she was preoccupied, he was chivalrous enough not to say so.

"Stop at that supermarket!" Libby blurted when they'd been driving for some minutes.

Jess gave her a quizzical look. "Supermarket?"

"Yes. They sell food there, among other necessary items."

Jess frowned. "Why can't we just eat in restaurants? There are several good ones—"

"Restaurants?" Libby cried with mock disdain. "How can I prove what a great catch I am if I don't cook something for you?"

Jess's right hand left the steering wheel to slide languorously up and down Libby's linen-skirted thigh. "Relax, sweetheart," he said in a rather good imitation of Humphrey Bogart. "I already know you're good in the kitchen."

The obvious reference to last night's episode in that room unsettled Libby. "You delight in saying outrageous things, don't you?" she snapped.

"I delight in *doing* outrageous things."

"You'll get no argument on that score, fella," she retorted acidly.

The car came to a stop in front of the supermarket, which was in the center of a small shopping mall. Libby noticed that Jess's gaze strayed to a jewelry store down the way.

"I'll meet you inside," he said, and then he was gone.

Though Libby told herself that she was being silly and sentimental, she was pleased to think that Jess might be shopping for a ring.

The giddy, romantic feeling faded when she selected a shopping cart inside the supermarket, however. She was wallowing in gushy dreams, behaving like a seventeen-year-old virgin. Of *course* Jess would buy a ring, but only because it would be expected of him.

Glumly Libby went about selecting items from a mental grocery list she had been composing since she'd checked the refrigerator and cupboards at the condominium and found them all but empty.

Taking refuge in practical matters, she frowned at a display of cabbage and wondered how much food to buy. Jess hadn't said how long they would be staying in Kalispell, beyond the time it would take to find the car he wanted.

Shrugging slightly, Libby decided to buy provisions for three days. Because that was the required waiting period for a marriage license, they would probably be in town at least that long.

She looked down at her slacks and brightly colored peasant blouse. The wedding ceremony was going to be an informal one, obviously, but she would still need a new dress, and she wanted to buy a wedding band for Jess, too.

She pushed her cart along the produce aisle, woodenly selecting bean sprouts, fresh broccoli, onions. Her first wedding had been a quiet one, too, devoid of lace and flowers and music, and something within her mourned those things.

They hadn't even discussed a honeymoon, and what kind of ceremony would this be, without Ken, without Cathy, without Senator Barlowe and Marion Bradshaw, the housekeeper?

A box seemed to float up out of the cart, but Libby soon saw that it was clasped in a strong sun-browned hand.

"I hate cereals that crunch," Jess said, and his eyes seemed to be looking inside Libby, seeing the dull ache she would rather have kept hidden. "What's wrong, love?"

Libby fought back the sudden silly tears that ached in her throat and throbbed behind her eyes. "Nothing," she lied.

Jess was not fooled. "You want Ken to come to the wedding," he guessed.

Libby lowered her head slightly. "He was hurt when Aaron and I got married without even telling him first," she said.

There was a short silence before a housewife, tagged by two preschoolers, gave Libby's cart a surreptitious bump with her own, tacitly demanding access to the cereal display. Libby wrestled her groceries out of the way and looked up at Jess, waiting for his response.

He smiled, touched her cheek. "Tell you what. We'll call the ranch and let everybody know we're getting married. That way, if they want to be there, they can. And if you want frills and flash, princess, we can have a formal wedding later."

The idea of a second wedding, complete with the trimmings, appealed to Libby's romantic soul. She smiled at the thought. "You would do that? You would go through it all over again, just for show?"

"Not for show, princess. For you."

The housewife made an appreciative sound and Libby started a little, having completely forgotten their surroundings.

Jess laughed and the subject was dropped. They walked up one aisle and down another, dropping the occasional pertinent item into the cart, arguing good-naturedly about who would do the cooking after they were married.

The telephone was ringing as Libby unlocked the front door of the condo, so she left Jess to carry in their bags of groceries and ran to answer it, expecting to hear Ken's voice, or Marion Bradshaw's, relaying some message from Cathy.

A cruel wave of *déjà vu* washed over her when she heard Aaron's smooth, confident greeting. "Hello, Libby."

"What do you want?" Libby rasped, too stunned to hang up. How on earth had he gotten that number?

"I told you before, dear heart," said Aaron smoothly. "I want a child."

Libby was conscious of Jess standing at her elbow, the shopping bags clasped in his arms. "You're insane!" she cried into the receiver.

"Maybe so, but not insane enough to let my grandmother hand over an empire to someone else. She has doubts, you know, about my dependability."

"I wonder why!"

"Don't be sarcastic, sugarplum. My request isn't really all that unreasonable, considering all I stand to lose."

"It is unreasonable, Aaron! In fact, it's sick!" At this point Libby slammed down the receiver with a vengeance. She was trembling so hard that Jess hastily shunted the grocery bags onto a side table and took her into his arms.

"What was that all about?" he asked when Libby had recovered herself a little.

"He's horrible," Libby answered, distracted and very much afraid. "Oh, Jess, he's a monster—"

"What did he say?" Jess pressed quietly.

"Aaron wants me to have his baby! Jess, he actually had the gall to ask me to come back, just so he can produce an heir and please his grandmother!"

Jess's hand was entangled in her hair now, comforting her. "It's all right, Lib. Everything will be all right."

Then why am I so damned scared? Libby asked herself, but she put on a brave face for Jess and even managed a smile. "Let's call my dad," she said.

Jess nodded, kissed her forehead. And then he took up the grocery bags again and carried them into the kitchen while Libby dialed her father's telephone number.

There was no answer, which was not surprising, considering that it was still early. Ken would be working, and because of the wide range of his responsibilities, he could be anywhere on the 150,000 acres that made up the Circle Bar B.

Sounds from the kitchen indicated that Jess was putting the food away, and Libby wandered in, needing to be near him.

"No answer?" he asked, tossing a package of frozen egg rolls into the refrigerator-freezer.

"No answer," confirmed Libby. "I should have known, I guess."

Jess turned, gave her a gentle grin. "You did know, Libby. But you needed to touch base just then, and going through the motions was better than nothing."

"When did you get so smart?"

"Last Tuesday, I think," he answered ponderously. "Know something? You look a little tired. Why don't you climb up that ladder that bugs you so much and take a nap?"

Libby arched one eyebrow. "While you do what?"

His answer was somewhat disappointing. "While I go back to town for a few hours," he said. "I have some things to do."

"Like what?"

He grinned. "Like picking up some travel brochures, so we can decide where to take our honeymoon."

Libby felt a rush of pleasure despite the weariness she was suddenly very aware of. Had it been there all along, or was she tired simply because this subtle hypnotist had suggested it to her? "Does it matter where we honeymoon?"

"Not really," Jess replied, coming disturbingly close, kissing Libby's forehead. "But I like having you all to myself. I can't help thinking that the farther we get from home right now, the better off we're going to be."

A tremor of fear brushed against Libby's heart, but it was quickly stilled when Jess caught her right earlobe between gentle teeth and then told her in bluntly erotic terms what he had wanted to do to her on the supermarket checkout counter.

When he'd finished, Libby was wildly aroused and, at the same time, resigned to the fact that when she crawled into that sun-washed bed up in the loft, she would be alone. "Rat," she said.

Jess swatted her backside playfully. "Later," he promised, and then calmly left the condo to attend to his errands.

Libby went obediently up to the bedroom, using the stairs rather than the ladder, and yawned as she stripped down to her lacy camisole and tap pants. She shouldn't be having a nap now, she told herself, when she had things of her own to do— choosing Jess's ring, for one thing, and buying a special dress, for another....

She was asleep only seconds after slipping beneath the covers.

LIBBY STIRRED, indulged in a deliciously lazy stretch. Someone was trailing soft, warm kisses across her collarbone—or was she dreaming? Just in case she was, she did not open her eyes.

Cool air washed over her breasts as the camisole was gently displaced. "Ummm," she said.

"Good dream?" asked Jess, moistening one pulsing nipple to crisp attention with his tongue.

"Oooooh," answered Libby, arching her back slightly, her eyes still closed, her head pressed into the silken pillow in eager, soft surrender. "Very good."

Jess left that nipple to subject its twin to a tender plundering that caused Libby to moan with delight. Her hips writhed slightly, calling to their powerful counterpart.

Jess heard their silent plea, slid the satiny tap pants down, down, away. "You're so warm, Libby," he said in a ragged whisper. "So soft and delicious." The camisole was unlaced, laid aside reverently, like the wrapping on some splendid gift. Kisses rained down on Libby's sleep-warmed, swollen breasts, her stomach, her thighs.

At last she opened her eyes, saw Jess's wondrous nakedness through a haze of sweet, sleepy need. As he ventured nearer and nearer to the silk-sheltered sanction of her womanhood, she instinctively reached up to clasp the brass railings on the headboard of the bed, anchoring herself to earth.

Jess parted the soft veil, admired its secret with a throaty exclamation of desire and a searing kiss.

A plea was wrenched from Libby, and she tightened her grasp on the headboard.

For a few mind-sundering minutes Jess enjoyed the swelling morsel with his tongue. "More?" he asked, teasing her, knowing that she was already half-mad with the need of him.

"More," she whimpered as his fingers strayed to the pebblelike peaks of her breasts, plying them, sending an exquisite lacelike net of passion knitting its way through her body.

Another tormenting flick of his tongue. "Sweet," he said. And then he lifted Libby's legs, placing one over each of his shoulders, making her totally, beautifully vulnerable to him.

She cried out in senseless delirium as he took his pleasure, and she was certain that she would have been flung beyond the dark sky if not for her desperate grasp on the headboard.

Even after the highest peak had been scaled, Libby's sated body convulsed again and again, caught in the throes of other, smaller releases.

Still dazed, Libby felt Jess's length stretch out upon her, seeking that sweetest and most intimate solace. In a burst of tender rebellion, she thrust him off and demanded loving revenge.

Soon enough, it was Jess who grasped the gleaming brass railings lest he soar away, Jess who chanted a desperate litany. Wickedly, Libby took her time, savoring him, taking outrageous liberties with him. Finally she conquered him, and his cry of joyous surrender filled her with love almost beyond bearing.

His breathing still ragged, his face full of wonder, Jess drew Libby down, so that she lay beside him. With his hands he explored her, igniting tiny silver fires in every curve and hollow of her body.

This time, when he came to her, she welcomed him with a ferocious thrust of her hips, alternately setting the pace and following Jess's lead. When the pinnacle was reached, each was lost in the echoing, triumphant cry of the other, and bits of a broken rainbow showered down around them.

SITTING INDIAN-STYLE on the living-room sofa, Libby twisted the telephone cord between her fingers and waited for her father's response to her announcement.

It was a soft chuckle.

"You aren't the least bit surprised!" Libby accused, marveling.

"I figured anybody that fought and jawed as much as you two did had to end up hitched," replied Ken Kincaid in his colorful way. "Did you let Cleave know yet?"

"Jess will, in a few minutes. Will you tell Cathy for me, please?"

Ken promised that he would.

Libby swallowed hard, gave Jess a warning glare as he moved to slide an exploring hand inside the top of her bathrobe. "Aren't you going to say that we're rushing into this or something like that? Some people will think it's too soon—"

"It was damned near too late," quipped Ken. "What time is the ceremony again?"

There were tears in Libby's eyes, though she had never been happier. "Two o'clock on Friday, at the courthouse."

"I'll be there, dumplin'. Be happy."

The whole room was distorted into a joyous blur. "I will, Dad. I love you."

"I love you, too," he answered with an ease that was typical of him. "Take care and I'll see you Friday."

"Right," said Libby, sniffling as she gently replaced the receiver.

Jess chuckled, touched her chin. "Tears? I'm insulted."

Libby made a face and shoved the telephone into his lap. "Call your father," she said.

Jess settled back in the sofa as he dialed the number of the senator's house in Washington, balancing the telephone on one blue-jeaned knee. While he tried to talk to his father in normal tones, Libby ran impudent fingertips over his bare chest, twining dark hair into tight curls, making hard buttons of deliciously vulnerable nipples.

With a mock-glare and a motion of his free arm, Jess tried to field her blatant advances. She simply knelt astraddle of his lap and had her way with him, her fingers tracing a path of fire around his mouth, along his neck, over his nipples.

Jess caught the errant hand in a desperate hold, only to be immediately assaulted by the other. Mischief flashed in his jade eyes, followed by an I'll-get-you-for-this look. "See you then," he said to his father, his voice a little deeper than usual and very carefully modulated. There was a pause, and then he added, "Oh, don't worry, I will. In about five seconds, I'm going to lay Libby on the coffee table and kiss her in all the best places. Yes, sir, by the time I get through with her, she'll be—"

Falling into the trap, Libby colored, snatched the receiver out of Jess's hand and pressed it to her ear. The line was, of course, dead.

Jess laughed as she assessed him murderously. "You deserved that," he said.

Libby moved to struggle off his lap, still crimson in the face, her heart pounding with embarrassment. But Jess's hands were strong on her upper arms, holding her in place.

"Oh, no you don't, princess. You're not getting out of this so easily."

"What—"

Jess smiled languidly, still holding her fast with one hand, undoing his jeans with the other. "You let this horse out of the barn, lady. Now you're going to ride it."

Libby gasped as she felt him prod her, hard and insistent, and fierce needs surged through her even as she raged at the affront. She was powerless, both physically and emotionally, to break away from him.

Just barely inside her, Jess reached out and calmly untied her bathrobe, baring her breasts, her stomach, her captured hips. His green eyes glittered as he stroked each satiny expanse in turn, allowing Libby more and more of him until she was fully his.

Seemingly unmoved himself, Jess took wicked delight in Libby's capture and began guiding her soft, trim hips up and down, endlessly up and down, upon him. All the while, he used soft words to lead her through flurries of silver snow to the tumultuous release beyond.

When her vision cleared, Libby saw that Jess had been caught in his own treachery. She watched in love and wonder as he gave himself up to raging sensation—his head fell back, his throat worked, his eyes were sightless.

Gruffly Jess pleaded with Libby, and she accelerated the up-and-down motion of her hips until he shuddered violently beneath her, stiffened and growled her name.

"Mess with me, will you?" she mocked, grinning down at him.

Jess began to laugh, between rasping breaths. When his mirth had subsided and he didn't have to drag air into his lungs, he caressed her with his eyes. In fact, it was almost as though he'd said he loved her.

Libby was still incredibly moved by the sweet spectacle she had seen played out in his face as he submitted to her, and she understood then why he so loved to watch her respond while pleasuring her.

Jess reached up, touched away the tear that tickled on her cheek. It would have been a perfect time for those three special words she so wanted to hear, but he did not say them.

Hurt and disappointed, Libby wrenched her bathrobe closed and tried to rise from his lap, only to be easily thwarted. Jess's hands opened the robe again, his eyes perused her and then came back to her face, silently daring her to hide any part of her body or soul from him.

With an insolent finger he brushed the pink buttons at the tips of her full breasts, smiled as they instantly obeyed him. Apparently satisfied with their pert allegiance, Jess moved on to trace patterns of fire on Libby's stomach, the rounding of her hips, the sensitive hollow at the base of her throat.

Jess seemed determined to prove that he could subdue Libby at will, and he only smiled at the startled gasp she gave when it became apparent that all his prowess had returned in full and glorious force.

He slid her robe off her shoulders then and removed it entirely. They were still joined, and Libby shivered as he toyed idly with her breasts, weighing them in his hands, pressing them together, thumbing their aching tips until they performed for him.

Presently Jess left his sumptuous playthings to tamper elsewhere, wreaking still more havoc, eliciting little anxious cries from a bedazzled Libby.

"What do you want, princess?" he asked in a voice of liquid steel.

Libby was wild upon him, her hands clutching desperately at his shoulders, her knees wide. "I want to be...under you. Oh, Jess...under you..."

In a swift and graceful motion, he turned her, was upon her. The movement unleashed the passion Jess had been able to contain until then, and he began to move over her and within her, his thrusts deep and powerful, his words ragged and incoherent.

As their very souls collided and then fused together, imitating their bodies, it was impossible to tell who had prevailed over whom.

LIBBY AWAKENED FIRST, entangled with Jess, amazed that they could have slept the whole night on that narrow couch.

A smile lifted one corner of her mouth as she kissed Jess's temple tenderly and then disengaged herself, careful not to disturb him. Heaven knew, he had a right to be tired.

Twenty minutes later, when Libby returned from her shower, dressed in sandals, white slacks and a lightweight yellow sweater, Jess was still sleeping. She could empathize, for her own slumber had been fathomless.

"I love you," she said, and then she went to the kitchen and wrote a quick note on the blackboard there, explaining that she had gone shopping and would be back within a few hours.

Getting into the rented car, which was parked in the gravel driveway near the front door, Libby spotted a cluster of colorful travel brochures fanned out on the opposite seat. Each one touted a different paradise: Acapulco, the Bahamas, Maui.

As Libby slid the key into the ignition and started the car, she grinned. She had it on good authority that paradise was only a few yards away, on the couch where Jess lay sleeping.

The day was a rich mixture of blue and green, set off by the fierce green of pine trees and the riotous blooms of crocuses and daffodils in quiet front yards. Downtown, Libby found a parking place immediately, locked the car and hurried on about her business.

Her first stop was a jewelry store, and while she had anticipated a great quandary, the decision of which wedding band to buy for Jess proved an easy one. Her eyes were immediately drawn to one particular ring, forged of silver, inset with polished chips of turquoise.

Once the jeweler had assured her the band could be resized if it didn't fit Jess's finger, Libby bought it.

In an art-supply store she purchased a sketching pad and a gum eraser and some charcoal pencils. Sweet as this interlude with Jess had been, Libby missed her work and her fingers itched to draw. Too, there were all sorts of new ideas for the comic strip bubbling in her mind.

From the art store, Libby pressed on to a good-sized department store. None of the dresses there quite struck her fancy, and she moved on to one boutique and then another.

Finally, in a small and wickedly expensive shop, she found that special dress, that dress of dresses, the one she would wear when she married Jess Barlowe.

It was a clingy creation of burgundy silk, showing off her

figure, bringing a glow of color to her cheeks. There were no ruffles of lace or fancy buttons—only a narrow belt made of the same fabric as the dress itself. It was the last word in elegant simplicity, that garment, and Libby adored it.

Carrying the dress box and the heavy bag of art supplies, she hurried back to the car and locked her purchases inside. It was only a little after ten, and Libby wanted to find shoes that would match her dress.

The shoes proved very elusive, and only after almost an hour of searching did she find a pair that would do. Tired of shopping and anxious to see Jess again, Libby started home.

Some intuitive feeling made her uneasy as she drove toward the elegant condominium hidden in the tall trees. After crossing the wooden bridge and making the last turn, she knew why—Stacey's ice-blue Ferrari was parked in the driveway.

Don't be silly, Libby reprimanded herself, but she still felt alarmed. What if Stacey had come to try to talk her out of marrying Jess? What if Cathy was with him, and there was an unpleasant scene?

Determined not to let her imagination get the upper hand, Libby gathered up her loot from the shopping trip and got out of the car. As she approached the house, she caught sight of a familiar face at the window and was surprised all over again. Monica! What on earth was she doing here? Hadn't she left for Washington, D.C., with the senator?

Now Libby really hesitated. She remembered the proprietary looks the woman had given Jess as he swam that day in the pool at the main ranch house. Looks that had implied intimacy.

Libby sighed. So what if Jess and Monica had slept together? She could hardly have expected a man like him to live like a monk, and it wasn't as if Libby hadn't had a prior relationship herself, however unsatisfactory.

Despite the cool sanity of this logic, it hurt to imagine Jess making love with Monica—or with any other woman, for that matter.

Libby grappled with her purchases at the front door, reached for the knob. Before she could clasp it, the door opened.

Jess was standing there, shirtless, wearing jeans, his hair and suntanned chest still damp from a recent shower. Instead of greeting Libby with a smile, let alone a kiss, he scowled at her and stepped back almost grudgingly, as though he had considered refusing her entrance.

Bewildered and hurt, Libby resisted a primal instinct urging her to flee and walked in.

Monica had left the window and was now seated comfortably on the couch, her shapely legs crossed at the knee, a cocktail in her hand.

Libby took in the woman's sleek designer suit and felt shabby by comparison in her casual attire. "Hello, Monica."

"Libby," replied Monica with a polite nod.

The formalities dispensed with, Libby flung a hesitant look at Jess. Why was he glaring at her like that, as though he wanted to do her bodily harm? Why was his jawline so tight, and why was it that he clenched the towel draped around his neck in white-knuckled hands?

Before Libby could voice any of her questions, Stacey came out of the kitchen, raked her with guileless caramel eyes and smiled.

"Hello," he said, as though his very presence, under the circumstances, was not an outrage.

Libby only stared at him. She was very conscious of Jess, seething somewhere on the periphery of her vision, and of Monica, taking in the whole scene with detached amusement.

Suddenly Stacey was coming toward Libby, speaking words she couldn't seem to hear. Then he had the outright gall to kiss her, and Libby's inertia was broken.

She drew back her hand and slapped him, her dress box, purse and bag of art supplies falling to the floor.

Stacey reached out for her, caught her waist in his hands. She squirmed and flung one appealing look in Jess's direction.

Though he looked anything but chivalrous, he did intercede. "Leave Libby alone, Stacey."

Stacey paled. "I've left Cathy," he said, as though that settled everything. "Libby, we can be together now!"

Libby stumbled backward, stunned. Only when she came up against the hard barrier of Jess's soap-scented body did she stop. Wild relief went through her as he enclosed her in a steel-like protective embrace.

"Get out," he said flatly, addressing his brother.

Stacey hesitated, but then he reddened and left the condo in a huff, pulling Monica Summers behind him.

CHAPTER TEN

FURIOUS AND SHAKEN, Libby turned to glare at Jess. It was all too clear what had happened—Stacey had been telling more of his outrageous lies and Jess had believed them.

For a few moments he stubbornly returned her angry regard, but then he spread his hands in a gesture of concession and said, "I'm sorry."

Libby was trembling now, but she stooped to pick up her dress box, and the art-store bag. She couldn't look at Jess or he would see the tears that had clouded her eyes. "After all we've done and planned, how could you, Jess? How could you believe Stacey?"

He was near, very near—Libby was conscious of him in every sense. He moved to touch her, instantly stopped himself. "I said I was sorry."

Libby forgot that she'd meant to hide her tears and looked him full in the face. Her voice shook with anger when she spoke. "Sometimes being sorry isn't enough, Jess!" She carried the things she'd bought across the room, tossed them onto the couch. "Is this what our marriage is going to be like? Are we going to do just fine as long as we aren't around Stacey?"

Jess was standing behind her; his hands came to rest on her shoulders. "What can I say, Libby? I was jealous. That may not be right, but it's human."

Perhaps because she wanted so desperately to believe that everything would turn out all right, that a marriage to this wonderful, contradictory man would succeed, Libby set aside her doubts and turned to face Jess. The depth of her love for this erstwhile enemy still staggered her. "What did Stacey tell you?"

Jess drew in an audible breath, and for a moment there was a tightness in his jaw. Then he sighed and said, "He was sharing the glorious details of your supposed affair. And he had a remarkable grasp on what you like in bed, Libby.''

The words were wounding, but Libby was strong. ''Did it ever occur to you that maybe all women like essentially the same things?''

Jess didn't answer, but Libby could see that she had made her mark, and she rushed on.

''Exactly what was Monica's part in all this?'' she demanded hotly. ''Was she here to moderate your sexual discussion? Why the hell isn't she in Washington, where she belongs?''

Jess shrugged, obviously puzzled. ''I'm not sure why she was here.''

''I am! Once you were diverted from your disastrous course—marrying me—she was going to take you by the hand and lead you home!''

One side of Jess's mouth lifted in a grin. ''I'm not the only one who is prone to jealousy, it appears.''

''You were involved with her, weren't you?''

''Yes.''

The bluntness of the answer took Libby unawares, but only for a moment. After all, had Jess said no, she would have known he was lying and that would have been devastating. ''Did you love Monica?''

''No. If I had, I would have married her.''

The possible portent of those words buoyed Libby's flagging spirits. ''Passion wouldn't be enough?'' she ventured.

''To base a marriage on? Never. Now, let's see what you bought today.''

Let's see what you bought today. Libby's frustration knew no bounds, but she was damned if she was going to pry those three longed-for words out of him—she'd fished enough as it was. ''I bought a wedding dress, for your information. And you're not going to see it until tomorrow, so don't pester me about it.''

He laughed. ''I like a woman who is loyal to her superstitions. What else did you purchase, milady?''

Libby's sense of financial independence, nurtured during the insecure days with Aaron, chafed under the question. "I didn't use your money, so what do you care?" she snapped.

Jess arched one eyebrow. "Another touchy subject rears its ugly head. I was merely curious, my love—I didn't ask for a meeting with your accountant."

Feeling foolish, Libby made a great project of opening the art-store bag and spreading its contents out on the couch.

Jess was grinning as he assessed the array of pencils, the large sketchbook. "Have I been boring you, princess?"

Libby pulled a face at him. "You could be called many things, Jess Barlowe, but you are definitely not boring."

"Thank you—I think. Shall we brave the car dealers of Kalispell again, or are you going to be busy?" The question was guileless, indicating that Jess would have understood if she wanted to stay and block out some of the ideas that had come to her.

After Aaron, who had viewed her cartooning as a childish hobby, Jess's attitude was a luxury. "I think I'd rather go with you," she said with a teasing smile. "If I don't you might come home with some motorized horror that has horns on its hood."

"Your faith in my good taste is positively underwhelming," he replied, walking toward the ladder, climbing its rungs to the loft in search of a shirt.

"You were right!" Libby called after him. "The view from down here is marvelous!"

During that foray into the jungle of car salesmen and gasoline-fed beasts, Libby spent most of her time in the passenger seat of Jess's rented car, sketching. Instead of drawing Liberated Lizzie, her cartoon character, however, she found herself reproducing Jess's image.

She imagined him looking out over the stunning view of prairies and mountains at home and drew him in profile, the wind ruffling his hair, a pensive look to his eyes and the set of his face. Another sketch showed him laughing, and still another, hidden away in the middle of the drawing pad, not meant for anyone else to see, mirrored the way Jess looked when he wanted her.

To field the responses the drawing evoked in her, Libby

quickly sketched Cathy's portrait, and then Ken's. After that, strictly from memory, she drew a picture of Jonathan, full face, as he'd looked before his illness, then, on the same piece of paper, in a profile that revealed the full ravages of his disease.

She supposed it was morbid, including this aspect of the child, but to leave out his pain would have meant leaving out his courage, and Jonathan deserved better.

Touching his charcoal image with gentle, remembering fingers, Libby heard the echo of his voice in her mind. *Naturally I'm brave,* he'd told her once, at the end of a particularly difficult day. *I'm a Jedi knight, like Luke Skywalker.*

Smiling through a mist of tears, Libby added another touch to the sketch—a tiny figure of Jonathan, well and strong, wielding a light saber in valiant defense of the Rebel Alliance.

"That's terrific," observed a gentle voice.

Libby looked up quickly, surprised that she hadn't heard Jess get into the car, hadn't sensed his presence somehow. Because she couldn't speak just yet, she bit her lower lip and nodded an acknowledgment of the compliment.

"Could I take a closer look? Please?"

Libby extended the notebook and it was a gesture of trust, for these sketches were different from the panels for her comic strip. They were large pieces of her soul.

Jess was pensive as he examined the portraits of himself, Cathy, Ken. But the study of Jonathan was clearly his favorite, and he returned to it at intervals, taking in each line, each bit of shading, each unspoken cry of grief.

Finally, with a tenderness that made Libby love him even more than she had before, Jess handed the sketchbook back to her. "You are remarkably talented," he said, and then he had the good grace to look away while Libby recomposed herself.

"D-did you find a car you like?" she asked finally.

Jess smiled at her. "Actually, yes. That's why I came back—to get you."

"Me? Why?"

"Well, I don't want to buy the thing without your checking it out first. Suppose you hated it?"

It amazed Libby that such a thing mattered to him. She set

the sketchbook carefully in the back seat and opened her car door to get out. "Lead on," she said, and the clean spring breeze braced her as it touched her face.

The vehicle in question was neither car nor truck, but a Land Rover. It was perfectly suited to the kind of life Jess led, and Libby approved of it with enthusiasm.

The deal was made, much to the relief of a salesman they had been plaguing, on and off, since the day before.

After some discussion, it was decided that they would keep the rental car until after the wedding, in case Libby needed it. Over a luncheon of steak and salad, which did much to settle her shaky nerves, Jess suggested that they start shopping all over again, for a second car.

Practical as it was, the thought exhausted Libby.

"You'll need transportation," Jess argued.

"I don't think I could face all those plaid sport jackets and test drives again," Libby replied with a sigh.

Jess laughed. "But you would like to have a car, wouldn't you?"

Libby shrugged. In New York, she had depended on taxis for transportation, but the ranch was different, of course. "I suppose."

"Aren't you choosy about the make, model—all that?"

"Wheels are wheels," she answered with another shrug.

"Hmmmm," Jess said speculatively, and then the subject was changed. "What about our honeymoon? Any place in particular you'd like to go?"

"Your couch," Libby said, shocked at her own audacity.

Again Jess laughed. "That is patently unimaginative."

"Hardly, considering the things we did there," Libby replied, immediately lifting a hand to her mouth. What was wrong with her? Why was she suddenly spouting these outlandish remarks?

Jess bent forward, conjured up a comical leer. "I wish we were on the ranch," he said in a low voice. "I'd take you somewhere private and make violent love to you."

Libby felt a familiar heat simmering inside her, melting through her pelvis. "Jess."

He drew some bills from his wallet, tossed them onto the table. "Let's get out of here while I can still walk," he muttered.

Libby laughed. "I think it's a good thing we're driving separate cars today," she teased, though secretly she was just as anxious for privacy as Jess was.

He groaned. "One more word, lady, and I'll spread you out on this table."

Libby's heart thudded at the bold suggestion and pumped color over her breasts and into her face. She tried to look indignant, but the fact was that she had been aroused by the remark and Jess knew it—his grin was proof of that.

As they left the restaurant, he bent close to her and described the fantasy in vivid detail, sparing nothing. And later, on the table in the condo's kitchen, he turned it into a wildly satisfying reality.

THAT AFTERNOON, Libby took another nap. Due to the episode just past, her dreams were deliciously erotic.

As he had before, Jess awakened her with strategic kisses. "Hi," he said when she opened her eyes.

She touched his hair, noted that he was wearing his brown leather jacket. "You've been out." She yawned.

Jess kissed the tip of her nose. "I have indeed. Bought you a present or two, as a matter of fact."

The glee in Jess's eyes made Libby's heart twist in a spasm of tenderness; whatever he'd purchased, he was very pleased with. She slipped languid arms around his neck. "I like presents," she said.

Jess drew back, tugged her camisole down so that her breasts were bared to him. Almost idly he kissed each dusty-rose peak and then covered them again. "Sorry," he muttered, his mouth a fraction of an inch from hers. "I couldn't resist."

That strange, magical heat was surging from Libby's just-greeted breasts to her middle, down into her thighs and even her knees. She felt as though every muscle and bone in her body had melted. "You m-mentioned presents?"

He chuckled, kissed her softly, groaned under his breath. "I was momentarily distracted. Get out of bed, princess. Said presents await.''

"Can't you just...bring them here?''

"Hardly.'' Jess withdrew from the bed to stand at its side and wrench back the covers. His green eyes smoldered as he took in the sleep-pinkened glow of her curves, and he bent to swat her satin-covered backside. "Get up,'' he repeated.

Libby obeyed, curious about the gifts but disappointed that Jess hadn't joined her in the bed, too. She found a floaty cotton caftan and slipped it on over her camisole and tap pants.

Jess looked at her, made a low growling sound in his throat, and caught her hand in his. "Come on, before I give in to my baser instincts,'' he said, pulling her down the stairs.

Libby looked around curiously as he dragged her across the living room but saw nothing out of the ordinary.

Jess opened the front door, pulled her outside. There, beside his maroon Land Rover, sat a sleek yellow Corvette with a huge rosette of silver ribbon affixed to its windshield.

Libby gaped at the car, her eyes wide.

"Like it?'' Jess asked softly, his mouth close to her ear.

"Like it?'' Libby bounded toward the car, heedless of her bare feet. "I love it!''

Jess followed, opened the door on the driver's side so that Libby could slide behind the wheel. When she did that, she got a second surprise. Taped to the gearshift knob was a ring of white gold, and the diamond setting formed the Circle Bar B brand.

"I'll hog-tie you later,'' Jess said.

Libby's hand trembled as she reached for the ring; it blurred and shifted before her eyes as she looked at it. "Oh, Jess.''

"Listen, if you hate it...''

Libby ripped away the strip of tape, slid the ring onto her finger. "Hate it? Sacrilege! It's the most beautiful thing I've ever seen.''

"Does it fit?''

The ring was a little loose, but Libby wasn't ready to part with it, not even to let a jeweler size it. "No,'' she said, overwhelmed, "but I don't care.''

Gently Jess lifted her chin with his hand, bent to sample her mouth with his. Beneath the hastily donned caftan and her camisole, Libby's nipples hardened in pert response.

"There's only one drawback to this car," Jess breathed, his lips teasing Libby's, shaping them. "It would be impossible to make love in it."

Libby laughed and pretended to shove him. "Scoundrel!"

"You don't know the half of it," he replied hoarsely, drawing Libby out of the beautiful car and back inside the house.

There she gravitated toward the front windows, where she could alternately admire her new car and watch the late-afternoon sun catch in the very special ring on her finger. Standing behind her, Jess wrapped his arms around her waist and held her close, bending to nip at her earlobe.

"Thank you, Jess," Libby said.

He laughed, and his breath moved in Libby's hair and sent warm tingles through her body. "No need for thanks. I'll nibble on your ears anytime."

"You know what I meant!"

His hands had risen to close over her breasts, fully possessing them. "What? What did you mean?" he teased in a throaty whisper.

Libby could barely breathe. "The car...the ring..."

Letting his hands slip from her breasts to her elbows, Jess ushered Libby over to face the mirror above the fireplace. As she watched his reflection in wonder, he undid the caftan's few buttons and slid it slowly down over her shoulders. Then he drew the camisole up over her head and tossed it away.

Libby saw a pink glow rise over her breasts to shine in her face, saw the passion sparking in her dark blue eyes, saw Jess's hands brush upward over her rib cage toward her breasts. The novelty of watching her own reactions to the sensations he was stirring inside her was erotic.

She groaned as she saw—and felt—masculine fingers rise to her waiting nipples and pluck then gently to attention.

"See?" Jess whispered at her ear. "See how beautiful you are, Libby? Especially when I'm loving you."

Libby had never thought of herself as beautiful, but now,

looking at her image in the mirror, seeing how passion darkened her eyes to indigo and painted her cheeks with its own special apricot shade, she felt ravishing.

She tilted her head back against the hard breadth of Jess's shoulder, moaned as he softly plundered her nipples.

He spoke with a gruff, choked sort of sternness. "Don't close your eyes, Libby. Watch. You're beautiful—so beautiful—and I want you to know it."

It was hard for Libby not to close her eyes and give herself up to the incredible sensations that were raging through her, but she managed it even as Jess came from behind her to bend his head and take suckle at one breast.

Watching him do this, watching the heightened color in her own face, gave a new intensity to the searing needs that were like storm winds within Libby. Her eyes were fires of ink-blue, and there was a proud, even regal lift to her chin as she watched herself pleasing the man she loved.

Jess drank deeply of one breast, turned to the other. It was an earthy communion between one man and one woman, each one giving and taking.

Presently Jess's mouth slid down over Libby's slightly damp stomach, and then he was kneeling, no longer visible in the magic mirror. "Don't close your eyes," he repeated, and Libby felt her satiny tap pants sliding slowly down over her hips, her knees, her ankles.

The wide-eyed sprite in the mirror gasped, and Libby was forced to brace herself with both hands against the mantel piece, just to keep from falling. Her breathing quickened to a rasp as Jess ran skilled hands over her bare bottom, her thighs, the backs of her knees. He heightened her pleasure by telling her precisely what he meant to do.

And then he did it.

Libby's release was a maelstrom of soft sobs that finally melded together into one lusty cry of pleasure. Jess was right, she thought, in the midst of all this and during the silvery descent that followed: she *was* beautiful.

Standing again, Jess lifted Libby up into his arms. Still feeling like some wanton Gypsy princess, she let her head fall back and gloried in the liberties his mouth took with the breasts that were thrust into easy reach.

Libby was conscious of an other-worldly floating sensation as she and Jess glided downward, together, to the floor.

RAIN PATTERED AND DANCED on the glass ceiling above the bed, a dismal heralding of what promised to be the happiest day of Libby Kincaid's life.

Jess slept beside her, beautifully naked, his breathing deep and even. If he hadn't actually spoken of his love, he had shown it in a dozen ways. So why did the pit of Libby's stomach jiggle, as though something awful was about to happen?

The insistent ringing of the doorbell brought Jess up from his stomach, push-up style, grumbling. His dark hair hopelessly rumpled, his eyes glazed, he stumbled around the bedroom until he found his robe and managed to struggle into it.

Libby laughed at him as he started down the stairs. "So much for being happy in the mornings, Barlowe," she taunted.

His answer was a terse word that Libby couldn't quite make out.

She heard the door open downstairs, heard Senator Barlowe's deep laugh and exuberant greeting. The sounds eased the feeling of dread that had plagued Libby earlier, and she got out of bed and hurried to the bathroom for a shower.

Periodically, as Libby shampooed her hair and washed, she laughed. Having his father arrive unexpectedly from Washington, probably with Ken and Cathy soon to follow, would certainly throw cold water on any plans the groom might have had for prenuptial frolicking.

When Libby went downstairs, her hair blown dry, her makeup in place, she was delighted to see that Cathy was with the senator. They were both, in fact, seated comfortably on the couch, drinking coffee.

"Where's Dad?" Libby asked when hugs and kisses had been exchanged.

Cleave Barlowe, with his elegant, old-fashioned manners, waited for Libby to sit down before returning to his own seat near Cathy. "He'll be here in time for the ceremony," he said.

"When we left the ranch, he was heading out with that bear patrol of his."

Libby frowned and fussed with her crisp pink sundress, feeling uneasy again. Jess had gone upstairs, and she could hear the water running in the shower. "Bear patrol?"

"We've lost a few calves to a rogue grizzly," Cleave said easily, as though such a thing were an everyday occurrence. "Ken and half a dozen of his best men have been tracking him, but they haven't had any luck so far."

Cathy, sitting at her father-in-law's elbow, seemed to sense her cousin's apprehension and signed that she wanted a better look at Libby's ring.

The tactic worked, but as Libby offered her hand, she at last looked into Cathy's face and saw the ravages of her marital problems. There were dark smudges under the green eyes, and a hollow ache pulsed inside them.

Libby reprimanded herself for being so caught up in her own tumultuous romance with Jess as to forget that during his visit the day before, Stacey had said he'd left Cathy. It shamed Libby that she hadn't thought more about her cousin, made it a point to find out how she was.

"Are you all right?" she signed, knowing that Cathy was always more comfortable with this form of communication than with lip reading.

Cathy's responding smile was real, if wan. She nodded and with mischievous interest assessed the ring Jess had had specially designed.

Cleave demanded a look at this piece of jewelry that was causing such an "all-fired" stir and laughed with appreciation when he saw his own brand in the setting.

Cathy lifted her hands. "I want to see your dress."

After Jess had come downstairs, dressed in jeans and the scandalous T-shirt Libby had given him, the two women went up to look at the new burgundy dress.

The haunted look was back in Cathy's eyes as she approved the garment. "I can hardly believe you're marrying Jess," she said in the halting, hesitant voice she would allow only Libby to hear.

Libby sat down on the rumpled bed beside her cousin. "That should settle any doubts you might have had about my relationship with Stacey," she said gently.

Cathy's pain was a visible spasm in her face. "He's living at the main house now," she confessed. "Libby, Stacey says he wants a divorce."

Libby's anger with Stacey was equal only to her sympathy for his wife. "I'm sure he doesn't mean any of the things he's been saying, Cathy. If only you would talk to him…"

The emerald eyes flashed. "So Stacey could laugh at me, Libby? No, thanks!"

Libby drew a deep breath. "I can't help thinking that this problem stems from a lack of communication and trust," she persisted, careful to face toward her cousin. "Stacey loves you. I know he does."

"How can you be so sure?" whispered Cathy. "How, Libby? Marriages end every day of the week."

"No one knows that better than I do. But some things are a matter of instinct, and mine tells me that Stacey is doing this to make you notice him, Cathy. And maybe because you won't risk having a baby."

"Having a baby would be pretty stupid, wouldn't it? Even if I wanted to take the risk, as you call it. After all, my husband moved out of our house!"

"I'm not saying that you should rush back to the ranch and get yourself pregnant, Cathy. But couldn't you just talk to Stacey, the way you talk to me?"

"I told you—I'd be embarrassed!"

"Embarrassed! You are married to the man, Cathy—you share his bed! How can you be embarrassed to let him hear your voice?"

Cathy knotted her fingers together in her lap and lowered her head. From downstairs Libby could hear Jess and the senator talking quietly about the vote Cleave had cast before coming back to Montana for the wedding.

Finally Cathy looked up again. "I couldn't talk to anyone but you, Libby. I don't even talk to Jess or Ken."

"That's your own fault," Libby said, still angry. "Have you

kept your silence all this time—all during the years I've been away?''

Cathy shook her head. "I ride up into the foothills sometimes and talk to the wind and the trees, for practice. Do you think that's silly?"

"No, and stop being so afraid that someone is going to think you're silly, dammit! So what if they do? What do you suppose people thought about me when I stayed with a man who had girlfriends?"

Cathy's mouth fell open. "Girlfriends?"

"Yes," snapped Libby, stung by the memory. "And don't tell my dad. He'd faint."

"I doubt it," replied Cathy. "But it must have hurt terribly. I'm so sorry, Libby."

"And I'm sorry if I was harsh with you," Libby answered. "I just want you to be happy, Cathy—that's all. Will you promise me that you'll talk to Stacey? Please?"

"I...I'll try."

Libby hugged her cousin. "That's good enough for me."

There was again a flash of delight in Cathy's eyes, indicating an imminent change of subject. "Is that car outside yours?"

Libby's answer was a nod. "Isn't it beautiful?"

"Will you take me for a ride in it? When the wedding is over and you're home on the ranch?"

"You know I will. We'll be the terror of the back roads— legends in our own time!"

Cathy laughed. "Legends? We'll be memories if we aren't careful."

Libby rose from her seat on the bed, taking up the pretty burgundy dress, slipping it carefully onto a hanger, hanging it in the back of the closet.

When that was done, the two women went downstairs together. By this time Jess and his father were embroiled in one of their famous political arguments.

Feeling uneasy again, Libby went to the telephone with as much nonchalance as she could and dialed Ken's number. There was no answer, of course—she had been almost certain that there wouldn't be—but the effort itself comforted her a little.

"Try the main house," Jess suggested softly from just behind her.

Libby glanced back at him, touched by his perception. Consoled by it. "How is it," she teased in a whisper, "that you managed to look elegant in jeans and a T-shirt that says 'If it feels good, do it'?"

Jess laughed and went back to his father and Cathy.

Libby called the main house and got a somewhat flustered Marion Bradshaw. "Hello!" barked the woman.

"Mrs. Bradshaw, this is Libby. Have you seen my father this morning?"

There was a long sigh, as though the woman was relieved to learn that the caller was not someone else. "No, dear, I haven't. He and the crew are out looking for that darned bear. Don't you worry, though—Ken told me he'd be in town for your wedding in plenty of time."

Libby knew that her father's word was good. If he said he'd be there, he would, come hell or high water. Still, something in Mrs. Bradshaw's manner was disturbing. "Is something the matter, Marion?"

Another sigh, this one full of chagrin. "Libby, one of the maids told me that a Mr. Aaron Strand called here, asking where you could be reached. Without so much as a by-your-leave, that woman came right out and told him you were in Kalispell and gave him the number. I'm so sorry."

So that was how Aaron had known where to call. Libby sighed. "It's all right, Marion—it wasn't your fault."

"I feel responsible all the same," said the woman firmly, "but I'll kick myself on my own time. I just wanted to let you know what happened. Did Miss Cathy and the senator get there all right?"

Libby smiled. "Yes, they're here. Any messages?"

"No, but I'd like a word with Jess, if it's all right."

Libby turned and gestured to the man in question. He came to the phone, took the receiver, greeted Marion Bradshaw warmly. Their conversation was a brief one, and when Jess hung up, he was laughing.

"What's so funny?" the senator wanted to know.

Jess slid an arm around Libby and gave her a quick squeeze. "Dare I say it in front of the creator of Liberated Lizzie, cartoon cave-woman? I just got Marion's blessing—she says I branded the right heifer."

CHAPTER ELEVEN

LIBBY STOOD AT A WINDOW overlooking the courthouse parking lot, peering through the gray drizzle, anxiously scanning each vehicle that pulled in.

"He'll be here," Cathy assured her, joining Libby at the rain-sheeted window.

Libby sighed. She knew that Ken would come if he possibly could, but the rain would make the roads hazardous, and there was the matter of that rogue grizzly bear. "I hope so," she said.

Cathy stood back a little to admire the flowing silken lines of Libby's dress. "You look wonderful. Here—let's see if the flowers match."

"Flowers?" Libby hadn't thought about flowers, hadn't thought about much at all, beyond contemplating the wondrous event about to take place. Her reason said that it was insanity to marry again, especially to marry Jess Barlowe, but her heart sang a very different song.

Cathy beamed and indicated a cardboard box sitting on a nearby table.

At last Libby left her post at the window, bemused. "But I didn't..."

Cathy was already removing a cellophane-wrapped corsage, several boutonnieres, an enormous bouquet made up of burgundy rosebuds, baby's breath, and white carnations. "This is yours, of course."

Libby reached out for her bridal bouquet, pleased and very surprised. "Did you order these, Cathy?"

"No," replied Cathy, "but I did nudge Jess in the florist's direction, after seeing what color your dress was."

Moved that such a detail had been taken into consideration, Libby hugged her cousin. "Thank you."

"Thank Jess. He's the one that browbeat the florist into filling a last-minute order." Cathy found a corsage labeled with her name. "Pin this on, will you?"

Libby happily complied. There were boutonnieres for Jess and the senator and Ken, too, and she turned this last one wistfully in her hands. It was almost time for the ceremony to begin—where was her father?

A light tap at the door made Libby's heart do a jittery flip. "Yes?"

"It's me," Jess said in a low, teasing voice. "Are the flowers in there?"

Cathy gathered up the boutonnieres, white carnations wrapped in clear, crackly paper, made her way to the door. Opening it just far enough to reach through, she held out the requested flowers.

Jess chuckled but made no move to step past the barrier and see his bride before the designated moment. "Five minutes, Libby," he said, and then she heard him walking away, his heels clicking on the marble courthouse floor.

Libby went back to the window, spotted a familiar truck racing into the parking lot, lurching to a stop. Two men in rain slickers got out and hurried toward the building.

Ken had arrived, and at last Libby was prepared to join Jess in Judge Henderson's office down the hall. She saw that august room through a haze of happiness, noticing a desk, a flag, a portrait of George Washington. In front of the rain-beaded windows, with their heavy, threadbare velvet draperies, stood Jess and his father.

Everyone seemed to move in slow motion. The judge took his place, and Jess, looking quietly magnificent in a tailored three-piece suit of dark blue, took his. His eyes caressed Libby, even from that distance, and somehow drew her toward him. At his side stood the senator, clearly tired from his unexpected cross-country trip, but proud and pleased, too.

Like a person strolling through a sweet dream, Libby let Jess draw her to him. At her side was Cathy, standing up very straight, her green eyes glistening with joyous tears.

Libby's sense of her father's presence was so strong that she did not need to look back and confirm it with her eyes. She tucked her arm through Jess's and the ceremony began.

When all the familiar words had been said, Jess bent toward Libby and kissed her tenderly. The haze lifted and the bride and groom turned, arm in arm, to face their few but much-loved guests.

Instead of congratulations, they met the pain-filled stares of two cowboys dressed in muddy jeans, sodden shirts and rain-coats.

Suddenly frantic, Libby scanned the small chamber for her father's face. She'd been so sure that he was there; he had seemed near enough to touch.

"Where—" she began, but her question was broken off because Jess left her side to stride toward the emissaries from the ranch, the senator close behind him.

"The bear..." said one of them in answer to Jess's clipped question. "We had him cornered and"—the cowboy's Adam's apple moved up and down in his throat—"and he was a mean one, Mr. Barlowe. Meaner'n the devil's kid brother."

Libby knew what was coming and the worn courthouse carpeting seemed to buckle and shift beneath her high-heeled burgundy sandals. Had it not been for Cathy, who gripped her elbow and maneuvered her into a nearby chair, she would have fallen.

"Just tell us what happened!" Jess rasped.

"The bear worked Ken over pretty good," the second cowboy confessed.

Libby gave a strangled cry and felt Cathy's arm slide around her shoulders.

"Is Ken dead?" demanded Cleave Barlowe, and as far as Libby was concerned, the whole universe hinged on the answer to that question.

"No, sir—we got Mr. Kincaid to the hospital fast as we could. But...but."

"But what?" hissed Jess.

"The bear got away, Mr. Barlowe."

Jess came slowly toward Libby, or at least it seemed so to

her. As he crouched before her chair and took her chilled hands into his, his words were gentle. "Are you all right?"

Libby was too frightened and sick to speak, but she did manage a nod. Jess helped her to her feet, supported her as they left the room.

She was conscious of the cowboys, behind her, babbling an account of the incident with the bear to Senator Barlowe, of Cathy's quiet sobs, of Jess's steel arm around her waist. The trip to the hospital, made in the senator's limousine, seemed hellishly long.

At the hospital's admissions desk, they were told by a harried, soft-voiced nurse that there was no news yet and directed to the nearest waiting room.

Stacey was there, and Cathy ran to him. He embraced her without hesitation, crooning to her, smoothing her hair with one hand.

"Ken?" barked the senator, his eyes anxious on his elder son's pale face.

"He's in surgery," replied Stacey. And though he still held Cathy, his gaze shifted, full of pain and disbelief, to Libby. "It's bad," he said.

Libby shuddered, more afraid than she'd ever been in her life, her arms and legs useless. Jess was holding her up—Jess and some instinct that had lain dormant within her since Jonathan's death. "Were you there when it happened, Stacey?" she asked dully.

Stacey was rocking Cathy gently in his arms, his chin propped in her hair. "Yes," he replied.

Suddenly rage surged through Libby—a senseless, shrieking tornado of rage. "You had guns!" she screamed. "I know you had guns! Why didn't you stop the bear? Why didn't you kill it?"

Jess's arm tightened around her. "Libby—"

Stacey broke in calmly, his voice full of compassion even in the face of Libby's verbal attack. "There was too much chance that Ken would be hit," he answered. "We hollered and fired shots in the air and that finally scared the grizzly off." There was a hollow look in Stacey's eyes as they moved to his fa-

ther's face and then Jess's, looking for the same understanding
he had just given to Libby.

"What about the bear?" the senator wanted to know.

Stacey averted his eyes for a moment. "He got away," he
breathed, confirming what one of the cowboys had said earlier
at the courthouse. "Jenkins got him in the hind flank, but he
got away. Ran like a racehorse, that son of a bitch. Anyway,
we were more concerned with Ken at the moment."

The senator nodded, but Jess tensed beside Libby, his gaze
fierce. "You sent men after the grizzly, didn't you?"

Stacey looked pained and his hold on Cathy tightened as her
sobs ebbed to terrified little sniffles. "I...I didn't think—"

"*You didn't think?*" growled Jess. "Goddammit, Stacey,
now we've got a wounded bear on the loose—"

The senator interceded. "I'll call the ranch and make sure
the grizzly is tracked down," he said reasonably. "Stacey got
Ken to the hospital, Jess, and that was the most important
thing."

An uncomfortable silence settled over the waiting room then.
The senator went to the window to stand, hands clasped behind
his back, looking out. The cowboys went back to the ranch,
and Stacey and Jess maneuvered their stricken wives into
chairs.

The sounds and smells peculiar to a hospital were a torment
to Libby, who had endured the worst minutes, hours, days, and
weeks of her life in just such a place. She had lost Jonathan in
an institution like this one—would she lose Ken, too?

"I can't stand it," she whispered, breaking the awful silence.

Jess took her chin in his hand, his eyes locking with hers,
sharing badly needed strength. "Whatever happens, Libby,
we'll deal with it together."

Libby shivered violently, looked at Jess's tailored suit, her
own dress, the formal garb of Cathy and the senator. Only
Stacey, in his muddy jeans, boots, shirt and sodden denim
jacket, seemed dressed for the horrible occasion. The rest of
the party was at ludicrous variance with the situation.

My father may be dying, she thought in quiet hysteria, *and
we're wearing flowers.* The smell of her bouquet suddenly sick-

ened Libby, bringing back memories of Jonathan's funeral, and she flung it away. It slid under a couch upholstered in green plastic and cowered there against the wall.

Jess's grip tightened on her hand, but no one made a comment.

Presently the senator wandered out, returning some minutes later with cups of vending-machine coffee balanced on a small tray. "Ken is my best friend," he announced in befuddled tones to the group in general.

The words brought a startling cry of grief from Cathy, who had been huddled in her chair until that moment, behind a curtain of tangled, rain-dampened hair. "I won't let him die!" she shrieked, to the openmouthed amazement of everyone except Libby.

Stacey, draped over the arm and back of Cathy's chair, stared down at her, his throat working. "Cathy?" he choked out.

Because Cathy was not looking at him, could not see her name on his lips, she did not answer. Her small hands flew to cover her face and she wept for the man who had loved her as his own child, raised her as his own, been her strength as well as Libby's.

"She can't hear you," Libby said woodenly.

"But she talked!" gasped Jess.

Libby lifted one shoulder in a broken shrug. "Cathy has been talking for years. To me, anyway."

"Good God," breathed the senator, his gaze sweeping over his shattered daughter-in-law. "Why didn't she speak to any of us?"

Libby was sorry for Stacey, reading the pain in his face, the shock. Of course, it was a blow to him to realize that his own wife had kept such a secret for so long.

"Cathy was afraid," Libby explained quietly. "She is very self-conscious about the way her voice sounds to hearing people."

"That's ridiculous!" barked Stacey, looking angry now, paler than before. He bolted away from Cathy's chair to stand at the windows, his back to the room. "For God's sake, I'm her husband!"

"Some of us had a few doubts about that," remarked Jess in an acid undertone.

Stacey whirled, full of fury, but the senator stepped between his two sons before the situation could get out of hand. "This is no time for arguments," he said evenly but firmly. "Libby and Cathy don't need it, and neither do I."

Both brothers receded, Stacey lowering his head a little, Jess averting a gaze that was still bright with anger. Libby watched a muscle leap in her husband's jaw and stifled a crazy urge to touch it with her finger, to still it.

"Was Dad conscious when you brought him here?" she asked of Stacey in a voice too calm and rational to be her own.

Stacey nodded, remembering. "He said that bear was almost as tough as a Mexican he fought once, down in Juarez."

The tears Libby had not been able to cry before suddenly came to the surface, and Jess held her until they passed. "Ken is strong," he reminded her. "Have faith in him."

Libby tried to believe the best, but the fact remained that Ken Kincaid was a mortal man, strong or not. And he'd been mauled viciously by a bear. Even if he survived, he might be crippled.

It seemed that Jess was reading her mind, as he so often did. His hand came up to stroke away her tears, smooth her hair back from her face. "Don't borrow trouble," he said gently. "We've got enough now."

Trying to follow this advice, Libby deliberately reviewed pleasant memories: Ken cursing a tangle of Christmas-tree lights; Ken sitting proudly in the audience while Cathy and Libby accepted their high school diplomas; Ken trying, and somehow managing, to be both mother and father.

More than two hours went by before a doctor appeared in the waiting room doorway, still wearing a surgical cap, his mask hanging from his neck. "Are you people here for Ken Kincaid?" he asked, and the simple words had the electrifying effect of a cattle prod on everyone there.

Both Libby and Cathy stiffened in their chairs, unable to speak. It was Jess who answered the doctor's question.

"Mr. Kincaid was severely injured," the surgeon said, "but we think he'll be all right, if he rests."

Libby was all but convulsed by relief. "I'm his daughter," she managed to say finally. "Do you think I could see him, just for a few minutes?"

The middle-aged physician smiled reluctantly. "He'll be in Recovery for some time," he said. "Perhaps it would be better if you visited your father tomorrow."

Libby was steadfast. It didn't matter that Ken was still under anesthetic; if she could touch his hand or speak to him, he would know that she was near. Another vigil had taught her the value of that. "I must see him," she insisted.

"She won't leave you alone until you say yes," Jess put in, his arm tight around Libby's shoulders.

Before the doctor could answer, Cathy was gripping Libby's hands, searching her cousin's face. "Libby?" she pleaded desperately. "Libby?"

It was clear that Cathy hadn't discerned the verdict on Ken's condition, and Libby's heart ached for her cousin as she freed her hands, quickly motioned the reassurances needed.

When that was done, Libby turned back to the doctor. "My cousin will want to see my father too."

"Now, just a minute..."

Stubbornly Libby lifted her chin.

Three hours later, Ken Kincaid was moved from the recovery room to a bed in the intensive-care unit. As soon as he had been settled there, Cathy and Libby were allowed into his room.

Ken was unconscious, and there were tubes going into his nostrils, an IV needle in one of his hands. His chest and right shoulder were heavily bandaged, and there were stitches running from his right temple to his neck in a crooked, gruesome line.

"Oh, God," whimpered Cathy.

Libby caught her cousin's arm firmly in her hand and faced her. "Don't you *dare* fall apart in here, Cathy Barlowe," she ordered. "He would sense how upset you are, and that would be bad for him."

Cathy trembled, but she squared her shoulders, drew a deep breath and then nodded. "We'll be strong," she said.

Libby went to the bedside, barely able to reach her father for all the equipment that was monitoring and sustaining him. "I hear you beat up on a bear," she whispered.

There was no sign that Ken had heard her, of course, but Libby knew that humor reached this man as nothing else could, and she went on talking, berating him softly for cruelty to animals, informing him that the next time he wanted to waltz, he ought to choose a partner that didn't have fur.

Before an insistent nurse came to collect Ken's visitors, both Libby and Cathy planted tender kisses on his forehead.

Stacey, Jess and Cleave were waiting anxiously when they reached the waiting room again.

"He's going to live," Libby said, and then the room danced and her knees buckled and everything went dark.

She awakened to find herself on a table in one of the hospital examining rooms, Jess holding her hand.

"Thanks for scaring the hell out of me," he said softly, a relieved grin tilting one corner of his mouth. "I needed that."

"Sorry," Libby managed, touching the wilting boutonniere that was still pinned to the lapel of his suit jacket. "Some wedding day, huh, handsome?"

"That's the wild west for you. We like excitement out here. How do you feel, princess?"

Libby tried to sit up, but the room began to swirl, so she fell back down. "I'm okay," she insisted. "Or I will be in a few minutes. How is Cathy?"

Jess smiled, kissed her forehead. "Cathy reacted a little differently to the good news than you did."

Libby frowned, still worried. "How do you mean?"

"After she'd been assured that you had fainted and not dropped dead of a coronary, she lit into Stacey like a whirlwind. It seems that my timid little sister-in-law is through being mute—once and for all."

Libby's eyes rounded. "You mean she was yelling at him?"

"Was she ever. When they left, he was yelling back."

Despite everything, Libby smiled. "In this case, I think a good loud argument might be just what the doctor ordered."

"I agree. But the condo will probably be a war zone by the time we get there."

Libby remembered that this was her wedding night, and with a little help from Jess, managed to sit up. "The condo? They're staying there?"

"Yes. The couch makes out into a bed, and Cathy wants to be near the hospital."

Libby reached out, touched Jess's strong face. "I'm sorry," she said.

"About what?"

"About everything. Especially about tonight."

Jess's green eyes laughed at her, gentle, bright with understanding. "Don't worry about tonight, princess. There will be plenty of other nights."

"But—"

He stilled her protests with an index finger. "You are in no condition to consummate a marriage, Mrs. Barlowe. You need to sleep. So let's go home and get you tucked into bed—with a little luck, Stacey and Cathy won't keep us awake all night while they throw pots and pans at each other."

Jess's remark turned out to be remarkably apt, for when they reached the condo, Stacey and his wife were bellowing at each other and the floor was littered with sofa pillows and bric-a-brac.

"Don't mind us," Jess said with a companionable smile as he ushered his exhausted bride across the war-torn living room. "We're just mild-mannered honeymooners, passing through."

Jess and Libby might have been invisible, for all the notice they got.

"Maybe we should have stayed in a motel," Libby yawned as she snuggled into Jess's strong shoulder, minutes later, in the loft bed.

Something shattered downstairs, and Jess laughed. "And miss this? No chance."

Cathy and Stacey were yelling again, and Libby winced. "You don't think they'll hurt each other, do you?"

"They'll be all right, princess. Rest."

Too tired to discuss the matter further, Libby sighed and fell asleep, lulled by Jess's nearness and the soft sound of rain on the glass roof overhead. She awakened once, in the depths of the night, and heard the sounds of another kind of passion from the darkened living room. A smile curved her lips as she closed her eyes.

CATHY WAS BLUSHING as she tried to neaten up the demolished living room and avoid Libby's gaze at the same time. Stacey, dead to the world, was sprawled out on the sofa bed, a silly smile shaping his mouth.

Libby made her way to the telephone in silence, called the hospital for a report on her father. He was still unconscious, the nurse on duty told her, but his vital signs were strong and stable.

Cathy was waiting, wide-eyed, when Libby turned away from the telephone.

Gently Libby repeated what the nurse had told her. After that, the two women went into the kitchen and began preparing a quick breakfast.

"I'm sorry about last night," Cathy said.

Standing at the stove, spatula in hand, Libby waited for her cousin to look at her and then asked, "Did you settle anything?"

Cathy's cheeks were a glorious shade of hot pink. "You heard!" she moaned.

Libby had been referring to the fight, not the lovemaking that had obviously followed, but there was no way she could clarify this without embarrassing her cousin further. She bit her lower lip and concentrated on the eggs she was scrambling.

"It was crazy," Cathy blurted, remembering. "I was *yelling* at Stacey! I wanted to hurt him, Libby—I really wanted to hurt him!"

Libby was putting slices of bread into the toaster and she offered no comment, knowing that Cathy needed to talk.

"I even threw things at him," confessed Cathy, taking orange juice from the refrigerator and putting it in the middle of the table. "I can't believe I acted like that, especially when Ken had just been hurt so badly."

Libby met her cousin's gaze and smiled. "I don't see what one thing has to do with the other, Cathy. You were angry with your husband—justifiably so, I'd say—and you couldn't hold it in any longer."

"I wasn't even worried about the way I sounded," Cathy reflected, shaking her head. "I suppose what happened to Ken triggered something inside me—I don't know."

"The important thing is that you stood up for yourself," Libby said, scraping the scrambled eggs out of the pan and onto a platter. "I was proud of you, Cathy."

"Proud? I acted like a fool!"

"You acted like an angry woman. How about calling those lazy husbands of ours to breakfast while I butter the toast?"

Cathy hesitated, wrestling with her old fear of being ridiculed, and then squared her shoulders and left the kitchen to do Libby's bidding.

Tears filled Libby's eyes at the sound of her cousin's voice. However ordinary the task was, it was a big step forward for Cathy.

The men came to the table, Stacey wearing only jeans and looking sheepish, Jess clad in slacks and a neatly pressed shirt, his green eyes full of mischief.

"Any word about Ken?" he asked.

Libby told him what the report had been and loved him the more for the relief in his face. He nodded and then executed a theatrical yawn.

Cathy blushed and looked down at her plate, while Stacey glared at his brother. "Didn't you sleep well, Jess?" he drawled.

Jess rolled his eyes.

Stacey looked like an angry little boy; Libby had forgotten how he hated to be teased. "I'll fight with my wife if I want to!" he snapped.

Both Libby and Jess laughed.

"Fight?" gibed Jess good-naturedly. "Was that what you two were doing? Fighting?"

"*Somebody* had to celebrate your wedding night," Stacey retorted, but then he gave in and laughed too.

When the meal was over, Cathy and Libby left the dirty dishes to their husbands and went off to get ready for the day.

They were allowed only a brief visit with Ken, and even though his doctor assured them that he was steadily gaining ground, they were both disheartened as they returned to the waiting room.

Senator Barlowe was there, with Jess and Stacey, looking as wan and worried as either of his daughters-in-law. Unaware of their approach, he was saying, "We've got every available man tracking that bear, plus hands from the Three Star and the Rocking C. All we've found so far is paw-prints and dead calves."

Libby was brought up short, not by the mention of the bear but by the look on Jess's face. He muttered something she couldn't hear.

Stacey sliced an ironic look in his brother's direction. "I suppose you think you can find that son of Satan when the hands from three of the biggest ranches in the state can't turn up a trace?"

"I know I can," Jess answered coldly.

"Dammit, we scoured the foothills, the ranges..."

Jess's voice was low, thick with contempt. "And when you had the chance to bring the bastard down, you let him trot away instead—wounded."

"What was I supposed to do? Ken was bleeding to death!"

"Somebody should have gone after the bear," Jess insisted relentlessly. "There were more than enough people around to see that Ken got to the hospital."

Stacey swore.

"Were you scared?" Jess taunted. "Did the big bad bear scare away our steak-house cowboy?"

At this, Stacey lunged toward Jess and Jess bolted out of his chair, clearly spoiling for a fight.

Again, as he had before, the senator averted disaster. "Stop it!" he hissed. "If you two have to brawl, kindly do it somewhere else!"

"You can bank on that," Jess said bitterly, his green gaze moving over Stacey and then dismissing him.

"What's gotten into the two of you?" Senator Barlowe rasped in quiet frustration. "This is a hospital! And have you forgotten that you're brothers?"

Libby cleared her throat discreetly, to let the men know that she and Cathy had returned. She was disturbed by the barely controlled hostility between Jess and his brother, but with Ken in the condition that he was, she had no inclination to pursue the issue.

It was later, in the Land Rover, when she and Jess were alone, that Libby voiced a subject that had been bothering her. "You plan to go looking for that bear, don't you?"

Jess appeared to be concentrating on the traffic, but a muscle in his cheek twitched. "Yes."

"You're going back to the ranch and track him down," Libby went on woodenly.

"That's right."

She sank back against the seat and closed her eyes. "Let the others do it."

There was a short, ominous silence. "No way."

Libby swallowed the sickness and fear that roiled in her throat. God in heaven, wasn't it enough that she'd nearly lost her father to that vicious beast? Did she have to risk losing her husband too? "Why?" she whispered miserably. "Why do you want to do this?"

"It's my job," he answered flatly, and Libby knew that there was no point in trying to dissuade him.

She squeezed her eyes even more tightly shut, but the tears escaped anyway. When they reached the condo again, Stacey's car and Cleave's pulling in behind them, Jess turned to her, brushed the evidence of her fear from her cheeks with gentle thumbs and kissed her.

"I promise not to get killed," he said softly.

Libby stiffened in his arms, furious and full of terror. "That's comforting!"

He kissed the tip of her nose. "You can handle this alone, can't you? Going to the hospital, I mean?"

Libby bit her lower lip. Here was her chance. She could say that she needed Jess now, she could keep him from hunting that bear. She did need him, especially now, but in the end, she couldn't use weakness to hold him close. "I can handle it."

An hour later, when Stacey and the senator left for the ranch, Jess went with them. Libby was now keeping two vigils instead of one.

Understanding Libby's feelings but unable to help, Cathy built a fire in the fireplace, brewed cocoa, and tried to interest her cousin in a closed-caption movie on television.

Libby watched for a while, then got out her sketchbook and began to draw with furious, angry strokes: Jess on horseback, a rifle in the scabbard of his saddle; a full-grown grizzly, towering on its hind legs, ominous muscles rolling beneath its hide, teeth bared. Try though she did, Libby could not bring herself to put Jess and that bear in the same picture, either mentally or on paper.

That evening, when Libby and Cathy went to the hospital, Ken was awake. He managed a weak smile as they came to his bedside to bestow tearful kisses.

"Sorry about missin' the wedding," he said, and for all his obvious pain, there was mirth in his blue eyes.

Libby dashed away the mist from her own eyes and smiled a shaky smile, shrugging. "You've seen one, cowboy, you've seen them all."

Ken laughed and the sound was beautiful.

CHAPTER TWELVE

HAVING ASSURED HERSELF that Ken was indeed recovering, Cathy slipped out to allow Libby a few minutes alone with her father.

"Thanks for scaring me half to death," she said.

Ken tried to shrug, winced instead. "You must have known I was too mean to go under," he answered. "Libby, did they get the bear?"

Libby stiffened. The bear, the bear—she was so damned sick of hearing about the bear! "No," she said after several moments, averting her eyes.

Ken sighed. He was pale and obviously tired. "Jess went after him, didn't he?"

Libby fought back tears of fear. Was Jess face to face with that creature even now? Was he suffering injuries like Ken's, or even worse? "Yes," she admitted.

"Jess will be all right, Libby."

"Like you were?" Libby retorted sharply, without thinking.

Ken studied her for a moment, managed a partial grin. "He's younger than I am. Tougher. No grizzly in his right mind would tangle with him."

"But this grizzly isn't in his right mind, is he?" Libby whispered, numb. "He's wounded, Dad."

"All the more reason to find him," Ken answered firmly. "That bear was dangerous before, Libby. He's deadly now."

Libby shuddered. "You'd think the beast would just crawl off and die somewhere."

"That would be real handy, but he won't do it, Lib. Grizzlies have nasty dispositions as it is—their eyesight is poor and their teeth hurt all the time. When they're wounded, they can rampage for days before they finally give out."

"The Barlowes can afford to lose a few cows!"

"Yes, but they can't afford to lose people, Lib, and that's what'll happen if that animal isn't found."

There was no arguing that; Ken was proof of how dangerous a bear could be. "The men from the Three Star and the Rocking C are helping with the hunt, anyway," Libby said, taking little if any consolation from the knowledge.

"That's good," Ken said, closing his eyes.

Libby bent, kissed his forehead and left the room.

Cathy was pacing the hallway, her lower lip caught in her teeth, her eyes wide. Libby chastised herself for not realizing that Stacey was probably hunting the bear too, and that her cousin was as worried as she was.

When Libby suggested a trip to the Circle Bar B, Cathy agreed immediately.

During the long drive, Libby made excuses to herself. She wasn't going just to check on Jess—she absolutely was not. She needed her drawing board, her pens and inks, jeans and blouses.

The fact that she could have bought any or all of these items in Kalispell was carefully ignored.

By the time Libby and Cathy drew the Corvette to a stop in the wide driveway of the main ranch house, the sun was starting to go down. There must have been fifty horsemen converging on the stables, all of them looking tired and discouraged.

Libby's heart wedged itself into her throat when she spotted Jess. He was dismounting, wrenching a high-powered rifle from the scabbard on his saddle.

She literally ran to him, but then she stopped short, her shoes encased in the thick, gooey mud Montanans call gumbo, her vocal cords no more mobile than her feet.

"Ken?" he asked in a hoarse whisper.

Libby was quick to reassure him. "Dad's doing very well."

"Then what are you doing here?"

Libby smiled, pried one of her feet out of the mud, only to have it succumb again when she set it down. "I had to see if you were all right," she admitted. "May I say that you look terrible?"

Jess chuckled, rubbed the stubble of beard on his chin, assessed the dirty clothes he wore in one downward glance. "You should have stayed in town."

Libby lifted her chin. "I'll go back in the morning," she said, daring him to argue.

Jess surrendered his horse to one of the ranch hands, but the rifle swung at his side as he started toward the big, well-lighted house. Libby slogged along at his side.

"Is that gun loaded?" she demanded.

"No," he replied. "Any more questions?"

"Yes. Did you see the bear?"

They had reached the spacious screened-in porch, where Mrs. Bradshaw had prudently laid out newspapers to accommodate dozens of mud-caked boots.

"No," Jess rasped, lifting his eyes to some distant thing that Libby could not see. "That sucker might as well be invisible."

Libby watched as Jess kicked off his boots, flung his sodden denim jacket aside, dispensed with his hat. "Maybe he's dead, Jess," she blurted out hopefully, resorting to the optimism her father had tacitly warned her against. "Maybe he collapsed somewhere—"

"Wrong," Jess bit out. "We found more cattle."

"Calves?"

"A bull and two heifers," Jess answered. "And the hell of it is, he didn't even kill them to eat. He just ripped them apart."

Libby shivered. "He must be enormous!"

"The men that were with Stacey and Ken said he stood over eight feet," Jess replied, and his green eyes moved wearily over Libby's face. "I don't suppose I need to say this, but I will. I don't like having you here, not now. For God's sake, don't go wandering off by yourself—not even to walk down to the mailboxes. The same goes for Cathy."

It seemed ludicrous that one beast could restrict the normal activities of human beings—in fact, the bear didn't seem real to Libby, even after what had happened to Ken. Instead, it was as though Jess was telling one of the delicious, scary stories he'd loved to terrify Libby with when they were children.

"That means, little one," he went on sternly, "that you don't go out to the barn and you don't go over to Ken's to sit and moon by that pond. Am I making myself clear?''

"Too clear," snapped Libby, following him as he carried the rifle through the kitchen, down a long hallway and into the massive billiard room where the gun cabinets were.

Jess locked the weapon away and turned to his wife. "I'm a little bit glad you're here," he confessed with a weary grin.

"Even tough cowboys need a little spoiling now and then," she replied, "so hie thyself to an upstairs bathroom, husband of mine, and get yourself a shower. I'll bring dinner to your room."

"And how do you know where my room is, Mrs. Barlowe?"

Libby colored a little. "I used to help Marion Bradshaw with the cleaning sometimes, remember?"

"I remember. I used to watch you bending over to tuck in sheets and smooth pillows and think what a great rear end you had."

She arched one eyebrow. "Had?"

Jess caught her bottom in strong hands, pressed her close to him. "Have," he clarified.

"Go take your shower!" Libby huffed, suddenly conscious of all the cowboys that would be gathering in the house for supper that night.

"Join me?" drawled Jess, persistent to the end.

"Absolutely not. You're exhausted." Libby broke away, headed toward the kitchen.

"Not *that* exhausted," Jess called after her.

Libby did not respond, but as she went in to prepare a dinner tray for her husband, she was smiling.

Minutes later, entering Jess's boyhood bedroom, she set the tray down on a long table under a line of windows. The door of the adjoining bathroom was open and steam billowed out like the mist in a spooky movie.

Presently Libby heard the shower shut off, the rustling sound of a towel being pulled from a rack. She sat down on the edge of Jess's bed and then bounded up again.

"Libby?"

She went cautiously to the doorway, looked in. Jess was

peering into a steamy mirror, trying to shave. "Your dinner is getting cold," she said.

After flinging one devilish look at his wife, Jess grabbed the towel that had been wrapped around his hips and calmly used it to wipe the mirror. "I'll hurry," he replied.

Libby swallowed hard, as stunned by the splendor of his naked, muscle-corded frame as she had been on that first stormy night when they'd made love in the bedroom at Jess's house, the fevered motions of their bodies metered by the raging elements outside.

Jess finished shaving, rinsed his face, turned toward Libby like a proud savage. She could not look away, even though she wanted to. Her eyes were fixed on the rising, swelling shaft of his manhood.

Jess laughed. "I used to fantasize about this."

"What?" Libby croaked, her throat tight.

"Bringing the foreman's pretty daughter up here and having my way with her."

Libby's eyes were, at last, freed, and they shot upward to his face. "Oh, yeah?"

"Yeah."

"I thought you liked Cathy then."

He nodded. "I did. But even before she married Stacey, I thought of her as a sister."

"And what, pray tell, did you think of me as?"

"A hellion. But I wanted to be your lover, all the same. Since I didn't dare, I settled for making your life miserable."

"How very chivalrous of you!"

Jess was walking toward her now, holding her with the scorching assessment of those jade-green eyes even before his hands touched her. "Teenage boys are not chivalrous, Libby."

Libby closed her eyes as he reached her, drew her close. "Neither are men," she managed to say.

Her blouse was coming untucked from her jeans, rising until she felt the steamy air on her stomach and back. Finally it was bunched under her arms and Jess was tracing a brazen finger over the lines of her scanty lace bra. Beneath the fabric, her nipples sprang into full bloom, coy flowers offering their nectar.

"Y-your dinner," she reminded Jess, floating on the sensations he was stirring within her, too bedazzled even to open her eyes.

The bra slipped down, just on one side, freeing a hardpeaked, eager breast. "Yes," Jess breathed evilly, "my dinner."

"Not that. I mean—"

His mouth closed over the delicate morsel, drawing at it softly. With a pleased and somewhat triumphant chuckle, Jess drew back from the tender treat and Libby's eyes flew open as he began removing her blouse and then her bra, leaving her jeans as they were.

He led her slowly to the bed, but instead of laying her down there, as she had expected, Jess stretched out on his back and positioned her so that she was sitting up, astraddle of his hips.

Gripping her waist, he pulled her forward and lifted, so that her breasts were suspended within easy reach of his mouth.

"The age-old quandary," he breathed.

Libby was dazed. "What qu-quandary?"

"Which one," Jess mused. "How like nature to offer two when a man has only one mouth."

Libby blushed hotly as Jess nuzzled a knotted peak, a peak that ached to nourish him. "Oh, God, Jess," she whispered. "Take it...take it!"

He chuckled, flicked the nipple in question with an impertinent tongue. "I love it when you beg."

Both rage and passion moved inside Libby. "I'm...not... begging!" she gasped, but even as she spoke she was bracing herself with her hands, brushing her breast back and forth across Jess's lips, seeking admission.

"You will," he said, and then he caught the pulsing nipple between careful teeth, raking it to an almost unendurable state of wanting.

"Not on your wretched life!" moaned Libby.

"We'll see," he replied.

The opposite breast was found and thoroughly teased and

Libby had to bite her lower lip to keep from giving in and pleading senselessly for the suckling Jess promised but would not give. He played with her, using his tongue and his lips, delighting in the rocking motion of her body and the soft whimpers that came from her throat.

The sweet torment became keener, and Libby both loved and hated Jess for being able to drive her to such lengths. "Make love to me…oh, Jess…make love…to me."

The concession elicited a hoarse growl from Jess, and Libby found herself spinning down to lie flat on the bed. Her remaining clothes were soon stripped away, her legs were parted.

Libby gasped and arched her back as he entered her in one ferocious, needing thrust. After gaining this warm and hidden place, Jess paused, his hard frame shuddering with restraint.

As bedazzled as she was, Libby saw her chance to set the pace, to take command, and she took it. Acting on an age-old instinct, she wrapped her legs around his hips in a fierce claiming and muttered, "Give me all of you, Jess—all of you."

He groaned in lusty surrender and plunged deep within her, seeking solace in the velvety heat of her womanhood. They were locked together for several glittering moments, each afraid to move. Soon enough, however, their bodies demanded more and began a desperate, swift rhythm.

Straining together, both moaning in fevered need, Libby and Jess reached their shattering pinnacle at the same moment, crying out as their two souls flared as one golden fire.

Twice after Jess lay still upon her, his broad back moist beneath her hands, Libby convulsed softly, whimpering.

"Some people are really greedy," he teased when, at last, her body had ceased its spasmodic clenching and unclenching.

Libby stretched, sated, cosseted in delicious appeasement. "More," she purred.

"What did I tell you?" Jess sighed. "The lady is greedy."

"Very."

He rolled, still joined with Libby, bringing her with him so that she once again sat astraddle of him. They talked, in hushed and gentle voices, of very ordinary things.

After some minutes had passed, however, Libby began to

trace his nipples with feather-light fingertips. "I've always wanted to have my way with the boss's son," she crooned, teasing him as he had teased her earlier.

She bent forward, tasted those hardening nipples, each in turn, with only the merest flick of her tongue. Jess groaned and grew hard within her, by degrees, as she continued to torment him.

"How like nature," she gibed tenderly, "to offer two when a woman has only one mouth."

Jess grasped her hips in inescapable hands and thrust his own upward in a savage demand.

Libby's release came swiftly; it was soft and warm, rather than violent, and its passing left her free to bring Jess to exquisite heights. She set a slow pace for him, delighting in the look in his eyes, the back-and-forth motion of his head on the pillow, the obvious effort it took for him to lie still beneath her.

He pleaded for release, but Libby was impervious, guiding him gently, reveling in the sweet power she held over this man she so completely loved. "I'm going to love you in my own way," she told him. "And in my own time."

His head pressed back into the pillows in magnificent surrender, Jess closed his eyes and moaned. His control was awesome, but soon enough it slipped and he began to move beneath Libby, slowly at first and then quickly. Finally, his hands tangling in her hair, he cried out and his body spasmed as she purposely intensified his pleasure. His triumph seemed endless.

When Jess was still at last, his eyes closed, his body glistening with perspiration, Libby tenderly stroked a lock of hair back from his forehead and whispered, "Some people are really greedy."

Jess chuckled and was asleep before Libby withdrew from him to make her way into the bathroom for a shower of her own.

THE DREAM WAS very sexy. In it, a blue-gray dawn was swelling at the bedroom windows and Libby's breast was full in Jess's hand, the nipple stroked to a pleading state.

She groaned as she felt his hard length upon her, his manhood seeking to sheathe itself in her warmth. Jess entered her, and his strokes were slow and gentle, evoking an immediate series of tremulous, velvet-smooth responses.

"Good," she sighed, giving herself up to the dream. "So good..."

The easy strokes became demanding thrusts. "Yes," said the dream Jess gruffly. "Good."

"Ooooooh," moaned Libby, as a sudden and piercing release rocked her, thrusting her into wakefulness.

And Jess was there, upon her, his face inches from her own. She watched in wonder and in love as his features grew taut and his splendid body flexed, more rapidly now. She thrust herself up to receive the fullness of his love.

Libby's hands clasped Jess's taut buttocks as he shuddered and delved deep, his manhood rippling powerfully within her, his rasping moan filling Libby's heart.

Minutes later, a languid, hazy sleep overtook Libby and she rolled over onto her stomach and settled back into her dreams. She stirred only slightly when Jess patted her derriere and left the bed.

Hours later, when she awakened fully, Libby was not entirely certain that she hadn't dreamed the whole gratifying episode. As she got out of bed, though, to take a bath and get dressed, Libby knew that Jess had loved her—the feeling of lush well-being she enjoyed was proof of that.

The pampered sensation was short-lived. When Libby went downstairs to search out a light breakfast, she found Monica Summers sitting in the kitchen, sipping coffee and reading a weekly newsmagazine.

Even though Monica smiled, her dark gray eyes betrayed her malice. "Hello...Mrs. Barlowe."

Libby nodded uneasily and opened the refrigerator to take out an apple and a carton of yogurt. "Good morning," she said.

"I was very sorry to hear about your father," Monica went on, the tone of her voice totally belying her expression. "Is he recovering?"

Libby got a spoon for her yogurt and sat down at the table. "Yes, thank you, he is."

"Will you be staying here with us, or going back to Kalispell?"

There was something annoyingly proprietary in the way Monica said the word "us," as though Libby were somehow invading territory where she didn't belong. She lifted her chin and met the woman's stormy-sky gaze directly. "I'll be going back to Kalispell," she said.

"You must hate leaving Jess."

The pit of Libby's stomach developed an unsettling twitch. She took a forceful bite from her apple and said nothing.

"Of course, I'll be happy to…look after him," sighed Monica, striking a flame to the fuse she had been uncoiling. "It's an old habit, you know."

Libby suppressed an unladylike urge to fly over the table, teeth bared, fists flying. "Sometimes old habits have to be broken," she said, sitting very still, reminding herself that she was a grown woman now, not the foreman's little brat. Furthermore, she was Jess's wife and she didn't have to take this kind of subtle abuse in any case.

Monica arched one perfect eyebrow. "Do they?"

Libby leaned forward. "Oh, yes. You see, Ms. Summers, if you mess with my husband, I'll not only break the habit for you, I'll break a few of your bones for good measure."

Monica paled, muttered something about country girls.

"I am not a girl," Libby pointed out. "I'm a woman, and you'd better remember it."

"Oh, I will," blustered Monica, recovering quickly. "But will Jess? That's the question, isn't it?"

If there was one thing in the world Libby had absolutely no doubts about, at that moment anyway, it was her ability to please her husband in the way Monica was referring to. "I don't see how he could possibly forget," she said, and then she finished her apple and her yogurt, dropped the remnants into the trash, and left the room.

Marion Bradshaw was sweeping away residual dried mud

when Libby reached the screened porch, hoping for one glimpse of Jess before she had to go back to Kalispell.

He was nowhere in sight, of course—Libby had not really expected him to be.

"How's Ken getting on?" Marion asked.

Libby smiled. "He's doing very well."

The housekeeper sighed, leaning on her broom. "Thank the good Lord for that. Me and Ken Kincaid run this place, and I sure couldn't manage it alone!"

Libby laughed and asked if Cathy was around.

Sheer delight danced in Mrs. Bradshaw's eyes. "She's where she belongs—upstairs in her husband's bed."

Libby blushed. She had forgotten how much this astute woman knew about the goings-on on the ranch. Did she know, too, why Jess had never gotten around to eating his dinner the night before?

"No shame in loving your man," Mrs. Bradshaw twinkled.

Libby swallowed. "Do you know if Stacey went with the others this morning?"

"He did. You go ahead and wake Miss Cathy right now, if you want to."

Libby was grateful for an excuse to hurry away.

Finding Stacey's room from memory, in just the way she'd found Jess's, she knocked briskly at the closed door, realized the foolishness of that, and turned the knob.

Cathy was curled up like a kitten in the middle of a bed as mussed and tangled as the one Libby had shared with Jess.

Libby bent to give Cathy's bare shoulder a gentle shake. Her cousin sat up, mumbling, her face lost behind a glistening profusion of tangled hair. "Libby? What…?"

Libby laughed and signed, "I'm going back to town as soon as I pick up some of my things at the other house. Do you want to go with me?"

Cathy's full lips curved into a mischievous smile and she shook her head.

"Things are going well between you and Stacey, then?"

Cathy's hands moved in a scandalously explicit answer.

"I'm shocked!" Libby signed, beaming. And then she gave

her cousin a quick kiss on the forehead, promised to call Mrs. Bradshaw if there was any sort of change in Ken's condition, and left the room.

In Jess's room she found paper and a pen, and probably because of the tempestuous night spent in his bed, dared to write, "Jess. I love you. Sorry I couldn't stay for a proper good-bye, but I've got to get back to Dad. Take care and come to me if you can. Smiles and sunshine, Libby."

On the way downstairs, Libby almost lost her courage and ran back to rip up the note. Telling Jess outright that she loved him! What if he laughed? What if he was derisive or, even worse, pitying?

Libby denied herself the cowardice of hiding her feelings any longer. It was time she took responsibility for her own emotions, wasn't it?

The weather was crisp and bright that day, and Libby hummed as she drove the relatively short distance to her father's house, parked her car behind his truck and went in to get the things she needed.

Fitting extra clothes and her special set of pens and inks into the back of the Corvette proved easy enough, but the drawing board was another matter. She turned it this way and that way and it just wouldn't fit.

Finally Libby took it back inside the house and left it there. She would just have to make do with the kitchen table at the condo for the time being.

Libby was just passing the passenger side of Ken's truck when she heard the sound; it was a sort of shifting rustle, coming from the direction of the lilac hedge on the far side of the yard. There followed a low, ominous grunt.

Instinctively Libby froze, the hair tingling on the nape of her neck. Dear God, it couldn't be... Not here—not when there were men with rifles searching every inch of the ranch...

She turned slowly, and her heart leapt into her throat and then spun back down into the pit of her stomach. The bear stood within ten feet of her, on its hind legs.

The beast growled and lolled its massive head to one side.

Its mangy, lusterless hide seemed loose over the rolling muscles beneath, and on its flank was a bloodcrusted, seeping wound.

In that moment, it was as though Libby became two people, one hysterically afraid, one calm and in control. Fortunately, it was this second Libby that took command. Slowly, ever so slowly, she eased her hand back behind her, to the door handle, opened it. Just as the bear lunged toward her, making a sound more horrifying than she could ever have imagined, she leapt inside the truck and slammed the door after her.

The raging beast shook the whole vehicle as it flung its great bulk against its side, and Libby allowed herself the luxury of one high-pitched scream before reaching for Ken's CB radio under the dashboard.

Again and again, the furious bear pummeled the side of the truck, while Libby tried frantically to make the CB radio work. She knew that the cowboys would be carrying receivers, in order to communicate with each other, and they were her only hope.

Fingers trembling, Libby finally managed to lift the microphone to her mouth and press the button. Her mind skittered over a series of movies she'd seen, books she'd read. *Mayday,* she thought with triumphant terror. *Mayday!* But the magic word would not come past her tight throat.

Suddenly a giant claw thundered across the windshield, shattering it into a glittering cobweb of cracks. One more blow, just one, and the bear would reach her easily, even though she was now crouching on the floorboard.

At last she found her voice. "Cujo!" she screamed into the radio receiver. "Cujo!" She closed her eyes, gasping, tried to get a hold on herself. *This is not a Stephen King movie,* she reminded herself. *This is reality. And that bear out there is going to tear you apart if you don't do something!*

"Libby!" the radio squawked suddenly. "Libby, come in!"

The voice was Jess's. "Th-the bear," she croaked, remembering to hold in the button on the receiver when she talked. "Jess, the bear!"

"Where are you?"

Libby closed her eyes as the beast again threw itself against the truck. "My dad's house—in his truck."

"Hold on. Please, baby, hold on. We're not far away."

"Hurry!" Libby cried, as the bear battered the windshield again and tiny bits of glass rained down on her head.

Another voice came in over the radio, this one belonging to Stacey. "Libby," he said evenly, "honk the horn. Can you do that?"

Libby couldn't speak. There were tears pouring down her face and every muscle in her body seemed inert, but she did reach up to the center of the wheel and press the truck's horn.

The bear bellowed with rage, as though the sound had hurt him, but he stopped striking the truck and withdrew a little way. Libby knew he wasn't gone, for she could hear him lumbering nearby, growling in frustration.

JESS'S MEN CONVERGED with Stacey's at the end of the rutted country road leading to Ken's house. When the pickup truck was in sight, they reined in their horses.

"He's mine," Jess breathed, reaching for the rifle in his scabbard, drawing it out, cocking it. He was conscious of the other men and their nervous, nickering horses, but only vaguely. Libby was inside that truck—his whole being seemed to focus on that one fact.

The bear rose up in full view suddenly, its enormous head visible even over the top of the pickup's cab. Even over the repeated honking of the truck's horn, the beast's hideous, echoing growl was audible.

"Sweet Jesus," Stacey whispered.

"Easy," said Jess, to himself more than the men around him, as he lifted the rifle, sighted in carefully, pulled back the trigger.

The thunderous shot struck the bear in the center of its nose, and the animal shrieked as it went down. The impact of its body was so solid that it seemed to shake the ground.

Instantly Jess was out of the saddle. "Make sure he's dead," he called over one shoulder as he ran toward the truck.

Stacey and several of his men reached the bear just as Jess wrenched open the door on the driver's side.

Libby scrambled out from under the steering wheel, her hair a wild, glass-spattered tangle, to fling herself, sobbing, into his arms. Jess cradled her in his arms, carried her away from the demolished truck and inside the house. His own knees suddenly weak, he fell into the first available chair and buried his face in Libby's neck.

"It's over, sweetheart," he said. "It's over."

Libby shuddered and wailed with terror.

When she was calmer, Jess caught her chin in his hand and lifted it. "What the hell did you mean, yelling 'Cujo! Cujo!'"

Libby sniffled, and the fight was back in her eyes, a glorious, snapping blue. "There was this book about a mad dog...and then there was a movie..."

Jess lifted his eyebrows and grinned.

"Oh, never mind!" hissed Libby.

CHAPTER THIRTEEN

LIBBY FROZE IN THE DOORWAY of Ken's room in the intensive-care unit, her mouth open, her heart racing as fast as it had earlier, when she'd been trapped by the bear.

"Where is he?" she finally managed to whisper. "Oh, Jess, where is my father?"

Standing behind Libby, Jess lifted his hands to her shoulders and gently ushered her back into the hallway, out of sight of the empty bed. "Don't panic," he said quietly.

Libby trembled, looked frantically toward the nurses' station. "Jess, what if he...?"

There was a gentle lecture forming in Jess's features, but before he could deliver it, an attractive red-headed nurse approached, trim in her uniform. "Mrs. Barlowe?"

Libby nodded, holding her breath.

"Your father is fine. We moved Mr. Kincaid to another floor earlier today, since he no longer needs such careful monitoring. If you will just come back to the desk with me, I'll be happy to find out which room he's in."

Libby's breath escaped in one long sigh. What with spending perilous minutes cowering inside a truck, with a rogue bear doing its best to get inside and tear her to bits, and then rushing to the hospital to find her father's bed empty, she had had more than enough stress for one day. "Thank you," she said, giving Jess a relieved look.

He got rather familiar during the elevator ride down to the second floor, but desisted when the doors opened again.

"You're incorrigible," Libby whispered, only half in anger.

"Snatching my wife from the jaws of death has that effect on me," he whispered back. "I keep thinking that I might never have gotten the chance to touch you like that again."

Libby paused, in the quest for Room 223, to search Jess's face. "Were you scared?"

"Scared? Sweet thing, I was *terrified*."

"You seemed so calm!"

He lifted one eyebrow. "Somebody had to be."

Libby considered that and then sighed. "I don't suppose we should tell Dad what actually happened. Not yet, at least."

Jess chuckled. "We'll tell a partial truth—that the bear is dead. The rest had better wait until he's stronger."

"Right," agreed Libby.

When they reached Ken's new room, another surprise was in store. A good-looking dark-haired woman was there plumping the patient's pillows, fussing with his covers. She wore well-cut jeans and a western shirt trimmed with a rippling snow-white fringe, and the way she laughed, low in her throat, said more about her relationship with Ken Kincaid than all her other attentions combined.

"Hello, Becky," said Jess, smiling.

Becky was one of those people, it seemed, who smile not just with the mouth but with the whole face. "Jess Barlowe," she crowed, "you black-hearted son-of-a-gun! Where ya been?"

Libby drew a deep breath and worked up a smile of her own. Was this the woman who had written that intriguing farewell on the condo's kitchen blackboard?

Deliberately she turned her attention on her father, who looked downright rakish as he favored his startled daughter with a slow grin and a wink.

"Who's this pretty little gal?" demanded Becky, giving Libby a friendly once-over.

For the first time, Ken spoke. "This is my daughter, Libby. Libby, Becky Stafford."

"I'll be!" cried Becky, clearly delighted. "Glad to meet ya!"

Libby found the woman's boisterous good nature appealing, and despite a few lingering twinges of surprise, she responded warmly.

"Did you get that bear?" Ken asked of Jess, once the women had made their exchange.

"Yes," Jess replied, after one glance at Libby.

Ken gave a hoot of delight and triumph. "Nail that son-of-a...nail that devil's hide to the barn door for me, will you?"

"Done," answered Jess with a grin.

A few minutes later, Jess and the energetic Becky left the room to have coffee in the hospital cafeteria. Libby lifted her hands to her hips, fixed her father with a loving glare and demanded, "Is there something you haven't told me?"

Ken laughed. "Maybe. But I'll wager that there are a few things you haven't told me, either, dumplin'."

"Who is Becky, exactly?"

Ken thought for a moment before speaking. "She's a good friend of mine, Libby. An old friend."

For some reason, Libby was determined to find something to dislike about Becky Stafford, difficult as it was. "Why does she dress like that? Is she a rodeo performer or something?"

"She's a cocktail waitress," Ken replied patiently.

"Oh," said Libby. And then she couldn't sustain her petty jealousy any longer, because Becky Stafford was a nice person and Ken had a right to like her. He was more than just her father, after all, more than just Senator Barlowe's general foreman. He was a man.

There was a brief silence, which Ken broke with a very direct question. "Do you like Becky, Lib?"

Like her? The warmth and humor of the woman still lingered in that otherwise dreary room, as did the earthy, unpretentious scent of her perfume. "Sure I do," said Libby. "Anybody with the perception to call Jess Barlowe a 'black-hearted son-of-a-gun' is okay in my book!"

Ken chuckled, but there was relief in his face, and his expression revealed that he knew how much Libby loved her husband. "How's Cathy?" he asked.

Remembering that morning's brief conversation with her cousin, Libby grinned. "She's doing fine, as far as I can tell. Bad as it was, your tussle with that bear seems to have brought

Cathy and Stacey both to a point where they can open up to each other. Cathy actually talked to him.''

Ken did not seem surprised by this last; perhaps he'd known all along that Cathy still had use of her voice. "I don't imagine it was peaceable," he observed dryly.

"Not in the least," confirmed Libby, "but they're communicating and...and, well, let's just say they're closer.''

"That's good," answered Ken, smiling at his daughter's words. "That's real good.''

Seeing that her father was getting very tired, Libby quickly kissed him and took her leave. When she reached the cafeteria, Becky was sitting alone at a table, staring sadly into her coffee cup.

Libby scanned the large room for Jess and failed to see him, but she wasn't worried. Probably he had gone back to Ken's room and missed seeing Libby on the way. Noticing the pensive look on Becky's face, she was glad for a few minutes alone with the woman her father obviously liked and perhaps even loved.

"May I sit down?" she asked, standing behind the chair that had probably been Jess's.

Becky looked up, smiled. "Sure," she said, and there was surprise in her dark eyes.

Libby sat down with a sigh. "I hate hospitals," she said, filled to aching with the memory of Jonathan's confinement.

"Me too," answered Becky, but her eyes were watchful. Hopeful, in a touchingly open way.

Libby swallowed. "My...my father has been very lonely, and I'm glad you're his friend.''

Becky's smile was almost cosmic in scope. "That's good to hear," she answered. "Lordy, that man did scare the life out of me, going a round with that damned bear that way.''

Libby thought of her own chance meeting with the creature and shivered. She hoped that she would never know that kind of numbing fear gain.

Becky's hand came to pat hers. "It's all right now, though, isn't it? That hairy booger is dead, thanks to Jess.''

Libby laughed. Indeed, that "hairy booger" was dead, and

she did have Jess to thank for her life. When she'd tried to voice her gratitude earlier, he had brushed away her words and said that she was his wife and, therefore, saving her from bears, fire-breathing dragons and the like was just part of the bargain.

As if conjured by her thoughts of him, Jess appeared to take Libby home.

THE COMING DAYS were happy ones for Libby, if hectic. She visited her father morning and evening and worked on her cartoon strip and the panels for the book between times, her drawing board having been transported from the ranch by Jess and set up in the middle of the condo's living room.

Jess commuted between Kalispell and the ranch; many of Ken's duties had fallen to him. Instead of being exhausted by the crazy pace, however, he seemed to thrive on it and his reports on the stormy reconciliation taking place between Cathy and Stacey were encouraging. It appeared that, with the help of the marriage counselor they were seeing, their problems might be worked out.

The irrepressible Becky Stafford rapidly became Libby's friend. Vastly different, the two women nevertheless enjoyed each other—Libby found that Becky could draw her out when she became too burrowed down in her work, and just as quickly drive her back if she tried to neglect it.

"You did what?" Jess demanded archly one early-summer evening as he and Libby sat on the living-room floor consuming the take-out Chinese food they both loved.

Libby laughed with glee and a measure of pride. "I rode the mechanical bull at the bar where Becky works," she repeated.

Jess worked up an unconvincing scowl. "Hanging around bars these days, are you?" he demanded, waving a fortune cookie for emphasis.

Libby batted her eyelashes demurely. "Don't you worry one little bit," she said, feigning a musical southern drawl. "Becky guards mah virtue, y'all."

Jess's green eyes slipped to the V neck of Libby's white sweater, which left a generous portion of cleavage in full and enticing view. "Does she now? And where is she, at this very moment, when said virtue is in immediate peril?"

An anticipatory thrill gyrated in the pit of Libby's stomach and warmed her breasts, which were bare beneath her light-weight sweater. Jess had loved her often, and well, but he could still stir that sweet, needing tension with remarkable ease. "What sort of peril am I in, exactly?"

Jess grinned and hooked one finger in the V of her sweater, slid it downward into the warmth between her breasts. "Oh, the most scandalous sort, Mrs. Barlowe."

Libby's breath quickened, despite stubborn efforts to keep it even. "Your attentions are quite unseemly, Mr. Barlowe," she replied.

He moved the wanton finger up and down between the swelling softness that was Libby, and sharp responses ached in other parts of her. "Absolutely," he said. "I mean to do several unseemly things to you."

Libby tensed with delicious sensation as Jess's exploring finger slid aside, explored a still-hidden nipple.

"I want to see your breast, Libby. This breast. Show it to me."

The outrageous request made Libby color slightly, but she knew she would comply. She was a strong, independent person, but now, in this sweet, aching moment, she was Jess's woman. With one motion of her hand, she tugged the sweater's neckline down and to one side, so that it made a sort of sling for the breast that had been softly demanded.

Not touching the rounded pink-tipped treasure in any way, Jess admired it, rewarding it with an approving smile when the confectionlike peak tightened into an enticing point.

Libby was kneeling now, resting on her heels, the cartons littering the coffee table completely forgotten. She was at once too proud to plead for Jess's mouth and too needing of it to cover herself.

Knowing that, Jess chuckled hoarsely and bent to flick at the exposed nipple with just the tip of his tongue. Libby moaned and let her head fall back, making the captured breast even more vulnerable.

"Unseemly," breathed Jess, nibbling, drawing at the straining morsel with his lips.

Libby felt the universe sway in time with his tender plundering, but she bit down hard on the garbled pleas that were rising in her throat. They escaped through her parted lips, all the same, as small gasps.

Her heartbeat grew louder and louder as Jess finally took suckle; it muffled the sounds of his greed, of the cartons being swept from the surface of the coffee table in a motion of one of his arms.

The coolness of the air battled with the heat of Libby's flesh as she was stripped of her sweater, her white slacks, her panties. Gently he placed her on the coffee table.

Entranced, Libby allowed him to position her legs wide of each other, one on one side of the low table, one on the other. Beyond the glass roof, in the dark, dark sky, a million silvery stars surged toward her and then melted back into the folds of heaven, becoming pinpoints.

Jess found the silken nest of her passion and attended it lovingly, stroking, kissing, finding, losing. Libby's hips moved wildly, struggling even as she gave herself up.

And when she had to have this singular gratification or die, Jess understood and feasted unreservedly, his hands firm under her bottom, lifting her, the breadth of his shoulders making it impossible for her to deny him what he would have from her.

At last, when the tumult broke on a lusty cry of triumph from Libby, she saw the stars above plummet toward her—or had she risen to meet them?

"OF COURSE YOUR'RE GOING to the powwow!" cried Becky, folding her arms and leaning over the platter of french fries in front of her. "You can't miss that and call yourself a Barlowe!"

Libby shrank down a little in the benchlike steak-house seat. As this restaurant was a part of the Barlowe chain, the name drew immediate attention from all the waiters and a number of the other diners, too. "Becky," she began patiently, "even though Dad's getting out of the hospital this afternoon, he won't be up to something like that, and I wouldn't feel right about leaving him behind.''

"Leaving Ken behind?" scoffed Becky in a more discreet tone of voice. "You just try keeping him away—he hasn't missed a powwow in fifteen years."

Libby's memories of the last Indian powwow and all-day rodeo she had attended were hardly conducive to nostalgia. She remembered the dust, the hot glare of the summer sun, the seemingly endless rodeo events, the drunks—Indian and white alike—draped over the hoods of parked cars and sprawled on the sidewalks. She sighed.

"Jess'll go," Becky prodded.

Libby had no doubt of that, and having spent so much time away from Jess of late, what with him running the ranch while she stayed in Kalispell, she was inclined to attend the powwow after all.

Becky saw that she had relented and beamed. "Wait'll you see those Sioux Indians doing their war dances," she enthused. "There'll be Blackfoot, too, and Flathead."

Libby consoled herself with the thought of Indians doing their dances and wearing their powwow finery of feathers and buckskin and beads. She could take her sketchbook along and draw, at least.

Becky wasn't through with her conversation. "Did you tell Jess how you rode that electric bull over at the Golden Buckle?"

Libby tried to look dignified in the wake of several molten memories. "I told him," she said shyly.

Her friend laughed. "If that wasn't a sight! I wish I woulda took your picture. Maybe you should enter some of the events at the powwow, Libby." Her face took on a disturbingly serious expression. "Maybe barrel racing, or women's calf roping—"

"Hold it," Libby interceded with a grin. "Riding a mechanical bull is one thing and calf roping is quite another. The only sport I'm going to take part in is stepping over drunks."

"Stepping over what?" inquired a third voice, masculine and amused, from the table side.

Libby looked and saw Stacey. "What are you doing here?"

He laughed, turning his expensive silver-banded cowboy hat in both hands. "I own the place, remember?"

"Where's Cathy?" Becky wanted to know. As she had become Libby's friend, she had also become Cathy's—she was even learning to sign.

Stacey slid into the bench seat beside Libby. "She's seeing the doctor," he said, and for all his smiling good manners, he seemed nervous.

Libby elbowed her brother-in-law lightly. "Why didn't you stay there and wait for her?"

"She wouldn't let me."

Just then Becky stood up, saying that she had to get to work. A moment later, eyes twinkling over some secret, she left.

Libby felt self-conscious with Stacey, though he hadn't made any more advances or disturbing comments. She wished that Becky had been able to stay a little longer. "What's going on? Is Cathy sick?"

"She's just having a checkup. Libby..."

Libby braced herself inwardly and moved a little closer to the wall of the enclosed booth, so that Stacey's thigh wasn't touching hers. "Yes?" she prompted when he hesitated to go on.

"I owe you an apology," he said, meeting her eyes. "I acted like a damned fool and I'm sorry."

Knowing that he was referring to the rumors he'd started about their friendship in New York, Libby chafed a little. "I accept your apology, Stacey, but I truly don't understand why you said what you did in the first place."

He sighed heavily. "I love Cathy very much, Libby," he said. "But we do have our problems. At that time, things were a lot worse, and I started thinking about the way you'd leaned on me when you were going through all that trouble in New York. I liked having somebody need me like that, and I guess I worked the whole thing up into more than it was."

Tentatively Libby touched his hand. "Cathy needs you, Stacey."

"No," he answered gruffly, looking at the flickering bowl

candle in the center of the table. "She won't allow herself to need me. After some of the things I've put her through, I can't say I blame her."

"She'll trust you again, if you're worthy of it," Libby ventured. "Just be there for Cathy, Stace. The way you were there for me when my whole life seemed to be falling apart. I don't think I could have gotten through those days without you."

At that moment Jess appeared out of nowhere and slid into the seat Becky had occupied before. "Now, that," he drawled acidly, "is really touching."

Libby stared at him, stunned by his presence and by the angry set of his face. Then she realized that both she and Stacey were sitting on the same side of the booth and knew that it gave an impression of intimacy. "Jess..."

He looked down at his watch, a muscle dancing furiously in his jaw. "Are you going to pick your father up at the hospital, or do you have more interesting things to do?"

Stacey, who had been as shocked by his brother's arrival as Libby had, was suddenly, angrily vocal. The candle leapt a little when he slammed one fist down on the tabletop and hissed, "Dammit, Jess, you're deliberately misunderstanding this!"

"Am I?"

"Yes!" Libby put in, on the verge of tears. "Becky and I were having lunch and then Stacey came in and—"

"Stop it, Libby," Stacey broke in. "You didn't do anything wrong. Jess is the one who's out of line here."

The long muscle in Jess's neck corded, and his lips were edged with white, but his voice was still low, still controlled. "I came here, Libby, because I wanted to be with you when you brought Ken home," he said, and his green eyes, dark with passion only the night before, were coldly indifferent now. "Are we going to collect him or would you rather stay here and carry on?"

Libby was shaking. "Carry on? *Carry on?*"

Stacey groaned, probably considering the scandal a scene in this particular restaurant would cause. "Couldn't we settle this somewhere else?"

"We'll settle it, all right," Jess replied.

Stacey's jaw was rock-hard as he stood up to let a shaken Libby out of the booth. "I'll be on the ranch," he said.

"So will I," replied Jess, rising, taking a firm grip on Libby's arm. "See you there."

"Count on it."

Jess nodded and calmly propelled Libby out of the restaurant and into the bright sunlight, where her shiny Corvette was parked. Probably he had seen the car from the highway and known that she was inside the steak house.

Now, completely ignoring her protests, he dragged her past her car and thrust her into the Land Rover beside it.

"Jess—damn you—will you *listen* to me?"

Jess started the engine, shifted it into reverse with a swift motion of his hand. "I'm afraid storytime will have to wait," he informed her. "We've got to go and get Ken, and I don't want him upset."

"Do you think I do?"

Jess sliced one menacing look in her direction but said nothing.

Libby felt a need to reach him, even though, the way he was acting, he didn't deserve reassurances. "Jess, how can you...after last night, how could you..."

"Last night," he bit out. "Yes. Tell me, Libby, do you do that trick for everybody, or just a favored few?"

It took all her determination not to physically attack him. "Take me back to my car, Jess," she said evenly. "Right now. I'll pick Dad up myself, and we'll go back to his house—"

"Correction, Mrs. Barlowe. *He* will go to his house. You, my little vixen, will go to mine."

"I will not!"

"Oh, but you will. Despite your obvious attraction to my brother, you are still my wife."

"I am not attracted to your brother!"

They had reached the hospital parking lot, and the Land Rover lurched to a stop. Jess smiled insolently and patted Libby's cheek in a way so patronizing that it made her screaming mad. "That's the spirit, Mrs. Barlowe. Walk in there and show your daddy what a pillar of morality you are."

Going into that hospital and pretending that nothing was wrong was one of the hardest things Libby had ever had to do.

PREPARATIONS FOR KEN'S RETURN had obviously been going on for some time. As Libby pulled her reclaimed Corvette in behind Jess's Land Rover, she saw that the front lawn had been mowed and the truck had been repaired.

Ken, still not knowing the story of his daughter, his truck, and the bear, paused after stepping out of Jess's Land Rover, his arm still in a sling. He looked his own vehicle over quizzically. "Looks different," he reflected.

Jess rose to the occasion promptly, smoothly. "The boys washed and waxed it," he said.

To say the very least, thought Libby, who would never forget, try though she might, how that truck had looked before the repair people in Kalispell had fixed and painted it. She opened her mouth to tell her father what had happened, but Jess stopped her with a look and a shake of his head.

The inside of the house had been cleaned by Mrs. Bradshaw and her band of elves; every floor and stick of furniture had been either dusted or polished or both. The refrigerator had been stocked and a supply of the paperback westerns Ken loved to read had been laid in.

As if all this wasn't enough to make Libby's services completely superfluous, it turned out that Becky was there too. She had strung streamers and dozens of brightly colored balloons from the ceiling of Ken's bedroom.

Her father was obviously pleased, and Libby's last hopes of drumming up an excuse to stay the night, at least, were dashed. Becky, however, was delighted with her surprise.

"I thought you were working!" Libby accused.

"I lied," replied Becky, undaunted. "After I left you and Stacey at the steak house, I got a friend to bring me out here."

Libby shot a glance in Jess's direction, knew sweet triumph as she saw that Becky's words had registered with him. After only a moment's chagrin, however, he tightened his jaw and looked away.

While Becky was getting Ken settled in his room and generally spoiling him rotten, Libby edged over to her husband. "You heard her," she whispered tersely, "so where's my apology?"

"Apology?" Jess whispered back, and there was nothing in his face to indicate that he felt any remorse at all. "Why should I apologize?"

"Because I was obviously telling the truth! Becky said—"

"Becky said that she left you and Stacey at the steak house. It must have been a big relief when she did."

Heedless of everything but the brutal effect of Jess's unfair words, Libby raised one hand and slapped him, hard.

Stubbornly, he refused her the satisfaction of any response at all, beyond an imperious glare, which she returned.

"Hey, do you guys…?" Becky's voice fell away when she became aware of the charged atmosphere of the living room. She swallowed and began again. "I was going to ask if you wanted to stay for supper, but maybe that wouldn't be such a good idea."

"You can say that again," rasped Jess, catching Libby's arm in a grasp she couldn't have broken without making an even more embarrassing scene. "Make our excuses to Ken, will you, please?"

After a moment's hesitation and a concerned look at Libby, Becky nodded.

"You overbearing bastard!" Libby hissed as her husband squired her out of the house and toward his Land Rover.

Jess opened the door, helped her inside, met her fiery blue gaze with one of molten green. Neither spoke to the other, but the messages flashing between them were all too clear anyway.

Jess still believed that Libby had been either planning or carrying on a romantic tryst with Stacey, and Libby was too proud and too angry to try to convince him otherwise. She was also too smart to get out of his vehicle and make a run for hers.

Jess would never hurt her, she knew that. But he would not allow her a dramatic exit, either. And she couldn't risk a screaming fight in the driveway of her father's house.

Because she was helpless and she hated that, she began to cry.

Jess ignored her tears, but he too was considerate of Ken—he did not gun the Land Rover's engine or back out at a speed that would fling gravel in every direction, as he might have at another time.

When they passed his house, with its window walls, and started up a steep road leading into the foothills beyond, Libby was still not afraid. For all his fury, this man was too tender a lover to touch her in anger.

"Where are we going?" she demanded.

He ground the Land Rover into a low gear and left the road, now little more than a cow path, for the rugged hillside. "On our honeymoon, Mrs. Barlowe."

Libby swallowed, unnerved by his quiet rage and the jostling, jolting ascent of the Land Rover itself. "If you take me in anger, Jess Barlowe, I'll never forgive you. Never. That would be rape."

The word "rape" got through Jess's hard armor and stung him visibly. He paled as he stopped the Land Rover with a lurch and wrenched on the emergency brake. "Goddammit, you *know* I wouldn't do anything like that!"

"Do I?" They were parked at an almost vertical angle, it seemed to Libby. Didn't he realize that they were almost straight up and down? "You've been acting like a maniac all afternoon!"

Jess's face contorted and he raised his fists and brought them down hard on the steering wheel. "Dammit it all to hell," he raged, "you drive me crazy! Why the devil do I love you so much when *you drive me crazy?*"

Libby stared at him, almost unable to believe what she had heard. Not even in their wildest moments of passion had he said he loved her, and if he had found that note she'd left for him, betraying her own feelings, the day the bear was killed, he'd never mentioned it.

"What did you say?"

Jess sighed, tilted his head back, closed his eyes. "That you drive me crazy."

"Before that."

"I said I loved you," he breathed, as though there was nothing out of the ordinary in that.

"Do you?"

"Hell, yes." The muscles in his sun-browned neck corded as he swallowed, his head still back, his eyes still closed. "Isn't that a joke?"

The words tore at Libby's heart. "A joke?"

"Yes." The word came, raw, from deep within him, like a sob.

"You idiot!" yelled Libby, struggling with the door, climbing out of the Land Rover to stalk up the steep hillside. She trembled, and tears poured down her face, and for once she didn't care who saw them.

At the top of the rise, she sat down on a huge log, her vision too blurred to take in the breathtaking view of mountains and prairies and an endless, sweeping sky.

She sensed Jess's approach, tried to ignore him.

"Why am I an idiot, Libby?"

Though the day was warm, Libby shivered. "You're too stupid to know when a woman loves you, that's why!" she blurted out, sobbing now. "Damn! You've had me every way but hanging from a chandelier, and you still don't know!"

Jess straddled the log, drew Libby into his arms and held her. Suddenly he laughed, and the sound was a shout of joy.

CHAPTER FOURTEEN

DRUNKEN COWBOYS AND INDIANS notwithstanding, the pow-wow of the Sioux, Flathead and Blackfoot was a spectacle to remember. Held annually in the same small and otherwise unremarkable town, the meeting of these three tribes was a tradition that reached back to days of mist and shadow, days recorded on no calendar but that of the red man's legends.

Now, on a hot July morning, the erstwhile cow pasture and ramshackle grandstands were churning with activity, and Libby Barlowe's fingers ached to make use of the sketchbook and pencils she carried.

Craning her neck to see the authentic tepees and their colorfully clad inhabitants, she could hardly stand still long enough for the plump woman at the admission gate to stamp her hand.

There was so much noise—laughter, the tinkle of change in the coin box, the neighing and nickering of horses that would be part of the rodeo. Underlying all this was the steady beat of tom-toms and guttural chants of Indian braves.

"Enjoy yourself now, honey," enjoined the woman tending the cashbox, and Libby jumped, realizing that she was holding up the line behind her. After one questioning look at the hat the woman wore, which consisted of panels cut from various beer cans and crocheted together, she hurried through the gate.

Jess chuckled at the absorbed expression on Libby's face. There was so much to see that a person didn't know where to look first.

"I think I see a fit of creativity coming on," he said.

Libby was already gravitating toward the tepees, plotting light angles and shading techniques as she went. In her heart was a dream, growing bigger with every beat of the tom-toms.

"I want to see, Jess," she answered distractedly. "I've got to *see*."

There was love in the sound of Jess's laughter, but no disdain. "All right, all right—but at least let me get you a hat. This sun is too hot for you to go around bareheaded."

"Get me a hat, get me a hat," babbled Libby, zeroing in on a group of small Indian children, who wore little more than loincloths and feathers as they sat watching fathers, uncles and elder brothers perform the ancient rites for rain or success in warfare or hunting.

Libby was taken with the flash of their coppery skin, the midnight black of their hair, the solemn, stalwart expressions in their dark eyes. Flipping open her sketchbook, she squatted in the lush summer grass and began to rough in the image of one particular little boy.

Her pencil flew, as did her mind. She was thinking in terms of oil paints—vivid, primitive shades that would do justice to the child's coloring and the peacock splendor of his headdress.

"Hello," she said when the dark eyes turned to her in dour question. "My name is Libby, what's yours?"

"Jimmy," the little boy responded, but then he must have remembered the majesty of his ancestry, for he squared his small shoulders and amended, "Jim Little Eagle."

Libby made a hasty note in the corner of his sketch. "I wish I had a name like that," she said.

"You'll have to settle for 'Barlowe,'" put in a familiar voice from behind her, and a lightweight hat landed on the top of her head.

Libby looked up into Jess's face and smiled. "I guess I can make do with that," she answered.

Jess dropped to his haunches, assessed the sketch she'd just finished with admiring eyes. "Wow," he said.

Libby laughed. "I love it when you're profound," she teased. And then she took off the hat he'd given her and inspected it thoroughly. It was a standard western hat, made of straw, and it boasted a trailing tangle of turquoise feathers and crystal beads.

Jess took the hat and put it firmly back on, then arranged the feathers so that they rested on her right shoulder, tickling the bare, sun-gilded flesh there in a pleasant way. "Did you wear that blouse to drive me insane, or are you trying to set a world record for blistering sunburns?" he asked unromantically.

Libby looked down at the brief white eyelet suntop and wondered if she shouldn't have worn a western shirt, the way Becky and Cathy had. The garment she had on had no shoulders or sleeves; it was just a series of broad ruffles falling from an elasticized band that fitted around her chest, just beneath her collarbone. Not even wanting to think about the tortures of a sunburn, she crinkled her nose and said, "I wore it to drive you insane, of course."

Jess was going to insist on being practical; she saw it in his face. "They're selling T-shirts on the fairway—buy one."

"Now?" complained Libby, not wanting to leave the splendors of the recreated Indian village even for a few minutes.

Jess looked down at his watch. "Within half an hour," he said flatly. "I'm going to find Ken and the others in the grandstands, Rembrandt. I'll see you later."

Libby squinted as he rose against the sun, towering and magnificent even in his ordinary jeans and worn cowboy shirt. "No kiss?"

Jess crouched again, kissed her. "Remember. Half an hour."

"Half an hour," promised Libby, turning to a fresh page in her sketchbook and pondering a little girl with coal-black braids and a fringed buckskin shift. She took a new pencil from the case inside her purse and began to draw again, her hand racing to keep up with the pace set by her heart.

When the sketch was finished, Libby thought about what she meant to do and how the syndicate that carried her cartoon strip would react. No doubt they would be furious.

"*Portraits!*" her agent would cry. "Libby, Libby, there is no *money* in portraits."

Libby sighed, biting her lower lip. Money wasn't a factor really, since she had plenty of that as it was, not only because she had married a wealthy man but also because of prior successes in her career.

She was tired of doing cartoons, yearning to delve into other

mediums—especially oils. She wanted color, depth, nuance—
she wanted and needed to grow.

"Where the hell is that T-shirt I asked you to buy?"

Libby started, but the dream was still glowing in her face
when she looked up to meet Jess's gaze. "Still on the fairway,
I would imagine," she said.

His mouth looked very stern, but Jess's eyes were dancing
beneath the brim of his battered western hat. "I don't know
why I let you out of my sight," he teased. And then he extended a hand. "Come on, woman. Let's get you properly
dressed."

Libby allowed herself to be pulled through the crowd to one
of the concession stands. Here there were such thrilling offer-
ings as ashtrays shaped like the state of Montana and gaudy
scarves commemorating the powwow itself.

"Your secret is out," she told Jess out of the corner of her
mouth, gesturing toward a display of hats exactly like her own.
The colors of their feather-and-bead plumage ranged from a
pastel yellow to deep, rich purple. "This hat is not a designer
original!"

Jess worked up an expression of horrified chagrin and then
laughed and began rifling through a stack of colorful T-shirts.
"What size do you wear?"

Libby stood on tiptoe, letting her breath fan against his ear,
delighting as that appendage reddened visibly. "About the size
of the palm of your hand, cowboy."

"Damn," Jess chuckled, and the red moved out from his ear
to churn under his suntan. "Unless you want me to drag you
off somewhere and make love to you right now, you'd better
not make any more remarks like that."

Suddenly Libby was as pink as the T-shirt he was measuring
against her chest. Coming from Jess, this was no idle threat—
since their new understanding, reached several weeks before on
the top of the hill behind his house, they had made love in
some very unconventional places. It would be like him to take
her to one of the small trailers brought by some of the cowboys
from the Circle Bar B and follow through.

Having apparently deemed the pink T-shirt appropriate, Jess

bought it and gripped Libby's hand, fairly dragging her across the sawdust-covered fairgrounds. From the grandstands came the deafening shouts and boot-stompings of more than a thousand excited rodeo fans.

Reaching the rest rooms, which were housed in a building of their own, Jess gave an exasperated sigh. There must have been a hundred women waiting to use the facilities, and he clearly didn't want to stand around in the sun just so Libby could exchange her suntop for a T-shirt.

Before she could offer to wait alone so that Jess could go back and watch the rodeo, he was hauling her toward the nest of Circle Bar B trailers at such a fast pace that she had to scramble to keep up with him.

Thrusting her inside the smallest, which was littered with boots, beer cans and dirty clothes, he ordered, "Put on the shirt."

Libby's color was so high that she was sure he could see it, even in the cool darkness of that camper-trailer. "This is Jake Peterson's camper, isn't it? What if he comes back?"

"He won't come back—he's entered in the bull-riding competition. Just change, will you?"

Libby knew only too well what would happen if she removed that suntop. "Jess…"

He closed the camper door, flipped the inadequate-looking lock. Then he reached out, collected her befeathered hat, her sketchbook, her purse. He laid all these items on a small, messy table and waited.

In the distance, over the loudspeaker system, the rodeo announcer exalted, "This cowboy, folks, has been riding bulls longer'n he's been tying his shoes."

There was a thunderous communal cry as the cowboy and his bull apparently came out of their chute, but it was strangely quiet in that tiny trailer where Jess and Libby stood staring at each other.

Finally, in one defiant motion of her hands, Libby wrenched the suntop off over the top of her head and stood still before her husband, her breasts high and proud and completely bare. "Are you satisfied?" she snapped.

"Not yet," Jess retorted.

He came to stand very close, his hands gentle on her breasts. "You were right," he said into her hair. "You just fit the palms of my hands."

"Oh," said Libby in sweet despair.

Jess's hands continued their tender work, lulling her. It was so cool inside that trailer, so intimate and shadowy.

Presently Libby felt the snap on her jeans, and then the zipper, give way. She was conscious of a shivering heat as the fabric glided downward. Protesting was quite beyond her powers now; she was bewitched.

Jess laid her on the narrow camper bed, joining her within moments. Stretched out upon her, he entered her with one deft thrust.

Their triumph was a simultaneous one, reached after they'd both traveled through a glittering mine field of physical and spiritual sensation, and it was of such dizzying scope that it seemed natural for the unknowing crowd in the grandstands to cheer.

FURIOUSLY LIBBY FASTENED her jeans and pulled on the T-shirt that had caused this situation in the first place. She gathered up her things, plopped her hat onto her head, and glared into Jess's amused face.

He dressed at a leisurely pace, as though they weren't trespassing.

"If Jake Peterson ever finds out about his, I'll die," Libby said, casting anxious, impatient looks at the locked door.

Jess pulled on one boot, then the other, ran a hand through his rumpled hair. His eyes smoldering with mischief and lingering pleasure, he stood up, pulled Libby into his arms and kissed her. "I love you," he said. "And your shameful secret is safe with me, Mrs. Barlowe."

Libby's natural good nature was overcoming her anger. "Sure," she retorted tartly. "All the same, I think you should know that every man who had ever compromised me in a ranch hand's trailer has said that selfsame thing."

Jess laughed, kissed her again, and then released her. "Go back to your Indians, you little hellion. I'll find you later."

"That's what I'm afraid of," Libby tossed back over one shoulder as she stepped out of the camper into the bright July sunshine. Almost before her eyes had adjusted to the change, she was sketching again.

Libby hardly noticed the passing of the hours, so intent was she on recording the scenes that so fascinated her: braves festooned with colorful feathers, doing their war and rain dances; squaws, plump in their worn buckskin dresses, demonstrating the grinding of corn or making their beaded belts and moccasins; children playing games that were almost as old as the distant mountains and the big sky.

Between the residual effects of that scandalous bout of lovemaking in the trailer and the feast of color and sound assaulting her now, Libby's senses were reeling. She was almost relieved when Cathy came and signed that it was time to leave.

As they walked back to find the others in the still-dense crowd, Libby studied her cousin out of the corner of her eye. Cathy and Stacey were living together again, but there was a wistfulness about Cathy that was disturbing.

There would be no chance to talk with her now—there were too many distractions for that—but Libby made a mental vow to get Cathy alone later, perhaps during the birthday party that was being held on the ranch for Senator Barlowe that evening, and find out what was bothering her.

As the group made plans to stop at a favorite café for an early supper, Libby grew more and more uneasy about Cathy. What was it about her that was different, besides her obviously downhearted mood?

Before Libby could even begin to work out that complex question, Ken and Becky were off to their truck, Stacey and Cathy to their car. Libby was still staring into space when Jess gently tugged at her hand.

She got into the Land Rover, feeling pensive, and laid her sketchbook and purse on the seat.

"Another fit of creativity?" Jess asked quietly, driving carefully through a maze of other cars, staggering cowboys and beleaguered sheriff's deputies.

"I was thinking about Cathy," Libby replied. "Have you noticed a change in her?"

He thought, shook his head. "Not really."

"She doesn't talk to me anymore, Jess."

"Did you have an argument?"

Libby sighed. "No. I've been so busy lately, what with finishing the book and everything, I haven't spent much time with her. I'm ashamed to say that I didn't even notice the change in her until just a little while ago."

Jess gave her a gentle look. "Don't start beating yourself up Libby. You're not responsible for Cathy's happiness or unhappiness."

Surprised, Libby stared at him. "That sounds strange, coming from you."

They were pulling out onto the main highway, which was narrow and almost as choked with cars as the parking area had been. "I'm beginning to think it was a mistake, our being so protective of Cathy. We all meant well, but I wonder sometimes if we didn't hurt her instead."

"Hurt her?"

One of Jess's shoulders lifted in a shrug. "In a lot of ways, Cathy's still a little girl. She's never had to be a grown-up, Libby, because one of us was always there to fight her battles for her. I think she uses her deafness as an excuse not to take risks."

Libby was silent, reflecting on Cathy's fear of being a mother.

As though he'd looked into her mind, Jess went on to say, "Both Cathy and Stacey want children—did you know that? But Cathy won't take the chance."

"I knew she was scared—she told me that. She's scared of so many things, Jess—especially of losing Stacey."

"She loves him."

"I know. I just wish she had something more—something of her own so that her security as a person wouldn't hinge entirely on what Stacey does."

"You mean the way your security doesn't hinge on what I do?" Jess ventured, his tone devoid of any challenge or rancor.

Libby turned, took off her hat and set it down between them with the other things. "I love you very, very much, Jess, but I could live without you. It would hurt unbearably, but I could do it."

He looked away from the traffic only long enough to flash her one devilish grin. "Who would take shameful liberties with your body, if it weren't for me?"

"I guess I would have to do without shameful liberties," she said primly.

"Thank you for sidestepping my delicate male ego," he replied, "but the fact of the matter is, there's no way a woman as beautiful and talented as you are would be alone for very long."

"Don't say that!"

Jess glanced at her in surprise. "Don't say what?"

It was his meaning that had concerned Libby, not his exact words. "I don't even want to think about another man touching me the way you do."

Jess's attention was firmly fixed on the road ahead. "If you're trying to make me feel secure, princess, it's working."

"I'm not trying to make you feel anything. Jess, before we made love that first time, when you said I was really a virgin, you were right. Even the books I've read couldn't have prepared me for the things I feel when you love me."

"It might interest you to know, Mrs. Barlowe, that my feelings toward you are quite similar. Before we made love, sex was just something my body demanded, like food or exercise. Now it's magic."

She stretched to plant a noisy kiss on her husband's cheek. "Magic, is it? Well, you're something of a sorcerer yourself, Jess Barlowe. You cast spells over me and make me behave like a wanton."

He gave an exaggerated evil chuckle. "I hope I can remember the hex that made you give in to me back there at the fairgrounds."

Libby moved the things that were between them into the

backseat and slid closer, taking a mischievous nip at his ear-lobe. "I'm sure you can," she whispered.

Jess shuddered involuntarily and snapped, "Dammit, Libby, I'm driving."

She was exploring the sensitive place just beneath his ear with the tip of her tongue. "Umm. You like getting me into situations where I'm really vulnerable, don't you, Jess?" she breathed, sliding one hand inside his shirt. "Like today, for instance."

"Libby..."

"Revenge is sweet."

And it was.

SHYLY LIBBY EXTENDED the carefully wrapped package that contained her personal birthday gift to Senator Barlowe. She had not shown it to anyone else, not even Jess, and now she was uncertain. After all, Monica had given Cleave gold cuf-flinks and Stacey and Cathy planned to present him with a bottle of rare wine. By comparison, would her offering seem tacky and homemade?

With the gentle smile that had won him so many hearts and so many votes over the years, he took the parcel, which was revealingly large and flat, and turned it in his hands. "May I?" he asked softly, his kind eyes twinkling with affection.

"Please do," replied Libby.

It seemed to take Cleave forever to remove the ribbons and wrapping paper and lift the lid from the box inside, but there was genuine emotion in his face when he saw the framed pen-and-ink drawing Libby had been working on, in secret, for days. "My sons," he said.

"That's us, all right," commented Jess, who had appeared at the senator's side. "Personally, I think I'm considerably handsomer than that."

Cleave was examining the drawing closely. It showed Jess looking forward, Stacey in profile. When the senator looked up, Libby saw the love he bore his two sons in his eyes. "Thank you," he said. "This is one of the finest gifts I've ever received." He assessed the drawing again, and when his gaze came back to meet hers, it was full of mischief. "But where are my daughters? Where are you and Cathy?"

Libby smiled and kissed his cheek. "I guess you'll have to wait until your *next* birthday for that."

"In that case," rejoined the senator, "why not throw in a couple of grandchildren for good measure?"

Libby grinned. "I might be able to come up with one, but a couple?"

"Cathy will just have to do her part," came the immediate reply. "Now, if you'll excuse me, I want to take this picture around and show all my guests what a talented daughter-in-law I have."

Once his father had gone, Jess lifted his champagne glass and one eyebrow. "'Talented' is definitely the word," he said.

Libby knew that he was not referring to her artwork and hastily changed the subject. "You look so splendid in that tuxedo that I think I'd like to dance with you."

Jess worked one index finger under the tight collar of his formal shirt, obviously uncomfortable. "Dance?" he echoed dryly. "Lead me to the organ grinder and we're in business."

Laughing, Libby caught at his free hand and dragged him into the spacious living room, which had been prepared for dancing. There was a small string band to provide the music.

Libby took Jess's champagne glass and set it aside, then rested both hands on his elegant satin lapels. The other guests—and there were dozens—might not have existed at all.

"Dance with me," she said.

Jess took her into his arms, his eyes never leaving hers. "You know," he said softly, "you look so wonderful in that silvery dress that I'm tempted to take you home and make damned sure my father gets that grandchild he wants."

"When we start a baby," she replied seriously, "I want it to be for us."

Jess's mouth quirked into a grin and his eyes were alight with love. "I wasn't going to tape a bow to the little stinker's head and hand it over to him, Libby."

Libby giggled at the picture this prompted in her mind. "Babies are so funny," she dreamed aloud.

"I know," Jess replied. "I love that look of drunken wonder they get when you lift them up high and talk to them. About that time, they usually barf in your hair."

Before she could answer, Ken and Becky came into the magical mist that had heretofore surrounded Libby and Jess.

"All right if I cut in?" Ken asked.

"How soon do you want a grandchild?" Jess countered.

"Sooner the better," retorted Ken. "And, Jess?"

"What?" demanded his son-in-law, eyes still locked with Libby's.

"The music stopped."

Jess and Libby both came to a startled halt, and Becky was so delighted by their expressions that her laughter pealed through the large room.

When the band started playing again, Libby found herself dancing with her father, while Jess and Becky waltzed nearby.

"You look real pretty," Ken said, beaming down at her.

"You're pretty fancy yourself," Libby answered. "In fact, you look downright handsome in that tuxedo."

"She says that to everybody," put in Jess, who happened to be whirling past with Becky.

Ken's laugh was low and throaty. "He never gets too far away from you, does he?"

"About as far as white gets from rice. And I like it that way."

"That's what I figured. Libby…"

The serious, tentative way he'd said her name gave Libby pause. "Yes?"

"Becky and I are going to get married," he blurted out, without taking a single breath.

Libby felt her eyes fill. "You were afraid to tell me that? Afraid to tell me something wonderful?"

Ken stopped, his arms still around his daughter, his blue eyes bright with relief and delight. Then, with a raucous shout that was far more typical of him than tuxedos and fancy parties, her father lifted her so high that she was afraid she would fall out of the top of her dress.

"THAT WAS CERTAINLY rustic," remarked Monica, five minutes later, at the refreshment table.

Libby saw Jess approaching through the crowd of guests and smiled down at the buttery crab puff in her fingers. "Are you making fun of my father, Ms. Summers?"

Monica sighed in exasperation. "This *is* a formal party, after all—not a kegger at the Golden Buckle. I don't know why the senator insists on inviting the help to important affairs."

Slowly, and with great deliberation, Libby tucked her crab puff into Monica's artfully displayed cleavage. "Will you hold this, please?" she trilled, and then walked toward her husband.

"The foreman's brat strikes again," Jess chuckled, pulling her into another waltz.

CATHY WAS SITTING alone in the dimly lit kitchen, her eyes fixed on something far in the distance. Libby was careful to let her cousin see her, rather than startle her with a touch.

"Hi," she said.

Cathy replied listlessly.

Libby took a chair opposite Cathy's and signed, "I'd like to help if I can."

Cathy's face crumbled suddenly and she gave a soft cry that tore at Libby's heart. Her hands flew as she replied, "Nobody can help me!"

"Don't I even get to try?"

A tendril of Cathy's hair fell from the soft knot at the back of her head and danced against a shoulder left bare by her Grecian evening gown. "I'm pregnant," she whispered. "Oh, Libby, I'm pregnant!"

Libby felt confusion and just a touch of envy. "Is that so terrible? I know you were scared before, but—"

"I'm still scared!" Cathy broke in, her voice unusually loud.

Libby drew a deep breath. "Why, Cathy? You're strong and healthy. And your deafness won't be the problem you think it will—you and Stacey can afford to hire help, if you feel it's necessary."

"All of that is so easy for you to say, Libby!" Cathy flared with sudden and startling anger. "You can hear! You're a whole person!"

Libby felt her own temper, always suppressed when dealing with her handicapped cousin, surge into life. "You know something?" she said furiously. "I'm sick of your 'Poor Cathy' number! A child is just about the best thing that can happen to a person and instead of rejoicing, you're standing here complaining!"

"I have a reason to complain!"

Libby's arms flew out from her side in a gesture of wild annoyance. "All right! You're deaf, you can't hear! Poor, poor Cathy! Now, can we get past singing your sad song? Dammit, Cathy, I know how hard it must be to live in silence, but can't you look on the positive side for once? You're married to a successful, gentle-hearted man who loves you very much. You have everything!"

"Said the woman who could hear!" shouted Cathy.

Libby sighed and sat back in her chair. "We're all handicapped in some way—Jess told me that once, and I think it's true."

Cathy was not going to be placated. "What's your handicap, Libby?" she snapped. "Your short fingernails? The fact that you freckle in the summer instead of getting tan?"

The derisive sarcasm of her cousin's words stung Libby. "I'm as uncertain of myself at times as you are, Cathy," she said softly. "Aaron—"

"Aaron!" spouted Cathy with contempt. "Don't hand me that, Libby! So he ran around a little—I had to stand by and watch my husband adore my own cousin for months! And I'll bet Jess has made any traumas you had about going to bed with a man all better!"

"Cathy, please..."

Cathy gave a guttural, furious cry of frustration. "I'm so damned tired of you, Libby, with your career and your loving father and your..."

Libby was mad again, and she bounded to her feet. "And my what?" she cried. "I can't help that you don't have a father—Dad tried to make up for that and I think he did a damned good job! As for a career—don't you dare hassle me about that! I worked like a slave to get where I am! If you want a career, Cathy, get off your backside and start one!''

Cathy stared at her, stunned, and then burst into tears. And, of course, Jess chose exactly that moment to walk in.

Giving Libby one scalding, reproachful look, he gathered Cathy into his arms and held her.

CHAPTER FIFTEEN

AFTER ONE MOMENT of feeling absolutely shattered, Libby lifted her chin and turned from Jess's annoyance and Cathy's veiled triumph to walk out of the kitchen with dignity.

She encountered a worried-looking Marion Bradshaw just on the other side of the door. "Libby...Mrs. Barlowe...that man is here!"

Libby drew a deep breath. "What man?" she managed to ask halfheartedly.

"Mr. Aaron Strand, that's who!" whispered Marion. "He had the nerve to walk right up and ring the bell..."

Libby was instantly alert, alive in every part of her being, like a creature being stalked in the wilds. "Where is he now?"

"He's in the senator's study," answered the flushed, quietly outraged housekeeper. "He says he won't leave till he talks with you, Libby. I didn't want a scene, what with all these people here, so I didn't argue."

Wearily Libby patted Marion's shoulder. Facing Aaron Strand, especially now, was the last thing in the world she wanted to do. But she knew that he would create an awful fuss if his request was denied, and besides, what real harm could he do with so many people in the house? "I'll talk to him," she said.

"I'll get Jess," mused Mrs. Bradshaw, "and your daddy, too."

Libby shook her head quickly, and warm color surged up over her face. Jess was busy lending a strong shoulder to Cathy, and she was damned if she was going to ask for his help now, even indirectly. And though Ken was almost fully recovered from his confrontation with the bear, Libby had no intention of subjecting him to the stress that could result from a verbal round with his former son-in-law. "I'll handle this myself," she said firmly, and then, without waiting for a reply, she started for the senator's study.

Aaron was there, tall and handsome in his formal clothes.

"At least when you crash a party, you dress for it," observed Libby dryly from the doorway.

Aaron set down the paperweight he had been examining and smiled. His eyes moved over her in a way that made her want to stride across the room and slap him with all her might. "That dress is classy, sugarplum," he said in acid tones. "You're definitely bunkhouse-calendar material."

Libby bit her lower lip, counted mentally until the urge to scream passed. "What do you want, Aaron?" she asked finally.

"Want?" he echoed, pretending pleasant confusion.

"Yes!" hissed Libby. "You flew two thousand miles—you must want something."

He sighed, leaned back against the senator's desk, folded his arms. "Are you happy?"

"Yes," answered Libby with a lift of her chin.

Again he assessed her shiny silver dress, the hint of cleavage it revealed. "I imagine the cowboy is pretty happy with you, too," he said. "Which Barlowe is it, Libby? The steak-house king or the lawyer?"

Libby's head began to ache; she sighed and closed her eyes for just a moment. "What do you want?" she asked again insistently.

His shoulders moved in a shrug. "A baby," he answered, as though he was asking for a cup of coffee or the time of day. "I know you're not going to give me that, so relax."

"Why did you come here, then?"

"I just wanted a look at this ranch. Pretty fancy spread, Lib. You do know how to land on your feet, don't you?"

"Get out, Aaron."

"Without meeting your husband? Your paragon of a father? I wouldn't think of it, Mrs. Barlowe."

Libby was off balance, trying to figure out what reason Aaron could have for coming all the way to Montana besides causing her added grief. Incredible as it seemed, he had apparently done just that. "You can't hurt me anymore, Aaron," she said. "I won't let you. Now, get out of here, please."

"Oh, no. I lost everything because of you—everything. And I'll have my pound of flesh, Libby—you can be sure of that."

"If your grandmother relieved you of your company responsibilities, Aaron, that's your fault, not mine. I should think you would be glad—now you won't have anything to keep you from your wine, women and song."

Aaron's face was tense. Gone was his easy, gentlemanly manner. "With the company went most of my money, Libby. And let's not pretend, sweetness—I can make your bright, shiny new life miserable, and we both know it."

"How?" asked Libby, poised to turn and walk out of the study.

"By generating shame and scandal, of course. Your father-in-law is a prominent United States senator, isn't he? I should think negative publicity could hurt him very badly—and you know how good I am at stirring that up."

Rage made Libby tremble. "You can't hurt Cleave Barlowe, Aaron. You can't hurt me. Now, get out before I have you thrown out!"

He crossed the room at an alarming speed, had a hold on Libby's upper arms before she could grasp what was happening. He thrust her back against the heavy door of the study and covered her mouth with his own.

Libby squirmed, shocked and repulsed. She tried to push Aaron away, but he had trapped her hands between his chest and her own. And the kiss went on, ugly and wet, obscene because it was forced upon her, because it was Aaron's.

Finally he drew back, smirking down at her, grasping her wrists in both hands when she tried to wriggle away from him. And suddenly Libby was oddly detached, calm even. Mrs. Bradshaw had been right when she'd wanted to let Jess know that Aaron was here, so very right.

Libby had demurred because of her pride, because she was mad at Jess; she'd thought she could handle Aaron Strand. Pride be damned, she thought, and then she threw back her head and gave a piercing, defiant scream.

Aaron chuckled. "Do you think I'm afraid of your husband, Libby?" he drawled. Incredibly, he was about to kiss her again, it appeared, when he was suddenly wrenched away.

Libby dared one look at Jess's green eyes and saw murder flashing there. She reached for his arm, but he shook her hand away.

"Strand," he said, his gaze fixed on a startled but affably recovering Aaron.

Aaron gave a mocking half-bow. It didn't seem to bother him that Jess was coldly furious, that half the guests at the senator's party, Ken Kincaid included, were jammed into the study doorway.

"Is this the part," Aaron drawled, "where we fight over the fair lady?"

"This is the part," Jess confirmed icily.

Aaron shrugged. "I feel honor-bound to warn you," he said smugly, "that I am a fifth-degree black belt."

Jess spared him an evil smile, but said nothing.

Libby was afraid; again she grasped at Jess's arm. "Jess, he really is a black belt."

Jess did not so much as look at Libby; he was out of her reach, and not just physically. She felt terror thick in her throat, and flung an appealing look at Ken, who was standing beside her, one arm around her waist.

Reading the plea in his daughter's eyes, he denied it with an almost imperceptible shake of his head.

Libby was frantic. As Jess and Aaron drew closer to each other, circling like powerful beasts, she struggled to free herself from her father's restraining arm. For all his weaknesses of character, Aaron Strand was agile and strong, and if he could hurt Jess, he would, without qualms of any kind.

"Jess, no!" she cried.

Jess turned toward her, his jaw tight with cold annoyance, and Aaron struck in that moment. His foot came up in a graceful arc and caught Jess in the side of the neck. Too sick to stand by herself or run away, Libby buried her face in Ken's tuxedo jacket in horror.

There were sounds—terrible sounds. Why didn't someone

stop the fight? Why were they all standing around like Romans thrilling to the exploits of gladiators? Why?

When the sounds ceased and Libby dared to look, Jess was still standing. Aaron was sitting on the floor, groaning theatrically, one corner of his lip bleeding. It was obvious that he wasn't badly hurt, for all his carrying on.

Rage and relief mingled within Libby in one dizzying sweep. "Animals!" she screamed, and when she whirled to flee the ugliness, no one moved to stop her.

LIBBY SAT ON THE COUCH in the condo's living room, her arms wrapped around her knees, stubbornly ignoring the ringing of the telephone. She couldn't help counting, though—that had become something of a game in the two days since she'd left the ranch to take refuge here. Twenty-six rings. It was a record.

She stood up shakily, made her way into the kitchen, where she had been trying to sketch out the panels for her cartoon strip. "Back to the old drawing board," she said to the empty room, and the stale joke fell flat because there was no one there to laugh.

The telephone rang again and, worn down, Libby reached out for the receiver affixed to the kitchen wall and snapped, "Hello!"

"Lib?" The voice belonged to her father, and it was full of concern. "Libby, are you all right?"

"No," she answered honestly, letting a sigh carry the word. "As a matter of fact, I'm not all right. How are you?"

"Never mind me—why did you run off like that?"

"You know why."

"Are you coming back to the ranch?"

"Why?" countered Libby, annoyed. "Am I missing some bloody spectacle?"

Ken gave a gruff sigh. "Dammit, Libby, do you love Jess Barlowe or not?"

Tears stung her eyes. Love him? These two days away from him had been hell, but she wasn't about to admit that. "What does it matter?" she shot back. "He's probably so busy holding Cathy's hand that he hasn't even noticed I'm gone."

"That's it. Cathy. Standing up for her is a habit with Jess, Lib—you know that."

Libby did know; in two days she'd had plenty of time to come to the conclusion that she had overreacted in the kitchen the night of the party when Jess had seemed to take Cathy's part against her. She shouldn't have walked out that way. "There is still the fight—"

"You screamed, Libby. What would you have done, if you'd been in Jess's place?" Without waiting for an answer, her father went on, "You're just being stubborn, and so is Jess. Do you love him enough to make the first move, Lib? Do you have the gumption?"

Libby reached out for a kitchen chair, sank into it. "Where is he?"

There was a smile in her father's voice. "Up on that ridge behind your place," he answered. "He's got a camp up there."

Libby knew mild disappointment; if Jess was camping, he hadn't been calling. She had been ignoring the telephone for two days for nothing. "It's nice to know he misses me so much," she muttered petulantly.

Having said his piece, Ken was silent.

"He does miss me, doesn't he?" demanded Libby.

"He misses you," chuckled Ken. "He wouldn't be doing his hermit routine if he didn't."

Libby sighed. "The ridge, huh?"

"The ridge," confirmed Ken with amusement. And then he hung up.

I SHOULDN'T BE DOING THIS in my condition, Libby complained to herself as she made her way up the steep hillside. *But since the mountain won't come to me...*

She stopped, looked up. The smoke from Jess's campfire was curling toward the sky; the sun was hot and bright. What the devil did he need with a fire, anyway? It was broad daylight, for heaven's sake.

Muttering, holding on to her waning courage tenaciously, Libby made her way up over the rise to the top of the ridge. Jess was standing with his back to her, looking in the opposite direction, but the stiffness of his shoulders revealed that he knew she was there.

And suddenly she was furious. Hadn't she climbed up this cursed mountain, her heart in her throat, her pride God-only-knew-where? Wasn't the current situation as much his fault as her own? Hadn't she found out, the very day after she'd left him, that she was going to have his baby?

"Damn you, Jess Barlowe," she hissed, "don't you dare ignore me!"

He turned very slowly to face her. "I'm sorry," he said stiffly and with annoying effort.

"For what?" pressed Libby. Damned if she was going to make it easy!

Jess sighed, idly kicked dirt over his campfire with one booted foot. There was a small tent pitched a few feet away, and a coffeepot sat on a fallen log, along with a paperback book and a half-eaten sandwich. "For assuming that the scene with Cathy was your fault," he said.

Libby huffed over to the log, which was a fair distance from Jess, and sat down, folding her arms. "Well, praise be!" she murmured. "What about that stupid fistfight in your father's study?"

His green eyes shot to her face. "You'll grow horns, lady, before you hear me apologize for that!"

Libby bit her lower lip. Fighting wasn't the ideal way to settle things, it was true, but she couldn't help recalling the pleasure she herself had taken in stuffing that crab puff down the front of Monica Summers' dress at the party. If Monica had made one move to retaliate, she would have gladly tangled with her. "Fair enough," she said.

There was an uncomfortable silence, which Libby finally felt compelled to break. "Why did you have a fire going in the middle of the day?"

Jess laughed. "I wanted to make damned sure you found my camp," he replied.

"Dad told you I was coming!"

He came to sit beside her on the log and even though he didn't touch her, she was conscious of his nearness in every fiber of her flesh and spirit. "Yeah," he admitted, and he looked so sad that Libby wanted to cry.

She eased closer to him. "Jess?"

"What?" he asked, looking her squarely in the eyes now.

"I'm sorry."

He said nothing.

Libby drew a deep breath. "I'm not only sorry," she went on bravely, "I'm pregnant, too."

He was quiet for so long that Libby feared she'd been wrong to tell him about their child—at least for now. It was possible that he wanted to ask for a separation or even a divorce, but he might stay with her out of duty now that he knew. To hold him in that manner would break Libby's heart.

"When did you find out?" he asked finally, and the lack of emotion in his face and in his voice made Libby feel bereft.

"Day before yesterday. After Cathy said she was pregnant, I got to thinking and realized that I had a few symptoms myself."

Jess was silent, looking out over the trees, the ranges, the far mountains. After what seemed like an eternity, he turned to her again, his green eyes full of pain. "You weren't going to tell me?"

"Of course I was going to tell you, Jess. But, well, the time didn't seem to be right."

"You're not going to leave, are you?"

"Would I have climbed a stupid mountain, for pity's sake, if I wanted to leave you?"

A slow grin spread across Jess's face, and then he gave a startling hoot of delight and shot to his feet, his hands gripping Libby's and pulling her with him. If he hadn't caught her in his arms and held her, she would probably have fallen into the lush summer grass.

"Is it safe to assume you're happy about this announcement?" Libby teased, looking up at him and loving him all the more because there were tears on his face.

He lifted her into his arms, kissed her deeply in reply.

"Excuse me, sir," she said when he drew back, "but I was

wondering if you would mind making love to me. You see, I'd like to find out if I'm welcome here.''

In answer, Jess carried her to the tent, set her on her feet. ''My tent is your tent,'' he said.

Libby blushed a little and bent to go inside the small canvas shelter. Since there wasn't room enough to stand, she sat on the rumpled sleeping bag and waited as Jess joined her.

She was never sure exactly how it came about, but within moments they were both lying down, facing each other. The weight of his hand was bliss on her breast, and so were the hoarse words he said.

''I love you, Libby. I need you. No matter how mad I make you, please don't leave me again.''

Libby traced the strong lines of his jaw with a fingertip. ''I won't, Jess. I might scream and yell, but I won't leave. I love you too much to be away from you—if I learned anything in the last two days, it was that.''

He was propped up on one elbow now, very close, and he was idly unbuttoning her blouse. ''I want you.''

Libby feigned shock. ''In a tent, sir?''

''And other novel places.'' He paused, undid the front catch of her bra.

Libby sighed, then gasped as the warmth of his mouth closed over the straining peak of her breast. The sensation was exquisite, sweeping through her, pushing away the weariness and confusion and pain. She tangled her fingers in his rumpled hair, holding him close.

Jess finally left the breast he had so gently plundered to remove his clothes, and then, more slowly, Libby's. When she lay naked before him in the cool shadows of the tiny tent, he took in her waiting body with a look of rapt wonder. ''Little enchantress,'' he breathed, ''let me worship you.

Libby could not bear to be separate from him any longer. ''Be close to me, Jess,'' she pleaded softly, ''be part of me.''

With a groan, he fell to her, his mouth moist and commanding upon hers. His tongue mated with Libby's and his manhood touched her with fire, prodding, taking only partial shelter inside her.

At last Jess broke the kiss and lifted his head, and Libby saw, through a shifting haze, that he was savoring her passion as well as his own. She was aware of every muscle in his body as he struggled to defy forces that do not brook the rebellion of mere mortals.

Finally these forces prevailed, and Jess was thrust, with a raspy cry, into Libby's depths. They moved together wildly, seeking and reaching and finally breaking through the barriers that divide this world from the glories of the next.

CATHY ASSESSED the large oil painting of Jim Little Eagle, the Indian child Libby had seen at the powwow months before, her hands resting on her protruding stomach.

Libby, whose stomach was as large as Cathy's, was wiping her hands on a rag reserved for the purpose. The painting was a personal triumph, and she was proud of it. "What do you think?" she signed, after setting aside the cloth.

Cathy grinned. "What do I think?" she asked aloud, sitting down on the tall stool behind Libby's drawing board. "I'll tell you what I think. I think you should sell it to me instead of letting that gallery in Great Falls handle it. After all, they've got your pen-and-ink drawings and the other paintings you did."

Libby tried to look stern. "Are you asking for special favors, Cathy Barlowe?"

Cathy laughed. "Yes!" Her sparkling green eyes fell to the sketch affixed to Libby's drawing board and she exclaimed in delighted surprise. "This is great!"

Libby came to stand behind her, but her gaze touched only briefly on the drawing. Instead, she was looking out at the snow through the windows of her studio in Ken and Becky's house.

"What are you going to do with this?" Cathy demanded, tugging at Libby's arm.

Libby smiled, looking at the drawing. It showed her cartoon character, given over to the care of another artist now. Liberated Lizzie was in an advanced state of pregnancy, and the blurb read, "If it feels good, do it."

"I'm going to give it to Jess," she said with a slight blush. "It's a private joke."

Cathy laughed again, then assessed the spacious, well-equipped studio with happy eyes. "I'm surprised you work down here at your dad's place. Especially with Jess home almost every day, doing paperwork and things."

Libby's mouth quirked in a grin. "That's *why* I work down here. If I tried to paint there, I wouldn't get anything done."

"You're really happy, aren't you?"

"Completely."

Cathy enfolded her in a hug. "Me, too," she said. And when her eyes came to Libby's face, they were dancing with mischief. "Of course, you and Jess have to understand that you will never win the Race. Stacey and I are ahead by at least a nose."

Libby stood straight and tried to look imperious. "We will not concede defeat," she said.

Before Cathy could reply to this, Stacey came into the room, pretending to see only Libby. "Pardon me, pudgy person," he began, "but has my wife waddled by lately?"

"Is she kind of short, with long, pretty hair and big green eyes and a stomach shaped rather like a watermelon?"

Stacey snapped his fingers and a light seemed to go on in his face. "That's a pretty good description."

"Haven't seen her," said Libby.

Cathy gave her a delighted shove and flung herself at her husband, laughing. A moment later they were on their way out, loudly vowing to win what Jess and Stacey had dubbed the Great Barlowe Baby Race.

Through with her work for the day and eager to get home to Jess, Libby cleaned her brushes and put them away, washed her hands again, and went out to find her coat. The first pain struck just as she was getting into the car.

At home, Jess was standing pensively in the kitchen, staring out at the heavy layer of snow blanketing the hillside behind the house. Libby came up as close behind him as her stomach would allow and wrapped her arms around his lean waist.

"I've just had a pretty good tip on the Baby Race," she said.

The muscles beneath his bulky woolen sweater tightened, and he turned to look down at her, his jade eyes dark with wonder. "What did you say?"

"We're on the homestretch, Jess. I need to go to the hospital. Soon."

He paled, this man who had hunted wounded bears and fire-breathing dragons. "My God!" he yelled, and suddenly they were both caught up in a whirlwind of activity. Phone calls were made, suitcases were snatched from the coat-closet floor, and then Jess was dragging Libby toward his Land Rover.

"Wait, I'm sure we have time—"

"I'm not taking any chances!" barked Jess, hoisting her pear-shaped and unwieldy form into the car seat.

"Jess," Libby scolded, grasping at his arm. "You're panicking!"

"You're damned right I'm panicking!" he cried, and then they were driving over the snowy, rutted roads of the ranch at the fastest pace he dared.

When they reached the airstrip, the Cessna had been brought out of the small hangar where it was kept and fuel was being pumped into it. After wrestling Libby into the front passenger seat, Jess quickly checked the engine and the landing gear. These were tasks, she had learned, that he never trusted to anyone else.

"Jess, this is ridiculous!" she protested when he scrambled into the pilot's seat and began a preflight test there. "We have plenty of time to drive to the hospital."

Jess ignored her, and less than a minute later the plane was taxiing down the runway. Out of the corner of one eye Libby saw a flash of ice blue.

"Jess, wait!" she cried. "The Ferrari!"

The plane braked and Jess craned his neck to see around Libby. Sure enough, Stacey and Cathy were running toward them, if Cathy's peculiar gait could be called a run.

Stacey leapt up onto the wing and opened the door. "Going

our way?'' he quipped, but his eyes were wide and his face was white.

"Get in,'' replied Jess impatiently, but his eyes were gentle as they touched Cathy and then Libby. "The race is on,'' he added.

Cathy was the first to deliver, streaking over the finish line with a healthy baby girl, but Libby produced twin sons soon after. Following much discussion, the Great Barlowe Baby Race was declared a draw.

THE DREAM UNFOLDS

Barbara Delinsky

CHAPTER ONE

THEY WERE THREE MEN with a mission late on a September afternoon. Purposefully they climbed from their cars, slammed their doors in quick succession and fell into broad stride on the brick walk leading to Elizabeth Abbott's front door. Gordon Hale rang the doorbell. It had been decided, back in his office at the bank, that he would be the primary speaker. He was the senior member of the group, the one who had organized the Crosslyn Rise consortium, the one who posed the least threat to Elizabeth Abbott.

Carter Malloy posed a threat because he was a brilliant architect, a rising star in his hometown, with a project in the works that stood to bring big bucks to the town. But there was more to his threat than that. He had known Elizabeth Abbott when they'd been kids, when he'd been the bad boy of the lot. The bad boy no longer, his biggest mistake in recent years had been bedding the vengeful Ms. Abbott. It had only happened once, he swore, and years before, despite Elizabeth's continued interest. Now, though, Carter was in love and on the verge of marrying Jessica Crosslyn, and Elizabeth had her tool for revenge. As chairman of the zoning commission, she was denying Crosslyn Rise the building permit it needed to break ground on its project.

Gideon Lowe was the builder for that project, and he had lots riding on its success. For one thing, the conversion of Crosslyn Rise from a single mansion on acres of land to an elegant condominium community promised to be the most challenging project he'd ever worked on. For another, it was the most visible. A job well-done there would be like a gold star on his résumé. But there was another reason why he wanted the project to be a success. He was an investor in it. For the first time, he had money at stake, *big* money. He knew he was taking a gamble, risking so much of his personal savings, but if things went well, he would have established himself as a businessman, a man of brain, as well as brawn. That was what he wanted, a change of image. And that was why he'd allowed himself to be talked into trading a beer with the guys after work for this mission.

A butler opened the door. "Yes?"

Gordon drew his stocky body to its full five-foot-ten-inch height. "My name is Gordon Hale. These gentlemen are Carter Malloy and Gideon Lowe. We're here to see Miss Abbott. I believe she's expecting us."

"Yes, sir, she is," the butler answered, and stood back to gesture them into the house. "If you'll come this way," he said as soon as they were all in the spacious front hall with the door closed behind them.

Gideon followed the others through the hall, then the living room and into the parlor, all the while fighting the urge to either laugh or say something crude. He hated phoniness. He also hated formality. He was used to it, he supposed, just as he was used to wearing a shirt and tie when the occasion called for it, as this one did. Still he couldn't help but feel scorn for the woman who was now rising, like a queen receiving her court, from a chintz-covered wingback chair.

"Gordon," she said with a smile, and extended her hand, "how nice to see you."

Gordon took her hand in his. "The pleasure's mine, Elizabeth." He turned and said nonchalantly, "I believe you know Carter."

"Yes," she acknowledged, and Gideon had to hand it to her. For a woman who had once lain naked and hot under Carter, she was cool as a cucumber now. "How are you, Carter?"

Carter wasn't quite as cool. Losing himself to the opportunity, he said, "I'd have been better without this misunderstanding."

"Misunderstanding?" Elizabeth asked innocently. "Is there a misunderstanding here?" She looked at Gordon. "I thought we'd been quite clear."

Gordon cleared his throat. "About denying us the building

permit, yes. About why you've denied it, no. That's why we requested this meeting. But before we start—'' he gestured toward Gideon ''—I don't believe you've met Gideon Lowe. He's both a member of the consortium and our general contractor.''

Elizabeth turned the force of her impeccably made-up blue eyes on Gideon. She nodded, then seemed to look a second time and with interest, after which she extended her hand. ''Gideon Lowe? Have I heard that name before?''

''I doubt it, ma'am,'' Gideon said. Her hand felt as cool as that cuke, and nearly as hard. He guessed she was made of steel and could understand why once had been enough for Carter. He knew then and there that he wasn't interested even in once, himself, but he had every intention of playing the game. ''Most of my work has been out in the western counties. I'm new to these parts.'' If he sounded like a nice country boy, even a little Southern, that was fine for now. Women liked that. They found it sweet, even charming, particularly when the man was as tall as Gideon was, and—he only thought it because, after thirty-nine years of hearing people say it, he supposed he had the right—as handsome.

''Welcome, then,'' she said with a smile. ''But how did you come to be associated with these two rogues?''

''That's a damn good question,'' he said, returning the smile, even putting a little extra shine in it. ''Seems I might have been taken in by promises of smooth sailing. We builders are used to delays, but that doesn't mean we like them. I've got my trucks ready to roll and my men champing at the bit. You're one powerful lady to control a group of guys that way.''

Elizabeth did something with her mouth that said she loved the thought of that, though she said a bit demurely, ''I'm afraid I can't take all the credit. I'm only one of a committee.''

''But you're its chairman,'' Gordon put in, picking up the ball. ''May we sit, Elizabeth?''

Elizabeth turned to him with a look of mild indignance. ''Be my guest, though it won't do you much good. We've made our decision. As a courtesy, I've agreed to see you, but the committee's next formal meeting won't be until February. I thought I explained all that to Jessica."

At mention of Jessica's name, Carter stiffened. "You explained just enough on the phone to upset her. Why don't you go over it once more, face-to-face, with us."

"What Carter means," Gordon rushed to explain, "is that we're a little confused. Until yesterday afternoon, we'd been under the impression that everything was approved. I've been in close touch with Donald Swett, who assured me that all was well."

"Donald shouldn't have said that. I suppose he can be excused, since he's new to the committee this year, but all is never 'well,' as you put it, until the last of the information has been studied. As it turns out, we have serious doubts about the benefit of your project to this community."

"Are you kidding?" Carter asked.

Gordon held up a hand to him. To Elizabeth, he said, "The proposal we submitted to your committee went through the issue of community impact, point by point. The town has lots to gain, not the least of which is new tax revenue."

Elizabeth tipped her head. "We have lots to lose, too."

"Like what?" Carter asked, though a bit more civilly.

"Like crowding on the waterfront."

Gordon shook his head. "The marina will be limited in size and exclusive, at that. The price of the slips, alone, will discourage crowds."

"That price will discourage the local residents, too," Elizabeth argued, "who, I might add, also pay taxes to this town."

"Oh, my God," Carter muttered, "you're worried about the common folk. Since when, Elizabeth? You never used to give a damn about anyone or anything—"

"Carter—" Gordon interrupted, only to be interrupted in turn by Elizabeth, who was glaring at Carter.

"I've moved up in the hierarchy of this town. It's become my responsibility to think of everyone here." When Carter snorted in disbelief, she deliberately looked back at Gordon. "There's also the matter of your shops and their effect on those we already have. The town owes something to the shopkeepers who've been loyal to us all these years. So you see, it's not just a matter of money.''

"That's the most honest thing you've said so far," Carter fumed. "In fact, it doesn't have a damn *thing* to do with money. Or with crowding the waterfront or squeezing out shops. It has to do with you and me—''

Gordon interrupted. "I think we're losing it a little, here.''

"Did you expect anything different?" Elizabeth said in a superior way. "Some people never change. Carter certainly hasn't. He was a troublemaker as a boy, and he's a troublemaker now. Maybe *that's* one of the reservations my committee has—''

Carter sliced a hand through the air. "Your 'committee' has no reservations. You're the only one who does. I'd venture to guess that your 'committee' was as surprised as we were by this sudden withholding of a permit. Face it, Lizzie. You're acting on a personal vendetta. I wonder what your 'committee' would say, or the townspeople, for that matter, if they were to learn that you and I—''

"Carter!" Gordon snapped at the very same time that Gideon decided things had gone far enough.

"Whoa," Gideon said in a firm but slow and slightly raspy voice. "Let's take it easy here." He knew Carter. When the man felt passionately about something, there was no stopping him. It had been that way with Jessica, whom he had wooed doggedly for months until finally, just the day before, she agreed to marry him. It was that way with Crosslyn Rise, where he had spent part of his childhood. Apparently it was that way, albeit negatively, with Elizabeth Abbott. But Gideon knew Elizabeth's type, too. Over the years, he had done enough work for people like her to know that the more she was pushed, the more she would dig in her heels. Reason had nothing to do with it; pride did.

But pride wouldn't get the consortium the building permit it needed, and the permit was all Gideon wanted. "I think," he went on in the same slow and raspy voice, "that we ought to cool it a second." He scratched his head. "Maybe we ought to cool it longer than that. It's late. I don't know about you

guys, but I've been working all day. I'm tired. We're all tired.'
He looked beseechingly at Elizabeth. "Maybe this discussion
would be better saved for tomorrow morning."

"I don't believe I can make it then," she said.

Gordon added, "Tomorrow morning's booked for me, too.'

Carter scowled. "I have meetings in Springfield."

"Then dinner now," Gideon suggested. "I'm starved."

Again Gordon shook his head. "Mary's expecting me home
I'm already late."

Carter simply said, "Bad night."

Gideon slid a look at Elizabeth. "We could talk over dinner
you and I. I know as much about this project as these bozos.
It'd be a hell of a lot more peaceful. And pleasant," he added
more softly. "What do you say?"

Elizabeth was interested. He could see that. But she wasn't
about to accept his invitation too quickly, lest she look eager.
So she regarded him contemplatively for a minute, then looked
at Gordon and at Carter, the latter in a dismissive way, before
meeting Gideon's gaze again.

"I say that would be a refreshing change. You're right. It
would be more peaceful. You seem like a reasonable man.
We'll be able to talk." She glanced at the slender gold watch
on her wrist. "But we ought to leave soon. I have an engage-
ment at nine."

As announcements went, it was a bitchy one. But Gideon
was glad she'd made it for several reasons. For one thing, he
doubted it was true, which dented her credibility considerably,
which made him feel less guilty for the sweet talking he was
about to do. For another, it gave him an out. He was more than
willing to wine and dine Elizabeth Abbott for the sake of the
project, but he wasn't going beyond that. Hopefully, he'd have
the concessions he wanted by the time dessert was done.

Actually he did even better than that. Around and between
sexy smiles, the doling out of small tidbits of personal information and the withholding of enough else to make Elizabeth
immensely curious, he got her to agree that though some of her
reservations had merit, the pluses of the Crosslyn Rise conversion outweighed the minuses. In a golden twist of fate—not

entirely bizarre, Gideon knew, since the restaurant they were at was the only place for fine evening dining in town—two other members of the zoning commission were eating there with their wives. Unable to resist showing Gideon how influential she was, Elizabeth insisted on threading her arm through his and leading him to their table, introducing him around, then announcing that she had decided not to veto the Crosslyn Rise conversion after all. The men from the commission seemed pleased. They vigorously shook hands with Gideon and welcomed him to their town, while their wives looked on with smiles. Gideon smiled as charmingly at the wives as he did at Elizabeth. He knew it would be hard for her to renege after she'd declared her intentions before so many witnesses.

Feeling proud of himself for handling things with such aplomb, he sent a wink to a waitress whose looks tickled his fancy, as he escorted Elizabeth from the restaurant. At her front door, he graciously thanked her for the pleasure of her company.

"Will we do it again?" she asked.

"By all means. Though I feel a little guilty."

"About what?"

"Seeing you, given our business dealings. There are some who would say we have a conflict of interest."

"They won't say it to me," Elizabeth claimed. "I do what I want."

"In this town, yes. But I work all over the state. I won't have you as my guardian angel other places."

Elizabeth frowned. "Are you saying that we shouldn't see each other until you're done with all of Crosslyn Rise? But that's ridiculous! The project could take years!"

In a soft, very gentle, slightly naughty voice, he said, "That's not what I'm saying at all. I'm just suggesting we wait until my work with the zoning commission is done."

Her frown vanished, replaced by a smug smile. "It's done. You'll have your permit by ten tomorrow morning." She tugged at his lapel. "Any more problems?"

He gave her his most lecherous grin and looked at her mouth. "None at all, ma'am. What say I call you later in the week.

I'm busy this weekend, but I'm sure we'll be able to find another time when we're both free." He glanced at his watch. "Almost nine. Gotta run before I turn into a mouse." He winked. "See ya."

"SO WHAT WAS she like?" Johnny McCaffrey asked him the next afternoon after work.

They were at Sully's, where they went most days when Gideon was home in Worcester. Sully's was a diner when the sun shone and a bar at night, the watering spot for the local rednecks. Gideon's neck wasn't as red as some, but he'd grown up with these guys. They were his framers, his plasterers, his masons. They were his teammates—softball in the summer, basketball the rest of the year. They were also his friends.

Johnny was the closest of those and had been since they were eight and pinching apples from Drattles' orchard on the outskirts of town. Ugly as sin, Johnny had a heart of gold, which was probably why he had a terrific wife, Gideon mused. He was as loyal as loyal came, and every bit as trustworthy. That didn't mean he didn't live a little vicariously through Gideon.

"She was incredible," Gideon said now of Elizabeth, and it wasn't a compliment. "She has everything going for her— blond hair, blue eyes, nice bod, great legs—then she opens her mouth and the arrogance pours out. And dim-witted? Man, she's amazing. What woman in this day and age wouldn't have seen right through me? I mean, I wasn't subtle about wanting that permit—and wanting it before I touched her. Hell, I didn't even have to *kiss* her for it."

"Too bad."

"Nah. She didn't turn *me* on." He took a swig of his beer.

Johnny tipped his own mug and found it empty. "That type used to. You must be getting old, pal. Used to be you'd take most anything, and the more hoity-toity the better." He punctuated the statement with two raps of his mug on the bar.

Gideon drew himself straighter on his stool and said with a self-mocking grin, "That was before I got hoity-toity myself. I don't need other people's flash no more. I got my own."

"Watch out you don't start believing that," Johnny teased.

"Give me another, Jinko," he told the bartender. To Gideon, he said, "I bumped into Sara Thayer today. She wanted to know how you've been. She'd love a call."

Gideon winced. "Come on, Johnny. She's a kid."

"She's twenty-one."

"I don't fool with kids."

"She doesn't look like a kid. She's got everything right where it's supposed to be. And she ain't gonna wait forever."

Sara Thayer was Johnny's wife's cousin. She'd developed a crush on Gideon at a Christmas party two years before, and Johnny, bless his soul, had been a would-be matchmaker ever since. Sara was a nice girl, Gideon thought. But she *was* far too young, and in ways beyond her age.

As though answering a call, the waitress chose that moment to come close and drape an arm around Gideon's shoulder. He slid his own around her waist and pulled her close. "Now this," he told Johnny, "is the kind of woman for me. Solid and mature. Dedicated. Appreciative." He turned to her. "What do you say, Cookie? Want to go for a ride, you and me?"

Cookie snapped her gum while she thought about it, then planted a kiss on his nose. "Not tonight, big guy. I gotta work till twelve, and you'll be sound asleep by then. Hear you landed a big new job."

"Yup."

"Hear it's on the coast."

"Yup."

"Now why'd you do that for, Gideon Lowe? Every time you sign up to build something off somewhere, we don't see you so much. How long is this one gonna take?"

"A while. But I'm commuting. I'll be around."

Cookie snorted. "You better be. If I've gotta look at this guy—" she hitched her chin toward Johnny "—sittin' here with the weight of all your other jobs on his shoulders for long, I'll go nuts."

"John can handle it," Gideon said with confidence. Johnny had been his foreman for years and had never once let him down. "You just be good to him, babe, and he'll smile. Right John?"

"Right," Johnny said.

Cookie snapped her gum by way of punctuation, then said, "You guys hungry? I got some great hash out back. Whaddya say?"

"Not for me," Johnny said. "I'm headin' home in another five."

Gideon was heading home, too, but not to a woman waiting with dinner. He was heading toward a deskful of paperwork. The idea of putting that off for just a little longer was mighty appealing.

"Is it fresh, the hash?" he asked.

Cookie cuffed him on the head.

"I'll have some," he said. "Fast." He gave Cookie a pat on the rump and sent her off.

"So you're all set to get started up there now that the permit's through?" Johnny asked.

"Yup. We'll break ground on Monday, get the foundation poured the week after, then start framing. October can be a bitch of a month if we get rain, but I really want to get everything up and closed in before the snows come."

"Think you can?"

Gideon thought about that, thought about the complex designs of the condominium clusters and the fact that the crews he used would be commuting better than an hour each way, just like he would. He'd debated using local subs, but he really wanted his own men. He trusted his own men. They knew him, knew what he demanded, and, in turn, he knew they could produce. Of course, if the weather went bad, or they dug into ledge and had to blast, things would be delayed. But with the permit now in hand, they had a chance.

"We're sure as hell gonna try," he said.

THEY DID just that. With Gideon supervising every move, dump trucks and trailers bearing bulldozers and backhoes moved as carefully as possible over the virgin soil of Crosslyn Rise toward the duck pond, which was the first of three areas on the property being developed. After a cluster of eight condominiums was built there, another eight would be built in the pine grove, then another eight in the meadow. The duck pond had the most charm, Gideon thought and was pleased it was being developed first. Done right, it would be a powerful selling tool. That fact was foremost in his mind as the large machines were unloaded and the work began.

Fortunately, he and Carter had paved the way by having things cited, measured and staked well before the heavy equipment arrived. Though they were both determined to remove the least number of trees, several did have to come down to make room for the housing. A separate specialty crew had already done the cutting and chipping, leaving only stumping for the bulldozers when they arrived.

Once the best of the topsoil had been scraped off the top of the land and piled to the side, the bulldozers began the actual digging. Carter came often to watch, sometimes with Jessica, though the marring of the land tore her apart. She had total faith in Carter's plans and even, thanks to Carter's conviction, in Gideon's ability to give those plans form. Still, she had lived on Crosslyn Rise all her life, as had her father before her. The duck pond was only one of the spots she found precious.

Gideon could understand her feelings for the Rise. From the first time he'd walked through the land, he'd been able to appreciate its rare beauty. Being intimately involved in the work process, though, he had enough on his mind to keep sentimentality in check.

Contrary to Jessica, the deeper the hole got, the more excited he was. There was some rock that could be removed without blasting, some that couldn't but that could be circumvented by moving the entire cluster over just a bit and making a small section of one basement a bit more shallow. But they hadn't hit water, and water was what Gideon had feared. The tests had said they wouldn't, but he'd done tests before and been wrong; a test done in one spot didn't always reveal what was in another. They'd lucked out, which meant that the foundation could be sunk as deeply as originally planned, which meant less grading later and a far more aesthetically pleasing result.

The cellar hole was completed and the forms for the foundation set up. Then, as though things were going too smoothly, just when the cement was to be poured, the rains came. They lasted only three days, but they came with such force—and on a Monday, Tuesday and Wednesday—that it wasn't until the following Monday that Gideon felt the hole had dried out enough to pour the foundation.

He mightn't have minded the layoff, since there were plenty of other things to be done on plenty of other projects that his crews were involved in, had it not been for Elizabeth Abbott's calls.

"SHE WANTS TO SEE ME," he told Gordon the following Saturday at Jessica and Carter's wedding reception. He'd cornered the banker at one end of the long living room of the mansion at Crosslyn Rise. They were sipping champagne, which Gideon rather enjoyed. He wasn't particularly enjoying his tuxedo, though. He felt slightly strangled in it, but Jessica had insisted. She wanted her wedding to be elegant, and Carter, lovesick fool that he was, had gone right along with her. When Gideon got married—*if* he ever did—he intended to wear jeans.

At the moment, though, that wasn't his primary concern; Elizabeth Abbott was. "I've already put her off two or three times, but she keeps calling. I'm telling you, the woman is either stubborn or desperate. She doesn't take a hint."

"Maybe you have to be more blunt," Gordon suggested. He was pursing his lips in a way that told Gideon he found some humor in the situation.

Gideon didn't find any humor in it at all. He felt a little guilty about what he'd done, leading Elizabeth on. Granted, he'd gotten his permit, which had made the entire eight-member consortium, plus numerous on-call construction workers very happy. None of the others, though, were getting suggestive phone calls.

"Oh, I can be more blunt," he said. "The question is whether there's anything else she can do to slow us down from here on. She's a dangerous woman. She's already shown us that. I wouldn't want to do or say anything to jeopardize this project.''

Gordon seemed to take that part a bit more seriously. He thought about it for a minute while he watched Carter lead Jessica in a graceful waltz to the accompaniment of a string quartet. "There's not much she can do now," he said finally. "We have written permits for each of the different phases of this project. She could decide to rescind one or the other, but I don't think she'd dare. Not after she pulled back last time, then changed her mind. I don't think she'd want people knowing that it was Carter last time and you this time.''

"It *isn't* me," Gideon said quickly. "I haven't slept with her. I haven't even gone *out* with her, other than that first dinner, and that was business.''

"Apparently not completely," Gordon remarked dryly.

"It was business. The rest was all innuendo." His eyes were glued to the bride and groom, moving so smoothly with just the occasional dip and twirl. "Where in the hell did Carter learn to do that? He was born on the same side of the tracks as me. The son of a bitch must've taken lessons.''

Gordon chuckled. "Must've.''

Gideon followed them a bit longer. "They look happy.''

"I'd agree with that.''

"He's a lucky guy. She's a sweetie.''

"You bet.''

"She got any sisters?''

"Sorry.''

Gideon sighed. "Then I guess I'll have to mosey over and see if I can't charm that redheaded cutie in the sparkly dress into swaying a little with me. I'm great at swaying." He took a long sip of his champagne. After it had gone down, he put a finger under his collar to give him a moment's free breath, set his empty glass on a passing tray, cleared his throat and was off.

THE REDHEADED CUTIE in the sparkly dress turned out to be a colleague of Jessica's at Harvard. She swayed with Gideon a whole lot that night, then saw him two subsequent times. Gideon liked her. She had a spark he wouldn't have imagined a professor of Russian history to have. She also had a tendency to lecture, and when she did that, he felt as though he were seventeen again and hanging on by his bare teeth, just trying to make it through to graduation so that he could start doing, full-time, what he'd always wanted, which was to build houses.

So he let their relationship, what of it there had been, die a very natural death. Elizabeth Abbott, though, wasn't so easy to dispose of. The first time she called after the wedding, he said that he had a previously arranged date. The second time, he said he was seeing the same woman and that they were getting pretty involved. The third time, he said he just couldn't date other women until he knew what was happening with this first.

"I'm not saying we have to *date*," Elizabeth had the gall to say in a slithery purr. "You could just drop over here one evening and we could let nature take its course."

He mustered a laugh. "I don't know, Elizabeth. Nature hasn't been real kind to me lately. First we had rain, now an early frost. Maybe we shouldn't push our luck."

The purr was suddenly gone, yielding to impatience. "You know, Gideon, this whole thing is beginning to smell. Have you been leading me on all this time?"

He figured she'd catch on at some point. Fortunately, he'd thought out his answer. "No. I really enjoyed the dinner we had. You're one pretty and sexy lady. It's just that I was madly in love with Marie for years before she up and married someone else. Now she's getting a divorce. I was sure there wouldn't be anything left between us, but I was wrong. So I could agree to go out with you, or drop in at your place some night, but that wouldn't be fair to you. You deserve more than a man with half a heart." *Half a heart.* Not bad, bucko.

Elizabeth wasn't at all impressed. "If she's married and divorced, she's a loser. Weak women make weak marriages. You're looking for trouble, Gideon."

"Maybe," he said, leaving allowance for that should the day come when Elizabeth found out there wasn't anyone special in his life after all, "but I have to see it through. If not, I'll be haunted forever. I have to know, once and for all, whether she and I have a chance.''

She accepted his decision, though only temporarily. She continued to call every few nights to check on the status of his romance with Marie. Gideon wasn't naturally a liar and certainly didn't enjoy doing it over and over again, but Elizabeth pushed him into a corner. There were times when he thought he was taking the wrong tactic, when he half wanted to take her up on her invitation, show up at her house, then proceed to be the worst lover in the world. But he couldn't do it. He couldn't demean her—or himself—that way.

So she continued to call, and he continued to lie, all the while cursing himself for doing it, cursing Carter and Gordon for setting him up, cursing Elizabeth for being so goddamned persistent. He was fit to be tied, wondering where it would end, when suddenly, one day, at the very worst possible moment, she appeared at the site.

At least he thought it was her. The hair was blond, the clothes conservative, the figure shapely, the legs long. But it had rained the night before, and the air was heavy with mist, reducing most everything to blandly generic forms.

He was standing on the platform that would be the second floor of one of the houses in the cluster and had been hammering right along with his crew, getting an end piece ready to raise. The work was done. The men had positioned themselves. They were slowly hoisting the large, heavy piece when the creamy figure emerged from the mist.

"Jeez, what's that?" one of the men breathed, diverting the attention of a buddy. That diversion, fractional though it was, was enough to upset the alignment of the skeletal piece. It wobbled and swayed as they tried to right it.

"Easy," Gideon shouted, every muscle straining as he struggled to steady the wood. "Ea-sy." But the balance was lost, and, in the next instant, the piece toppled over the side of the house to the ground.

Gideon swore loudly, then did it again to be heard above the ducks on the pond. He made a quick check to assure himself that none of his men had gone over with the frame. He stalked to the edge of the platform and glared at the splintered piece. Then he raised his eyes and focused on the woman responsible.

CHAPTER TWO

SHE WAS DRESSED all in beige, but Gideon saw red. Whirling around, he stormed to the rough stairway, clattered down to the first floor, half walked, half ran out of the house and, amid fast-scattering ducks, around to where she stood. Elizabeth Abbott had been a pain in the butt for weeks, but she hadn't disturbed his work until now. He intended to make sure she didn't do it again.

The only thing was that when he came face-to-face with her, he saw that it wasn't Elizabeth. At first glance, though, it could have been her twin, the coloring was so similar. His anger was easily transferred. The fact was that *regardless* of who she was, she was standing where she didn't belong.

"What in the hell do you think you're doing, just popping up out of thin air like that?" he bellowed with his hands on his hips and fury in his voice. Disturbed by his tone, the ducks around the pond quacked louder. "In case you didn't see the sign out front, this is private property. That means that people don't just go wandering around—" he tossed an angry hand back toward the ruined framework "—and for good reason. Look what you've done. My men spent the better half of a day working on that piece, and it'll have to be done over now, which isn't real great, since we were racing to get it up before the rain started again this afternoon. And that's totally aside from the fact that someone could have been hurt in this little fiasco. I carry insurance, lady, but I don't count on people tempting fate. You could have been killed. *I* could have been killed. Any of my *men* could have been killed. A whole god-damned feast worth of *ducks* could have been killed. This is no place for tourists!"

It wasn't that he ran out of breath. He could have ranted on for a while, venting everything negative that he was feeling, only something stopped him, something to do with the woman herself and the way she looked.

Yes, her coloring was like Elizabeth's. She had fair skin, blue eyes, and blond hair that was pulled back into a neat knot. And to some extent, she was dressed as he imagined Elizabeth might have been, though he'd only seen her that one time, when she'd been wearing a dress. This woman was wearing a long pleated skirt of the same cream color as her scarf, which was knotted around the neck of a jacket that looked an awful lot like his old baseball jacket, but of a softer, finer fabric. The jacket was taupe, as were her boots. She wore large button earrings that could have been either ivory or plastic—he wasn't a good judge of things like that in the best of times, and this wasn't the best of times. He was still deeply shaken from what had happened. The look on her face, the way her eyes were wide and her hands were tucked tightly into her pockets, said that she was shaken, too.

"I'm not a tourist," she said quietly. "I know the owner of Crosslyn Rise."

"Well, if you were hoping to find her out here in the rain, you won't. She's working. If you were really a friend of hers, you'd know that."

"I know it. But I didn't come to see Jessica. I came to see what was happening here. She said I could. She was the one who suggested I do it."

If there was one thing Gideon hated, it was people who managed to hold it together when he was feeling strewn. This woman was doing just that, which didn't endear her to him in the least. "Well, she should have let me know first," he barked. "I'm the one in charge here, I ought to know what's going on. If we're having visitors to the site, I can alert my men. There's no reason why they should be shocked the way they were."

"You're right," she agreed. "What's wrong with them? Haven't they ever seen a woman before?"

She was totally innocent, totally direct and quite cutting with that last statement. Gideon shifted her closer in ilk to Elizabeth again. "Oh, they've seen women. They've seen lots of them, and in great and frequent intimacy, I'd wager. But what you just did was like a woman showing up in the men's john.''

She had the gall to laugh, but it, too, had an innocent ring. ''Cute analogy, though it's not quite appropriate. The sign out front says Private Way. It doesn't say No Women Allowed. Is it my fault if your men get so rattled by the sight of a woman that they become unglued? Face it. You should be yelling at them, not me.''

She had a point, he supposed, but he wasn't about to admit it. She had a quiet confidence to her that didn't need stroking. ''The fact is that your appearance here has messed us up.''

''I'm sorry for that.''

''Fine for you to be sorry, after the fact.''

''It's better than nothing, which is what I'm getting from you. You could try an apology, too.''

''For what?''

''Nearly killing me. If I'd been a little closer, or that piece had shattered and bounced, I'd be lying on the ground bleeding right now.''

He gave her a once-over, then drawled, ''That wouldn't do much for your outfit.''

''It wouldn't do much for your future, unless you have a fondness for lawsuits.''

''You don't have the basis for any lawsuit.''

''I don't know about that. You and your men were clearly negligent in this case.''

Gideon drew himself straighter, making the most of his six-foot-four-inch frame. ''So you're judge and jury rolled into one?''

She drew herself straighter to match, though she didn't have more than five foot seven to work with. ''Actually, I'm an interior designer. It may well be that I'll be working on this project.''

''Not if I can help it,'' he said, because she was a little too sure of herself, he thought.

''Well, then,'' she turned to leave, ''it's a good thing you're not anyone who counts. If I take this job, I'll be answerable to the Crosslyn Rise consortium, not to some job foreman who can't control his men." With a final direct look, she started off.

Gideon almost let her go. After all, they were far enough from the building that his men hadn't heard what she'd said, so he didn't have to think about saving face, at least, not before them. There was, of course, the matter of his own pride. For years he'd been fighting for respect, and he was doing it now, on several levels, with this project. The final barrier to fall would be with people like this one, who were educated and cultured and arrogant enough to choke a horse.

"You really think you're something, don't you?" he called.

She stopped but didn't turn. "No. Not really. I'm just stating the facts."

"You don't know the facts."

"I know that the consortium controls this project. It isn't some sort of workmen's cooperative."

"In some ways it is. Carter Malloy is in the consortium, and he's the architect of record. Nina Stone is in the consortium, and she'll be marketing us."

There was an expectancy to her quiet. "So?"

He savored the impending satisfaction. "So I'm not just 'some job foreman.' I'm the general contractor here. I also happen to be a member of that consortium."

For another minute, she didn't move. Then, very slowly she turned her head and looked at him, in a new light, he thought.

He touched a finger to the nonexistent visor of the wool cap perched on the top of his head. "Name's Gideon Lowe. See y'in the boardroom." With that, he turned back to his men, yelled, "Let's get this mess cleaned up," and set about doing just that with a definitive spring to his step.

CHRISTINE GILLETTE was appalled. She hadn't imagined that the man who'd blasted her so unfairly was a member of the consortium. Granted, he was better spoken than some of the laborers she'd met. But he'd been bullheaded and rough-hewn, not at all in keeping with the image she had of polished men sitting around a boardroom table with Jessica Crosslyn Malloy at its head.

Unsure as to what to say or do, she turned and left when he returned to his work. During the forty-minute drive back to her Belmont office, she replayed their conversation over and over in her mind and never failed to feel badly at its end. She wasn't normally the kind to cut down other people with words, though she did feel she'd had provocation. She also felt that she was right. She *had* apologized. What more could she do?

The fact remained, though, that in several weeks' time she'd be making a presentation to the Crosslyn Rise consortium. Gideon Lowe would be there, no doubt wearing a smug smile on his handsome face. She was sure he'd be the first to vote against her. Smug, handsome, physical men were like that, she knew. They defined the world in macho terms and were perfectly capable of acting on that principle alone. No way would he willingly allow her to work on his project.

She wished she could say that she didn't care, that Crosslyn Rise was just another project, that something else as good would come along. But Crosslyn Rise was special, not only in terms of the project itself but what it would mean to her. She'd been a designer for nearly ten years, working her way up from the most modest jobs—even freebies, at first—to jobs that were larger and more prestigious. This job, if she got it, would be the largest and most prestigious yet. From a designer's standpoint, given the possibilities between the condominium clusters and the mansion, it was exciting. In terms of her career, it was even more so.

Her mind was filled with these thoughts and others when she arrived at her office. Margie Dow, her secretary, greeted her with a wave, then an ominous, "Sybil Thompson's on the warpath. She's called three times in the last two hours. She says she *needs* to talk with you."

Chris rolled her eyes, took the other pink slips that Margie handed her and headed into her office. Knowing that waiting wouldn't make things any better, she dialed Sybil's number. "Hi, Sybil. It's Chris. I just this minute got back to the office. Margie tells me you have a problem."

"*I* have a problem?" Sybil asked, giving Chris a premoni-

tion of what was coming. "*You* have a problem. I just came
from Stanley's. Your people put down the wrong rug."

Stanley was Sybil's husband and a lawyer, and the carpeting
in question was for his new suite of offices. Chris had been
hired as the decorator one short month before and had been
quite blunt, when Stanley and his partners had said that they
wanted the place looking great within the week, about saying
that quality outfittings were hard to find off the rack. They'd
agreed to the month, and she'd done her best, running back
and forth with pictures and swatches and samples, placing rush
orders on some items, calling around to locate others in less
well-traveled outlets. Now Sybil was saying that one of those
items wasn't right.

Propping a shoulder to the phone to hold it at her ear, Chris
went around her desk to the file cabinet, opened it and thumbed
through. "I was there yesterday afternoon when it was installed, Sybil. It's the one we ordered."

"But it's too dark. Every tiny little bit of lint shows. It'll
look filthy all the time."

"No. It's elegant." She extracted a file. It held order forms,
sales receipts and invoices relating to the Thompsons' account.
"It goes perfectly with the rest of the decor." She began flipping through.

"It's too dark. It really is. I'm sure we chose something
lighter. Check the order form and you'll see."

"That's what I'm doing right now. According to this," Chris
studied the slip, "we ordered Bold Burgundy, and Bold Burgundy is the color we installed yesterday."

"It can't be."

"It is." She spoke gently, easily understanding Sybil's confusion. "Everything was done quickly. You looked at samples
of carpeting, chose what you wanted, and I ordered it. When
things move fast like that, with as much done at one time as
you did, it's only natural to remember some things one way
and some things another way. I'd do it myself, if I didn't write
everything down." Of course, that wasn't the only reason she
wrote everything down. The major reason was to protect herself
from clients who ordered one thing, saw it installed, then de-

cided that it wasn't what they wanted after all. She didn't know whether Sybil fell into that category or whether this was an innocent mix-up. But Chris did have the papers to back up her case.

"I suppose you're right," Sybil said. "Still, that carpet's going to look awful."

"It won't. The cleaning people come through to vacuum every night. Besides, you don't get half the lint in a lawyer's office as you get at home, especially when you're dealing with the upscale clientele that your husband is. Trust me. Bold Burgundy looks great."

Sybil was weakening. "You think so?"

"I know so. Just wait. Give it a few weeks and see what the clients say. They'll rave about it. I'm sure. That carpeting gives a rich look. They'll feel privileged to be there, without knowing why."

Sybil agreed to wait. Satisfied, Chris hung up the phone and returned the folder to the cabinet. Then she opened another drawer, removed a thick cardboard tube, slid out the blueprints for Crosslyn Rise and spread them on her desk.

Carter was brilliant. She had to hand it to him. What he'd done—taking the Georgian colonial theme from the mansion, modifying columns and balconies, elongating the roof and adding skylights to give just a hint of something more contemporary—was perfect. The housing clusters were subtle and elegant, nestling into the setting as though they'd been there forever.

She sighed. She wanted to work on this project in one regard that had nothing to do with either challenge, prestige or money. It had to do with Crosslyn Rise itself. She thought it was gorgeous, real dream material. If ever she pictured a place she would have liked to call home, it was the mansion on the rise. Doing the decorating for it was the next best thing to living there.

She wanted that job.

Picking up the phone, she dialed Jessica Malloy's Harvard office. Despite what she'd told Gideon, Jessica and she were less friends than acquaintances. They had a mutual friend, who was actually the one to suggest to Jessica that Chris do the work on the Rise. They had met after that and hit it off. Though Chris knew that other designers were being considered for the job, she was sure she could compete—unless Gideon Lowe blackballed her.

"Hi," she said to the secretary who answered, "this is Christine Gillette. I'm looking for Jessica. Has she come back from her honeymoon?"

"She certainly has," the woman said. "Hold on, please."

Less than a minute later, Jessica came on the phone. "Christine, how are you?"

"I'm fine, but, hey, congratulations on your marriage." Last time they'd talked, Jessica had been up to her ears in plans. Apparently the wedding had been something of a last-minute affair thanks to Carter, who had refused to wait once Jessica had finally agreed to marry him. "I take it everything went well?"

"Perfectly," Jessica said.

Chris could hear her smile and was envious. "And the trip to Paris?"

"Too short, but sweet."

And terribly romantic, Chris was sure. Paris was that way, or so she was told. She'd never been there herself. "I'm sure you'll get back some day. Maybe for your fiftieth anniversary?"

"Lord, we'll be doddering by then," Jessica said, laughing, and again Chris was envious. To have someone special, like Jessica had Carter, was precious. So was growing old with that someone special. She hoped Jessica knew how lucky she was.

"I wouldn't worry about doddering. You have years of happiness ahead. I wish you both all the best."

"Thanks, Chris. But enough about me. Tell me what's doing with you. You are getting a presentation ready for us, aren't you?"

"Definitely," Chris said and took a breath, "but I had a small problem this morning. I'm afraid I went out to the Rise to walk around, and I upset some of the men working there."

"You upset them? I'd have thought it'd be the other way around. What they're doing to my gorgeous land upsets me to no end."

"But the mess is only temporary. You know that."

"I know, and I'm really excited about Carter's plans and about what the Rise will be, and I know this was my only out, since I couldn't afford the upkeep, not to mention repairs and renovations—" She caught her breath. "Still, I have such sentimental feelings for the place that it's hard for me when even the smallest tree is felled."

"I can understand that," Chris said with a smile. She really liked Jessica, among other things for the fact that she wasn't a money grubber. In that sense, Chris identified with her. Yes, the conversion of Crosslyn Rise would be profitable, but it was a means to an end, the end being the preservation of the Rise, rather than the enhancement of Jessica's bank account. Likewise, Chris sought lucrative jobs like decorating Stanley Thompson's law firm, redecorating the Howard family compound on the Vineyard, and yes, doing Crosslyn Rise, for a greater cause than her own. Her personal needs were modest and had always been so.

"Tell me what happened to you, though," Jessica was saying, returning to the events of that morning.

Chris told her about appearing at the site and jinxing Gideon's crew. "It was an innocent mistake, Jessica. Honestly. I never dreamed I'd disturb them, or I never would have gone. I thought I was being unobtrusive. I just stood there, watching without saying a word, but one of the guys saw me and two others looked and then the damage was done. I really am sorry. I tried to tell your contractor that, but I'm not sure I got through."

"To Gideon? I'm sure you did. He's a sensible guy."

"Maybe when he's cool, but he was pretty hot under the collar when that framework fell, and I don't blame him. Someone could have been hurt, and then there's the time lost in having to redo the piece, and the rain that he was trying to beat. I, uh, think we may have gotten off on the wrong foot,

Gideon and I. He was annoyed and said some things that irked me, so I said some irksome things back, and I may have sounded arrogant. I'm not usually like that.''

''And now you're worried that he'll stand in the way of your getting this job.''

''That, and that if I do get the job, he and I will have trouble working together. He's a macho type. I don't do well with macho types. I kind of pull in and get intimidated, so I guess I put up a wall, and then I come off sounding snotty. I'm sure that's what he thinks.''

''He'll change his mind when he meets you in a more controlled setting.''

''When there are other people, *civilized* people around, sure. But if we work together, it won't always be in that kind of controlled setting. There won't always be other people around. We'll be spending a lot of time at the site. His subs and their crews may be around, but if today was any indication, they won't be much help.''

The telephone line was quiet for a minute before Jessica asked, ''Are you saying that you don't want to try for the job?''

''Oh, no!'' Chris cried. ''Not at all! I *want* the job. I want it a *lot*!''

Jessica sounded genuinely relieved. ''That's good, because I really like what I've seen of your work. It has a sensitivity that I haven't found in some of the others' things. I don't want the Rise to look done up, or glossy. I don't want a 'decorated' look. I want something different and special, something with feeling. Your work has that. *You* have that, I think.''

''I hope so, at least as far as my work goes,'' and she was deeply gratified to hear Jessica say it. But that wasn't why she'd called. ''As far as this business with Gideon Lowe goes—''

''Don't think twice about it, Chris. You may not believe it, but Gideon is really a pretty easygoing kind of guy.''

''You're right. I don't believe it.''

Jessica laughed. ''He is. Really. But he takes his work very seriously. He may have overreacted this morning, in which case he's probably feeling like a heel, but he'll get over it. This project means a lot to him. He has money invested in it. He'd be the first one to say that when we pick people to do the work, we have to pick the best.''

"Is that why he picked himself as the builder?" Chris couldn't resist tossing out. She barely had to close her eyes to picture his smug smile or the broad set of his shoulders or the tight-hipped way he'd walked away from her.

"He's good. I've seen his things. Carter has worked with him before, and *he* says he's good. Gideon's reputation's at stake here, along with his money. He wants the best. And if the best turns out to be you, once we hear all the presentations, he'll go along with it.''

"Graciously?" Somehow Chris couldn't see it.

"Graciously. He's a professional.''

CHRIS THOUGHT A LOT that in the days following. She figured Jessica might be right. Gideon was a professional. But a professional what? A professional builder? A professional businessman? A professional bruiser? A professional lover? No doubt he had a wife stashed away somewhere, waiting with the television warmed and the beer chilled for the time when he got home from work and collapsed into his vinyl recliner. Chris could picture it. He looked like that type. Large, brawny, physical, he'd be the king of whatever castle he stormed.

Then again, he was a member of the consortium. Somehow that didn't jibe with the image. To be a member of a consortium, one needed money and brains. Chris knew there was good money in building, at least for the savvy builder, and the savvy builder had to be bright. But there were brains, and there were brains. Some were limited to one narrow field, while others were broader. She didn't picture Gideon Lowe being broad in any respect but his shoulders.

That was one of the reasons why she grew more nervous as the day of the presentation drew near. She burned the midnight oil doing drawings, then redoing them, trying to get them just right. She sat back and rethought her concept, then altered the drawings yet again to accommodate even the slightest shift. She knew that, given Gideon's predisposition, she'd have to impress the others in the group in a big way if she wanted the job.

THE DAY OF THE MEETING was a beautiful one, cool and clear as the best of November days were along the North Atlantic shore. Gideon felt good. The first roof section had gone up despite a last-minute glitch that had kept Carter and him sweating over the plans the weekend before. But things had finally fit, and if all went well, the second, third and fourth roof sections would be up by the end of the week. Once that was done, the snows could come and Gideon wouldn't give a hoot.

It had also been eight whole days since he'd last heard from Elizabeth Abbott.

So he was in a plucky mood when the eight members of the consortium held their weekly meeting at seven that evening in Gordon's office. It occurred to Gideon as he greeted the others and took his place at the table, that he was comfortable with the group. It hadn't been so at first. He had felt self-conscious, almost like an imposter, as though he didn't have any business being there and they all knew it. Over the weeks that they'd been meeting, though, he'd found himself accepted as a peer. More than that, his status as the general contractor actually gave him a boost in their eyes. He was the one member of the group most closely aligned with the reality of the project.

There were Carter and Jessica, sitting side by side, then the three men Gordon had brought in from other areas—Bill Nolan, from the Nolan Paper Mill family in Maine, Ben Heavey, a real estate developer well-known in the East, and Zach Gould, a retired banker with time and money on his hands, who visited the site often. Rounding out the group were John Sawyer, a local bookseller, and Nina Stone, the realtor who would one day market the project.

Being single, Gideon had taken notice of Nina at the start. They'd even gone out to dinner once, but neither had wanted a follow-up, certainly not as a prelude to something deeper. Nina was a tough cookie, an aggressive woman, almost driven.

Petite and a little bizarre, she wasn't Gideon's type at all. By mutual agreement, they were simply friends.

After calling the meeting to order, Gordon, who always sat in as an advisor of sorts, gave them a rundown of the money situation, then handed the meeting over to Carter, who called in, one by one, the interior designers vying for the project.

The first was a woman who worked out of Boston and had done several of the more notable condo projects there in recent years. Gideon thought her plans were pretentious.

The second was a man who talked a blue streak about glass and marble and monotonic values. Gideon thought everything about him sounded sterile.

The third was Christine Gillette, and Gideon didn't take his eyes off her once. She was wearing beige again, a suit this time, with a tweedy blazer over a solid-colored blouse and skirt, and he had to admit that she looked elegant. She also looked slightly nervous, if the faint shimmer of her silk blouse was any indication of the thudding of her heart. But she was composed, and obviously well rehearsed. She made her presentation, exchanging one drawing for another with slender fingers as she talked about recreating the ambience that she believed made Crosslyn Rise special. Her voice was soft, but it held conviction. She clearly believed in what she was saying.

Quite against his wishes, Gideon was impressed. Her eyes had glanced across his from time to time, but if she was remembering their last encounter, she didn't let on. She was cool, but in a positive way. Not haughty, but self-assured. She didn't remind him at all of Elizabeth Abbott.

At the end of her presentation she left, sent home, as the others had been, with word that a decision would be made within the week. It was obvious, though, where the group's sentiment lay.

"Christine's plans were the warmest," John Sawyer said. "I like the feeling she captured."

Zach Gould agreed. "I liked her, too. She wasn't heavy-handed like the first, or slick like the second."

"Her estimates are high," Ben Heavey reminded them. He was the most conservative of the group.

"All three are high," Nina said, "but the fact is that if we want this done right, we'll have to shell out. I have a feeling that Christine, more than the others, will be able to get us the most for the least. She seems the most inventive, the least programmed."

"I want to know what Gideon thinks," Carter said, looking straight at him. "He'll be spending more time with the decorator than the rest of us. There are things like moldings, doors, flooring and deck work that I specified in my plans but that are fully changeable if something else fits better with the decor. So, Gideon, what are your thoughts?"

Gideon, who had been slouched with an elbow on the arm of his chair and his chin on his fist, wasn't sure *what* those thoughts were. Christine was the best of the three, without a doubt, but he wasn't sure he wanted to work with her. There was something about her that unsettled him, though he couldn't put his finger on what it was.

"She's the least experienced of the lot," he finally said, lowering the fist and sitting straighter. "What's the setup of her firm?"

Jessica answered. "She's something of a single practitioner. Her office is small. She has one full-time secretary and two part-time assistants, both with degrees in decorating, both with small children. They're job-sharing. It works out well for them, and from what she says, it works out well for Chris."

"Job-sharing," John mused with a grin. "I like that." They all knew that he was a single parent, and that though he owned his bookstore, he only manned the cash register during those hours when he had a sitter for his son. He had a woman who sold books for him the rest of the time, so he was basically job-sharing, himself.

Job-sharing didn't mean a whole lot to Gideon. Men did the work in his field, and even if their bosses allowed it, which they didn't, they weren't the types to leave at one in the afternoon to take a toddler to gym-and-swim.

He wondered what the story was on Christine Gillette. The résumé she'd handed out said nothing whatsoever about her personal life. He hadn't seen a wedding band, though that didn't mean anything in this day and age. He wondered whether she had a husband at home, and was vaguely annoyed at the thought.

"Does *she* have little kids who she'll have to miss work for each time they get a cold?" he asked, looking slightly miffed.

"Whoa," said John. "Be compassionate, my friend."

But Gideon wasn't a father, and as for compassion, there seemed to be plenty in the room for Christine Gillette without his. "Carter's right. If we decide to use this woman, I'm the one who'll be working most closely with her. Job-sharing may be well and good in certain areas, but construction isn't one. If I have to order bathroom fixtures, and she's off taking the kid to Disney World over school vacation so she can't meet with me, we'll be held back." He thought the argument was completely valid and he was justified to raise it. Christine might be able to charm the pants off this consortium, but if she couldn't come through when *he* needed her, he didn't want her at all! "I keep things moving. That's the way I work. I need people who'll be there."

"Chris will be there," Jessica assured him. "There are no little ones at home. From what I've been told—and from more than one source—she puts in fifty-hour weeks."

"Still," he cautioned, "if she's a single practitioner—"

"With a secretary and assistants," Jessica put in.

"Okay, with a secretary and assistants, but she's the main mover. Both of the other candidates for this position have partners, full partners, people who could take over if something happened."

"What could happen?" Jessica asked. "Chris is in good health. She has a reputation for finishing jobs on time, if not ahead. She's efficient and effective. And she needs this job." She held up a hand before he could comment on that. "I know, I know. You're going to ask me why she's so desperate, and she's not. Not desperate. But this job could give her career a boost, and she wants that. She deserves it.''

Gideon didn't want to think that Christine, with her fair-haired freshness, her poise, and legs long enough to drive a man wild, deserved a thing. "Hey, this isn't a charity. We're not in the business of on-the-job training.''

"Gideon,'' Jessica said with a mocking scowl, "I know that. More than *anyone* here, I know it. I've lived on Crosslyn Rise all my life. I'm the one who's being torn apart that I can't leave it the way it always was—'' She stopped for a minute when Carter put a hand on her arm. She nodded, took a calming breath. "I want the Rise to be the best it can possibly be, and if Chris wasn't the best, I wouldn't be recommending her.''

"She's a friend,'' Gideon accused, recalling what Chris had told him.

"She's a friend of a friend, but I have no personal interest in her getting this job. If anything, I was wary when my friend mentioned her to me, because I'm *not* in the business of doing favors. Then I looked at pictures of other jobs Chris has done. Now, looking at what she's come up with for us, I'm more convinced than ever that she's the right one.'' She stopped, had another thought, went on. "Besides, there's a definite advantage to working with someone with a smaller client list. It's the old issue of being a small fish in a big pond, or vice versa. Personally, I'd rather be the big fish in Chris's pond, than a small fish in someone else's, particularly since no one else's ideas for this project are anywhere near as good as hers.''

Gideon might have said more, but didn't. Clearly the others agreed with Jessica, as the vote they took several minutes later proved. Christine was approved as the decorator for Crosslyn Rise by a unanimous vote. Or a nearly unanimous one. Gideon abstained.

"Why did you do that?'' Carter asked quietly after the meeting had adjourned and most of the others had left.

Gideon didn't have a ready answer. "I don't know. Maybe

because she didn't need my vote. She had the rest of you wowed.''

"But you like her ideas."

"Yes, I like her ideas."

"Think you can work with her?"

Gideon jammed his fists into his pockets and rocked back on his heels. "Work with her? I suppose."

"So what bothers you?"

"I don't know."

Carter was beginning to have his suspicions, if the look on Gideon's face went for anything. "She's pretty, and she's single."

"Single?" Somehow that made Gideon feel worse.

"Single. Available. Is that a threat?"

"Only if she's on the make. Is she looking for it?"

"Not that I know of." Carter leaned closer. "Word has it she lives like a monk."

Gideon glowered. "Is that supposed to impress me?"

"If you're worried about being attacked, it should."

"Attacked? Me? By *her*? That's the last thing I'm worried about. Listen, man, I've got plenty of women to call when I get the urge. Snap my fingers, there they are."

"Christine isn't likely to do that."

"Don't you know it. She's the kind to snap *her* fingers. Well, I don't come running so fast, and I don't give a damn *how* pretty she is. Long legs are a dime a dozen. So are breasts, bottoms and big blue eyes, and as far as that blond hair of hers goes, it's probably right out of a bottle." He paused only for the quickest breath. "I can work with her. As long as she produces, I can work with her. But if she starts playing games, acting high and mighty and superior, and botching things up so *my* work starts looking shabby, we'll be in trouble. Big trouble."

ACTUALLY GIDEON WAS in big trouble already, but it wasn't until three weeks had passed, during which time he couldn't get Christine Gillette out of his mind for more than a few hours at a stretch, that he realized it. The realization was driven home when she called to make an appointment to see him and he hung up the phone with a pounding heart and a racing pulse.

CHAPTER THREE

CHRISTINE WAS HAVING a few small physical problems of her own as she left Belmont early that Thursday morning and headed north toward Crosslyn Rise. Her stomach was jumpy. Tea hadn't helped. Nor had a dish of oatmeal. Worse, the jitters seemed to echo through her body, leaving a fine tremor in her hands.

It was excitement, she told herself. She'd been flying high since receiving the call from Jessica that she'd landed the Crosslyn Rise job. She'd also been working her tail off since then to get ahead on other projects so that she'd have plenty of time to devote to the Rise. So maybe, she speculated as she turned onto Route 128, the trembling was from fatigue.

Then again, maybe it was nervousness. She didn't like to think so, because she'd never felt nervous this way about her work, but she'd never worked with anyone like Gideon Lowe before. She'd always managed to keep her cool, at least outwardly, with even the most intimidating of clients, but Gideon was something else. He was large, though she'd worked with larger men. He was quick-tempered, though she'd worked with some even more so. He was chauvinistic, though heaven knows she'd met worse. But he got to her as the others hadn't. He stuck in her mind. She wasn't quite sure why.

As the car cruised northward on the highway, she pondered that, just as she had been doing practically every free minute since her interview at the bank three weeks before.

She'd been slightly stunned to see him there—not to see him, per se, but to see how he looked. At the site, he'd been a craftsman. His work boots had been crusted with dirt, his jeans faded and worn. He'd been wearing a down vest, open over a plaid flannel shirt, which was open over a gray T-shirt dotted with sweat in spite of the cold. His dark hair had stuck out in a mess around the wool cap he wore. He needed a shower and a shave.

When she saw him at the bank, he'd had both. His hair was neatly combed, still longer than that of the other men in the room, though cut well. His jaw was smooth and tanned. His shoulders looked every bit as broad under a camel hair blazer as under a down vest. He knew how to knot a tie, even how to pick one, if indeed he'd picked out the paisley one he wore. And in the quick look she'd had, when the men had briefly stood as she entered then left the room, his gray slacks had fit his lean hips nearly as nicely as had a pair of jeans.

He was an extremely good-looking man, she had to admit, though she refused to believe that had anything to do with her nervousness. After all, she'd already decided that he was married, and anyway, she wasn't on the lookout for a man. She had one, a very nice one named Anthony Haskell, who was even-tempered and kind and took her to a show or a movie or to dinner whenever she had the time, which wasn't often. She didn't see him more than two or three times a month. But he was pleasant. He was an amiable escort. That was all she asked, all she wanted from a man—light companionship from time to time as a break from the rest of her life.

So, Gideon Lowe wasn't any sort of threat to her in that regard. Still he was so *physical*. A woman couldn't be within arm's reach of him and not feel his force. Hell, she'd been farther away than that in the boardroom at the bank, and she'd felt it. It started with his eyes and was powerful.

So he was slightly intimidating, she admitted with a sigh, and that was why she was feeling shaky. Of course, she couldn't let him know that. She'd taken the bull by the horns and called him for an appointment, making sure to sound fully composed, for that reason. Gideon looked to be the predatory type. If he sensed weakness, he'd zoom right in for the kill.

Fortifying herself with the determination to do the very best job for Crosslyn Rise that she possibly could, she turned off the highway and followed the shore road. Actually she would have preferred meeting Gideon at the bank or at Carter's office, either of which were safer places, given what had happened on that last misty morning. But Gideon had said that they should see what they were discussing, and she supposed he had a point.

The good news was that the day was sunny and bright, not at all like that other misty one. The bad news was that it was well below freezing, as was perfectly normal for December. There had already been snow, though barely enough to shovel. She couldn't help but wonder how Gideon's men kept from freezing as they worked.

As for her, she'd dressed for the occasion. She was wearing wool tights under wool slacks, a heavy cowl-neck sweater and a long wool coat. Beside her on the seat were a pair of mittens and some earmuffs. It had occurred to her that Gideon was testing her mettle, deliberately subjecting her to adverse conditions, but if so, she wasn't going to come up short. She could handle subfreezing weather. She'd done it many times before.

Of course, that didn't mean that she was thrilled to be riding in her car dressed as heavily as she was. If it hadn't been for the seat belt, she'd have shrugged out of her coat. She'd long since turned down the heat, and even then, by the time she arrived at Crosslyn Rise, she felt a trickle of perspiration between her breasts.

She drove directly to the duck pond over the trail that the trucks had made, but when she reached it, it looked deserted. There wasn't a car or truck in sight. She sat for a minute, then glanced at her watch. They'd agreed on eight-thirty, which it was on the nose. Gideon had told her, a bit arrogantly, she thought, that his men started work an hour before that. But she didn't see a soul working on this cold, crisp morning. She opened her door and stepped out. The only noise came from the ducks, their soft, random quacks a far cry from the sharp sounds of construction.

Slipping back into the car, she turned it around and retraced the trail to the point where the main driveway led to the mansion. She followed it, parked and went up the brick walk, under the ivy-draped portico, to the door. Putting her face to the sidelight, she peered inside.

The place was empty. Jessica and Carter had finally finished clearing things out, putting some in storage, selling others in a huge estate sale held several weekends before. The idea was for Gideon's men to spend the worst of the winter months inside, working on the renovations that would eventually make the mansion into a central clubhouse, health center and restaurant for the condominium complex. Whether Jessica and Carter would buy one of the condo units was still undecided. For the time being, they were living in Carter's place in Boston.

Reaching into her pocket, Chris took out the key Jessica had given her and let herself into the mansion. Seconds later, she was standing in the middle of the rotundalike foyer. Ahead of her was the broad sweeping staircase that she found so breathtaking, to the right the spacious living room lit by knee-to-ceiling windows bare of drapes, to the left the similarly bright dining room.

That was the direction in which she walked, her footsteps echoing through the silent house. As she stood under the open arch, looking from window to window, chandelier to wall sconce, spot to spot where paintings had so recently hung, she imagined the long, carved mahogany table dominating the room once more. The last time it had been used was for the wedding, and though she hadn't been there, she could easily picture its surface covered with fine linen, then silver tray after silver tray of elegantly presented food. Giving herself up to a moment of fancy, she felt the excitement, heard the sounds of happiness. Then she blinked, and those happy sounds were replaced by the loud and repeated honking of a horn.

She hurried back to the front door in time to see Gideon climb from his truck. He was wearing his work clothes with nothing more than the same down vest, which surprised her, given the weather. So he was hot-blooded. She should have guessed that.

"I thought we agreed to meet down there," he said by way of greeting. He looked annoyed. "I've been waiting for ten minutes."

She checked her watch. "Not ten minutes, because I was there five minutes ago. When you didn't show, I thought I'd take a look around here. Where is everyone? It's a gorgeous day. I thought for sure there'd be work going on one place or the other.''

''There will be,'' Gideon said, holding her gaze as he approached. Stopping a few feet away, he hooked his hands on his hips. ''The men are picking up supplies. They'll be along.'' He smirked. ''This works out really well, don't you think? We can talk about whatever it is you want to talk about, then you can be long gone by the time they get here, so they can work undisturbed.''

His reference to what had happened the last time was barely veiled. The look in his eye took it a step further with the implication that she'd been the one at fault. That bothered her. ''You deliberately planned it this way, I take it.''

He scratched his head, which was hatless, though from the looks of his hair, he'd just tumbled out of bed, stuck on his clothes and come. The thought made her feel warmer than she already was.

''Actually,'' he said, ''the guys had to pick up the stuff either today or tomorrow anyway. After you and I arranged to meet, today sounded real good.''

''It's a shame. I was hoping they'd be here. They'll have to get used to seeing me around. I will be, more and more, once things get going.''

His smirk deteriorated. ''Yeah. Well...''

''They won't bother *me* if that's got you worried,'' she went on, gaining strength from her own reassuring tone. ''I'm with workmen all the time. It's part of my job. Plumbers, plasterers, painters—you name it, I've seen it. They may not love having me poking around, but at least if they know I'll be wandering in from time to time, they won't be alarmed when it happens.''

''My men weren't alarmed,'' Gideon argued, ''just distracted at a very critical time.''

''Because they weren't expecting me. They had no idea who I was. Maybe it would help if I met them.''

''It wouldn't help at all! You don't have any business with them. You have business with *me*!'' He eyed her with sudden suspicion. ''You want them around for protection, I think. You don't like being alone with me. Is that it? Is that what this is about? Because if it is—'' he held both hands up ''—I can assure you, you're safe. I don't fool with the hired help. And I don't fool with blondes.''

''I'm relieved to hear *that*,'' she said, deliberately ignoring the business about ''hired help'' because it was a potential firecracker. The other was easier to handle. ''What's wrong with blondes?''

''They're phony.''

''Like rednecks are crude?''

Gideon glared at her for a minute, looking as though there were a dozen other derogatory things he wanted to say. Before he could get any out, though, she relented and said, ''Look, I'm sorry. I'm not here to fight. I have a job to do, just like you. Name-calling won't help.''

He continued to glare. ''*Do* I make you nervous?''

''Of course not. Why would you think that?''

''You were nervous at the meeting at the bank.''

And she thought she'd looked so calm. So much for show. ''There were eight people—nine, counting the banker—at that meeting. I was auditioning for a job I really wanted. I had a right to be nervous.'' She wondered how he'd known, whether they'd all seen it or whether those dark gray eyes were just more keen than most.

''Were you surprised when you got the job?'' he asked innocently enough.

''In a way. The others have bigger names than I do.''

Again, innocently, he asked, ''Did you think that I'd vote against you?''

''That thought did cross my mind.''

''I didn't.''

''Thank you.''

''I abstained.''

''Oh.'' She felt strangely hurt, then annoyed. ''Well. I appreciate your telling me that. I'm glad to know you think so highly of my work.''

He didn't blink. ''I think your work is just fine, but I don't relish the idea of working with you. We rub each other the wrong way, you and me. I don't know why, but we do.''

That about said it all. There wasn't much she could add. So she stood with her hands buried deep in the pockets of her coat, wondering what he'd say next. He seemed bent on throwing darts at her. She imagined that if she let him do it enough, let him get every little gripe off his chest, they might finally be able to work together.

Unfortunately, the darts stung.

He stared at her for a long, silent time, just stared. Holding her chin steady and her spine straight, she stared right back.

"Nothing to say?" he asked finally.

"No."

He arched a brow. "Nothing at all?"

She shook her head.

"Then why are we here?"

Chris felt a sudden rush of color to her face. "Uh, we're here to discuss business," she said, and hurried to gather her thoughts. Something had happened. Gideon's eyes must have momentarily numbed her mind. "I want to see where you're at with the condos. I thought maybe I could get a bead on things like roofing materials, stairway styles and so on." She stopped, took a deep breath, recomposed herself. "But I told you all that when I called. You were the one who said we should walk through what you've done." She gestured in the direction of the duck pond. "Can we?"

He shrugged. "Sure." He turned back toward his truck. "Climb in. I'll drive you down."

"Thanks, but I'll follow in my car."

He stopped and turned back. "Climb *in*. I'll drive you back here when we're done."

"That's not necessary," she said, but there was a challenge in his look. She wasn't sure whether it had to do with the idea of their being alone in the cab of a pickup or the idea of her climbing into a pickup, period, but in either case she had a point to make. "Okay. Let me get my purse." Crossing the driveway to her car, she took the large leather satchel in which she carried pen and paper, along with other necessities of life such as a wallet, tissues, lip gloss and appointment book. Hitching the bag to her shoulder, she grabbed her earmuffs and mittens. Then, putting on a show of confidence, she walked to the passenger's side of the truck, opened the door and climbed up.

"That was smooth," Gideon remarked.

She settled herself as comfortably as she could, given that she felt rattled. "My father is an electrician. I've been riding around in trucks all my life." And she knew how intimate they could be. A truck was like a man's office, filled with personal belongings, small doodads, tokens of that man's life. It also had his scent. Gideon's was clean, vaguely leathery, distantly coffee flavored, thanks to a half-filled cup on the console, and overwhelmingly male. She felt surrounded by it, so much so that it was a struggle to concentrate on what he was saying.

"Funny, you don't look like the type."

She swallowed. "What type?"

"To have an electrician for a father. I'd have thought your old man would be the CEO of some multinational corporation. Not an electrician."

Another dart hit home. She bristled. "There's nothing wrong with being an electrician. My father is honest and hardworking. He takes pride in what he does. *I'm* proud of what he does. And who are *you* to say something like that?"

"You asked. I answered." He shrugged. "I still don't peg you as the type to be around trucks."

"You think I'm lying?"

"No. But I think you could."

"What's *that* supposed to mean?"

"That I'd more easily believe you if you said you've had a silver spoon in your mouth for most of your life, got bored with doing nothing, so decided to dabble around as a decorator. Real estate and interior decorating—those are the two fields women go into when they want people to think they're aggressive little workers."

That dart hurt more than the others, no doubt because she was already bruised. "You don't know what you're talking about," she said.

"If the shoe fits, wear it."

His smug look did it. Turning to face him head-on, she said, "Well, it doesn't. And, quite frankly, I resent your even suggesting it. I work hard, probably harder than you do, and so do most of the women I know in *either* of the fields you mentioned. We have to work twice as hard to get half the respect, thanks to people like you." She took a fast breath. "And as for 'types,' I didn't have a silver spoon in my mouth at birth or at any *other* time in my life. My parents couldn't afford silver, or silk, or velvet, but they gave me lots and lots of love, which is clearly something you know nothing about. I feel badly for your wife, or your woman, whoever the hell it is you go home to at night." She reached for the door. "I'll take my own car, after all. Being cooped up in a truck with you is oppressive." In a second, she was out the door and looking back at him. "Better still, I think maybe we'd better do this another time. I'm feeling a little sick to my stomach."

Slamming the door, she stalked back to her car. She was trembling, and though she doubted he could see, she wouldn't have cared. She felt pervasive anger and incredible hurt, neither of which abated much as she sped back to Belmont. By the time she was back in her office, sitting at her desk with the door closed on the rest of the world, she was also feeling humiliated.

He'd won. He'd badgered her and she'd crumbled. She couldn't believe she'd done that. She prided herself on being strong. Lord knows, she'd had to overcome adversity to get where she was. She'd faced critics far more personal and cutting than Gideon Lowe and survived. With him, though, she'd fallen apart.

She was ashamed of herself.

She was also frightened. She wanted, *needed* to do Crosslyn Rise. By running, she may well have blown her credibility. If she'd thought working with Gideon was going to be hard before, it could well be impossible now. He'd seen her weakness. He could take advantage of it.

He could also spread word among the consortium members about what had happened, but she doubted he'd do that. He wasn't exactly an innocent party. He wouldn't want the others to know of his part. He had an image to protect, too.

Then again, he could lie. He could tell them that she made

appointments, showed up, then took off minutes later. He could say that she wasted his time. He could suggest that she was mentally unbalanced.

If he spread that kind of word around, she'd be in a serious fix. Crosslyn Rise was supposed to make her career, not break it!

What to do, what to do. She sat at her desk with her feet flat on the floor, her knees pressed together, her elbows on the glass surface, her clasped hands pressed to her mouth, and wondered about that. She could call Jessica, she supposed. But she'd done that once regarding Gideon. To do it again would be tattling. Worse, it would smack of cowardice. Jessica might well begin to wonder what kind of woman she'd hired.

Nor could she call Carter. Gideon was his friend.

And she certainly couldn't call Gideon. They'd only get into another fight.

But she had to do something. She'd committed herself to Crosslyn Rise. Her reputation, her future was on the line.

The phone rang. She watched the flashing light turn solid when Margie picked it up. Distractedly she glanced at the handful of pink slips on the desk, all telephone messages waiting to be answered. She shuffled them around. Nothing interesting caught her eye.

The intercom buzzed. "Chris, you have a call from a Gideon Lowe. Do you want to take it, or should I take a message?"

Gideon Lowe. Chris's pulse skittered, then shot ahead. She didn't want to talk with him now. She was still stinging from his last shots. And embarrassed. And confused. And feeling less sure of herself than she had in years and years.

Did she want to take the phone? *No!* But that was foolish.

Bolstering herself with a deep breath, she said to Margie, "I'll take it." But she didn't pick up Gideon's call immediately. It took a few deep breaths, plus several seconds with her eyes shut tight before she felt composed enough. Even then, her finger shook when she punched in the button.

"Yes, Gideon." She wanted to sound all business. To her own ear though, she sounded frightened, just as she was feeling inside. She waited for him to blast her about driving off, leaving their meeting almost before it had begun. But he didn't say a thing. She looked at the telephone, thinking that maybe they'd been cut off. "Hello?"

"I'm sorry," he said in as quiet a tone as she'd heard from him yet. "That was not very nice of me. I shouldn't have said those things. Any of them."

"Then why did you?" she cried, only then realizing how personally she'd taken his barbs. She didn't understand *why* they bothered her so, since she and Gideon weren't anything more to each other than two people temporarily working together. But the fact was that they did, and she was upset enough to lose the cool she'd struggled to gain in the moments before she'd picked up the phone.

"Do you have something special against me?" she asked. "Have I ever done anything to you that warrants what you've been doing? I mean, I wandered innocently onto the site one day and was standing there, minding my own business, when your men saw me and botched the work they were doing. Forget that it wasn't my fault. I apologized, but it didn't make any difference. You've had it in for me ever since. Am I missing something here? Do I remind you of someone else, maybe someone unpleasant, someone who hurt you once, or who let you down? Why do you *hate* me?"

She ran out of breath. In the silence that ensued, she heard all that she'd blurted out and was appalled. She'd blown professionalism to bits, but then, that was something she seemed to do a lot in Gideon's company. She was debating hanging up the phone and burying her head in the trash can when he spoke again. His voice was still low. He actually sounded troubled.

"I don't hate you. I just look at you and...something happens. I can't explain it. Believe me, I've been trying. I've worked with lots of people over the years, lots of women, and I've never been this way before. People usually think I'm easygoing."

Chris recalled Jessica saying something to that extent. She hadn't believed it then, and she didn't believe it now. "Easygoing, like an angry bull," she murmured.

"I heard that. But it's okay. I deserve it."

In response to the confession, she softened a bit. "If you've never been this way before, then it's me. What is it I'm doing wrong? I'm trying. Really I am. I'm trying to be agreeable. I felt we should talk, because that's part of my job, and when you wanted to meet at the site, I agreed, even though it wasn't my first choice. I try to overlook some of the things you say, but they hurt, you know. I'm not a shallow person. I haven't gotten anything in life for free. I work hard at what I do, and I'm proud of that. So why do I annoy you so much?"

He was a minute in answering, and then he didn't get out more than a word when he was cut off by the operator. "All right, all right," he muttered. "Hold on Chris."

She was puzzled. "Where are you?"

She heard the clink of coins, then, "At a pay phone in town. The phones have been taken out at the Rise, and none of the ones on the street take credit cards. Can you believe that? We're building a complex that's state-of-the-art as far as living goes, in the middle of a town that's old-fashioned as hell. I'm probably gonna have to get a car phone before this project is done."

"Truck phone."

"Hmm?"

She sat back in her chair. "You drive a truck. Wouldn't you call it a truck phone?"

"I don't know. Do they? The guys who make them?"

"Beats me."

"You don't have a phone in your car?"

"No. They're expensive. Besides, I like silence when I drive. It gives me a chance to think."

"Aren't you worried about making the most of every minute?" he asked.

"I am. Making the most, that is. Thinking is important."

"Yeah, but all I hear from people is that I could be answering phone calls, communicating with clients, even getting new jobs if I had a phone in my car. Don't all those things apply to you?"

Chris had heard the arguments, too. "If someone is so desperate for my work that they can't wait until I get back into my office to talk with me, I don't want the job. You can bet it would be a nightmare. Even the most simple jobs run into snags. But one where the client wants instant satisfaction? I'll pass those up, thanks. I'm no miracle worker.'' She tacked on a quiet, ''I wish I was.''

''If you were, what would you do?''

She took another deep breath, a calmer one this time. She'd settled down, she realized. When he wasn't yelling at her, Gideon's deep voice was strangely soothing. ''Wave my magic wand over you so that whatever it is that bugs you about me would disappear. I want to do a good job at Crosslyn Rise. I'm a perfectionist. But I'm also a pacifist. I can't work in an atmosphere of hostility.''

''I'm not feeling hostile now.''

She thought about the conversation they were having, thought about the civility that they'd somehow momentarily managed to achieve. Her heart started beating faster, in relief, she figured. ''Neither am I.''

''That's 'cause we're talking on the phone. We're not face-to-face.''

''What is it about my *face* that bugs you, then?''

''Nothing. It's beautiful.''

The unexpected compliment left Chris speechless. Before she had a chance to start stammering simply to fill in the silence, Gideon said, ''You guessed right, though. That first time, I thought you were someone else. She'd been such a royal pain in the butt that I guess I took my frustration out on you.'' Elizabeth had called the week before; he told her he was still seeing Marie. ''After that, I couldn't confuse you with her. You're different.''

Chris didn't know whether that was a compliment or not. She was still basking in the first, though she felt foolish for that. What did it matter that Gideon thought she was beautiful? He was someone she'd be working with. By all rights, she should be furious that he was thinking of her in terms of looks rather than ability. He was as sexist as they came. And as deceitful, if indeed he was married.

''Uh, Chris?'' He sounded hesitant.

"Yes."

"I think there's something we ought to get straight right about now. What you said before in the truck about me and a wife or a woman or whoever—"

Her heart was hammering again. "Yes?"

"There isn't any wife. I'm not married. I was once, for a real short time, years ago. But I liked having fun more than I liked being married. So it died."

Chris felt a heat in the area of her breasts that had nothing to do with her heavy cowl-neck sweater. She almost resented his saying what he'd said, though deep down she'd known he wasn't married. But they had actually been getting along. Now, having his availability open and confirmed threw a glitch into the works. "Why are you telling me this?"

"Because I think it's part of the problem. For me, at least. I'm single, and you're single. Every time I look at you I get a little bothered."

"Bothered?" If he meant what she thought he meant, they were in trouble. Suddenly she didn't want to know. "Listen, if you're worried about me, don't be. I won't accost you. I'm not in this business to pick up men."

"That's not what I meant—"

"In fact," she cut in, "I'm not looking for a man at all. There's someone I've been seeing for a while, and he's a really nice guy, but to tell you the truth, I don't even have much time for him. I spend all my free time working."

"What fun is *that*?" Gideon asked indignantly.

On the defensive again, she sat straighter. "It's plenty of fun. I enjoy my work—except for those times when I get cut to ribbons by builders who take pleasure in making other people miserable."

"I don't do it on purpose. That's what I'm trying to tell you."

"Well, try something else. Try changing. Don't assume things about me, or make value judgments. Just because I think or act differently from you, doesn't mean that I'm wrong. I don't tell you what to like. Don't tell *me* what to like."

"I'm not *doing* that," Gideon insisted. "I'm just expressing my opinion. So I express it in a way that you find offensive. Well, maybe you're too sensitive.''

"Maybe I'm human! Maybe I like to get along with people. Maybe I like to please them. Maybe I like to have their respect every once in a while.''

"How can you have my respect,'' he threw back, "if you don't hang around long enough for me to get to know you? You got upset by what I said, so instead of sticking around and fighting it out, you took off. That doesn't solve anything, Chris.''

Her hand tightened on the phone. "Ah. I knew we'd get around to that sooner or later. Okay. Why don't you say what you think, just get it off your chest. I'm already feeling crushed. A little more won't hurt.''

He didn't say a word.

"Go on, Gideon. Say something. I know you're dying to. Tell me that I'm a coward. Tell me that you were being overly optimistic when you abstained in that vote. Tell me that you seriously doubt whether I have the wherewithal to make it through the decorating of Crosslyn Rise.'' She paused, waiting. "Tell me I'm in the wrong field. Tell me I should be doing something like secretarial work. Or teaching. Or waitressing.'' She paused again. "Go ahead. Be my guest. I'm steeled for it.'' A third time, she paused. Then, cautiously she said, "Gideon?''

"Are you done?''

She was relieved that he hadn't hung up. "Yes.''

"Want to meet me for lunch tomorrow?''

That wasn't what she'd expected to hear. She was taken totally off guard. "Uh, uh—''

"Maybe you were right. Maybe what we need is a neutral place to talk. So you choose it. Wherever you want to go, we'll go. I can drive down there, you can drive up here, we can meet somewhere in the middle. But we both have to eat lunch. We can even go dutch if you want. I'm perfectly willing to pay, but you women have a thing about a man treating you. Heaven forbid you might feel a little indebted to him.''

"That's not why we do it. We do it because it's the professional thing to do."

"If that's so, why is it that when I go out for a business lunch with another guy, one of us usually pays, with the understanding that the other'll do it the next time? Sometimes it's easier just to charge it rather than split the bill in two. But modern women have to make things so hard."

"Then why do you bother with us?"

"I don't, usually. On my own time, I steer as far away from you as I can get. Give me the secretary or the teacher or the waitress any day. They're not hung up on proving themselves. They like it when a man opens the door for them, or helps them with their coat, or holds their chair. They like to be treated like women."

"So do I."

"Could've fooled me."

"You were the one who suggested we go dutch. If you want to pay for lunch, be my guest. You probably make a whole lot more money than I do, anyway."

"What makes you think that?" he asked.

"You've invested in Crosslyn Rise, haven't you?"

"Yeah. With every last cent I had to my name. As far as cash flow goes, I'm just about up the creek."

"Was that a wise thing to do?"

"Ask me that two years from now and I may have an answer. I've got a whole lot riding on—" The telephone clicked, cutting him off. He came back in ripe form. "Damn, I'm out of change. Look, Chris, will you meet me or not?"

"Uh, tomorrow?" She looked at her calendar. "I wouldn't be able to make it until two. My morning's wild."

The phone clicked again. "Two is fine," he said hurriedly. "Name the place."

"Joe's Grille. It's in Burlington. Right off the Middlesex Turnpike."

"Joe's Grille at two. See you then."

She wasn't sure whether he hung up the phone or the operator cut him off, but after a minute of silence, she heard a dial tone. As the seconds passed, it seemed to grow louder and more blaring, almost like an alarm, and well it might have been. She'd arranged to see Gideon again. Granted, the conditions were more to her liking this time, but still she felt uneasy.

He was a very, very confusing man, annoying her most of the time, then, in the strangest ways and when she least expected it, showing charm. Not that she was susceptible to the charm. She'd made it clear that she wasn't available, and it was true. Still, she wished he was married. She'd have felt safer that way.

But he wasn't. And the fact was that they'd be working together. It helped some to know how much Crosslyn Rise meant to him. If he was telling the truth about his financial involvement, he couldn't afford to have anything go wrong, which ruled out his sabotaging her work. And he hadn't suggested that she pull out of the project. She'd given him the chance, had all but put the words into his mouth, but he hadn't used them.

That was the up side of the situation. The downside was the lunch that she'd stupidly agreed to. A meeting at the bank would have been better. Being in a restaurant, having lunch with Gideon seemed so...personal.

But she was a professional with a job to do. So she'd meet him, and she'd be in full control, and she'd show him that she was done being bullied. She could stand up to him. It was all a matter of determination.

CHAPTER FOUR

GIDEON WAS LOOKING forward to lunch. He felt really good after their phone conversation, as though they'd finally connected, and that mattered to him. Despite everything that he found wrong with Chris, she intrigued him. She wasn't what he'd first assumed her to be. He suspected she wasn't what, even now, he assumed her to be. She was a mystery, and he was challenged.

He was also excited in a way that had nothing to do with making progress on Crosslyn Rise and everything to do with having a date with an attractive woman. Because it was a date. Chris could call it a professional lunch, and it was, a little, but in his mind it was first and foremost a date. His motives were far from professional. He wanted to get to know Chris, wanted to start to unravel the mystery that she was. "Start" was the operative word, of course, because he envisioned this as only the first of many dates. She had already proclaimed that she wasn't looking for a man, so clearly she wasn't going to be rushed. But there'd be fun in that. Gideon was anticipating the slow, increasingly pleasant evolution of their relationship.

This first date was very important in that it would be laying the groundwork for those to come. For that reason, he was determined to be on his best, most civil and urbane behavior. He would have liked to add sophisticated or cultured to that, only he wasn't either of those things. Pretending might have worked with Elizabeth, but it wouldn't work with Chris. She'd see through him in a minute. She was sharp that way—knew damn well that he hadn't been waiting at the duck pond for ten minutes and caught him on it, though he'd only exaggerated a little. But he didn't want to be caught again, not when he wanted to impress. So he'd be himself, or that part of himself that would be most apt to please her.

For starters, he dressed for the occasion. Though he was at Crosslyn Rise at seven-thirty with the rest of his men and put in a full morning of work, he left them on their own at midday and drove all the way home to clean up. After showering and shaving, he put on a pair of gray slacks, a pink shirt, a sweater that picked up variations of those shades, and loafers. It was his yuppie outfit, the one he'd bought in Cambridge on the day he had decided to invest in Crosslyn Rise. He figured that he owed himself a small extravagance before the big splurge, and that he could use the clothes. He hated shopping. But he had to look the part of the intelligent investor, and so he'd bought the outfit, plus a blazer, two ties and a blue shirt. But he liked the pink one, at least to wear for Chris. She'd appreciate the touch.

After all, rednecks didn't wear pink.

He also put on the leather jacket that his mother had sent him several birthdays ago. It was one of the few gifts she'd given him that he liked. Most of the others were too prissy, reminding him of all she wanted him to be that he wasn't. The leather jacket, though, was perfect. It was conservative in style and of the richest brown leather he'd ever seen. He wore it a lot.

Leaving his truck in the yard, he took the Bronco, allowing plenty of time for traffic, and headed for Burlington. The route was the same to Crosslyn Rise. There were times when he felt he could do it in his sleep, except that he liked driving. Chris used her road time to think; he used his to relax, which was why he resisted getting a car phone, himself. A phone would interfere with his music. With sophisticated stereo setups in both of his vehicles, his idea of heaven was cruising along the highway at the fastest speed the traffic would bear, listening to Hank Jr., Willie or Waylon.

He didn't listen to anyone now, though, because he was too busy thinking about Chris. She really was a knockout, pretty in a soft-as-woman kind of way, despite the air of professionalism she tried to maintain. She turned him on. Oh, yeah. There was no mistaking the heat she generated. He was old enough and experienced enough—and blunt enough—to call a spade a spade. Sure, he was a little nervous to see her. Sure, it was cold outside. Sure, he hadn't eaten since six that morning. But the tiny tremors he felt inside weren't from any of those things. They were from pure, unadulterated lust.

That was the last thing he wanted Chris to know. And since it got worse the longer he thought about her—and since she was probably sharp enough to see *that* first thing, if he didn't do something to cool off—he opened the windows, turned on the music and began to sing at the top of his lungs. By the time he turned off the Middlesex Turnpike into the parking lot of Joe's Grille, his cheeks were red from the cold, his voice faintly hoarse, and his hands, as they pushed a comb through his wind-blown hair, slightly unsteady. He pulled on his jacket, checked the rearview mirror one last time to make sure he looked all right, took a breath and stepped out.

He was early. They were supposed to meet at two, and it was ten before the hour. He went into the restaurant just to make sure she hadn't arrived, gave his name to the hostess, along with a five for a good table and a wink for good cheer, then entered the adjoining mall and, hands stashed in his pockets, started walking around. With less than three weeks to go before Christmas, the holiday season was in full bloom. One store window was more festive, more glittery, more creative than the next. Almost as an escape from tinsel overload, he found himself gravitating toward the center of the mall, where a huge tree stood, decorated not with the usual ornaments, but with live flowers.

He stood there for a while, looking at the tree, thinking how pretty it was and that he didn't think he'd ever seen one quite like it before.

"I'm sorry," someone gasped beside him. He looked quickly down to see Chris. Her cheeks were flushed, and she was trying to catch her breath, but there was the hint of a smile on her face, even as she pressed a hand to her chest. "I got here a few minutes early, so I thought I'd pick up a gift or two, only the salesperson messed things up at the register and didn't know how to correct it, so I had to stand around waiting while he got his supervisor. The store was at the other end of the mall. I had to race back.'' She barely paused. ''Have you been here long?''

''Not long,'' he said. He wondered if she was babbling because she was nervous, and hoped it was a good sign. ''I was just wandering around. Everything's so pretty.'' But Chris took the cake. She was wearing a navy sweater and slacks and a long beige coat with a wool scarf hanging down the lapels. She might have pulled off the business look if it hadn't been for her cheeks and her hair, a few wisps of which had escaped its knot and were curling around her face, and her mouth, which looked soft, and her eyes, which were blue as the sky on a clear summer's day.

It struck him that she was more beautiful than the tree, but he wasn't about to say it. She thought she was here on business, and business partners didn't drool over each other. So he looked back at the tree. ''I've never seen one decorated this way. The flowers are pretty. How do they stay so fresh?''

He hadn't actually been expecting an answer, but Chris had one nonetheless. ''The stem of each is in a little tube that holds enough water to keep the flowers alive. If they're cut at the right time, lilies last a while.''

''Those are lilies?''

''Uh-huh. Stargazers. I use them a lot in silk arrangements for front foyers or buffets or dining room tables. They're elegant.''

He eyed her guardedly. ''You do silk arrangements?''

''No. Someone does them for me. She's the artist, but whenever I see an arrangement of fresh-cuts that I like, I make a note and tell her about it later.''

''I hate silk arrangements. They look fake.''

''Then you've never seen good ones. Good silks are hard to tell from the real thing.''

''I can tell. I can always tell.''

''You've seen that many?''

''Enough to know that it's a matter of moisture.'' His gaze fell to her mouth. ''I don't care how good the silk is, it doesn't breathe the way a real flower does. It doesn't shine or sweat. A real flower is like human skin that way.'' He brushed her cheek with the pad of his thumb, feeling the smoothness, the warmth, the dewiness that her run down the mall had brought. He also felt his own body responding almost instantaneously, so he cleared his throat, stuck his hand back into his pocket and said, "Are you hungry?"

She nodded.

"Wanna get lunch?"

"Uh-huh." She sounded breathless still.

Gideon wasn't rushing to attribute that breathlessness to anything other than the most innocent of causes, but he hadn't missed the way her eyes had widened just a fraction when he'd touched her face or the fact that she seemed glued to the spot.

He hitched his chin toward the restaurant.

With an effort, it seemed, Chris nodded again, then looked down to make sure that she had her bundle safely tucked under her arm.

"Can I carry that for you?" he asked.

"Uh, no. It's okay."

They started off. "What did you buy, anyway? Or is it a secret, maybe something black and sexy for your mom?" He faltered, suddenly wondering whether he'd put his foot in his mouth. "Uh, she's still around, isn't she?"

Chris smiled. The affection she so clearly felt for her mother brought added warmth to her eyes. "Quite. She's an energetic fifty-five. But she'd be embarrassed out of her mind to get something black and sexy. She doesn't define herself that way. No, this is for another relative. Something totally different. As a matter of fact, I don't know *what* to get my mother."

"What does she do?" Gideon asked, hoping to get hints about Chris through this mother she cared for.

"She reads, but books are so impersonal."

"What else does she do?"

"Needlepoint, but she's already in the middle of three projects and doesn't need a fourth."

"What else?"

"She cleans and cooks—" this was offered facetiously "—but I don't think she'd appreciate either a bottle of window cleaner or a tin of garlic salt."

Gideon was picturing a delightful homebody, someone he'd feel comfortable with in a minute. "How about a clay pot?"

Chris drew in her chin. "Clay pot?"

He'd seen them advertised on the back of one of the dozens of unsolicited catalogues that came in the mail every week. Rolled tight, those catalogues were kindling for his fire. Once in a while, something registered while he was doing the rolling. "You know, the kind you cook a whole meal in, kind of like a Crockpot, but clay." They'd reached the restaurant. He held the door for her to go through first.

"How do you know about clay pots?" she asked, shooting him a curious glance as she passed.

He shrugged. With a light hand on her waist, he guided her toward the hostess, who promptly led them to the quietest table in the house. Unfortunately, that wasn't saying a whole lot. The restaurant was filled, even at two, with a cross of business types from nearby office buildings and shoppers with kids. The business types were no problem, but the kids and their mothers were loud. Noting that the table the hostess had given them—a table for four, at that—was set slightly apart from the others, Gideon felt his money had been well spent. Every little bit of privacy helped when a man was pursuing his cause.

"Would you like me to hang up your coat?" he asked just before Chris slid into her seat.

She glanced at the nearby hooks. "Uh, okay." Depositing her bag and purse on one of the free chairs, she started to slip the coat off. Gideon took it from her shoulders and hung it up, then put his own jacket beside it. When he returned to the table, she was already seated. He took the chair to the right of hers, which was where the hostess had set the second menu, but no sooner had he settled in than he wondered if he'd made a mistake. Chris was sitting back in the pine captain's chair with her hands folded in her lap, looking awkward.

"Is this where I'm supposed to sit for a business lunch?" he asked, making light of it. "Or should I be sitting across from you?"

"I think," she said, glancing out at the crowd, "that if you sit across from me, I won't be able to hear a word you say. I thought most of the kids would be gone by now, but I guess at Christmastime anything goes.''

''I take it you've been here before.''

''Uh-huh. My family comes a lot.''

''Family,'' he prodded nonchalantly, ''as in mother and father?''

''And the rest. I'm the oldest. The youngest is just fifteen. It's harder now than it used to be, but we still try to do things together whenever we can.'' She opened her menu, but rather than looking at it, she took a drink of water. ''The club sandwiches are good here. So are the ribs. I usually go for one of the salads. There's a great Cobb salad, and a spinach one.''

''I hate spinach.''

The blunt statement brought her eyes finally to his. ''Like you hate silk flowers?''

''Pretty much.'' He paused, held her gaze, watched her cheeks turn a little pink and her slender fingers tuck a wisp of hair behind her ear. Unable to help himself, he said, ''I like your outfit. You look nice in navy.'' He paused again. ''Or aren't I supposed to say that at a business lunch?''

She looked at him for another minute, then seemed to relax. ''Technically, it is a sexist thing to say.''

''It's a compliment.''

''Would you give a compliment like that to one of your men?''

''Like that? Of course not. He'd think I was coming on to him.''

She arched an eloquent brow.

''I'm not coming on to you,'' Gideon told her, and in one sense it was true. He'd complimented her because he really *did* like the way she looked, and he was used to saying what he thought. ''I'm just telling you you look pretty. It's a fact. Besides, I do give my men compliments. Just not like that.''

''Like what, then?''

''Like...hey, man, that's a wild shirt...or...cool hat, bucko.''

''Ah,'' she said gravely. ''Man talk.'' She lowered her eyes to his shirt, then his sweater, and the corner of her mouth twitched. "I'll bet they had choice words to say about what you're wearing now."

Feeling a stab of disappointment, he looked down at himself. "What's wrong with what I'm wearing?"

"Nothing. It's a gorgeous outfit. But it's way different from what I've seen you wearing at the Rise."

It's a gorgeous outfit. Did that ever make him feel good! "Thanks, but I wasn't working in this." He snickered. "You're right. The guys would have kidded me off the lot. No, I went home to change."

She was silent, almost deliberative, for a minute before asking, "Where's home?"

"Worcester."

Her eyes went wide. "Worcester? That's halfway across the state. You're not actually commuting from there to Crosslyn Rise every day, are you?"

He nodded. "I can do it in an hour and a quarter."

"Speeding."

He shrugged.

"And you drove all that way this morning, then drove home, then drove all the way back to meet me?"

"I couldn't very well meet you in my work clothes. You wouldn't have wanted to sit across from me, much less next to me. Besides, I didn't have to drive *all* the way back. Crosslyn Rise is still farther on up."

"But I would have picked some place even closer, if I'd known." Her voice grew softer. "I'm sorry."

"Hey," he said with a puzzled smile, "it's no big thing. I asked you to name the place, and you named it." He looked around. "This is a nice place."

"Hello," the waitress said, materializing between them as though on cue. "My name is Melissa, and I'll be serving you today. May I get you something from the bar?"

Gideon raised his brows toward Chris.

She shook her head. "Tea for me, please."

"And you, sir?"

He wanted a beer, but that wasn't part of the image. Then again, he couldn't see himself ordering wine. So he settled for a Coke. "And maybe something to munch on," he said, waving his fingers a little. "What do you have?"

Chris spoke before Melissa could. "We'll have an order of skins, please. Loaded."

The minute Melissa left, he asked, "How do you know I like skins?"

"Do you?"

"Sure."

"Loaded?"

"Sure."

There was satisfaction in her smile. "So do my father and brothers, and they're all big and physical like you."

Gideon was thinking that being like her father and brothers was a good thing, since she clearly liked them, when he had a different thought. "What about your boyfriend? Does he like them?"

"My boyfriend? Oh, you mean Anthony. Uh, actually, he doesn't."

"So what does he eat when he comes here?"

"He doesn't."

"Doesn't eat?"

"Doesn't come here. He lives in Boston. And he's really not my boyfriend. Just a friend. I don't have time for a boyfriend. I told you that. I'm not interested."

"A girlfriend then?" he asked before he could think to hold his tongue.

She scowled at him. "Why *are* you so offensive." It wasn't a question.

He held up a hand and said softly, "Hey, I'm sorry. It's just that I like to know what's going on. I mean, why is a woman as beautiful and talented as you are still single?"

She threw the ball right back at him. "You're still single. What's *your* excuse?"

"I told you. I blew marriage once."

"A long time ago, you said. But you haven't tried again."

"But I date. I date a whole lot. There's just no one I like well enough to want to wake up to in the morning." He let the suggestiveness of that sink in, along with all the sexy images it brought. He could picture Chris in his bed, could picture it easily, and wondered if she could picture it, too.

She didn't look to be panting. Nor did she speak right away. Finally, slowly she said, "Then you live alone?"

He fancied he detected interest and grabbed onto the thought. "That's right."

"In an apartment?"

"A house. That I built."

A small smile touched the edge of her mouth. "Mmm. I should have guessed." She paused, seemed deliberative again. He guessed that she wasn't sure how personal to get.

"Go on," he coaxed gently. "Ask. I'll answer."

Given permission, she didn't waste any time. "You live all alone in a big house?"

"It's not big. But it's nice. And it's all I need."

"And you take care of yourself—cook, clean, do laundry?"

"I cook. I have someone come in to do the rest." He didn't see anything wrong with that. She couldn't expect that he'd do everything for himself when he had important work to do every day.

"You really do cook?"

"Enough to stay alive." He wondered what she was getting at. "Why?"

"Because you know about clay pots," she mused, and seemed suddenly, seriously pleased. "That's not a bad idea. My mother doesn't have anything like it. It's really a *good* idea. Thank you."

Gideon grinned. "Glad to be of help." Then his eyes widened at the sight of the skins that suddenly appeared on the table. They looked incredible and he was famished.

"Are you ready to order the rest?" Melissa asked.

Chris looked inquiringly at Gideon, but he hadn't even opened his menu. "Some kind of sandwich," he said softly. "You choose. You know what's good."

She ordered a triple-decker turkey club for him and a Cobb salad for herself. Then she hesitated, seeming unsure for a minute.

"Sounds great," he assured her, and winked at Melissa, who

blushed and left. When he looked back at Chris, she was reaching into her purse and pulling out a notebook. Tugging a pen from its spiral binding, she opened to a page marked by a clip.

"What are you doing?" Gideon asked. He was being the gentleman, waiting for her to help herself to a potato skin before he dug in.

"I have questions for you. I want to make notes."

"About me?"

"About Crosslyn Rise."

"Oh." He looked longingly at the skins. Taking the two large spoons resting beside them, he transferred one to Chris's plate.

She protested instantly. "Uh-uh. Those are for you."

"I can't eat them all."

"Then you'll have to take them home for supper. All I want is a salad."

"Aha," he breathed, "you're one of those women who's always on a diet." He shot a quick look at her hips. "I don't see any fat."

"It's there."

"Where?"

"There." She sat back in her chair and stared at him.

Fantasize all he might, but that stare told him she wasn't saying a word about her thighs or her bottom or her waist or her breasts, if those were the spots where she imagined there was fat. So he helped himself to a skin and said, "Okay, what are your questions?" He figured that while he was eating, they could take care of business, so that by the time he was done they could move on to more interesting topics.

He had to hand it to her. She was prepared. She knew exactly what she wanted to ask and went right to it. "Will you consider putting wood shingles on the roof?"

"No." He said. "Next question." He forked half a skin into his mouth.

"Why not?"

"Mmm. These are great."

"Why not wood shingles?" she repeated patiently.

"Because they're expensive and impractical."

"But they look so nice."

"Brick does, too, but it's expensive as hell."

She held his gaze without so much as a blink. "That was my next question. Couldn't we use brick in a few select areas?"

"That's not part of Carter's concept. He wants clapboard."

"What do you think?"

"I think you should talk with Carter."

"What do *you* think?"

"I think we can do very well without that expense, too. Next question." He took another skin, cut it in two, downed the half.

"Windows. What about some half-rounds?"

"What about them?"

"They'd look spectacular over the French doors in the back."

Gideon had to agree with her there, but he was a realist. "It's still a matter of cost," he said when he'd finished what was in his mouth. "I based my bid on the plans Carter gave me. Half-rounds are expensive. If I go over budget, it's money out of my pocket any way you see it."

"Maybe you won't have to go over budget," she said hopefully, "not if you get a good deal from a supplier."

"You know a supplier who'll give us that kind of deal?"

Her hope seemed to fade. "I thought you might."

He looked down at his plate as he cut another skin, arching little more than a brow in her direction. "You're the one with connections in the business. Me, I'm on my own." He popped the skin into his mouth.

"You don't have any relatives in construction?"

After a minute of chewing, he said, "None living. My dad was a housepainter. But he's been gone for ten years now."

She sobered. "Ten years. He must have been very young."

"Not so young overall, but too young to die. There was an accident on the job. He never recovered." Gideon sent her a pointed look. "That's one of the reasons I go berserk when I see carelessness at my sites."

After a minute's quiet, she said, "I can understand that." She'd put down the notebook, had her elbows on the arms of the chair and was making no attempt to look anywhere but at him. "Were you working with him at the time?"

"No. I worked with him when I was a kid, but I was already into construction when the accident happened. He did a lot of work for me in those last years, but when he fell, it was on another job. The scaffolding collapsed."

"I'm sorry," she said, and sounded it. "Were you two close?"

"Growing up, he was all I had."

"Your mother?"

"Left when I was three."

"Just left?" Chris asked, looking appalled.

"She met someone else, someone with more promise. So she divorced my dad, married the other guy and moved to California." He put down his fork. "She did well. I have to give her that. She's become a very nice society lady—with silk arrangements all over her house."

"Ah, but not *good* silks, if you thought they looked fake." She smiled for a second, then sobered again. "Do you see her often?"

"Once, maybe twice a year. She keeps in touch. She even wanted me to come live with her at one point, but I wasn't about to betray my dad that way. Then, after he died, I wasn't about to move. My roots are here. My business is here." He smirked. "She isn't wild about what I do. Thinks it's a little pedestrian. But that's okay. California doesn't tempt me, anyway. I'm not the beach boy type."

Chris mirrored his smirk. "Not into surfing?"

"Not quite. Softball and basketball. That's it."

"That's enough," she said with feeling.

"Your father and brothers, too?" he guessed.

"Brothers," she answered. "They're basketball fanatics."

"How about you? Are you into exercise?"

"Uh-huh. I do ballet."

Ballet. He might have known. He had about as much appreciation for ballet as he did for Godiva chocolates. He was a Hershey man all the way. "Do you dance in shows?"

"Oh, no. Even if I were good enough, which I'm not, and

even if I were young enough, which I'm not, I wouldn't have the time. I go to class twice a week, for the fun and the exercise of it. In a slow and controlled kind of way, it's a rigorous workout." She took a fast breath. "So why did you move from painting to construction?"

He wanted to know more about her, but she kept turning the questions back at him, which bothered him, on the one hand, because he wasn't used to talking about himself so much, at least not on really personal matters. For instance, he didn't usually tell people about his mother. Then again, Chris seemed genuinely interested, which made it easy to talk. She wasn't critical. Just curious. As though he were a puzzle she wanted to figure out.

So he'd be her puzzle. Maybe she'd be as intrigued with him as he was with her.

"Painting to construction?" He thought back to the time he'd made the switch, which had been hard, given his father's preference. "Money was part of it. The construction business was booming, while painting just went along on the same even keel. I also had a thing for independence. I didn't want to be just my dad's son. But I guess most of it had to do with challenge." He narrowed an eye. "Ever spend day after day after day painting a house? When I first started, I thought it was great. I could stand up there on a ladder, goin' back and forth with a brush, listening to my music from morning to night. Then the monotony set in. I used to feel like I was dryin' up inside. I mean, I didn't have to *think*."

"You certainly have to do that now."

"Thank you."

"I mean it."

"I know. Believe me, I *know* how much I have to think every day. There are times when it's a major pain in the butt, but I wouldn't trade what I do for any other job."

Chris looked puzzled at that. "But you've invested in Crosslyn Rise. You're a member of the consortium. Isn't that like stepping over the line?"

"I'm kind of straddling it right now."

"Then it's not a permanent move into development?"

Gideon thought about it for a minute. A month before, he'd have had a ready answer, but he didn't have one now. "I invested in the Rise because I've never invested in a project before. It was a step up the ladder, something I wanted to try, something I *had* to try." He frowned down at his plate, nudging it back and forth by tiny degrees. "So I'm trying it, and I'm finding that I really want it to work, I mean, *really* want it to work, and there's pressure that goes with that." His eyes sought hers. "Do you know what I mean?"

She nodded, but he wasn't done. "The pressure isn't all fun. And then there's the thing about working in an office, versus working at a site. I like the meetings at the bank. I like being involved at that level. But when the meetings adjourn and we all shake hands, there isn't the feeling of accomplishment that I get at the end of a day when I stand back and see the progress that's been made on a house. Or the feeling," he said, coming alive just at the thought, "of standing back and seeing the finished product, seeing people move in, seeing them live in a place I've built and loving it. I could never give up building. I could never give up that kind of satisfaction."

He said back quietly in his chair, thinking about what he'd said, feeling sheepish. "Funny, I hadn't quite put all those thoughts into words before. You're a positive influence."

"No," she said softly. "You'd have said those things, or recognized that you felt them, sooner or later. I just happened to ask the question that triggered it, that's all."

"I'll bet you do that a lot for people. It takes a good listener to ask a good question. You're a good listener."

She shrugged, then looked quickly up and removed a hand from the table when Melissa delivered their lunches. When they were alone again, she said, "Listening is important in my line of work. If I don't hear what a client is saying, I can't deliver." She dunked her tea bag into the minicarafe of hot water. "Speaking of which, I have more questions about Crosslyn Rise."

"If they involve spending money—"

"Of course they involve spending money," she teased, her blue eyes simultaneously dead serious and mischievous.

"Then you might as well save your breath," he warned, but gently. "We're locked into our budget, says Ben Heavey. He's one of the men you met at the bank that night, and a tightwad? He gives new meaning to the word."

"But what if I can save money here—" she held out her right hand, then her left "—and use it there?"

He pointed his fork at her plate. "Eat your salad."

"Take the flooring. Carter's blueprints call for oak flooring throughout the place, but the fact is that in practically every home I've decorated, the people want carpeting in the bedrooms. If we were to do that, substituting underlayment for oak in the bedrooms, even just the upstairs bedrooms, with the money we'd save, we could pickle the oak downstairs. *That* would look *spectacular*."

"Pickled oak is a bitch to keep clean."

"Only if you have little kids—"

"*I'd* have trouble with it—"

"Or big kids who don't know how to wipe their feet, but how many of those will we attract at Crosslyn Rise? Think about it, Gideon. Or ask Nina Stone. She'll be the first one to tell you that we're aiming at a mature buyer. Not a retiree, exactly, but certainly not a young couple with a whole gang of kids."

"How many kids did you say were in your family?"

"I didn't. But there are six."

"Six kids." He grinned. "That's fun. From what to fifteen?"

She saw through the ruse at once and told him so with a look. "Thirty-three. I'm thirty-three. Is that supposed to have something to do with Crosslyn Rise?"

"Would you move there?"

"If I wanted to live on the North Shore, which I don't, because my business is in Belmont."

"Where do you live now?" Of the information he wanted, that was one vital piece.

She hesitated for just a minute before saying, "Belmont."

"To be near your family?"

She nodded slowly. "You could say that."

"Because you're all so close," he said quickly, so that she

wouldn't think he was interested, *personally* interested, in where she lived. "Do you know how lucky you are about that? I've never had any brothers or sisters. Thanksgiving was my dad and me. Christmas was my dad and me. Fourth of July was my dad and me."

"Didn't you have any friends?"

"Sure, lots of them, and we were invited places and *went* places all the time. But that's different from being home for the holidays." He grew still, picked up his sandwich and took a bite.

Chris speared a piece of lettuce. For a minute she seemed lost in her thoughts. Then, quietly she said, "My family means the world to me. I don't know what I'd do without them."

"Is that why you haven't married?"

She raised her head. "I told you why. Marriage just isn't high on my list of priorities."

"Because you're too busy. But you made time to have lunch with me."

"This is business."

"It's also fun. At least, I think so. It's the most fun I've had at lunch in a while." It was true, he realized. He'd had more bawdy lunches, certainly wilder ones, but never one that excited him more. Even aside from the sexual attraction, he liked Chris. She was intelligent. Interesting.

Concentrating on her salad, she began to eat, first a piece of lettuce, then a slice of olive, then some chicken and a crumble of blue cheese. Gideon, too, ate in silence, but he was watching her all the while.

"Well?" he said when he couldn't stand it any longer.

She looked up. "Well what?"

"Are you enjoying yourself?"

"Right now, no. I'm feeling very awkward."

"Because I'm watching you eat?"

"Because you're waiting for me to say something that I don't want to say." With care, she set down her fork. "Gideon, I'm not looking for a relationship. I thought I made that clear."

"Well, you said it, but do I have to take it for gospel?"

"Yes."

"Come on, Chris. I like you."

"I'm glad. That'll make it easier for us to work together."

"What about after work? Can I see you?"

"No. I told you. I don't have the time or desire for something like that."

Sitting back in his chair, he gave her a long, hard look. "I think you're bluffing," he said, and to some extent he was himself. He wasn't a psychologist. He wasn't into analyzing people's motives. But he was trying to understand Chris, to understand why she wouldn't date him, when he had a gut feeling they'd be good together. "I think you're protecting yourself, because maybe, just maybe you're afraid of involvement. You've got your family, and that's great, and I imagine it's time-consuming to give a big family a hunk of yourself. But I think that if the right thing came along, you'd have all the time in the world for it—" he leaned close enough to breathe in the gentle floral scent that clung to her skin "—and more desire than a man could begin to hope for." He stayed close for a minute, because he just couldn't leave her so soon. Unable to resist, he planted a soft kiss on her cheek. Then he straightened and sat back.

"I'm not giving up, Chris." His voice was thick, vibrating in response to all he felt inside. "I'll wait as long as it takes. I've got all the time in the world, too—and more desire than you could ever want."

CHAPTER FIVE

CHRIS NEVER KNEW how she made it through the rest of lunch. She felt warm all over, her insides were humming, and even after Gideon took pity on her and changed the subject, she was shockingly aware of him—shockingly, because the things she kept noticing she hadn't noticed in any man, *any* man since she'd been eighteen years old, and even then, it was different.

Brant had been eighteen, too. He'd been big and brawny, a football player, far from the best on the team but good enough to earn a college scholarship. She remembered the nights they'd spent before graduation, parked in the shadowy grove behind the reservoir in his secondhand Chevy. She'd worshiped him then, had thought him the most beautiful creature on earth. With his sable hair and eyes, his strong neck and shoulders, and hands that knew just what to do with her breasts, he excited her beyond belief. Wanting only to please him, she let him open her blouse and bra to touch her naked flesh, and when that wasn't enough, she let him slip a hand inside her jeans, and when even that wasn't enough, she wore a skirt, so that all he had to do was take off her panties, unzip his pants and push inside her. It had hurt the first time, and she bled, but after that it was better, then better still.

Looking back, trying to remember how she could have been so taken in, she wondered if she wasn't half-turned-on by the illicitness of what they were doing. She hadn't ever been a rebel, but she was a senior in high school and feeling very grown-up in a houseful of far younger siblings. And then, yes, there was Brant. Looking back, she saw that he was a shallow cad, but at the time he was every cheerleader's dream with his thick hair, his flexing muscles, his tiny backside and his large strong thighs.

Gideon Lowe put her memory of Brant Conway to shame

Gideon was mature, richly so, a freewheeling individual with a wealth of character, all of which was reflected in his physicality. The things she noticed about him—that stuck in her mind long after she left Joe's Grille—were the dark shadow of a mustache over his clean-shaven upper lip, the neat, narrow lobe of his ear and the way his hair swept vibrantly behind it, the length of his fingers and their strength, their newly scrubbed look, the scar on the smallest of them. She noticed the tan— albeit fading with the season—on his neck and his face, the crinkles radiating outward from the corners of his eyes, the small indentation on his cheek that should have been a dimple but wasn't. She remembered his size—not only his largeness, but the way he leaned close, making her feel enveloped and protected. And his scent, she remembered that with every breath she took. It was clean, very male and very enticing.

The problem, of course, was resisting the enticement, which she was determined to do above all else. She meant what she told him. She didn't have time for a serious man in her life. Her career was moving, and when she wasn't working, her time was happily filled with family. Thanksgiving had been larger— now that Jason was married, Evan engaged, and Mark and Steven bringing friends home from college—and more fun than ever. Christmas promised to be the same. She wanted to enjoy the holiday bustle. And then, there was work, which felt the Christmas crunch, too. Clients wanted everything delivered and looking great for the holidays. That meant extra phone calls on Chris's part, extra appointments, extra deliveries, extra installations. She *really* didn't have time for Gideon Lowe.

Of course, trying to explain that to Gideon was like beating her head against a brick wall. He called an hour after she returned to the office, on the day they met for lunch, to make sure she'd gotten back safely. He called two days later to say that, though he couldn't promise anything, he was getting estimates on half-round windows. He called three days after that to ask her to dinner.

Just hearing his voice sparked the heat in her veins. She couldn't possibly go to dinner with him. Couldn't *possibly*. "I'm sorry, Gideon, but I can't."

"Can't, or won't?"

"Can't. I have other plans." Fortunately, she did.

"Break them."

"I can't do that." The Christmas concert was being held at the high school that night. She wouldn't miss it for the world.

"Then tomorrow night. We could take in a movie or something."

She squeezed her eyes shut and said more softly, "No. I'm sorry."

He was silent for a minute. "You won't see me at all?"

"I don't think it would be a good idea. We work together. Let's leave it at that."

"But I'm lonely."

She cast a helpless glance at the ceiling. When he was blunt that way, there was something so endearing about the man that she wanted to strangle him. He was making things hard for her. "I thought you said you date. In fact, you said you date *a whole lot*." She remembered that quite clearly.

"I did, and I do, but those women are just friends. They're fine for fast fun, but they don't do anything for loneliness. They don't fill my senses the way you do."

"For *God's* sake, Gideon," she breathed. He was being corny as hell, but she liked it. It wasn't fair.

"Say you'll see me this weekend. Sometime. Anytime."

"I have a better idea," she said, trying to regain control of herself and the situation. "I'll talk with you on the phone again next week. There are questions that I didn't get around to asking you when we had lunch—" questions that she hadn't had the presence of mind to ask after he'd leaned close and kissed her "—and I've had other thoughts on the Rise since then. What do you say we talk a week from today?"

"A week!"

"This is an awful season for me. I'm up to my ears in promises and commitments. A week from today? Please?"

Mercifully her plea got through to him, because he did agree to call her the following Thursday. She was therefore unprepared when, on that Tuesday, between calls to a furniture factory in North Carolina, a ceramic tile importer in Delaware and an independent carpenter in Bangor, Maine, she heard an unmistakably familiar male voice coming from the outer office.

After listening to it for a minute, she knew just what was happening. She had told Margie that she needed an uninterrupted hour to make all her calls. So Margie was giving Gideon a hard time. But Gideon wasn't giving up.

Leaving her chair, Chris opened the office door, crossed her arms over her breasts and leaned against the jamb. "What are you doing here, Gideon?" she asked in as stern a voice as she could produce, given the way her heart was thudding at first sound, then sight of him. He was wearing jeans, a sweater and a hip-length parka. His hair was combed, but he hadn't shaved, which suggested that he'd come straight from work, with the benefit of only cursory repairs in the truck. The image of that unsettled her even more. But the worst was the way his eyes lit up when she appeared.

"Hey, Chris," he said, as though finding her here were a total surprise, "what's up?"

"What are you doing here?" she repeated, but she was having trouble keeping a straight face. For a big, burly, bullheaded guy, he looked adorably innocent.

Sticking his hands into the pockets of his jeans—knowingly or unknowingly pushing his parka in the process to reveal the faithful gloving of his lower limbs—he shrugged and said, "I was in the neighborhood and thought I'd drop in. How've you been?"

She steeled herself against his charm. "Just fine since we talked last week."

"Have a good weekend?"

"Uh-huh. And you?"

"Lonely. Very lonely. But I told you it would be." The look in his eye told her that if she didn't invite him into her office, he'd elaborate on that in front of Margie.

Chris didn't want even the slightest elaboration. She didn't trust where he'd stop, and it wasn't only Margie who'd hear, but Andrea, who was with a client in the second office and would no doubt be out before long. Then there would be comments and questions and suggestions the minute he left, and she couldn't bear that. No, the less attention drawn to Gideon, the better.

Dropping her arms, she nodded him into her office. The minute he was inside with the door closed, she sent him a baleful stare. "I told you I couldn't see you, and I mean it, Gideon. I have work to do. I'm *swamped*." She shook a hand at her desk. "See that mess? That's what the Christmas rush is about. I don't have time to play." Her eyes widened. "What are you doing?"

"Taking off my jacket. It's warm in here."

Didn't she know it. Something about the two of them closed in the same room sent the temperature soaring. She felt the rise vividly, and it didn't help that he looked to be bare under his sweater, which fell over his pectorals with taunting grace.

"Put that jacket back on," she ordered, and would have helped him with it if she dared touch him, which she didn't. "You're not staying."

"I thought we could talk about the Rise."

"Baloney. You're not here about the Rise, and you know it," she scolded, but she seemed to have lost his attention. He was looking around her office, taking in the apricot, pale gray and chrome decor.

"Not bad," he decided. Crossing to the upholstered sofa, he pushed at one of the cushions with a testing hand, then turned and lowered his long frame onto the piece. He stretched out his arms, one across the back of the sofa, the other along its arm, and looked as though he'd be pleased to stay there a week.

Chris had her share of male clients, many of whom had been in her office, but none had ever looked as comfortable on that sofa as Gideon did. He was that kind of man, comfortable and unpretentious—neither of which helped her peace of mind any more than his sweater did, or his jeans. "I have to work, Gideon," she pleaded softly.

He gestured toward the desk. "Be my guest. I won't say a word."

"I can't work with you here."

"Why not?"

"You'll distract me."

"You don't have to look at me."

"I'll see you anyway."

"Ahh." He sighed. "A confession at last."

She blushed, then scowled in an attempt to hide it. "Gideon. Please."

Coming forward, he put his elbows on his spread thighs and linked his hands loosely between his knees. His voice went lower, his eyes more soulful. "It's been just over a week since I've seen you, but it feels like a month. You look so pretty."

Chris was wearing a burgundy jumper that she'd pulled from the closet, and a simple cream-colored blouse with a large pin at the throat. It was one of her oldest outfits. She didn't think she looked pretty at all and was embarrassed that he should say it. "Please, Gideon."

But he wasn't taking back the words. "I think about you a lot. I think about what you're doing and who you're with. I think about—wonder about—whether you're thinking of me."

She shut her eyes tight against the lure of his voice. "I told you. Things have been wild."

"But when you're home alone at night, do you think about me then?"

She pressed two fingers to her lips, where, just the night before, she'd dreamed he'd kissed her. From behind the fingers, she breathed a soft, "This isn't what I want."

"It's not what I want, either, but it's happening, and I can't ignore it. I feel an attraction to you the likes of which I haven't felt in years. I've tried to hold back, Chris. I tried not to come today because I know how you feel. But I'm not real good at waiting around. Call it impatient or domineering or macho, but I'm used to taking the lead. I want to see you again."

Anthony Haskell waited around, Chris realized. Anthony waited around all the time for her to beckon him on, but when she did, there was never any heat. There was heat now, with Gideon. She felt it running from her head to her toes, stalling and pooling at strategic spots in between.

Needing a buffer, she took refuge in the large chair behind the desk. "I thought we agreed to talk on Thursday," she said a little shakily.

"We did. And we can. But you're right. I didn't come to talk about the Rise. And I don't really want to talk about it on Thursday. There's nothing pressing there, certainly nothing that can't wait until the beginning of January, especially if you're as busy now as you say."

"I *am* busy."

"I believe you," he said genially. "But you have to take a break sometime. Why can't you take one with me?"

"I don't *want* to."

"Why not?"

She could think of dozens of answers, none of which she was ready to share.

Gideon didn't have that problem. "Don't you like me?"

She scowled. "Of course, I like you. If I didn't, I'd have already called the police to kick you out. You're interfering with my business."

"Do I still make you nervous?"

"Not nervous. Exasperated. Gideon," she begged, "I have to work."

"Do I excite you?"

"Yeah, to thoughts of mayhem." She glowered at him. "This isn't the time or place for a discussion like this."

"You're right. Let me take you to dinner tonight."

She shook her head.

"Tomorrow night, then. Come on, Chris, you have to eat."

"I do eat. With my family."

"Can't they spare you for one night?"

She shook her head.

"Then let me come eat with you." He seemed to warm to the idea once it was out. "I'd like that. I mean, I'd really like it. Big family dinners are something I always wanted but never had. I'll bring flowers for your mom. I'll bring cigars for your dad—"

"He doesn't smoke."

"Then beer."

"He doesn't drink."

"Then cashew nuts."

She shook her head. "Sorry. Doctor's orders."

Gideon looked appalled. "The poor guy. What does he *do* for the little joys in life?"

"He sneaks out to the kitchen when he thinks none of us is looking and steals kisses from my mom while she does the dishes."

That shut Gideon up. For a minute he just stared at her as though he couldn't grasp the image. Then his expression slid from soft to longing. "That's nice," he finally said, his voice a little thick. "I'm envious of you all."

Chris was beginning to feel like the worst kind of heel. If she was to believe Gideon's act, he was all alone in the world. But he dated, he dated *a lot*. And he had a mother in California. Maybe even a stepfamily. No doubt there would be numerous brightly wrapped gifts under his Christmas tree. So why did he look as though spending a little time with her family might be the best gift of all?

"Look," she said with a helpless sigh, "my parents have a Christmas open house every year." It would be packed. She could do her good deed, ease her conscience and be protected by sheer numbers. "It's this Sunday. If you want, you could come."

He brightened. "I'll come. Tell me where and when."

Taking a business card—deliberately, as a reminder of the nature of their relationship—she printed the address on the back. "It runs from three to seven, with the best of the food hitting the table at six."

"What should I wear?" he asked as he rose from the sofa to take the card.

"Something casual. Like what you wore to lunch last week."

He looked at the card, then stretched a little to slide it into the front pocket of his jeans. Chris was barely recovering from the way that stretch had lengthened his body when he turned, grabbed his coat and threw it on. For a split second his sweater rose high enough to uncover a sliver of skin just above his jeans. In the middle of that sliver, directly above the snap, was a belly button surrounded by whorls of dark hair.

She felt as though she'd been hit by a truck.

Oblivious to her turmoil, Gideon made for the door. Once there, he turned and gave her an ear-to-ear grin. "You've made my day. Made my *week*. Thanks, Chris. I'll see you Sunday." With a wink, he was gone.

FIVE DAYS WAS far too soon to see him again, Chris decided on Sunday morning as she pulled on a sweatshirt and sweatpants and went to help her mother prepare for the party. He was still too fresh in her mind—or rather, the effect he had on her was too fresh. Every time she thought of him, her palms itched. Itched to touch. Itched to touch hair-spattered male flesh. And every time she thought of doing it, she burned.

She didn't know what was wrong with her. For fifteen years, she hadn't felt the least attraction to a man, and it hadn't been deliberate. She was with men when she worked. Her dad had men over. So did her brothers. But none had ever turned her on, it was as simple, as blunt as that.

What she felt for Gideon Lowe made up for all those chaste years, so much so that she was frightened. She sensed she'd need far more than crowds to lessen the impact he had on her. She only prayed he'd arrive late to coincide with the food. The less time he stayed, the better.

GIDEON WOULD HAVE ARRIVED at three on the nose if it hadn't been for his truck, which coughed and choked and balked at having to go out in the cold. He called it every name in the book as he worked under its hood, finally even threatened to trade it in for a sports car. That must have hit home, because the next time he tried it, the engine turned smoothly over and hummed nicely along while he went back into the house to scrub his hands clean.

It was three-thirty when he pulled into the closest spot he could find to the address Chris had written down. The street was pretty and tree lined, though the trees were bare, in a neighborhood that was old and well loved. Wood-frame houses stood, one after another, on scant quarter-acre lots. Their closeness gave a cozy feeling that was reinforced by wreaths decorating each and every door and Christmas lights shining from nearly every window. None of the houses was large, including Chris's parents', but that added to the coziness.

From the looks of things, the party was in full swing. The front door was open, there were people preceding him up the walk, and the side stoop was occupied by a group of college-age kids who seemed oblivious to the cold.

Leaving his truck, he followed the walk to the door, dodging two young girls who darted out of the house to join their friends. Once on the threshold, he felt a little unsure for the first time since he'd bulldozed the invitation from Chris. He'd gone to parties at the homes of people far more wealthy and influential, but none mattered more to him than this one.

He assumed that he was looking a little lost, because he barely had time to take more than two steps into the house when he was greeted by a tall gray-haired man. "Welcome," the man said in a voice loud enough to be heard above the din. "Come on in."

Gideon extended his hand. "Mr. Gillette?"

"That I am," the man said, giving him a hearty shake, "but probably not the one you want. I'm Peter. If you're looking for my brother Frank, he's mixing the eggnog, which is real serious business, so I'd advise you to leave him be. If he messes up, we all lose out, if you get my drift."

"Actually," Gideon said, searching for a blond head among those crowded into the living room, "I'm looking for Christine. I'm a friend of hers, Gideon Lowe."

"Even better," Peter said with a broad grin. "Tell you what. Why don't you hang your coat up in the closet while I go find her."

Gideon was already working his way out of the leather jacket. "That's okay. I'll go." Spotting a hook at the end of the closet, he freed himself of the jacket. "Which direction?"

Peter looked first toward the dining room on the left, then the living room on the right, then back toward the dining room. "The kitchen, I guess. If she's not helping Frank, she'll be helping Mellie." He pointed through the dining room. "That way."

With a nod, Gideon started off. The dining room was filled

with people helping themselves to drinks and the small holiday cookies and cakes that covered plate after plate on the table. At one end was a huge punch bowl, into which a man Gideon assumed to be Frank was alternately pouring eggnog and brandy. He was a good-looking man, Gideon thought, tall and stocky, with salt-and-pepper hair and a ruddy complexion. Despite the good-natured coaxing and wheedling of several onlookers, he was concentrating solely on his work.

Gideon inched between two people here, three others there, until he'd made his way to the far end of the dining room and slipped through the door into a small pantry that led to the kitchen. There he saw Chris. She was standing at the counter by the sink with her back to him. Beside her was the woman who had to be her mother, if the similarity of height, build and coloring were any indication. They were slicing hot kielbasa, putting toothpicks in each slice, arranging the slices on a platter.

Coming up close behind Chris, he bent and put a gentle kiss beneath her ear.

She cried out and jumped a mile, then whirled on him in a fury. "Gideon! Don't *ever* do that again! My God—" she pressed her hand to her heart "—you've aged me fifteen years."

He gestured toward her mother, who was eyeing him curiously. "If this lovely lady is any indication of what you'll look like fifteen years from now, you've got it made." He extended his hand toward Mellie. "Mrs. Gillette?" There was no mistaking it. The eyes were the same, the hair, the mouth. Chris was slimmer and, wearing loose pants with a tunic top, more stylishly dressed, but they were very definitely mother and daughter.

"Gideon…?"

"Gideon Lowe, Mom. He's the builder for Crosslyn Rise and may well be the death of me before I even get to the project." She scolded him with her eyes, then her voice. "I thought you were coming later."

"You suggested six if I was starved. I figured I'd give myself a while to build up to that." He shook Mellie's hand warmly.

"It's nice to meet you, Mr. Lowe."

"Gideon. Nice to meet you, too, ma'am." He let her take her hand back and return to her work. "This is quite some party." He looked down at the platter. "Can I help?"

"No," both women said at the same time.

Chris elaborated. "Men don't cook in my mother's kitchen. My father does the eggnog, but not in here. Men are good for cleaning up. That's all."

"And a few other things," Mellie added softly, almost under her breath. Then she looked straight at Gideon and spoke up, "But I don't want you in here. You're a guest. Christine, leave these now. I'll finish up. Take Gideon out and introduce him around."

Gideon thought Chris was going to argue, but even he could see that Mellie wasn't taking no for an answer. So she washed and dried her hands, then led him through another door into a hallway that led back to the front. This hallway, too, was crammed with people, giving Gideon ample excuse to stay close to Chris.

"You look fantastic," he murmured into her ear as they inched their way along.

"Thanks," she murmured back.

"You taste even better."

"Oh, please," she whispered, but before he had a chance to come back with anything wickedly witty, she half turned, took his elbow and drew him alongside her. "Gideon, this is my brother Steven. He's a junior at U. of Mass. Steven, meet Gideon Lowe, a builder I work with."

Gideon shook hands with a blond-haired young man who also had the family features. "You must be one of the basketball fanatics," he said, noting that Steven stood nearly as tall as he did.

Steven grinned. "You got it. You, too?"

"You bet. If not for this gorgeous sister of yours, I'd be at the game right now." Leaning close, he asked out of the corner of his mouth, "Any fix on the score?"

In every bit as low a tone, Steven answered, "Last time I

checked, the Celts were up by eight. Game's on upstairs, if you want.''

Gideon slapped his shoulder and straightened. ''Thanks for the word. Maybe later.''

''Don't you dare go up and watch that game,'' Chris warned, leading him on by the hand. ''That would be very rude.''

''Keep holding my hand,'' he whispered, ''and I'll stay right by your side.'' He raised his voice. ''Ah, here comes another brother.''

Chris shot him an amused grin. ''This is Jason. He works with Dad. His wife's over there—'' She stood on tiptoe, looking around, ''Jase, where's Cheryl?''

Jason shook hands with Gideon. ''Upstairs nursing the baby.''

''Gideon Lowe,'' Gideon said. ''What baby?''

''A little boy,'' Chris explained. ''He's their first.''

''Hey, congratulations.''

''Thanks,'' Jason said, but he had something else on his mind. ''Chrissie, you seen Mark? He parked that rattletrap of his in the driveway in back of the Davissons and they have to leave.''

''Try the front steps. Last I knew he was holding court out there.'' Jason promptly made for the door, but before Chris and Gideon could make any progress, a loud cheer came from the dining room. Seconds later, a grinning Frank Gillette emerged through a gauntlet of backslapping friends. When he caught sight of Chris, his eyes lit up even more.

''Go on in and try it, honey. They say it's better than ever.''

''I will,'' Chris said. Her hand tightened on Gideon's. ''Dad, I'd like you to meet Gideon Lowe. He and I work together.''

''Nice to meet you,'' Frank said, ''and glad you could come.''

''It's kind of you all to welcome me.''

''Any friend of Chrissie's, as they say. Hey, Evan,'' he called, ''get over here.'' Seconds later, he was joined by another fair-haired son. ''Evan, say hello to Gideon Lowe. Gideon, this is my second oldest son, and his fiancée, Tina.''

Gideon smiled and nodded to them. Waving, they continued

on into the living room. Gideon was beginning to wonder how Chris kept her brothers apart when yet another stole by. This one was younger and faster. He would have made it out the front door if Frank hadn't reached out and grabbed his arm. "Where you off to so fast?"

"I want to see Mark's friends. Steve says there're a couple'a cool girls out there."

Chris grinned up at Gideon. "That's Alex, the baby."

Alex looked instantly grieved. "Come on, Chris. That's not fair. I'm fifteen. Besides, I'm not the baby. Jill is."

"Jill?" Gideon asked. Chris had said there were six kids in the family. He was sure he'd already met ten. "There's another one?"

"Yeah," Alex said, "and there she is." He pointed to the girl coming down the stairs. While everyone looked that way, he escaped out the door.

"Come over here, girl," Frank said, but it was to Chris's side that the girl came.

Accordingly Chris was the one to make the introduction. "Say hi to Gideon," she told Jill. "He's the builder for Crosslyn Rise, but be careful what you say. He's also on the consortium."

Jill grinned. "Ah, he's the one?"

"He's the one."

Gideon couldn't take his eyes off Jill. With her long brown hair and her large brown eyes, she was different from every other Gillette he'd met. A beauty, she looked to be at least seventeen, yet Alex had called her the baby, and he was fifteen. Gideon wondered if they were twins, with Jill the younger of the two by mere minutes. She couldn't possibly be *fourteen*.

He stuck out his free hand. "Hi, Jill."

For a split second she seemed a little shy, and in that second he almost imagined she could be younger. Then she composed herself and gave him her hand, along with Chris's smile. "Nice to meet you."

"The pleasure's mine. It's not often that I get to hang around with *two* gorgeous women."

Chris arched a brow at Jill. "Didn't I tell you?"

Grinning back, Jill nodded.

"What?" Gideon asked.

"You know how to throw it around," Jill said.

Gideon looked at Frank. "Was that bull? Are these two women gorgeous, or are they gorgeous?"

"They're gorgeous," Frank confirmed, "but who'm I to judge. I got a vested interest in them."

Gideon considered that interest as he looked from Chris's face to Jill's and back. "All those blondes and one brunette," he said to no one in particular. To Jill he said, "How old are you?"

"Fifteen."

To Chris, he said, "I thought Alex was fifteen."

"He is."

"Then they're twins?"

"Not exactly."

"Irish twins?"

Chris slid an amused glance at Jill before saying, "No. Jill is five months younger."

"Five months?" He frowned. "No, that can't be—" He stopped when Chris and Jill burst out laughing, then looked questioningly at Frank, who was scowling at Chris.

"That's not real nice, Chris. I told you not to do it. It isn't fair to put people on the spot like that."

"Thank you," Gideon told him, and directed his gaze at Chris. It was Jill, though, who offered the explanation he sought.

"I'm not his," she said, tossing her dark head toward Frank. "I'm *hers*." Her head bobbed toward Chris.

Hers? For a long minute, Gideon didn't make the connection. When he did, he ruled it out as quickly as it had come.

Chris squeezed his hand, which she hadn't let go of once. She was looking up at him, her eyes surprisingly serious. "Say something."

Gideon said the first thing that came to mind. "You're too young, and she's too old."

"I was eighteen when she was born."

"You look like sisters."

"If she were my sister, she'd be blond."

"But she has the Gillette smile."

"That's my smile. She's my daughter."

Daughter. Somehow, the word did it—that, and the fact that with two witnesses, one of whom had originally made the claim and the other of whom wasn't opening his mouth to rebut it, Gideon figured it had to be true. "Wow," he breathed. "A daughter."

"Does that shock you?"

"Yeah," he said, then felt it worth repeating. "Yeah."

"Kind of throws things into a new light?" Chris asked, but before he could answer, she released his hand, said a soft, "Excuse me, I want to check on Mom," and escaped into the crowd.

"Chris—"

Frank put a tempering hand on his arm. "Let her go. She'll be back."

But Gideon's eyes continued to follow her blond head as it moved farther away. "She'll misinterpret what I just said. I know she will. She'll think I don't want any part of her because she has a child, but that's not what I'm feeling at all. I'm feeling that, my God, she's done this wonderful thing in life, and I haven't ever done anything that even comes *close* in importance to it."

"This is getting heavy," Jill drawled.

Gideon's eyes flew to hers. He'd forgotten she was there, and was appalled. "Hey, I'm sorry. I didn't mean to offend you, too. I really like...your mom. If you're her daughter, I like you, too. Hell, I like the whole damned family. I don't have *any* family."

Jill's eyes widened. "None?"

But before he could answer, there was an uproar at the door. Frank turned around, then, wearing a broad grin, turned back and leaned close to Gideon. "See that bald-headed son of a bitch who just walked in? I haven't seen him in twenty years." To Jill, he said, "Take Gideon around, honey. If you run out of things to say, point him toward the game. He's a fan."

"Chris said I couldn't," Gideon told him.

Frank made a face. "Mellie says I can't, but do I listen?" Slapping his shoulder, he went off to greet his friend.

"You don't have *any* family?" Jill repeated, picking up right where she'd left off.

He shook his head. His hand felt empty without Chris's, so he slipped it into his pocket.

"No family."

"That's awful. Do you live all alone?"

"All alone."

"Wow, I don't think I could do that. I'd miss having people around and things happening."

Gideon was trying to think back to what Chris had said about herself. There wasn't a whole lot. She had evaded some questions and turned others right back to him. He didn't think she had ever lied to him, per se, but she'd obviously chosen every word with care.

When it came to where she lived, he had the distinct impression that she had her own place close to her family's. He suddenly wondered whether, there too, she'd stretched the words. "You don't live *here*, do you?"

"Oh, no. We're next-door. But we're here all the time."

"Next-door?" He was trying to remember what that house had looked like. "To the right or the left?"

"Behind. We're in the garage."

"The *garage*."

She nodded. "Uh-huh."

"You're stuck in the *garage*?"

She shot him a mischievous grin. "Want to see?"

"Yeah, I want to see." It occurred to him that Chris's daughter was a treasure trove of information on Chris, and that he wasn't adverse to getting what he could.

Jill led him around the crowd at the door, out and across the frozen lawn to the driveway. "My friends love my place," she said when he'd come up alongside her. "They keep bugging their parents to do something like it for them."

From what Gideon could see, the garage was like any other. Detached from the house, it was set far back at the end of a long driveway, with a single large door that would raise and ower to allow two cars inside. His builder's mind went to work imagining all the possibilities, but when Jill opened a side door and beckoned him inside, he wasn't prepared for what he found.

The garage had been elongated at the rear and converted into a small house, with an open living-room-kitchen-dining area, then a balcony above, off which two doors led, he assumed, to bedrooms. To compensate for a dearth of windows, there were indirect lights aplenty, as befitted the home of the daughter and granddaughter of an electrician. But what impressed Gideon even more than that was the decor. Nearly everything was white, and what wasn't white was a soft shade of blue. There was a light, bright, clean feel to the place. He couldn't believe he was in a garage.

"This is fantastic," he said.

Jill beamed. "Mom designed it, and Gramp's friends did it. I was just a baby and Mom was still in school, so it meant she could leave me with Gramma and Alex during the day, then have me to herself here at night."

Gideon was still looking around, taking in the small, sweet touches—like pictures of Jill at every imaginable age, in frames that were unique, one from the other—but he heard what she said. "So you grew up right alongside Alex?"

"Uh-huh. He's not bad for an uncle."

Gideon looked at her to find a very dry, very mature grin on her face. Narrowing an eye, he said, "You get a kick out of that, don't you?"

"Kinda." She dropped onto the arm of a nearby sofa with her legs planted straight to the floor. "People don't know what to think when they meet Alex and me. I mean, we're in the same grade and we have the same last name but we look so different. They don't believe it when we tell them the truth. They get the funniest looks on their faces—like you did before."

He wondered what explanation she gave for where her own father was. He wanted to ask about that himself, but figured it was something better asked of Chris. "Do you mind your mom working?"

Jill shrugged. "She has to earn a living."

"But you must miss her."

"Yes and no. I have Gramma. She's always around. And I have a house full of uncles. And then Mom comes home at night and tells me about everything she did at work that day."

"Everything?"

Jill nodded. "We're very close."

He had the odd feeling that it was a warning. Cautiously he asked, "What did she say about me?"

Without any hesitancy—as though she'd been wanting the question and he'd done nothing more than follow her lead—she said, "That you were a builder, that you were on the committee that interviewed her, and that you were a real jerk." When Gideon's face fell, she burst out laughing. "Just kidding. She didn't say that. She did say that you were very good-looking and very confident and that she wasn't sure how easy it'd be working with you." Jill paused, then added, "She likes you, I think."

"I know she likes me—"

"I mean, *likes* you."

Gideon studied her hesitantly. "Think so?" When she nodded, he said, "How do you know?"

"The way she ran off after we told you about me. She was nervous about what you'd think. She wouldn't have been if she didn't care. And then there was the thing with the hands."

"What thing?"

"She was holding yours. Or letting you hold hers. She doesn't usually do that with men. She's very prim."

"But you noticed the hands."

"I sure did."

Gideon ran a finger inside the collar of his shirt. "How old did you say you were?"

"It was only hands," she said in a long-suffering way. "And I *ought* to notice things like that. She's my mother. I care about what she does with her life."

He could see that she did, and had the oddest sense of talking with Chris's parent rather than her child. "Would it bother you if I dated her?"

"No. She ought to have more fun. She works too hard."

"What about Anthony?"

"Anthony is a total dweeb."

"Oh." That about said it. "Okay. Then he isn't competition?"

"Are you kidding?" she said with a look of such absurdity on her face that he would have laughed if they'd been talking about anything else. But his future with Chris was no laughing matter.

"So we rule out Anthony. Are there any others I should know about?"

"Did she say there were?"

"No."

Jill tipped her head. "There's your answer."

"And you wouldn't mind it if I took her out sometimes?"

The head straightened and there was a return hint of absurdity in her expression. "Why would I mind?"

"If I took her out, it would be taking her away from time spent with you."

Jill didn't have to consider that for long. "There are times when I want to do things with friends, but I feel so guilty going out and leaving Mom alone here. She can go over to the house and be with everyone there, but it's not the same. I mean, I love her and all, but my friends go shopping or to the movies on the weekends, and it's fun to do that. And then there's college. I want to go away. I've never *been* away. But how can I do that if it means leaving her alone?"

Gideon scratched his head. "Y'know, if I didn't know better, I'd wonder whether you're trying to marry her off."

"I'm not," Jill protested, and came off the sofa. "I wouldn't be saying this to just anyone, but you like her, and she likes you, and what I'm saying is that you can't use me as an excuse for not taking her out. I'm a good kid. I don't drink or do drugs or smoke. I'll be gone in three years. I won't be in the way."

Gideon hadn't had much experience with fifteen-year-old girls, but he knew without doubt that this one had a soft and sensitive side. She might be totally adjusted to the fact of her parentage; she might be far more mature than her years. But only in some respects. In others, she was still a girl wanting to please the adults in her life.

The fact that she considered him one of those adults touched him to the core. Crossing to where she stood, he tipped her chin up and said, "You could never be in the way, Jill. I don' know what'll happen between your mother and me. Our relationship has barely gotten off the ground. But believe me when I say that your existence is a plus. A big, big plus. I've been alone most of my life. I *like* the idea of being with someone who has family."

"Family can get in the way sometimes."

"You wouldn't say that if you've been without the way have."

"Are you gonna tell Mom that?"

"As soon as I can get her alone long enough to talk."

"What's going on here?" Chris asked from the door.

Jill slipped away from his hand. "Whoops. Looks like you'll have that chance sooner'n you thought." She grinned. "Hi Mom. I think I'll go back to the house and get something to drink. I'm parched." She was halfway past Chris when she said, "Invite him for Christmas dinner. He's nice." Before Chris could begin to scold, she was gone.

CHAPTER SIX

"WHOSE IDEA WAS IT to come back here?" Chris asked. She wasn't quite angry, wasn't quite pleased. In fact, she wasn't quite sure *what* she was feeling, and hadn't been since she'd shocked Gideon with the fact of Jill.

"Uh, I'm not sure. I think it was kind of mutual."

"Uh-huh." Chris understood. "It was Jill's idea. You're protecting her."

Gideon held up a cautioning hand. "Look, she may have suggested it, but only after I started pestering her about where you two lived." Dropping the hand to his pocket, he looked around. "It's a super place, Chris. I like it a lot."

"So do I, but it's only a place. Jill's a person. She means more to me than anything else on earth. I don't want her hurt."

Gideon straightened. "You think I could *hurt* her?"

That was exactly what Chris thought. "You could get real close, then lose interest. When I said that she throws a new light on things, I meant it."

"Hold on a minute. I'm not romancing Jill. It's you—"

"But she's part of the package," Chris interrupted, feeling the urgency of the message. "That's what I'm trying to tell you. You say you want to date me. You hoodwinked me into inviting you here today. Well, okay, you're here, and I'll date you, but you have to know where my priorities lie. I'm not like some women who flit around wherever the mood takes them. I'm not an independent agent. I'm not a free spirit."

"I never thought you were," Gideon said soberly. "From the start, you've been serious and down-to-earth. You made it clear how much your family means to you."

"Jill is more than family. She's someone I created—"

"Not alone."

"Someone I *chose* to bring into this world. I have a responsibility to her."

"And you think you're unique?" Gideon challenged impulsively. "Doesn't every mother feel that responsibility? Doesn' every single mother feel it even more strongly, just like you do? For God's sake, Chris, I'm not trying to come between you and your daughter. Maybe I'm trying to add something to both of your lives. Ever thought of it that way? I sure as hell know I'm trying to add something to mine." He swore again, this time under his breath. "*Trying* is the operative word here. You get so goddamned prickly that I'm not making a helluva lot o headway." He stopped, then started right back up in the next breath. "And as far as Jill's existence throwing a new light or things, let me tell you that I find the fact that you have a daughter to be incredibly wonderful—which you would have known sooner if you hadn't run off so fast. You do that a lot, Chris. It's a bad habit. You run off before things can be settled."

"There's nothing to be settled here," Chris informed him staunchly sticking to her guns, "since nothing's open for dis cussion. Jill is my daughter. For the past fifteen years, she' been the first thought on my mind when I wake up in the morning and the last thought before I fall asleep at night."

"Is that healthy?" Gideon asked innocently, but the word: set her off.

"Healthy or not, that's the way it is," she snapped. "A woman with a child isn't the same as one without. You ough to think really hard about that before you do any more sweet talking around here." She turned and made for the door, but Gideon was across the floor with lightning speed, catching her arm, drawing her back into the living room and shoving the door shut.

"Not so fast. Not this time. This time we talk."

"I can't talk now," she cried. "I have a house full of Christ mas guests to entertain."

But Gideon was shaking his head. "Those guests entertair themselves, and besides, there are a dozen other hosts in tha house." His voice softened, as did his hand on her arm, though

1e didn't release her. "Just for a minute, Chris. I won't keep
ou long, but I want to make something very clear."

She glanced up at him, and her heart lurched. The look in
1is eyes was gentle, almost exquisitely so.

"I like you," he said. "God only knows why, because you
give me a hard time, but I like you a lot. You could've had
ive kids, with half of them in diapers, and I wouldn't care.
Knowing about Jill now, I respect you even more for what
you've done with your business, and you've obviously done
something right with her, or she wouldn't be as nice a kid as
she seems to be." He paused. "When I said I was shocked
oack there, it was because you never let on—I didn't expect it.
You just didn't strike me as the type to—"

"Get knocked up?"

"Have a baby so young. Okay, yeah, maybe be with a guy
so young." A tiny crease appeared between his brows. Quietly
1e asked, "Who was he?"

"It doesn't matter," Chris said, and tried to turn back toward
he door only to have Gideon lock a grip on her other arm, too.

"Did you love him?" he asked, still quietly, even unsurely.

Chris had been prepared for criticism, which was what she'd
gotten most often when she'd first become pregnant. *Didn't you
know what you were doing? Didn't you* use *anything? Didn't
you stop to consider the consequences?* Rarely had she been
asked what Gideon just asked her. Looking up into his deep
charcoal eyes, she almost imagined he was worried.

"I thought I did," she told him in a voice as quiet as his.
"We were both seniors. He was handsome and popular, full of
charm and fun. I was totally snowed. We didn't have anywhere
to go, so we used to park up behind the reservoir. That's where
Jill was conceived."

She thought Gideon started to wince, but he caught himself.
"What happened after?"

"He didn't want me or the baby," she said bluntly. She'd
long since passed the time when she blamed herself for that.
She might have loved Brant at the time, or thought she did,

but the only person Brant had loved was himself. "He denied it was his."

This time Gideon's wince was for real. "What kind of selfish bastard was he?"

Chris shrugged. "He was going to college on a scholarship and didn't want anyone or anything to slow him down."

"So he left you in the lurch. You must have been furious."

"Furious, hurt, frightened."

"I'd be angry still."

"Why? I got the better part of the deal. I got Jill."

Gideon seemed momentarily stunned, as though that idea had never occurred to him. Finally, in a hoarse whisper, he said, "That's what I think I like about you so much. You feel things. You love."

Chris too was stunned, nearly as much by his whispered awe as by the reverence in his eyes. Then she didn't have time to think of either, because he lowered his head to kiss her. At least, that was what she thought he was going to do. She felt the approach of his mouth, the warmth of his breath—then he pulled back and looked at her again, and in the look, something gave inside her.

"Do it," she whispered, suddenly wanting his kiss more than anything else.

His lips were smooth and firm. They touched hers lightly, rubbed them open in a back and forth caress, then, just as his hands left her arms and framed her face, came in more surely.

Chris was overwhelmed by the warmth of the kiss, its wetness, and by Gideon's fresh male scent that seemed to fill her and overflow. Needs that had lain dormant for better than fifteen years suddenly came to life, touching off an explosion of awareness inside her. Her limbs tingled, her heart pounded, her blood rushed hot through her veins. Feeling dizzy and hungry at the same time, she clasped fistfuls of sweater at his waist, gave a tiny moan and opened her mouth to his silent demand.

The demand went on and on, sometimes pressing, sometimes hovering, sometimes sucking so strongly that she was sure she'd never emerge whole again. When, with several last, lingering touches, the kiss ended, she felt bereft.

It was a minute before she realized exactly what had happened, and by that time, Gideon had his mouth pressed to her temple and his arms wrapped tightly around her. With her slow return to reality came the awareness of a fine tremor snaking through his large frame.

"Gideon?" she whispered, shaky herself.

"Shh," he whispered back. "Give me a minute."

She knew all too well why he needed the time. She could feel the reason pressing insistently against her thigh, and while the strength of it shocked her, it also excited her beyond belief. She wanted another kiss. She wanted some touching. She wanted something even harder, something to relieve the deep ache she was feeling.

"I knew it'd be like that," he whispered again.

"I didn't know it *could* be."

He made a low, longing sound and crushed her even closer.

"That's not helping," she whispered, but neither was breathing against his neck the way she was doing. His skin was firm and hot and smelled wonderfully of man.

"I know, but I need it. I can't let you go just yet."

"You'll have to soon. Someone's apt to come looking."

Raising his head, he caught her eyes. His voice remained little more than a ragged train of breath. "Know what I'd do if I had my way?" When she shook her head, he said, "I'd back you right up to that door and make love to you here and now."

She felt a searing heat deep in her belly and had to swallow before she could get a word out. "You can't."

"Yes, I can. I'm hard. Can't you feel?" Slipping his hands to her bottom, he manipulated her hips against his. His arousal was electrifying.

She had to close her eyes against its force. "Don't, Gideon," she cried, her breath coming in shallow gusts. She lowered her forehead to his throat.

His mouth touched her ear. "Right against that door. Then,

after that, on your bed. You've never done it on a bed, have
you?''

"No." She tugged at his sweater, which she was still clutching for dear life. "Don't talk."

"Why not?"

"Because you're making things harder."

"I'll say," he muttered with the nudge of his hips.

Moaning against the fire that small movement sparked, she
slipped her arms around his neck, drawing herself up on tiptoe
and hung on tight. Her body felt foreign but wonderful. It knew
what it wanted. Her mind wasn't so sure. "I have to get back
to the house."

"You don't want to."

"I have to." But she moved against him, needing the friction
to ease the knot between her legs.

"You want to stay here and make love with me."

"Oh, Gideon!" she cried.

"You do. I'd make it so good, baby, so good. I wouldn't
rush you, wouldn't hurt you, and it'd be so incredibly good."
He slipped a hand from her bottom to her thigh, then moved
upward and inward.

"Don't," she begged, but the plea was empty. Between his
words and his closeness, she was floating, then soaring, burning
up from the inside out. When he touched her where she was
most sensitive, she cried out, and when he began to caress her,
she held on tighter to his neck.

"You're so hot here," he whispered.

"Gideon," she moaned. "Oh, no." She was arching into his
hand, coming apart with no way to stop it.

His stroking grew bolder. "That's it, baby. That's it. Feel it.
Let it come."

She was lost. In a moment of blinding bliss, she convulsed
into an orgasm that left her gasping for air. She couldn't speak,
could only make small, throaty sounds. Gradually they eased.
The next sound she made was a humiliated sob. Twisting away
from Gideon with such suddenness that he was taken off guard,

she stumbled around the sofa and collapsed into its corner, pressing her knees together and huddling low over them.

"It's okay, sweetheart," Gideon said, reaching out to stroke her hair.

She felt his hand and would have pulled away if there was anywhere to pull to. "That shouldn't have happened," she cried. "I'm so embarrassed."

Barely removing his hand, Gideon came around the end of the sofa and squatted close before her. "Don't be," he said. "I'm not. I feel so *good*."

"You can't feel good. You didn't…get anything."

"Wrong. Way wrong. I got a whole lot." His strong hands were framing her neck, and his voice, though hoarse, was astonishingly tender. He leaned forward so that his breath brushed her cheek. "Was that the first time since—"

She gave a sharp, quick nod against her knees.

"The first time since Jill's father?"

She repeated the same sharp nod.

"You've never done it yourself?"

She kicked his leg.

"Chris?" When she didn't answer, he said again, "Chris?"

Her voice was small. "What?"

"I think I'm falling in love with you."

"Don't *say* that."

"But it's true."

She pressed her hands to her ears and shook her head.

Forcibly removing her hands, he raised her head until she was sitting up, looking at him. "I won't say it again, if it makes you uncomfortable. It shakes me a little, too. We don't know each other much, do we?"

Unable to take her eyes from his, she gave a feeble shake of her head.

"But there's a remedy for that," he went on. "You can stop cooking up cockamamy excuses for why you can't see me."

Chris pulled back as much as his hands would allow. "They're not cockamamy excuses. This is the busiest time of the year for me. Between work and all the things I want to do with Jill—"

"Invite me along. We don't have to be alone all the time."

She made a disbelieving face. "What kind of man wants to put up with that?"

His voice went low and husky again. "The kind of man who knows his woman is made of fire. As long as I know it's coming, I can wait."

Chris felt her cheeks go red. "I won't ever live that down, will I?"

"Not if I can help it. It was the most beautiful, most sensual, most natural and spontaneous response I've ever experienced with a woman."

She had to look away. His eyes were too intense. Very softly she said, "You've been with lots of women, haven't you?"

"Over the years? Enough." He paused. "But if it's the health thing that's got you worried, don't be. I've always used a rubber. Always. For birth control, as much as anything. I'm clean, Chris."

Focusing on a cable twist in his sweater, she murmured. "I wasn't worried about that." She was actually worried about the issue of experience, because, other than with Brant, she was very much without.

"I don't want to use anything with you."

Her eyes shot to his. "You have to. I don't have—I'm not taking—"

His mouth cut off the words, kissing her gently, then less gently, before he regained control and drew up his head. "If you got pregnant by me, I wouldn't run away. I'd want you and the baby and Jill and your family. I'd marry you in a minute."

Chris was having trouble breathing again. "This conversation is very premature."

"Just so you know how I feel."

"How can you feel that way so soon?"

"Beats me, but I do."

"I think you're getting carried away on some kind of fantasy."

"No fantasy. Just you."

How was she supposed to answer *that*? She swallowed. "I have to get back to the house."

Gideon sat on his heels. "I'm staying till the party's over. Can we talk more then?"

"Maybe we shouldn't. Maybe we should let things cool off a little."

"It won't help. The fire's there, whether we're together or not. It's there even when I sleep. I had a wet dream last night—"

"Gideon, for goodness' sakes!"

"I did."

"But don't *tell* me."

"Why not?" he asked reasonably. "I know damned well you're going to think back on what happened here and be embarrassed, and I just want you to know that you're not the only one who loses control sometimes. You had far more reason to than I did, what with the way I was touching you—"

She pressed a hand to his mouth. "Please," she begged in a whisper, "don't say another word." She waited. He was silent. She moved her fingers very lightly over his lips. "I'm going to get up now and go back to the house. If you'd like, you can come, too. You can talk with people—Jessica and Carter may be here by now—or even watch the game if it isn't over."

"The Lakers come on next," he murmured against her fingers.

"Okay. The Lakers. My brothers will be watching. You can get something to eat and stay as long as you want, but I can't go out with you afterward. I want to help my mother clean up. Then I want to spend some time with Jill. Then I want to go to bed. Tomorrow's as busy as Mondays get." Her hand slid from his mouth to the shirt collar that rose above the crew neck of his sweater.

"What's on for tomorrow night?"

"I have deliveries to supervise until eight."

"So Jill will be here with your folks?"

"She has Driver Ed on Monday nights. I'll pick her up on my way home."

"What about supper?"

"I'll grab something when I get home."

"Why don't I pick up Chinese and stop by your office?"

"Because I won't be at my office."

"So I'll go where you are."

"You can't. Not with food. My clients would die."

"Okay. What about Tuesday night? No, forget Tuesday night. I have a game." His eyes lit up. "Come see me play."

For an instant, he was so eager that she actually wished she could. But the logistics wouldn't work. "In Worcester?"

"Too far, hmm?"

"And I have ballet."

"Okay. What's on for Wednesday night?"

"Jill's piano recital."

"I'll come."

"You will not. She's nervous enough at recitals without having to worry about her mother's new boyfriend showing up."

Gideon grinned. "New boyfriend. I like that. It's better than the builder." His grin vanished. "But I won't make her nervous. She likes me."

"She likes you here, now, today. That's because you're one of lots of people coming to party. She's apt to be threatened when she realizes something's going on between us."

"She already does. And she won't be threatened. She *likes* me. Besides, she wants you to date. She told me so."

"She told you?"

"Yes."

Chris felt just the slightest bit betrayed. "What else did she tell you?"

"Not much. You came along before she had a chance. But, damn it, Chris, we haven't settled anything here. When can I see you again? We're up to Thursday."

"Thursday's no good. I have ballet again, and then we're going shopping."

"I'll go with you."

But she shook her head. Last-minute Christmas shopping was something that had become almost traditional with Jill and her. Chris wasn't ready to let someone else intrude.

"Okay," Gideon said, "that brings us to the weekend, and to Christmas Eve. So are you inviting me over, or what?"

Chris didn't know what to do. Christmas Eve, then Christmas Day were every bit as personal and special and traditional for the whole family as last-minute shopping was for Jill and her alone.

"Jill said you should," he reminded her.

"Jill was out of line."

"What are all your plans?"

"Dinner, caroling, then Midnight Mass on Christmas Eve, and a huge meal on Christmas Day."

"Is it all just family?"

"No," Chris answered truthfully. "Friends come, too." She sighed and sent him a beseeching look. "But this is happening too fast, Gideon. Can't we slow it down?"

"Some things won't be slowed down—like what happened a little while ago."

She squeezed her eyes shut.

"What are you afraid of, Chris? What's holding you back?"

She had asked herself the same question more than once in recent weeks. Slowly she opened her eyes and met his. "Being hurt. I'm afraid of that. Jill may be the highlight of my life, but what Brant did hurt. I got over it. I came back and built a life, and I think I've been a great mother. Things are going smoothly. I don't want that to change."

"Not even for the better?"

"I don't *need* things to be better."

The look on Gideon's face contradicted her even before he spoke. "I think you do. There's a closeness only a man can give that I think you crave. It's like the way you held my hand back at the house, and the way you came apart before, even the way you're touching me right now."

"I'm not—"

"You are. Look at your hand."

Chris did. Her hand was folded over his collar, her fingers against the warm skin on the inside. Very carefully she removed them and put her hand into her lap. "I didn't know I was doing that," she said meekly.

"Like I didn't know what was happening until I woke up panting this morning. There's something to be said for the subconscious. It's more honest than we are sometimes."

He had a point, she supposed. She could deny that she wanted him, deny that she wanted any kind of relationship, but it wouldn't be the truth. Still, despite his arguments, she meant what she'd said about slowing things down.

"New Year's Eve," she said, focusing on her lap. "You probably already have plans—"

"I don't, and I accept. What would you like to do? We can work around Jill's plans or your family's plans. Just tell me. I'm open."

Hesitantly she raised her eyes. "Jill is going to a party at a friend's house. I have to drop her there, then pick her up. She's bringing two other friends home for a sleep-over."

"A sleep-over? Wow, that'd be fun!"

"Gideon, you're not invited to the sleep-over."

"So what *do* I get?"

"Four hours, while she's at the party. We could go somewhere to eat, maybe dance. Or we could go to First Night."

"First Night is loud and cold and crowded. I vote for the other."

"We may have trouble getting reservations this late."

"I don't want reservations. I want to eat here."

She didn't know whether to laugh or cry. "I didn't *invite* you to eat here."

"But it makes sense, doesn't it?" he argued. "Go to a restaurant on New Year's Eve, and it's crowded and overpriced and slow. You'll be nervous about getting back in time, so you won't be able to relax. On the other hand, if we eat here, we can talk all we want. We really need to do that, Chris, just talk. Besides, if we go somewhere fancy, I'll have to go shopping. You've already seen the sum total of my fancy wardrobe, and I hate shopping. Don't make me do it, not until after Christmas at least.''

"If you hate shopping, why did you offer to go with Jill and me?''

"Because that would be fun. It's shopping for *me* that I hate.''

She was bemused. "Why?''

"Because it's so damned hard to get things that fit. I'm broad up here, and long down there, so things have to be tailored, which means having some salesclerk feel me up.''

She sputtered out a laugh. "That's terrific.''

"No, it's sickening. Anybody feels me up, I want it to be you. So what do you say? Dinner here on New Year's Eve? Nice and quiet and relaxed? I'll bring some food if you want. Better still, give me a list and I'll pick up groceries so we can make dinner together. Now *that's* a good idea.''

Chris had to admit that it was. She wasn't a big one for public New Year's Eves and had always spent hers quietly. The idea of being with Gideon for those few hours while Jill was at her party was appealing.

"Okay,'' she said.

He broke out into a smile. Standing, he tugged her to her feet and wrapped an arm around her waist as he started for the door. "What time should I come? Four? Five?''

"Try eight-thirty.'' Jill's party began at eight. That would give Chris time to come home, change, get things ready.

"No way am I waiting around until eight-thirty, when everything closes at midafternoon. Five-thirty. I'll come at five-thirty. Then I can talk with Jill before she leaves.''

"Jill will be totally preoccupied with her hair.''

"So I'll be here to tell her how great it looks.''

"Come at seven-thirty. You can go with me when I drive her to the party.''

"Six. We can have appetizers early."

"Seven, and that's the earliest, the absolute earliest you can come."

"Can I bring champagne?"

"Wine. I like it better. And wear your fancy outfit. Is that the one you were wearing that day at the bank?" She wanted to see it again. Even through her nervousness his handsomeness that day had registered.

"Yeah," he protested, "but that defeats the purpose of staying in."

She shook her head and said softly, "It's New Year's Eve. If we're having a nice dinner with wine, we have to dress the part. And don't say I've already seen it, because I don't work that way. You don't have to wear something different every time you see me. I'm not that shallow."

"I didn't say you were. But it's me. My pride."

"Your pride is misplaced if you're hung up on clothes. Wear the blazer and slacks."

"The blazer and slacks?"

"Yes."

He sighed, gave her a squeeze and opened the door. "Okay. The blazer and slacks it is." He inhaled a hearty breathful of the fast-falling winter's night. "Wow, do I feel good."

Chris was surprised to realize that she did, too.

THE FEELING persisted. On the one hand, she could say it was the Christmas spirit. Her family always made the holiday a happy time. Deep down, though, she knew there were other reasons this year. Jill was happy. The business was going well. And Gideon had come on the scene.

He didn't let her forget that last fact. He called her every night, usually around ten, when he knew she'd be home, and though he never kept her on the phone for long—just wanted to see how her day had been or tell her something about his— the calls were sweet.

Jill was aware of them. She was the one who sat by the phone doing her homework when the ring pierced the quiet night, or talking with a friend when the call-waiting clicked. Sometimes Chris took the call in the same room, sometimes in another room. Each time, Jill acknowledged it afterward.

Not that Chris would have tried to hide anything. She knew that if she wanted Jill to be open and communicative with her, she had to be the same way right back. Their relationship had always been honest that way. And besides, there wasn't anything to hide. Gideon liked her. So he was calling her.

Of course, Jill wanted to know more. "Do you like him?" she asked, wandering down to the kitchen after one of the calls.

In a burst of late-night energy, Chris was making wreath cookies, which required a minimum of brain and a modicum of brawn. She was vigorously stirring the butter and marshmallows that she'd unceremoniously dumped into a pot.

"He's nice," she answered. "I didn't expect him to be after what happened at the Rise that first day." She'd told Jill about that when it happened, albeit more philosophically than she'd felt at the moment of confrontation. "So I'm surprised. But I still don't know him very well."

"It sounds like he wants to change that."

"Uh-huh." Chris felt the same shimmer of excitement she always felt when she anticipated seeing Gideon again.

"Why isn't he coming for Christmas?"

Chris kept stirring. "Because I didn't invite him."

"Why not?"

"Because he's too new. Christmas is for people we're really close to. Our family is special. If you're not one of us, you have to *earn* a place at our table." She'd been trying for a little dry wit. It went right past Jill.

"But he's alone. He'll be sitting there in a lonely apartment all by himself. He probably doesn't even have a tree."

Chris felt a moment's unease, wondering just how thickly Gideon had poured it on. If there was one thing she wouldn't abide, it was his using Jill to get to her. "Did he mention a lonely apartment?"

"No, but he said he had no family."

"Okay, that's true. But he doesn't live in an apartment, to begin with. He lives in a house that he built himself—"

"So he's sitting in a lonely house."

"He is not. Jill, he has lots of friends. I'm sure he's doing something with them." She hadn't asked, exactly, but she assumed that was the case. He was a really friendly guy, and he said he dated, he dated *a lot*. Chris didn't believe that he'd left all of his holiday time free.

Of course, he would have come for Christmas if she'd invited him, and he jumped at her first mention of New Year's Eve, so apparently whatever plans he had weren't etched in stone. She didn't want to think a woman was involved, didn't want to think he would break a date and disappoint someone. Better, she decided, to imagine that if he wasn't with her, he'd be with a large group of friends.

Maybe some of his workmen.

Maybe his basketball teammates.

She wondered what he wore on the court and how he looked.

"Do you think you could like him?"

Brought back from a small distance, Chris stirred the melting marshmallows with greater force. The roughness of the wooden spoon against the bottom of the pot told her that there was some sticking, apt punishment for a wandering mind. "I do like him. I told you that."

"Love him?"

Though she couldn't help but remember what Gideon had said about falling in love with her, Chris shook her head. "Too soon. Way too soon. Ask me that in another year or two."

"That's not how love happens. It happens quickly."

"Says the authority. Sweetheart, I forgot to take out the food coloring. Can you get it for me? Green?"

Jill took the small vial from the baking supply shelf and removed its lid. "How many drops?" She held it poised.

"Start with four."

Jill squeezed. Chris stirred. Gradually the thick white stuff turned a faintly minty shade.

"A little more, I think."

Jill squeezed, she stirred, but if she had hoped Jill would let the matter of love go, she was mistaken.

"You loved my father when I was conceived."

"Uh-huh." They had discussed that at length several years before, when Chris had sat down with Jill and explained what getting a period was about. Given the slightest encouragement, Jill had asked questions about making babies and making love. She knew who her father was, that he had left Massachusetts before her birth, that he was selling real estate in Arizona. At that time, she had wanted to know about Chris's relationship with him.

Chris had been forthright in telling her about feeling love and the specialness of the moment. She never wanted Jill to feel unwanted, though in essence Brant had made it clear that she was. His whole family had moved away—conveniently, a job transfer had come through for his father—and, to Chris's knowledge, none of them had been back. Outside of family, few people knew who Jill's father was.

"But you'd only been dating him for two months."

"I was young. When you're young, you're more quickly taken with things like love. Another drop, maybe?"

Jill added it, while Chris kept stirring.

"Don't you think it's more romantic when it's fast? I mean, I think what happened to you was *really* romantic. You saw each other in English, started doing homework together, fell in love and did it. Do you think he's married now?"

"Probably."

"Do you think he ever wonders about me?"

Chris sent her an affectionate smile. "He must. You're that strong a being."

"Think he ever wants to see me?"

"I think he doesn't dare." She tried to keep it light. "Seeing you, he'll realize all he's missed. He'll hate himself."

Jill frowned. "But what kind of parent isn't curious about his own child?"

Chris had asked herself that question dozens of times, and in many of those times she'd thought the lowliest things about

Brant. But she'd vowed many years ago not to bad-mouth him in front of Jill. "The kind who may not be able to forgive himself for leaving you behind. He knows you exist. I imagine—" it was a wild guess, giving Brant a big benefit of the doubt "—that knowledge has been with him a lot."

Jill thought about that, standing back while Chris dumped the premeasured cups of corn flakes into the pot with the melted marshmallows that were now a comfortable Christmas green. Finally Jill said, "Do you ever imagine that you might open the front door one day and find him there?"

"No." That was the last thing Chris wanted. She had no desire to see Brant, no desire to have Brant see Jill. Jill was *hers*. She felt vehemently about that. For Jill's sake alone, she tempered her feelings. "He's probably very involved with his own life. His family only lived here for three years. They were midwesterners to begin with. They have no ties here."

"That didn't mean he couldn't have married you if he loved you."

Chris had to work hard stirring the mess in the pot, but she appreciated the physical demand. It was a good outlet. "He had plans. He was going to college. He had a scholarship."

But Jill was insistent. "If he loved you, he could have married you."

Her petulance, far more than the words themselves, stopped Chris. Leaving the wooden spoon sticking straight up, she turned and took Jill's face in her hands. "Then I guess he didn't love me," she said softly, "at least, not as much as I thought. And in that sense, it's a good thing we didn't get married. The marriage wouldn't have been good. We'd have been unhappy together. And you would have suffered." She paused. "Do you miss having a father so much?"

"No. Not so much. You know that." They'd talked about it before. "There are times when I wonder, that's all. There are times when I think it would be nice to go places, just the three of us."

"So what would Gramma and Gramps do?" she teased. "And Alex? And the others?"

Jill thought about that for a minute, gave a small smile of concession and shrugged, at which point Chris planted a kiss in the middle of her forehead. She was about to turn back to the pot when Jill said, "I still think you should have invited Gideon for Christmas dinner."

"Uh-oh. We're on this again?"

"It was just a thought."

"Well, here's another one. I think that sticky stuff in the pot may have hardened. You gonna clean up the mess?"

In a blink, Jill was the picture of innocence. "Me? I still have homework to do." She slipped smoothly away and was up the stairs before Chris could think to scold. Not that she would have. All too soon, Jill would be slipping smoothly away to college, then beyond. Chris wasn't about to scold away their time together, not when it was so dear.

CHAPTER SEVEN

COME NEW YEAR'S EVE, Chris wasn't thinking of spending time with Jill, but spending time without her. Christmas with the family had been wonderfully fun and absorbing—her mother had *loved* the clay pot—but in the week that followed, in all the little in-between moments when her mind might have been on something else but wasn't, Chris thought of Gideon. Each time, she felt a warm suffusion of desire.

He continued to call every night, "just to make sure you don't forget me," he teased, which was a laugh. She couldn't have forgotten him if she'd tried. He was like a string tied around her finger, a tightness around her insides, cinching deeply and pleasantly.

Had anyone read her mind during that week, she would have been mortified, so carnal were her thoughts. Rather than picturing Gideon in his blazer and slacks, she pictured him in every state of undress imaginable. It didn't help that she was haunted by glimpses of a sliver of skin, a whorl of dark hair and a belly button. When he called at night, she pictured him lying in bed wearing briefs, or nothing. She pictured his body, pictured the dark hair that would mat it, clustering more thickly at some places than others. She pictured him coming to her on New Year's Eve, unbuttoning his shirt, removing it, opening his pants, removing them, baring himself to her, a man at the height of his virility and proud of it.

At times, she wondered if there was something wrong with her, if she was so sex starved that anyone would do. But the courier, who stopped by the office several times that week and was very attractive, didn't turn her on. Nor did her hairdresser, who was surprisingly straight. Nor did Anthony Haskell, who called several times wanting to see her and whom she turned down as gently as she could.

She didn't remember ever feeling quite so alive in quite as feminine a way as she did with the approach of New Year's Eve. Like an alarm that kept going off every few minutes, the buzz of arousal in the pit of her stomach had her counting the minutes until Gideon arrived.

Seven, she had told him. Fortunately, she was ready early, because when the bell rang at six-forty-five, she had no doubt who it was. Pulling the door open, she sent him a chiding look.

He shrugged. "I left extra time in case there was traffic, but there wasn't."

How could she get angry when the mere sight of him took her breath away? He was wearing a topcoat with the collar up against the cold, and between the lapels she caught sight of his blazer and slacks, but he looked far more handsome than he had that day at the bank. No doubt, she decided, it had to do with the ruddy hue on his cheeks.

That hue bemused her. "You look like you've been out in the cold." But he'd been in a heated car.

"Had the windows open," he said, not taking his eyes from her. She looked bright, almost glowing, sophisticated, but young and fresh. He decided that the young part had to do with her hair. Rather than pinning it in its usual knot, she'd left it down. It was shiny and smooth, swept from a side part, its blunt-cut ends dancing on her shoulders. "It was the only way I could keep my mind on the road."

She didn't have to ask where his mind would have been otherwise. The hunger in his eyes answered that quite well. It made her glad that she'd splurged on a new dress, though the splurging hadn't been painful. Contrary to Gideon, she loved to shop. She kept herself on a budget, but she'd been due for a treat. His appreciation made the effort more than worth it.

"May I come in?" he asked.

She blushed. "Of course. I'm sorry. Here, let me take that." She reached for the grocery bag he held in one arm. They had agreed that he would bring fresh French bread and some kind of dessert, since there was a bakery not far from his house. But he held tight to the bag and, instead, handed her the two bottles of wine that he was grasping by the neck with the fingers of one hand. She peered suspiciously at the bag, which seemed filled and heavy. "What's in there?"

"I got carried away," he confessed, thinking about sweets for the sweet and other trite expressions, but loath to voice them lest she think him a jerk. Elbowing the door shut behind him, he headed for the kitchen. He set the bag on the counter, relieved her of the wine and stood it beside the bag, then gave her a slow up and down.

"You look great," he said in an understatement that he hoped his appreciative tone would correct.

Her temperature was up ten degrees, making her words breathy and warm. "Thanks. You, too." Feeling a dire urge to touch him, she laced her fingers together in the area of her lap. "Please, take your coat off." When he'd done so, she hung it in the closet, then turned to find him directly behind her.

"Where's Jill?" he whispered.

"Upstairs," she whispered back.

"Does she know I'm here?"

"She must have heard the bell."

"Do we have time for a kiss?"

"If it's a quick one."

"I don't know if I can make it quick. I've been dreaming about it for more than ten days." His whisper was growing progressively rough. He felt desperately in need. "What I had in mind was something slow and deep and wet—"

"Hey, you guys," came Jill's full voice from halfway down the stairs. She trotted down the rest, her steps muted by the carpet. "What're you whispering about?"

Chris felt she'd been caught in the act of doing something naughty. It was a minute before she could compose herself enough to realize that she hadn't—and that even if she had, she was the mother and had that right. "Gideon was saying things that *definitely* shouldn't be heard by tender ears such as yours," she drawled, and made for the kitchen. "Do me a favor, sweetie? Keep him company while I get these hors d'oeuvres?"

Gideon put his hands into the pockets of his blazer and angled them forward to hide his arousal from Jill. "Can I help?"

he called after Chris. To Jill, he said, "You may think I'm one of those helpless males, but believe me, I'm not. I'm a very handy man to have around the house. I know how to crack eggs, whip cream and brew coffee."

"We could've used you around here earlier," Jill said. "Mom ruined two batches of stuffed mushrooms before she finally got one that was edible. They're supposed to be her specialty. So she thought she knew the ingredients by heart, only she blew it. That was the first time. The second time she burned the meat."

"Distracted, huh?" Gideon asked, pleased by the thought.

"You could say that." She took a step back. "How do I look?"

He checked her over. "Spectacular. Great jeans skirt. Great sweater. Great legs. Is this a boy-girl party you're going to?"

She tossed a glance at the ceiling. "Of course! I am old enough for that, y'know."

He knew all too well. Where he'd grown up, fifteen-year-old girls did far more than go to parties. Instinct told him, though, that Jill wasn't that way. Common sense told him that Chris wouldn't have stood for it. "You're gonna knock 'em dead," he told her, feeling a pride he had no right to feel. "And your hair looks great, too."

"I'm not done with my hair."

"But it looks perfect."

"It looks blah," she maintained, drawing up a thick side swath with two fingers. "I think I need a clasp or something. And some earrings. Mom—" she called, only to be interrupted when Chris approached.

"No need to yell. I'm right here." To Gideon she said apologetically, "They weren't hot enough. They'll be ready in a minute."

"I need something large and silver, Mom."

"For her hair and ears," Gideon prompted in a soft voice to Chris, who was looking a bit helplessly at Jill.

"The last time I lent you something silver," she said, thinking of a bangle bracelet that she hadn't seen in months, "I didn't get it back. You can borrow something *only* if it's re-turned in the morning."

"She's so fussy," Jill said to Gideon. Then she turned and went back up the stairs, leaving Gideon and Chris momentarily alone.

Gideon started whispering again. "How long do you think she'll stay up there?"

"Five seconds," Chris whispered back.

Jill yelled down, "Can I wear the enamel hair clip you bought at the Vineyard last summer?"

"I thought you wanted something silver," Chris called back.

"But the enamel one has earrings to match."

"It also," Chris murmured for Gideon's benefit, "cost an arm and a leg. She's been wanting to wear that set since I bought it. I think she's taking advantage of the company and the night."

"You can always tell her no," Gideon suggested.

Chris snorted softly, then called to Jill, "If you're very, very, *very* careful." She caught Gideon's eye. "Don't look at me that way."

"Are you always such a pushover?"

"No. But we're talking a hair clip and some earrings here. If she asked for a quart of gin, I'd say no. Same for cigarettes or dope, if I had either around the house, which I don't. The way I see it, you have to pick and chose your battles."

Gideon considered that, then nodded. "Sounds right." He shot a glance over her shoulder toward the stove. "Think your mushrooms are hot yet?"

"It's only been a minute since I last checked."

"Check again," he said, and ushered her to the farthest reaches of the kitchen. Once there, he backed her to the counter, lowered his head and captured her lips in what would have been a deep, devouring kiss had not Jill's call intruded.

"Mom?"

With a low groan, he wrenched his mouth away and stepped back.

Chris felt she was spinning around, twisting at the end of a

long, spiraling line. She was hot, dizzy and frustrated. It was
a minute before she could steady herself to answer. "Yes?"

"Where *is* the set?"

Chris made a small sound and closed her eyes for a minute.
Then, shaking her head, she sent Gideon an apologetic look
and pushed off from the counter. Jill was at the top of the stairs.

"Just tell me where it is," she called down.

But Chris didn't remember exactly where it was. "I'm coming," she said lightly. Once upstairs, it took several minutes of
searching through drawers before she finally located the clip
and earrings. She handed them over with a repeat of the warning, "You'll be very, very, *very* careful."

"I will. See?" She held the earrings in her hand. "They're
perfect with what I'm wearing."

Chris knew that just about anything would go with a blue
denim skirt. But Jill had a point. The swirls of blue-and-green
enamel picked up the color of her sweater beautifully.

Rubbing her hands together, she took a deep breath. "Okay.
Are you all set now? Anything else you need?"

"Nope. Thanks, Mom."

"If you're using my perfume—" which happened often
"—remember, a little goes a long way. You don't want to hit
the party smelling like a whorehouse."

"Okay."

"I'll be downstairs. Come on down when you're ready and
have some hors d'oeuvres."

"If there are any left. Gideon looks hungry."

You should only know, Chris thought, then was grateful Jill
didn't. Too soon, she'd be into serious dating. Too soon, she
would know about hunger, about the urges that drove men and
women together at times that weren't always the wisest. What
Chris had done with Brant sixteen years before hadn't been
smart at all, though she'd never had cause to regret having Jill.
She meant what she'd told Gideon, that she was happy with
her life.

Would she be happier with a man in the picture? She didn't
know. She did know that she was drawn to Gideon in an elemental way that refused to be ignored. She was older and wiser.

Still, she was drawn. Even now, returning to the kitchen to find that he'd opened the wine and was filling two glasses, she felt a flare of excitement. For a split second, she was at the end of that truncated kiss again, spinning on a spiral of desire, feeling the frustration.

"Is Jill all set?" he asked, handing her one of the glasses.

"Uh-huh."

"To us, then," he said, raising the other.

Chris touched her glass to his, then took a sip. "Mmm. This is nice." Focusing on the amber liquid, she whispered, "Sorry about before. The timing was unfortunate."

"Did I complain?" he whispered back, coming in close to her side. "It just lengthens the foreplay, that's all."

Chris felt a soft shuddering inside. "Uh, maybe we ought to sit down."

"Maybe we ought to have something to eat."

"Right." Setting her wine on the counter, she put on mitts and removed the tray of mushrooms from the oven. She arranged half of them on a dish that also held a wedge of cheese and some crackers, then put the rest back. "So they'll stay warm."

Gideon carried the dish to the low glass table in front of the living room sofa. When Chris joined him there, he popped a mushroom into his mouth. "Whoa," he drawled when it was gone, "that was worth two wasted batches."

Chris went red. "I wasn't paying attention to what I was doing."

"Like my men weren't that day at Crosslyn Rise?" he teased, because he couldn't resist, and leaned close. "Was I the cause of your distraction?"

She focused on his tie, which was silk and striped diagonally in blue, yellow and purple. "Of course not. I was thinking about work."

"I'm work, aren't I?"

"Not actively. Not yet."

"I got some half-rounds."

Her eyes flew to his, wide and pleased. "You did?"

He nodded. "Above the French doors, like you wanted. Put them in last week."

"All those phone calls, and you didn't tell me?"

"I wanted to surprise you." His gaze fell to her mouth and stuck there. "Thought if I saved it for a special time, it might win me a kiss." His voice was rough. "How about it?"

Without a moment's hesitancy, Chris reached up and put a soft kiss on his mouth. Then, because it had been so sweet and too short, she followed it with a second.

"You smell good," he whispered against her lips. "I'll bet you smell like this all over." When she caught in a small gasp, he sealed it in with the full pressure of his mouth, giving her the kind of hard, hungry kiss he craved.

Chris wanted the hardness and more. She opened to the sweep of his tongue, but he was barely done when he ended the kiss. She felt she was hanging in midair. "What's wrong?"

"Too fast," he whispered, breathing heavily. "Too hot." He shot a glance toward the stairs. "Too public." Pulling away from her, he bent over, propping his elbows on his knees. The low sounds that escaped his throat as he tried to steady his breathing told her of his discomfort.

Chris felt dismayed. In the moment when he'd kissed her, she'd forgotten that Jill was still upstairs. "I should have realized," she whispered.

"Not your fault alone. It takes two to tango."

It was a figure of speech, but she latched on to it as a diversion from desire. "Do you tango?"

"Nope. Can't dance much at all. But I make love real good."

She moaned, picturing that with far too great an ease. In desperation, she reached for the dish of mushrooms. "Here. Have another. And tell me what else is happening at the Rise."

With a slightly shaky but nonetheless deep breath, Gideon straightened. He ate another mushroom, then a third. "These are really good." He glanced back toward the kitchen. "And something else smells good." He frowned, trying to identify it.

"Rock Cornish Hens," she said. "It's the orange sauce that you smell." But she wasn't feeling at all hungry for that. "Tell me about the Rise," she repeated. She needed to think of something settling.

Gideon understood and agreed. He really hadn't intended to start things off hot and heavy. It had just happened. For both of them. But the civil thing was to talk and visit and eat first.

Casually crossing an ankle over his knee as he would have done if he'd been with the guys, he began to talk. He told Chris about the progress his crew had made, the few problems they'd run into, the solutions they'd found, that they'd moved inside. The diversion worked. When Jill joined them some fifteen minutes later, they were involved in a discussion of staircase options.

"You look great, honey," Chris told her with a smile.

"Better than great," Gideon added. "Those poor guys won't be able to keep their hands off you."

Chris shot him a dirty look. "They'd better." To Jill, she said, "One swift kick you know where."

Jill seemed embarrassed. She glanced at Gideon before sitting close to Chris and saying quietly, "My hair looks awful."

"Your hair looks great."

"I should have had it cut."

"If you had, you'd be tugging at the ends to make it longer."

"It never curls the way I want. I've been fiddling with it for an hour, and it's still twisting the wrong way."

"You're the only one who knows that. To everyone else, me included, it looks great."

"You're just saying that because you're my mother."

"I'm not your mother," Gideon said, "and I say it, too."

Jill eyed him warily. "You'd say anything to please Mom."

"No way," he argued. "If you'd been down sooner, you'd have heard me telling her that she could grovel all night if she wanted, but I was not putting in winding staircases at Crosslyn Rise."

"This man," Chris told Jill, "is a cheapskate. There's a huge winding staircase in the mansion. It would be *perfect* to have smaller versions in the condos. Don't you think so?"

Jill crinkled her nose. "Winding staircases are good for long, sweeping dresses, but modern people don't wear them."

"That's right," Gideon chimed in. "They spend their money on skylights and Jacuzzis and Sub-Zero refrigerators instead. Face it, Chris, you're outvoted."

But Chris shook her head. "I still think they'd be great, and I'm the decorator."

"Well, I'm the builder, and I say they're too expensive. We can't fit them into the budget. That's all there is to it."

"You won't even *try*?"

"We're talking *ten grand* per staircase! I just can't do it."

Chris sensed that she could argue until she was blue in the face and she wouldn't get anywhere. She arched a brow Jill's way. "So much for trying to please me."

Jill's gaze bounced from Chris to Gideon and back. "Did I cause that fight?"

"Of course not—"

"It wasn't a fight—"

"You both look pretty ticked off."

"I'm not ticked off—"

"I never get ticked off—"

"Maybe you shouldn't be talking work on New Year's Eve."

"I don't know—"

"Yeah, well—"

Jill looked at her watch. "Hey, can we leave now?"

"Have something to eat first," Chris told her, escaping into the role of mother with ease.

"They'll have food at the party."

"Uh-huh. Pizza, but not for a few hours, I'd wager."

"They'll have munchies," Jill argued, and rose to get her coat. "We're picking up Jenny and Laura on the way, so they can put their stuff right in the car." She grew hesitant, again looking back and forth. "Uh, whose car?"

"My Bronco," Gideon said, "if that's okay with you. And it's fine about the stuff. We'll bring it in when we get back here."

Chris hadn't known they were picking up the two other girls and sensed that it had been a last-minute deal. She wondered if it had anything to do with Gideon being there, or more spe-

cifically, with the fact that Chris was seeing him. None of Jill'
friends had ever seen Chris with a man. Maybe Jill wanted he
friends to know that her mother was human.

Oh, she was human, all right, human and female. Once in
the truck, sitting in the front seat with Gideon, she was a
keenly aware of him as she'd been back in the house. Each
move he made seemed to register. Fortunately, he kept up a
steady conversation with Jill, asking about the party, who was
going, who of those going she was closest to. That led into a
fast discussion about school, what she was taking, what she
liked best and worst. By the time they reached Jenny's house
Chris had picked up several tidbits even she hadn't known.

Jill and Jenny talked softly in back from there. They were
soon joined by Laura, who directed Gideon the short distance
from her house to the one where the party was being held
When they arrived, and Jenny and Laura climbed out, Jill hung
back for a minute.

"So, you guys are going back home for dinner?"

"Uh-huh," Chris said.

"You're not going out to a movie or anything later?"

Chris gave her cheek a reassuring touch. "We'll be home
If there's any problem, just call and we'll be right here. Otherwise, we'll be back to pick you up at twelve-thirty." She
kissed her. "Have a super time, honey."

"You, too, Mom," Jill said softly, then raised her voice
"You, too, Gideon."

"Thanks, Jill. Have fun. We'll be back."

With the slam of the door, she was gone. She glanced back
once on the way to join her friends, then disappeared with them
into the house.

"Was that nervousness?" Gideon asked as he shifted into
gear and started off.

"I'm not sure. I think so. She's so grown-up in some ways.
then in others…"

He knew just what she meant. Jill was physically mature.
She was personable and poised. But the look in her eye from
time to time told the truth. "She's only fifteen. That's pretty
young."

"Sometimes I forget. We're such good friends."

"She's a really nice girl." He reached for Chris's hand, needing her warmth. "Even if she did interrupt what was promising to be one of the best kisses of my life."

Chris closed her fingers around his, but she didn't say a word. Left hanging, of course, was the fact that they could resume that kiss the minute they got home without worry of interruption.

"What are your parents doing tonight?" he asked a drop too casually. He was thinking of interruptions, too, but it seemed crass to let on. Hadn't he decided that they should talk and eat first?

"They're having dinner with friends. There's a local group that's been spending their New Year's Eves together for years. It used to be Mom and Dad would make a point to be home before midnight to be with us—Jill and me and anyone else who was home—but everyone's out this year."

"Except you," he said softly.

"Except me." She held more tightly to his hand. When he gave a tug, she slid closer to him.

"Are *you* nervous?" he asked. He supposed it was a form of talk, though it was getting right to the point.

She studied his face. Muted in the dark, his expression was strangely dear. "A little."

He drove quietly for a time before saying, "Does it help to know I am, too?"

"You? Buy why?"

"Because you're special. I want to make things good for you."

A light tremor shimmered through her insides. Swallowing, she said, "I think you could do that with your eyes closed."

"I don't want them closed. There's too much to see."

Like frames of a movie, the images that had haunted her flicked one after another through her mind. "Uh, Gideon?" she whispered. "I think there's something you should know."

"Don't tell me you're a virgin."

"I'm not, but—"

"You've had a baby, Chris."

"I know that," she said quickly, quietly, putting her cheek against his arm, "but the sum total of my experience with a man took place in the back seat of a '72 Chevy."

He was amused by that. "The back seat, eh?"

"It was dark. I didn't see much."

"I never did it in a car." Most everywhere else when he'd been younger, but never in a car. He'd gotten too big too fast. "What was it like?"

"That's not the point."

"But I want to know." He flattened her hand on his thigh and held it there. "Wouldn't I have to be kind of crunched up?"

"Gideon—"

"I'm too tall for a car."

She sighed. "No, you're not. You could do it. It'd just take a little ingenuity."

He began moving her hand around. "Like with positions?"

She nodded, still against his arm. She was picturing the wildest things. "You'd have to be kind of half on, half off the seat."

"I'd be on top?"

That was the only position Chris had ever known, but she'd read of others. "Or under," she murmured.

"Would we be undressed?"

"Just…vaguely."

"Could I touch your breasts?"

She sucked in a breath. "If you wanted to."

"Bare? Could I open your bra?"

"It might be cold."

His low voice, angled into her hair, was like liquid fire, which was precisely what was searing his gut. "I'd want to do it anyway. I want to see what you look like all over, then I'd warm you up."

She pressed her face into his arm. "Gideon—"

He slid her hand upward, urging it back and forth at the very top of his thigh. "Heating up?"

"Oh, yes."

"It doesn't take much with us."

"I know. I don't understand it. All these years, and I haven't been attracted to any other man." But she could feel the heat in him searing her palm and curling right through her. Later, thinking back on it, she wouldn't know which of them moved first, but suddenly she was covering his sex, shaping her fingers to his arousal, cupping the heaviness beneath.

"Chris." He made a deep, choking sound. She started to take her hand away, but he held it fast. "It's okay, okay." He made another sound when he swallowed. "How much longer till we're home?"

Chris looked out the window. It was a minute before she could focus, a minute more before she could identify the street they were on. "Two more blocks." She glanced up at his face, where the tension was marked. A surge of feeling welled up from inside, propelling her mouth to his jaw. She kissed it once, moved an inch, kissed it again. Her voice was like down against his rough skin. "Can you make it?"

"Oh, yeah," he gritted, and released her hand. "Loosen my tie, Chris? I'm being strangled."

She loosened it and unbuttoned the top button. "Better?"

"Yes...listen, Chris, if you think there's even the slightest chance that you may get cold feet on me and want to call this off, better tell me now so I can run around the block a couple of times before we go inside." He didn't think they were going to get in much talking or visiting or eating. They'd already passed that point.

"I won't get cold feet," she said, and knew she wouldn't, couldn't. She was too hot.

"What about the food?"

"It'll hold." She took a shallow breath. "Gideon, what I said the other night about birth control? I still don't have anything. I was thinking I should see my doctor, then I didn't know whether we'd really, uh, get together, and I felt funny. Do you have something?"

Turning into her street, he nodded. In a gritty whisper, he said, "Will you help me put it on?"

Her insides grew swollen at the thought. "I don't know how."

"I'll show you."

"So we'll be sharing the responsibility?"

"I wasn't thinking of it that way."

"What were you thinking of?"

"The turn-on. Having you touch me—having you look at me—" He was torturing himself, unable to stop.

"Gideon, what I was trying to tell you before—"

"Jeez, I've never talked about making love this way. Does it sound calculated?" He turned onto the driveway.

"It sounds hot."

"I *feel* hot." He pulled as close to the garage as he could.

"Gideon, there's something I want to *tell* you." She rushed the words out, fearful of being cut off again. "I may have had a baby, but I'm pretty new at this. I haven't even—"

"Shh," he whispered, pressing his fingers to her mouth. Opening the door, he slid out, drawing her along in nearly the same motion. A supportive arm circled her shoulders and hugged her to him as he guided her quickly toward the door. Once inside, with the cold air and all of humanity locked out, he pressed her to the wall, ran his mouth from her forehead, down her nose to her lips. She smelled sweet, almost innocent, and was soft to match. That softness burned into him, from the spot, waist high, where their bodies met to the one at the knee where they parted. She was giving, yielding. Her chin tipped up under the light urging of his thumbs. Her mouth opened to his, welcoming him inside. Every move she made was untutored, purely instinctive, intensely feminine. Each one called to the man in him that craved her possession.

"The nice thing," he breathed against her forehead as he pushed away the shoulders of her coat, "would have been to wait on this until later, but I can't, Chris." The coat slipped to the floor. "If that makes me a not-nice man, I guess that's what I am, but I need you too much now." His fingers met at her throat, touched the collar of her dress and the top buttons, then separated and slid over silk to her breasts. It was the first time he'd touched her there. She was full and firm. Even through her dress and a bra, he could feel the tightness of her nipples.

The sensation of being touched and held was so charged,

Chris thought she'd die—just explode. With a small sound, she covered his hands.

He was instantly concerned. As aroused as he was, he had promised to make it good for her, and if it killed him, he intended to do just that. "Hurt?"

"Not enough." She felt impatient and greedy. Transferring her hands from her chest to his, she ran her open palms over him while he worked at the buttons of her dress. When it was open to the waist, she felt him part the fabric, then release the center clasp of her bra. She was holding him at the hips by that time, needing an anchor, feeling momentarily shy when he peeled back the lace and cool air hit her breasts.

Gideon sensed her shyness, and it fueled his fire. In the past, he'd had the most experienced of women, but none sparked him as Chris did. Angling his upper body away, he took pleasure in what he'd unclothed. Her breasts were pale, strawberry at their crests, quivering with each shallow breath she took.

He was smitten. Never in his life had he seen anything as beautiful as Chris against that door with her fingers clutching his hips, her eyes lowered to his belt, her dress open and her breasts bare and waiting. Unable to resist, he ducked his head and put his mouth to one. He drew it in. His tongue raked its turgid tip.

She cried out, a frantic whisper of his name.

"I want you so badly," he moaned. Dragging himself from her breast, he straightened and tore off his blazer. Holding her gaze, which had risen with him, he tugged off his tie, unbuttoned his shirt and unfastened his pants. Then he slid his fingers into her hair, held her head still and took her mouth in a strong, sucking kiss.

Chris wanted more than that. "Upstairs," she gasped when he finally allowed her a breath. "I want you in my bed." She took his hand, but no leading was necessary. He was right beside her, half-running up the stairs, stopping midway for another deep kiss before continuing to the top.

Her room was shadowed, lit only from the hall, though neither of them seemed aware. They were kissing again within seconds, but this time their hands were at work, fumbling with buttons, zippers and sleeves. Their fingers tangled. They alternately laughed, moaned and gasped. She was sitting on the edge of the bed pulling the stockings from her feet when he came down beside her.

"Help me," he said, fiddling with a small foil pack.

For a minute, she couldn't breathe. He was stark naked and fully aroused. She'd known he would be, of course, still her startled eyes were drawn to the thickly thatched spot from which his arousal jutted so tall and straight.

At her utter stillness, Gideon raised his head. He didn't have to follow her gaze to know what she was looking at. The thought that she might be afraid gave him the control he wouldn't otherwise have had. "It won't hurt," he whispered, drawing her close. "You know that. You've done this before."

"But I've never seen it before," she whispered back. "That was what I've been trying to tell you. I have lots of brothers, but by the time they reached puberty, I was out of the house. And with Brant it was always so dark." Tremulously she touched his stomach. "I'm not afraid. You're very beautiful." From his navel, she brushed the back of her fingers down the thin, dark line to where the hair grew more dense, then on to his velvety strength. Satin on steel, it seemed to her. She explored it lightly, felt it flex and grow.

Gideon croaked out her name.

She looked up. "Too much?"

"Too little." He reached again for the foil pack, but no sooner had he removed the condom than she took it from him.

"Tell me how," she whispered.

He told her. With surprising ease, given her trembling and his hardness, she had the condom on. Then, feeling proud and excited and filled with something else that was nearly overwhelming, she slipped her arms around his neck and put her mouth to his. "Love me?"

"I do," he muttered, near the end of his tether. With an arm around her slender waist, he fell over onto the bed, sweeping her beneath him as he drew them both up toward the pillows.

That was when Chris felt the full force of his nakedness. He was man through and through, from the luxury of his weight to the friction of his limbs. His hands seemed everywhere, touching her in large sweeps from her breasts to her hips, then the hot spot between her legs. Suddenly without patience, she opened for him.

"Hurry!"

Taut and trembling, Gideon lifted himself, positioned himself and slowly, slowly sank into the tightest sheath that had ever encased him. "There. Ah. Chris, you're so small."

She felt it. Small, feminine and cherished. And she loved it.

"Am I hurting you?" he asked.

"Oh, no. You feel so new. So special. So big."

Gideon nearly came. He went very still for a minute, shut his eyes tight, gritted his teeth until he'd regained control. "What you do to me."

Chris was thinking the same thing about him, because the small pinching she'd first felt at his entry was gone, leaving only a yearning to be stroked. Grasping his hair, she looked up at him and said, "Make love to me now, Gideon. Do it."

He didn't need any more urging than that. Withdrawing nearly all the way, he surged back with a cry of triumph, then repeated the pattern in a rhythm that seemed to anticipate, then mirror her need. Chris surrendered to that need, letting it take her higher and higher until, closing her eyes and arching her back, she tumbled head-on into a mindless riot of sensation.

Somewhere at the tail end of the riot, a low light came on, but awareness was slow to return. When her breathing had finally slowed and she opened her eyes, she found Gideon propped above her, looking down with a smile. He'd managed to light the lamp beside the bed without leaving her; he was as rigid as ever inside her. But that didn't seem to be bothering him. Though the muscles of his upper arms were taut beneath her hands and his breathing was heavy, something pleased him immensely.

"What?" she whispered with a shy smile.

"You wouldn't ask that if you could see what I do," he replied. His voice was low and husky, as tight as his body, but he wasn't rushing toward his own release. There was too much pleasure to be gained just in looking at Chris, with her blond hair mussed, her cheeks pink, her skin aglow with a light sheen of sweat, her lips rosy and full. There was too much pleasure to be gained just in holding himself inside her, knowing that for a short time she was all his. He felt more loved than he ever had in his life. "Was it good?"

She nodded. "You touch me, and...poof!"

His grin broadened. "That's good. I want it like that."

"But you haven't come."

"I will." He took a deep, shuddering breath. "I do love you, y'know."

She felt a burst of heat in the area of her heart. "How can you tell?"

"Because of what I feel, like I could stay this way forever and be perfectly happy. Before, when we were downstairs and then in the car, I thought I'd die if I didn't get into you fast, and maybe I would have. But now that I'm here, there's no rush. What you looked like when you came—what that look did to me—was more satisfying than any climax I've ever had."

Chris felt tears pool in the outside corners of her eyes. "That's beautiful," she whispered. She touched his chest, running a finger by his small, dark nipple. "You're beautiful." Giving more freedom to her hands, she let them familiarize themselves with the wedge of fine hair beneath his collarbone, the muscular ridges of his shoulders, the tapering strength of his back. She was entranced by his perfection, his mix of hard and soft, ragged and smooth, flat and curved. "You *are* beautiful," she whispered again. Curving her hands to his backside, she arched her back and rose off the bed to put her mouth to his throat.

Gideon lost it then. In her slow, gentle way, she was driving him to distraction. Unable to wait any longer, he began to make love to her again. He tempered himself only at the end, when he felt her coming so close, and when her senses erupted for a second time, he gave in to his own powerful release.

LATER, much later that night, after the New Year had been welcomed in with toasts and kisses, after Jill and her friends had been fetched and settled, after Gideon had left for the ride back to Worcester and Chris was in bed, she thought about all that had happened.

Gideon had been incredible. He'd made love to her yet another time in her bed, then once in the shower before they dressed. It wasn't the fact of his physical prowess that impressed her as much as the soft things he'd said, the adoring look in his eye and the cherished way he'd made her feel.

Brant had never done that.

More than once, as she lay in bed that night, then on subsequent nights after talking with Gideon on the phone, she wondered if she loved him. The thought was a sobering one. She didn't have faith in herself when it came to love. She'd misjudged once before, and had spent fifteen years trying to make up for it to Jill. If she loved Gideon now, if she became more deeply involved with him than she already was, Jill was bound to be affected. Worse, if the involvement deepened and Jill came to love him, too, and then something happened, Chris would never forgive herself.

The dilemma was whether to take the chance or leave things the way they were. The answer eluded her.

CHAPTER EIGHT

OF ALL THE MONTHS of the year, Chris liked January the least. It was the coldest and most bleak, physically and emotionally, a necessary evil to be suffered through to reach February, which had a vacation, at least. And then March came with its lengthening days, and April with its promise of rebirth, and by then she had it made.

This year, January was fun. For one thing, she got down to serious work on Crosslyn Rise, poring over Carter's plans, visiting the site at least once a week to check on the progress, wading through swatches of wallpaper and carpeting, studying furniture and cabinetry designs, pondering electrical and bathroom fixtures, and kitchen appliances.

Though she would be working with buyers as they came along later that summer, the plan was to completely outfit a model apartment in one of the units for potential clients to see. Moreover, she would be decorating the entire mansion, once it was subdivided into a restaurant, a health club and a meeting place. For that, she would be calling in experts to help, but she was the coordinator.

There was lots to think about, but she loved it. She also loved spending time with Gideon, which was probably why she went to the Rise so often, given the season and the relatively slow rate of the work. They argued often, but within reason. Though she'd yielded on the issue of winding stairways, she wanted marble tiles in the bathrooms, Corian in the kitchens, and full walls of brick where the fireplaces would go. Invariably Gideon rebelled at the cost, just as inevitably he went out of his way to try to accommodate her. Sometimes he made it, sometimes he didn't. But he tried. She couldn't ask for more.

January was also bright because she saw him after work. She

kept it to once a week, on the weekend when Jill might have other plans, but the anticipation of that one night, along with his regular phone calls, kept her feeling alive in ways she hadn't known she'd been missing.

Come February, he asked to stay the weekend at her place, but she was uncomfortable with that. "Jill will be in and out. I just can't."

They were lying face-to-face on a bed in a small motel off the highway not far from Crosslyn Rise. It was three o'clock on a Thursday afternoon. Working together at the Rise shortly before, they'd suffered a sharp desire attack. The motel had been Gideon's suggestion. Chris hadn't protested.

Now, in the afterglow of what had been more hot and exciting than ever, Gideon only knew that he needed more of her. "Jill knows what's going on."

"She doesn't know that we sleep together." They'd been careful about that, choosing their time together with care.

"She knows," he insisted. "She's a perceptive kid. She sees the way we look at each other, the way we touch. She was the one who noticed the hand-holding that first day. You think she doesn't suspect that there's more than hands involved now?"

"I don't know what she suspects," Chris replied, feeling unsettled because it was true. And it was her own fault. She didn't have the courage to ask. "But I think it would be awkward for her if you slept over. It's too soon."

Nothing could be too soon for Gideon, whose love for Chris kept growing. Although he sensed she wasn't really ready, he wanted to ask her to marry him, which was a *really* big step. He'd been footloose and fancy-free for a good long time. But he was willing to give it all up for Chris. He *had* given it all up. Since meeting her, he hadn't dated another woman. Footloose and fancy-free had lost its lure.

He did agree, though, that Jill was a concern. "Does she ask you questions about what we do?"

"Surface ones, like where we ate and what we had for dinner."

"Do you think she accepts me?" He knew that Jill liked

him, and remembered all too clearly the permission she'd given him to date Chris. But that had been before he'd started doing it. Faced with the reality of having someone to compete with for her mother's time, she might have had second thoughts.

Chris moved her hand through the hair on his chest. "She accepts you as someone I have a good time with on the weekends."

"But not as my lover?"

"She doesn't know you are."

"You think."

After a minute, she admitted, "I think."

"Maybe you should tell her. You're young. You're healthy. You're an adult. You have every right to want to be with a man."

"I'm supposed to set an example for her."

The sound of that gave Gideon a chill. He drew her closer to ward it off. "You're not doing anything illegal or immoral. You're making love with a man you care deeply about." His voice lowered. "You do care that way, don't you?"

Her eyes were soft, as was her voice. "You know I do." For a minute, secure in his arms, enveloped by his scent and lost in his gaze, she was engulfed by a longing for forever. Then the minute passed and reality returned. "But you have to understand, Gideon. You're the first man I've dated, really dated, in Jill's memory, and we haven't been doing it for long. If I suddenly have you staying the night, she's apt to think that it's okay to do that after a couple of dates."

"It is. Sometimes."

"She's only fifteen!"

"And you're thirty-three. She's bright enough to see the difference. It's okay for you to be doing what we're doing, Chris. It's *right* for you to be doing it, given what you feel. You're a passionate woman." How well he knew. Each time they made love, she was more hungry, more aggressive. "How you kept it locked away for so long is beyond me."

"It wasn't any big thing. I never wanted another man the way I do you."

"Not even Brant?" he couldn't resist asking.

"Not even Brant," she said, and knew it was true. What she felt for Gideon, what she did with him, had nothing to do with growing up, experimenting, feeling her oats or rebelling. It had to do with mature desires and deep inner feelings. "We were young. Too young. I don't want Jill doing what we did."

"You can't put a chastity belt on her."

"No, but I can teach her the importance of waiting."

"Would you have her be a virgin at her wedding?"

"I wouldn't mind it."

"That's unrealistic, Chris."

"I know. But it's not unrealistic to encourage her to wait until someone important to her comes along. I've tried to teach her that lovemaking is special."

"It is. So why can't you tell her that we do it?"

"I can't. She'll jump to conclusions."

"So talk to her. Explain."

But Chris wasn't ready for that. "She's always come first in my life. She may get nervous."

"So you'll talk to her more. You'll explain more. You two are close. You talk about everything else. Why not this?"

She wished she could make him understand. "Because it's so *basic*."

"You're right about that," Gideon drawled, then grew intense. "Lord, Chris, do you know how much I want to sleep with you? Not make love. *Sleep*. Roll over with you tucked up against me. Wake up that way, too."

"And then what would happen?" she asked knowingly.

"We'd make love."

"Right. With Jill in the next room, listening to the headboard bang rhythmically against the wall."

"So we'll pull the bed out."

"The *frame* squeaks."

"I'm a handyman. I'll fix it."

"You're missing the *point*."

"So we won't make love. I'll just go through the rest of the day suffering silently—"

"Gideon," she pleaded softly, "I need time. That's all. I need time to get Jill accustomed to a man in my life. I owe it to her, don't you see?"

As he saw it, she owed things to herself, too. But, then, he'd never been a parent. He'd never felt the kind of responsibility for another human being that Chris felt so keenly for Jill. Loving Chris as he did, he had to respect her feelings.

"Okay," he said in surrender, "then we go to plan B."

"Plan B?"

"We go away together."

Chris was dumbfounded. "Did you hear *anything* I said?"

"All three of us. Jill has school vacation coming up in two weeks. So we'll make reservations and go somewhere together. That way, she'll be able to get used to the idea of our being together."

"But that'll be no different than having you over at the house! The same problem exists."

"Not if we book separate rooms." When Chris seemed to listen at that, he went on. "You and Jill room together. I'll have my own. We could either go north to ski or south to sun and swim."

Chris wanted to tell him he was crazy, except that idea wasn't bad. In fact, the more she thought of it, the more she liked it. "Do you ski?" she asked.

"Sure, I ski," he answered. "I mean, I may not do my turns as neatly as I do my lay-ups, but neither do I make a fool out of myself." He could see she was tempted. "Ever been to Stowe?"

She shook her head against his shoulder. "Only to Woodstock, and not for skiing. Stowe is farther north. I never wanted to drive that long."

"Would you want to with me?"

"I wouldn't mind it."

"What about Jill?"

"She'd be game. She's dying to go skiing."

"Does she know how?"

"Barely."

"No sweat. The instructors are good. Would you prefer a condo or an inn?"

"An inn."

"Separate rooms?"

She nodded.

"Would you visit me in mine?"

She grinned. "Maybe."

With a grin of his own, he slid an arm around her hips, which was where, by a stretch of the imagination, there was a touch of fullness. "Maybe?"

"If it isn't too hard."

"It'll definitely be hard."

"Is that a warning," she asked softly, "or a promise?"

Eyes smoldering, he rolled to his back and drew her on top. His large hands cupped her head, directing her down for his kiss. It was the only answer he gave.

WHEN CHRIS TOLD JILL that they were going skiing, her eyes lit up. When she told her that Gideon would be coming, the light faded a little. "I didn't know he skied," she said with reluctant interest.

"I didn't, either. But he does. And he's been to Stowe before, so he knows the good places to eat."

"Will we rent a condo?"

"I thought we'd go to an inn." She paused. "I thought you'd be more comfortable that way."

"Will I have my own room?"

"We'll share, you and me."

Jill seemed surprised by that, and relieved. "You're not rooming with Gideon?"

Chris shook her head. "I'm rooming with you."

"Won't he mind?"

"He knows that's the way it has to be."

Jill considered that. "Do you wish it was different?"

"In what sense?"

"That you two were going away alone?"

"Of course not. You're my best friend."

"And what's he?"

"He's a man I'm seeing, who I like a lot."

"Do you love him?"

"You've asked me that before. What did I tell you then?"

"That it was too soon to ask you, but you've seen him a lo since then. You must have some idea what you feel. Or wha you think you can feel. If we're going skiing with him—"

"We're doing it because it sounds like fun."

"We could drive up there, you and me, just ourselves."

"But it was Gideon's idea." She gave Jill a funny look "Weren't you the one who felt so badly that he had to spen Christmas all by himself in a lonely house?"

"Yeah, but this is different. This is purely voluntary. It's m vacation time. Not his."

Chris felt a stab of concern. "Would you rather he not go?

"No. He can go."

"Such enthusiasm," she teased, trying to hide her uneas "I thought you liked him."

"I *do*. And I'm *glad* we're going skiing with him. I ju want to know if you love him."

Chris thought about it for a minute before finally, truthfull saying, "I don't know. There are times when I think I do, b then there are so many considerations—"

"Like what?"

"Like whether he's prepared to play second fiddle to yo You come first, Jill. You always have and always will."

"But that's not fair to you. Maybe you want to be wit Gideon. Maybe you *should* be with him."

"How would you feel if I were?"

Jill was awhile in answering. The words were cautious whe they came. "Happy for you. Happy for Gideon."

"And for you?"

"Happy, too, I guess."

"You don't sound convinced."

She looked at her hands. "I don't know. It just takes som getting used to. I mean, I'd really like it because then you' have things to do, yourself, and I wouldn't feel badly leaving you home all alone.''

Chris hadn't realized. ''Do you do that?''

''Sometimes. But then I like knowing you're here. I like knowing you're waiting for me. Selfish, huh?''

Brushing a wisp of dark hair from Jill's cheek, Chris said, ''Not selfish at all. Just a little worried. You've been used to one thing, and now you see the possibility of things changing. Don't you think the idea of change frightens me, too? Don't you think it comes into play when you ask if I love Gideon?''

''Does it?''

''Sure, it does. I'm used to my life, our life. I like it. I'm not sure I want anything to disturb it.''

''But if you love Gideon—''

''I don't know for sure that I do, which is one of the reasons why I really want the three of us to go on this trip. If I'm going to love any man, you'll have to feel comfortable with him—and vice versa—because no matter what else happens, I'm your mother. Always. I'll be here for you even if I love *ten* guys.''

Jill smirked. ''Ten guys? Fat chance. You're such a prude.''

''What is that supposed to mean?'' Chris asked with an indignance that was only half-feigned.

''You haven't even gone to bed with Gideon! I mean, look at him. He's gorgeous. Jenny and Laura are *still* drooling over him. Why aren't you?''

''Why aren't I drooling?''

''Why aren't you sleeping with him?''

Chris swallowed. As openings went, it was perfect. Remembering the conversation she'd had such a short time before with Gideon, she knew he was right. She and Jill were close. She'd always prided herself on forthrightness. She could explain her feelings. They could talk. It was time.

''How do you know I'm not?'' she asked gently.

While Jill didn't jump immediately at the suggestion, she grew more alert. ''When do you have time?''

''You make time for what you want.''

''I mean, when have you had the *chance*?''

"You find chances, if you want them."

Jill was quiet. After a minute, she blurted out, "So have you—or haven't you?"

"Is it important to you to know?"

She backed down. "Not if you don't want to tell me."

"I do. I want to tell you. I want to, because some of the things Gideon and I have shared have been very, very beautiful. I've always told you that. With the right person, making love is precious."

Jill seemed suddenly shy, as though this Chris was a new and different person from the one she'd known moments before. "So you have," she whispered.

Chris nodded. "He is...very special."

"Does he love you?"

"Yes."

"Do you think you'll marry him?"

Chris had taught her that lovemaking should be with someone special, that marriage should be with someone special. So Jill had made the connection, as the mother in Chris wanted her to. Now Chris was caught in the middle.

"I don't know, honey. If what I feel for him proves to be love, I might. But that would be a long way off."

"Why?"

"Because I wouldn't do anything until you went to college."

"Will a man like Gideon wait around that long?"

"If he loves me enough. Maybe that's the test."

"What if you get pregnant before that?"

"Pregnant. Jill, I've taught *you* about using birth control. Don't you think I practice it myself?" She'd seen her doctor right after New Year's.

"What do you use?"

"*Jill.*"

"I'm not supposed to ask that?"

Chris closed her eyes for a second, then reached for her daughter's hand. "Of course you can. This is new for me. That's all."

"Birth control is?"

"Telling you about *my* using it is."

"Wouldn't you want to know what I used?"

"Jill, you're not—"

"No! But if I were, wouldn't you want me to discuss it with you?"

"Definitely."

"So?"

Chris sighed. "I got a diaphragm."

"Do you like it?"

"Uh, well, uh, it's okay, I mean, it's safe and effective, and if you, uh, if you have to use something—"

Jill started to laugh.

"What's so funny?"

"You. You're all red."

"This is *embarrassing*."

"Why? You've told me so many other things without getting embarrassed."

"This is different." She searched for the words. "It's like you're my mother, but I've never had this kind of discussion with my mother."

"That's why I came along."

"And the very best thing you were. I've never, *never* regretted having you, though there are times when I wished my timing had been better. There are times when I wish I could have given you a family of your own, maybe brothers and sisters."

"You could have more babies."

"Hey, I just said I was using birth control."

"But you could stop. Any time you wanted to. You're young enough to have lots more kids. Does Gideon want them?"

"I don't know. We haven't gotten that far."

"Do you?"

"I don't know. You'd be a pretty hard act to follow."

"Naturally," Jill said with a grin.

Chris grinned right back. "Naturally." She took a breath. "So. What do you say? Want to go skiing?"

THE INN WAS small and quaint, with six guest rooms on the second floor and two baths. If she'd wanted to be secretive, Chris would have stolen into Gideon's room, which was down the hall from hers and Jill's, when she was supposedly using the bathroom. But Jill would have known. Besides, she wanted more time.

So she and Gideon returned to his room shortly after Jill had joined an afternoon ski class. Knowing that it would be three hours before she was done, they felt they had all the time in the world.

Chris never failed to marvel at Gideon's body, and this time was no exception. Wearing ski garb—navy stretch pants that clung to him like static and a lime-green turtleneck sweater that matched his navy-and-green parka—he presented the kind of figure that was regularly photographed for the pages of *W*. When that garb came off, though, slowly revealing broad shoulders, a lean stomach and long, long legs, he was Chris's own very personal fantasy come to life.

Dropping her panties onto the floor by the rest of her things, she approached him. Her hands found his shoulders, then moved down and around and back. "When we're out on the slopes," she said in a sultry whisper, "women do double takes when you pass. Your moves may not be studied, but you have a natural grace." She moved closer, bringing her breasts, her belly, her thighs into contact with his. "You do this way, too," she said. Opening her mouth on his neck, she dragged her lips over that corded column. "You are an incredible male." Her palms chafed his thighs, moving slowly in to frame his sex.

Gideon was sure he'd died and gone to heaven. "You make me this way," he said. "It's all for you." Lowering his head, he caught her lips at the same time that he lifted her legs to his hips. He slid into her with the comfort and ease of an old lover and the excitement of a new one.

Familiarity gave them the confidence to be inventive, and a boundless hunger gave them the fuel. Gideon loved her standing up, then sitting on the edge of the bed, then, with Chris astride, on the sheets. He paused midway to love her with his tongue until she was wild with need, then shot back into her with a speed and force that she welcomed. The quiet in the room was broken by gasps and cries. By the time those finally eased, they were both sated, their bodies slick with sweat, tangled but limp.

"Marry me, Chris."

She was half-asleep. "Hmm?"

"I want to marry you."

"I know," she mumbled.

"Will you?"

Eyes closed, she kissed the smooth, soft spot just before his armpit. "Ask me later. Can't think now."

Gideon gave her ten minutes. Then he nudged her partly awake, tipped up her face with a finger and kissed her the rest of the way.

She grinned. "Hi."

"Hi, yourself." He looked at her, then looked some more. Never in a million years would he tire of seeing her after they made love, when she was warm and wet and sensual. He had never before had the stamina to make love three or four times in a night, but he had it with Chris. She inspired him to great heights. "Are you up?"

Sleepily she nodded. "This is so nice. I'm *so* glad we came here."

"Me, too." He paused, figuring he'd take a different, less direct tack this time. "Hard to believe the week's almost done. I could take this on a regular basis for the next thirty or forty years."

Even in her half-dreamy state, Chris knew what he meant. "There's something about ski country. The air is so clear. So cold. So invigorating. It's so warm coming inside."

"When I grow up," Gideon said, "I'm going to buy a place, maybe not as far north as this, but closer, so I can use it on weekends." He ran the pad of his thumb over her eyebrows, first one, then the other. "What do you think? Make any sense?"

Chris thought the idea sounded divine. "What kind of place?" she asked, dreaming wide awake now.

"Something old. With charm."

"A Victorian on the edge of a town green, with the white spire of a church at one end and the stone chimney of the local library at the other."

"You got it. I'd do the place over inside myself, so that it had every modern convenience. I'd break down walls so everything was open, and redo the fireplace so you could see the fire front and back. I'd put in lofts and skylights and spiral stairways and—"

"A Jacuzzi."

"You'd like one?"

"Definitely."

"We've never made love in a Jacuzzi."

"I know." Chris let herself imagine it. "I'd like to."

He was getting hard just thinking of it. "So would I."

"You should have put one in when you built your house."

"But I hadn't met you then. Real men don't soak in tubs unless there's a woman with them, and you're the only woman I've ever entertained at my house."

"The only one?"

"Only one. I love you."

She smiled helplessly. "I know."

"How 'bout you?"

"I'm workin' on it," she teased.

But he was serious. "How far have you come?"

"I'm at the point," she said, "of being happier with you than I've ever been before in my life." There were times when she felt delirious inside, so pleased and excited that she didn't know what to do with her excess energy.

"How far is that from being in love?"

"Pretty close, I guess."

"How long will it take to make 'pretty close' *there*?"

"I don't know." That was where things got hairy, because she knew what was coming next.

"I need you, Chris," he said in the slow, rumbling voice

that she'd come to associate with Gideon at his most intense. "I want to be with you morning and night for the rest of my life. I want us to get married."

She'd heard him ask her before, of course, but in the afterglow of loving, she'd pushed it from her mind. She couldn't do that now. She looked up at him to answer, then was momentarily stunned by the look in his eyes. They were so filled with love—and desperation—that she had to fight for a breath.

Coming up over him, she kissed him softly. Her forearms, resting on his chest, held her in position to meet his gaze. "I never thought I'd say this, I really didn't, because marriage wasn't something I ever spent much time considering, but I could almost see myself marrying you, Gideon. I could. I feel so much for you that it overwhelms me sometimes."

"That's love."

"Maybe. But I have to be sure. For me, and for you, and for Jill. I have to know it'll last."

"It'll last."

"So says every couple when they exchange wedding vows, but look at the statistics. I thought I was in love once, and I wasn't."

"You were too young to know what love was about. You're older now."

"We're both older. Look at you. You're almost forty. You were married once, and it didn't work, and now you've been single for years. Is what you feel for me different from what you felt for your first wife?"

"Totally," he said with conviction. "I never wanted to spend all my time with her, not even at the beginning. She had a limited time and place in my life. I had my friends, my business, my games, and I didn't want her to have any part of them. With you, I'm passing up all those other things just to be with you."

"You shouldn't—"

"I *want* to. I'd much *rather* be with you than be with anyone else. I'd much rather be with you than be alone. My first marriage wasn't fun. Being with you is. Know what I want?'' The look in his eyes was precious in its enthusiasm.

"What?"

"I want us to work together all the time. We'd be partners. I build, you decorate. Would you like that?"

She would, a whole lot, but her throat was so tight that she could only nod her answer.

He ran his finger over her lips. "I want to make you happy, Chris, and that's another thing that's different from the first time. I never thought about making Julie happy. I was almost defiant about going on with my life as though marriage didn't change it at all.'' He made a small sound. "I'm not even married to you yet, and my life has changed. Everything I do is geared to when I'll be seeing you again, and I love it that way.'' He gave her a lopsided grin. "Johnny thinks I'm sick. We were having a sandwich at the diner the other day and these two women came in. Ten, fifteen, twenty minutes went by and he started looking at me strangely."

"Why?"

"Because he thought they were real lookers and I wasn't even interested. I guess they were pretty, but that's all. Hell, I don't even wink at Cookie anymore!"

"Poor Cookie."

"Yeah, she was kinda hurt."

"You have my permission to wink. There's no harm in that."

"But winking is a kind of come-on. It's like me saying, 'I'm a man, and I think you're cute.' But I'm not thinking about anyone else being cute anymore. No one but you."

"Oh, Gideon."

"I've even thought about living arrangements. We could buy a piece of land halfway between Worcester and Belmont, something really pretty, big and wooded. There're lots of bedroom communities with good schools for Jill—"

"I can't change her."

"Why not?"

"Because she's in high school. She's with friends she's

grown up with, and they're just getting to the fun years. It'd be cruel to take her away from that.''

"Then we'll live in Belmont until she's done with high school, and in the meanwhile we can be building our dream house—''

She pressed a hand to his mouth. "Shh.''

"What?''

"You're being too accommodating.''

"That's the point. I love you, so I *want* to be accommodating.''

"But I can't be accommodating back!'' she cried. "Don't you see? You're right about love meaning that, but I'm not free to love that way. I have Jill. I want things to be so right for her in the next few years.''

Gideon felt that they had circled around and were right back to the point where they'd been weeks before. It was frustrating, but he wasn't about to give up. "I want things right for her, too. My coming into your life doesn't have to change anything.''

"But it will. It will. And then if something goes wrong—''

"What something?''

"With our relationship, and there'd be tension and upset. I don't want to subject Jill to that. She's been so good about not having a father.''

"But that's *another* thing,'' he went on. "You could *give* her a father, if you wanted. Me.''

"It's not the same.''

Gideon let the words sink in, along with the look on Chris's face. The moment was enlightening. "You feel guilty about that, don't you?''

"Yes, I feel guilty.''

Wrapping his arms around her, he hugged her. "After all you've given Jill, the last thing you should be feeling is guilty. My God, Chris, you've been a saint.''

"Not quite,'' she murmured, though she liked hearing him say it.

"Jill has had more love than most kids with *two* parents get. She wouldn't be as well adjusted if that weren't so."

"I want her to stay well adjusted."

"So do I," he said, and let it go at that. He knew from experience that where Jill's welfare was concerned, Chris was unyielding. It was simply going to be up to him, over the next weeks and months, to show her that he'd be good for Jill, too.

CHAPTER NINE

GIDEON HAD THE BEST of intentions. When he took Chris to a movie, he suggested Jill bring a friend along. When a foot of snow fell and school was canceled, he drove in from Worcester with a toboggan and took them all sliding. When Jill wanted to buy a gift for Chris's birthday, he took her to not one mall, not two, but *three* before she found what she wanted. And he was thrilled to do it. He genuinely enjoyed Jill. And he thought she enjoyed him.

Chris did, too. Jill looked forward to seeing him. At other times, though, she was more quiet than usual. More than once, when she was at the kitchen table doing homework at night and Chris was nearby, talking softly on the phone to Gideon, she sensed Jill looking at her, sensed a pensiveness that had nothing to do with schoolwork. At times, she thought that pensiveness was brooding, but when she asked, Jill shook her head in denial.

March came, then April, and Chris began to worry in earnest. Jill just wasn't herself. She was doing fine in school, and her social life was as active as ever, but at home she was definitely distracted. She continued to deny there was a problem, and Chris could only push so far. She thought, though, that it might be wise for them to spend some time alone together. They hadn't done it much of late, what with Chris's work—she was up to her ears with orders both for the model condo at Crosslyn Rise and the mansion, itself—and Gideon's presence. So, over dinner at home one midweek night, she broached the topic.

"Any thoughts on vacation, Jill?" When Jill set down her fork, alert but silent, Chris said, "I was thinking that we could go down to New York for a few days."

"New York?"

"Uh-huh. Just the two of us. We could shop, eat out, maybe take in a show or two. Would you like that?"

Jill lifted her fork again and pushed a piece of chicken around the plate.

"Jill?"

The fork settled. Looking young and vulnerable, Jill met her gaze. "I was thinking I'd use that vacation for something else."

"What's that?"

"I want to meet my father."

Chris felt the blood leave her face. Of all the things she'd imagined Jill wanting to do, that wasn't one. "Your father?"

"He's out there. I want to meet him."

"Uh, uh, what—" she cleared her throat "—what brought this on?"

Jill shrugged. "I'm curious."

"Is this what's been getting you down lately?"

"Not getting me down. But I've been thinking about it a lot. I really want to know who he is. I want to see him."

Chris felt dizzy. She took a deep breath to steady herself. "Uh, honey, I don't know where he is."

"You said he was in Arizona," Jill shot back in an accusing tone.

Chris tried to be conciliatory. "He was, last time I heard, but that was second- or thirdhand, and years ago."

"Where in Arizona?"

"Phoenix."

"So I could start looking there."

"In *person*?"

"Of course not. I'd call Directory Assistance. How many Brant Conways can there be?"

"Lots."

"Okay. You said he sells real estate. There must be some state list of people who do that. If he was there even ten years ago, he must have worked with someone who's kept in touch with him. I could find all that out on the phone."

Chris realized that Jill had given the possibilities a certain amount of very adult thought. She wondered how far that adult thought had gone. "And then what?"

"Then I'll call him, then fly out to see him during vacation."

"What if he doesn't want that?"

"Then we'll arrange another time to meet."

"What if he doesn't want that, either?"

"Then we'll arrange something else. There has to be *some* way we can get together."

Chris studied the napkin she was clutching so tightly in her lap. "Has it occurred to you that he might not want to see you?"

Sounding defiant but subdued, Jill said, "Yes. And if he doesn't, I won't go."

"But you'll be hurt in the process. I don't want that, Jill. I've tried to protect you from hurt. You don't *need* Brant. Trust me. You have everything that's good for you here, without him."

"But he's my father."

"Biologically, yes. Beyond that, he's nothing to you."

"He may be a very nice man."

"He may be, but he has his own life and you have yours."

"I don't want to be *in* his life. I just want to *meet* him."

Chris had always recognized the possibility of that, but she had kept it a very distant thought. Suddenly it was real and near, and she wasn't prepared to handle it.

She felt betrayed. She knew it was wrong. But that was how she felt.

"Why now?" she asked, half to herself.

"I already told you that."

But she had a sudden, awful suspicion. "It has something to do with Gideon, doesn't it?"

"What could it have to do with him?"

"He's the first man I've been interested in. In the past few weeks, he's probably come as close as you've ever come to having a father around." She'd known it. Damn it, she'd *known* something would happen. "I'm right, aren't I?"

"I like Gideon. I like being with him."

"But he's made you think of your father."

"It's not *Gideon's* fault."

But Chris had known. She'd *known*. Bolting from the table, she started pacing the room. "I told him it was too much, too fast. I asked him to slow things down, but did he? No. *He* knew what was best."

"Mom—"

"Over and over, I asked him to be patient. I told him I didn't want anything upsetting you. I told him you needed time."

"Mom—"

"The big expert, sticking his nose into other people's business."

"*Mom.*" She was twisted around in her chair. When Chris looked at her, she said, "This is *not Gideon's fault*! I love Gideon. He loves you, and you love him."

"I don't—"

"You do! I see it every night. It's written all over your face when you talk to him on the phone. And I think it's great. I *want* you to love him. I *want* you to marry him. I think it'd be fun to be a family. That's something I could never have with my father, and I accept that. I don't want anything with him. I like what I have. I just want to meet the man, so that I'll know who he is and who I am. Then I can be a stepdaughter to Gideon."

There had been certain times over the years when Chris had found motherhood to be overwhelmingly emotional. One had been when she'd first been presented her gooey, scrunched-up baby girl, another when Jill had gone off on the school bus for the very first time, another when Jill had had the lead in the middle school's musical production of *Snow White and the Seven Dwarfs*. Intense pride always affected Chris.

Intense pride was what she felt at that moment, along with a bit of humility. Fighting back tears, she put her arm around Jill and gave her a tight hug. "You are incredible."

Jill hugged her back. "I do love you, Mom. I'll always love you. I don't think I could ever love *him*, but I want to know who he is."

Regaining a modicum of composure, Chris slid back into her chair. She wanted to think clearly, wanted Jill to do the same. "I don't really know much about him. If he has a slew of other children, how will you feel?"

"Okay."

"What if he's big and bald and fat?"

"Haven't you been the one to always tell me not to judge a book by its cover?"

"But this is your father. You may be fantasizing that he's some kind of god—"

"If he were that, he'd have come for me, not the other way around." She took a breath, seeming strong now that she'd aired what had clearly been weighing so heavily on her mind. "Mom, I'm not looking for someone to take your place, and I'm *not* looking for another place to live. I just want to meet my father. Once I've seen him, I'll know who he is and that he exists, and that he knows *I* exist. Then I can go on with my life."

THE WORDS WERE all correct. They were grown-up and sensible. Chris knew that, but the knowledge was small solace for the fear she felt. Jill had been her whole life, and vice versa, for so long, that the thought of Brant intruding in any way was upsetting. She sensed that, for the first time, there was a crack in her relationship with Jill—not a crack as in hostility, but one as in growing up and separating. That too was inevitable, but Chris wasn't ready for it.

Nor was she ready for Gideon when he called that night. "I'm really tired. Why don't we connect later in the week."

He was immediately concerned. "Aren't you feeling well?"

"I'm fine. Just tired."

When he called the next night, she didn't claim fatigue, but she was quiet, answering his questions as briefly as possible, not offering anything extra. "Is something wrong?" he finally asked after five minutes of trying to pull her usual enthusiasm from her.

"Of course not. What could be wrong?"

He didn't know. But he knew she wasn't herself, and he feared that what was upsetting her had to do with him. "You sound angry."

"Not angry. Just busy."

"At ten o'clock at night?"

"I'm trying to get some papers in order. I have a slew of deliveries coming for five different jobs, and if the invoices get messed up—"

"I thought Margie took care of paperwork like that."

"Margie isn't involved the way I am, and I want these things to be right. If there are screwups, I'll have to be cleaning them up at the same time that Crosslyn Rise is picking up—"

Gideon interrupted. "Chris, why are you working so hard?"

"Because I'm a professional. I have commitments."

"But you don't have to work *this* hard."

"I have bills to pay," she snapped. "In case you've forgotten, I have a teenage daughter to support."

"I haven't forgotten," Gideon said quietly. "I want to help you do that."

"You've done enough!"

A heavy silence stretched between them before he said, "What's that supposed to mean?"

"Nothing."

"*What*, Chris?"

She sighed and rubbed the back of her neck. "*Nothing*. Listen, I'm tired and short-tempered. You'd probably be best to avoid me for a little while."

He didn't like the sound of that at all. "A little while?"

"A few days."

"No way. We have a date for dinner tomorrow night."

"Look, maybe that's not such a good idea."

"I think it is." He paused. "You're angry. What have I done? Damn it, Chris, if you don't tell me, I won't know and I can't do a goddamned thing about remedying it. Come on. *Talk* to me."

"Not tonight," she said firmly. "I'll be back in the office

sometime after three tomorrow. Call me then and we'll decide what to do about dinner.''

GIDEON DIDN'T call. True to form, he was there, waiting in her office when she returned. She stopped at the door when she saw him, feeling an overwhelming rush of sensation. He could arouse that, whether she was annoyed with him or not, and it wasn't only physical. Her heart swelled at the sight of him, which was probably why she hadn't wanted to see him. Looking at him, feeling the warm embrace of his eyes and the love that was so clearly behind it, she was more confused than ever about the anger she felt.

"Hi, doll," he said with a gentle smile. He went to her and kissed her cheek, then leaned back. "Uh-oh. I'm still in the doghouse?"

She slipped past him to her desk, where she deposited her briefcase and the folders she carried.

"Chris." He drew her name out in a way that said he knew something was wrong and wanted to know what it was before he lost his patience.

Knowing that she wouldn't have a chance of keeping still with him right there—and realizing she didn't *want* to—she sat down at her desk, linked her hands tightly in her lap, and said, "Jill wants to contact her father."

Gideon hadn't been expecting that, but he wasn't surprised. "Ahh. And that upsets you."

To put it mildly. "Of course, it upsets me! She wants to go off and find a man who, for all intents and purposes, doesn't want her around."

"How do you know that?"

"Because she's fifteen, and he's never once made the slightest attempt to see her—" she held up both hands "—and that's okay by me, because she doesn't need him in her life, but she's suddenly decided that she wants to know who he is. She's going to be hurt. I know it." Her fingers knotted again. "*That's* what I don't want!"

Knowing Chris the way he did, knowing what she wanted

in life for Jill, Gideon could understand why she was upset, though he didn't completely agree. "She doesn't have to be hurt. He may be cordial. He may even welcome her."

Chris felt deep, dark fears rush to the surface. "And if that happens, she may want to see him again and again, and that'll mess her up completely."

"Her, or you?"

"What?"

"Are you afraid for her," Gideon repeated patiently, "or for you?"

Chris was furious that he was so calm when she felt as if the bottom of her world were falling away. "For *me*?" Emotional stress brought her out of her chair. "You think I'm being selfish?"

"No, that's not—"

"How *dare* you suggest that!" she fumed. "I've spent the better half of my life doing and thinking and feeling for that child. I've sacrificed a whole lot, and I'd do the same thing again in a minute." Trembling, she steadied her fingertips on the chrome rim of her desk. "Selfish? Who in the *hell* are you to tell me I'm selfish? You've never sacrificed for a child. You've never sacrificed for anyone!"

Gideon was on the verge of coming to his own defense, when Chris raced on. She needed to air what she was feeling, he realized. He also realized that he wanted to know it all. He'd been a nervous wreck wondering what was wrong with her. So, much as it hurt him, he leaned back against the wall, arms folded on his chest, and listened.

"You've lived life for your own pleasure and enjoyment," she charged. "You wanted something, you took it, and that included me. But that wasn't enough, was it? It wasn't enough that we started dating, even though I didn't want to, or that we kept *on* dating, even though I didn't want to, or that we started sleeping together. That wasn't enough for you. You wanted marriage, and you wanted it fast. When I said I was worried about Jill, you said, 'No sweat, she loves me,' and maybe she does. But it's thinking about you and wondering about us and whether we're getting married that's now making her think about Brant!''

Gideon remained quiet, waiting. When she didn't say anything, simply glared at him—albeit with tears in her eyes now, and that tore through him—he said, ''Are you done?''

''If it hadn't been for you, pushing your way into our lives, it wouldn't have *occurred* to her to think of him!''

Again Gideon was quiet, though it was harder to remain so with each word she said. In the old days, he wouldn't have put up with a woman throwing unjust claims at him. He'd either have thrown them right back or walked out the door. So maybe he was sacrificing for Chris now. If so, he was more than happy to do it.

''Can I speak?'' he asked, but again his quiet words spurred her on.

''Everything was so good! We had our lives together, she was well adjusted and happy, not going for alcohol or drugs the way some of the kids at her school are, I was beginning to earn some real money. Then you came along—'' she caught her breath, a single trickle of tears escaping from each eye ''—then you came along and upset it all!''

It was the trickle of tears that did it. Unable to stand still any longer, he left the wall and went to her. ''Honey, I think you're confusing the issues,'' he said softly, but when he reached for her, she batted his hands away.

''I'm not! I've done nothing but go over and over every single aspect of this for the past two days.''

''You've lost perspective.''

''I have *not*!''

''Maybe if you'd shared it sooner, you would have seen—''

''Seen what?'' she cut in shakily. ''That you're the answer to my problems? That all I have to do is marry you and let you take me away from here, so Jill can find herself with her father?''

''Of course not!'' Gideon argued. ''Jill is part of our lives. It's you, me and her. It has been right from the start.''

''But it's *not* her,'' Chris cried, and her chin began to wobble. "She's going off to Arizona to see Brant." Her breathing grew choppy. "Things won't ever be the same again!"

Gideon had had enough. He pulled her into his arms, then held her tighter when she struggled. Within seconds, she went limp against him, and within seconds of that, clutching his sweater, she began to cry softly.

"Oh, baby," he said, crushed by the sound of her sobs. He stroked her blond hair, rubbed her slender back, held her as close as he could until her weeping began to abate. Then he sat against the edge of the desk and propped her between his thighs. Her head was still down, her cheek against his chest. Quietly he began to speak.

"You're right, Chris. Things won't ever be the same again. We've found each other, Jill's growing up, Crosslyn Rise has been gutted. That's growth. It's progress. And you're afraid, because for the first time in a long time things are changing in your life, and that makes you nervous. It would make me nervous, too, I suppose, but that's just a guess, because you're right, I haven't been in your shoes. I haven't had a child. I haven't raised that child and poured every bit of myself into it. So I don't know what it's really like when suddenly something appears to threaten that relationship."

"I'm so scared," Chris whimpered.

He tightened his arms around her. "I know, baby, I know, but there are a couple of things you're not taking into consideration. First off, just because Jill wants to see Brant, that doesn't mean she'll have an ongoing relationship with him."

"She will. I know she will."

"How do you know?" he challenged. When she didn't answer, he gentled his voice again. "You don't know, because you don't know who Brant is now, and because you're underestimating Jill. She wouldn't do anything to hurt you."

"She wants to see him!"

"She *needs* to see him. It's part of growing up. It's part of forming her identity. She's been wondering about him for a long time, now she needs to finally see who he is, so that she can put the wondering aside and go on living."

The thoughts sounded strangely familiar. In a slow, suspicious voice, Chris asked, "Did you discuss this with her?" The idea that Jill would go to Gideon before she went to her own mother was cutting.

But Gideon was quick to deny it. "Are you kidding? She wouldn't open to me that way. At least, not yet."

"But she said nearly the same thing you just did."

"That's because it's what she's feeling."

Chris looked up. "How would you know what she's feeling?"

He brushed at tear tracks with the pads of his thumbs. "Because I felt those same things myself when I was a kid. I was younger than she is. I didn't understand it the way she probably does, but after the fact I could see it. My mother came to visit me when I was little, but it wasn't the same. I couldn't put her in any kind of context. I reached a point of wanting—no, *needing*—to go to her, to see where she lived and who she lived with." He arched a dark brow. "You think my dad was pleased? He was *furious*! Couldn't understand why I'd spend all that money to fly all the way across the country to see a woman who hadn't cared enough to hang around. He yelled and yelled and carried on for a good long time until it finally hit me that he was jealous."

"I'm not jealous," Chris claimed, but more quietly. Her mind had been so muddled since Jill had mentioned Brant that she hadn't realized—hadn't remembered—that Gideon had been in a situation not unlike the one Jill was in. "I'm just scared."

"Well, my dad was, too. He was scared that I'd take a look at her life and reject him the way she had. He was scared that I'd pick up and move out to California to live with her, and that he'd be left all alone. He didn't even have family, the way you do."

Needing the cushion, she returned her head to his chest. "That doesn't make it any easier."

"I know," he crooned against her hair, "I know. The loss of a child like that would be traumatic in any case. But the fact was that he didn't lose me. I saw where my mother lived, and sure, she had plenty of money and could have given me a hell of a lot if I'd gone out there to live with her, but the fact is that I wouldn't have traded my father's love for a penny of her money in a million years.''

It was a minute before his words penetrated fully and sank deep into her soul. Moaning, she slipped her arms around his waist. He was so dear.

But he wasn't done talking. "Don't you think Jill knows what a good thing she has in you? Don't you think she knows how much she loves you?''

"Yes, but she doesn't know how much I love *her*. She doesn't know that I'd be destroyed if she ever decided to live with Brant. He was so horrible doing what he did to me—and to her. One part of me is absolutely infuriated that she even wants to *see* him.''

His breath was warm against her forehead. "But you can't tell her that—or show her, because that's not the way you are— so you took your anger out on me. And that's okay, Chris. I'd rather you took it out on me than on her. But you owed me an explanation, at least. It's not fair to refuse to talk to me, like you've done for two nights on the phone. If you want to scream and yell at me, fine. That's what I'm here for. Screaming and yelling is sometimes the only way to get anger out of your system. Or fear. Or worry.'' His voice grew more fierce. "Just don't shut me out, damn it. Don't shut me out.''

Slipping her arms higher on his back, Chris buried her face against his neck. "I'm sorry,'' she whispered. "I guess you were the only scapegoat around. I've just been so miserable since she brought it up. I keep thinking of all the possibilities—''

"Not all of them. Only the worst ones.''

He was probably right, she knew. "I keep thinking that she'll find him and like him and want to stay, or that she'll hate him but he'll like her and want a part of her, even, God forbid, sue for visitation rights. I keep worrying that her going after Brant will open a whole can of worms. She's such a terrific kid. I don't want her messed up."

"She won't be messed up."

Chris raised her eyes to his. "Look at all the kids whose parents are divorced."

"What about them?"

"They're messed up."

"Not all of them. But your situation isn't the same."

"If there's suddenly a tug-of-war between Brant and me, it's the same."

"There won't be any tug-of-war. Jill won't want to live with him. She's happy here, with you and all the friends she's grown up with. You said that yourself when I suggested we build a house somewhere other than Belmont, and it made sense. She isn't about to want to pick up and relocate all of a sudden."

"What if Brant wants it?"

"He won't want it. Not at this late date."

"But what if he does?"

"You'll tell him no."

"What if he fights?"

"You mean, goes to court? He won't do that." He snorted. "Talk about cans of worms. If he goes to court, you can sue him for back child support. Think he'll pay up?"

"What if he does? What if he does, and then wants visitation rights?"

"He won't have much of a chance of getting them. He knew he had a child fifteen years ago. He chose to ignore her. He didn't give money, and he didn't give time. No court is going to feel terribly sympathetic toward him. Besides, Jill isn't a baby. She's old enough to express her feelings and to have them taken into account."

"In court. Oh, God. I don't want her dragged through anything like that."

"She *won't* be." He took her face in his hands and put conviction into his words. "The chances of anything like that happening are so remote that it's absurd to even be thinking of it now."

"It's not absurd to me. I'm her mother. I *care*."

"So do I, Chris," he stated fiercely, "but it won't do her any good if you're a basket case worrying about worst-case scenarios. Chances are she'll meet the man, and that'll be it."

For the first time, hearing his words and the confidence behind them, Chris let herself believe it might be true. "I'd give anything for that."

He kissed her nose. "She's a good, sensible young woman, her mother's daughter all the way. My guess is that if she ever knew how upset you've been, she'd cancel her plans."

"If she did that, she'd always wonder."

"Uh-huh."

Though she could have done without his agreement, she felt herself beginning to relax. The breath she took was only slightly shaky, a vague reminder of her recent crying jag. "You don't think I'll lose her?"

"No *way* could you lose her. She'll probably go see Brant and then come back and be her good old self." He frowned. "You say the guy's in Arizona?"

"He was in Phoenix last time I heard. I told Jill we'd make some calls this weekend."

"Then you'll help her."

"Of course. I wouldn't put her through this alone. I wouldn't trust *him* alone with her."

"And you'll go out there with her?"

Chris nodded.

"It'll be the first time you've seen him since—"

She nodded again.

"Think you'll feel anything?"

Even if she hadn't sensed his unsureness, she would have said the same thing. "I'll feel exactly what I felt when he told me he didn't know if the baby was his and walked away— anger, frustration and fear." She touched Gideon's lean cheek and said softly. "But you have nothing to worry about. He won't interest me in the least."

"Maybe I could come with you."

"That might put more pressure on Jill."

"Then maybe I can help you find him. I have a friend who lives out there—" He stopped when she shook her head. "Why not? It might speed things up."

"It might tell her you're trying to get rid of her."

Gideon couldn't believe his ears. "Are you kidding? She knows better than that!" But Chris was wearing a strange expression. "But maybe you don't." He swore against the anguish that shot through him. "When will you accept the fact that I want her with us?"

"Some men wouldn't."

"I'm not some men," he barked.

"You've been a bachelor for a long time. It's one thing to live with a woman, another to suddenly inherit her teenage daughter."

He was hurt. "Have I ever complained? Have I ever suggested, even in the slightest way, that I didn't want her around?"

"I remember a few very frustrating times—"

"Yeah, I remember them, too, and I'd have felt that frustration whether it was Jill we had to behave for or a child that you and I had ourselves, but that doesn't mean I don't want her. Or them. I want kids, Chris. We're using birth control because we're not married yet, and because we want you to have a choice this time, but I do want kids. I want them for us, and I want them for Jill. She'd love some brothers and sisters. She told me so."

"She did?"

He nodded. "When we were out shopping the other week. She said that you were a great mother, and that she hoped you'd have some children so you'd have someone to take care of when she went off to school."

Chris's face fell. "Off to school. College."

"She is going."

"I know. It's creeping up so fast." Closing her eyes, she made a small, helpless sound. "Why do things have to change?" It was the question she'd been asking herself over and over again.

Gideon had never pretended to be a philosopher. All he could do was to speak from the heart. "Because we grow. We move on to things that are even better. Hey, listen, I know it's scary. Change always is. But just think—if Jill goes to see Brant and gets him out of her system, you won't have to worry about that anymore. Then, if you and I get married and have a few kids who adore Jill so much that they raise holy hell when she goes off to college, you'll have something else to think about besides an empty nest."

"Empty nest—hah. From the sounds of it, you've got the nest so full, there may not be room for any of us to breathe!"

"Not to worry," was his smug response. "I'm a builder. I'll enlarge the nest." He doubted it was the time or place, still he couldn't resist pressing his point. "So, what do you think?"

"About what?"

"Having kids."

"What about my career?"

"You'll cut back a few hours. So will I. Between the two of us, we'll handle things." He paused, wanting to believe but afraid to. "Are you considering it?"

"Not now. All I can do now is to get through this thing with Jill and Brant."

"You'll get through it," he said. Ducking his head, he kissed her on the lips. When she didn't resist, he did it again, more persuasively this time, more deeply. Just as he felt the beginning of her response, he tore his mouth away. "Do you still blame me for Jill wanting to go?"

Closing her eyes against his chin, Chris whispered, "How can I blame you for anything when you kiss me that way?"

"Are you gonna shut me out again?"

"You'll only barge your way back in."

"How about dinner tonight?"

"Goin' for broke, hmm?"

"Damn right."

She opened her eyes and slowly met his. "Okay, but I have to be home early. Jill will be back from her friend's at nine, and I want to be there."

Understanding why, Gideon nodded.

Chris studied his face, feature by handsome feature, for another minute before wrapping her arms around his neck. "Thank you, Gideon."

"For what?"

"Being my friend."

"My pleasure."

She was silent for a minute, thinking about how very much she did love him and how, surprisingly, she was coming to depend on him. She hadn't wanted that at all, but just then, she wasn't sorry. Having someone to lean on was a luxury. Sure, she had her parents and brothers, but it wasn't the same. Gideon was a man. Her man. Holding on to him, being held in return, was the nicest thing that had happened to her in two whole days.

CHAPTER TEN

GIDEON WOULD HAVE LIKED to have been there when Chris made the call to Brant Conway. He knew the call was, in some respects, a pivotal point in her life, and he wanted to be part of it. But he also knew how worried she was about Jill. He could appreciate how sensitive a time it was for her. The last thing he wanted was to complicate things with his presence.

That didn't mean he couldn't keep in close contact by phone. He wanted to give Chris support, to show her that he could listen and comfort, even absorb her anger and frustration.

Actually, there was far less anger and frustration than he expected. When she finally contacted Brant, then called to tell him about it, she was more tired than anything else.

"It was so easy," she said in a quiet voice, talking in the privacy of her bedroom after Jill had finally gone to sleep. "One call to Directory Assistance did it. He's still living in Phoenix, still selling real estate."

Gideon wanted to know everything. "Who talked, you or Jill?"

"Me," Chris said emphatically. "Jill wanted to do it, but I put my foot down. Can you imagine what she'd have felt if he'd denied he was her father?"

"Did he?"

"I didn't give him a chance. He was slightly stunned when I told him my name. He never expected to hear from me. So I had an advantage to start with, and I pressed it. I told him Jill was fifteen, that she looked just like him, and that she wanted to see him. I told him we'd be flying out during April vacation."

"What'd he say?"

"He stammered a little. Then he said that he had a wife an

two little boys, and that Jill's showing up out of nowhere would upset them."

"The bastard," Gideon muttered.

"Uh-huh."

"So what'd you say?"

"I wanted to tell him that he was the scum of the earth and the last person I wanted my daughter to see, but Jill was sitting right there beside me, hanging on my every word. So I just repeated what I'd said, that she wanted to see him. I made it sound as if we were coming whether he liked it or not. I suggested that we would stay in a hotel and that he could visit with her there."

"Did he agree?"

"Reluctantly. He must have figured that he had no choice. We'd gotten his phone number. We could get his address. I doubt he wants us showing up at his house and surprising the wife and kids."

Gideon heard bitterness at the last. "Does it bother you— the idea that he has a family?"

"I kind of figured he did," Chris said. She didn't have to think long about her feelings on that score. "I'm not personally bothered in the least. I wouldn't want the creep if he was presented to me on a silver platter. What does bother me is that he's given legitimacy to two other children, while denying it to Jill."

"She's better off without him. You know that."

"I do." Chris sighed. "I just wish she did."

"She will. Give her time." His thoughts jumped ahead. "When will you go?"

"A week from Monday. We'll come back Wednesday. That leaves Tuesday to see Brant."

Gideon remembered the trips he'd made to see his mother, when he'd flown west, visited and flown home. Years later, he wished he'd taken greater advantage of the cross-country flight. "What about seeing the Southwest? I hear it's beautiful. Maybe you could kind of make it a treat for Jill. I mean, since you're going so far—"

"I thought of doing that, and one part of me would like to. The other part doesn't think it would be so good."

"Why not?"

"Two reasons." She really had thought it out. "First, I don't want her directly associating Brant with that part of the country. I'd rather she see it at a separate time."

"The second reason?"

"You," Chris said softly. "I'd rather not be away from here so long."

Gideon swore. "Damn it, Chris, how can you say something like that on the phone, when I can't hold you or kiss you or love you?" The mere thought of doing all that made his body tighten.

"You asked."

"Right." And since she was in an answering mode, he went for it all. "You do love me, don't you?"

She sighed. "Yes, Gideon, I do love you."

"Since when?"

"I don't know since when. I knew I was in trouble way back at the beginning when you bothered me so much. You kept zinging me with these little darts. I think they had some kind of potion on them."

"Will you marry me?"

"Uh-huh."

"When?"

"Someday."

"'Someday'? What's *that* supposed to mean?"

"I have to get this business with Jill straightened out first."

Gideon's mind started working fast. "Okay. This is April. The trip's comin' right up. Can we plan on a wedding in May?"

"We can't plan on *anything*. We'll have to take it day by day."

"But you will marry me?" He was so desperate for it he'd even wear a tux if she asked. "Marry me, Chris?"

"Yes." And she knew she would. With his enthusiasm, his sense of humor, adventure and compassion, his gentleness and s fire, he had become a vital part of her life. "I do love you," he said, knowing he wanted to hear the words again, knowing e deserved them.

"Ahh." He let out his breath and grinned. "You've just ade me a very happy man, Christine Gillette. Horny, but appy."

OTH THE FEELINGS persisted through the next day, which was aturday. The first was remedied that night, in the coziness of hris's bed, while Jill was at a movie with friends. The second st grew.

Sunday night, though, Chris phoned him in a state of re-rained panic. Her sentences were short and fast, her voice gher than usual. "Brant called a little while ago. Jill answered e phone. I was in the bath. You won't believe what he did, ideon! I still can't believe it myself! He is such a snake," e hissed, "such a snake!"

"Shh." His heart was pounding, but he said, "Take it slow, oney. Tell me."

"Instead of waiting until I could get to the phone, he talked irectly to her. He said that his parents want her to stay with em. Her. Not me. Just her. He said that I shouldn't even other coming out, that he would meet the plane himself and en deliver Jill to her grandparents." She nearly choked on e words. "Her grandparents. Well, at least he acknowledges at she's his, but to call those people her grandparents when ey haven't given any more of a damn than he has all these ears—"

"Chris, shh, Chris. Maybe they didn't know."

She was trembling, though whether from anger or fear she idn't know. "That's beside the point. They don't have any ght to her. *He* doesn't have any right to her. She's mine. He ould have made his plans through *me*." She caught in a livid reath. "Can you believe the *audacity* of the man to go over y head that way?"

"You'll tell him no."

"That's what I told Jill, and she got really upset. She said

that he sounded nice, that she was old enough to travel alon
and that that was what she'd been planning to do in the fir
place." Her voice dropped to a desperate whisper. Though sl
had her door shut, she didn't want to take the chance that Ji
might hear. "But how can I *let* her, Gideon? How can I let he
fly all that way alone, then face a man who—for all I know—
is strange or sadistic? It's been more than fifteen years sinc
I've seen him. We were kids ourselves. I have no idea wha
kind of person he's become."

"Did you know his parents?"

"I met them once or twice, but that was all." She coul
barely picture what they looked like. "What should I do, Gic
eon? This is my *baby*."

Gideon was silent for a bit. She wanted his opinion, but h
was still a fledgling, as parents went. Talk about trial by fire.

"Have you run this by your parents?"

"Not yet. I want to know what *you* think."

"I think," he said slowly, "that you need more informatio
before you can make any kind of judgment."

"Sure, I do," she returned facetiously. "I need a complet
dossier on the man, but there's no way I can get that withou
hiring an investigator, and I refuse to do that! I shouldn't hav
to pay the money, and we don't have the time."

"I have a friend in Phoenix," Gideon reminded her. "He'
a builder there. If he hasn't run across Conway himself, he'
bound to know people who have. Let me call him. He may b
able to tell us something about what kind of person he is."

"What kind of person is your friend?"

"A trustworthy one."

Chris wasn't about to look a gift horse in the mouth. Sh
agreed to let Gideon do it and was grateful for his offer. Lat
the next day, he called with the information his friend ha
provided.

"According to Paul, Brant Conway has made a good nam
for himself. He's successful in his field, has some dough, live
in a nice house in Scottsdale. He isn't exactly a fixture in hig

society but he's respected and liked. His parents live in Scottsdale, too. They all do well for themselves.''

Chris had mixed feelings about that. She was pleased for Jill,
not so pleased for herself. If the report had come back in any
way negative, she might have been able to cancel the trip. It
looked as though she didn't have any grounds for that.

''And your friend is reliable?'' she asked.

''Fraid so,'' Gideon answered.

She paused. ''Do you think I should let her go?''

''I think that if you don't, Jill may resent it. The fact is that
if she wants to go, she'll go anyway, whether it's now or later.
It would be awful if your refusal put a wedge between you. I
think you have to trust that you've raised her the right way,
and that she'll be able to take care of herself and know to call
if there's any problem.''

That was pretty much what Chris's parents had said when
she'd talked it over with them that morning. She had wanted
to argue then, just as she wanted to argue now, but she knew
that they were all right. Jill wasn't a small child. She would be
met at the airport and cared for by her grandparents, who possibly felt far more for her than Brant. Most importantly, Jill
had a sane head on her shoulders. If something went wrong,
she would know to get herself to the nearest phone.

HEART IN HER MOUTH, Chris saw Jill off for Phoenix on the
Monday of her school vacation. Brant had suggested that she
stay until Friday—another suggestion that Chris resented but
that she was helpless to deny.

She did deny Gideon the chance of going to the airport. ''My
folks want to drive us. Any more people and it'll be a major
production.'' But he was on the phone with her as soon as she
returned to the office, and when she got home that night, he
was waiting with his overnight bag in the bedroom.

Deliberately that first night, he didn't make love to her. Sex
wasn't the reason he'd come. He was there to be with her, to
hold her, to talk through her unease and help her pass the time
until she heard from Jill.

Jill called late Monday night to say that the flight was fine, that Brant's parents' house was pretty and that Brant had been nice. Chris would have been reassured if she felt that Jill had been making the call in private. She could tell from the conversation, though, that Jill wasn't alone.

"Do you think she's hiding something?" Chris asked Gideon fearfully the minute they'd hung up.

Gideon had no way of knowing that, but he felt he had a handle on Jill. "Your daughter is no wilting violet. If there's something she wanted to tell you but couldn't, she'll find another time to call."

"What if they won't let her?"

"She'll find a way." Taking her in his arms, he hugged her tightly. "Chris, don't expect the worst. You have no reason to believe that Brant's parents are anything but lovely people just discovering a very beautiful granddaughter. Jill sounded well. She's doing fine."

The call that came from Phoenix Tuesday night was like the first, sweet and correct. This one held news on the weather, which was warm, the desert, which was in bloom, and her grandparents' swimming pool, which was "radical."

"See?" Gideon said when they hung up the phone this time. "She's being treated very well." He said it as much for Chris's benefit as for his own. Living with Chris, being part of her daily life, anticipating what it would be like when they married, he was approaching things from a new angle. He missed Jill. In truth, though he kept telling himself there was no cause, he was worried, too. "If they took her on a Jeep tour of the desert, they're obviously making an effort to show her the sights."

"Brant's parents are," Chris conceded reluctantly. "She doesn't say much about Brant."

"Maybe that's just as well. If she's seen him, her curiosity is satisfied. If there's going to be any kind of continuing relationship, let it be with his parents."

Chris couldn't imagine going through the hell of that kind of visit several times a year, but she knew Gideon was right.

Grandparents were often kinder than parents. She supposed, if she was looking to the positive, she should be grateful they were there.

Clinging to that thought, she calmed herself some, enough so that she didn't fall apart when Jill called on Wednesday night sounding like she wanted to cry.

"What's wrong, baby?" she said softly. She could recognize throat-tight talk when she heard it, particularly in the daughter she knew so well.

After an agonizing minute, Jill said, "I miss you."

Tears came to Chris's eyes. "Oh, sweetheart, sweetheart, I miss you, too." She clutched Gideon's hand, wishing Jill had one as strong to hold. "Aren't you having a good time?"

Jill's voice fell to a murmur. "It's okay. But they're strangers. I don't think they knew I existed at all until he told them, after you called. They don't know what to do with me." Her murmur caught. "I wish you were here. You were right. We should have both come. We could have stayed at a hotel. Then it wouldn't have been so awkward."

Chris swallowed her tears. "Day after tomorrow you'll be home."

"I wish I was now."

"Hang in there, sweetheart. We'll be at the airport Friday to pick you up."

"Gideon, too?"

"Yeah. He misses you."

"Mom?"

"What?"

The murmur dropped to a whisper. "I'm glad you didn't marry Brant. Gideon's so much better."

"Oh, honey." Pressing her hands to her lips, Chris looked at Gideon through a pool of tears.

"What?" he whispered. He'd about had it with sitting still, trying to catch the gist of the conversation from Chris's short words and now her tears. Clearly Jill was upset. He wanted to snatch the phone away and talk to her himself, only he didn't know how appropriate it was. Chris might think he was butting in where he didn't belong, and though *he* knew he belonged there, he didn't know if Chris saw that yet.

In place of an answer, Chris transferred her fingers from her lips to his. To Jill, she said a soft, "Thanks, honey. Maybe you'll tell him that when you get home."

"I sure will," Jill said, sounding better.

"Are you okay, now?"

"I think so."

"If you want to call again, just call."

"I will."

"Don't forget."

"I won't."

"Bye-bye, sweetheart. I love you."

"I love you, too, Mom. Bye."

Chris hung up the phone, all the while looking at Gideon with eyes still moist with tears. "She's special."

"Damn it, I know that," Gideon said crossly. He was feeling shut out. "What's wrong out there?"

"She's lonesome. They're not what she's used to. She wished I'd gone with her."

Gideon stared at her for another minute before snatching up the phone. By the time he was done with his call, he was feeling defiant. "That's what I should have done in the first place," he told Chris.

Her mouth was agape and had been since the start of his call. "You made reservations to fly to Phoenix?"

"For two." His finger wagged between them. "You and me. I can't take this sitting around, worrying about her. We're leaving at dawn tomorrow, we'll be there by noon, so we'll have the rest of the day to pack her up and take her off and decide what we want to do for the rest of the week. I vote for the Grand Canyon. I've never been there. Jill will love it. And there are some great places to see along the way. Then we can fly home on Sunday."

Chris couldn't believe what he'd done. More than that, she couldn't believe the feeling she saw in his eyes. "But—but you have work," was all she could manage to say.

"I have Johnny, and even if I didn't, work'll wait. We're right on schedule, even a little ahead at the Rise, which is the one project I've been worried about. I could use a vacation."

"You took one in February."

"So did most of my men, so it didn't matter then, and we're only talking two days here. I deserve it." Scowling, he stuck his hands on his hips. "I should have suggested this when the plans were first made. It would have made things a whole lot more enjoyable for all of us. But I was afraid to say anything, because Jill's not my daughter, she's yours, and I'm not even your husband. But damn it, if we're gonna be a family, we're gonna be a family. That means good times and bad. It means we stick together. It means we share things." He held up a hand and arched a brow in warning. "Now, if that's not what you want, I think you'd better tell me right away, because if it isn't, I'm not the guy for you. If it is, let's get married—now. I have no intention of sitting at home by myself for the next three years until Jill goes off to college and you decide you're lonesome. Either you want me or you don't. Either you love me, or you don't. I've waited almost forty years for a woman as warm and giving and bright and sweet and sexy as you, and I can't wait any longer. I just can't." He took a deep breath. "So, what'll it be, Chris? Do we get married, or do we call the whole thing off?"

Chris eyed him askance. "You're giving me an ultimatum?"

"That's right," he said, returning his hand to his hip. "Not only that, but I want an answer now. And don't tell me that I'm rushing you or pressuring you, because you either feel it here—" he knocked a fist to his heart "—or you don't. If you love me, and you know I love you, we'll be able to handle anything that comes up with Jill." His face went beseeching. "Don't you see, it's the love that counts?"

At that moment, Chris would have had to be blind not to see, ignorant not to know, heartless not to feel. Gideon Lowe, master-builder, macho flirt, notorious bachelor, rabid Celtics fan, was also a man of sensitivity and insight. If she'd ever wanted a stepfather for Jill, she couldn't have asked for a better one. But Gideon was more, even than that. Far more. He was kind and caring and generous. Yes, he'd upset the applecart of her life, but in such a way that the apples would never taste as sweet without him. When she was with him, she felt the kind of wholeness she'd seen in her parents. If she'd ever wanted a lover, she couldn't have asked for a better one. And if she'd ever wanted a husband...

"Yes," she said softly, and went to him. "I see. I do see." She slipped her arms around his neck, leaning into him in such a way that their physical fit was as perfect as everything else. "The love's there. Let's do it."

Gideon's eyes lit up in the endearingly naughty way that she loved. "*Do* it?"

She grinned, feeling, with the commitment, suddenly happier and more light-headed than she ever had before. "Get married." She paused. Her grin tilted. "And the other, too."

He didn't need to hear any more. Scooping her up in his arms, he made for the stairs.

"Put me down, Gideon Lowe," she cried, laughing. "Put me down. I can walk. This is embarrassing."

He didn't miss a step. "Embarrassing? It's supposed to be romantic."

"It's totally tough and macho."

He did stop then, just shy of the top step, and met her gaze. "The irony of that is really too much."

"What irony?"

"Crosslyn Rise. I went into the project to shake the image."

"What image?"

"Brawn versus brain. And here I am, carting you off to bed like the best of my big-rig buddies." His grin grew wicked. "Know something?" When she shook her head, he said, "This is the *smartest* damn thing I've ever done in my life." Still grinning, he took the last step.

WHISTLEBLOWER

Tess Gerritsen

To Fien and Frans

PROLOGUE

BRANCHES WHIPPED HIS FACE, and his heart was pounding so hard he thought his chest would explode, but he couldn't stop running. Already, he could hear the man gaining on him, could almost imagine the bullet slicing through the night and slamming into his back. Maybe it already had. Maybe he was trailing a river of blood; he was too numb with terror to feel anything now, except the desperate hunger to live. The rain was pouring down his face, icy, blinding sheets of it, rattling on the dead leaves of winter. He stumbled through a pool of darkness and found himself sprawled flat on his belly in the mud. The sound of his fall was deafening. His pursuer, alerted by the sharp crack of branches, altered course and was now headed straight for him. The thud of a silencer, the zing of a bullet past his cheek, told him he'd been spotted. He forced himself to his feet and made a sharp right, zigzagging back toward the highway. Here in the woods, he was a dead man. But if he could flag down a car, if he could draw someone's attention, he might have a chance.

A crash of branches, a coarse oath, told him his pursuer had stumbled. He'd gained a few precious seconds. He kept running, moving only by an instinctive sense of direction. There was no light to guide his way, nothing except the dim glow of the clouds in the night sky. The road had to be just ahead. Any second now, his feet would hit pavement.

And then what? What if there's no car to flag down, no one to help me?

Then, through the trees ahead, he saw a faint flickering, two watery beams of light.

With a desperate burst of speed, he sprinted toward the car. His lungs were on fire, his eyes blinded by the lash of branches and rain. Another bullet whipped past him and thudded into a tree trunk, but the gunman behind him had suddenly lost all importance. All that mattered was those lights, beckoning him through the darkness, taunting him with the promise of salvation.

When his feet suddenly hit the pavement, he was shocked. The lights were still ahead, bobbing somewhere beyond the trees. Had he missed the car? Was it already moving away, around a curve? No, there it was, brighter now. It was coming this way. He ran to meet it, following the bend of the road and knowing all the time that here in the open, he was an easy target. The sound of his shoes slapping the wet road filled his ears. The lights twisted toward him. At that instant, he heard the gun fire a third time. The force of the impact made him stumble to his knees, and he was vaguely aware of the bullet tearing through his shoulder, of the warmth of his own blood dribbling down his arm, but he was oblivious to pain. He could focus only on staying alive. He struggled back to his feet, took a stumbling step forward…

And was blinded by the onrush of headlights. There was no time to throw himself out of the way, no time even to register panic. Tires screamed across the pavement, throwing up a spray of water.

He didn't feel the impact. All he knew was that he was suddenly lying on the ground and the rain was pouring into his mouth and he was very, very cold.

And that he had something to do, something important.

Feebly, he reached into the pocket of his windbreaker, and his fingers curled around the small plastic cylinder. He couldn't quite remember why it mattered so much, but it was still there and he was relieved. He clutched it tightly in his palm.

Someone was calling to him. A woman. He couldn't see her face through the rain, but he could hear her voice, hoarse with panic, floating through the buzz in his head. He tried to speak, tried to warn her that they had to get away, that death was waiting in the woods. But all that came out was a groan.

CHAPTER ONE

THREE MILES OUT of Redwood Valley, a tree had fallen across the road, and with the heavy rains and backed-up cars, it took Catherine Weaver nearly three hours to get past the town of Willits. By then it was already ten o'clock and she knew she wouldn't reach Garberville till midnight. She hoped Sarah wouldn't sit up all night waiting for her. But knowing Sarah, there'd be a supper still warm in the oven and a fire blazing in the hearth. She wondered how pregnancy suited her friend. Wonderfully, of course. Sarah had talked about this baby for years, had chosen its name—Sam or Emma—long before it was conceived. The fact she no longer had a husband was a minor point. "You can only wait around so long for the right father," Sarah had said. "Then you have to take matters into your own hands."

And she had. With her biological clock furiously ticking its last years away, Sarah had driven down to visit Cathy in San Francisco and had calmly selected a fertility clinic from the yellow pages. A liberal-minded one, of course. One that would understand the desperate longings of a thirty-nine-year-old single woman. The insemination itself had been a coolly clinical affair, she'd said later. Hop on the table, slip your feet into the stirrups, and five minutes later, you were pregnant. Well, almost. But it was a simple procedure, the donors were certifiably healthy, and best of all, a woman could fulfill her maternal instincts without all that foolishness about marriage.

Yes, the old marriage game. They'd both suffered through it. And after their divorces, they'd both carried on, albeit with battle scars.

Brave Sarah, thought Cathy. *At least she has the courage to go through with this on her own.*

The old anger washed through her, still potent enough to

make her mouth tighten. She could forgive her ex-husband Jack for a lot of things. For his selfishness. His demands. His infidelity. But she could never forgive him for denying her the chance to have a child. Oh, she could have gone against his wishes and had a baby anyway, but she'd wanted him to want one as well. So she'd waited for the time to be right. But during their ten years of marriage, he'd never been ''ready,'' never felt it was the ''right time.''

What he should have told her was the truth: that he was too self-centered to be bothered with a baby.

I'm thirty-seven years old, she thought. *I no longer have a husband. I don't even have a steady boyfriend. But I could be content, if only I could hold my own child in my arms.*

At least Sarah would soon be blessed.

Four months to go and then the baby was due. Sarah's baby. Cathy had to smile at that thought, despite the rain now pouring over her windshield. It was coming down harder now; even with the wipers thrashing at full speed, she could barely make out the road. She glanced at her watch and saw it was already eleven-thirty; there were no other cars in sight. If she had engine trouble out here, she'd probably have to spend the night huddled in the backseat, waiting for help to arrive.

Peering ahead, she tried to make out the road's dividing line and saw nothing but a solid wall of rain. This was ridiculous. She really should have stopped at that motel in Willits, but she hated the thought of being only fifty miles from her goal, especially when she'd already driven so far.

She spotted a sign ahead: Garberville, 10 Miles. So she was closer than she'd thought. Twenty-five miles more, then there'd be a turnoff and a five-mile drive through dense woods to Sarah's cedar house. The thought of being so close fueled her impatience. She fed the old Datsun some gas and sped up to forty-five miles an hour. It was a reckless thing to do, especially in these conditions, but the thought of a warm house and hot chocolate was just too tempting.

The road curved unexpectedly; startled, she jerked the wheel to the right and the car slid sideways, tobogganing wildly across the rain-slicked pavement. She knew enough not to slam on the brakes. Instead, she clutched the wheel, fighting to regain control. The tires skidded a few feet, a heart-stopping ride that took her to the very edge of the road. Just as she thought she'd clip the trees, the tires gripped the pavement. The car was still moving twenty miles an hour, but at least it was headed in a straight line. With clammy hands, she managed to negotiate the rest of the curve.

What happened next caught her completely by surprise. One instant she was congratulating herself for averting disaster, the next, she was staring ahead in disbelief.

The man had appeared out of nowhere. He was crouched in the road, captured like a wild animal in the glare of her headlights. Reflexes took over. She slammed on the brakes, but it was already too late. The screech of her tires was punctuated by the thud of the man's body against the hood of her car.

For what seemed like eternity, she sat frozen and unable to do anything but clutch the steering wheel and stare at the windshield wipers skating back and forth. Then, as the reality of what she'd just done sank in, she shoved the door open and dashed out into the rain.

At first she could see nothing through the downpour, only a glistening strip of blacktop lit by the dim glow of her taillights. *Where is he?* she thought frantically. With water streaming past her eyes, she traced the road backward, struggling to see in the darkness. Then, through the pounding rain, she heard a low moan. It came from somewhere off to the side, near the trees.

Shifting direction, she plunged into the shadows and sank ankle-deep in mud and pine needles. Again she heard the moan, closer now, almost within reach.

"Where are you?" she screamed. "Help me find you!"

"Here…" The answer was so weak she barely heard it, but it was all she needed. Turning, she took a few steps and practically stumbled over his crumpled body in the darkness. At first, he seemed to be only a confusing jumble of soaked clothes, then she managed to locate his hand and feel for his pulse. It was fast but steady, probably steadier than her own pulse, which was skipping wildly. His fingers suddenly closed over hers in a desperate grip. He rolled against her and struggled to sit up.

"Please! Don't move!" she said.

"Can't—can't stay here—"

"Where are you hurt?"

"No time. Help me. Hurry—"

"Not till you tell me where you're hurt!"

He reached out and grabbed her shoulder in a clumsy attempt to rise to his feet. To her amazement, he managed to pull himself halfway up. For an instant they wobbled against each other, then his strength seemed to collapse and they both slid to their knees in the mud. His breathing had turned harsh and irregular and she wondered about his injuries. If he was bleeding internally he could die within minutes. She had to get him to a hospital now, even if it meant dragging him back to the car.

"Okay. Let's try again," she said, grabbing his left arm and draping it around her neck. She was startled by his gasp of agony. Immediately she released him. His arm left a sticky trail of warmth around her neck. *Blood.*

"My other side's okay," he grunted. "Try again."

She shifted to his right side and pulled his arm over her neck. If she weren't so frantic, it would have struck her as a comical scene, the two of them struggling like drunkards to stand up. When at last he was on his feet and they stood swaying together in the mud, she wondered if he even had the strength to put one foot in front of the other. She certainly couldn't move them both. Though he was slender, he was also a great deal taller than she'd expected, and much more than her five-foot-five frame could support.

But something seemed to compel him forward, a kindling of some hidden reserves. Even through their soaked clothes, she could feel the heat of his body and could sense the urgency driving him onward. A dozen questions formed in her head, but she was breathing too hard to voice them. Her every effort had to be concentrated on getting him to the car, and then to a hospital.

Gripping him around the waist, she latched her fingers through his belt. Painfully they made their way to the road, struggling step by step. His arm felt taut as wire over her neck. It seemed everything about him was wound up tight. There was something desperate about the way his muscles strained to move forward. His urgency penetrated right through to her skin. It was a panic as palpable as the warmth of his body, and she was suddenly infected with his need to flee, a need made more desperate by the fact they could move no faster than they already were. Every few feet she had to stop and shove back her dripping hair just to see where she was going. And all around them, the rain and darkness closed off all view of whatever danger pursued.

The taillights of her car glowed ahead like ruby eyes winking in the night. With every step the man grew heavier and her legs felt so rubbery she thought they'd both topple in the road. If they did, she wouldn't have the strength to haul him back up again. Already, his head was sagging against her cheek and water trickled from his rain-matted hair down her neck. The simple act of putting one foot in front of the other was so automatic that she never even considered dropping him on the road and backing the car to him instead. And the taillights were already so close, just beyond the next veil of rain.

By the time she'd guided him to the passenger side, her arm felt ready to fall off. With the man on the verge of sliding from her grasp, she barely managed to wrench the door open. She had no strength left to be gentle; she simply shoved him inside.

He flopped onto the front seat with his legs still hanging out. She bent down, grabbed his ankles, and heaved them one by one into the car, noting with a sense of detachment that no man with feet this big could possibly be graceful.

As she slid into the driver's seat, he made a feeble attempt to raise his head, then let it sink back again. "Hurry," he whispered.

At the first turn of the key in the ignition, the engine sputtered and died. Dear God, she pleaded. Start. *Start!* She switched the key off, counted slowly to three, and tried again. This time the engine caught. Almost shouting with relief, she jammed it into gear and made a tire-screeching takeoff toward Garberville. Even a town that small must have a hospital or, at the very least, an emergency clinic. The question was: could she find it in this downpour? And what if she was wrong? What if the nearest medical help was in Willits, the other direction? She might be wasting precious minutes on the road while the man bled to death.

Suddenly panicked by that thought, she glanced at her passenger. By the glow of the dashboard, she saw that his head was still flopped back against the seat. He wasn't moving.

"Hey! Are you all right?" she cried.

The answer came back in a whisper. "I'm still here."

"Dear God. For a minute I thought…" She looked back at the road, her heart pounding. "There's got to be a clinic somewhere—"

"Near Garberville—there's a hospital—"

"Do you know how to find it?"

"I drove past it—fifteen miles…"

If he drove here, where's his car? she thought. "What happened?" she asked. "Did you have an accident?"

He started to speak but his answer was cut off by a sudden flicker of light. Struggling to sit up, he turned and stared at the headlights of another car far behind them. His whispered oath made her look sideways in alarm.

"What is it?"

"That car."

She glanced in the rearview mirror. "What about it?"

"How long's it been following us?"

"I don't know. A few miles. Why?"

The effort of keeping his head up suddenly seemed too much for him, and he let it sink back down with a groan. "Can't think," he whispered. "Christ, I can't think…"

He's lost too much blood, she thought. In a panic, she shoved hard on the gas pedal. The car seemed to leap through the rain the steering wheel vibrating wildly as sheets of spray flew up from the tires. Darkness flew at dizzying speed against their windshield. *Slow down, slow down! Or I'll get us both killed.*

Easing back on the gas, she let the speedometer fall to a more manageable forty-five miles per hour. The man was struggling to sit up again.

"Please, keep your head down!" she pleaded.

"That car—"

"It's not there anymore."

"Are you sure?"

She looked at the rearview mirror. Through the rain, she saw only a faint twinkling of light, but nothing as definite as headlights. "I'm sure," she lied and was relieved to see him slowly settle back again. *How much farther?* she thought. *Five miles? Ten?* And then the next thought forced its way into her mind: *He might die before we get there.*

His silence terrified her. She needed to hear his voice, needed to be reassured that he hadn't slipped into oblivion. "Talk to me," she urged. "Please."

"I'm tired...."

"Don't stop. Keep talking. What—what's your name?"

The answer was a mere whisper: "Victor."

"Victor. That's a great name. I like that name. What do you do, Victor?"

His silence told her he was too weak to carry on any conversation. She couldn't let him lose consciousness! For some reason it suddenly seemed crucial to keep him awake, to keep him in touch with a living voice. If that fragile connection was broken, she feared he might slip away entirely.

"All right," she said, forcing her voice to remain low and steady. "Then *I'll* talk. You don't have to say a thing. Just listen. Keep listening. My name is Catherine. Cathy Weaver. I live in San Francisco, the Richmond district. Do you know the city?" There was no answer, but she sensed some movement in his head, a silent acknowledgement of her words. "Okay," she went on, mindlessly filling the silence. "Maybe you don't know the city. It really doesn't matter. I work with an independent film company. Actually, it's Jack's company. My ex-husband. We make horror films. Grade B, really, but they turn a profit. Our last one was *Reptilian.* I did the special-effects makeup. Really gruesome stuff. Lots of green scales and slime..." She laughed—it was a strange, panicked sound. It had an unmistakable note of hysteria.

She had to fight to regain control.

A wink of light made her glance up sharply at the rearview mirror. A pair of headlights was barely discernible through the rain. For a few seconds she watched them, debating whether to say anything to Victor. Then, like phantoms, the lights flickered off and vanished.

"Victor?" she called softly. He responded with an unintelligible grunt, but it was all she needed to be reassured that he was still alive. That he was listening. *I've got to keep him awake,* she thought, her mind scrambling for some new topic of conversation. She'd never been good at the glib sort of chitchat so highly valued at filmmakers' cocktail parties. What she needed was a joke, however stupid, as long as it was vaguely funny. *Laughter heals.* Hadn't she read it somewhere? That a steady barrage of comedy could shrink tumors? *Oh sure,* she chided herself. *Just make him laugh and the bleeding will miraculously stop....*

But she couldn't think of a joke, anyway, not a single damn one. So she returned to the topic that had first come to mind: her work.

"Our next project's slated for January. *Ghouls.* We'll be filming in Mexico, which I hate, because the damn heat always melts the makeup...."

She looked at Victor but saw no response, not even a flicker of movement. Terrified that she was losing him, she reached out to feel for his pulse and discovered that his hand was buried deep in the pocket of his windbreaker. She tried to tug it free, and to her amazement he reacted to her invasion with immediate and savage resistance. Lurching awake, he blindly lashed at her, trying to force her away.

"Victor, it's all right!" she cried, fighting to steer the car and protect herself at the same time. "It's all right! It's me, Cathy. I'm only trying to help!"

At the sound of her voice, his struggles weakened. As the tension eased from his body, she felt his head settle slowly against her shoulder. "Cathy," he whispered. It was a sound of wonder, of relief. "Cathy..."

"That's right. It's only me." Gently, she reached up and brushed back the tendrils of his wet hair. She wondered what color it was, a concern that struck her as totally irrelevant but nonetheless compelling. He reached for her hand. His fingers closed around hers in a grip that was surprisingly strong and steadying. *I'm still here,* it said. *I'm warm and alive and breathing.* He pressed her palm to his lips. So tender was the gesture, she was startled by the roughness of his unshaven jaw against her skin. It was a caress between strangers, and it left her shaken and trembling.

She returned her grip to the steering wheel and shifted her full attention back to the road. He had fallen silent again, but she couldn't ignore the weight of his head on her shoulder or the heat of his breath in her hair.

The torrent eased to a slow but steady rain, and she coaxed the car to fifty. The Sunnyside Up cafe whipped past, a drab little box beneath a single streetlight, and she caught a glimpse of Victor's face in the brief glow of light. She saw him only in profile: a high forehead, sharp nose, a jutting chin, and then the light was gone and he was only a shadow breathing softly against her. But she'd seen enough to know she'd never forget that face. Even as she peered through the darkness, his profile floated before her like an image burned into her memory.

"We have to be getting close," she said, as much to reassure herself as him. "Where a cafe appears, a town is sure to follow." There was no response. "Victor?" Still no response. Swallowing her panic, she sped up to fifty-five.

Though they'd passed the Sunnyside Up over a mile ago, she could still make out the streetlight winking on and off in her mirror. It took her a few seconds to realize it wasn't just one light she was watching but two, and that they were moving—a pair of headlights, winding along the highway. Was it the same car she'd spotted earlier?

Mesmerized, she watched the lights dance like twin wraiths among the trees, then, suddenly, they vanished and she saw only darkness. A ghost? she wondered irrationally. Any instant she expected the lights to rematerialize, to resume their phantom twinkling in the woods. She was watching the mirror so intently that she almost missed the road sign:

Garberville, Pop, 5,750
Gas—Food—Lodging

A half mile later streetlights appeared, glowing a hazy yellow in the drizzle; a flatbed truck splashed by, headed in the other direction. Though the speed limit had dropped to thirty-five, she kept her foot firmly on the gas pedal and for once in her life prayed for a police car to give chase.

The *Hospital* road sign seemed to leap out at her from nowhere. She braked and swerved onto the turnoff. A quarter mile away, a red *Emergency* sign directed her up a driveway to a side entrance. Leaving Victor in the front seat, she ran inside, through a deserted waiting room, and cried to a nurse sitting at her desk: "Please, help me! I've got a man in my car...."

The nurse responded instantly. She followed Cathy outside, took one look at the man slumped in the front seat, and yelled for assistance.

Even with the help of a burly ER physician, they had difficulty pulling Victor out of the car. He had slid sideways, and his arm was wedged under the emergency hand brake.

"Hey, Miss!" the doctor barked at Cathy. "Climb in the other side and free up his arm!"

Cathy scrambled to the driver's seat. There she hesitated. She would have to manipulate his injured arm. She took his elbow and tried to unhook it from around the brake, but discovered his wristwatch was snagged in the pocket of his windbreaker. After unsnapping the watchband, she took hold of his arm and lifted it over the brake. He responded with a groan of pure agony. The arm slid limply toward the floor.

"Okay!" said the doctor. "Arm's free! Now, just ease him toward me and we'll take it from there."

Gingerly, she guided Victor's head and shoulders safely past the emergency brake. Then she scrambled back outside to help load him onto the wheeled stretcher. Three straps were buckled into place. Everything became a blur of noise and motion as the stretcher was wheeled through the open double doors into the building.

"What happened?" the doctor barked over his shoulder at Cathy.

"I hit him—on the road—"

"When?"

"Fifteen—twenty minutes ago."

"How fast were you driving?"

"About thirty-five."

"Was he conscious when you found him?"

"For about ten minutes—then he sort of faded—"

A nurse said: "Shirt's soaked with blood. He's got broken glass in his shoulder."

In that mad dash beneath harsh fluorescent lights, Cathy had her first clear look at Victor, and she saw a lean, mud-streaked face, a jaw tightly squared in pain, a broad forehead matted damply with light brown hair. He reached out to her, grasping for her hand.

"Cathy—"

"I'm here, Victor."

He held on tightly, refusing to break contact. The pressure of his fingers in her flesh was almost painful. Squinting through the pain, he focused on her face. "I have to—have to tell you—"

"Later!" snapped the doctor.

"No, wait!" Victor was fighting to keep her in view, to hold her beside him. He struggled to speak, agony etching lines on his face.

Cathy bent close, drawn by the desperation of his gaze. "Yes, Victor," she whispered, stroking his hair, longing to ease his pain. This link between their hands, their gazes, felt forged in timeless steel. "Tell me."

"We can't delay!" barked the doctor. "Get him in the room."

All at once, Victor's hand was wrenched away from her as they whisked him into the trauma suite, a nightmarish room of stainless steel and blindingly bright lights. He was lifted onto the surgical table.

"Pulse 110," said a nurse. "Blood pressure eight-five over fifty!"

The doctor ordered, "Let's get two IVs in. Type and cross six units of blood. And get hold of a surgeon. We're going to need help...."

The machine-gun fire of voices, the metallic clang of cabinets and IV poles and instruments was deafening. No one seemed to notice Cathy standing in the doorway, watching in horrified fascination as a nurse pulled out a knife and began to tear off Victor's bloody clothing. With each rip, more and more flesh was exposed, until the shirt and windbreaker were shredded off, revealing a broad chest thickly matted with tawny hair. To the doctors and nurses, this was just another body to labor over, another patient to be saved. To Cathy, this was a living, breathing man, a man she cared about, if only because they had shared those last harrowing moments. The nurse shifted her attention to his belt, which she quickly unbuckled. With a few firm tugs, she peeled off his trousers and shorts and threw them into a pile with the other soiled clothing. Cathy scarcely noticed the man's nakedness, or the nurses and technicians shoving past her into the room. Her shocked gaze had focused on Victor's left shoulder, which was oozing fresh blood onto the table. She remembered how his whole body had resonated with pain when she'd grabbed that shoulder; only now did she understand how much he must have suffered.

A sour taste flooded her throat. She was going to be sick.

Struggling against the nausea, she somehow managed to stumble away and sink into a nearby chair. There she sat for a few minutes, oblivious to the chaos whirling around her. Looking down, she noted with instinctive horror the blood on her hands.

"There you are," someone said. A nurse had just emerged from the trauma room, carrying a bundle of the patient's belongings. She motioned Cathy over to a desk. "We'll need your name and address in case the doctors have any more questions. And the police will have to be notified. Have you called them?"

Cathy shook her head numbly. "I—I guess I should..."

"You can use this phone."

"Thank you."

It rang eight times before anyone answered. The voice that greeted her was raspy with sleep. Obviously, Garberville provided little late-night stimulation, even for the local police. The desk officer took down Cathy's report and told her he'd be in touch with her later, after they'd checked the accident scene.

The nurse had opened Victor's wallet and was flipping through the various ID cards for information. Cathy watched her fill in the blanks on a patient admission form: *Name: Victor Holland. Age: 41. Occupation: Biochemist. Next of kin: Unknown.*

So that was his full name. Victor Holland. Cathy stared down at the stack of ID cards and focused on what appeared to be a security pass for some company called Viratek. A color photograph showed Victor's quietly sober face, its green eyes gazing straight into the camera. Even if she had never seen his face, this was exactly how she would have pictured him, his expression unyielding, his gaze unflinchingly direct. She touched her palm, where he had kissed her. She could still recall how his beard had stung her flesh.

Softly, she asked, "Is he going to be all right?"

The nurse continued writing. "He's lost a lot of blood. But he looks like a pretty tough guy...."

Cathy nodded, remembering how, even in his agony, Victor had somehow dredged up the strength to keep moving through the rain. Yes, she knew just how tough a man he was.

The nurse handed her a pen and the information sheet. "If you could write your name and address at the bottom. In case the doctor has any more questions."

Cathy fished out Sarah's address and phone number from her purse and copied them onto the form. "My name's Cathy Weaver. You can get hold of me at this number."

"You're staying in Garberville?"

"For three weeks. I'm just visiting."

"Oh. Terrific way to start a vacation, huh?"

Cathy sighed as she rose to leave. "Yeah. Terrific."

She paused outside the trauma room, wondering what was happening inside, knowing that Victor was fighting for his life.

She wondered if he was still conscious, if he would remember her. It seemed important that he *did* remember her.

Cathy turned to the nurse. "You will call me, won't you? I mean, you'll let me know if he..."

The nurse nodded. "We'll keep you informed."

Outside, the rain had finally stopped and a belt of stars twinkled through a parting in the clouds. To Cathy's weary eyes, it was an exhilarating sight, that first glimpse of the storm's end. As she drove out of the hospital parking lot, she was shaking from fatigue. She never noticed the car parked across the street or the brief glow of the cigarette before it was snuffed out.

CHAPTER TWO

BARELY A MINUTE after Cathy left the hospital, a man walked into the emergency room, sweeping the smells of a stormy night in with him through the double doors. The nurse on duty was busy with the new patient's admission papers. At the sudden rush of cold air, she looked up to see a man approach her desk. He was about thirty-five, gaunt-faced, silent, his dark hair lightly feathered by gray. Droplets of water sparkled on his tan Burberry raincoat.

"Can I help you, sir?" she asked, focusing on his eyes, which were as black and polished as pebbles in a pond.

Nodding, he said quietly, "Was there a man brought in a short time ago? Victor Holland?"

The nurse glanced down at the papers on her desk. That was the name. Victor Holland. "Yes," she said. "Are you a relative?"

"I'm his brother. How is he?"

"He just arrived, sir. They're working on him now. If you'll wait, I can check on how he's doing—" She stopped to answer the ringing telephone. It was a technician calling with the new patient's laboratory results. As she jotted down the numbers, she noticed out of the corner of her eye that the man had turned and was gazing at the closed door to the trauma room. It suddenly swung open as an orderly emerged carrying a bulging plastic bag streaked with blood. The clamor of voices spilled from the room:

"Pressure up to 110 over 70!"

"OR says they're ready to go."

"Where's that surgeon?"

"On his way. He had car trouble."

"Ready for X rays! Everyone back!"

Slowly the door closed, muffling the voices. The nurse hung

up just as the orderly deposited the plastic bag on her desk. "What's this?" she asked.

"Patient's clothes. They're a mess. Should I just toss 'em?"

"I'll take them home," the man in the raincoat cut in. "Is everything here?"

The orderly flashed the nurse an uncomfortable glance. "I'm not sure he'd want to...I mean, they're kind of...uh, dirty...."

The nurse said quickly, "Mr. Holland, why don't you let us dispose of the clothes for you? There's nothing worth keeping in there. I've already collected his valuables." She unlocked a drawer and pulled out a sealed manila envelope labeled: Holland, Victor. Contents: Wallet, Wristwatch. "You can take these home. Just sign this receipt."

The man nodded and signed his name: David Holland. "Tell me," he said, sliding the envelope in his pocket. "Is Victor awake? Has he said anything?"

"I'm afraid not. He was semiconscious when he arrived."

The man took this information in silence, a silence that the nurse found suddenly and profoundly disturbing. "Excuse me, Mr. Holland?" she asked. "How did you hear your brother was hurt? I didn't get a chance to contact any relatives...."

"The police called me. Victor was driving my car. They found it smashed up at the side of the road."

"Oh. What an awful way to be notified."

"Yes. The stuff of nightmares."

"At least someone was able to get in touch with you." She sifted through the sheaf of papers on her desk. "Can we get your address and phone number? In case we need to reach you?"

"Of course." The man took the ER papers, which he quickly scanned before scrawling his name and phone number on the blank marked Next of Kin. "Who's this Catherine Weaver?" he asked, pointing to the name and address at the bottom of the page.

"She's the woman who brought him in."

"I'll have to thank her." He handed back the papers.

"Nurse?"

She looked around and saw that the doctor was calling to her from the trauma room doorway. "Yes?"

"I want you to call the police. Tell them to get in here as soon as possible."

"They've been called, Doctor. They know about the accident—"

"Call them again. This is no accident."

"What?"

"We just got the X rays. The man's got a bullet in his shoulder."

"A *bullet?*" A chill went through the nurse's body, like a cold wind sweeping in from the night. Slowly, she turned toward the man in the raincoat, the man who'd claimed to be Victor Holland's brother. To her amazement, no one was there. She felt only a cold puff of night air, and then she saw the double doors quietly slide shut.

"Where the hell did he go?" the orderly whispered.

For a few seconds she could only stare at the closed doors. Then her gaze dropped and she focused on the empty spot on her desk. The bag containing Victor Holland's clothes had vanished.

"WHY DID THE POLICE call again?"

Cathy slowly replaced the telephone receiver. Even though she was bundled in a warm terry-cloth robe, she was shivering. She turned and stared across the kitchen at Sarah. "That man on the road—they found a bullet in his shoulder."

In the midst of pouring tea, Sarah glanced up in surprise. "You mean—someone *shot* him?"

Cathy sank down at the kitchen table and gazed numbly at the cup of cinnamon tea that Sarah had just slid in front of her. A hot bath and a soothing hour of sitting by the fireplace had made the night's events seem like nothing more than a bad dream. Here in Sarah's kitchen, with its chintz curtains and its cinnamon and spice smells, the violence of the real world seemed a million miles away.

Sarah leaned toward her. "Do they know what happened? Has he said anything?"

"He just got out of surgery." She turned and glanced at the telephone. "I should call the hospital again—"

"No. You shouldn't. You've done everything you possibly can." Sarah gently touched her arm. "And your tea's getting cold."

With a shaking hand, Cathy brushed back a strand of damp hair and settled uneasily in her chair. A bullet in his shoulder, she thought. Why? Had it been a random attack, a highway gunslinger blasting out the car window at a total stranger? She'd read about it in the newspapers, the stories of freeway arguments settled by the pulling of a trigger.

Or had it been a deliberate attack? Had Victor Holland been targeted for death?

Outside, something rattled and clanged against the house. Cathy sat up sharply. "What was that?"

"Believe me, it's not the bogeyman," said Sarah, laughing. She went to the kitchen door and reached for the bolt.

"Sarah!" Cathy called in panic as the bold slid open. "Wait!"

"Take a look for yourself." Sarah opened the door. The kitchen light swung across a cluster of trash cans sitting in the carport. A shadow slid to the ground and scurried away, trailing food wrappers across the driveway. "Raccoons," said Sarah. "If I don't tie the lids down, those pests'll scatter trash all over the yard." Another shadow popped its head out of a can and stared at her, its eyes glowing in the darkness. Sarah clapped her hands and yelled, "Go on, get lost!" The raccoon didn't budge. "Don't you have a home to go to?" At last, the raccoon dropped to the ground and ambled off into the trees. "They get bolder every year," Sarah sighed, closing the door. She turned and winked at Cathy. "So take it easy. This isn't the big city."

"Keep reminding me." Cathy took a slice of banana bread and began to spread it with sweet butter. "You know, Sarah, I think it'll be a lot nicer spending Christmas with you than it ever was with old Jack."

"Uh-oh. Since we're now speaking of ex-husbands—" Sarah shuffled over to a cabinet "—we might as well get in the right frame of mind. And tea just won't cut it.'' She grinned and waved a bottle of brandy.

"Sarah, you're not drinking alcohol, are you?''

"It's not for *me*.'' Sarah set the bottle and a single wine glass in front of Cathy. "But I think *you* could use a nip. After all, it's been a cold, traumatic night. And here we are, talking about turkeys of the male variety.''

"Well, since you put it that way...'' Cathy poured out a generous shot of brandy. "To the turkeys of the world,'' she declared and took a sip. It felt just right going down.

"So how *is* old Jack?'' asked Sarah.

"Same as always.''

"Blondes?''

"He's moved on to brunettes.''

"It took him only a year to go through the world's supply of blondes?''

Cathy shrugged. "He might have missed a few.''

They both laughed then, light and easy laughter that told them their wounds were well on the way to healing, that men were now creatures to be discussed without pain, without sorrow.

Cathy regarded her glass of brandy. "Do you suppose there *are* any good men left in the world? I mean, shouldn't there be *one* floating around somewhere? Maybe a mutation or something? One measly decent guy?''

"Sure. Somewhere in Siberia. But he's a hundred-and-twenty years old.''

"I've always liked older men.''

They laughed again, but this time the sound wasn't as light-hearted. So many years had passed since their college days together, the days when they had *known,* had never doubted, that Prince Charmings abounded in the world.

Cathy drained her glass of brandy and set it down. "What a lousy friend I am. Keeping a pregnant lady up all night! What time is it, anyway?''

"Only two-thirty in the morning.''

"Oh, Sarah! Go to bed!'' Cathy went to the sink and began wetting a handful of paper towels.

"And what are you going to do?" Sarah asked.

"I just want to clean up the car. I didn't get all the blood off the seat."

"I already did it."

"What? When?"

"While you were taking a bath."

"Sarah, you idiot."

"Hey, I didn't have a miscarriage or anything. Oh, I almost forgot." Sarah pointed to a tiny film canister on the counter. "I found that on the floor of your car."

Cathy shook her head and sighed. "It's Hickey's."

"Hickey! Now *there's* a waste of a man."

'He's also a good friend of mine."

"That's all Hickey will ever be to a woman. A *friend*. So what's on the roll of film? Naked women, as usual?"

"I don't even want to know. When I dropped him off at the airport, he handed me a half-dozen rolls and told me he'd pick them up when he got back. Guess he didn't want to lug 'em all the way to Nairobi."

"Is that where he went? Nairobi?"

"He's shooting 'gorgeous ladies of Africa' or something." Cathy slipped the film canister into her bathrobe pocket. "This must've dropped out of the glove compartment. Gee. I hope it's not pornographic."

"Knowing Hickey, it probably is."

They both laughed at the irony of it all. Hickman Von Trapp, whose only job it was to photograph naked females in erotic poses, had absolutely no interest in the opposite sex, with the possible exception of his mother.

"A guy like Hickey only goes to prove my point," Sarah said over her shoulder as she headed up the hall to bed.

"What point is that?"

"There really *are* no good men left in the world!"

IT WAS THE LIGHT that dragged Victor up from the depths of unconsciousness, a light brighter than a dozen suns, beating against his closed eyelids. He didn't want to wake up; he knew, in some dim, scarcely functioning part of his brain, that if he continued to struggle against this blessed oblivion he would feel pain and nausea and something else, something much, much worse: terror. Of what, he couldn't remember. Of death? No, no, this was death, or as close as one could come to it, and it was warm and black and comfortable. But he had something important to do, something that he couldn't allow himself to forget. He tried to think, but all he could remember was a hand, gentle but somehow strong, brushing his forehead, and a voice, reaching to him softly in the darkness.

My name is Catherine....

As her touch, her voice, flooded his memory, so too did the fear. Not for himself (he was dead, wasn't he?) but for her. Strong, gentle Catherine. He'd seen her face only briefly, could scarcely remember it, but somehow he knew she was beautiful, the way a blind man knows, without benefit of vision, that a rainbow or the sky or his own dear child's face is beautiful. And now he was afraid for her.

Where are you? he wanted to cry out.

"He's coming around," said a female voice (not Catherine's, it was too hard, too crisp) followed by a confusing rush of other voices.

"Watch that IV!"

"Mr. Holland, hold still. Everything's going to be all right—"

"I said, watch the IV!"

"Hand me that second unit of blood—"

"Don't move, Mr. Holland—"

Where are you, Catherine? The shout exploded in his head. Fighting the temptation to sink back into unconsciousness, he struggled to lift his eyelids. At first, there was only a blur of light and color, so harsh he felt it stab through his sockets straight to his brain. Gradually the blur took the shape of faces, strangers in blue, frowning down at him. He tried to focus but the effort made his stomach rebel.

"Mr. Holland, take it easy," said a quietly gruff voice. "You're in the hospital—the recovery room. They've just operated on your shoulder. You just rest and go back to sleep...."

No. No, I can't, he tried to say.

"Five milligrams of morphine going in," someone said, and Victor felt a warm flush creep up his arm and spread across his chest.

"That should help," he heard. "Now, sleep. Everything went just fine...."

You don't understand, he wanted to scream. *I have to warn her*—It was the last conscious thought he had before the lights once again were swallowed by the gentle darkness.

ALONE IN HER husbandless bed, Sarah lay smiling. No, laughing! Her whole body seemed filled with laughter tonight. She wanted to sing, to dance. To stand at the open window and shout out her joy! It was all hormonal, she'd been told, this chemical pandemonium of pregnancy, dragging her body on a roller coaster of emotions. She knew she should rest, she should work toward serenity, but tonight she wasn't tired at all. Poor exhausted Cathy had dragged herself up the attic steps to bed. But here was Sarah, still wide awake.

She closed her eyes and focused her thoughts on the child resting in her belly. *How are you, my love? Are you asleep? Or are you listening, hearing my thoughts even now?*

The baby wiggled in her belly, then fell silent. It was a reply, secret words shared only between them. Sarah was almost glad there was no husband to distract her from this silent conversation, to lie here in jealousy, an outsider. There was only mother and child, the ancient bond, the mystical link.

Poor Cathy, she thought, riding those roller coaster emotions from joy to sadness for her friend. She knew Cathy yearned just as deeply for a child, but eventually time would snatch the chance away from her. Cathy was too much of a romantic to realize that the man, the circumstances, might never be right. Hadn't it taken Cathy ten long years to finally acknowledge that her marriage was a miserable failure? Not that Cathy hadn't tried to make it work. She had tried to the point of developing a monumental blind spot to Jack's faults, primarily his selfishness. It was surprising how a woman so bright, so intuitive, could have let things drag on as long as she did. But that was Cathy. Even at thirty-seven she was open and trusting and loyal to the point of idiocy.

The clatter of gravel outside on the driveway pricked Sarah's awareness. Lying perfectly still, she listened and for a moment heard only the familiar creak of the trees, the rustle of branches against the shake roof. Then—there it was again. Stones skittering across the road, and then the faint squeal of metal. Those raccoons again. If she didn't shoo them off now, they'd litter garbage all over the driveway.

Sighing, she sat up and hunted in the darkness for her slippers. Shuffling quietly out of her bedroom, she navigated instinctively down the hallway and into the kitchen. Her eyes found the night too comfortable; she didn't want to assault them with light. Instead of flipping on the carport switch, she grabbed the flashlight from its usual spot on the kitchen shelf and unlocked the door.

Outside, moonlight glowed dimly through the clouds. She pointed the flashlight at the trash cans, but her beam caught no raccoon eyes, no telltale scattering of garbage, only the dull reflection of stainless steel. Puzzled, she crossed the carport and paused next to the Datsun that Cathy had parked in the driveway.

That was when she noticed the light glowing faintly inside the car. Glancing through the window, she saw that the glove compartment was open. Her first thought was that it had somehow fallen open by itself or that she or Cathy had forgotten to close it. Then she spotted the road maps strewn haphazardly across the front seat.

With fear suddenly hissing in her ear, she backed away, but terror made her legs slow and stiff. Only then did she sense that someone was nearby, waiting in the darkness; she could feel his presence, like a chill wind in the night.

She wheeled around for the house. As she turned, the beam of her flashlight swung around in a wild arc, only to freeze on the face of a man. The eyes that stared down at her were as slick and as black as pebbles. She scarcely focused on the rest of his face: the hawk nose, the thin, bloodless lips. It was only the eyes she saw. They were the eyes of a man without a soul.

"Hello, Catherine," he whispered, and she heard, in his voice, the greeting of death.

Please, she wanted to cry out as she felt him wrench her hair backward, exposing her neck. *Let me live!*

But no sound escaped. The words, like his blade, were buried in her throat.

ATHY WOKE UP TO the quarreling of blue jays outside her window, a sound that brought a smile to her lips for it struck her as somehow whimsical, this flap and flutter of wings across the panes, this maniacal crackling of feathered enemies. So unlike the morning roar of buses and cars she was accustomed to. The blue jays' quarrel moved to the rooftop, and she heard their claws scratching across the shakes in a dance of combat. She trailed their progress across the ceiling, up one side of the roof and down the other. Then, tired of the battle, she focused on the window.

Morning sunlight cascaded in, bathing the attic room in a soft haze. Such a perfect room for a nursery! She could see all the changes Sarah had already made here—the Jack-and-Jill curtains, the watercolor animal portraits. The very prospect of a baby sleeping in this room filled her with such joy that she sat up, grinning, and hugged the covers to her knees. Then she glanced at her watch on the nightstand and saw it was already nine-thirty—half the morning gone!

Reluctantly, she left the warmth of her bed and poked around in her suitcase for a sweater and jeans. She dressed to the thrashing of blue jays in the branches, the battle having moved from the roof to the treetops. From the window, she watched them dart from twig to twig until one finally hoisted up the feathered version of a white flag and took off, defeated. The victor, his authority no longer in question, gave one last screech and settled back to preen his feathers.

Only then did Cathy notice the silence of the house, a stillness that magnified her every heartbeat, her every breath.

Leaving the room, she descended the attic steps and confronted the empty living room. Ashes from last night's fire mounded the grate. A silver garland drooped from the Christmas tree. A cardboard angel with glittery wings winked on the mantelpiece. She followed the hallway to Sarah's room and frowned at the rumpled bed, the coverlet flung aside. "Sarah?"

Her voice was swallowed up in the stillness. How could a cottage seem so immense? She wandered back through the living room and into the kitchen. Last night's teacups still sat in the sink. On the windowsill, an asparagus fern trembled, stirred by a breeze through the open door.

Cathy stepped out into the carport where Sarah's old Dodge was parked. "Sarah?" she called.

Something skittered across the roof. Startled, Cathy looked up and suddenly laughed as she heard the blue jay chattering in the tree above—a victory speech, no doubt. Even the animal kingdom had its conceits.

She started to head back into the house when her gaze swept past a stain on the gravel near the car's rear tire. For a few seconds she stared at the blot of rust-brown, unable to comprehend its meaning. Slowly, she moved alongside the car, her gaze tracing the stain backward along its meandering course.

As she rounded the rear of the car, the driveway came into full view. The dried rivulet of brown became a crimson lake in which a single swimmer lay open-eyed and still.

The blue jay's chatter abruptly ceased as another sound rose up and filled the trees. It was Cathy, screaming.

"HEY, MISTER. Hey, mister."

Victor tried to brush off the sound but it kept buzzing in his ear, like a fly that can't be shooed away.

"Hey, mister. You awake?"

Victor opened his eyes and focused painfully on a wry little face stubbled with gray whiskers. The apparition grinned, and darkness gaped where teeth should have been. Victor stared into that foul black hole of a mouth and thought: *I've died and gone to hell.*

"Hey, mister, you got a cigarette?"

Victor shook his head and barely managed to whisper: "I don't think so."

"Well, you got a dollar I could borrow?"

"Go away," groaned Victor, shutting his eyes against the daylight. He tried to think, tried to remember where he was, but his head ached and the little man's voice kept distracting him.

"Can't get no cigarettes in this place. Like a jail in here. Don't know why I don't just get up and walk out. But y'know, streets are cold this time of year. Been rainin' all night long. Least in here it's warm...."

Raining all night long... Suddenly Victor remembered. The rain. Running and running through the rain.

Victor's eyes shot open. "Where am I?"

"Three East. Land o' the bitches."

He struggled to sit up and almost gasped from the pain. Dizzily, he focused on the metal pole with its bag of fluid dripping slowly into the plastic intravenous tube, then stared at the bandages on his left shoulder. Through the window, he saw that the day was already drenched in sunshine. "What time is it?"

"Dunno. Nine o'clock, I guess. You missed breakfast."

"I've got to get out of here." Victor swung his legs out of bed and discovered that, except for a flimsy hospital gown, he was stark naked. "Where's my clothes? My wallet?"

The old man shrugged. "Nurse'd know. Ask her."

Victor found the call button buried among the bed sheets. He stabbed it a few times, then turned his attention to peeling off the tape affixing the IV tube to his arm.

The door hissed open and a woman's voice barked, *"Mr. Holland! What do you think you're doing?"*

"I'm getting out of here, that's what I'm doing," said Victor as he stripped off the last piece of tape. Before he could pull the IV out, the nurse rushed across the room as fast as her stout legs could carry her and slapped a piece of gauze over the catheter.

"Don't blame me, Miss Redfern!" screeched the little man.

"Lenny, go back to your own bed this instant! And as for you, Mr. Holland," she said, turning her steel-blue eyes on Victor, "you've lost too much blood." Trapping his arm against her massive biceps, she began to retape the catheter firmly in place.

"Just get me my clothes."

"Don't argue, Mr. Holland. You have to stay."

"Why?"

"Because you've got an IV, that's why!" she snapped, as if the plastic tube itself was some sort of irreversible condition.

"I want my clothes."

"I'd have to check with the ER. Nothing of yours came up to the floor."

"Then call the ER, damn you!" At Miss Redfern's disapproving scowl, he added with strained politeness, "*If* you don't mind."

It was another half hour before a woman showed up from the business office to explain what had happened to Victor's belongings.

"I'm afraid we—well, we seem to have…lost your clothes, Mr. Holland," she said, fidgeting under his astonished gaze.

"What do you mean, *lost?*"

"They were—" she cleared her throat "—er, stolen. From the emergency room. Believe me, this has never happened before. We're really very sorry about this, Mr. Holland, and I'm sure we'll be able to arrange a purchase of replacement clothing…."

She was too busy trying to make excuses to notice that Victor's face had frozen in alarm. That his mind was racing as he tried to remember, through the blur of last night's events, just what had happened to the film canister. He knew he'd had it in his pocket during the endless drive to the hospital. He remembered clutching it there, remembered flailing senselessly at the woman when she'd tried to pull his hand from his pocket. After that, nothing was clear, nothing was certain. *Have I lost it?* he thought. *Have I lost my only evidence?*

"…While the money's missing, your credit cards seem to be all there, so I guess that's something to be thankful for."

He looked at her blankly. "What?"

"Your valuables, Mr. Holland." She pointed to the wallet and watch she'd just placed on the bedside table. "The security guard found them in the trash bin outside the hospital. Looks like the thief only wanted your cash."

"And my clothes. Right."

The instant the woman left, Victor pressed the button for Miss Redfern. She walked in carrying a breakfast tray. "Eat, Mr. Holland" she said. "Maybe your behavior's all due to hypoglycemia."

"A woman brought me to the ER," he said. "Her first name was Catherine. I have to get hold of her."

"Oh, look! Eggs and Rice Krispies! Here's your fork—"

"Miss Redfern, will you forget the damned Rice Krispies!"

Miss Redfern slapped down the cereal box. "There is no need for profanity!"

"I have to find that woman!"

Without a word, Miss Redfern spun around and marched out of the room. A few minutes later she returned and brusquely handed him a slip of paper. On it was written the name Catherine Weaver followed by a local address.

"You'd better eat fast," she said. "There's a policeman coming over to talk to you."

"Fine," he grunted, stuffing a forkful of cold, rubbery egg in his mouth.

"And some man from the FBI called. He's on his way, too."

Victor's head jerked up in alarm. "The FBI? What was his name?"

"Oh, for heaven's sake, how should I know? Something Polish, I think."

Staring at her, Victor slowly put down his fork. "Polowski," he said softly.

"That sounds like it. Polowski." She turned and headed out of the room. "The FBI indeed," she muttered. "Wonder what he did to get *their* attention...."

Before the door had even swung shut behind her, Victor was out of bed and tearing at his IV. He scarcely felt the sting of the tape wrenching the hair off his arm; he had to concentrate on getting the hell out of this hospital before Polowski showed up. He was certain the FBI agent had set him up for that ambush last night, and he wasn't about to wait around for another attack.

He turned and snapped at his roommate, "Lenny, where are your clothes?"

Lenny's gaze traveled reluctantly to a cabinet near the sink. "Don't got no other clothes. Besides, they wouldn't fit you, mister…"

Victor yanked open the cabinet door and pulled out a frayed cotton shirt and a pair of baggy polyester pants. The pants were too short and about six inches of Victor's hairy legs stuck out below the cuffs, but he had no trouble fastening the belt. The real trouble was going to be finding a pair of size twelve shoes. To his relief, he discovered that the cabinet also contained a pair of Lenny's thongs. His heels hung at least an inch over the back edge, but at least he wouldn't be barefoot.

"Those are mine!" protested Lenny.

"Here. You can have this." Victor tossed his wristwatch to the old man. "You should be able to hock that for a whole new outfit."

Suspicious, Lenny put the watch up against his ear. "Piece of junk. It's not ticking."

"It's quartz."

"Oh. Yeah. I knew that."

Victor pocketed his wallet and went to the door. Opening it just a crack, he peered down the hall toward the nurses' station. The coast was clear. He glanced back at Lenny. "So long, buddy. Give my regards to Miss Redfern."

Slipping out of the room, Victor headed quietly down the hall, away from the nurses' station. The emergency stairwell door was at the far end, marked by the warning painted in red: Alarm Will Sound If Opened. He walked steadily towards it, willing himself not to run, not to attract attention. But just as he neared the door, a familiar voice echoed in the hall.

"Mr. Holland! You come back here this instant!"

Victor lunged for the door, slammed against the closing bar, and dashed into the stairwell.

His footsteps echoed against the concrete as he pounded down the stairs. By the time he heard Miss Redfern scramble after him into the stairwell, he'd already reached the first floor and was pushing through the last door to freedom.

"Mr. Holland!" yelled Miss Redfern.

Even as he dashed across the parking lot, he could still hear Miss Redfern's outraged voice echoing in his ears.

Eight blocks away he turned into a K Mart, and within ten minutes had bought a shirt, blue jeans, underwear, socks and a pair of size-twelve tennis shoes, all of which he paid for with his credit card. He tossed Lenny's old clothes into a trash can.

Before emerging back outside, he peered through the store window at the street. It seemed like a perfectly normal mid-December morning in a small town, shoppers strolling beneath a tacky garland of Christmas decorations, a half-dozen cars waiting patiently at a red light. He was just about to step out the door when he spotted the police car creeping down the road. Immediately he ducked behind an undressed mannequin and watched through the nude plastic limbs as the police car made its way slowly past the K Mart and continued in the direction of the hospital. They were obviously searching for someone. Was he the one they wanted?

He couldn't afford to risk a stroll down Main Street. There was no way of knowing who else besides Polowski was involved in the double cross.

It took him at least an hour on foot to reach the outskirts of town, and by then he was so weak and wobbly he could barely stand. The surge of adrenaline that had sent him dashing from the hospital was at last petering out. Too tired to take another step, he sank onto a boulder at the side of the highway and halfheartedly held out his thumb. To his immense relief, the next vehicle to come along—a pickup truck loaded with fire-wood—pulled over. Victor climbed in and collapsed gratefully on the seat.

The driver spat out the window, then squinted at Victor from beneath an Agway Seeds cap. "Goin' far?"

"Just a few miles. Oak Hill Road."

"Yep. I go right past it." The driver pulled back onto the road. The truck spewed black exhaust as they roared down the highway, country music blaring from the radio.

Through the plucked strains of guitar music, Victor heard a sound that made him sit up sharply. A siren. Whipping his head around, he saw a patrol car zooming up fast behind them. *That's it,* thought Victor. *They've found me. They're going to stop this truck and arrest me....*

But for what? For walking away from the hospital? For insulting Miss Redfern? Or had Polowski fabricated some charge against him?

With a sense of impending doom, he waited for the patrol car to overtake them and start flashing its signal to pull over. In fact, he was so certain they *would* be pulled over that when the police car sped right past them and roared off down the highway, he could only stare ahead in amazement.

"Must be some kinda trouble," his companion said blandly, nodding at the rapidly vanishing police car.

Victor managed to clear his throat. "Trouble?"

"Yep. Don't get much of a chance to use that siren of theirs but when they do, boy oh boy, do they go to town with it."

With his heart hammering against his ribs, Victor sat back and forced himself to calm down. He had nothing to worry about. The police weren't after him, they were busy with some other concern. He wondered what sort of small-town catastrophe could warrant blaring sirens. Probably nothing more exciting than a few kids out on a joyride.

By the time they reached the turnoff to Oak Hill Road, Victor's pulse had settled back to normal. He thanked the driver, climbed out, and began the trek to Catherine Weaver's house. It was a long walk, and the road wound through a forest of pines. Every so often he'd pass a mailbox along the road and, peering through the trees, would spot a house. Catherine's address was coming up fast.

What on earth should he say to her? Up till now he'd concentrated only on reaching her house. Now that he was almost there, he had to come up with some reasonable explanation for why he'd dragged himself out of a hospital bed and trudged all this way to see her. A simple *thanks for saving my life* just wouldn't do it. He had to find out if she had the film canister.

But she, of course, would want to know why the damn thing was so important.

You could tell her the truth.

No, forget that. He could imagine her reaction if he were to launch into his wild tale about viruses and dead scientists and double-crossing FBI agents. *The FBI is out to get you? I see. And who else is after you, Mr. Holland?* It was so absurdly paranoid he almost felt like laughing. No, he couldn't tell her any of it or he'd end up right back in a hospital, and this time in a ward that would make Miss Redfern's Three East look like paradise.

She didn't need to know any of it. In fact, she was better off ignorant. The woman had saved his life, and the last thing he wanted to do was put her in any danger. The film was all he wanted from her. After today, she'd never see him again.

He was so busy debating what to tell her that he didn't notice the police cars until well after he'd rounded the road's bend. Suddenly he froze, confronted by three squad cars—probably the entire police fleet of Garberville—parked in front of a rustic cedar house. A half-dozen neighbors lingered in the gravel driveway, shaking their heads in disbelief. Good God, had something happened to Catherine?

Swallowing the urge to turn and flee, Victor propelled himself forward, past the squad cars and through the loose gathering of onlookers, only to be stopped by a uniformed officer.

"I'm sorry, sir. No one's allowed past this point."

Dazed, Victor stared down and saw that the police had strung out a perimeter of red tape. Slowly, his gaze moved beyond the tape, to the old Datsun parked near the carport. Was that Catherine's car? He tried desperately to remember if she'd driven a Datsun, but last night it had been so dark and he'd been in so much pain that he hadn't bothered to pay attention. All he could remember was that it was a compact model, with scarcely enough room for his legs. Then he noticed the faded parking sticker on the rear bumper: Parking Permit, Studio Lot A.

I work for an independent film company, she'd told him last night.

It was Catherine's car.

Unwillingly, he focused on the stained gravel just beside the Datsun, and even though the rational part of him knew that that peculiar brick red could only be dried blood, he wanted to deny it. He wanted to believe there was some other explanation for that stain, for this ominous gathering of police.

He tried to speak, but his voice sounded like something dragged up through gravel.

"What did you say, sir?" the police officer asked.

"What—what happened?"

The officer shook his head sadly. "Woman was killed here last night. Our first murder in ten years."

"*Murder?*" Victor's gaze was still fixed in horror on the bloodstained gravel. "But—*why?*"

The officer shrugged. "Don't know yet. Maybe robbery, though I don't think he got much." He nodded at the Datsun. "Car was the only thing broken into."

If Victor said anything at that point, he never remembered what it was. He was vaguely aware of his legs carrying him back through the onlookers, past the three police cars, toward the road. The sunshine was so brilliant it hurt his eyes and he could barely see where he was going.

I killed her, he thought. *She saved my life and I killed her....*

Guilt slashed its way to his throat and he could scarcely breathe, could barely take another step for the pain. For a long time he stood there at the side of the road, his head bent in the sunshine, his ears filled with the sound of blue jays, and mourned a woman he'd never known.

When at last he was able to raise his head again, rage fueled the rest of his walk back to the highway, rage against Catherine's murderer. Rage at himself for having put her in such danger. It was the film the killer had been searching for, and he'd probably found it in the Datsun. If he hadn't, the house would have been ransacked, as well.

Now what? thought Victor. He dismissed the possibility that his briefcase—with most of the evidence—might still be in his wrecked car. That was the first place the killer would have searched. Without the film, Victor was left with no evidence at all. It would all come down to his word against Viratek's. The newspapers would dismiss him as nothing more than a disgruntled ex-employee. And after Polowski's double cross, he couldn't trust the FBI.

At that last thought, he quickened his pace. The sooner he got out of Garberville, the better. When he got back to the highway, he'd hitch another ride. Once safely out of town, he could take the time to plan his next move.

He decided to head south, to San Francisco.

CHAPTER THREE

FROM THE WINDOW of his office at Viratek, Archibald Black watched the limousine glide up the tree-lined driveway and pull to a stop at the front entrance. Black snorted derisively. The cowboy was back in town, damn him. And after all the man's fussing about the importance of secrecy, about keeping his little visit discreet, the idiot had the gall to show up in a limousine—with a uniformed driver, no less.

Black turned from the window and paced over to his desk. Despite his contempt for the visitor, he had to acknowledge the man made him uneasy, the way all so-called men of action made him uneasy. Not enough brains behind all that muscle. Too much power in the hands of imbeciles, he thought. Is this an example of who we have running the country?

The intercom buzzed. "Mr. Black?" said his secretary. "A Mr. Tyrone is here to see you."

"Send him in, please," said Black, smoothing the scorn from his expression. He was wearing a look of polite deference when the door opened and Matthew Tyrone walked into the office.

They shook hands. Tyrone's grip was unreasonably firm, as though he was trying to remind Black of their relative positions of power. His bearing had all the spit and polish of an ex-marine, which Tyrone was. Only the thickening waist betrayed the fact that Tyrone's marine days had been left far behind.

"How was the flight from Washington?" inquired Black as they sat down.

"Terrible service. I tell you, commercial flights aren't what they used to be. To think the average American pays good money for the privilege."

"I imagine it can't compare with Air Force One."

Tyrone smiled. "Let's get down to business. Tell me where things stand with this little crisis of yours."

Black noted Tyrone's use of the word *yours. So now it's my problem,* he thought. Naturally. That's what they meant by deniability: When things go wrong, the other guy gets the blame. If any of this leaked out, Black's head would be the one to fall. But then, that's why this contract was so lucrative—because he—meaning Viratek—was willing to take that risk.

"We've recovered the documents," said Black. "And the film canisters. The negatives are being developed now."

"And your two employees?"

Black cleared his throat. "There's no need to take this any further."

"They're a risk to national security."

"You can't just kill them off!"

"Can't we?" Tyrone's eyes were a cold, gun-metal gray. An appropriate color for someone who called himself "the Cowboy." You didn't argue with anyone who had eyes like that. Not if you had an instinct for self-preservation.

Black dipped his head deferentially. "I'm not accustomed to this sort of…business. And I don't like dealing with your man Savitch."

"Mr. Savitch has performed well for us before."

"He killed one of my senior scientists!"

"I assume it was necessary."

Black looked down unhappily at his desk. Just the thought of that monster Savitch made him shudder.

"Why, exactly, did Martinique go bad?"

Because he had a conscience, thought Black. He looked at Tyrone. "There was no way to predict it. He'd worked in commercial R and D for ten years. He'd never presented a security problem before. We only found out last week that he'd taken classified documents. And then Victor Holland got involved…."

"How much does Holland know?"

"Holland wasn't involved with the project. But he's clever. If he looked over those papers, he might have pieced it together."

Now Tyrone was agitated, his fingers drumming the desktop. "Tell me about Holland. What do you know about him?"

"I've gone over his personnel file. He's forty-one years old, born and raised in San Diego. Entered the seminary but dropped out after a year. Went on to Stanford, then MIT. Doctorate in biochemistry. He was with Viratek for four years. One of our most promising researchers."

"What about his personal life?"

"His wife died three years ago of leukemia. Keeps pretty much to himself these days. Quiet kind of guy, likes classical jazz. Plays the saxophone in some amateur group."

Tyrone laughed. "Your typical nerd scientist." It was just the sort of moronic comment an ex-marine like Tyrone would make. It was an insult that grated on Black. Years ago, before he created Viratek Industries, Black too had been a research biochemist.

"He should be a simple matter to dispose of," said Tyrone. "Inexperienced. And probably scared." He reached for his briefcase. "Mr. Savitch is an expert on these matters. I suggest you let him take care of the problem."

"Of course." In truth, Black didn't think he had any choice. Nicholas Savitch was like some evil, frightening force that, once unleashed, could not be controlled.

The intercom buzzed. "Mr. Gregorian's here from the photo lab," said the secretary.

"Send him in." Black glanced at Tyrone. "The film's been developed. Let's see just what Martinique managed to photograph."

Gregorian walked in carrying a bulky envelope. "Here are those contact prints you requested," he said, handing the bundle across the desk to Black. Then he cupped his hand over his mouth, muffling a sound suspiciously like laughter.

"Yes, Mr. Gregorian?" inquired Black.

"Nothing, sir."

Tyrone cut in, "Well, let's see them!"

Black removed the five contact sheets and lay them out on the desk for everyone to see. The men stared.

For a long time, no one spoke. Then Tyrone said, "Is this some sort of joke?"

Gregorian burst out laughing.

Black said, "What the hell is this?"

"Those are the negatives you gave me, sir," Gregorian insisted. "I processed them myself."

"These are the photos you got back from Victor Holland?" Tyrone's voice started soft and rose slowly to a roar. "Five rolls of *naked women?*"

"There's been a mistake," said Black. "It's the wrong film—"

Gregorian laughed harder.

"Shut up!" yelled Black. He looked at Tyrone. "I don't know how this happened."

"Then the roll we want is still out there?"

Black nodded wearily.

Tyrone reached for the phone. "We need to clean things up. Fast."

"Who are you calling?" asked Black.

"The man who can do the job," said Tyrone as he punched in the numbers. "Savitch."

IN HIS MOTEL ROOM on Lombard Street, Victor paced the avocado-green carpet, wracking his brain for a plan. Any plan. His well-organized scientist's mind had already distilled the situation into the elements of a research project. Identify the problem: someone is out to kill me. State your hypothesis: Jerry Martinique uncovered something dangerous and he was killed for it. Now they think I have the information—and the evidence. Which I don't. Goal: Stay alive. Method: *Any damn way I can!*

For the last two days, his only strategy had consisted of holing up in various cheap motel rooms and pacing the carpets. He couldn't hide out forever. If the feds were involved, and he had reason to believe they were, they'd soon have his credit card charges traced, would know exactly where to find him.

I need a plan of attack.

Going to the FBI was definitely out. Sam Polowski was the agent Victor had contacted, the one who'd arranged to meet him in Garberville. No one else should have known about that meeting. Sam Polowski had never shown up.

But someone else had. Victor's aching shoulder was a constant reminder of that near-disastrous rendezvous.

I could go to the newspapers. But how would he convince some skeptical reporter? Who would believe his stories of a project so dangerous it could kill millions? They would think his tale was some fabrication of a paranoid mind.

And I am not paranoid.

He paced over to the TV and switched it on to the five o'clock news. A perfectly coiffed anchorwoman smiled from the screen as she read a piece of fluff about the last day of school, happy children, Christmas vacation. Then her expression sobered. Transition. Victor found himself staring at the TV as the next story came on.

"And in Garberville, California, there have been no new leads in the murder investigation of a woman found slain Wednesday morning. A houseguest found Sarah Boylan, 39, lying in the driveway, dead of stab wounds to the neck. The victim was five months pregnant. Police say they are puzzled by the lack of motive in this terrible tragedy, and at the present time there are no suspects. Moving on to national news..."

No, no, no! Victor thought. She wasn't pregnant. Her name wasn't Sarah. It's a mistake....

Or was it?

My name is Catherine, she had told him.

Catherine Weaver. Yes, he was sure of the name. He'd remember it till the day he died.

He sat on the bed, the facts spinning around in his brain. Sarah. Cathy. A murder in Garberville.

When at last he rose to his feet, it was with a swelling sense of urgency, even panic. He grabbed the hotel room phone book and flipped to the *W*s. He understood now. The killer had made a mistake. If Cathy Weaver was still alive, she might have that roll of film—or know where to find it. Victor had to reach her.

Before someone else did.

NOTHING COULD HAVE prepared Cathy for the indescribable sense of gloom she felt upon returning to her flat in San Francisco. She had thought she'd cried out all her tears that night in the Garberville motel, the night after Sarah's death. But here she was, still bursting into tears, then sinking into deep, dark meditations. The drive to the city had been temporarily numbing. But as soon as she'd climbed the steps to her door and confronted the deathly silence of her second-story flat, she felt overwhelmed once again by grief. And bewilderment. Of all the people in the world to die, why Sarah?

She made a feeble attempt at unpacking. Then, forcing herself to stay busy, she surveyed the refrigerator and saw that her shelves were practically empty. It was all the excuse she needed to flee her apartment. She pulled a sweater over her jeans and, with a sense of escape, walked the four blocks to the neighborhood grocery store. She bought only the essentials, bread and eggs and fruit. Enough to tide her over for a few days, until she was back on her feet and could think clearly about any sort of menu.

Carrying a sack of groceries in each arm, she walked through the gathering darkness back to her apartment building. The night was chilly, and she regretted not wearing a coat. Through an open window, a woman called, "Time for dinner!" and two children playing kickball in the street turned and scampered for home.

By the time Cathy reached her building, she was shivering and her arms were aching from the weight of the groceries. She trudged up the steps and, balancing one sack on her hip, managed to pull out her keys and unlock the security door. Just as she swung through, she heard footsteps, then glimpsed a blur of movement rushing toward her from the side. She was swept through the doorway, into the building. A grocery bag tumbled from her arms, spilling apples across the floor. She stumbled forward, catching herself on the wood banister. The door slammed shut behind her.

She spun around, ready to fight off her attacker.

It was Victor Holland.

"You!" she whispered in amazement.

He didn't seem so sure of *her* identity. He was frantically searching her face, as though trying to confirm he had the right woman. "Cathy Weaver?"

"What do you think you're—"

"Where's your apartment?" he cut in.

"What?"

"We can't stand around out here."

"It's—it's upstairs—"

"Let's go." He reached for her arm but she pulled away.

"My groceries," she said, glancing down at the scattered apples.

He quickly scooped up the fruit, tossed it in one of the bags, and nudged her toward the stairs. "We don't have a lot of time."

Cathy allowed herself to be herded up the stairs and halfway down the hall before she stopped dead in her tracks. "Wait a minute. You tell me what this is all about, Mr. Holland, and you tell me right now or I don't move another step!"

"Give me your keys."

"You can't just—"

"Give me your keys!"

She stared at him, shocked by the command. Suddenly she realized that what she saw in his eyes was panic. They were the eyes of a hunted man.

Automatically she handed him her keys.

"Wait here," he said. "Let me check the apartment first."

She watched in bewilderment as he unlocked her door and cautiously eased his way inside. For a few moments she heard nothing. She pictured him moving through the flat, tried to estimate how many seconds each room would require for inspection. It was a small flat, so why was he taking so long?

Slowly she moved toward the doorway. Just as she reached it, his head popped out. She let out a little squeak of surprise. He barely caught the bag of groceries as it slipped from her grasp.

"It's okay," he said. "Come on inside."

The instant she stepped over the threshold, he had the door locked and bolted behind her. Then he quickly circled the living room, closing the drapes, locking windows.

"Are you going to tell me what's going on?" she asked, following him around the room.

"We're in trouble."

"You mean *you're* in trouble."

"No. I mean *we*. Both of us." He turned to her, his gaze clear and steady. "Do you have the film?"

"What are you talking about?" she asked, utterly confused by the sudden shift of conversation.

"A roll of film. Thirty-five millimeter. In a black plastic container. Do you have it?"

She didn't answer. But an image from that last night with Sarah had already taken shape in her mind: a roll of film on the kitchen counter. Film she'd thought belonged to her friend Hickey. Film she'd slipped into her bathrobe pocket and later into her purse. But she wasn't about to reveal any of this, not until she found out why he wanted it. The gaze she returned to him was purposefully blank and unrevealing.

Frustrated, he forced himself to take a deep breath, and started over. "That night you found me—on the highway—I had it in my pocket. It wasn't with me when I woke up in the hospital. I might have dropped it in your car."

"Why do you want this roll of film?"

"I need it. As evidence—"

"For what?"

"It would take too long to explain."

She shrugged. "I've got nothing better to do at the moment—"

"*Damn it!*" He stalked over to her. Taking her by the shoulders, he forced her to look at him. "Don't you understand? That's why your friend was killed! The night they broke into your car, they were looking for that film!"

She stared at him, a look of sudden comprehension and horror. "Sarah..."

"Was in the wrong place at the wrong time. The killer must have thought she was *you*."

Cathy felt trapped by his unrelenting gaze. And by the inescapable threat of his revelation. Her knees wobbled, gave way. She sank into the nearest chair and sat there in numb silence.

"You have to get out of here," he said. "Before they find

you. Before they figure out you're the Cathy Weaver they're looking for.''

She didn't move. She couldn't move.

''Come on, Cathy. There isn't much time!''

''What was on that roll of film?'' she asked softly.

''I told you. Evidence. Against a company called Viratek.''

She frowned. ''Isn't—isn't that the company you work for?''

''Used to work for.''

''What did they do?''

''They're involved in some sort of illegal research project. I can't tell you the particulars.''

''Why not?''

''Because I don't know them. I'm not the one who gathered the evidence. A colleague—a friend—passed it to me, just before he was killed.''

''What do you mean by killed?''

''The police called it an accident. I think otherwise.''

''You're saying he was murdered over a research project?'' She shook her head. ''Must have been dangerous stuff he was working on.''

''I know this much. It involves biological weapons. Which makes the research illegal. And incredibly dangerous.''

''Weapons? For what government?''

''Ours.''

''I don't understand. If this is a federal project, that makes it all legal, right?''

''Not by a long shot. People in high places have been known to break the rules.''

''How high are we talking about?''

''I don't know. I can't be sure of anyone. Not the police, not the Justice Department. Not the FBI.''

Her eyes narrowed. The words she was hearing sounded like paranoid ravings. But the voice—and the eyes—were perfectly sane. They were sea-green, those eyes. They held an honesty, a steadiness that should have been all the assurance she needed.

It wasn't. Not by a long shot.

Quietly she said, ''So you're telling me the FBI is after you. Is that correct?''

Sudden anger flared in his eyes, then just as quickly, it was gone. Groaning, he sank onto the couch and ran his hands through his hair. "I don't blame you for thinking I'm nuts. Sometimes I wonder if I'm all there. I thought if I could trust anyone, it'd be you...."

"Why me?"

He looked at her. "Because you're the one who saved my life. You're the one they'll try to kill next."

She froze. No, no, this was insane. Now he was pulling her into his delusion, making her believe in his nightmare world of murder and conspiracy. She wouldn't let him! She stood up and started to walk away, but his voice made her stop again.

"Cathy, think about it. Why was your friend Sarah killed? Because they thought she was *you*. By now they've figured out they killed the wrong woman. They'll have to come back and do the job right. Just in case you know something. In case you have evidence—"

"This is crazy!" she cried, clapping her hands over her ears. "No one's going to—"

"They already have!" He whipped out a scrap of newspaper from his shirt pocket. "On my way over here, I happened to pass a newsstand. This was on the front page." He handed her the piece of paper.

She stared in bewilderment at the photograph of a middle-aged woman, a total stranger. "San Francisco woman shot to death on front doorstep," read the accompanying headline.

"This has nothing to do with me," she said.

"Look at her name."

Cathy's gaze slid to the third paragraph, which identified the victim.

Her name was Catherine Weaver.

The scrap of newsprint slipped from her grasp and fluttered to the floor.

"There are three Catherine Weavers in the San Francisco phone book," he said. "That one was shot to death at nine o'clock this morning. I don't know what's happened to the second. She might already be dead. Which makes you next on the list. They've had enough time to locate you."

"I've been out of town—I only got back an hour ago—"

"Which explains why you're still alive. Maybe they came here earlier. Maybe they decided to check out the other two women first."

She shot to her feet, suddenly frantic with the need to flee. "I have to pack my things—"

"No. Let's just get the hell out of here."

Yes, do what he says! an inner voice screamed at her.

She nodded. Turning, she headed blindly for the door. Halfway there, she halted. "My purse—"

"Where is it?"

She headed back, past a curtained window. "I think I left it by the—"

Her next words were cut off by an explosion of shattering glass. Only the closed curtains kept the shards from piercing her flesh. Pure reflex sent Cathy diving to the floor just as the second gun blast went off. An instant later she found Victor Holland sprawled on top of her, covering her body with his as the third bullet slammed into the far wall, splintering wood and plaster.

The curtains shuddered, then hung still.

For a few seconds Cathy was paralyzed by terror, by the weight of Victor's body on hers. Then panic took hold. She squirmed free, intent on fleeing the apartment.

"Stay down!" Victor snapped.

"They're trying to kill us!"

"Don't make it easy for them!" He dragged her back to the floor. "We're getting out. But not through the front door."

"How—"

"Where's your fire escape?"

"My bedroom window."

"Does it go to the roof?"

"I'm not sure—I think so—"

"Then let's move it."

On hands and knees they crawled down the hall, into Cathy's unlit bedroom. Beneath the window they paused, listening. Outside, in the darkness, there was no sound. Then, from downstairs in the lobby, came the tinkle of breaking glass.

"He's already in the building!" hissed Victor. He yanked open the window. "Out, out!"

Cathy didn't need to be prodded. Hands shaking, she scrambled out and lowered herself onto the fire escape. Victor was right behind her.

"Up," he whispered. "To the roof."

And then what? she wondered, climbing the ladder to the third floor, past Mrs. Chang's flat. Mrs. Chang was out of town this week, visiting her son in New Jersey. The apartment was dark, the windows locked tight. No way in there.

"Keep going," said Victor, nudging her forward.

Only a few more rungs to go.

At last, she pulled herself up and over the edge and onto the asphalt roof. A second later, Victor dropped down beside her. Potted plants shuddered in the darkness. It was Mrs. Chang's rooftop garden, a fragrant mélange of Chinese herbs and vegetables.

Together, Victor and Cathy weaved their way through the plants and crossed to the opposite edge of the roof, where the next building abutted theirs.

"All the way?" said Cathy.

"All the way."

They hopped onto the adjoining roof and ran across to the other side, where three feet of emptiness separated them from the next building. She didn't pause to think of the perils of that leap, she simply flung herself across the gap and kept running, aware that every step took her farther and farther from danger.

On the roof of the fourth building, Cathy finally halted and stared over the edge at the street below. End of the line. It suddenly occurred to her that it was a very long drop to the ground below. The fire escape looked as sturdy as a Tinkertoy.

She swallowed. "This probably isn't a good time to tell you this, but—"

"Tell me what?"

"I'm afraid of heights."

He clambered over the edge. "Then don't look down."

Right, she thought, slithering onto the fire escape. *Don't look down.* Her palms were so slick with sweat she could barely grip the rungs. Suddenly seized by an attack of vertigo, she froze there, clinging desperately to that flimsy steel skeleton.

"Don't stop now!" Victor whispered up to her. "Just keep moving!"

Still she didn't move. She pressed her face against the rung, so hard she felt the rough edge bite into her flesh.

"You're okay, Cathy!" he said. "Come on."

The pain became all-encompassing, blocking out the dizziness, even the fear. When she opened her eyes again, the world had steadied. On rubbery legs, she descended the ladder, pausing on the third floor landing to wipe her sweaty palms on her jeans. She continued downward, to the second-floor landing. It was still a good fifteen-foot drop to the ground. She unlatched the extension ladder and started to slide it down, but it let out such a screech that Victor immediately stopped her.

"Too noisy. We have to jump!"

"But—"

To her astonishment, he scrambled over the railing and dropped to the ground. "Come on!" he hissed from below. "It's not that far. I'll catch you."

Murmuring a prayer, she lowered herself over the side and let go.

To her surprise he did catch her—but held on only for a second. The bullet wound had left his injured shoulder too weak to hold on. They both tumbled to the ground. She landed smack on top of him, her legs astride his hips, their faces inches apart. They stared at each other, so stunned they could scarcely breathe.

Upstairs, a window slid open and someone yelled, "Hey, you bums! If you don't clear out this instant, I'm calling the cops!"

Instantly Cathy rolled off Victor, only to stagger into a trash can. The lid fell off and slammed like a cymbal against the sidewalk.

"That's it for rest stops," Victor grunted and scrambled to his feet. *"Move it."*

They took off at a wild dash down the street, turned up an

alley, and kept running. It was a good five blocks before they finally stopped to catch their breath. They glanced back.

The street was deserted.

They were safe!

NICHOLAS SAVITCH STOOD BESIDE the neatly made bed and surveyed the room. It was every inch a woman's room, from the closet hung with a half-dozen simple but elegant dresses, to the sweetly scented powders and lotions lined up on the vanity table. It took only a single circuit around the room to tell him about the woman whose bedroom this was. She was slim, a size seven dress, size six-and-a-half shoe. The hairs on the brush were brown and shoulder-length. She owned only a few pieces of jewelry, and she favored natural scents, rosewater and lavender. Her favorite color was green.

Back in the living room, he continued to gather information. The woman subscribed to the Hollywood trade journals. Her taste in music, like her taste in books, was eclectic. He noticed a scrap of newspaper lying on the floor. He picked it up and glanced at the article. Now this was interesting. The death of Catherine Weaver I had not gone unnoticed by Catherine Weaver III.

He pocketed the article. Then he saw the purse, lying on the floor near the shattered window.

Bingo.

He emptied the contents on the coffee table. Out tumbled a wallet, checkbook, pens, loose change, and…an address book. He opened it to the *B*s. There he found the name he was looking for: Sarah Boylan.

He now knew this was the Catherine Weaver he'd been seeking. What a shame he'd wasted his time hunting down the other two.

He flipped through the address book and spotted a half dozen or so San Francisco listings. The woman may have been clever enough to slip away from him this time. But staying out of sight was a more difficult matter. And this little book, with its names of friends and relatives and colleagues, could lead him straight to her.

Somewhere in the distance, a police siren was wailing.

It was time to leave.

Savitch took the address book and the woman's wallet and headed out the door. Outside, his breath misted in the cold air as he walked at a leisurely pace down the street,

He could afford to take his time.

But for Catherine Weaver and Victor Holland, time was running out.

CHAPTER FOUR

THERE WAS NO TIME to rest. They jogged for the next six blocks, miles and miles, it seemed to Cathy. Victor moved tirelessly, leading her down side streets, avoiding busy intersections. She let him do the thinking and navigating. Her terror slowly gave way to numbness and a disorienting sense of unreality. The city itself seemed little more than a dreamscape, asphalt and streetlights and endless twists and turns of concrete. The only reality was the man striding close beside her, his gaze alert, his movements swift and sure. She knew he too must be afraid, but she couldn't see his fear.

He took her hand; the warmth of that grasp, the strength of those fingers, seemed to flow into her cold, exhausted limbs.

She quickened her pace. "I think there's a police substation down that street," she said. "If we go a block or two further—"

"We're not going to the police."

"What?" She stopped dead, staring at him.

"Not yet. Not until I've had a chance to think this through."

"Victor," she said slowly. "Someone is trying to kill us. Trying to kill *me*. What do you mean, you need time to *think this through?*"

"Look, we can't stand around talking about it. We have to get off the streets." He grabbed her hand again. "Come on."

"Where?"

"I have a room. It's only a few blocks away."

She let him drag her only a few yards before she mustered the will to pull free. "Wait a minute. Just *wait*."

He turned, his face a mask of frustration, and confronted her. "Wait for what? For that maniac to catch up? For the bullet to start flying again?"

"For an explanation!"

"I'll explain it all. When we're safe."

She backed away. "Why are you afraid of the police?"

"I can't be sure of them."

"Do you have a reason to be afraid? What have you done?"

With two steps he closed the gap between them and grabbed her hard by the shoulders. "I just pulled you out of a death trap, remember? The bullets were going through your window, not mine!"

"Maybe they were aimed at you!"

"Okay!" He let her go, let her back away from him. "You want to try it on your own? Do it. Maybe the police'll be a help. Maybe not. But I can't risk it. Not until I know all the players behind this."

"You—you're letting me go?"

"You were never my prisoner."

"No." She took a breath—it misted in the cold air. She glanced down the street, toward the police substation. "It's...the reasonable thing to do," she muttered, almost to reassure herself. "That's what they're there for."

"Right."

She frowned, anticipating what lay ahead. "They'll ask a lot of questions."

"What are you going to tell them?"

She looked at him, her gaze unflinchingly meeting his. "The truth."

"Which'll be at best, incomplete. And at worst, unbelievable."

"I have broken glass all over my apartment to prove it."

"A drive-by shooting. Purely random."

"It's their job to protect me."

"What if they don't think you need protection?"

"I'll tell them about you! About Sarah."

"They may or may not take you seriously."

"They have to take me seriously! Someone's trying to kill me!" Her voice, shrill with desperation, seemed to echo endlessly through the maze of streets.

Quietly he said, "I know."

She glanced back toward the substation. "I'm going."

He said nothing.

"Where will you be?" she asked.

"On my own. For now."

She took two steps away, then stopped. "Victor?"

"I'm still here."

"You did save my life. Thank you."

He didn't respond. She heard his footsteps slowly walk away. She stood there thinking, wondering if she was doing the right thing. Of course she was. A man afraid of the police—with a story as paranoid as his was—had to be dangerous.

But he saved my life.

And once, on a rainy night in Garberville, she had saved his.

She replayed all the events of the last week. Sarah's murder, never explained. The other Catherine Weaver, shot to death on her front doorstep. The film canister that Sarah had retrieved from the car, the one Cathy had slipped into her bathrobe pocket...

Victor's footsteps had faded.

In that instant she realized she'd lost the only man who could help her find the answers to all those questions, the one man who'd stood by her in her darkest moment of terror. The one man she knew, by some strange intuition, she could trust. Facing that deserted street, she felt abandoned and utterly friendless. In sudden panic, she whirled around and called out: "Victor!"

At the far end of the block, a silhouette stopped and turned. He seemed an island of refuge in that crazy, dangerous world. She started toward him, her legs moving her faster and faster, until she was running, yearning for the safety of his arms, the arms of a man she scarcely knew. Yet it didn't feel like a stranger's arms gathering her to his chest, welcoming her into his protective embrace. She felt the pounding of his heart, the grip of his fingers against her back, and something told her that this was a man she could depend upon, a man who wouldn't fold when she needed him most.

"I'm right here," he murmured. "Right here." He stroked through her windblown hair, his fingers burying deep in the tangled strands. She felt the heat of his breath against her face, felt her own quick and shuddering response. And then, all at once, his mouth hungrily sought hers and he was kissing her. She responded with a kiss just as desperate, just as needy. Stranger though he was, he had been there for her and he was still here, his arms sheltering her from the terrors of the night.

She burrowed her face against his chest, longing to press ever deeper, ever closer. "I don't know what to do! I'm so afraid, Victor, and I don't know what to do...."

"We'll work this out together. Okay?" He cupped her face in his hands and tilted it up to his. "You and I, we'll beat this thing."

She nodded. Searching his eyes, connecting with that rock-solid gaze, she found all the assurance she needed.

A wind gusted down the street. She shivered in its wake. "What do we do first?" she whispered.

"First," he said, pulling off his windbreaker and draping it over her shoulders, "We get you warmed up. And inside." He took her hand. "Come on. A hot bath, a good supper, and you'll be operating on all cylinders again."

It was another five blocks to the Kon-Tiki Motel. Though not exactly a five-star establishment, the Kon-Tiki was comfortingly drab and anonymous, one of a dozen on motel row. They climbed the steps to Room 214, overlooking the half-empty parking lot. He unlocked the door and motioned her inside.

The rush of warmth against her cheeks was delicious. She stood in the center of that utterly charmless space and marveled at how good it felt to be safely surrounded by four walls. The furnishings were spare: a double bed, a dresser, two nightstands with lamps, and a single chair. On the wall was a framed print of some nameless South Pacific island. The only luggage she saw was a cheap nylon bag on the floor. The bedcovers were rumpled, recently napped in, the pillows punched up against the headboard.

"Not much," he said. "But it's warm. And it's paid for." He turned on the TV. "We'd better keep an eye on the news. Maybe they'll have something on the Weaver woman."

The Weaver woman, she thought. *It could have been me.* She was shivering again, but now it wasn't from the cold. Settling onto the bed she stared numbly at the TV, not really seeing what was on the screen. She was more aware of *him*. He was circling the room, checking the windows, fiddling with the lock on the door. He moved quietly, efficiently, his silence a testimony to the dangers of their situation. Most men she knew began to babble nonsense when they were scared; Victor Holland simply turned quiet. His mere presence was overwhelming. He seemed to fill the room.

He moved to her side. She flinched as he took her hands and gently inspected them, palm side up. Looking down, she saw the bloodied scratches, the flakes of rust from the fire escape embedded in her skin.

"I guess I'm a mess," she murmured.

He smiled and stroked her face. "You could use some washing up. Go ahead. I'll get us something to eat."

She retreated into the bathroom. Through the door she could hear the drone of the TV, the sound of Victor's voice ordering a pizza over the phone. She ran hot water over her cold, numb hands. In the mirror over the sink she caught an unflattering glimpse of herself, her hair a tangled mess, her chin smudged with dirt. She washed her face, rubbing new life, new circulation into those frigid cheeks. Glancing down, she noticed Victor's razor on the counter. The sight of that blade cast her situation into a new focus—a frightening one. She picked up the razor, thinking how lethal that blade looked, how vulnerable she would be tonight. Victor was a large man, at least six foot two, with powerful arms. She was scarcely five foot five, a comparative weakling. There was only one bed in the next room. She had come here voluntarily. What would he assume about her? That she was a willing victim? She thought of all the ways a man could hurt her, kill her. It wouldn't take a razor to finish the job. Victor could use his bare hands. *What am I doing here?* she wondered. *Spending the night with a man I scarcely know?*

This was not the time to have doubts. She'd made the decision. She had to go by her instincts, and her instincts told her Victor Holland would never hurt her.

Deliberately she set down the razor. She would have to trust him. She was afraid not to.

In the other room, a door slammed shut. Had he left?

Opening the door a crack, she peered out. The TV was still on. There was no sign of Victor. Slowly she emerged, to find she was alone. She began to circle the room, searching for clues, anything that would tell her more about the man. The bureau drawers were empty, and so was the closet. Obviously he had not moved into this room for a long stay. He'd planned only one night, maybe two. She went to the nylon bag and glanced inside. She saw a clean pair of socks, an unopened package of underwear, and a day-old edition of the *San Francisco Chronicle*. All it told her was that the man kept himself informed and he traveled light.

Like a man on the run.

She dug deeper and came up with a receipt from an automatic teller machine. Yesterday he'd tried to withdraw cash. The machine had printed out the message: *Transaction cannot be completed. Please contact your bank.* Why had it refused him the cash? she wondered. Was he overdrawn? Had the machine been out of order?

The sound of a key grating in the lock caught her by surprise. She glanced up as the door swung open.

The look he gave her made her cheeks flush with guilt. Slowly she rose to her feet, unable to answer that look of accusation in his eyes.

The door swung shut behind him.

"I suppose it's a reasonable thing for you to do," he said. "Search my things."

"I'm sorry. I was just..." She swallowed. "I had to know more about you."

"And what terrible things have you dug up?"

"Nothing!"

"No deep dark secrets? Don't be afraid. Tell me, Cathy."

"Only...only that you had trouble getting cash out of your account."

He nodded. "A frustrating state of affairs. Since by my estimate I have a balance of six thousand dollars. And now I can't seem to touch it.'' He sat down in the chair, his gaze still on her face. ''What else did you learn?''

''You—you read the newspaper.''

''So do a lot of people. What else?''

She shrugged. ''You wear boxer shorts.''

Amusement flickered in his eyes. ''Now we're getting personal.''

''You...'' She took a deep breath. ''You're on the run.''

He looked at her a long time without saying a word.

''That's why you won't go to the police,'' she said. ''Isn't it?''

He turned away, gazing not at her but at the far wall. ''There are reasons.''

''Give me one, Victor. One good reason is all I need and then I'll shut up.''

He sighed. ''I doubt it.''

''Try me. I have every reason to believe you.''

''You have every reason to think I'm paranoid.'' Leaning forward, he ran his hands over his face. ''Lord, sometimes *I* think I must be.''

Quietly she went to him and knelt down beside his chair. ''Victor, these people who are trying to kill me—who are they?''

''I don't know.''

''You said it might involve people in high places.''

''It's just a guess. It's a case of federal money going to illegal research. Deadly research.''

''And federal money has to be doled out by someone in authority.''

He nodded. ''This is someone who's bent the rules. Someone who could be hurt by a political scandal. He just might try to protect himself by manipulating the Bureau. Or even your local police. That's why I won't go to them. That's why I left the room to make my call.''

''When?''

''While you were in the bathroom. I went to a pay phone and called the police. I didn't want it traced.''

''You just said you don't want them involved.''

"This call I had to make. There's a third Catherine Weaver in that phone book. Remember?"

A third victim on the list. Suddenly weak, she sat down on the bed. "What did you say?" she asked softly.

"That I had reason to think she might be in danger. That she wasn't answering her phone."

"You tried it?"

"Twice."

"Did they listen to you?"

"Not only did they listen, they demanded to know my name. That's when I picked up the cue that something must already have happened to her. At that point I hung up and hightailed it out of the booth. A call can be traced in seconds. They could've had me surrounded."

"That makes three," she whispered. "Those two other women. And me."

"They have no way of finding you. Not as long as you stay away from your apartment. Stay out of—"

They both froze in panic.

Someone was knocking on the door.

They stared at each other, fear mirrored in their eyes. Then, after a moment's hesitation, Victor said: "Who is it?"

"Domino's," called a thin voice.

Cautiously, Victor eased open the door. A teenage boy stood outside, wielding a bag and a flat cardboard box.

"Hi!" chirped the boy. "A large combo with the works, two Cokes and extra napkins. Right?"

"Right." Victor handed the boy a few bills. "Keep the change," he said and closed the door. Turning, he gave Cathy a sheepish look. "Well," he admitted. "Just goes to show you. Sometimes a knock at the door really is just the pizza man."

They both laughed, a sound not of humor but of frayed nerves. The release of tension seemed to transform his face, melted his wariness to warmth. Erase those haggard lines, she thought, and he could almost be called a handsome man.

"I tell you what," he said. "Let's not think about this mess right now. Why don't we just get right down to the really important issue of the day. Food."

Nodding, she reached out for the box. "Better hand it over. Before I eat the damn bedspread."

While the ten o'clock news droned from the television set, they tore into the pizza like two ravenous animals. It was a greasy and utterly satisfying banquet on a motel bed. They scarcely bothered with conversation—their mouths were too busy devouring cheese and pepperoni. On the TV, a dapper anchorman announced a shakeup in the mayor's office, the resignation of the city manager, news that, given their current situation, seemed ridiculously trivial. Scarcely thirty seconds were devoted to that morning's killing of Catherine Weaver I; as yet, no suspects were in custody. No mention was made of any second victim by the same name.

Victor frowned. "Looks like the other woman didn't make it to the news."

"Or nothing's happened to her." She glanced at him questioningly. "What if the second Cathy Weaver is all right? When you called the police, they might've been asking you routine questions. When you're on edge, it's easy to—"

"Imagine things?" The look he gave her almost made her bite her tongue.

"No," she said quietly. "Misinterpret. The police can't respond to every anonymous call. It's natural they'd ask for your name."

"It was more than a request, Cathy. They were champing at the bit to interrogate me."

"I'm not doubting your word. I'm just playing devil's advocate. Trying to keep things level and sane in a crazy situation."

He looked at her long and hard. At last he nodded. "The voice of a rational woman," he sighed. "Exactly what I need right now. To keep me from jumping at my own shadow."

"And remind you to eat." She held out another slice of pizza. "You ordered this giant thing. You'd better help me finish it."

The tension between them instantly evaporated. He settled onto the bed and accepted the proferred slice. "That maternal look becomes you," he noted wryly. "So does the pizza sauce."

"What?" She swiped at her chin.

"You look like a two-year-old who's decided to fingerpaint her face."

"Good grief, can you hand me the napkins?"

"Let me do it." Leaning forward, he gently dabbed away the sauce. As he did, she studied his face, saw the laugh lines creasing the corners of his eyes, the strands of silver intertwined with the brown hair. She remembered the photo of that very face, pasted on a Viratek badge. How somber he'd looked, the unsmiling portrait of a scientist. Now he appeared young and alive and almost happy.

Suddenly aware that she was watching him, he looked up and met her gaze. Slowly his smile faded. They both went very still, as though seeing, in each other's eyes, something they had not noticed before. The voices on the television seemed to fade into a far-off dimension. She felt his fingers trace lightly down her cheek. It was only a touch, but it left her shivering.

She asked, softly, "What happens now, Victor? Where do we go from here?"

"We have several choices."

"Such as?"

"I have friends in Palo Alto. We could turn to them."

"Or?"

"Or we could stay right where we are. For a while."

Right where we are. In this room, on this bed. She wouldn't mind that. Not at all.

She felt herself leaning toward him, drawn by a force against which she could offer no resistance. Both his hands came up to cradle her face, such large hands, but so infinitely gentle. She closed her eyes, knowing that this kiss, too, would be a gentle one.

And it was. This wasn't a kiss driven by fear or desperation. This was a quiet melting together of warmth, of souls. She swayed against him, felt his arms circle behind her to pull her inescapably close. It was a dangerous moment. She could feel herself tottering on the edge of total surrender to this man she scarcely knew. Already, her arms had found their way around his neck and her hands were roaming through the silver-streaked thickness of his hair.

His kisses dropped to her neck, exploring all the tender rises and hollows of her throat. All the needs that had lain dormant these past few years, all the hungers and desires, seemed to stir inside her, awakening at his touch.

And then, in an instant, the magic slipped away. At first she didn't understand why he suddenly pulled back. He sat bolt upright. The expression on his face was one of frozen astonishment. Bewildered, she followed his gaze and saw that he was focused on the television set behind her. She turned to see what had captured his attention.

A disturbingly familiar face stared back from the screen. She recognized the Viratek logo at the top, the straight-ahead gaze of the man in the photo. Why on earth would they be broadcasting Victor Holland's ID badge?

"...Sought on charges of industrial espionage. Evidence now links Dr. Holland to the death of a fellow Viratek researcher, Dr. Gerald Martinique. Investigators fear the suspect has already sold extensive research data to a European competitor...."

Neither one of them seemed able to move from the bed. They could only stare in disbelief at the newscaster with the Ken doll haircut. The station switched to a commercial break, raisins dancing crazily on a field, proclaiming the wonders of California sunshine. The lilting music was unbearable.

Victor rose to his feet and flicked off the television.

Slowly he turned to look at her. The silence between them grew agonizing.

"It's not true," he said quietly. "None of it."

She tried to read those unfathomable green eyes, wanting desperately to believe him. The taste of his kisses were still warm on her lips. The kisses of a con artist? *Is this just another lie? Has everything you've told me been nothing but lies? Who and what are you, Victor Holland?*

She glanced sideways, at the telephone on the bedside stand.

It was so close. One call to the police, that's all it would take to end this nightmare.

"It's a frame-up," he said. "Viratek's releasing false information."

"Why?"

"To corner me. What easier way to find me than to have the police help them?"

She edged toward the phone.

"Don't, Cathy."

She froze, startled by the threat in his voice.

He saw the instant fear in her eyes. Gently he said, "Please. Don't call. I won't hurt you. I promise you can walk right out that door if you want. But first listen to me. Let me tell you what happened. Give me a chance."

His gaze was steady and absolutely believable. And he was right beside her, ready to stop her from making a move. Or to break her arm, if need be. She had no other choice. Nodding, she settled back down on the bed.

He began to pace, his feet tracing a path in the dull green carpet.

"It's all some—some incredible lie," he said. "It's crazy to think I'd kill him. Jerry Martinique and I were the best of friends. We both worked at Viratek. I was in vaccine development, he was a microbiologist. His specialty was viral studies. Genome research."

"You mean—like chromosomes?"

"The viral equivalent. Anyway, Jerry and I, we helped each other through some bad times. He'd gone through a painful divorce and I..." He paused, his voice dropping. "I lost my wife three years ago. To leukemia."

So he'd been married. Somehow it surprised her. He seemed like the sort of man who was far too independent to have ever said, "I do."

"About two months ago," he continued, "Jerry was transferred to a new research department. Viratek had been awarded a grant for some defense project. It was top security—Jerry couldn't talk about it. But I could see he was bothered by something that was going on in that lab. All he'd say to me was, 'They don't understand the danger. They don't know what they're getting into.' Jerry's field was the alteration of viral genes. So I assume the project had something to do with viruses as weapons. Jerry was fully aware that those weapons are outlawed by international agreement.''

"If he knew it was illegal, why did he take part in it?''

"Maybe he didn't realize at first what the project was aiming for. Maybe they sold it to him as purely defensive research. In any event, he got upset enough to resign from the project. He went right to the top—the founder of Viratek. Walked into Archibald Black's office and threatened to go public if the project wasn't terminated. Four days later he had an accident.'' Anger flashed in Victor's eyes. It wasn't directed at her, but the fury in that gaze was frightening all the same.

"What happened to him?'' she asked.

"His wrecked car was found at the side of the road. Jerry was still inside. Dead, of course.'' Suddenly, the anger was gone, replaced by overwhelming weariness. He sank onto the bed. "I thought the accident investigation would blow everything into the open. It was a farce. The local cops did their best, but then some federal transportation ''expert'' showed up on the scene and took over. He said Jerry must've fallen asleep at the wheel. Case closed. That's when I realized just how deep this went. I didn't know who to go to, so I called the FBI in San Francisco. Told them I had evidence.''

"You mean the film?'' asked Cathy.

Victor nodded. "Just before he was killed, Jerry told me about some duplicate papers he'd stashed away in his garden shed. After the…accident, I went over to his house. Found the place ransacked. But they never bothered to search the shed. That's how I got hold of the evidence, a single file and a roll of film. I arranged a meeting with one of the San Francisco agents, a guy named Sam Polowski. I'd already talked to him a few times on the phone. He offered to meet me in Garberville. We wanted to keep it private, so we agreed to a spot just outside of town. I drove down, fully expecting him to show. Well someone showed up, all right. Someone who ran me off the road." He paused and looked straight at her. "That's the night you found me."

The night my whole life changed, she thought.

"You have to believe me," he said.

She studied him, her instincts battling against logic. The story was just barely plausible, halfway between truth and fantasy. But the man looked solid as stone.

Wearily she nodded. "I do believe you, Victor. Maybe I'm crazy. Or just gullible. But I do."

The bed shifted as he sat down beside her. They didn't touch, yet she could almost feel the warmth radiating between them.

"That's all that matters to me right now," he said. "That you know, in your heart, I'm telling the truth."

"In my heart?" She shook her head and laughed. "My heart's always been a lousy judge of character. No, I'm guessing. I'm going by the fact you kept me alive. By the fact there's another Cathy Weaver who's now dead..."

Remembering the face of that other woman, the face in the newspaper, she suddenly began to shake. It all added up to the terrible truth. The gun blasts into her apartment, the other dead Cathy. And Sarah, poor Sarah.

She was gulping in shaky breaths, hovering on the verge of tears.

She let him take her in his arms, let him pull her down on the bed beside him. He murmured into her hair, gentle words of comfort and reassurance. He turned off the lamp. In darkness they held each other, two frightened souls joined against a terrifying world. She felt safe there, tucked away against his chest. This was a place where no one could hurt her. It was a stranger's arms, but from the smell of his shirt to the beat of his heart, it all seemed somehow familiar. She never wanted to leave that spot, ever.

She trembled as his lips brushed her forehead. He was stroking her face now, her neck, warming her with his touch. When his hand slipped beneath her blouse, she didn't protest. Somehow it seemed so natural, that that hand would come to lie at her breast. It wasn't the touch of a marauder, it was simply a gentle reminder that she was in safekeeping.

And yet, she found herself responding....

Her nipple tingled and grew taut beneath his cupping hand. The tingling spread, a warmth that crept to her face and flushed her cheeks. She reached for his shirt and began to unbutton it. In the darkness she was slow and clumsy. By the time she finally slid her hand under the fabric, they were both breathing hard and fast with anticipation.

She brushed through the coarse mat of hair, stroking her way across that broad chest. He took in a sharp breath as her fingers skimmed a delicate circle around his nipple.

If playing with fire had been her intention, then she had just struck the match.

His mouth was suddenly on hers, seeking, devouring. The force of his kiss pressed her onto her back, trapping her head against the pillows. For a dizzy eternity she was swimming in sensations, the scent of male heat, the unyielding grip of his hands imprisoning her face. Only when he at last drew away did they both come up for air.

He stared down at her, as though hovering on the edge of temptation.

"This is crazy," he whispered.

"Yes. Yes, it is—"

"I never meant to do this—"

"Neither did I."

"It's just that you're scared. We're both scared. And we don't know what the hell we're doing."

"No." She closed her eyes, felt the unexpected bite of tears. "We don't. But I *am* scared. And I just want to be held. Please, Victor. Hold me, that's all. Just hold me."

He pulled her close, murmuring her name. This time the embrace was gentle, without the fever of desire. His shirt was still unbuttoned, his chest bared. And that's where she lay her head, against that curling nest of hair. Yes, he was right, so wise. They were crazy to be making love when they both knew it was fear, nothing else, that had driven their desire. And now the fever had broken.

A sense of peace fell over her. She curled up against him. Exhaustion robbed them both of speech. Her muscles graduall fell limp as sleep tugged her into its shadow. Even if she tried to, she could not move her arms or legs. Instead she was drifting free, like a wraith in the darkness, floating somewhere in a warm and inky sea.

Vaguely she was aware of light sliding past her eyelids.

The warmth encircling her body seemed to melt away. No, she wanted it back, wanted *him* back! An instant later she felt him shaking her.

"Cathy. Come on, wake up!"

Through drowsy eyes she peered at him. "Victor?"

"Something's going on outside."

She tumbled out of bed and followed him to the window. Through a slit in the curtains she spotted what had alarmed him: a patrol car, its radio crackling faintly, parked by the motel registration door. At once she snapped wide awake, her mind going over the exits from their room. There was only one.

"Out, now!" he ordered. "Before we're trapped."

He eased open the door. They scrambled out onto the walkway. The frigid night air was like a slap in the face. She was already shivering, more from fear than from the cold. Running at a crouch, they moved along the walkway, away from the stairs, and ducked past the ice machine.

Below, they heard the lobby door open and the voice of the motel manager: "Yeah, that'll be right upstairs. Gee, he sure seemed like a nice-enough guy...."

Tires screeched as another patrol car pulled up, lights flashing.

Victor gave her a push. *"Go!"*

They slipped into a breezeway and scurried through, to the other side of the building. No stairways there! They climbed over the walkway railing and dropped into the parking lot.

Faintly they heard a banging, then the command: "Open up! This is the police."

At once they were sprinting instinctively for the shadows. No one spotted them, no one gave chase. Still they kept running, until they'd left the Kon-Tiki Motel blocks and blocks behind them, until they were so tired they were stumbling.

At last Cathy slowed to a halt and leaned back against a

doorway, her breath coming out in clouds of cold mist. "How did they find you?" she said between gasps.

"It couldn't have been the call...." Suddenly he groaned. "My credit card! I had to use it to pay the bill."

"Where now? Should we try another motel?"

He shook his head. "I'm down to my last forty bucks. I can't risk a credit card again."

"And I left my purse at the apartment. I—I'm not sure I want to—"

"We're not going back for it. They'll be watching the place."

They. Meaning the killers.

"So we're broke," she said weakly.

He didn't answer. He stood with his hands in his pockets, his whole body a study in frustration. "You have friends you can go to?"

"I think so. Uh, no. She's out of town till Friday. And what would I tell her? How would I explain you?"

"You can't. And we can't handle any questions right now."

That leaves out most of my friends, she thought. Nowhere to go, no one to turn to. Unless...

No, she'd promised herself never to sink that low, never to beg for *that* particular source of help.

Victor glanced up the street. "There's a bus stop over there." He reached in his pocket and took out a handful of money. "Here," he said. "Take it and get out of the city. Go visit some friends on your own."

"What about you?"

"I'll be okay."

"Broke? With everyone after you?" She shook her head.

"I'll only make things more dangerous for you." He pressed the money into her hand.

She stared down at the wad of bills, thinking: *This is all he has. And he's giving it to me.* "I can't," she said.

"You have to."

"But—"

"Don't argue with me." The look in his eyes left no alternative.

Reluctantly she closed her fingers around the money.

"I'll wait till you get on the bus. It should take you right past the station."

"Victor?"

He silenced her with a single look. Placing both hands on her shoulders, he stood her before him. "You'll be fine," he said. Then he pressed a kiss to her forehead. For a moment his lips lingered, and the warmth of his breath in her hair left her trembling. "I wouldn't leave you if I thought otherwise."

The roar of a bus down the block made them both turn.

"There's your limousine," he whispered. "Go." He gave her a nudge. "Take care of yourself, Cathy."

She started toward the bus stop. Three steps, four. She slowed and came to a halt. Turning, she saw that he had already edged away into the shadows.

"Get on it!" he called.

She looked at the bus. *I won't do it,* she thought.

She turned back to Victor. "I know a place! A place we can both stay!"

"What?"

"I didn't want to use it but—"

Her words were drowned out as the bus wheezed to the stop, then roared away.

"It's a bit of a walk," she said. "But we'd have beds and a meal. And I can guarantee no one would call the police."

He came out of the shadows. "Why didn't you think of this earlier?"

"I did think of it. But up till now, things weren't, well... desperate enough."

"Not desperate enough," he repeated slowly. He moved toward her, his face taut with incredulity. "Not *desperate* enough? Hell, lady. I'd like to know exactly what kind of crisis would qualify!"

"You have to understand, this is a last resort. It's not an easy place for me to turn to."

His eyes narrowed in suspicion. "This place is beginning to sound worse and worse. What are we talking about? A flophouse?"

"No, it's in Pacific Heights. You could even call the place a mansion."

"Who lives there? A friend?"

"Quite the opposite."

His eyebrow shot up. "An enemy?"

"Close." She let out a sigh of resignation. "My ex-husband."

CHAPTER FIVE

"JACK, OPEN UP! Jack!" Cathy banged again and again on the door of the formidable Pacific Heights home. There was no answer. Through the windows they saw only darkness.

"Damn you, Jack!" She gave the door a slap of frustration. "Why aren't you *ever* home when I need you?"

Victor glanced around at the neighborhood of elegant homes and neatly trimmed shrubbery. "We can't stand around out here all night."

"We're not going to," she muttered. Crouching on her knees, she began to dig around in a red-brick planter.

"What are you doing?"

"Something I swore I'd never do." Her fingers raked the loamy soil, searching for the key Jack kept buried under the geraniums. Sure enough, there it was, right where it had always been. She rose to her feet, clapping the dirt off her hands. "But there are limits to my pride. Threat of death being one of them." She inserted the key and felt a momentary dart of panic when it didn't turn. But with a little jiggling, the lock at last gave way. The door swung open to the faint gleam of a polished wood floor, a massive bannister.

She motioned Victor inside. The solid thunk of the door closing behind them seemed to shut out all the dangers of the night. Cloaked in the darkness, they both let out a sigh of relief.

"Just what kind of terms are you on with your ex-husband?" Victor asked, following her blindly through the unlit foyer.

"Speaking. Barely."

"He doesn't mind you wandering around his house?"

"Why not?" She snorted. "Jack lets half the human race wander through his bedroom. The only prerequisite being XX chromosomes."

She felt her way into the pitch-dark living room and flipped on the light switch. There she froze in astonishment and stared at the two naked bodies intertwined on the polar bear rug.

"*Jack!*" she blurted out.

The larger of the two bodies extricated himself and sat up. "Hello, Cathy!" He raked his hand through his dark hair and grinned. "Seems like old times."

The woman lying next to him spat out a shocking obscenity, scrambled to her feet, and stormed off in a blur of wild red hair and bare bottom toward the bedroom.

"That's Lulu," yawned Jack, by way of introduction.

Cathy sighed. "I see your taste in women hasn't improved."

"No, sweetheart, my taste in women hit a high point when I married you." Unmindful of his state of nudity, Jack rose to his feet and regarded Victor. The contrast between the two men was instantly apparent. Though both were tall and lean, it was Jack who possessed the striking good looks, and he knew it. He'd always known it. Vanity wasn't a label one could ever pin on Victor Holland.

"I see you brought a fourth," said Jack, giving Victor the once-over. "So, what'll it be, folks? Bridge or poker?"

"Neither," said Cathy.

"That opens up all *sorts* of possibilities."

"Jack, I need your help."

He turned and looked at her with mock incredulity. "*No!*"

"You know damn well I wouldn't be here if I could avoid it!"

He winked at Victor. "Don't believe her. She's still madly in love with me."

"Can we get serious?"

"Darling, you never did have a sense of humor."

"*Damn you,* Jack!" Everyone had a breaking point and Cathy had reached hers. She couldn't help it; without warning she burst into tears. "For once in your life will you *listen* to me?"

That's when Victor's patience finally snapped. He didn' need a degree in psychology to know this Jack character wa a first-class jerk. Couldn't he see that Cathy was exhausted and terrified? Up till this moment, Victor had admired her for he strength. Now he ached at the sight of her vulnerability.

It was only natural to pull her into his arms, to ease her tear-streaked face against his chest. Over her shoulder, he growled out an oath that impugned not only Jack's name but that of Jack's mother as well.

The other man didn't seem to take offense, probably because he'd been called far worse names, and on a regular basis. He simply crossed his arms and regarded Victor with a raised eyebrow. "Being protective, are we?"

"She needs protection."

"From what, pray tell?"

"Maybe you haven't heard. Three days ago, someone murdered her friend Sarah."

"Sarah...Boylan?"

Victor nodded. "Tonight, someone tried to kill Cathy."

Jack stared at him. He looked at his ex-wife. "Is this true? What he's saying?"

Cathy, wiping away tears, nodded.

"Why didn't you tell me this to begin with?"

"Because you were acting like an ass to begin with!" she shot back.

Down the hall came the *click-click* of high-heeled shoes. "She's absolutely right!" yelled a female voice from the foyer. "You *are* an ass, Jack Zuckerman!" The front door opened and slammed shut again. The thud seemed to echo endlessly through the mansion.

There was a long silence.

Suddenly, through her tears, Cathy laughed. "You know what, Jack? I *like* that woman."

Jack crossed his arms and gave his ex-wife the critical once-over. "Either I'm going senile or you forgot to tell me something. Why haven't you gone to the police? Why bother old Jack about this?"

Cathy and Victor glanced at each other.

"We can't go to the police," Cathy said.

"I assume this has to do with *him?*" He cocked a thumb at Victor.

Cathy let out a breath. "It's a complicated story...."

"It must be. If you're afraid to go to the police."

"I can explain it," said Victor.

"Mm-hm. Well." Jack reached for the bathrobe lying in a heap by the polar bear rug. "Well," he said again, calmly tying the sash. "I've always enjoyed watching creativity at work. So let's have it." He sat down on the leather couch and smiled at Victor. "I'm waiting. It's showtime."

SPECIAL AGENT SAM POLOWSKI lay shivering in his bed, watching the eleven o'clock news. Every muscle in his body ached, his head pounded, and the thermometer at his bedside read an irrefutable 101 degrees. So much for changing flat tires in the pouring rain. He wished he could get his hands on the joker who'd punched that nail in his tire while he was grabbing a quick bite at that roadside cafe. Not only had the culprit managed to keep Sam from his appointment in Garberville, thereby shredding the Viratek case into confetti, Sam had also lost track of his only contact in the affair: Victor Holland. And now, the flu.

Sam reached over for the bottle of aspirin. To hell with the ulcer. His head hurt. And when it came to headaches, there was nothing like Mom's time-tested remedy.

He was in the midst of gulping down three tablets when the news about Victor Holland flashed on the screen.

"...New evidence links the suspect to the murder of fellow Viratek researcher, Dr. Gerald Martinique...."

Sam sat up straight in bed. "What the hell?" he growled at the TV.

Then he grabbed the telephone.

It took six rings for his supervisor to answer. "Dafoe?" Sam said. "This is Polowski."

"Do you know what time it is?"

"Have you seen the late-night news?"

"I happen to be in bed."

"There's a story on Viratek."

A pause. "Yeah, I know. I cleared it."

"What's with this crap about industrial espionage? They're making Holland out to be a—"

"Polowski, drop it."

"Since when did he become a murder suspect?"

"Look, just consider it a cover story. I want him brought in. For his own good."

"So you sic him with a bunch of trigger-happy cops?"

"I said drop it."

"But—"

"You're off the case." Dafoe hung up.

Sam stared in disbelief at the receiver, then at the television, then back at the receiver.

Pull me off the case? He slammed the receiver down so hard the bottle of aspirin tumbled off the nightstand.

That's what you think.

"I THINK I'VE HEARD about enough," said Jack, rising to his feet. "I want this man out of my house. And I want him out now."

"Jack, please!" said Cathy. "Give him a chance—"

"You're buying this ridiculous tale?"

"I believe him."

"Why?"

She looked at Victor and saw the clear fire of honesty burning in his eyes. "Because he saved my life."

"You're a fool, babycakes." Jack reached for the phone. "You yourself saw the TV. He's wanted for murder. If you don't call the police, I will."

But as Jack picked up the receiver, Victor grabbed his arm. "No," he said. Though his voice was quiet, it held the unmistakable note of authority.

The two men stared at each other, neither willing to back down.

"This is more than just a case of murder," said Victor. "This is deadly research. The manufacture of illegal weapons. This could reach all the way to Washington."

"Who in Washington?"

"Someone in control. Someone with the federal funds to authorize that research."

"I see. Some lofty public servant is out knocking off scientists. With the help of the FBI."

"Jerry wasn't just any scientist. He had a conscience. He was a whistleblower who would've taken this to the press to stop that research. The political fallout would've been disastrous, for the whole administration."

"Wait. Are we talking Pennsylvania Avenue?"

"Maybe."

Jack snorted. "Holland, I *make* Grade B horror films. I don't live them."

"This isn't a film. This is real. Real bullets, real bodies."

"Then that's all the more reason I want nothing to do with it." Jack turned to Cathy. "Sorry, sweetcakes. It's nothing personal, but I detest the company you keep."

"Jack," she said. "You have to help us!"

"You, I'll help. Him—no way. I draw the line at lunatics and felons."

"You heard what he said! It's a frame-up!"

"You are so gullible."

"Only about you."

"Cathy, it's all right," said Victor. He was standing very still, very calm. "I'll leave."

"No, you won't." Cathy shot to her feet and stalked over to her ex-husband. She stared him straight in the eye, a gaze so direct, so accusing, he seemed to wilt right down into a chair. "You owe it to me, Jack. You owe me for all the years we were married. All the years I put into *your* career, *your* company, *your* idiotic flicks. I haven't asked for anything. You have the house. The Jaguar. The bank account. I never asked because I didn't want to take a damn thing from this marriage except my own soul. But now I'm asking. This man saved my life tonight. If you ever cared about me, if you ever loved me, even a little, then you'll do me this favor."

"Harbor a criminal?"

"Only until we figure out what to do next."

"And how long might that take? Weeks? Months?"

"I don't know."

"Just the kind of definite answer I like."

Victor said, "I need time to find out what Jerry was trying to prove. What it is Viratek's working on—"

"You had one of his files," said Jack. "Why didn't you read the blasted thing?"

"I'm not a virologist. I couldn't interpret the data. It was some sort of RNA sequence, probably a viral genome. A lot of the data was coded. All I can be sure of is the name: Project Cerberus."

"Where is all this vital evidence now?"

"I lost the file. It was in my car the night I was shot. I'm sure they have it back."

"And the film?"

Victor sank into a chair, his face suddenly lined by weariness. "I don't have it. I was hoping that Cathy…" Sighing, he ran his hands through his hair. "I've lost that, too."

"Well," said Jack. "Give or take a few miracles, I'd say this puts your chances at just about zero. And I'm known as an optimist."

"I know where the film is," said Cathy.

There was a long silence. Victor raised his head and stared at her. "What?"

"I wasn't sure about you—not at first. I didn't want to tell you until I could be certain—"

Victor shot to his feet. *"Where is it?"*

She flinched at the sharpness of his voice. He must have noticed how startled she was—his next words were quiet but urgent. "I need that film, Cathy. Before they find it. Where is it?"

"Sarah found it in my car. I didn't know it was yours! I thought it was Hickey's."

"Who's Hickey?"

"A photographer—a friend of mine—"

Jack snorted. "Hickey. Now *there's* a ladies' man."

"He was in a rush to get to the airport," she continued. "At the last minute he left me with some rolls of film. Asked me to take care of them till he got back from Nairobi. But all his film was stolen from my car."

"And my roll?" asked Victor.

"It was in my bathrobe pocket the night Sarah—the night she—" She paused, swallowing at the mention of her friend. "When I got back here, to the city, I mailed it to Hickey's studio."

"Where's the studio?"

"Over on Union Street. I mailed it this afternoon—"

"So it should be there sometime tomorrow." He began to pace the room. "All we have to do is wait for the mail to arrive."

"I don't have a key."

"We'll find a way in."

"Terrific," sighed Jack. "Now he's turning my ex-wife into a burglar."

"We're only after the film!" said Cathy.

"It's still breaking and entering, sweetie."

"You don't have to get involved."

"But you're asking me to harbor the breakers and enterers."

"Just one night, Jack. That's all I'm asking."

"That sounds like one of *my* lines."

"And your lines always work, don't they?"

"Not this time."

"Then here's another line to chew on: 1988. Your federal tax return. Or lack of one."

Jack froze. He glowered at Victor, then at Cathy. "That's below the belt."

"Your most vulnerable spot."

"I'll get around to filing—"

"More words to chew on. Audit. IRS. Jail."

"Okay, okay!" Jack threw his arms up in surrender. "God, I *hate* that word."

"What, *jail?*"

"Don't laugh, babycakes. The word could soon apply to all of us." He turned and headed for the stairs.

"Where are you going?" Cathy demanded.

"To make up the spare beds. Seems I have houseguests for the night...."

"Can we trust him?" Victor asked after Jack had vanished upstairs.

Cathy sank back on the couch, all the energy suddenly drained from her body, and closed her eyes. "We have to. I can't think of anywhere else to go...."

She was suddenly aware of his approach, and then he was sitting beside her, so close she could feel the overwhelming strength of his presence. He didn't say a word, yet she knew he was watching her.

She opened her eyes and met his gaze. So steady, so intense, it seemed to infuse her with new strength.

"I know it wasn't easy for you," he said. "Asking Jack for favors."

She smiled. "I've always wanted to talk tough with Jack." Ruefully she added, "Until tonight, I've never quite been able to pull it off."

"My guess is, talking tough isn't in your repertoire."

"No, it isn't. When it comes to confrontation, I'm a gutless wonder."

"For a gutless wonder, you did pretty well. In fact, you were magnificent."

"That's because I wasn't fighting for me. I was fighting for you."

"You don't consider yourself worth fighting for?"

She shrugged. "It's the way I was raised. I was always told that sticking up for yourself was unladylike. Whereas sticking up for other people was okay."

He nodded gravely. "Self-sacrifice. A fine feminine tradition."

That made her laugh. "Spoken like a man who knows women well."

"Only two women. My mother and my wife."

At the mention of his dead wife, she fell silent. She wondered what the woman's name was, what she'd looked like, how much he'd loved her. He must have loved her a great deal—she'd heard the pain in his voice earlier that evening when he'd mentioned her death. She felt an unexpected stab of envy that this unnamed wife had been so loved. What Cathy would give to be as dearly loved by a man! Just as quickly she suppressed the thought, appalled that she could be jealous of a dead woman.

She turned away, her face tinged with guilt. "I think Jack will go along," she said. "Tonight, at least."

"That was blackmail, wasn't it? That stuff about the tax return?"

"He's a careless man. I just reminded him of his oversight."

Victor shook his head. "You are amazing. Jumping along rooftops one minute, blackmailing ex-husbands the next."

"You're so right," said Jack, who'd reappeared at the bottom of the stairs. "She is an amazing woman. I can't wait to see what she'll do next."

Cathy rose wearily to her feet. "At this point I'll do anything." She slipped past Jack and headed up the stairs. "Anything I have to to stay alive."

The two men listened to her footsteps recede along the hall. Then they regarded each other in silence.

"Well," said Jack with forced cheerfulness. "What's next on the agenda? Scrabble?"

"Try solitaire," said Victor, hauling himself off the couch. He was in no mood to share pleasantries with Jack Zuckerman. The man was slick and self-centered and he obviously went through women the way most men went through socks. Victor had a hard time imagining what Cathy had ever seen in the man. That is, aside from Jack's good looks and obvious wealth. There was no denying the fact he was a classic hunk, with the added attraction of money thrown in. Maybe it was that combination that had dazzled her.

A combination I'll certainly never possess, he thought.

He crossed the room, then stopped and turned. "Zuckerman?" he asked. "Do you still love your wife?"

Jack looked faintly startled by the question. "Do I still love her? Well, let me see. No, not exactly. But I suppose I have a sentimental attachment, based on ten years of marriage. And I respect her."

"Respect her? You?"

"Yes. Her talents. Her technical skill. After all, she's my number-one makeup artist."

That's what she meant to him. An asset he could use. *Thinking of himself, the jerk.* If there was anyone else Victor could turn to, he would. But the one man he would've trusted—Jerry—was dead. His other friends might already be under observation. Plus, they weren't in the sort of tax brackets that allowed private little hideaways in the woods. Jack, on the other hand, had the resources to spirit Cathy away to a safe place. Victor could only hope the man's sentimental attachment was strong enough to make him watch out for her.

"I have a proposition," said Victor.

Jack instantly looked suspicious. "What might that be?"

"I'm the one they're really after. Not Cathy. I don't want to make things any more dangerous for her than I already have."

"Big of you."

"It's better if I go off on my own. If I leave her with you, will you keep her safe?"

Jack shifted, looked down at his feet. "Well, sure. I guess so."

"Don't guess. Can you?"

"Look, we start shooting a film in Mexico next month. Jungle scenes, black lagoons, that sort of stuff. Should be a safe-enough place."

"That's next month. What about now?"

"I'll think of something. But first you get yourself out of the picture. Since you're the reason she's in danger in the first place."

Victor couldn't disagree with that last point. *Since the night I met her I've caused her nothing but trouble.*

He nodded. "I'm out of here tomorrow."

"Good."

"Take care of Cathy. Get her out of the city. Out of the country. Don't wait."

"Yeah. Sure."

Something about the way Jack said it, his hasty, whatever-you-say tone, made Victor wonder if the man gave a damn about anyone but himself. But at this point Victor had no choice. He had to trust Jack Zuckerman.

As he climbed the stairs to the guest rooms, it occurred to him that, come morning, it would be goodbye. A quiet little bond had formed between them. He owed his life to her and she to him. That was the sort of link one could never break.

Even if we never see each other again.

In the upstairs hall, he paused outside her closed door. He could hear her moving around the room, opening and closing drawers, squeaking bedsprings.

He knocked on the door. "Cathy?"

There was a pause. Then, "Come in."

One dim lamp lit the room. She was sitting on the bed, dressed in a ridiculously huge man's shirt. Her hair hung in damp waves to her shoulders. The scent of soap and shampoo permeated the shadows. It reminded him of his wife, of the shower smells and feminine sweetness. He stood there, pierced by a sense of longing he hadn't felt in over a year, longing for the warmth, the love, of a woman. Not just any woman. He wasn't like Jack, to whom a soft body with the right equipment would be sufficient. What Victor wanted was the heart and soul; the package they came wrapped in was only of minor importance.

His own wife Lily hadn't been beautiful; neither had she been unattractive. Even at the end, when the ravages of illness had left her shrunken and bruised, there had been a light in her eyes, a gentle spirit's glow.

The same glow he'd seen in Catherine Weaver's eyes the night she'd saved his life. The same glow he saw now.

She sat with her back propped up on pillows. Her gaze was silently expectant, maybe a little fearful. She was clutching a handful of tissues. *Why were you crying?* he wondered.

He didn't approach; he stood just inside the doorway. Their gazes locked together in the gloom. "I've just talked with Jack," he said.

She nodded but said nothing.

"We both agree. It's better that I leave as soon as possible. So I'll be taking off in the morning."

"What about the film?"

"I'll get it. All I need is Hickey's address."

"Yes. Of course." She looked down at the tissues in her fist.

He could tell she wanted to say something. He went to the bed and sat down. Those sweet woman smells grew intoxicating. The neckline of her oversized shirt sagged low enough to reveal a tempting glimpse of shadow. He forced himself to focus on her face.

"Cathy, you'll be fine. Jack said he'd watch out for you. Get you out of the city."

"Jack?" What sounded like a laugh escaped her throat.

"You'll be safer with him. I don't even know where I'll be going. I don't want to drag you into this—"

"But you already have. You've dragged me in over my head, Victor. What am I supposed to do now? I can't just—just sit around and wait for you to fix things. I owe it to Sarah—"

"And I owe it to you not to let you get hurt."

"You think you can hand me over to Jack and make everything be fine again? Well, it won't be fine. Sarah's dead. Her baby's dead. And somehow it's not just your fault. It's mine as well."

"No, it's not. Cathy—"

"It is my fault! Did you know she was lying there in the driveway all night? In the rain. In the cold. There she was, lying, and I slept through the whole damn thing...." She dropped her face in her hands. The guilt that had been tormenting her since Sarah's death at last burst through. She began to cry, silently, ashamedly, unable to hold back the tears any longer.

Victor's response was automatic and instinctively male. He pulled her against him and gave her a warm, safe place to cry. As soon as he felt her settle into his arms, he knew it was a mistake. It was too perfect a fit. She felt as if she belonged here, against his heart, felt that if she ever pulled away there would be left a hole so gaping it could never be filled. He pressed his lips to her damp hair and inhaled her heady scent of soap and warm skin. That gentle fragrance was enough to drown a man with need. So was the softness of her face, the silken luster of that shoulder peeking out from beneath the shirt. And all the time he was stroking her hair, murmuring inane words of comfort, he was thinking: *I have to leave her. For her sake I have to abandon this woman. Or I'll get us both killed.*

"Cathy," he said. It took all the willpower he could muster to pull away. He placed his hands on her shoulders, made her look at him. Her gaze was confused and brimming with tears. "We have to talk about tomorrow."

She nodded and swiped at the tears on her cheeks.

"I want you out of the city, first thing in the morning. Go to Mexico with Jack. Anywhere. Just keep out of sight."

"What will you do?"

"I'm going to take a look at that roll of film, see what kind of evidence it has."

"And then?"

"I don't know yet. Maybe I'll take it to the newspapers. The FBI is definitely out."

"How will I know you're all right? How do I reach you?"

He thought hard, fighting the distraction of her scent, her hair. He found himself stroking the bare skin of her shoulder, marveling at how smooth it felt beneath his fingers.

He focused on her face, on the look of worry in her eyes "Every other Sunday I'll put an ad in the Personals. *Los Angeles Times.* It'll be addressed to, let's say, Cora. Anything need to tell you will be there."

"Cora." She nodded. "I'll remember."

They looked at each other, a silent acknowledgment that thi parting had to be. He cupped her face and pressed a kiss to he mouth. She barely responded; already, it seemed, she had sai her goodbyes.

He rose from the bed and started for the door. There h couldn't resist asking, one more time: "You'll be all right?"

She nodded, but it was too automatic. The sort of nod one gave to dismiss an unimportant question. "I'll be fine. After all, I'll have Jack to watch over me."

He didn't miss the faint note of irony in her reply. Jack, it seemed, didn't inspire confidence in either of them. *What's my alternative? Drag her along with me as a moving target?*

He gripped the doorknob. No, it was better this way. He'd already ripped her life apart; he wasn't going to scatter the pieces as well.

As he was leaving, he took one last backward glance. She was still huddled on the bed, her knees drawn up to her chest. The oversized shirt had slid off one bare shoulder. For a moment he thought she was crying. Then she raised her head and met his gaze. What he saw in her eyes wasn't tears. It was something far more moving, something pure and bright and beautiful.

Courage.

IN THE PALE LIGHT of dawn, Savitch stood outside Jack Zuckerman's house. Through the fingers of morning mist, Savitch studied the curtained windows, trying to picture the inhabitants within. He wondered who they were, in which room they slept, and whether Catherine Weaver was among them.

He'd find out soon.

He pocketed the black address book he'd taken from the woman's apartment. The name C. Zuckerman and this Pacific Heights address had been written on the inside front cover. Then the Zuckerman had been crossed out and replaced with Weaver. She was a divorcée, he concluded. Under Z, he'd found a prominent listing for a man named Jack, with various phone numbers and addresses, both foreign and domestic. Her ex-husband, he'd confirmed, after a brief chat with another name listed in the book. Pumping strangers for information was a simple matter. All it took was an air of authority and a cop's ID. The same ID he was planning to use now.

He gave the house one final perusal, taking in the manicured lawns and shrubbery, the trellis with its vines of winter-dormant wisteria. A successful man, this Jack Zuckerman. Savitch had always admired men of wealth. He gave his jacket a final tug to assure himself that the shoulder holster was concealed. Then he crossed the street to the front porch and rang the doorbell.

CHAPTER SIX

AT FIRST LIGHT, Cathy awakened. It wasn't a gentle return but a startling jerk back to consciousness. She was instantly aware that she was not in her own bed and that something was terribly wrong. It took her a few seconds to remember exactly what it was. And when she did remember, the sense of urgency was so compelling she rose at once from bed and began to dress in the semidarkness. *Have to be ready to run...*

The creak of floorboards in the next room told her that Victor was awake as well, probably planning his moves for the day. She rummaged through the closet, searching for things he might need in his flight. All she came up with was a zippered nylon bag and a raincoat. She searched the dresser next and found a few men's socks. She also found a collection of women's underwear. *Damn Jack and all his women,* she thought with sudden irritation and slammed the drawer shut. The thud was still resonating in the room when another sound echoed through the house.

The doorbell was ringing.

It was only seven o'clock, too early for visitors or deliverymen. Suddenly her door swung open. She turned to see Victor, his face etched with tension.

"What should we do?" she asked.

"Get ready to leave. Fast."

"There's a back door—"

"Let's go."

They hurried along the hall and had almost reached the top of the stairs when they heard Jack's sleepy voice below, grumbling: "I'm coming, dammit! Stop that racket, I'm coming!"

The doorbell rang again.

"Don't answer it!" hissed Cathy. "Not yet—"

Jack had already opened the door. Instantly Victor snatched

Cathy back up the hall, out of sight. They froze with their backs against the wall, listening to the voices below.

"Yeah," they heard Jack say. "I'm Jack Zuckerman. And who are you?"

The visitor's voice was soft. They could tell only that it was a man.

"Is that so?" said Jack, his voice suddenly edged with panic. "You're with the *FBI,* you say? And what on earth would the *FBI* want with my *ex-wife?*"

Cathy's gaze flew to Victor. She read the frantic message in his eyes: *Which way out?*

She pointed toward the bedroom at the end of the hall. He nodded. Together they tiptoed along the carpet, all the time aware that one misstep, one loud creak, might be enough to alert the agent downstairs.

"Where's your warrant?" they heard Jack demand of the visitor. "Hey, wait a minute! You can't just barge in here without a court order or something!"

No time left! thought Cathy in panic as she slipped into the last room. They closed the door behind them.

"The window!" she whispered.

"You mean jump?"

"No." She hurried across the room and gingerly eased the window open. "There's a trellis!"

He glanced down dubiously at the tangled vines of wisteria. "Are you sure it'll hold us?"

"I know it will," she said, swinging her leg over the sill. "I caught one of Jack's blondes hanging off it one night. And believe me, she was a *big* girl." She glanced down at the ground far below and felt a sudden wave of nausea as the old fear of heights washed through her. "God," she muttered "Why do we always seem to be hanging out of windows?"

From somewhere in the house came Jack's outraged shout "You can't go up there! You haven't shown me your warrant!"

"*Move!*" snapped Victor.

Cathy lowered herself onto the trellis. Branches clawed he

face as she scrambled down the vine. An instant after she landed on the dew-soaked grass, Victor dropped beside her.

At once they were on their feet and sprinting for the cover of shrubbery. Just as they rolled behind the azalea bushes, they heard a second-floor window slide open, and then Jack's voice complaining loudly: "I know my rights! This is an illegal search! I'm going to call my lawyer!"

Don't let him see us! prayed Cathy, burrowing frantically into the bush. She felt Victor's body curl around her back, his arms pulling her tightly to him, his breath hot and ragged against her neck. For an eternity they lay shivering in the grass as mist swirled around them.

"You see?" they heard Jack say. "There's no one here but me. Or would you like to check the garage?"

The window slid shut.

Victor gave Cathy a little push. "Go," he whispered. "The end of the hedge. We'll run from there."

On hands and knees she crawled along the row of azalea bushes. Her soaked jeans were icy and her palms scratched and bleeding, but she was too numbed by terror to feel any pain. All her attention was focused on moving forward. Victor was crawling close behind her. When she felt him bump up against her hip, it occurred to her what a ridiculous view he had, her rump swaying practically under his nose.

She reached the last bush and stopped to shove a handful of tangled hair off her face. "That house next?" she asked.

"Go for it!"

They both took off like scared rabbits, dashing across the twenty yards of lawn between houses. Once they reached the cover of the next house, they didn't stop. They kept running, past parked cars and early-morning pedestrians. Five blocks later, they ducked into a coffee shop. Through the front window, they glanced out at the street, watching for signs of pursuit. All they saw was the typical Monday morning bustle: the stop-and-go traffic, the passersby bundled up in scarves and overcoats.

From the grill behind them came the hiss and sizzle of bacon. The smell of freshly brewed coffee wafted from the counter burner. The aromas were almost painful; they reminded Cathy that she and Victor probably had a total of forty dollars between them. Damn it, why hadn't she begged, borrowed or stolen some cash from Jack?

"What now?" she asked, half hoping he'd suggest blowing the rest of their cash on breakfast.

He scanned the street. "Let's go on."

"Where?"

"Hickey's studio."

"Oh." She sighed. Another long walk, and all on an empty stomach.

Outside, a car passed by bearing the bumper sticker: Today is the First Day of the Rest of Your Life.

Lord, I hope it gets better than this, she thought. Then she followed Victor out the door and into the morning chill.

FIELD SUPERVISOR LARRY DAFOE was sitting at his desk, pumping away at his executive power chair. Upper body strength, he always said, was the key to success as a man. Bulk out those muscles *pull!*, fill out that size forty-four jacket *pull!*, and what you got was a pair of shoulders that'd impress any woman, intimidate any rival. And with this snazzy 700-buck model, you didn't even have to get out of your chair.

Sam Polowski watched his superior strain at the system of wires and pulleys and thought the device looked more like an exotic instrument of torture.

"What you gotta understand," gasped Dafoe, "is that there are other *pull!* issues at work here. Things you know nothing about."

"Like what?" asked Polowski.

Dafoe released the handles and looked up, his face sheened with a healthy sweat. "If I was at liberty to tell you, don't you think I already would've?"

Polowski looked at the gleaming black exercise handles, wondering whether he'd benefit from an executive power chair. Maybe a souped-up set of biceps was what he needed to get a little respect around this office.

"I still don't see what the point is," he said. "Putting Victor Holland in the hot seat."

"The point," said Dafoe, "is that you don't call the shots."

"I gave Holland my word he'd be left out of this mess."

"He's *part* of the mess! First he claims he has evidence, then he pulls a vanishing act."

"That's partly my fault. I never made it to the rendezvous."

"Why hasn't he tried to contact you?"

"I don't know." Polowski sighed and shook his head. "Maybe he's dead."

"Maybe we just need to find him." Dafoe reached for the exercise handles. "Maybe you need to get to work on the Lanzano file. Or maybe you should just go home. You look terrible."

"Yeah. Sure." Polowski turned. As he left the office, he could hear Dafoe once again huffing and puffing. He went to his desk, sat down and contemplated his collection of cold capsules, aspirin and cough syrup. He took a double dose of each. Then he reached in his briefcase and pulled out the Viratek file.

It was his own private collection of scrambled notes and phone numbers and news clippings. He sifted through them, stopping to ponder once again the link between Holland and the woman Catherine Weaver. He'd first seen her name on the hospital admission sheet, and had later been startled to hear of her connection to the murdered Garberville woman. Too many coincidences, too many twists and turns. Was there something obvious here he was missing? Might the woman have an answer or two?

He reached for the telephone and dialed the Garberville police department. They would know how to reach their witness. And maybe she would know how to find Victor Holland. It was a long shot but Sam Polowski was an inveterate horseplayer. He had a penchant for long shots.

THE MAN RINGING his doorbell looked like a tree stump dressed in a brown polyester suit. Jack opened the door and said, "Sorry, I'm not buying today."

"I'm not selling anything, Mr. Zuckerman," said the man. "I'm with the FBI."

Jack sighed. "Not again."

"I'm Special Agent Sam Polowski. I'm trying to locate a woman named Catherine Weaver, formerly Zuckerman. I believe she—"

"Don't you guys ever know when to quit?"

"Quit what?"

"One of your agents was here this morning. Talk to him!"

The man frowned. "One of *our* agents?"

"Yeah. And I just might register a complaint against him. Barged right in here without a warrant and started tramping all over my house."

"What did he look like?"

"Oh, I don't know! Dark hair, terrific build. But he could've used a course in charm school."

"Was he about my height?"

"Taller. Skinnier. Lots more hair."

"Did he give you his name? It wasn't Mac Braden, was it?"

"Naw, he didn't give me any name."

Polowski pulled out his badge. Jack squinted at the words: Federal Bureau of Investigation. "Did he show you one of these?" asked Polowski.

"No. He just asked about Cathy and some guy named Victor Holland. Whether I knew how to find them."

"Did you tell him?"

"That jerk?" Jack laughed. "I wouldn't bother to give him the time of day. I sure as hell wasn't going to tell him about—" Jack paused and cleared his throat. "I wasn't going to tell him anything. Even if I knew. Which I don't."

Polowski slipped his badge into his pocket, all the time gazing steadily at Jack. "I think we should talk, Mr. Zuckerman."

"What about?"

"About your ex-wife. About the fact she's in big trouble."

"That," sighed Jack, "I already know."

"She's going to get hurt. I can't fill you in on all the details because I'm still in the dark myself. But I do know one woman's already been hit. Your wife—"

"My ex-wife."

"Your ex-wife could be next."

Jack, unconvinced, merely looked at him.

"It's your duty as a citizen to tell me what you know," Polowski reminded him.

"My duty. Right."

"Look, cooperate, and you and me, we'll get along just fine. Give me grief, and I'll give *you* grief." Polowski smiled. Jack didn't. "Now, Mr. Zuckerman. Hey, can I call you Jack? Jack, why don't you tell me where she is? Before it's too late. For both of you."

Jack scowled at him. He drummed his fingers against the door frame. He debated. At last he stepped aside. "As a law-abiding citizen, I suppose it is my duty." Grudgingly, he waved the man in. "Oh, just come in, Polowski. I'll tell you what I know."

THE WINDOW SHATTERED, raining slivers into the gloomy space beyond.

Cathy winced at the sound. "Sorry, Hickey," she said under her breath.

"We'll make it up to him," said Victor, knocking off the remaining shards. "We'll send him a nice fat check. You see anyone?"

She glanced up and down the alley. Except for a crumpled newspaper tumbling past the trash cans, nothing moved. A few blocks away, car horns blared, the sounds of another Union Street traffic jam.

"All clear," she whispered.

"Okay." Victor draped his windbreaker over the sill. "Up you go."

He gave her a lift to the window. She clambered through and landed among the glass shards. Seconds later, Victor dropped down beside her.

They were standing in the studio dressing room. Against one wall hung a rack of women's lingerie; against the other were makeup tables and a long mirror.

Victor frowned at a cloud of peach silk flung over one of

the chairs. "What kind of photos does your friend take, anyway?"

"Hickey specializes in what's politely known as 'boudoir portraits.'"

Victor's startled gaze turned to a black lace negligee hanging from a wall hook. "Does that mean what I think it means?"

"What do you think it means?"

"You know."

She headed into the next room. "Hickey insists it's not pornography. It's tasteful erotic art...." She stopped in her tracks as she came face-to-face with a photo blowup on the wall. Naked limbs—eight, maybe more—were entwined in a sort of human octopus. Nothing was left to the imagination. Nothing at all.

"Tasteful," Victor said dryly.

"That must be one of his, uh, commercial assignments."

"I wonder what product they were selling."

She turned and found herself staring at another photograph. This time it was two women, drop-dead gorgeous and wearing not a stitch.

"Another commercial assignment?" Victor inquired politely over her shoulder.

She shook her head. "Don't ask."

In the front room they found a week's worth of mail piled up beneath the door slot, darkroom catalogues and advertising flyers. The roll of film Cathy had mailed the day before was not yet in the mound.

"I guess we just sit around and wait for the postman," she said.

He nodded. "Seems like a safe-enough place. Any chance your friend keeps food around?"

"I seem to remember a refrigerator in the other room."

She led Victor into what Hickey had dubbed his "shooting gallery." Cathy flipped the wall switch and the vast room was instantly illuminated by a dazzling array of spotlights.

"So this is where he does it," said Victor, blinking in the sudden glare. He stepped over a jumble of electrical cords and slowly circled the room, regarding with humorous disbelief the various props. It was a strange collection of objects: a genuine English phone booth, a street bench, an exercise bicycle. In a place of honor sat a four-poster bed. The ruffled coverlet was Victorian; the handcuffs dangling from the bedposts were not.

Victor picked up one of the cuffs and let it fall again. "Just how good a friend *is* this Hickey guy, anyway?"

"None of this stuff was here when he shot me a month ago."

"He photographed *you?*" Victor turned and stared at her.

She flushed, imagining the images that must be flashing through his mind. She could feel his gaze undressing her, posing her in a sprawl across that ridiculous four-poster bed. With the handcuffs, no less.

"It wasn't like—like these other photos," she protested. "I mean, I just did it as a favor...."

"A favor?"

"It was a purely *commercial* shot!"

"Oh."

"I was fully dressed. In overalls, as a matter of fact. I was supposed to be a plumber."

"A lady plumber?"

"I was an emergency stand-in. One of his models didn't show up that day, and he needed someone with an ordinary face. I guess that's me. Ordinary. And it really was just my face."

"And your overalls."

"Right."

They looked at each other and burst out laughing.

"I can guess what you were thinking," she said.

"I don't even want to *tell* you what I was thinking." He turned and glanced around the room. "Didn't you say there was some food around here?"

She crossed the room to the refrigerator. Inside she found a shelf of film plus a jar of sweet pickles, some rubbery carrots and half a salami. In the freezer they discovered real treasures: ground Sumatran coffee and a loaf of sourdough bread.

Grinning, she turned to him. "A feast!"

They sat together on the four-poster bed and gnawed on salami and half-frozen sourdough, all washed down with cups of coffee. It was a bizarre little picnic, paper plates with pickles and carrots resting in their laps, the spotlights glaring down like a dozen hot suns from the ceiling.

"Why did you say that about yourself?" he asked, watching her munch a carrot.

"Say what?"

"That you're ordinary. So ordinary that you get cast as the lady plumber?"

"Because I am ordinary."

"I don't think so. And I happen to be a pretty good judge of character."

She looked up at a wall poster featuring one of Hickey's super models. The woman stared back with a look of glossy confidence. "Well, I certainly don't measure up to *that*."

"*That*," he said, "is pure fantasy. *That* isn't a real woman, but an amalgam of makeup, hairspray and fake eyelashes."

"Oh, I know that. That's my job, turning actors into some moviegoer's fantasy. Or nightmare, as the case may be." She reached into the jar and fished out the last pickle. "No, I really meant *underneath* it all. Deep inside, I *feel* ordinary."

"I think you're quite extraordinary. And after last night, I should know."

She gazed down, at the limp carrot stretched out like a little corpse across the paper plate. "There was a time—I suppose there's always that time, for everyone, when we're still young, when we feel special. When we feel the world's meant just for us. The last time I felt that way was when I married Jack." She sighed. "It didn't last long."

"Why did you marry him?"

"I don't know. Dazzle? I was only twenty-three, a mere apprentice on the set. He was the director." She paused. "He was *God*."

"He impressed you, did he?"

"Jack can be very impressive. He can turn on the power, the charisma, and just overwhelm a gal. Then there was the champagne, the suppers, the flowers. I think what attracted him to me was that I didn't immediately fall for him. That I wasn't swooning at his every look. He thought of me as a challenge, the one he finally conquered.'' She gave him a rueful look. ''That accomplished, he moved onto bigger and better things. That's when I realized that I wasn't particularly special. That I'm really just a perfectly ordinary woman. It's not a bad feeling. It's not as if I go through life longing to be someone different, someone special.''

''Then who do you consider special?''

''Well, my grandmother. But she's dead.''

''Venerable grandmothers always make the list.''

''Okay, then. Mother Teresa.''

''She's on everyone's list.''

''Kate Hepburn. Gloria Steinem. My friend Sarah...'' Her voice faded. Looking down, she added softly: ''But she's dead, too.''

Gently he took her hand. With a strange sense of wonder she watched his long fingers close over hers and thought about how the strength she felt in that grasp reflected the strength of the man himself. Jack, for all his dazzle and polish, had never inspired a fraction of the confidence she now felt in Victor. No man ever had.

He was watching her with quiet sympathy. ''Tell me about Sarah,'' he said.

Cathy swallowed, trying to stem the tears. ''She was absolutely lovely. I don't mean in *that* way.'' She nodded at the photo of Hickey's picture-perfect model. ''I mean, in an inner sort of way. It was this look in her eyes. A perfect calmness. As though she'd found exactly what she wanted while all the rest of us were still grubbing around for lost treasure. I don't think she was born like that. She came to it, all by herself. In college, we were both pretty unsure of ourselves. Marriage certainly didn't help either of us. My divorce—it was nothing short of devastating. But Sarah's divorce only seemed to make her stronger. Better able to take care of herself. When she finally got pregnant, it was exactly as she planned it. There wasn't a father, you see, just a test tube. An anonymous donor. Sarah used to say that the primeval family unit wasn't man, woman and child. It was just woman and child. I thought she was brave, to take that step. She was a lot braver than I could ever be...." She cleared her throat. "Anyway, Sarah *was* special. Some people simply are."

"Yes," he said. "Some people are."

She looked up at him. He was staring off at the far wall, his gaze infinitely sad. What had etched those lines of pain in his face? She wondered if lines so deep could ever be erased. There were some losses one never got over, never accepted.

Softly she asked, "What was your wife like?"

He didn't answer at first. She thought: *Why did I ask that? Why did I have to bring up such terrible memories?*

He said, "She was a kind woman. That's what I'll always remember about her. Her kindness." He looked at Cathy and she sensed it wasn't sadness she saw in those eyes, but acceptance.

"What was her name?"

"Lily. Lillian Dorinda Cassidy. A mouthful for such a tiny woman." He smiled. "She was about five foot one, maybe ninety pounds sopping wet. It used to scare me, how small she always seemed. Almost breakable. Especially toward the end, when she'd lost all that weight. It seemed as if she'd shrunk down to nothing but a pair of big brown eyes."

"She must have been young when she died."

"Only thirty-eight. It seemed so unfair. All her life, she'd done everything right. Never smoked, hardly ever touched a glass of wine. She even refused to eat meat. After she was diagnosed, we kept trying to figure out how it could've happened. Then it occurred to us what might have caused it. She grew up in a small town in Massachusetts. Directly downwind from a nuclear power plant."

"You think that was it?"

"One can never be sure. But we asked around. And we learned that, just in her neighborhood, at least twenty families had someone with leukemia. It took four years and a class-action suit to force an investigation. What they found was a history of safety violations going back all the way to the plant's opening."

Cathy shook her head in disbelief. "And all those years they allowed it to operate?"

"No one knew about it. The violations were hushed up so well even the federal regulators were kept in the dark."

"They shut it down, didn't they?"

He nodded. "I can't say I got much satisfaction, seeing the plant finally close. By that time Lily was gone. And all the families, well, we were exhausted by the fight. Even though it sometimes felt as though we were banging our heads against a wall, we knew it was something we had to do. *Somebody* had to do it, for all the Lilys of the world." He looked up, at the spotlights shining above. "And here I am again, still banging my head against walls. Only this time, it feels like the Great Wall of China. And the lives at stake are yours and mine."

Their gazes met. She sat absolutely still as he lightly stroked down the curve of her cheek. She took his hand, pressed it to her lips. His fingers closed over hers, refusing to release her hand. Gently he tugged her close. Their lips met, a tentative kiss that left her longing for more.

"I'm sorry you were pulled into this," he murmured. "You and Sarah and those other Cathy Weavers. None of you asked to be part of it. And somehow I've managed to hurt you all."

"Not you, Victor. You're not the one to blame. It's this windmill you're tilting at. This giant, dangerous windmill. Anyone else would have dropped his lance and fled. You're still going at it."

"I didn't have much of a choice."

"But you did. You could have walked away from your friend's death. Turned a blind eye to whatever's going on at Viratek. That's what Jack would have done."

"But I'm not Jack. There are things I can't walk away from. I'd always be thinking of the Lilys. All the thousands of people who might get hurt."

At the mention once again of his dead wife, Cathy felt some unbreachable barrier form between them—the shadow of Lily, the wife she'd never met. Cathy drew back, at once aching from the loss of his touch.

"You think that many people could die?" she asked.

"Jerry must have thought so. There's no way to predict the outcome. The world's never seen the effects of all-out biological warfare. I like to think it's because we're too smart to play with our own self-destruction. Then I think of all the crazy things people have done over the years and it scares me...."

"Are viral weapons that dangerous?"

"If you alter a few genes, make it just a little more contagious, raise the kill ratio, you'd end up with a devastating strain. The research alone is hazardous. A single slip-up in lab security and you could have millions of people accidentally infected. And no means of treatment. It's the kind of worldwide disaster a scientist doesn't want to think about."

"Armageddon."

He nodded, his gaze frighteningly sane. "If you believe in such a thing. That's exactly what it'd be."

She shook her head. "I don't understand why these things are allowed."

"They aren't. By international agreement, they're outlawed. But there's always some madman lurking in the shadows who wants that extra bit of leverage, that weapon no one else has."

A madman. That's what one would have to be, to even think of unleashing such a weapon on the world. She thought of a novel she'd read, about just such a plague, how the cities had lain dead and decaying, how the very air had turned poisonous. But those were only the nightmares of science fiction. This was real.

From somewhere in the building came the sound of whistling.

Cathy and Victor both sat up straight. The melody traveled along the hall, closer and closer, until it stopped right outside Hickey's door. They heard a rustling, then the slap of magazines hitting the floor.

"It's here!" said Cathy, leaping to her feet.

Victor was right behind her as she hurried into the front room. She spotted it immediately, sitting atop the pile: a padded envelope, addressed in her handwriting. She scooped it up and ripped the envelope open. Out slid the roll of film. The note she'd scribbled to Hickey fluttered to the floor. Grinning in triumph, she held up the canister. "Here's your evidence!"

"We hope. Let's see what we've got on the roll. Where's the darkroom?"

"Next to the dressing room." She handed him the film. "Do you know how to process it?"

"I've done some amateur photography. As long as I've got the chemicals I can—" He stopped and glanced over at the desk.

The phone was ringing.

Victor shook his head. "Ignore it," he said and turned for the darkroom.

As they left the reception room, they heard the answering machine click on. Hickey's voice, smooth as silk, spoke on the recording. "This is the studio of Hickman Von Trapp, specializing in tasteful and artistic images of the female form...."

Victor laughed. "Tasteful?"

"It depends on your taste," said Cathy as she followed him up the hall.

They had just reached the darkroom when the recording ended and was followed by the message beep. An agitated voice rattled from the speaker. "Hello? Hello, Cathy? If you're there, answer me, will you? There's an FBI agent looking for you—some guy named Polowski—"

Cathy stopped dead. "It's Jack!" she said, turning to retrace her steps toward the front room.

The voice on the speaker had taken on a note of panic. "I couldn't help it—he made me tell him about Hickey. Get out of there now!"

The message clicked off just as Cathy grabbed the receiver. "Hello? *Jack?*"

She heard only the dial tone. He'd already hung up. Hands shaking, she began to punch in Jack's phone number.

"There's no time!" said Victor.

"I have to talk to him—"

He grabbed the receiver and slammed it down. "Later! We have to get out of here!"

She nodded numbly and started for the door. There she halted. "Wait. We need money!" She turned back to the reception desk and searched the drawers until she found the petty cash box. Twenty-two dollars was all it contained. "Always keep just enough for decent coffee beans," Hickey used to say. She pocketed the money. Then she reached up and yanked one of Hickey's old raincoats from the door hook. He wouldn't miss it. And she might need it for concealment. "Okay," she said, slipping on the coat. "Let's go."

They paused only a second to check the corridor. From another suite came the faint echo of laughter. Somewhere above, high heels clicked across a wooden floor. With Victor in the lead, they darted down the hall and out the front door.

The midday sun seemed to glare down on them like an accusing eye. Quickly they fell into step with the rest of the lunch crowd, the businessmen and artists, the Union Street chic. No one glanced their way. But even with people all around her, Cathy felt conspicuous. As though, in this bright cityscape of crowds and concrete, she was the focus of the painter's eye.

She huddled deeper into the raincoat, wishing it were a mantle of invisibility. Victor had quickened his pace, and she had to run to keep up.

"Where do we go now?" she whispered.

"We've got the film. Now I say we head for the bus station."

"And then?"

"Anywhere." He kept his gaze straight ahead. "As long as it's out of this city."

CHAPTER SEVEN

THAT PESKY FBI AGENT was ringing his doorbell again.

Sighing, Jack opened the front door. "Back already?"

"Damn right I'm back." Polowski stamped in and shoved the door closed behind him. "I want to know where to find 'em next."

"I told you, Mr. Polowski. Over on Union Street there's a studio owned by Mr. Hickman—"

"I've been to Von Whats-his-name's studio."

Jack swallowed. "You didn't find them?"

"You knew I wouldn't. You warned 'em, didn't you?"

"Really, I don't know why you're harrassing me. I've tried to be—"

"They left in a hurry. The door was wide open. Food was still lying around. They left the empty cash box just sitting on the desk."

Jack drew himself up in outrage. "Are you calling my ex-wife a petty thief?"

"I'm calling her a desperate woman. And I'm calling you an imbecile for screwing things up. Now where is she?"

"I don't know."

"Who would she turn to?"

"No one I know."

"Think harder."

Jack stared down at Polowski's turgid face and marveled that any human being could be so unattractive. Surely the process of natural selection would have dictated against such unacceptable genes?

Jack shook his head. "I honestly don't know."

It was the truth, and Polowski must have sensed it. After a moment of silent confrontation, he backed off. "Then maybe you can tell me this. Why did you warn them?"

"It—it was—" Jack shrugged helplessly. "Oh, I don't know! After you left, I wasn't sure I'd done the right thing. I wasn't sure whether to trust you. *He* doesn't trust you."

"Who?"

"Victor Holland. He thinks you're in on some conspiracy. Frankly, the man struck me as just the slightest bit paranoid."

"He has a right to be. Considering what's happened to him so far." Polowski turned for the door.

"Now what happens?"

"I keep looking for them."

"Where?"

"You think I'd tell *you?*" He stalked out. "Don't leave town, Zuckerman," he snapped over his shoulder. "I'll be back to see you later."

"I don't think so," Jack muttered softly as he watched the other man lumber back to his car. He looked up and saw there wasn't a cloud in the sky. Smiling to himself, he shut the door.

It would be sunny in Mexico, as well.

SOMEONE HAD LEFT in a hurry.

Savitch strolled through the rooms of the photo studio, which had been left unlocked. He noted the scraps of a meal on the four-poster bed: crumbs of sourdough bread, part of a salami, an empty pickle jar. He also took note of the coffee cups: there were two of them. Interesting, since Savitch had spotted only one person leaving the studio, a squat little man in a polyester suit. The man hadn't been there long. Savitch had observed him climb into a dark green Ford parked at a fifteen-minute meter. The meter still had three minutes remaining.

Savitch continued his tour of the studio, eyeing the tawdry photos, wondering if this wasn't another waste of his time. After all, every other address he'd pulled from the woman's black book had turned up no sign of her. Why should Hickman Von Trapp's address be any different?

Still, he couldn't shake the instinct that he was getting close. Clues were everywhere. He read them, put them together. To day, this studio had been visited by two hungry people. They' entered through a broken window in the dressing room. They' eaten scraps taken from the refrigerator. They (or the man in the polyester suit) had emptied the petty cash box.

Savitch completed his tour and returned to the front room. That's when he noticed the telephone message machine blinking on and off.

He pressed the play button. The string of messages seemed endless. The calls were for someone named Hickey—no doubt the Hickman Von Trapp of the address book. Savitch lazily circled the room, half listening to the succession of voices. Business calls for the most part, inquiring about appointments, asking when proofs would be ready and would he like to do the shoot for *Snoop* magazine? Near the door, Savitch halted and stooped down to sift through the pile of mail. It was boring stuff, all addressed to Von Trapp. Then he noticed, off to the side, a loose slip of paper. It was a note, addressed to Hickey.

"Feel awful about this, but someone stole all those rolls of film from my car. This was the only one left. Thought I'd get it to you before it's lost, as well. Hope it's enough to save your shoot from being a complete waste—"

It was signed "Cathy."

He stood up straight. Catherine Weaver? It had to be! The roll of film—where the hell was the roll of film?

He rifled through the mail, searching, searching. He turned up only a torn envelope with Cathy Weaver's return address. The film was gone. In frustration, he began to fling magazines across the room. Then, in mid-toss, he froze.

A new message was playing on the recorder.

"Hello? Hello, Cathy? If you're there, answer me, will you? There's an FBI agent looking for you—some guy named Polowski. I couldn't help it—he made me tell him about Hickey. Get out of there now!"

Savitch stalked over to the answering machine and stared down as the mechanism automatically whirred back to the beginning. He replayed it.

Get out of there now!

There was now no doubt. Catherine Weaver had been here, and Victor Holland was with her. But who was this agent Polowski and why was he searching for Holland? Savitch had

been assured that the Bureau was off the case. He would have
to check into the matter.

He crossed over to the window and stared out at the bright
sunshine, the crowded sidewalks. So many faces, so many
strangers. Where, in this city, would two terrified fugitives
hide? Finding them would be difficult, but not impossible.

He left the suite and went outside to a pay phone. There he
dialed a Washington, D.C., number. He wasn't fond of asking
the Cowboy for help, but now he had no choice. Victor Holland
had his hands on the evidence, and the stakes had shot sky-
high.

It was time to step up the pursuit.

THE CLERK YELLED, "Next window, please!" and closed the
grate.

"Wait!" cried Cathy, tapping at the pane. "My bus is leaving right now!"

"Which one?"

"Number 23 to Palo Alto—"

"There's another at seven o'clock."

"But—"

"I'm on my dinner break."

Cathy stared helplessly as the clerk walked away. Over the
PA system came the last call for the Palo Alto express. Cathy
glanced around just in time to see the Number 23 roar away
from the curb.

"Service just ain't what it used to be," an old man muttered
behind her. "Get there faster usin' yer damn thumb."

Sighing, Cathy shifted to the next line, which was eight-deep
and slow as molasses. The woman at the front was trying to
convince the clerk that her social security card was an acceptable ID for a check.

Okay, Cathy thought. *So we leave at seven o'clock. That puts
us in Palo Alto at eight. Then what? Camp in a park? Beg a
few scraps from a restaurant? What does Victor have in
mind…?*

She glanced around and spotted his broad back hunched inside one of the phone booths. Whom could he possibly be

calling? She saw him hang up and run his hand wearily through his hair. Then he picked up the receiver and dialed another number.

"Next!" Someone tapped Cathy on the shoulder. "Go ahead, Miss."

Cathy turned and saw that the ticket clerk was waiting. She stepped to the window.

"Where to?" asked the clerk.

"I need two tickets to…" Cathy's voice suddenly faded.

"Where?"

Cathy didn't speak. Her gaze had frozen on a poster tacked right beside the ticket window. The words Have You seen This Man? appeared above an unsmiling photo of Victor Holland. And at the bottom were listed the charges: Industrial espionage and murder. If you have any information about this man, please contact your local police or the FBI.

"Lady, you wanna go somewhere or not?"

"What?" Cathy's gaze jerked back to the clerk, who was watching her with obvious annoyance. "Oh. Yes, I'm—I'd like two tickets. To Palo Alto." Numbly she handed over a fistful of cash. "One way."

"Two to Palo Alto. That bus will depart at 7:00, Gate 11."

"Yes. Thank you…" Cathy took the tickets and turned to leave the line. That's when she spotted the two policemen, standing just inside the front entrance. They seemed to be scanning the terminal, searching—for what?

In a panic, her gaze shot to the phone booth. It was empty. She stared at it with a sense of abandonment. *You left me! You left me with two tickets to Palo Alto and five bucks in my pocket!*

Where are you, Victor?

She couldn't stand here like an idiot. She had to do something, had to move. She pulled the raincoat tightly around her shoulders and forced herself to stroll across the terminal. *Don't let them notice me,* she prayed. *Please. I'm nobody. Nothing.* She paused at a chair and picked up a discarded *San Francisco Chronicle.* Then, thumbing through the Want Ads, she sauntered right past the two policemen. They didn't even glance at her as she went out the front entrance.

Now what? she wondered, pausing amidst the confusion of a busy sidewalk. Automatically she started to walk and had taken only half a dozen steps down the street when she was wrenched sideways, into an alley.

She reeled back against the trash cans and almost sobbed with relief. "Victor!"

"Did they see you?"

"No. I mean, yes, but they didn't seem to care—"

"Are you sure?" She nodded. He turned and slapped the wall in frustration. "What the hell do we do now?"

"I have the tickets."

"We can't use them."

"How are we going to get out of town? Hitchhike? Victor, we're down to our last five dollars!"

"They'll be watching every bus that leaves. And they've got my face plastered all over the damn terminal!" He slumped back against the wall and groaned. "*Have you seen this man?* God, I looked like some two-bit gangster."

"It wasn't the most flattering photo."

He managed to laugh. "Have you *ever* seen a flattering wanted poster?"

She leaned back beside him, against the wall. "We've got to get out of this city, Victor."

"Amend that. *You've* got to get out."

"What's that supposed to mean?"

"The police aren't looking for you. So *you* take that bus to Palo Alto. I'll put you in touch with some old friends. They'll see you make it somewhere safe."

"No."

"Cathy, they've probably got my mug posted in every airport and car rental agency in town! We've spent almost all our money for those bus tickets. I say you use them!"

"I'm not leaving you."

"You don't have a choice."

"Yes I do. I choose to stick to you like glue. Because you're the only one I feel safe with. The only one I can count on!"

"I can move faster on my own. Without you slowing me down." He looked off, toward the street. "Hell, I don't even *want* you around."

"I don't believe that."

"Why should I care what you believe?"

"Look at me! Look at me and say that!" She grabbed his arm, willing him to face her. "Say you don't want me around!"

He started to speak, to repeat the lie. She knew then that it *was* a lie; she could see it in his eyes. And she saw something else in that gaze, something that took her breath away.

He said, "I don't—I won't have you—"

She just stood there, looking up at him, waiting for the truth to come.

What she didn't expect was the kiss. She never remembered how it happened. She only knew that all at once his arms were around her and she was being swept up into some warm and safe and wonderful place. It started as an embrace more of desperation than passion, a coming together of two terrified people. But the instant their lips met, it became something much more. This went beyond fear, beyond need. This was a souls' joining, one that wouldn't be broken, even after this embrace was over, even if they never touched again.

When at last they drew apart and stared at each other, the taste of him was still fresh on her lips.

"You see?" she whispered. "I was right. You do want me around. You do."

He smiled and touched her cheek. "I'm not a very good liar."

"And I'm not leaving you. You need me. You can't show your face, but I can! I can buy bus tickets, run errands—"

"What I really need," he sighed, "is a new face." He glanced out at the street. "Since there's no plastic surgeon handy, I suggest we hoof it over to the BART station. It'll be crowded at this hour. We might make it to the East Bay—"

"God, I'm such an *idiot!*" she groaned. "A new face is exactly what you need!" She turned toward the street. "Come on. There isn't much time...."

"Cathy?" He followed her up the alley. They both paused,

scanning the street for policemen. There were none in sight. "Where are we going?" he whispered.

"To find a phone booth."

"Oh. And who are we calling?"

She turned and the look she gave him was distinctly pained. "Someone we both know and love."

JACK WAS PACKING his suitcase when the phone rang. He considered not answering it, but something about the sound, an urgency that could only have been imagined, made him pick up the receiver. He was instantly sorry he had.

"Jack?"

He sighed. "Tell me I'm hearing things."

"Jack, I'm going to talk fast because your phone might be tapped—"

"You don't say."

"I need my kit. The whole shebang. And some cash. I swear I'll pay it all back. Get it for me right now. Then drop it off where we shot the last scene of *Cretinoid.* You know the spot."

"Cathy, you wait a minute! I'm in trouble enough as it is!"

"One hour. That's all I can wait."

"It's rush hour! I can't—"

"It's the last favor I'll ask of you." There was a pause. Then, softly, she added, "Please."

He let out a breath. "This is the absolute last time, right?"

"One hour, Jack. I'll be waiting."

Jack hung up and stared at his suitcase. It was only half packed, but it would have to do. He sure as hell wasn't coming back *here* tonight.

He closed the suitcase and carried it out to the Jaguar. As he drove away it suddenly occurred to him that he'd forgotten to cancel his date with Lulu tonight.

No time now, he thought. I've got more important things on my mind—like getting out of town.

Lulu would be mad as a hornet, but he'd make it up to her. Maybe a pair of diamond ear studs. Yeah, that would do the trick.

Good old Lulu, so easy to please. Now there was a woman he could understand.

THE CORNER OF Fifth and Mission was a hunker-down, chew-the-fat sort of gathering place for the street folk. At five forty-five it was even busier than usual. Rumor had it the soup kitchen down the block was fixing to serve beef Bourguignonne, which, as those who remembered better days and better meals could tell you, was made with red wine. No one passed up the chance for a taste of the grape, even if every drop of alcohol was simmered clean out of it. And so they stood around on the corner, talking of other meals they'd had, of the weather, of the long lines at the unemployment office.

No one noticed the two wretched souls huddled in the doorway of the pawnshop.

Lucky for us, thought Cathy, burying herself in the folds of the raincoat. The sad truth was, they were both beginning to fit right into this crowd. Just a moment earlier she'd caught sight of her own reflection in the pawnshop window and had almost failed to recognize the disheveled image staring back. *Has it been that long since I've combed my hair? That long since I've had a meal or a decent night's sleep?*

Victor looked no better. A torn shirt and two days' worth of stubble on his jaw only emphasized that unmistakable look of exhaustion. He could walk into that soup kitchen down the block and no one would look twice.

He's going to look a hell of a lot worse when I get through with him, she thought with a grim sense of humor.

If Jack ever showed up with the kit.

"It's 6:05," Victor muttered. "He's had an hour."

"Give him time."

"We're running out of time."

"We can still make the bus." She peered up the street, as though by force of will she could conjure up her ex-husband. But only a city bus barreled into view. *Come on, Jack, come on! Don't let me down this time....*

"Will ya lookit that!" came a low growl, followed by general murmurs of admiration from the crowd.

"Hey, pretty boy!" someone called as the group gathered on the corner to stare. "What'd you have to push to get yerself wheels like that?"

Through the gathering of men, Cathy spied the bright gleam of chrome and burgundy. "Get away from my car!" demanded a querulous voice. "I just had her waxed!"

"Looks like Pretty Boy got hisself lost. Turned down the wrong damn street, did ya?"

Cathy leaped to her feet. "He's here!"

She and Victor pushed through the crowd to find Jack standing guard over the Jaguar's gleaming finish.

"Don't—don't touch her!" he snapped as one man ran a grimy finger across the hood. "Why can't you people go find yourselves a job or something?"

"A job?" someone yelled. "What's that?"

"Jack!" called Cathy.

Jack let out a sigh of relief when he spotted her. "This is the last favor. The absolute *last* favor—"

"Where is it?" she asked.

Jack walked around to the trunk, where he slapped away another hand as it stroked the Jaguar's burgundy flank. "It's right here. The whole kit and kaboodle." He swung out the makeup case and handed it over. "Delivered as promised. Now I gotta run."

"Where are you going?" she called.

"I don't know." He climbed back into the car. "Somewhere. Anywhere!"

"Sounds like we're headed in the same direction."

"God, I hope not." He started the engine and revved it up a few times.

Someone yelled: "So long, Pretty Boy!"

Jack gazed out dryly at Cathy. "You know, you really should do something about the company you keep. Ciao, sweetcakes."

The Jaguar lurched away. With a screech of tires, it spun around the corner and vanished into traffic.

Cathy turned and saw that every eye was watching her. Automatically, Victor moved close beside her, one tired and hungry man facing a tired and hungry crowd.

Someone called out: "So who's the jerk in the Jag?"

"My ex-husband," said Cathy.

"Doin' a lot better than you are, honey."

"No kidding." She held up the makeup case and managed a careless laugh. "I ask the creep for my clothes, he throws me a change of underwear."

"Babe, now ain't that just the way it works?"

Already, the men were wandering away, regrouping in doorways, or over by the corner newsstands. The Jaguar was gone, and so was their interest.

Only one man stood before Cathy and Victor, and the look he gave them was distinctly sympathetic. "That's all he left you, huh? Him with that nice, fancy car?" He turned to leave, then glanced back at them. "Say, you two need a place to stay or somethin'? I got a lot of friends. And I hate to see a lady out in the cold."

"Thanks for the offer," said Victor, taking Cathy's hand. "But we've got a bus to catch."

The man nodded and shuffled away, a kind but unfortunate soul whom the streets had not robbed of decency.

"We have a half hour to get on that bus," said Victor, hurrying Cathy along. "Better get to work."

They were headed up the street, toward the cover of an alley, when Cathy suddenly halted. "Victor—"

"What's the matter?"

"Look." She pointed at the newsstand, her hand shaking.

Beneath the plastic cover was the afternoon edition of the *San Francisco Examiner.* The headline read: "Two Victims, Same Name. Police Probe Coincidence." Beside it was a photo of a young blond woman. The caption was hidden by the fold, but Cathy didn't need to read it. She could already guess the woman's name.

"Two of them," she whispered. "Victor, you were right...."

"All the more reason for us to get out of town." He pulled on her arm. "Hurry."

She let him lead her away. But even as they headed down

the street, even as they left the newsstand behind them, she carried that image in her mind: the photograph of a blond woman, the second victim.

The second Catherine Weaver.

PATROLMAN O'HANLEY WAS a helpful soul. Unlike too many of his colleagues, O'Hanley had joined the force out of a true desire to serve and protect. The "Boy Scout" was what the other men called him behind his back. The epithet both annoyed and pleased him. It told him he didn't fit in with the rough-and-tumble gang on the force. It also told him he was above it all, above the petty bribe-taking and backbiting and maneuverings for promotion. He wasn't out to glorify the badge on his chest. What he wanted was the chance to pat a kid on the head, rescue an old granny from a mugging.

That's why he found this particular assignment so frustrating. All this standing around in the bus depot, watching for a man some witness *might* have spotted a few hours ago. O'Hanley hadn't noticed any such character. He'd eyeballed every person who'd walked in the door. A sorry lot, most of them. Not surprising since, these days, anyone with the cash to spare took a plane. By the looks of these folks, none of 'em could spare much more than pennies. Take that pair over there, huddled together in the waiting area. A father and daughter, he figured, and both of 'em down on their luck. The daughter was bundled up in an old raincoat, the collar pulled up to reveal only a mop of windblown hair. The father was an even sorrier sight, gaunt-faced, white-whiskered, about as old as Methuselah. Still, there was a remnant of pride in the old codger—O'Hanley could see it in the way the man held himself, stiff and straight. Must've been an impressive fellow in his younger years since he was still well over six feet tall.

The public speaker announced final boarding for number fourteen to Palo Alto.

The old man and his daughter rose to their feet.

O'Hanley watched with concern as the pair shuffled across the terminal toward the departure gate. The woman was carrying only one small case, but it appeared to be a heavy one

And she already had her hands full, trying to guide the old man in the right direction. But they were making progress, and O'Hanley figured they'd make it to the bus okay.

That is, until the kid ran into them.

He was about six, the kind of kid no mother wants to admit she produced, the kind of kid who gives all six-year-olds a bad name. For the last half hour the boy had been tearing around the terminal, scattering ashtray sand, tipping over suitcases, banging locker doors. Now he was running. Only this kid was doing it *backward*.

O'Hanley saw it coming. The old man and his daughter were crossing slowly toward the departure gate. The kid was scuttling toward them. Intersecting paths, inevitable collision. The kid slammed into the woman's knees; the case flew out of her grasp. She stumbled against her companion. O'Hanley, paralyzed, expected the codger to keel over. To his surprise, the old man simply caught the woman in his arms and handily set her back on her feet.

By now O'Hanley was hurrying to their aid. He got to the woman just as she'd regained her footing. "You folks okay?" he asked.

The woman reacted as though he'd slapped her. She stared up at him with the eyes of a terrified animal. "What?" she said.

"Are you okay? Looked to me like he hit you pretty hard." She nodded.

"How 'bout you, Gramps?"

The woman glanced at her companion. It seemed to O'Hanley that there was a lot being said in that glance, a lot he wasn't privy to.

"We're both fine," the woman said quickly. "Come on, Pop. We'll miss our bus."

"Can I give you a hand with him?"

"That's mighty kind of you, officer, but we'll do fine." The woman smiled at O'Hanley. Something about that smile wasn't right. As he watched the pair shuffle off toward bus number fourteen, O'Hanley kept trying to figure it out. Kept trying to put his finger on what was wrong with that pair of travelers.

He turned away and almost tripped over the fallen case. The woman had forgotten it. He snatched it up and started to run for the bus. Too late; the number fourteen to Palo Alto was already pulling away. O'Hanley stood helplessly on the curb, watching the taillights vanish around the corner.

Oh, well.

He turned in the makeup case at Lost and Found. Then he stationed himself once again at the entrance. Seven o'clock already and still no sighting of the suspect Victor Holland.

O'Hanley sighed. What a waste of a policeman's time.

FIVE MINUTES OUT OF San Francisco, aboard the number fourteen bus, the old man turned to the woman in the raincoat and said, "This beard is killing me."

Laughing, Cathy reached up and gave the fake whiskers a tug. "It did the trick, didn't it?"

"No kidding. We practically got a police escort to the getaway bus." He scratched furiously at his chin. "Geez, how do those actors stand this stuff, anyway? The itch is driving me up a wall."

"Want me to take it off?"

"Better not. Not till we get to Palo Alto."

Another hour, she thought. She sat back and gazed out at the highway gliding past the bus window. "Then what?" she asked softly.

"I'll knock on a few doors. See if I can dig up an old friend or two. It's been a long time, but I think there are still a few in town."

"You used to live there?"

"Years ago. Back when I was in college."

"Oh." She sat up straight. "A *Stanford* man."

"Why do you make it sound just a tad disreputable?"

"I rooted for the Bears, myself."

"I'm consorting with the arch enemy?"

Giggling, she burrowed against his chest and inhaled the warm, familiar scent of his body. "It seems like another lifetime. Berkeley and blue jeans."

"Football. Wild parties."

"Wild parties?" she asked. "You?"

"Well, *rumors* of wild parties."

"Frisbee. Classes on the lawn..."

"Innocence," he said softly.

They both fell silent.

"Victor?" she asked. "What if your friends aren't there any longer? Or what if they won't take us in?"

"One step at a time. That's how we have to take it. Otherwise it'll all seem too overwhelming."

"It already does."

He squeezed her tightly against him. "Hey, we're doing okay. We made it out of the city. In fact, we waltzed out right under the nose of a cop. I'd call that pretty damn impressive."

Cathy couldn't help grinning at the memory of the earnest young Patrolman O'Hanley. "All policemen should be so helpful."

"Or blind," Victor snorted. "I can't believe he called me *Gramps*."

"When I set out to change a face, I do it right."

"Apparently."

She looped her arm through his and pressed a kiss to one scowling, bewhiskered cheek. "Can I tell you a secret?"

"What's that?"

"I'm crazy about older men."

The scowl melted away, slowly reformed into a dubious smile. "How much older are we talking about?"

She kissed him again, this time full on the lips. "Much older."

"Hm. Maybe these whiskers aren't so bad, after all." He took her face in his hands. This time he was the one kissing her, long and deeply, with no thought of where they were or where they were going. Cathy felt herself sliding back against the seat, into a space that was inescapable and infinitely safe.

Someone behind them hooted: "Way to go, Gramps!"

Reluctantly, they pulled apart. Through the flickering shadows of the bus, Cathy could see the twinkle in Victor's eyes, the gleam of a wry smile.

She smiled back and whispered, "Way to go, Gramps."

THE POSTERS WITH Victor Holland's face were plastered [
over the bus station.

Polowski couldn't help a snort of irritation as he gazed
that unflattering visage of what he knew in his gut was [
innocent man. A damn witchhunt, that's what this'd turned int
If Holland wasn't already scared enough, this public stalkir
would surely send him diving for cover, beyond the reach (
those who could help him. Polowski only hoped it'd also b
beyond the reach of those with less benign intentions.

With all these posters staring him in the face, Hollar
would've been a fool to stroll through this bus depot. Sti
Polowski had an instinct about these things, a sense of ho
people behaved when they were desperate. If he were in Ho
land's shoes, a killer on his trail and a woman companion
worry about, he knew what *he'd* do—get the hell out of Sa
Francisco. A plane was unlikely. According to Jack Zucke
man, Holland was operating on a thin wallet. A credit ca
would've been out of the question. That also knocked out
rental car. What was left? It was either hitchhike or take th
bus.

Polowski was betting on the bus.

His last piece of info supported that hunch. The tap on Zucl
erman's phone had picked up a call from Cathy Weaver. She'
arranged some sort of drop-off at a site Polowski couldn't ider
tify at first. He'd spent a frustrating hour asking around th
office, trying to locate someone who'd not only seen Zucke
man's forgettable film, *Cretinoid*, but could also pinpoint whe
the last scene was filmed. The Mission District, some movi
nut file clerk had finally told him. Yeah, she was sure of i
The monster came up through the manhole cover right at th
corner of Fifth and Mission and slurped down a derelict or tw
just before the hero smashed him with a crated piano. Polows}
hadn't stayed to hear the rest; he'd made a run for his car.

By that time, it was too late. Holland and the woman wer
gone, and Zuckerman had vanished. Polowski found himse
cruising down Mission, his doors locked, his windows rolle
up, wondering when the local police were going to clean u
the damn streets.

That's when he remembered the bus depot was only a few blocks away.

Now, standing among the tired and slack-jawed travelers at the bus station, he was beginning to think he'd wasted his time. All those wanted posters staring him in the face. And there was a cop standing over by the coffee machine, taking furtive sips from a foam cup.

Polowski strolled over to the cop. "FBI," he said, flashing his badge.

The cop—he was scarcely more than a boy—instantly straightened. "Patrolman O'Hanley, sir."

"Seeing much action?"

"Uh—you mean today?"

"Yeah. Here."

"No, sir." O'Hanley sighed. "Pretty much a bust. I mean, I could be out on patrol. Instead they got me hanging around here eyeballing faces."

"Surveillance?"

"Yes, sir." He nodded at the poster of Holland. "That guy. Everyone's hot to find him. They say he's a spy."

"Do they, now?" Polowski took a lazy glance around the room. "Seen anyone around here who looks like him?"

"Not a one. I been watching every minute."

Polowski didn't doubt it. O'Hanley was the kind of kid who, if you asked him to, would scrub the Captain's boots with a toothbrush. He'd do a good job of it, too.

Obviously Holland hadn't come through here. Polowski turned to leave. Then another thought came to mind, and he turned back to O'Hanley. "The suspect may be traveling with a woman," he said. He pulled out a photo of Cathy Weaver, one Jack Zuckerman had been persuaded to donate to the FBI. "Have you seen her come through here?"

O'Hanley frowned. "Gee. She sure does look like... Naw. That can't be her."

"Who?"

"Well, there was this woman in here 'bout an hour ago. Kind of a down and outer. Some little brat ran smack into her. I sort've brushed her off and sent her on her way. She looked a lot like this gal, only in a lot worse shape.''

''Was she traveling alone?''

''She had an old guy with her. Her pop, I think.''

Suddenly Polowski was all ears. That instinct again—it was telling him something. ''What did this old man look like?''

''Real old. Maybe seventy. Had this bushy beard, lot of white hair.''

''How tall?''

''Pretty tall. Over six feet...'' O'Hanley's voice trailed off as his gaze focused on the wanted poster. Victor Holland was six foot three. O'Hanley's face went white. ''Oh, God...''

''Was it him?''

''I—I can't be sure—''

''Come on, come on!''

''I just don't know... Wait. The woman, she dropped a makeup case! I turned it in at that window there—''

It took only a flash of an FBI badge for the clerk in Lost and Found to hand over the case. The instant Polowski opened the thing, he knew he'd hit pay dirt. It was filled with theatrical makeup supplies. Stenciled inside the lid was: Property of Jack Zuckerman Productions.

He slammed the lid shut. ''Where did they go?'' he snapped at O'Hanley.

''They—uh, they boarded a bus right over there. That gate. Around seven o'clock.''

Polowski glanced up at the departure schedule. At seven o'clock, the number fourteen had departed for Palo Alto.

It took him ten minutes to get hold of the Palo Alto depot manager, another five minutes to convince the man this wasn't just another Prince-Albert-in-the-can phone call.

''The number fourteen from San Francisco?'' came the answer. ''Arrived twenty minutes ago.''

''What about the passengers?'' pressed Polowski. ''You see any of 'em still around?''

The manager only laughed. ''Hey, man. If you had a choice would *you* hang around a stinking bus station?''

Muttering an oath, Polowski hung up.

"Sir?" It was O'Hanley. He looked sick. "I messed up, didn't I? I let him walk right past me. I can't believe—"

"Forget it."

"But—"

Polowski headed for the exit. "You're just a rookie," he called over his shoulder. "Chalk it up to experience."

"Should I call this in?"

"I'll take care of it. I'm headed there, anyway."

"Where?"

Polowski shoved open the station door. "Palo Alto."

CHAPTER EIGHT

THE FRONT DOOR was answered by an elderly oriental woman whose command of English was limited.

"Mrs. Lum? Remember me? Victor Holland. I used to know your son."

"Yes, yes!"

"Is he here?"

"Yes." Her gaze shifted to Cathy now, as though the woman didn't want her second visitor to feel left out of the conversation.

"I need to see him," said Victor. "Is Milo here?"

"Milo?" At last here was a word she seemed to know. She turned and called out loudly in Chinese.

Somewhere a door squealed open and footsteps stamped up the stairs. A fortyish oriental man in blue jeans and chambray shirt came to the front door. He was a dumpling of a fellow, and he brought with him the vague odor of chemicals, something sharp and acidic. He was wiping his hands on a rag.

"What can I do for you?" he asked.

Victor grinned. "Milo Lum! Are you still skulking around in your mother's basement?"

"Excuse me?" Milo inquired politely. "Am I supposed to know you, sir?"

"Don't recognize an old horn player from the Out of Tuners?"

Milo stared in disbelief. "Gershwin? That can't be *you?*"

"Yeah, I know," Victor said with a laugh. "The years haven't been kind."

"I didn't want to say anything, but..."

"I won't take it personally. Since—" Victor peeled off his false beard "—the face isn't all mine."

Milo gazed down at the lump of fake whispers, hanging like

a dead animal in Victor's grasp. Then he stared up at Victor's jaw, still blotchy with spirit gum. "This is some kind of joke on old Milo, right?" He stuck his head out the door, glancing past Victor at the sidewalk. "And the other guys are hiding out there somewhere, waiting to yell *surprise!* Aren't they? Some big practical joke."

"I wish it were a joke," said Victor.

Milo instantly caught the undertone of urgency in Victor's voice. He looked at Cathy, then back at Victor. Nodding, he stepped aside. "Come in, Gersh. Sounds like I have some catching up to do."

Over a late supper of duck noodle soup and jasmine tea, Milo heard the story. He said little; he seemed more intent on slurping down the last of his noodles. Only when the ever-smiling Mrs. Lum had bowed good-night and creaked off to bed did Milo offer his comment.

"When you get in trouble, man, you sure as hell do it right."

"Astute as always, Milo," sighed Victor.

"Too bad we can't say the same for the cops," Milo snorted. "If they'd just bothered to ask around, they would've learned you're harmless. Far as I know, you're guilty of only one serious crime."

Cathy looked up, startled. "What crime?"

"Assaulting the ears of victims unlucky enough to hear his saxophone."

"This from a piccolo player who practises with earplugs," observed Victor.

"That's to drown out extraneous noise."

"Yeah. Mainly your own."

Cathy grinned. "I'm beginning to understand why you called yourselves the Out of Tuners."

"Just some healthy self-deprecating humor," said Milo. "Something we needed after we failed to make the Stanford band." Milo rose, shoving away from the kitchen table. "Well, come on. Let's see what's on that mysterious roll of film."

He led them along the hall and down a rickety set of steps to the basement. The chemical tang of the air, the row of trays lined up on a stainless-steel countertop and the slow drip, drip of water from the faucet told Cathy she was standing in an enormous darkroom. Tacked on the walls was a jumble of photos. Faces, mostly, apparently snapped around the world. Here and there she spotted a newsworthy shot: soldiers storming an airport, protestors unfurling a banner.

"Is this your job, Milo?" she asked.

"I wish," said Milo, agitating the developing canister. "No, I just work in the ol' family business."

"Which is?"

"Shoes. Italian, Brazilian, leather, alligator, you name it, we import it." He cocked his head at the photos. "That's how I get my exotic faces. Shoe-buying trips. I'm an expert on the female arch."

"For that," said Victor, "he spent four years at Stanford."

"Why not? Good a place as any to study the fine feet of the fair sex." A timer rang. Milo poured out the developer, removed the roll of film, and hung it up to dry. "Actually," he said, squinting at the negatives, "it was my dad's dying request. He wanted a son with a Stanford degree. I wanted four years of nonstop partying. We both got our wishes." He paused and gazed off wistfully at his photos. "Too bad I can't say the same of the years since then."

"What do you mean?" asked Cathy.

"I mean the partying's long since over. Gotta earn those profits, keep up those sales. Never thought life'd come down to the bottom line. Whatever happened to all that rabble-rousing potential, hey, Gersh? We sort of lost it along the way. All of us, Bach and Ollie and Roger. The Out of Tuners finally stepped into line. Now we're all marching to the beat of the same boring drummer." He sighed and glanced at Victor. "You make out anything on those negatives?"

Victor shook his head. "We need prints."

Milo flipped off the lights, leaving only the red glow of the darkroom lamp. "Coming up."

As Milo laid out the photographic paper, Victor asked "What happened to the other guys? They still around?"

Milo flipped the exposure switch. "Roger's VP at some mul

tinational bank in Tokyo. Into silk suits and ties, the whole nine yards. Bach's got an electronics firm in San José.''

"And Ollie?''

"What can I say about Ollie?'' Milo slipped the first print into the bath. "He's still lurking around in that lab over at Stanford Med. I doubt he ever sees the light of day. I figure he's got some secret chamber in the basement where he keeps his assistant Igor chained to the wall.''

"This guy I have to meet,'' said Cathy.

"Oh, he'd love you.'' Victor laughed and gave her arm a squeeze. "Seeing as he's probably forgotten what the female of the species looks like.''

Milo slid the print into the next tray. "Yeah, Ollie's the one who never changed. Still the night owl. Still plays a mean clarinet.'' He glanced at Victor. "How's the sax, Gersh? You keeping it up?''

"Haven't played in months.''

"Lucky neighbors.''

"How did you ever get that name?'' asked Cathy. "Gersh?''

"Because,'' said Milo, wielding tongs as he transferred another batch of prints between trays, "he's a firm believer in the power of George Gershwin to win a lady's heart. 'Someone to Watch Over Me,' wasn't that the tune that made Lily say...'' Milo's voice suddenly faded. He looked at his friend with regret.

"You're right,'' said Victor quietly. "That was the tune. And Lily said yes.''

Milo shook his head. "Sorry. Guess I still have a hard time remembering she's gone.''

"Well, she is,'' said Victor, his voice matter-of-fact. Cathy knew there was pain buried in the undertones. But he hid it well. "And right now,'' Victor said, "we've got other things to think about.''

"Yeah.'' Milo, chastened, turned his attention back to the prints he'd just developed. He fished them out and clipped the first few sheets on the line to dry. "Okay, Gersh. Tell us what's on this roll that's worth killing for.''

Milo switched on the lights.

Victor stood in silence for a moment, frowning at the first five dripping prints. To Cathy, the data was meaningless, only a set of numbers and codes, recorded in an almost illegible hand.

"Well," grunted Milo. "That sure tells me a lot."

Victor's gaze shifted quickly from one page to the next. He paused at the fifth photo, where a column ran down the length of the page. It contained a series of twenty-seven entries, each one a date followed by the same three letters: EXP.

"Victor?" asked Cathy. "What does it mean?"

He turned to them. It was the look in his eyes that worried her. The stillness. Quietly he said, "We need to call Ollie."

"You mean tonight?" asked Milo. "Why?"

"This isn't just some experiment in test tubes and petri dishes. They've gone beyond that, to clinical trials." Victor pointed to the last page. "These are monkeys. Each one was infected with a new virus. A manmade virus. And in every case the results were the same."

"You mean this?" Milo pointed to the last column. "EXP?"

"It stands for expired," said Victor. "They all died."

SAM POLOWSKI SAT on a bench in the Palo Alto bus terminal and wondered: If I wanted to disappear, where would I go next? He watched a dozen or so passengers straggle off to board the 210 from San José, noting they were by and large the Birkenstock and backpack set. Probably Stanford students heading off for Christmas break. He wondered why it was that students who could afford such a pricey university couldn't seem to scrape up enough to buy a decent pair of jeans. Or even a decent haircut, for that matter.

At last Polowski rose and automatically dusted off his coat, a habit he'd picked up from his early years of hanging around the seamier side of town. Even if the grime wasn't actually visible, he'd always *felt* it was there, coating any surface he happened to brush against, ready to cling to him like wet paint.

He made one phone call—to Dafoe's answering machine, to tell him Victor Holland had moved on to Palo Alto. It was, after all, his responsibility to keep his supervisor informed. He was glad he only had to talk to a recording and not to the man himself.

He left the bus station and strolled down the street, heading Lord knew where, in search of a spark, a hunch. It was a nice-enough neighborhood, a nice-enough town. Palo Alto had its old professors' houses, its bookshops and coffee houses where university types, the ones with the beards and wire-rim glasses, liked to sit and argue the meaning of Proust and Brecht and Goethe. Polowski remembered his own university days, when, after being subjected to an hour of such crap from the students at the next table, he had finally stormed over to them and yelled, "Maybe Brecht meant it that way, maybe not. But can you guys answer this? *What the hell difference does it make?*"

This did not, needless to say, enhance his reputation as a serious scholar.

Now, as he paced along the street, no doubt in the footsteps of more serious philosophers, Polowski turned over in his head the question of Victor Holland. More specifically the question of where such a man, in his desperation, would hide. He stalked past the lit windows, the glow of TVs, the cars spilling from garages. Where in this warren of suburbia was the man hiding?

Holland was a scientist, a musician, a man of few but lasting friendships. He had a Ph.D. from MIT, a B.S. from Stanford. The university was right up the road. The man must know his way around here. Maybe he still had friends in the neighborhood, people who'd take him in, keep his secrets.

Polowski decided to take another look at Holland's file. Somewhere in the Viratek records, there had to be some employment reference, some recommendation from a Stanford contact. A friend Holland might turn to.

Sooner or later, he would have to turn to *someone*.

IT WAS AFTER MIDNIGHT when Dafoe and his wife returned home. He was in an excellent mood, his head pleasantly abuzz with champagne, his ears still ringing with the heart-wrenching aria from *Samson and Delilah*. Opera was a passion for him, a brilliant staging of courage and conflict and *amore,* a vision of life so much grander than the petty little world in which he found himself. It launched him to a plane of such thrilling intensity that even his own wife took on exciting new aspects. He watched her peel off her coat and kick off her shoes. Forty pounds overweight, hair streaked with silver, yet she had her attractions. *It's been three weeks. Surely she'll let me tonight....*

But his wife ignored his amorous looks and wandered off to the kitchen. A moment later, the rumble of the automatic dishwasher announced another of her fits of housecleaning.

In frustration, Dafoe turned and stabbed the blinking button on his answering machine. The message from Polowski completely destroyed any amorous intentions he had left.

"...Reason to believe Holland is in, or has just left, the Palo Alto area. Following leads. Will keep you informed...."

Polowski, you half-wit. Is following orders so damn difficult?

It was 3:00 a.m. Washington time. An ungodly hour, but he made the phone call.

The voice that answered was raspy with sleep. "Tyrone here."

"Cowboy, this is Dafoe. Sorry to wake you."

The voice became instantly alert, all sleep shaken from it. "What's up?"

"New lead on Holland. I don't know the particulars, but he's headed south, to Palo Alto. May still be there."

"The university?"

"It is the Stanford area."

"That may be a very big help."

"Anything for an old buddy. I'll keep you posted."

"One thing, Dafoe."

"Yeah?"

"I can't have any interference. Pull all your people out. We'll take it from here."

Dafoe paused. "I might...have a problem."

"A problem?" The voice, though quiet, took on a razor's edge.

"It's, uh, one of my men. Sort of a wild card. Sam Polowski. He's got this Holland case under his skin, wants to go after him."

"There's such a thing as a direct order."

"At the moment, Polowski's unreachable. He's in Palo Alto, digging around in God knows what."

"Loose cannons. I don't like them."

"I'll pull him back as soon as I can."

"Do that. And keep it quiet. It's a matter of utmost security."

After Dafoe hung up, his gaze shifted automatically to the photo on the mantelpiece. It was a '68 snapshot of him and the Cowboy: two young marines, both of them grinning, their rifles slung over their shoulders as they stood ankle-deep in a rice paddy. It was a crazy time, when one's very life depended on the loyalty of buddies. When Semper Fi applied not only to the corps in general but to each other in particular. Matt Tyrone was a hero then, and he was a hero now. Dafoe stared at that smiling face in the photo, disturbed by the threads of envy that had woven into his admiration for the man. Though Dafoe had much to be proud of—a solid eighteen years in the FBI, maybe even a shot at assistant director somewhere in his stars, he couldn't match the heady climb of Matt Tyrone in the NSA. Though Dafoe wasn't clear as to exactly what position the Cowboy held in the NSA, he had heard that Tyrone regularly attended cabinet meetings, that he held the trust of the president, that he dealt in secrets and shadows and security. He was the sort of man the country needed, a man for whom patriotism was more than mere flag-waving and rhetoric; it was a way of life. Matt Tyrone would do more than die for his country; he'd live for it.

Dafoe couldn't let such a man, such a friend, down.

He dialed Sam Polowski's home phone and left a message on the recorder.

This is a direct order. You are to withdraw from the Holland case immediately. Until further notice you are on suspension.

He was tempted to add, *by special request from my friends in Washington,* but thought better of it. No room for vanity here. The Cowboy had said national security was at stake.

Dafoe had no doubt it truly was. He'd gotten the word from Matt Tyrone. And Matt Tyrone's authority came direct from the President himself.

"THIS DOES NOT look good. This does not look good at all."

Ollie Wozniak squinted through his wire-rim glasses at the twenty-four photographs strewn across Milo's dining table. He held one up for a closer look. Through the bottle-glass lens, one pale blue eye stared out, enormous. One only saw Ollie's eyes; everything else, hollow cheeks, pencil lips and baby-fine hair, seemed to recede into the background pallor. He shook his head and picked up another photo.

"You're right, of course," he said. "Some of these I can't interpret. I'd like to study 'em later. But these here are definitely raw mortality data. Rhesus monkeys, I suspect." He paused and added quietly, "I hope."

"Surely they wouldn't use people for this sort of thing," said Cathy.

"Not officially." Ollie put down the photo and looked at her. "But it's been done."

"Maybe in Nazi Germany."

"Here, too," said Victor.

"What?" Cathy looked at him in disbelief.

"Army studies in germ warfare. They released colonies of Serratia Marcescens over San Francisco and waited to see how far the organism spread. Infections popped up in a number of Bay Area hospitals. Some of the cases were fatal."

"I can't believe it," murmured Cathy.

"The damage was unintentional, of course. But people died just the same."

"Don't forget Tuskegee," said Ollie. "People died in those experiments, too. And then there was that case in New York. Mentally retarded kids in a state hospital who were deliberately exposed to hepatitis. No one died there, but the ethics were just as shaky. So it's been done. Sometimes in the name of humanity."

"Sometimes not," said Victor.

Ollie nodded. "As in this particular case."

"What exactly are we talking about here?" asked Cathy nodding at the photos. "Is this medical research? Or weapon development?"

"Both." Ollie pointed to one of the photos on the table. "B

all appearances, Viratek's engaged in biological weapons research. They've dubbed it Project Cerberus. From what I can tell, the organism they're working on is an RNA virus, extremely virulent, highly contagious, producing over eighty-percent mortality in its lab animal hosts. This photo here—" he tapped one of the pages "—shows the organism produces vesicular skin lesions on the infected subjects."

"Vesicular?"

"Blisterlike. That could be one route of transmission, the fluid in those lesions." He sifted through the pile and pulled out another page. "This shows the time course of the illness. The viral counts, periods of infectiousness. In almost every case the course is the same. The subject's exposed here." He pointed to Day One on the time graph. "Minor signs of illness here at Day Seven. Full-blown pox on Day Twelve. And here—" he tapped the graph at Day Fourteen "—the deaths begin. The time varies, but the result's the same. They all die."

"You used the word *pox*," said Cathy.

Ollie turned to her, his eyes like blue glass. "Because that's what it is."

"You mean like chickenpox?"

"I wish it was. Then it wouldn't be so deadly. Almost everyone gets exposed to chickenpox as a kid, so most of us are immune. But this one's a different story."

"Is it a new virus?" asked Milo.

"Yes and no." He reached for an electron micrograph. "When I saw this I thought there was something weirdly familiar about all this. The appearance of the organism, the skin lesions, the course of illness. The whole damn picture. It reminded me of something I haven't read about in decades. Something I never dreamed I'd see again."

"You're saying it's an old virus?" said Milo.

"Ancient. But they've made some modifications. Made it more infectious. And deadlier. Which turns this into a real humdinger of a weapon, considering the millions of folks it's already killed."

"*Millions?*" Cathy stared at him. "What are we talking about?"

"A killer we've known for centuries. Smallpox."

"That's impossible!" said Cathy. "From what I've read, we conquered smallpox. It's supposed to be extinct."

"It was," said Victor. "For all practical purposes. World-wide vaccination wiped it out. Smallpox hasn't been reported in decades. I'm not even sure they still make the vaccine. Ollie?"

"Not available. No need for it since the virus has vanished."

"So where did *this* virus come from?" asked Cathy.

Ollie shrugged. "Probably someone's closet."

"Come on."

"I'm serious. After smallpox was eradicated, a few samples of virus were kept alive in government labs, just in case someone needed it for future research. It's the scientific skeleton in the closet, so to speak. I'd assume those labs are top security. Because if any of the virus got out, there could be a major epidemic." He looked at the stack of photos. "Looks like security's already been breached. Someone obviously got hold of the virus."

"Or had it handed to them," said Victor. "Courtesy of the U.S. government."

"I find that incredible, Gersh," said Ollie. "This is a pow derkeg experiment you're talking about. No committee would approve this sort of project."

"Right. That's why I think this is a maverick operation. It' easy to come up with a scenario. Bunch of hardliners cooking this up over at NSA. Or joint chiefs of staff. Or even the Ova Office. Someone says: 'World politics have changed. We can' get away with nuking the enemy. We need a new weapon option, one that'll work well against a Third World army. Let' find one.' And some guy in that room, some red, white an blue robot, will take that as the go-ahead. International law b damned."

"And since it's unofficial," said Cathy, "it'd be completel deniable."

"Right. The administration could claim it knew nothing."

"Sounds like Iran-Contra all over again."

"With one big difference," said Ollie. "When Iran-Cont

fell apart, all you had were a few ruined political careers. If Project Cerberus goes awry, what you'll have is a few million dead people."

"But Ollie," said Milo. "I got vaccinated for smallpox when I was a kid. Doesn't that mean I'm safe?"

"Probably. Assuming the virus hasn't been altered too much. In fact, everyone over 35 is probably okay. But remember, there's a whole generation after us that never got the vaccine. Young adults and kids. By the time you could manufacture enough vaccine for them all, we'd have a raging epidemic."

"I'm beginning to see the logic of this weapon," said Victor. "In any war, who makes up the bulk of combat soldiers? Young adults."

Ollie nodded. "They'd be hit bad. As would the kids."

"A whole generation," Cathy murmured. "And only the old would be spared." She glanced at Victor and saw, mirrored in his eyes, the horror she felt.

"They chose an appropriate name," said Milo.

Ollie frowned. "What?"

"Cerberus. The three-headed dog of Hades." Milo looked up, visibly shaken. "Guardian of the dead."

IT WASN'T UNTIL Cathy was fast asleep and Milo had retired upstairs that Victor finally broached the subject to Ollie. It had troubled him all evening, had shadowed his every moment since they'd arrived at Milo's house. He couldn't look at Cathy, couldn't listen to the sound of her voice or inhale the scent of her hair without thinking of the terrible possibilities. And in the deepest hours of night, when it seemed all the world was asleep except for him and Ollie, he made the decision.

"I need to ask you a favor," he said.

Ollie gazed at him across the dining table, steam wafting up from his fourth cup of coffee. "What sort of favor?"

"It has to do with Cathy."

Ollie's gaze shifted to the woman lying asleep on the living room floor. She looked very small, very defenseless, curled up beneath the comforter. Ollie said, "She's a nice woman, Gersh."

"I know."

"There hasn't really been anyone since Lily. Has there?"

Victor shook his head. "I guess I haven't felt ready for it. There were always other things to think about...."

Ollie smiled. "There are always excuses. I should know. People keep telling me there's a glut of unattached female baby boomers. I haven't noticed."

"And I never bothered to notice." Victor looked at Cathy. "Until now."

"What're you gonna do with her, Gersh?"

"That's what I need you for. I'm not the safest guy to hang around with these days. A woman could get hurt."

Ollie laughed. "Hell, a *guy* could get hurt."

"I feel responsible for her. And if something happened to her, I'm not sure I could ever..." He let out a long sigh and rubbed his bloodshot eyes. "Anyway, I think it's best if she leaves."

"For where?"

"She has an ex-husband. He'll be working down in Mexico for a few months. I think she'd be pretty safe."

"You're sending her to her ex-husband?"

"I've met him. He's a jerk, but at least she won't be alone down there."

"Does Cathy agree to this?"

"I didn't ask her."

"Maybe you should."

"I'm not giving her a choice."

"What if she wants the choice?"

"I'm not in the mood to take any crap, Okay? I'm doing this for her own good."

Ollie took off his glasses and cleaned them on the tablecloth. "Excuse me for saying this, Gersh, but if it was me, I'd want her nearby, where I could sort of keep an eye on her."

"You mean where I can watch her get killed?" Victor shook his head. "Lily was enough. I won't go through it with Cathy."

Ollie thought it over for a moment, then he nodded. "What do you want me to do?"

"Tomorrow I want you to take her to the airport. Buy her a

ticket to Mexico. Let her use your name. Mrs. Wozniak. Make sure she gets safely off the ground. I'll pay you back when I can."

"What if she won't get on the plane? Do I just shove her aboard?"

"Do whatever it takes, Ollie. I'm counting on you."

Ollie sighed. "I guess I can do it. I'll call in sick tomorrow. That'll free up my day." He looked at Victor. "I just hope you know what you're doing."

So do I, thought Victor.

Ollie rose to his feet and tucked the envelope with the photos under his arm. "I'll get back to you in the morning. After I show these last two photos to Bach. Maybe he can identify what those grids are."

"If it's anything electronic, Bach'll figure it out."

Together they walked to the door. There they paused and regarded each other, two old friends who'd grown a little grayer and, Victor hoped, a little wiser.

"Somehow it'll all work out," said Ollie. "Remember. The system's there to be beaten."

"Sounds like the old Stanford radical again."

"It's been a long time." Grinning, Ollie gave Victor a clap on the back. "But we're still not too old to raise a little hell, hey, Gersh? See you in the morning."

Victor waved as Ollie walked away into the darkness. Then he closed the door and turned off all the lights.

In the living room he sat beside Cathy and watched her sleep. The glow of a streetlight spilled in through the window onto her tumbled hair. *Ordinary,* she had called herself. Perhaps, if she'd been a stranger he'd merely passed on the street, he might have thought so, too. A chance meeting on a rainy highway in Garberville had made it impossible for him to ever consider this woman ordinary. In her gentleness, her kindness, she was very much like Lily.

In other ways, she was very different.

Though he'd cared about his wife, though they'd never stopped being good friends, he'd found Lily strangely passionless, a pristine, spiritual being trapped by human flesh. Lily had never been comfortable with her own body. She'd undress in the dark, make love—the rare times they did—in the dark. And then, the illness had robbed her of what little desire she had left.

Gazing at Cathy, he couldn't help wondering what passions might lie harbored in her still form.

He cut short the speculation. What did it matter now? Tomorrow, he'd send her away. *Get rid of her,* he thought brutally. It was necessary. He couldn't think straight while she was around. He couldn't stay focused on the business at hand: exposing Viratek. Jerry Martinique had counted on him. Thousands of potential victims counted on him. He was a scientist, a man who prided himself on logic. His attraction to this particular woman was, in the grand scheme of things, clearly unimportant.

That was what the scientist in him said.

That problem finally settled, he decided to get some rest while he could. He kicked off his shoes and stretched out beside her to sleep. The comforter was large enough—they could share it. He climbed beneath it and lay for a moment, not touching her, almost afraid to share her warmth.

She whimpered in her sleep and turned toward him, her silky hair tumbling against his face.

This was more than he could resist. Sighing, he wrapped his arms around her and felt her curl up against his chest. It was their last night together. They might as well spend it keeping each other warm.

That was how he fell asleep, with Cathy in his arms.

Only once during the night did he awaken. He had been dreaming of Lily. They were walking together, in a garden of pure white flowers. She said absolutely nothing. She simply looked at him with profound sadness, as if to say, *Here I am Victor. I've come back to you. Why doesn't that make you happy?* He couldn't answer her. So he simply took her in his arms and held her.

He'd awakened to find he was holding Cathy, instead.

Joy instantly flooded his heart, warmed the darkest corner of his soul. It took him by surprise, that burst of happiness;

also made him feel guilty. But there it was. And the joy was all too short-lived. He remembered that today she'd be going away.

Cathy, Cathy. What a complication you've become.

He turned on his side, away from her, mentally building a wall between them.

He concentrated on the dream, trying to remember what had happened. He and Lily had been walking. He tried to picture Lily's face, her brown eyes, her curly black hair. It was the face of the woman he'd been married to for ten years, a face he should know well.

But the only face he saw when he closed his eyes was that of Catherine Weaver.

IT TOOK NICHOLAS SAVITCH only two hours to pack his bags and drive down to Palo Alto. The word from Matt Tyrone was that Holland had slipped south to the Stanford area, perhaps to seek out old friends. Holland was, after all, a Stanford man. Maybe not the red-and-white rah-rah Cardinals type, but a Stanford man nonetheless. These old school ties could run deep. It was only a guess on Savitch's part; he'd never gone beyond high school. His education consisted of what a hungry and ambitious boy could pick up on Chicago's south side. Mainly a keen, almost uncanny knack for crawling into another man's head, for sensing what a particular man would think and do in a given situation. Call it advanced street psychology. Without spending a day in college, Savitch had earned his degree.

Now he was putting it to use.

The *finder,* they called him. He liked that name. He grinned as he drove, his leather-gloved hands expertly handling the wheel. Nicholas Savitch, diviner of human souls, the hunter who could ferret a man out of deepest hiding.

In most cases it was a simple matter of logic. Even while on the run, most people conformed to old patterns. It was the fear that did it. It made them seek out their old comforts, cling to their usual habits. In a strange town, the familiar was precious, even if it was only the sight of those ubiquitous golden arches.

Like every other fugitive, Victor Holland would seek the familiar.

Savitch turned his car onto Palm Drive and pulled up in front of the Stanford Arch. The campus was silent; it was 2:00 a.m. Savitch sat for a moment, regarding the silent buildings, Holland's alma mater. Here, in his former stomping grounds, Holland would turn to old friends, revisit old haunts. Savitch had already done his homework. He carried, in his briefcase, a list of names he'd culled from the man's file. In the morning he'd start in on those names, knock on neighbors' doors, flash his government ID, ask about new faces in the neighborhood.

The only possible complication was Sam Polowski. By last report, the FBI agent was also in town, also on Holland's trail. Polowski was a dogged operator. It'd be messy business, taking out a Bureau man. But then, Polowski was only a cog, the way the Weaver woman was only a cog, in a much bigger wheel.

Neither of them would be missed.

CHAPTER NINE

IN THE COLD, clear hours before dawn, Cathy woke up shaking, still trapped in the threads of a nightmare. She had been walking in a world of concrete and shadow, where doorways gaped and silhouettes huddled on street corners. She drifted among them, one among the faceless, taking refuge in obscurity, instinctively avoiding the light. No one pursued her; no attacker lunged from the alleys. The real terror lay in the unending maze of concrete, the hard echoes of the streets, the frantic search for a safe place.

And the certainty that she would never find it.

For a moment she lay in the darkness, curled up beneath a down comforter on Milo's living room floor. She barely remembered having crawled under the covers; it must have been sometime after three when she'd fallen asleep. The last she remembered, Ollie and Victor were still huddled in the dining room, discussing the photographs. Now there was only silence. The dining room, like the rest of the house, lay in shadow.

She turned on her back, and her shoulder thumped against something warm and solid. Victor. He stirred, murmuring something she couldn't understand.

"Are you awake?" she whispered.

He turned toward her and in his drowsiness enfolded her in his arms. She knew it was only instinct that drew him to her, the yearning of one warm body for another. Or perhaps it was the memory of his wife sleeping beside him, in his mind always there, always waiting to be held. For the moment, she let him cling to the dream. *While he's still half asleep, let him believe I'm Lily,* she thought. *What harm can there be? He needs the memory. And I need the comfort.*

She burrowed into his arms, into the safe spot that once had belonged to another. She took it without regard for the consequences, willing to be swept up into the fantasy of being, for this moment, the one woman in the world he loved. How good it felt, how protected and cared for. From the soap-and-sweat smell of his chest to the coarse fabric of his shirt, it was sanctuary. He was breathing warmly into her hair now, whispering words she knew were for another, pressing kisses to the top of her head. Then he trapped her face in his hands and pressed his lips to hers in a kiss so undeniably needy it ignited within her a hunger of her own. Her response was instinctive and filled with all the yearning of a woman too long a stranger to love.

She met his kiss with one just as deep, just as needy.

At once she was lost, whirled away into some grand and glorious vortex. He stroked down her face, her neck. His hands moved to the buttons of her blouse. She arched against him, her breasts suddenly aching to be touched. It had been so long, so long.

She didn't know how the blouse fell open. She knew only that one moment his fingers were skimming the fabric, and the next moment, they were cupping her flesh. It was that unexpected contact of skin on forbidden skin, the magic torment of his fingers caressing her nipple, that made any last resistance fall away. How many chances were left to them? How many nights together? She longed for so many more, an eternity, but this might be all they had. She welcomed it, welcomed him, with all the passion of a woman granted one last taste of love.

With a knowing touch, she slid her hands down his shirt, undoing buttons, stroking her way through the dense hair of his chest, to the top of his trousers. There she paused, feeling his startled intake of breath, knowing that he too was past retreat.

Together they fumbled at buttons and zippers, both of them suddenly feverish to be free. It all fell away in a tumult of cotton and lace. And when the last scrap of clothing was shed, when nothing came between them but the velvet darkness, she reached up and pulled him to her, on her.

It was a joyful filling, as if, in that first deep thrust within her, he also reached some long-empty hollow in her soul.

"Please," she murmured, her voice breaking into a whimper.

He fell instantly still. "Cathy?" he asked, his hands anxiously cupping her face. "What—"

"Please. Don't stop...."

His soft laughter was all the reassurance she needed. "I have no intention of stopping," he whispered. "None whatsoever..."

And he didn't stop. Not until he had taken her with him all the way, higher and further than any man ever could, to a place beyond thought or reason. Only when release came, wave flooding upon wave, did she know how very high and far they had climbed.

A sweet exhaustion claimed them.

Outside, in the grayness of dawn, a bird sang. Inside, the silence was broken only by the sound of their breathing.

She sighed into the warmth of his shoulder. "Thank you."

He touched her face. "For what?"

"For making me feel...wanted again."

"Oh, Cathy."

"It's been such a long time. Jack and I, we—we stopped making love way before the divorce. It was me, actually. I couldn't bear having him..." She swallowed. "When you don't love someone anymore, when they don't love you, it's hard to let yourself be...touched."

He brushed his fingers down her cheek. "Is it still hard? Being touched?"

"Not by you. Being touched by you is like...being touched the very first time."

By the window's pale light she saw him smile. "I hope your very first time wasn't too awful."

Now she smiled. "I don't remember it very well. It was such a frantic, ridiculous thing on the floor of a college dorm room."

He reached out and patted the carpet. "I see you've come a long way."

"Haven't I?" she laughed. "But floors can be terribly romantic places."

"Goodness. A carpet connoisseur. How do dorm room and living room floors compare?"

"I couldn't tell you. It's been such a long time since I was eighteen.'' She paused, hovering on the edge of baring the truth. ''In fact,'' she admitted, ''it's been a long time since I've been with anyone.''

Softly he said, ''It's been a long time for both of us.''

She let that revelation hang for a moment in the semi-darkness. ''Not—not since Lily?'' she finally asked.

''No.'' A single word, yet it revealed so much. The three years of loyalty to a dead woman. The grief, the loneliness. How she wanted to fill that womanless chasm for him! To be his savior, and he, hers. Could she make him forget? No, not forget; she couldn't expect him ever to forget Lily. But she wanted a space in his heart for herself, a very large space designed for a lifetime. A space to which no other woman, dead or alive, could ever lay claim.

''She must have been a very special woman,'' she said.

He ran a strand of her hair through his fingers. ''She was very wise, very aware. And she was kind. That's something I don't always find in a person.''

She's still part of you, isn't she? She's still the one you love.

''It's the same sort of kindness I find in you,'' he said.

His fingers had slid to her face and were now stroking her cheek. She closed her eyes, savoring his touch, his warmth. ''You hardly know me,'' she whispered.

''But I do. That night, after the accident, I survived purely on the sound of your voice. And the touch of your hand. I'd know them both, anywhere.''

She opened her eyes and gazed at him. ''Would you really?''

He pressed his lips to her forehead. ''Even in my sleep.''

''But I'm not Lily. I could never be Lily.''

''That's true. You can't be. No one can.''

''I can't replace what you lost.''

''What makes you think that's what I want? Some sort of replacement? She was my wife. And yes, I loved her.'' By the way he said it, his answer invited no exploration.

She didn't try.

From somewhere in the house came the jingle of a telephone. After two rings it stopped. Faintly they heard Milo's voice murmuring upstairs.

Cathy sat up and reached automatically for her clothes. She dressed in silence, her back turned to Victor. A new modesty had sprung up between them, the shyness of strangers.

"Cathy," he said. "People do move on."

"I know."

"You've gotten over Jack."

She laughed, a small, tired sound. "No woman ever really gets over Jack Zuckerman. Yes, I'm over the worst of it. But every time a woman falls in love, really falls in love, it takes something out of her. Something that can never be put back."

"It also gives her something."

"That depends on who you fall in love with, doesn't it?"

Footsteps thumped down the stairs, creaked across the dining room. A wide-awake Milo stood in the doorway, his uncombed hair standing out like a brush. "Hey, you two!" he hissed. "Get up! Hurry."

Cathy rose to her feet in alarm. "What is it?"

"That was Ollie on the phone. He called to say some guy's in the area, asking questions about you. He's already been down to Bach's neighborhood."

"What?" Now Victor was on his feet and hurriedly stuffing his legs into his trousers.

"Ollie figures the guy'll be knocking around here next. Guess they know who your friends are."

"Who was asking the questions?"

"Claimed he was FBI."

"Polowski," muttered Victor, pulling his shirt on. "Has to be."

"You know him?"

"The same guy who set me up. The guy who's been tailing us ever since."

"How did he know we're here?" said Cathy. "No one could've followed us—"

"No one had to. They have my profile. They know I have friends here." Victor glanced at Milo. "Sorry, buddy. Hope this doesn't get you into trouble."

Milo's laugh was distinctly tense. "Hey, I didn't do nothin' wrong. Just harbored a felon." The bravado suddenly melted away. He asked, "Exactly what kind of trouble should I expect?"

"Questions," said Victor, quickly buttoning his shirt. "Lots of 'em. Maybe they'll even take a look around. Just keep cool, tell 'em you haven't heard from me. Think you can do it?"

"Sure. But I don't know about Ma—"

"Your Ma's no problem. Just tell her to stick to Chinese." Victor grabbed the envelope of photos and glanced at Cathy. "Ready?"

"Let's get out of here. Please."

"Back door," Milo suggested.

They followed him through the kitchen. A glance told them the way was clear. As he opened the door, Milo added, "I almost forgot. Ollie wants to see you this afternoon. Something about those photos."

"Where?"

"The lake. Behind the boathouse. You know the place."

They stepped out into the chill dampness of morning. Fog-borne silence hung in the air. *Will we ever stop running?* thought Cathy. *Will we never stop listening for footsteps?*

Victor clapped his friend on the shoulder. "Thanks, Milo. I owe you a big one."

"And one of these days I plan to collect!" Milo hissed as they slipped away.

Victor held up his hand in farewell. "See you around."

"Yeah," Milo muttered into the mist. "Let's hope not in jail."

THE CHINESE MAN was lying. Though the man betrayed nothing in his voice, no hesitation, no guilty waver, still Savitch knew this Mr. Milo Lum was hiding something. His eyes betrayed him.

He was seated on the living room couch, across from Savitch. Off to the side sat Mrs. Lum in an easy chair, smiling uncomprehendingly. Savitch might be able to use the old biddy for now, it was the son who held his interest.

"I can't see why you'd be after him," said Milo. "Victor'

as clean as they come. At least, he was when I knew him. But that was a long time ago.''

"How far back?'' asked Savitch politely.

"Oh, years. Yeah. Haven't seen him since. No, sir.''

Savitch raised an eyebrow. Milo shifted on the couch, shuffled his feet, glanced pointlessly around the room.

"You and your mother live here alone?'' Savitch asked.

"Since my dad died.''

"No tenants? No one else lives here?''

"No. Why?''

"There were reports of a man fitting Holland's description in the neighborhood.''

"Believe me, if Victor was wanted by the police, he wouldn't hang around here. You think I'd let a murder suspect in the house? With just me and my old Ma?''

Savitch glanced at Mrs. Lum, who merely smiled. The old woman had sharp, all-seeing eyes. A survivor's eyes.

It was time for Savitch to confirm his hunch. "Excuse me,'' he said, rising to his feet. "I had a long drive from the city. May I use your restroom?''

"Uh, sure. Down that hall.''

Savitch headed into the bathroom and closed the door. Within seconds he'd spotted the evidence he was looking for. It was lying on the tiled floor: a long strand of brown hair. Very silky, very fine.

Catherine Weaver's shade.

It was all the proof he needed to proceed. He reached under his jacket for the shoulder holster and pulled out the semiautomatic. Then he gave his crisp white shirt a regretful pat. Messy business, interrogation. He would have to watch the bloodstains.

He stepped out into the hall, casually holding his pistol at his side. He'd go for the old woman first. Hold the barrel to her head, threaten to pull the trigger. There was an uncommonly strong bond between this mother and son. They would protect each other at all costs.

Savitch was halfway down the hall when the doorbell rang.

He halted. The front door was opened and a new voice said, "Mr. Milo Lum?"

"And who the hell are you?" came Milo's weary reply.

"The name's Sam Polowski. FBI."

Every muscle in Savitch's body snapped taut. No choice now; he had to take the man out.

He raised his pistol. Soundlessly, he made his way down the hall toward the living room.

"*Another* one?" came Milo's peevish voice. "Look, one of your guys is already here—"

"What?"

"Yeah, he's back in the—"

Savitch stepped out and was swinging his pistol toward the front doorway when Mrs. Lum shrieked.

Milo froze. Polowski didn't. He rolled sideways just as the bullet thudded into the door frame, splintering wood.

By the time Savitch got off a second shot, Polowski was crawling somewhere behind the couch and the bullet slammed uselessly into the stuffing. That was it for chances—Polowski was armed.

Savitch decided it was time to vanish.

He turned and darted back up the hall, into a far bedroom. It was the mother's room; it smelled of incense and old-lady perfume. The window slid open easily. Savitch kicked out the screen, scrambled over the sill and sank heel-deep into the muddy flower bed. Cursing, he slogged away, trailing clumps of mud across the lawn.

He heard, faintly, "Halt! FBI!" but continued running.

He nursed his rage all the way back to the car.

MILO STARED in bewilderment at the trampled pansies. "What the hell was that all about?" he demanded. "Is this some sort of FBI practical joke?"

Sam Polowski didn't answer; he was too busy tracking the footprints across the grass. They led to the sidewalk, then faded into the road's pebbly asphalt.

"Hey!" yelled Milo. "What's going on?"

Polowski turned. "I didn't really see him. What did he look like?"

Milo shrugged. "I dunno. Efrem Zimbalist-type."

"Meaning?"

"Tall, clean-cut, great build. Typical FBI."

There was a silence as Milo regarded Polowski's sagging belly.

"Well," amended Milo, "maybe not *typical*..."

"What about his face?"

"Lemme think. Brown hair? Maybe brown eyes?"

"You're not sure."

"You know how it is. All you white guys look alike to me."

An eruption of rapid Chinese made them both turn. Mrs. Lum had followed them out onto the lawn and was jabbering and gesticulating.

"What's she saying?" asked Polowski.

"She says the man was about six foot one, had straight dark brown hair parted on the left, brown eyes, almost black, a high forehead, a narrow nose and thin lips, and a small tattoo on his inside left wrist."

"Uh—is that all?"

"The tattoo read PJX."

Polowski shook his head in amazement. "Is she always this observant?"

"She can't exactly converse in English. So she does a lot of watching."

"Obviously." Polowski took out a pen and began to jot the information in a notebook.

"So who was this guy?" prodded Milo.

"Not FBI."

"How do I know *you're* FBI."

"Do I look like it?"

"No."

"Only proves my point."

"What?"

"If I wanted to pretend I was an agent, wouldn't I at least try to *look* like one? Whereas, if I *am* one, I wouldn't bother try and look like one."

"Oh."

"Now." Polowski slid the notebook in his pocket. "You're still going to insist you haven't seen, or heard from, Victor Holland?"

Milo straightened. "That's right."

"And you don't know how to get in touch with him?"

"I have no idea."

"That's too bad. Because I could be the one to save his life. I've already saved yours."

Milo said nothing.

"Just why the hell do you think that guy was here? To pay a social visit? No, he was after information." Polowski paused and added, ominously, "And believe me, he would've gotten it."

Milo shook his head. "I'm confused."

"So am I. That's why I need Holland. He has the answers. But I need him alive. That means I need to find him before the other guy does. Tell me where he is."

Polowski and Milo looked at each other long and hard.

"I don't know," said Milo. "I don't know what to do."

Mrs. Lum was chattering again. She pointed to Polowski and nodded.

"Now what's she saying?" asked Polowski.

"She says you have big ears."

"For that, I can look in the mirror."

"What she means is, the size of your ears indicates sagacity."

"Come again?"

"You're a smart dude. She thinks I should listen to you."

Polowski turned and grinned at Mrs. Lum. "Your mother a great judge of character." He looked back at Milo. ' wouldn't want anything to happen to her. Or you. You bo have to get out of town."

Milo nodded. "On that particular point, we both agree." H turned toward the house.

"What about Holland?" called Polowski. "Will you he me find him?"

Milo took his mother by the arm and guided her across t

lawn. Without even a backward look he said, "I'm thinking about it."

"IT WAS THOSE two photos. I just couldn't figure them out," said Ollie.

They were standing on the boathouse pier, overlooking the bed of Lake Lagunita. The lake was dry now, as it was every winter, drained to a reedy marsh until spring. They were alone, the three of them, sharing the lake with only an occasional duck. In the spring, this would be an idyllic spot, the water lapping the banks, lovers drifting in rowboats, here and there a poet lolling under the trees. But today, under black clouds, with a cold mist rising from the reeds, it was a place of utter desolation.

"I knew they weren't biological data," said Ollie. "I kept thinking they looked like some sort of electrical grid. So this morning, right after I left Milo's, I took 'em over to Bach's, down in San José. Caught him at breakfast."

"Bach?" asked Cathy.

"Another member of the Out of Tuners. Great bassoon player. Started an electronics firm a few years back and now he's working with the big boys. Anyway, the first thing he says as I walk in the door is, 'Hey, did the FBI get to you yet?' And I said, 'What?' and he says, 'They just called. For some reason they're looking for Gershwin. They'll probably get around to you next.' And that's when I knew I had to get you two out of Milo's house, stat."

"So what did he say about those photos?"

"Oh, yeah." Ollie reached into his briefcase and pulled out the photos. "Okay. This one here, it's a circuit diagram. An electronic alarm system. Very sophisticated, very secure. Designed to be breached by use of a keypad code, punched in at this point here. Probably at an entryway. You seen anything like it at Viratek?"

Victor nodded. "Building C-2. Where Jerry worked. The keypad's in the hall, right by the Special Projects door."

"Ever been inside that door?"

"No. Only those with top clearance can get through. Like Jerry."

"Then we'll have to visualize what comes next. Going by the diagram, there's another security point here, probably another keypad. Right inside the first door, they've stationed a camera system."

"You mean like a bank camera?" asked Cathy.

"Similar. Only I'd guess this one's being monitored twenty-four hours a day."

"They went first class, didn't they?" said Victor. "Two secured doors, plus inspection by a guard. Not to mention the guard at the outside gate."

"Don't forget the laser lattice."

"What?"

"This inner room here." Ollie pointed to the diagram's core. "Laser beams, directed at various angles. They'll detect movement of just about anything bigger than a rat."

"How do the lasers get switched off?"

"Has to be done by the security guard. The controls are on his panel."

"You can tell all this from the diagram?" asked Cathy. "I'm impressed."

"No problem." Ollie grinned. "Bach's firm designs security systems."

Victor shook his head. "This looks impossible. We can't get through all that."

Cathy frowned at him. "Wait a minute. What are you talking about? You aren't considering going into that building, are you?"

"We discussed it last night," said Victor. "It may be the only way—"

"Are you crazy? Viratek's out to kill us and you want to break in?"

"It's the proof we need," said Ollie. "You try going to the newspapers or the Justice Department and they'll demand evidence. You can bet Viratek's going to deny everything. Even if someone does launch an investigation, all Viratek has to do is toss the virus and, *poof!* your evidence is gone. No one can prove a thing.''

''You have photos—''

''Sure. A few pages of animal data. The virus is never identified. And all that evidence could've been fabricated by, say, some disgruntled ex-employee.''

''So what *is* proof? What do you need, another dead body? Victor's, for instance?''

''What we need is the virus—a virus that's supposed to be extinct. Just a single vial and the case against them is nailed shut.''

''Just a single vial. Right.'' Cathy shook her head. ''I don't know what I'm worried about. No one can get through those doors. Not without the keypad codes.''

''Ah, but those we have!'' Ollie flipped to the second photo. ''The mysterious numbers. See, they finally make sense. Two sets of seven digits. Not phone numbers at all! Jerry was pointing the way through Viratek's top security.''

''What about the lasers?'' she pointed out, her agitation growing. They couldn't be serious! Surely they could see the futility of this mission. She didn't care if her fear showed; she had to be their voice of reason. ''And then there's the guards,'' she said. ''Two of them. Do you have a way past them? Or did Jerry also leave you the formula for invisibility?''

Ollie glanced uneasily at Victor. ''Uh, maybe I should let you two discuss this first. Before we make any other plans.''

''I thought I was part of all this,'' said Cathy. ''Part of every decision. I guess I was wrong.''

Neither man said a thing. Their silence only fueled Cathy's anger. She thought: *So you left me out of this. You didn't respect my opinion enough to ask me what I think, what I want.*

Without a word she turned and walked away.

Moments later, Victor caught up with her. She was standing on the dirt path, hugging herself against the cold. She heard his approach, sensed his uncertainty, his struggle to find the right words. For a moment he simply stood beside her, not speaking.

''I think we should run,'' she said. She gazed over the dry

lake bed and shivered. The wind that swept across the reeds was raw and biting; it sliced right through her sweater. "I want to get away," she said. "I want to go somewhere warm. Some place where the sun's shining, where I can lie on a beach and not worry about who's watching me from the bushes...." Suddenly reminded of the terrible possibilities, she turned and glanced at the oaks hulking behind them. She saw only the fluttering of dead leaves.

"I agree with you," said Victor quietly.

"You do?" She turned to him, relieved. "Let's go, Victor! Let's leave now. Forget this crazy idea. We can catch the next bus south—"

"This very afternoon. You'll be on your way."

"*I* will?" She stared at him, at first not willing to accept what she'd heard. Then the meaning of his words sank in. "You're not coming."

Slowly he shook his head. "I can't."

"You mean you won't."

"Don't you see?" He took her by the shoulders, as though to shake some sense into her. "We're backed into a corner Unless we do something—I do something—we'll always be running."

"Then let's *run!*" She reached for him, her fingers clutching at his windbreaker. She wanted to scream at him, to tear away his cool mask of reason and get to the raw emotions beneath They had to be there, buried deep in that logical brain of his "We could go to Mexico," she said. "I know a place on th coast—in Baja. A little hotel near the beach. We could sta there a few months, wait until things are safer—"

"It'll never be safer."

"Yes, it will! They'll forget about us—"

"You're not thinking straight."

"I am. I'm thinking I want to stay alive."

"And that's exactly why I have to do this." He took he face in his hands, trapping it so she could look nowhere but him. No longer was he the lover, the friend—his voice no held the cold, steady note of authority and she hated the sour of it. "I'm trying to keep you alive," he said. "With a futu ahead of you. And the only way I can do that is to blow this thing wide open so the world knows about it. I owe it to you. And I owe it to Jerry.''

She wanted to argue with him, to plead with him to go with her, but she knew it was useless. What he said was true. Running would only be a temporary solution, one that would give them a few sweet months of safety, but a temporary one just the same.

"I'm sorry, Cathy," he said softly. "I can't think of any other way—"

"—But to get rid of me," she finished for him.

He released her. She stepped back, and the sudden gulf between them left her aching. She couldn't bear to look at him, knowing that the pain she felt wouldn't be reflected in his eyes. "So how does it work?" she said dully. "Do I leave tonight? Will it be plane, train or automobile?"

"Ollie will drive you to the airport. I've asked him to buy you the ticket under his name—Mrs. Wozniak. He'll have to be the one to see you off. We thought it'd be safer if I didn't come along to the airport."

"Of course."

"That'll get you to Mexico. Ollie'll give you enough cash to keep you going for a while. Enough to get you anywhere you want to go from there. Baja. Acapulco. Or just hang around with Jack if you think that's best."

"Jack." She turned away, unwilling to show her tears. "Right."

"Cathy." She felt his hand on her shoulder, as though he wanted to turn her toward him, to pull her back one last time into his arms. She refused to move.

Footsteps approached. They both glanced around to see Ollie, standing a few feet away. "Ready to go?" he asked.

There was a long silence. Then Victor nodded. "She's ready."

"Uh, look," Ollie mumbled, suddenly aware that he'd stepped in at a bad time. "My car's over by the boathouse. If you want, I can, uh, wait for you there...."

Cathy furiously dashed away her tears. "No," she said with sudden determination. "I'm coming."

Victor stood watching her, his gaze veiled by some cool, impenetrable mist.

"Goodbye, Victor," she said.

He didn't answer. He just kept looking at her through that terrible mist.

"If I—if I don't see you again..." She stopped, struggling to be just as brave, just as invulnerable. "Take care of yourself," she finished. Then she turned and followed Ollie down the path.

Through the car window, she glimpsed Victor, still standing on the lake path, his hands jammed in his pockets, his shoulders hunched against the wind. He didn't wave goodbye; he merely watched them drive away.

It was an image she'd carry with her forever, that last, fading view of the man she loved. The man who'd sent her away.

As Ollie turned the car onto the road, she sat stiff and silent, her fists balled in her lap, the pain in her throat so terrible she could scarcely breathe. Now he was behind them. She couldn't see him, but she knew he was still standing there, as unmoving as the oaks that surrounded him. *I love you,* she thought. *And I will never see you again.*

She turned to look out. He was a distant figure now, almost lost among the trees. In a gesture of farewell, she reached up and gently touched the window.

The glass was cold.

"I HAVE TO STOP OFF at the lab," said Ollie, turning into the hospital parking lot. "I just remembered I left the checkbook in my desk. Can't get you a plane ticket without it."

Cathy nodded dully. She was still in a state of shock, still trying to accept the fact that she was now on her own. That Victor had sent her away.

Ollie pulled into a stall marked Reserved, Wozniak. "This'll only take a sec."

"Shall I come in with you?"

"You'd better wait in the car. I work with a very nosy

bunch. They see me with a woman and they want to know everything. Not that there's ever anything to know." He climbed out and shut the door. "Be right back."

Cathy watched him stride away and vanish into a side entrance. She had to smile at the thought of Ollie Wozniak squiring around a woman—any woman. Unless it was someone with a Ph.D. who could sit through his scientific monologues.

A minute passed.

Outside, a bird screeched. Cathy glanced out at the trees lining the hospital driveway and spotted the jay, perched among the lower branches. Nothing else moved, not even the leaves.

She leaned back and closed her eyes.

Too little sleep, too much running, had taken its toll. Exhaustion settled over her, so profound she thought she would never again be able to move her limbs. *A beach,* she thought. *Warm sand. Waves washing at my feet...*

The jay's cry cut off in mid-screech. Only vaguely did Cathy register the sudden silence. Then, even through her half sleep, she sensed the shadowing of the window, like a cloud passing before the sun.

She opened her eyes. A face was staring at her through the glass.

Panic sent her lunging for the lock button. Before she could jam it down, the door was wrenched open. A badge was thrust up to her face.

"FBI!" the man barked. "Out of the car, please."

Slowly Cathy emerged, to stand weak-kneed against the door. *Ollie,* she thought, her gaze darting toward the hospital entrance. *Where are you?* If he appeared, she had to be ready to bolt, to flee across the parking lot and into the woods. She doubted the man with the badge would be able to keep up; his stubby legs and thick waist didn't go along with a star athlete.

But he must have a gun. If I bolt, would he shoot me in the back?

"Don't even think about it, Miss Weaver," the man said. He took her arm and gave her a nudge toward the hospital entrance. "Go on. Inside."

"But—"

"Dr. Wozniak's waiting for us in the lab."

Waiting didn't exactly describe Ollie's predicament. Bound and trussed would have been a better description. She found Ollie bent over double in his office, handcuffed to the foot of his desk, while three of his lab colleagues stood by gaping in amazement.

"Back to work, folks," said the agent as he herded the onlookers out of the office. "Just a routine matter." He shut the door and locked it. Then he turned to Cathy and Ollie. "I have to find Victor Holland," he said. "And I have to find him fast."

"Man," Ollie muttered into his chest. "This guy sounds like a broken record."

"Who are you?" demanded Cathy.

"The name's Sam Polowski. I work out of the San Francisco office." He pulled out his badge and slapped it on the desk. "Take a closer look if you want. It's official."

"Uh, excuse me?" called Ollie. "Could I maybe, possibly, get into a more comfortable position?"

Polowski ignored him. His attention was focused on Cathy. "I don't think I need to spell it out for you, Miss Weaver. Holland's in trouble."

"And you're one of his biggest problems," she retorted.

"That's where you're wrong." Polowski moved closer, his gaze unflinching, his voice absolutely steady. "I'm one of his hopes. Maybe his only hope."

"You're trying to kill him."

"Not me. Someone else, someone who's going to succeed. Unless I can stop it."

She shook her head. "I'm not stupid! I know about you. What you've been trying to—"

"Not me. The other guy." He reached for the telephone on the desk. "Here," he said, holding the receiver out to her. "Call Milo Lum. Ask him what happened at his house this morning. Maybe he'll convince you I'm on your side."

Cathy stared at the man, wondering what sort of game he was playing. Wondering why she was falling for it. *Because I want so much to believe him.*

"He's alone out there," said Polowski. "One man trying to buck the U.S. government. He's new to the game. Sooner or later he's going to slip, do something stupid. And that'll be it." He dialed the phone for her and again held out the receiver. "Go on. Talk to Lum."

She heard the phone ring three times, followed by Milo's answer "Hello? Hello?"

Slowly she took the receiver. "Milo?"

"Is that you? Cathy? God, I was hoping you'd call—"

"Listen, Milo. I need to ask you something. It's about a man named Polowski."

"I've met him."

"You *have?*" She looked up and saw Polowski nodding.

"Lucky for me," said Milo. "The guy's got the charm of an old shoe but he saved my life. I don't know what Gersh was talking about. Is Gersh around? I have to—"

"Thanks, Milo," she murmured. "Thanks a lot." She hung up.

Polowski was still looking at her.

"Okay," she said. "I want your side of it. From the beginning."

"You gonna help me out?"

"I haven't decided." She crossed her arms. "Convince me."

Polowski nodded. "That's just what I plan to do."

CHAPTER TEN

FOR VICTOR IT WAS a long and miserable afternoon. After leaving the lake, he wandered around the campus for a while, ending up at last in the main quad. There in the courtyard, standing among the buildings of sandstone and red tile, Victor struggled to keep his mind on the business at hand: exposing Viratek. But his thoughts kept shifting back to Cathy, to that look she'd given him, full of hurt abandonment.

As if I'd betrayed her.

If she could just see the good sense in his actions. He was a scientist, a man whose life and work was ruled by logic. Sending her away was the logical thing to do. The authorities were closing in, the noose was growing ever tighter. He could accept the danger to himself. After all, he'd chosen to take on Jerry's battle, to see this through to the end.

What he hadn't chosen was to put Cathy in danger. *Now she's out of the mess and on her way to a safe place. One less thing to worry about. Time to put her out of my mind.*

As if I could.

He stared up at one of the courtyard's Romanesque arches and reminded himself, once again, of the wisdom of his actions. Still, the uneasiness remained. Where was she? Was she safe? She'd been gone only an hour and he missed her already.

He gave a shrug, as though by that gesture, he could somehow cast off the fears. Still they remained, constant and gnawing. He found a place under the eaves and huddled on the steps to wait for Ollie's return.

At dusk he was still waiting. By the last feeble light of day he paced the stone courtyard. He counted and recounted the number of hours it should've taken Ollie to drive to San Jose Airport and return. He added in traffic time, red lights, ticket counter delays. Surely three hours was enough. Cathy had to be on a plane by now, jetting for warmer climes.

Where was Ollie?

At the sound of the first footstep, he spun around. For a moment he couldn't believe what he was seeing, couldn't understand how she could be standing there, silhouetted beneath the sandstone archway. "Cathy?" he said in amazement.

She stepped out, into the courtyard. "Victor," she said softly. She started toward him, slowly at first, and then, in a jubilant burst of flight, ran toward his waiting arms. He swept her up, swung her around, kissed her hair, her face. He didn't understand why she was here but he rejoiced that she was.

"I don't know if I've done the right thing," she murmured. "I hope to God I have."

"Why did you come back?"

"I wasn't sure—I'm still not sure—"

"Cathy, what are you doing here?"

"You can't fight this alone! And he can help you—"

"Who can?"

From out of the twilight came another voice, gruff and starling. "*I* can."

At once Victor stiffened. His gaze shifted back to the arch behind Cathy. A man emerged and walked slowly toward him. Not a tall man, he had the sort of body that, in a weight-loss ad, would've been labeled Before. He came up to Victor and planted himself squarely on the courtyard stones.

"Hello, Holland," he said. "I'm glad we've finally met. The name is Sam Polowski."

Victor turned and looked in disbelief at Cathy. "Why?" he asked in quiet fury. "Just tell me that. *Why?*"

She reacted as though he'd delivered a physical blow. Tentively she reached for his arm; he pulled away from her at once.

"He wants to help," she said, her voice wretched with pain. "*Listen* to him!"

"I'm not sure there's any point to listening. Not now." He let his whole body go slack in defeat. He didn't understand it, would never understand it. It was over, the running, the scraping along on fear and hope. All because Cathy had betrayed him. He turned matter-of-factly to Polowski. "I take it I'm under arrest," he said.

"Hardly," said Polowski, nodding toward the archway. "Seeing as he's got my gun."

"What?"

"Hey, Gersh! Over here!" Ollie yelled. "See, I got him covered!"

Polowski winced. "Geez, do ya have to wave the damn thing?"

"Sorry," said Ollie.

"Now, does that convince you, Holland?" asked Polowski. "You think I'd hand my piece over to an idiot like him if I didn't want to talk to you?"

"He's telling the truth," insisted Cathy. "He gave the gun to Ollie. He was willing to take the risk, just to meet you face-to-face."

"Bad move, Polowski," said Victor bitterly. "I'm wanted for murder, remember? Industrial espionage? How do you know I won't just blow you away?"

"'Cause I know you're innocent."

"That makes a difference, does it?"

"It does to me."

"Why?"

"You're caught up in something big, Holland. Something that's going to eat you up alive. Something that's got my supervisor doing backflips to keep me off the case. I don't like being pulled off a case. It hurts my delicate ego."

The two men gazed at each other through the gathering darkness, each sizing up the other.

At last Victor nodded. He looked at Cathy, a quiet plea for forgiveness, for not believing in her. When at last she came into his arms, he felt the world had suddenly gone right again.

He heard a deliberate clearing of a throat. Turning, he saw Polowski hold out his hand. Victor took it in a handshake that could very well be his doom—or his salvation.

"You've led me on a long, hard chase," said Polowski. "I think it's time we worked together."

"BASICALLY," said Ollie, "What we have here is just your simple, everyday mission impossible."

They were assembled in Polowski's hotel room, a five-member team that Milo had just dubbed the "Older, Crazier Out of Tuners," or Old COOTS for short. On the table in the center of the room lay potato chips, beer and the photos detailing Viratek's security system. There was also a map of the Viratek compound, forty acres of buildings and wooded grounds, all of it surrounded by an electrified fence. They had been studying the photos for an hour now, and the job that lay before them looked hopeless.

"No easy way in," said Ollie, shaking his head. "Even if those keypad codes are still valid, you're faced with the human element of recognition. Two guards, two positions. No way they're gonna let you pass."

"There has to be a way," said Polowski. "Come on, Holland. You're the egghead. Use that creative brain of yours."

Cathy looked at Victor. While the others had tossed ideas back and forth, he had said very little. *And he's the one with the most at stake—his life,* she thought. It took incredible courage—or foolhardiness—even to consider such a desperate move. Yet here he was, calmly scanning the map as though he were planning nothing more dangerous than a Sunday drive.

He must have felt her gaze, for he slung his arm around her and tugged her close. Now that they were reunited, she savored every moment they shared, committed to memory every look, every caress. Soon he could be wrenched away from her. Even now he was making plans to enter what looked like a death trap.

He pressed a kiss to the top of her head. Then, reluctantly, he turned his attention back to the map.

"The electronics I'm not worried about," he said. "It's the human element. The guards."

Milo cocked his head toward Polowski. "I still say ol' J. Edgar here should get a warrant and raid the place."

"Right," snorted Polowski. "By the time that order gets through the judge and Dafoe and your Aunt Minnie's cousin, Viratek'll have that lab turned into a baby-milk factory. No, we need to get in on our own. Without anyone getting word of it.'' He looked at Ollie. ''And you're sure this is the only evidence we'll need?''

Ollie nodded. ''One vial should do it. Then we take it to a reputable lab, have them confirm it's smallpox, and your case is airtight.''

''They'll have no way around it?''

''None. The virus is officially extinct. Any company caught playing with a live sample is, ipso facto, dead meat.''

''I like that,'' said Polowski. ''That ipso facto stuff. No fancy Viratek attorney can argue that one away.''

''But first you gotta get hold of a vial,'' said Ollie. ''And from where I'm standing, it looks impossible. Unless we're willing to try armed robbery.''

For one frightening moment, Polowski actually seemed to give that thought serious consideration. ''Naw,'' he conceded. ''Wouldn't go over well in court.''

''Besides which,'' said Ollie, ''I refuse to shoot another human being. It's against my principles.''

''Mine, too,'' said Milo.

''But theft,'' said Ollie, ''that's acceptable.''

Polowski looked at Victor. ''A group with high moral standards.''

Victor grinned. ''Holdovers from the sixties.''

''Sounds like we're back to the first option,'' said Cathy ''We have to steal the virus.'' She focused on the map of th compound, noting the electrified fence that circled the entir complex. The main road led straight to the front gate. Excep for an unpaved fire road, labeled *not maintained,* no other ap proaches were apparent.

''All right,'' she said. ''Assume you do get through the fron gate. You still have to get past two locked doors, two separa guards and a laser grid. Come on.''

''The doors are no problem,'' said Victor. ''It's the tw guards.''

''Maybe a diversion?'' suggested Milo. ''How about we s a fire?''

''And bring in the town fire department?'' said Victor. ''N

a good idea. Besides, I've dealt with this night guard at the front gate. I know him. And he goes strictly by the book. Never leaves the booth. At the first hint of anything suspicious, he'll hit the alarm button.''

''Maybe Milo could whip up a fake security pass,'' said Ollie. ''You know, the way he used to fix us up with those fake drivers' licenses.''

''He falsified IDs?'' said Polowski.

''Hey, I just changed the age to twenty-one!'' protested Milo.

''Made great passports, too,'' said Ollie. ''I had one from the kingdom of Booga Booga. It got me right past the customs official in Athens.''

''Yeah?'' Polowski looked impressed. ''So what about it, Holland? Would it work?''

''Not a chance. The guard has a master list of top-security employees. If he doesn't know the face, he'll do a double check.''

''But he does let some people through automatically?''

''Sure. The bigwigs. The ones he recognizes on—'' Victor suddenly paused and turned to stare at Cathy ''—on sight. Lord. It just might work.''

Cathy took one look at his face and immediately read his mind. ''No,'' she said. ''It's not that easy! I need to see the subject! I need molds of his face. Detailed photos from every angle—''

''But you *could* do it. You do it all the time.''

''On film it works! But this is face-to-face!''

''It's at night, through a car window. Or through a video camera. If you could just make me pass for one of the exec's—''

''What are you talking about?'' demanded Polowski.

''Cathy's a makeup artist. You know, horror films, special effects.''

''This is different!'' Cathy said. The difference being it was Victor's life on the line. No, he couldn't ask her to do this. If anything went wrong, she would be responsible. Having his death on her conscience would be more than she could live with.

She shook her head, praying he'd read the deadly earnestness in her gaze. "There's too much at stake," she insisted. "It's not as simple as—as filming *Slimelords*!"

"You did *Slimelords*?" asked Milo. "Terrific flick!"

"Besides," said Cathy, "it's not that easy, copying a face. I have to cast a mold, to get the features just right. For that I need a model."

"You mean the real guy?" asked Polowski.

"Right. The real guy. And I hardly think you're going to get some Viratek executive to sit down and let me slap plaster all over his face."

There was a long silence.

"That does present a problem," said Milo.

"Not necessarily."

They all turned and looked at Ollie.

"What are you thinking?" asked Victor.

"About this guy who works with me once in a while. Down in the lab…" Ollie looked up, and the grin on his face wa distinctly smug. "He's a veterinarian."

THE EVENTS OF the past few weeks had weighed heavily o Archibald Black, so heavily, in fact, that he found it difficu to carry on with those everyday tasks of life. Just driving t and from his office at Viratek was an ordeal. And then, to s down at his desk and face his secretary and pretend that notI ing, absolutely nothing, was wrong—that was almost more tha he could manage. He was a scientist, not an actor.

Not a criminal.

But that's what they would call him, if the experiments C wing ever came to light. His instinct was to shut the l down, to destroy the contents of those incubators. But Matthe Tyrone insisted the work continue. They were so close to co pletion. After all, Defense had underwritten the project, a Defense expected a product. This matter of Victor Holland w only a minor glitch, soon to be solved. The thing to do v carry on.

Easy for Tyrone to say, thought Black. *Tyrone had no conscience to bother him.*

These thoughts had plagued him all day. Now, as Black packed up his briefcase, he felt desperate to flee forever this teak-and-leather office, to take refuge in some safe and anonymous job. It was with a sigh of relief that he walked out the door.

It was dark when he pulled into his gravel driveway. The house, a saltbox of cedar and glass tucked among the trees, looked cold and empty and in need of a woman. Perhaps he should call his neighbor Muriel. She always seemed to appreciate an impromptu dinner together. Her snappy wit and green Jell-O salad almost made up for the fact she was 75. What a shame his generation didn't produce many Muriels.

He stepped out of his car and started up the path to the front door. Halfway there, he heard a soft *whht!* and almost simultaneously, a sharp pain stung his neck. Reflexively he slapped at it; something came away in his hands. In wonderment, he stared down at the dart, trying to understand where it had come from and how such a thing had managed to lodge in his neck. But he found he couldn't think straight. And then he found he was having trouble seeing, that the night had suddenly darkened to a dense blackness, that his legs were being sucked into some sort of quagmire. His briefcase slipped from his grasp and thudded to the ground.

I'm dying, he thought. And then, *Will anyone find me here?*

It was his last conscious thought before he collapsed onto the leaf-strewn path.

"Is he dead?"

Ollie bent forward and listened for Archibald Black's breathing. "He's definitely alive. But out cold." He looked up at Polowski and Victor. "Okay, let's move it. He'll be out for only an hour or so."

Victor grabbed the legs, Ollie and Polowski, the arms. Together they carried the unconscious man a few dozen yards through the woods, toward the clearing where the van was parked.

"You—you sure we got an hour?" gasped Polowski.

"Plus or minus," said Ollie. "The tranquilizer's designed for large animals, so the dose was only an estimate. And this guy's heavier than I expected." Ollie was panting now. "Hey, Polowski, he's slipping. Pull your weight, will ya?"

"I am! I think his right arm's heavier than his left."

The van's side door was already open for them. They rolled Black inside and slid the door closed. A bright light suddenly glared, but the unconscious man didn't even twitch.

Cathy knelt down at his side and critically examined the man's face.

"Can you do it?" asked Victor.

"Oh, I can do it," she said. "The question is, will you pass for him?" She glanced up and down the man's length, then back at Victor. "Looks about your size and build. We'll have to darken your hair, give you a widow's peak. I think you'll pass." She turned and glanced at Milo, who was already poised with his camera. "Take your photos. A few shots from every angle. I need lots of hair detail."

As Milo's strobe flashed again and again, Cathy donned gloves and an apron. She pointed to a sheet. "Drape him for me," she directed. "Everything but his face. I don't want him to wake up with plaster all over his clothes."

"Assuming he wakes up at all," said Milo, frowning down at Black's inert form.

"Oh, he'll wake up," said Ollie. "Right where we found him. And if we do the job right, Mr. Archibald Black will never know what hit him."

IT WAS THE RAIN that awakened him. The cold droplets pelted his face and dribbled into his open mouth. Groaning, Black turned over and felt gravel bite into his shoulder. Even in his groggy state it occurred to him that this did not make sense. Slowly he took stock of all the things that were not as they should be: the rain falling from the ceiling, the gravel in his bed, the fact he was still wearing his shoes...

At last he managed to shake himself fully awake. He found to his puzzlement that he was sitting in his driveway, and that his briefcase was lying right beside him. By now the rain had swelled to a downpour—he had to get out of the storm. Half crawling, half walking, Black managed to make it up the porch steps and into the house.

An hour later, huddled in his kitchen, a cup of coffee in hand, he tried to piece together what had happened. He remembered parking his car. He'd taken out his briefcase and apparently had managed to make it halfway up the path. And then…what?

A vague ache worried its way into his awareness. He rubbed his neck. That's when he remembered something strange had happened, just before he blacked out. Something associated with that ache in his neck.

He went to a mirror and looked. There it was, a small puncture in the skin. An absurd thought popped into his head: *Vampires*. Right. *Damn it, Archibald. You are a scientist. Come up with a rational explanation.*

He went to the laundry hamper and fished out his damp shirt. To his alarm he spotted a droplet of blood on the lapel. Then he saw what had caused it: a common, everyday tailor's pin. It was still lodged in the collar, no doubt left there by the dry cleaners. There was his rational explanation. He'd been pricked by a collar pin and the pain had sent him into a faint.

In disgust, he threw the shirt down. First thing in the morning, he was going to complain to the Tidy Girl cleaners and demand they do his suit for free.

Vampires, indeed.

"EVEN WITH BAD LIGHTING, you'll be lucky if you pass," said Cathy.

She stood back and gave Victor a long, critical look. Slowly she walked around him, eyeing the newly darkened hair, the resculpted face, the new eye color. It was as close as she could make it, but it wasn't good enough. It would never be good enough, not when Victor's life was at stake.

"I think he's the spitting image," said Polowski. "What's the problem now?"

"The problem is, I suddenly realize it's a crazy idea. I say we call it off."

"You've been working on him all afternoon. You got it right down to the damn freckles on his nose. What else can you improve on?"

"I don't know. I just don't feel *good* about this!"

There was a silence as she confronted the four men.

Ollie shook his head. "Women's intuition. That's a dangerous thing to disregard."

"Well, here's *my* intuition," said Polowski. "I think it'll work. And I think it's our best option. Our chance to nail the case."

Cathy turned to Victor. "You're the one who'll get hurt. It's your decision." What she really wanted to say was, *Please. Don't do it. Stay with me. Stay alive and safe and mine.* But she knew, looking into his eyes, that he'd already made his decision, and no matter how much she might wish for it, he would never really be hers.

"Cathy," he said. "It'll work. You have to believe that."

"The only thing I believe," she said, "is that you're going to get killed. And I don't want to be around to watch it."

Without another word, she turned and walked out the door.

Outside, in the parking lot of the Rockabye Motel, she stood in the darkness and hugged herself. She heard the door shut, and then his footsteps moved toward her across the blacktop.

"You don't have to stay," he said. "There's still that beach in Mexico. You could fly there tonight, be out of this mess."

"Do you want me to go?"

A pause, then, "Yes."

She shrugged, a poor attempt at nonchalance. "All right. I suppose it all makes perfect sense. I've done my part."

"You saved my life. At the very least, I owe you a measure of safety."

She turned to him. "Is that what weighs most on your mind, Victor? The fact that you *owe* me?"

"What weighs most on my mind is that you might get caught in the crossfire. I'm prepared to walk through those doors at Viratek. I'm prepared to do a lot of stupid things. But I'm not prepared to watch you get hurt. Does that make any sense?"

He pulled her against him, into a place that felt infinitely warm and safe. "Cathy, Cathy. I'm not crazy. I don't want to die. But I don't see any way around this...."

She pressed her face against his chest, felt his heartbeat, so steady, so regular. She was afraid to think of that heart not beating, of those arms no longer alive to hold her. He was brave enough to go through with this crazy scheme; couldn't she somehow dredge up the same courage? She thought, *I've come this far with you. How could I dream of walking away? Now that I know I love you?*

The motel door opened, and light arced across the parking lot. "Gersh?" said Ollie. "It's getting late. If we want to go ahead, we'll have to leave now."

Victor was still looking at her. "Well?" he said. "Do you want Ollie to take you to the airport?"

"No." She squared her shoulders. "I'm coming with you."

"Are you sure that's what you want to do?"

"I'm never sure of anything these days. But on this I've decided. I'll stick it out." She managed a smile. "Besides, you might need me on the set. In case your face falls off."

"I need you for a hell of a lot more than that."

"Gersh?"

Victor reached out for Cathy's hand. She let him take it. "We're coming," he said. "Both of us."

"I'M APPROACHING the front gate. One guard in the booth. No one else around. Copy?"

"Loud and clear," said Polowski.

"Okay. Here I go. Wish me luck."

"We'll be tuned in. Break a leg." Polowski clicked off the microphone and glanced at the others. "Well, folks, he's on his way."

To what? Cathy wondered. She glanced around at the other faces. There were four of them huddled in the van. They'd parked a half mile from Viratek's front gate. Close enough to hear Victor's transmissions, but too far away to do him much good. With the microphone link, they could mark his progress.

They could also mark his death.

In silence, they waited for the first hurdle.

"EVENING," said Victor, pulling up at the gate.

The guard peered out through the booth window. He was in his twenties, cap on straight, collar button fastened. This was Pete Zahn, Mr. By-the-book Extraordinaire. If anyone was to cut the operation short, it would be this man. Victor made a brave attempt at a smile and prayed his mask wouldn't crack. It seemed an eternity, that exchange of looks. Then, to Victor's relief, the man smiled back.

"Working late, Dr. Black?"

"Forgot something at the lab."

"Must be important, huh? To make a special trip at midnight."

"These government contracts. Gotta be done on time."

"Yeah." The guard waved him through. "Have a nice night."

Heart pounding, Victor pulled through the gate. Only when he'd rounded the curve into the empty parking lot did he manage a sigh of relief. "First base," he said into the microphone. "Come on, guys. Talk to me."

"We're here," came the response. It was Polowski.

"I'm heading into the building—can't be sure the signal will get through those walls. So if you don't hear from me—"

"We'll be listening."

"I've got a message for Cathy. Put her on."

There was a pause, then he heard, "I'm here, Victor."

"I just wanted to tell you this. I'm coming back. I promise. Copy?"

He wasn't sure if it was just the signal's waiver, but he thought he heard the beginning of tears in her reply. "I copy."

"I'm going in now. Don't leave without me."

IT TOOK PETE ZAHN only a minute to look up Archibald Black's license plate number. He kept a Rolodex in the booth, though he seldom referred to it as he had a good memory for numbers. He knew every executive's license by heart. It was his own little mind game, a test of his cleverness. And the plate on Dr. Black's car just didn't seem right.

He found the file card. The auto matched up okay: a gray

1991 Lincoln sedan. And he was fairly certain that *was* Dr. Black sitting in the driver's seat. But the license number was all wrong.

He sat back and thought about it for a while, trying to come up with all the possible explanations. That Black was simply driving a different auto. That Black was playing a joke on him, testing him.

That it hadn't been Archibald Black, at all.

Pete reached for the telephone. The way to find out was to call Black's home. It was after midnight, but it had to be done. If Black didn't answer the phone, then that must be him in the Lincoln. And if he *did* answer, then something was terribly wrong and Black would want to know about it.

Two rings. That's all it took before a groggy voice answered, "Hello?"

"This is Pete Zahn, night man at Viratek. Is this—is this Dr. Black?"

"Yes."

"Dr. *Archibald* Black?"

"Look, it's late! What is it?"

"I don't know how to tell you this, Dr. Black, but..." Pete cleared his throat. "Your double just drove through the gate...."

"I'M THROUGH the front door. Heading up the hall to the security wing. In case anyone's listening." Victor didn't expect a reply, and he heard none. The building was a concrete monstrosity, designed to last forever. He doubted a radio signal would make it through these walls. Though he'd been on his own from the moment he'd entered the front gate, at least he'd had the comfort of knowing his friends were listening in on the progress. Now he was truly alone.

He moved at a casual pace to the locked door marked Authorized Personnel Only. A camera hung from the ceiling, its lens pointed straight at him. He pointedly ignored it and turned his attention to the security keypad mounted on the wall. The numbers Jerry had given him had gotten him through the front door; would the second combination get him through this one?

His hands were sweating as he punched in the seven digits. He felt a dart of panic as a beep sounded and a message flashed on the screen: *Incorrect security code. Access denied.*

He could feel the sweat building up beneath the mask. Were the numbers wrong? Had he simply transposed two digits? He knew someone was watching him through the camera, wondering why he was taking so long. He took a deep breath and tried again. This time, he entered the digits slowly, deliberately. He braced himself for the warning beep. To his relief, it didn't go off.

Instead, a new message appeared. *Security code accepted. Please enter.*

He stepped through, into the next room.

Third hurdle, he thought in relief as the door closed behind him. Now for the home run.

Another camera, mounted in a corner, was pointed at him. Acutely conscious of that lens, he made his way across the room to the inner lab door. He turned the knob and a warning bell sounded.

Now what? he thought. Only then did he notice the red light glowing over the door, and the warning *Laser grid activated.* He needed a key to shut it off. He saw no other way to deactivate it, no way to get past it, into the room beyond.

It was time for desperate measures, time for a little chutzpah. He patted his pockets, then turned and faced the camera. "Hello?" He waved.

A voice answered over an intercom. "Is there a problem, Dr. Black?"

"Yes. I can't seem to find my keys. I must have left them at home...."

"I can cut the lasers from here."

"Thanks. Gee, I don't know how this happened."

"No problem."

At once the red warning light shut off. Cautiously Victor tried the door; it swung open. He gave the camera a goodbye wave and entered the last room.

Inside, to his relief, there were no cameras anywhere—at least, none that he could spot. A bit of breathing space, he thought. He moved into the lab and took a quick survey of his surroundings. What he saw was a mind-numbing display of space-age equipment—not just the expected centrifuges and microscopes, but instruments he'd never seen before, all of them brand-new and gleaming. He headed through the decontamination chamber, past the laminar flow unit, and went straight to the incubators. He opened the door.

Glass vials tinkled in their compartments. He took one out. Pink fluid glistened within. The label read Lot #341. Active.

This must be it, he thought. This was what Ollie had told him to look for. Here was the stuff of nightmares, the grim reaper distilled to sub-microscopic elements.

He removed two vials, fitted them into a specially padded cigarette case, and slipped it into his pocket. *Mission accomplished,* he thought in triumph as he headed back through the lab. All that lay before him was a casual stroll back to his car. Then the champagne...

He was halfway across the room when the alarm bell went off.

He froze, the harsh ring echoing in his ears.

"Dr. Black?" said the guard's voice over some hidden intercom. "Please don't leave. Stay right where you are."

Victor spun around wildly, trying to locate the speaker. "What's going on?"

"I've just been asked to detain you. If you'll hold on, I'll find out what—"

Victor didn't wait to hear the reason—he bolted for the door. Even as he reached it, he heard the whine of the lasers powering on, felt something slash his arm. He shoved through the first door, dashed across the anteroom and out the security door, into the hallway.

Everywhere, alarms were going off. The whole damn building had turned into an echo chamber of ringing bells. His gaze shot right, to the front entrance. No, not that way—the guard was stationed there.

He sprinted left, toward what he hoped was a fire exit. Somewhere behind him a voice yelled, "Halt!" He ignored it and kept running. At the end of the hall he slammed against the opening bar and found himself in a stairwell. No exit, only steps leading up and down. He wasn't about to be trapped like a rat in the basement. He headed up the stairs.

One flight into his climb, he heard the stairwell door slam open on the first floor. Again a voice commanded, "Halt or I'll shoot!"

A bluff, he thought.

A pistol shot exploded, echoing up the concrete stairwell.

Not a bluff. With new desperation, he pushed through the landing door, into the second-floor hallway. A line of closed doors stretched before him. Which one, which one? There was no time to think. He ducked into the third room and softly shut the door behind him.

In the semidarkness, he spotted the gleam of stainless steel and glass beakers. Another lab. Only this one had a large window, now shimmering with moonlight, looming over the far countertop.

From down the hall came the slam of a door being kicked open and the guard's shouted command: "Freeze!"

He was down to one last escape route. Victor grabbed a chair, raised it over his head, and flung it at the window. The glass shattered, raining moonlight-silvered shards into the darkness below. He scarcely bothered to look before he leapt. Bracing himself for the impact, he jumped from the window and landed in a tangle of shrubbery.

"Halt!" came a shout from above.

That was enough to jar Victor back to his feet. He sprinted off across a lawn, into the cover of trees. Glancing back, he saw no pursuing shadow. The guard wasn't about to risk his neck leaping out any window.

Got to make it out the gate...

Victor circled around the building, burrowing his way through bushes and trees to a stand of oaks. From there he could view the front gate, way off in the distance. What he saw made his heart sink.

Floodlights illuminated the entrance, glaring down on the four security cars blocking the driveway. Now a panel truck pulled up. The driver went around to the back and opened the doors. At his command two German shepherds leaped out and danced around, barking at his feet.

Victor backed away, stumbling deeper into the grove of oaks. *No way out,* he thought, glancing behind him at the fence, topped with coils of barbed wire. Already, the dogs' barking was moving closer. *Unless I can sprout wings and fly, I'm a dead man....*

CHAPTER ELEVEN

"SOMETHING'S WRONG!" Cathy cried as the first security car drove past.

Polowski touched her arm. "Easy. It could be just a routine patrol."

"No. Look!" Through the trees, they spotted three more cars, all roaring down the road at top speed toward Viratek.

Ollie muttered a surprisingly coarse oath and reached for the microphone.

"Wait!" Polowski grabbed his hand. "We can't risk a transmission. Let him contact us first."

"If he's in trouble—"

"Then he already knows it. Give him a chance to make it out on his own."

"What if he's trapped?" said Cathy. "Are we just going to sit here?"

"We don't have a choice. Not if they've blockaded the front gate—"

"We *do* have a choice!" said Cathy, scrambling forward into the driver's seat.

"What the hell are you doing?" demanded Polowski.

"Giving him a fighting chance. If we don't—"

They all fell instantly silent as a transmission suddenly hissed over the receiver. "Looks like I got myself in a bind, guys. Don't see a way out. You copy?"

Ollie snatched up the microphone. "Copy, Gersh. What's your situation?"

"Bad."

"Specify."

"Front gate's blocked and lit up like a football field. Big time alarms going off. They just brought in the dogs—"

"Can you get over the fence?"

"Negative. It's electrified. Low voltage, but more than I can handle. You guys better hit the road without me."

Polowski grabbed the microphone and barked, "Did you get the stuff?"

Cathy turned and snapped: "Forget that! Ask him where he is. *Ask him!*"

"Holland?" said Polowski. "Where are you?"

"At the northeast perimeter. Fence goes all the way around. Look, get moving. I'll manage—"

"Tell him to head for the east fence!" Cathy said. "Near the midpoint!"

"What?"

"Just tell him!"

"Go to the east fence," Polowski said into the microphone. "Midpoint."

"I copy."

Polowski looked up at Cathy in puzzlement. "What the hell are you thinking of?"

"This is a getaway car, right?" she muttered as she turned on the engine. "I say we put it to its intended use!" She threw the van into gear and spun it around, onto the road.

"Hey, you're going the wrong way!" yelled Milo.

"No, I'm not. There's a fire road, just off to the left somewhere. There it is." She made a sharp turn, onto what was little more than a dirt track. They bounced along, crashing through tree branches and shrubs, a ride so violently spine-shaking it was all they could do to hang on.

"How did you find this *wonderful* road?" Polowski managed to ask.

"It was on the map. I saw it when we were studying the plans for Viratek."

"Is this a scenic route? Or does it go somewhere?"

"The east fence. Used to be the construction entrance for he compound. I'm hoping it's still clear enough to get hrough...."

"And then what happens?"

Ollie sighed. "Don't ask."

Cathy steered around a bush that had sprung up in her path

and ran head-on into a sapling. Her passengers tumbled to the floor. "Sorry," she muttered. Reversing gear, she spun them back on the road. "It should be just ahead...."

A barrier of chain link suddenly loomed before them. Instantly she cut the lights. Through the darkness, they could hear dogs barking, moving in. Where was he?

Then they saw him, flitting through the moonlight. He was running. Somewhere off to the side, a man shouted and gunfire spat the ground.

"Brace yourselves!" yelled Cathy. She snapped on her seatbelt and gripped the steering wheel. Then she stepped on the gas.

The van jerked forward like a bronco, barreled through the underbrush, and slammed into the fence. The chain link sagged; electrical sparks hissed in the night. Cathy threw the gears into reverse, backed up, and hit the gas again.

The fence toppled; barbed wire scraped across the windshield.

"We're through!" said Ollie. He yanked open the sliding door and yelled: "Come on, Gersh! Come on!"

The running figure zigzagged across the grass. All around him, gunfire exploded. He made a last flying leap across the coil of barbed wire and stumbled.

"Come on, Gersh!"

Gunfire spattered the van.

Victor struggled back to his feet. They heard the rip of clothing, then he was reaching up to them, being dragged inside, to safety.

The door slammed shut. Cathy backed up, wheeled the van around and slammed on the gas pedal.

They leaped forward, bouncing through the bushes and across ruts. Another round of bullets pinged the van. Cathy was oblivious to it. She focused only on getting them back to the main road. The sound of gunfire receded. At last the trees gave way to a familiar band of blacktop. She turned left and gunned the engine, anxious to put as many miles as possible between them and Viratek.

Off in the distance, a siren wailed.

"We got company!" said Polowski.

"Which way now?" Cathy cried. Viratek lay behind them; the sirens were approaching from ahead.

"I don't know! Just get the hell out of here!"

As yet her view of the police cars was blocked by trees, but she could hear the sirens moving rapidly closer. *Will they let us pass? Or will they pull us over?*

Almost too late she spotted a clearing, off to the side. On sudden impulse she veered off the pavement, and the van bounced onto a stubbly field.

"Don't tell me," groaned Polowski. "Another fire road?"

"Shut up!" she snapped and steered straight for a clump of bushes. With a quick turn of the wheel, she circled behind the shrubbery and cut her lights.

It was just in time. Seconds later, two patrol cars, lights flashing, sped right past the concealing bushes. She sat frozen, listening as the sirens faded in the distance. Then, in the darkness, she heard Milo say softly, "Her name is Bond. Jane Bond."

Half laughing, half crying, Cathy turned as Victor scrambled beside her, onto the front seat. At once she was in his arms, her tears wetting his shirt, her sobs muffled in the depths of his embrace. He kissed her damp cheeks, her mouth. The touch of his lips stilled her tremors.

From the back came the sound of a throat being cleared. "Uh, Gersh?" inquired Ollie politely. "Don't you think we ought to get moving?"

Victor's mouth was still pressed against Cathy's. Reluctantly he broke contact but his gaze never left her face. "Sure," he murmured, just before he pulled her back for another kiss. "But could somebody else mind driving…?"

HERE'S THINGS get dangerous," said Polowski. He was at the wheel now, as they headed south toward San Francisco. Cathy and Victor sat in front with Polowski; in the back of the van, Milo and Ollie lay curled up asleep like two exhausted puppies. From the radio came the soft strains of a country western song. The dials glowed a vivid green in the darkness.

"We've finally got the evidence," said Polowski. "All we need to hang 'em. They'll be desperate. Ready to try anything. From here on out, folks, it's going to be a game of cat and mouse."

As if it wasn't already, thought Cathy as she huddled closer to Victor. She longed for a chance to be alone with him. There had been no time for tearful reunions, no time for any confessions of love. They'd spent the last two hours on a harrowing journey down backroads, always avoiding the police. By now the break-in at Viratek would have been reported to the authorities. The state police would be on the lookout for a van with frontal damage.

Polowski was right. Things were only getting more dangerous.

"Soon as we hit the city," said Polowski, "we'll get those vials off to separate labs. Independent confirmation. That should wipe any doubts away. You know names we can trust, Holland?"

"Fellow alum back in New Haven. Runs the hospital lab. I can trust him."

"Yale? Great. That'll have clout."

"Ollie has a pal at UCSF. They'll take care of the second vial."

"And when those reports get back, I know a certain journalist who loves to have a little birdie chirp in his ear." Polowski gave the steering wheel a satisfied slap. "Viratek, you are dead meat."

"You enjoy this, don't you?" said Cathy.

"Workin' the right side of the law? I say it's good for the soul. It keeps your mind sharp and your feet on their toes. helps you stay young."

"Or die young," said Cathy.

Polowski laughed. "Women. They just never understand the game."

"I don't understand it, at all."

"I bet Holland here does. He just had the adrenaline high his life. Didn't you?"

Victor didn't answer. He was gazing ahead at the blacktop stretching before their headlights.

"Well, wasn't it a high?" asked Polowski. "To claw your way to hell and back again? To know you made it through on nothing much more than your wits?"

"No," said Victor quietly. "Because it's not over yet."

Polowski's grin faded. He turned his attention back to the road. "Almost," he said. "It's almost over."

They passed a sign: San Francisco: 12 Miles.

FOUR IN THE MORNING. The stars were mere pinpricks in a sky washed out by streetlights. In a North Beach doughnut shop, five weary souls had gathered around steaming coffee and cheese Danish. Only one other table was occupied, by a man with bloodshot eyes and shaking hands. The girl behind the counter sat with her nose buried in a paperback. Behind her, the coffee machine hissed out a fresh brew.

"To the Old Coots," said Milo, raising his cup. "Still the best ensemble around."

They all raised their cups. "To the Old Coots!"

"And to our newest and fairest member," said Milo. "The beautiful—the intrepid—"

"Oh, *please*," said Cathy.

Victor wrapped his arm around her shoulder. "Relax and be honored. Not everyone gets into this highly selective group."

"The only requirement," said Ollie, "is that you have to play a musical instrument badly."

"But I don't play anything."

"No problem." Ollie fished out a piece of waxed paper from the pile of Danishes and wrapped it around his pocket comb. "Kazoo."

"Fitting," said Milo. "Since that was Lily's instrument."

"Oh." She took the comb. Lily's instrument. It always came back to *her,* the ghost who would forever be there. Suddenly the air of celebration was gone, as though swept away by the cold wind of dawn. She glanced at Victor. He was looking out the window, at the garishly lit streets. *What are you thinking?*

Are you wishing she was here? That it wasn't me being presented this silly kazoo, but her?

She put the comb to her lips and hummed an appropriately out-of-tune version of "Yankee Doodle." Everyone laughed and clapped, even Victor. But when the applause was over, she saw the sad and weary look in his eyes. Quietly she set the kazoo down on the table.

Outside, a delivery truck roared past. It was 5:00 a.m.; the city was stirring.

"Well, folks," said Polowski, slapping down a dollar tip. "We got a hotshot reporter to roust outta bed. And then you and I—" he looked at Victor "—have a few deliveries to make. When's United leave for New Haven?"

"At ten-fifteen," said Victor.

"Okay. I'll buy you the plane tickets. In the meantime, you see if you can't grow yourself a new mustache or something." Polowski glanced at Cathy. "You're going with him, right?"

"No," she said, looking at Victor.

She was hoping for a reaction, any reaction. What she saw was a look of relief. And, strangely, resignation.

He didn't try to change her mind. He simply asked, "Where will you be going?"

She shrugged. "Maybe I should stick to our original plan. You know, head south. Hang out with Jack for a while. What do you think?"

It was his chance to stop her. His chance to say, *No, I want you around. I won't let you leave, not now, not ever.* If he really loved her, that's exactly what he would say.

Her heart sank when he simply nodded and said, "I think it's a good idea."

She blinked back the tears before anyone could see them. With an indifferent smile she looked at Ollie. "So I guess I'll need a ride. When are you and Milo heading home?"

"Right now, I guess," said Ollie, looking bewildered. "Seeing as our job's pretty much done."

"Can I hitch along? I'll catch the bus at Palo Alto."

"No problem. In fact, you can sit in the honored front seat."

"Long as you don't let her behind the wheel," grumbled Milo. "I want a nice, quiet drive home if you don't mind."

Polowski rose to his feet. "Then we're all set. Everyone's got a place to go. Let's do it."

Outside, on a street rumbling with early-morning traffic, with their friends standing only a few yards away, Cathy and Victor said their goodbyes. It wasn't the place for sentimental farewells. Perhaps that was all for the best. At least she could leave with some trace of dignity. At least she could avoid hearing, from his lips, the brutal truth. She would simply walk away and hold on to the fantasy that he loved her. That in their brief time together she'd managed to work her way, just a little, into his heart.

"You'll be all right?" he asked.

"I'll be fine. And you?"

"I'll manage." He thrust his hands in his pockets and looked off at a bus idling near the corner. "I'll miss you," he said. "But I know it doesn't make sense for us to be together. Not under the circumstances."

I would stay with you, she thought. *Under any circumstances. If I only knew you wanted me.*

"Anyway," he said with a sigh, "I'll let you know when things are safe again. When you can come home."

"And then?"

"And then we'll take it from there," he said softly.

They kissed, a clumsy, polite kiss, all the more hurried because they knew their friends were watching. There was no passion here, only the cool, dry lips of a man saying goodbye. As they pulled apart, she saw his face blur away through the tears.

"Take care of yourself, Victor," she said. Then, shoulders squared, she turned and walked toward Ollie and Milo.

"Is that it?" asked Ollie.

"That's it." Brusquely she rubbed her hand across her eyes. "I'm ready to go."

"TELL ME ABOUT Lily," she said.

The first light of dawn was already streaking the sky as they drove past the boxy row homes of Pacifica, past the cliffs where sea waves crashed and gulls swooped and dove.

Ollie, his gaze on the road, asked: "What do you want to know?"

"What kind of woman was she?"

"She was a nice person," said Ollie. "And brainy. Though she never went out of her way to impress people, she was probably the smartest one of all of us. Definitely brighter than Milo."

"And a lot better-looking than Ollie," piped a voice from the backseat.

"A real kind, real decent woman. When she and Gersh got married, I remember thinking, 'he's got himself a saint.'" He glanced at Cathy, suddenly noticing her silence. "Of course," he added quickly, "not every man *wants* a saint. I know I'd be happier with a lady who can be a little goofy." He flashed Cathy a grin. "Someone who might, say, crash a van through an electrified fence, just for kicks."

It was a sweet thing to say, a comment designed to lift her spirits. It couldn't take the edge off her pain.

She settled back and watched dawn lighten the sky. How she needed to get away! She thought about Mexico, about warm water and hot sand and the tang of fresh fish and lime. She would throw herself into working on that new film. Of course, Jack would be on the set, Jack with his latest sweetie pie in tow, but she could handle that now. Jack would never be able to hurt her again. She was beyond that now, beyond being hurt by any man.

The drive to Milo's house seemed endless.

When at last they pulled up in the driveway, the dawn had already blossomed into a bright, cold morning. Milo climbed out and stood blinking in the sunshine.

"So, guys," he said through the car window. "Guess here's where we go our separate ways." He looked at Cathy. "Mexico, right?"

She nodded. "Puerto Vallarta. What about you?"

"I'm gonna catch up with Ma in Florida. Maybe get a look of Disney World. Wanna come, Ollie?"

"Some other time. I'm going to go get some sleep."

"Don't know what you're missing. Well, it's been some adventure. I'm almost sorry it's over." Milo turned and headed up the walk to his house. On the front porch he waved and yelled, "See you around!" Then he vanished through the front door.

Ollie laughed. "Milo and his ma, together? Disney World'll never be the same." He reached for the ignition. "Next stop, the bus station. I've got just enough gas to get us there and—"

He didn't get a chance to turn the key.

A gun barrel was thrust in the open car window. It came to rest squarely against Ollie's temple.

"Get out, Dr. Wozniak," said a voice.

Ollie's reply came out in a bare croak. "What—what do you want?"

"Do it now." The click of the hammer being cocked was all the coaxing Ollie needed.

"Okay, okay! I'm getting out!" Ollie scrambled out and backed away, his hands raised in surrender.

Cathy, too, started to climb out, but the gunman snapped, "Not you! You stay inside."

"Look," said Ollie, "You can have the damn car! You don't need her—"

"But I do. Tell Mr. Holland I'll be in contact. Regarding Ms. Weaver's future." He went around and opened the passenger door. "You, into the driver's seat!" he commanded her.

"No. Please—"

The gun barrel dug into her neck. "Need I ask again?"

Trembling, she moved behind the wheel. Her knee brushed the car keys, still dangling from the ignition. The man slid in beside her. Though the gun barrel was still thrust against her neck, it was the man's eyes she focused on. They were black, fathomless. If any spark of humanity lurked in those depths, she couldn't see it.

"Start the engine," he said.

"Where—where are we going?"

"For a drive. Somewhere scenic."

Her thoughts were racing, seeking some means of escape, but she came up with nothing. That gun was insurmountable.

She turned on the ignition.

"Hey!" yelled Ollie, grabbing at the door. "You can't do this!"

Cathy screamed, "Ollie, no!"

The gunman had already shifted his aim out the window.

"Let her go!" yelled Ollie. "Let her—"

The gun went off.

Ollie staggered backward, his face a mask of astonishment.

Cathy lunged at the gunman. Pure animal rage, fueled by the instinct to survive, sent her clawing first for his eyes. At the last split second he flinched away. Her nails scraped down his cheek, drawing blood. Before he could shift his aim, she grabbed his wrist, wrenching desperately for control of the gun. He held fast. Not with all her strength could she keep the gun at bay, keep the barrel from turning toward her.

It was the last image she registered: that black hole, slowly turning until it was pointed straight at her face.

Something lashed at her from the side. Pain exploded in her head, shattering the world into a thousand slivers of light.

They faded, one by one, into darkness.

CHAPTER TWELVE

"VICTOR'S HERE," said Milo.

It seemed to take Ollie forever to register their presence. Victor fought the urge to shake him to consciousness, to drag the words out of his friend's throat. He was forced to wait, the silence broken only by the hiss of oxygen, the gurgle of the suction tube. At last Ollie stirred and squinted through pain-glazed eyes at the three men standing beside his bed. "Gersh. I didn't—couldn't—" He stopped, exhausted by the effort just to talk.

"Easy, Ollie," said Milo. "Take it slow."

"Tried to stop him. Had a gun..." Ollie paused, gathering the strength to continue.

Victor listened fearfully for the next terrible words to come out. He was still in a state of disbelief, still hoping that what Milo had told him was one giant mistake, that Cathy was, at this very moment, on a bus somewhere to safety. Only two hours ago he'd been ready to board a plane for New Haven. Then he'd been handed a message at the United gate. It was addressed to passenger Sam Polowski, the name on his ticket. It had consisted of only three words: *Call Milo immediately.*

Passenger "Sam Polowski" never did board the plane.

Two hours, he thought in anguish. What have they done to her in those two long hours?

"This man—what did he look like?" asked Polowski.

"Didn't see him very well. Dark hair. Face sort of... thin."

"Tall? Short?"

"Tall."

"He drove off in your car?"

Ollie nodded.

"What about Cathy?" Victor blurted out, his control shattered. "He—didn't hurt her? She's all right?"

There was a pause that, to Victor, seemed like an eternity in hell. Ollie's gaze settled mournfully on Victor. "I don't know."

It was the best Victor could hope for. *I don't know.* It left open the possibility that she was still alive.

Suddenly agitated, he began to pace the floor. "I know what he wants," he said. "I know what I have to give him—"

"You can't be serious," said Polowski. "That's our evidence! You can't just hand it over—"

"That's exactly what I'm going to do."

"You don't even know how to contact him!"

"He'll contact *me.*" He spun around and looked at Milo. "He must've been watching your house all this time. Waiting for one of us to turn up. That's where he'll call."

"If he calls," said Polowski.

"He will." Victor touched his jacket pocket, where the two vials from Viratek still rested. "I have what he wants. He has what I want. I think we're both ready to make a trade."

THE SUN, glaring and relentless, was shining in her eyes. She tried to escape it, tried to close her lids tighter, to stop those rays from piercing through to her brain, but the light followed her.

"Wake up. *Wake up!*"

Icy water slapped her face. Cathy gasped awake, coughing, rivulets of water trickling from her hair. She struggled to make out the face hovering above her. At first all she saw was a dark oval against the blinding circle of light. Then the man moved away and she saw eyes like black agate, a slash of a mouth. A scream formed in her throat, to be instantly frozen by the cold barrel of a gun against her cheek.

"Not a sound," he said. "Got that?"

In silent terror she nodded.

"Good." The gun slid away from her cheek and was tucked under his jacket. "Sit up."

She obeyed. Instantly the room began to spin. She sat clutching her aching head, the fear temporarily overshadowed by waves of pain and nausea. The spell lasted for only a few moments. Then, as the nausea faded, she became aware of a second man in the room, a large, broad-shouldered man she'd never before seen. He sat off in a corner, saying nothing, but watching her every move. The room itself was small and windowless. She couldn't tell if it was day or night. The only furniture was a chair, a card table and the cot she was sitting on. The floor was a bare slab of concrete. *We're in a basement,* she thought. She heard no other sounds, either outside or in the building. Were they still in Palo Alto? Or were they a hundred miles away?

The man in the chair crossed his arms and smiled. Under different circumstances, she might have considered that smile a charming one. Now it struck her as frighteningly inhuman. "She seems awake enough," he said. "Why don't you proceed, Mr. Savitch?"

The man called Savitch loomed over her. "Where is he?"

"Who?" she said.

Her answer was met by a ringing slap to her cheek. She sprawled backwards on the cot.

"Try again," he said, dragging her back up to a sitting position. "Where is Victor Holland?"

"I don't know."

"You were with him."

"We—we split up."

"Why?"

She touched her mouth. The sight of blood on her fingers shocked her temporarily into silence.

"Why?"

"He—" She bowed her head. Softly she said, "He didn't want me around."

Savitch let out a snort. "Got tired of you pretty quick, did he?"

"Yes," she whispered. "I guess he did."

"I don't know why."

She shuddered as the man ran his finger down her cheek,

her throat. He stopped at the top button of her blouse. *No,* she thought. *Not that.*

To her relief, the man in the chair suddenly cut in. "This is getting us nowhere."

Savitch turned to the other man. "You have another suggestion, Mr. Tyrone?"

"Yes. Let's try using her in a different way." Fearfully Cathy watched as Tyrone moved to the card table and opened a satchel. "Since we can't go to him," he said, "we'll have Holland come to us." He turned and smiled at her. "With your help, of course."

She stared at the cellular telephone he was holding. "I told you. I don't know where he is."

"I'm sure one of his friends will track him down."

"He's not stupid. He wouldn't come for me—"

"You're right. He's not stupid." Tyrone began to punch in a phone number. "But he's a man of conscience. And that's a flaw that's every bit as fatal." He paused, then said into the telephone, "Hello? Mr. Milo Lum? I want you to pass this message to Victor Holland for me. Tell him I have something of his. Something that won't be around much longer..."

"IT'S HIM!" hissed Milo. "He wants to make a deal."

Victor shot to his feet. "Let me talk to him—"

"Wait!" Polowski grabbed his arm. "We have to take this slow. Think about what we're—"

Victor pulled his arm free and snatched the receiver from Milo. "This is Holland," he barked into the phone. "Where is she?"

The voice on the other end paused, a silence designed to emphasize just who held the upper hand. "She's with me. She's alive."

"How do I know that?"

"You'll have to take my word for it."

"Word, hell! I want proof!"

Again there was a silence. Then, through the crackle of the line, came another voice, so tremulous, so afraid, it almost broke his heart. "Victor, it's me."

"Cathy?" He almost shouted with relief. "Cathy, are you all right?"

"I'm...fine."

"Where are you?"

"I don't know—I think—" She stopped. The silence was agonizing. "I can't be sure."

"He hasn't hurt you?"

A pause. "No."

She's not telling me the truth, he thought. *He's done something to her...*

"Cathy, I promise. You'll be all right. I swear to you I'll—"

"Let's talk business." The man was back on the line.

Victor gripped the receiver in fury. "If you hurt her, if you just touch her, I swear I'll—"

"You're hardly in a position to bargain."

Victor felt a hand grasp his arm. He turned and met Polowski's gaze. *Keep your head* was the message he saw. *Go along with him. Make a bargain. It's the only way to buy time.*

Nodding, Victor fought to regain control. When he spoke again, his voice was calm. "Okay. You want the vials, they're yours."

"Not good enough."

"Then I'll throw myself into the bargain. A trade. Is that acceptable?"

"Acceptable. You and the vials in exchange for her life."

An anguished cry of *"No!"* pierced the dialogue. It was Cathy, somewhere in the background, shouting, "Don't, Victor! They're going to—"

Through the receiver, Victor heard the thud of a blow, followed by soft moans of pain. All his control shattered. He was screaming now, cursing, begging, anything to make the man stop hurting her. The words ran together, making no sense. He couldn't see straight, couldn't think straight.

Again, Polowski took his arm, gave it a shake. Victor, breathing hard, stared at him through a gaze blurred by tears. Polowski's eyes advised: *Make the deal. Go on.*

Victor swallowed and closed his eyes. *Give me strength,* he thought. He managed to ask, "When do we make the exchange?"

"Tonight. At 2:00 a.m."

"Where?"

"East Palo Alto. The old Saracen Theater."

"But it's closed. It's been closed for—"

"It'll be open. Just you, Holland. I spot anyone else and the first bullet has her name on it. Clear?"

"I want a guarantee! I want to know she'll be—"

He was answered by silence. And then, seconds later, he heard a dial tone.

Slowly he hung up.

"Well? What's the deal?" demanded Polowski.

"At 2:00 a.m. Saracen Theater."

"Half an hour. That barely gives us time to set up a—"

"I'm going alone."

Milo and Polowski stared at him. "Like hell," said Polowski.

Victor grabbed his jacket from out of the closet. He gave the pocket a quick pat; the cigarette case was right where he'd left it. He turned and reached for the door.

"But Gersh!" said Milo. "He's gonna kill you!"

Victor paused in the doorway. "Probably," he said softly. "But it's Cathy's only chance. And it's a chance I have to take."

"HE WON'T COME," said Cathy.

"Shut up," Matt Tyrone snapped and shoved her forward.

As they moved down the glass-strewn alley behind the Saracen Theater, Cathy frantically searched her mind for some way to sabotage this fatal meeting. It *would* be fatal, not just for Victor, but for her, as well. The two men now escorting her through the darkness had no intention of letting her live. The best she could hope for was that Victor would survive. She had to do what she could to better his chances.

"He's already got his evidence," she said. "You think he'd give that up just for me?"

Tyrone glanced at Savitch. "What if she's right?"

"Holland's coming," said Savitch. "I know how he thinks. He's not going to leave the little woman behind." Savitch gave Cathy's cheek a deceptively gentle caress. "Not when he knows exactly what we'll do to her."

Cathy flinched away, repelled by his touch. *What if he really doesn't come?* she thought. *What if he does the sensible thing and leaves me to die?*

She wouldn't blame him.

Tyrone gave her a push up the steps and into the building. "Inside. Move."

"I can't see," she protested, feeling her way along a pitch-black passage. She stumbled over boxes, brushed past what felt like heavy drapes. "It's too dark—"

"Then let there be light," said a new voice.

The lights suddenly sprang on, so bright she was temporarily blinded. She raised her hand to shield her eyes. Through the glare she could make out a third man, looming before her. Beyond him, the floor seemed to drop away into a vast blackness.

They were standing on a theater stage. It was obvious no performer had trod these boards in years. Ragged curtains hung like cobwebs from the rafters. Panels of an old set, the ivy-hung battlements of a medieval castle, still leaned at a crazy tilt against the back wall, framed by a pair of mops.

Tyrone said, "Any problems, Dafoe?"

"None," said the new man. "I've reconned the building. One door at the front, one backstage. The emergency side doors are padlocked. If we block both exits, he's trapped."

"I see the FBI deserves its fine reputation."

Dafoe grinned and dipped his head. "I knew the Cowboy would want the very best."

"Okay, Ms. Weaver." Tyrone shoved Cathy forward, toward a chair placed directly under the spotlight. "Let's put you right where he can see you. Center stage."

It was Savitch who tied her to the chair. He knew exactly what he was doing. She had no hope of working her hands free from such tight, professional knots.

He stepped back, satisfied with his job. "She's not going

anywhere," he said. Then, as an afterthought, he ripped off a strip of cloth tape and slapped it over her mouth. "So we don't have any surprises," he said.

Tyrone glanced at his watch. "Zero minus fifteen. Positions, gentlemen."

The three men slipped away into the shadows, leaving Cathy alone on the empty stage. The spotlight beating down on her face was hot as the midday sun. Already she could feel beads of sweat forming on her forehead. Though she couldn't see them, by their voices she could guess the positions of the three men. Tyrone was close by. Savitch was at the back of the theater, near the building's front entrance. And the man named Dafoe had stationed himself somewhere above, in one of the box seats. Three different lines of fire. No route of escape.

Victor, don't be a fool, she thought. *Stay away...*

And if he doesn't come? She couldn't bear to consider that possibility, either, for it meant he was abandoning her. It meant he didn't care enough even to make the effort to save her.

She closed her eyes against the spotlight, against the tears. *I love you. I could take anything, even this, if I only knew you loved me.*

Her hands were numb from the ropes. She tried to wriggle the bonds looser, but only succeeded in rubbing her wrists raw. She fought to remain calm, but with every minute that passed, her heart seemed to pound harder. A drop of sweat trickled down her temple.

Somewhere in the shadows ahead, a door squealed open and closed. Footsteps approached, their pace slow and deliberate. She strained to see against the spotlight's glare, but could make out only the hint of shadow moving through shadow.

The stage floorboards creaked behind her as Tyrone strolled out from the wings. "Stop right where you are, Mr. Holland," he said.

CHAPTER THIRTEEN

ANOTHER SPOTLIGHT suddenly sprang on, catching Victor in its glare. He stood halfway up the aisle, a lone figure trapped in a circle of brilliance.

You came for me! she thought. *I knew, somehow I knew, that you would....*

If only she could shout to him, warn him about the other two men. But the tape had been applied so tightly that the only sound she could produce was a whimper.

"Let her go," said Victor.

"You have something we want first."

"I said, *let her go!*"

"You're hardly in a position to bargain." Tyrone strolled out of the wings, onto the stage. Cathy flinched as the icy barrel of a gun pressed against her temple. "Let's see it, Holland," said Tyrone.

"Untie her first."

"I could shoot you both and be done with it."

"Is this what it's come to?" yelled Victor. "Federal dollars for the murder of civilians?"

"It's all a matter of cost and benefit. A few civilians may have to die now. But if this country goes to war, think of all the millions of Americans who'll be saved!"

"I'm thinking of the Americans you've already killed."

"Necessary deaths. But you don't understand that. You've never seen a fellow soldier die, have you, Holland? You don't know what a helpless feeling it is, to watch good boys from good American towns get cut to pieces. With this weapon, they won't have to. It'll be the enemy dying, not us."

"Who gave you the authority?"

"I gave myself the authority."

"And who the hell are *you?*"

"A patriot, Mr. Holland! I do the jobs no one else in the Administration'll touch. Someone says, 'Too bad our weapons don't have a higher kill ratio.' That's my cue to get one developed. They don't even have to ask me. They can claim total ignorance."

"So you're the fall guy."

Tyrone shrugged. "It's part of being a good soldier. The willingness to fall on one's sword. But I'm not ready to do that yet."

Cathy tensed as Tyrone clicked back the gun hammer. The barrel was still poised against her skull.

"As you can see," said Tyrone, "the cards aren't exactly stacked in her favor."

"On the other hand," Victor said calmly, "how do you know I've brought the vials? What if they're stashed somewhere, a publicity time bomb ticking away? Kill her now and you'll never find out."

Deadlock. Tyrone lowered the pistol. He and Victor faced each other for a moment. Then Tyrone reached into his pocket, and Cathy heard the click of a switchblade. "This round goes to you, Holland," he said as he cut the bindings. The sudden rush of circulation back into Cathy's hands was almost painful. Tyrone ripped the tape off her mouth and yanked her out of the chair. "She's all yours!"

Cathy scrambled off the stage. On unsteady legs, she moved up the aisle, toward the circle of the spotlight, toward Victor. He pulled her into his arms. Only by the thud of his racing heart did she know how close he was to panic.

"Your turn, Holland," called Tyrone.

"Go," Victor whispered to her. "Get out of here."

"Victor, he has two other men—"

"Let's have it!" yelled Tyrone.

Victor hesitated. Then he reached into his jacket and pulled out a cigarette case. "They'll be watching me," he whispered. "You move for the door. Go on. *Do it.*"

She stood paralyzed by indecision. She couldn't leave him to die. And she knew the other two gunmen were somewhere in the darkness, watching their every move.

"She stays where she is!" said Tyrone. "Come on, Holland. The vials!"

Victor took a step further, then another.

"No further!" commanded Tyrone.

Victor halted. "You want it, don't you?"

"Put it down on the floor."

Slowly Victor set the cigarette case down by his feet.

"Now slide it to me."

Victor gave the case a shove. It skimmed down the aisle and came to a rest in the orchestra pit.

Tyrone dropped from the stage.

Victor began to back away. Taking Cathy's hand, he edged her slowly up the aisle, toward the exit.

As if on cue, the click of pistol hammers being snapped back echoed through the theater. Reflexively, Victor spun around, trying to sight the other gunmen. It was impossible to see anything clearly against the glare of the spotlight.

"You're not leaving yet," said Tyrone, reaching down for the case. Gingerly he removed the lid. In silence he stared at the contents.

This is it, thought Cathy. *He has no reason to keep us alive, now that he has what he wants....*

Tyrone's head shot up. "Double cross," he said. Then, in a roar, *"Double cross! Kill them!"*

His voice was still reverberating through the far reaches of the theater when, all at once, the lights went out. Blackness fell, so impenetrable that Cathy had to reach out to get her bearings.

That's when Victor pulled her sideways, down a row of theater seats.

"Stop them!" screamed Tyrone in the darkness.

Gunfire seemed to erupt from everywhere at once. As Cathy and Victor scurried on hands and knees along the floor, they could hear bullets thudding into the velvet-backed seats. The gunfire quickly became random, a blind spraying of the theater.

"Hold your fire!" yelled Tyrone. "Listen for them!"

The gunfire stopped. Cathy and Victor froze in the darkness, afraid to give away their position. Except for the pounding of her own pulse, Cathy heard absolute silence. *We're trapped. We make a single move and they'll know where we are.*

Scarcely daring to breathe, she reached back and pulled off her shoe. With a mighty heave, she threw it blindly across the theater. The clatter of the shoe's landing instantly drew a new round of gunfire. In the din of ricocheting bullets, Victor and Cathy scurried along the remainder of the row and emerged in the side aisle.

Again, the gunfire stopped.

"No way out, Holland!" yelled Tyrone. "Both doors are covered! It's just a matter of time...."

Somewhere above, in a theater balcony, a light suddenly flickered on. It was Dafoe, holding aloft a cigarette lighter. As the flame leapt brightly, casting its terrible light against the shadows, Victor shoved Cathy to the floor behind a seat.

"I know they're here!" shouted Tyrone. "See 'em, Dafoe?"

As Dafoe moved the flame, the shadows shifted, revealing new forms, new secrets. "I'll spot 'em any second. Wait. I think I see—"

Dafoe suddenly jerked sideways as a shot rang out. The flame's light danced crazily on his face as he wobbled for a moment on the edge of the balcony. He reached out for the railing, but the rotten wood gave way under his weight. He pitched forward, his body tumbling into a row of seats.

"Dafoe!" screamed Tyrone. "Who the hell—"

A tongue of flame suddenly slithered up from the floor. Dafoe's lighter had set fire to the drapes! The flames spread quickly, dancing their way along the heavy velvet fabric, toward the rafters. As the first flames touched wood, the fire whooshed into a roar.

By the light of the inferno, all was revealed: Victor and Cathy, cowering in the aisle. Savitch, standing near the entrance, semiautomatic at the ready. And onstage, Tyrone, his expression demonic in the fire's glow.

"They're yours, Savitch!" ordered Tyrone.

Savitch aimed. This time there was no place for them to hide no shadows to scurry off to. Cathy felt Victor's arm encircle her in a last protective embrace.

The gun's explosion made them both flinch. Another shot; still she felt no pain. She glanced at Victor. He was staring at her, as though unable to believe they were both alive.

They looked up to see Savitch, his shirt stained in a spreading abstract of blood, drop to his knees.

"Now's your chance!" yelled a voice. *"Move, Holland!"*

They whirled around to see a familiar figure silhouetted against the flames. Somehow, Sam Polowski had magically appeared from behind the drapes. Now he pivoted, pistol clutched in both hands, and aimed at Tyrone.

He never got a chance to squeeze off the shot.

Tyrone fired first. The bullet knocked Polowski backward and sent him sprawling against the smoldering velvet seats.

"Get out of here!" barked Victor, giving Cathy a push toward the exit. "I'm going back for him—"

"Victor, you can't!"

But he was on his way. Through the swirling smoke she could see him moving at a half crouch between rows of seats. *He needs help. And time's running out....*

Already the air was so hot it seemed to sear its way into her throat. Coughing, she dropped to the floor and took in a few breaths of relatively smoke-free air. She still had time to escape. All she had to do was crawl up the aisle and out the theater door. Every instinct told her to flee now, while she had the chance.

Instead, she turned from the exit and followed Victor into the maelstrom.

She could just make out his figure, scrambling before a solid wall of fire. She raised her arm to shield her face against the heat. Squinting into the smoke, she crawled forward, moving ever closer to the flames. "Victor!" she screamed.

She was answered only by the fire's roar, and by a sound even more ominous: the creak of wood. She glanced up. To her horror she saw that the rafters were sagging and on the verge of collapse.

Panicked, she scurried blindly forward, toward where she'd last spotted Victor. He was no longer visible. In his place was a whirlwind of smoke and flame. Had he already escaped? Was she alone, trapped in this blazing tinderbox?

Something slapped against her cheek. She stared, at first uncomprehending, at the human hand dangling before her face. Slowly she followed it up, along the bloodied arm, to the lifeless eyes of Dafoe. Her cry of terror seemed to funnel into the fiery cyclone.

"Cathy?"

She turned at the sound of Victor's shout. That's when she saw him, crouching in the aisle just a few feet away. He had Polowski under the arms and was struggling to drag him toward the exit. But the heat and smoke had taken its toll; he was on the verge of collapse.

"The roof's about to fall!" she screamed.

"Get out!"

"Not without you!" She scrambled forward and grabbed Polowski's feet. Together they hauled their burden up the aisle, across carpet that was already alight with sparks. Step by step they neared the top of the aisle. Only a few yards to go!

"I've got him," gasped Victor. "Go—open the door—"

She rose to a half crouch and turned.

Matt Tyrone stood before her.

"Victor!" she sobbed.

Victor, his face a mask of soot and sweat, turned to meet Tyrone's gaze. Neither man said a word. They both knew the game had been played out. Now the time had come to finish it.

Tyrone raised his gun.

Just as he did, they heard the loud crack of splintering wood. Tyrone glanced up as one of the rafters sagged, spilling a shower of burning tinder.

That brief distraction was all the time Cathy needed. In an act of sheer desperation she lunged at Tyrone's legs, knocking him backward. The gun flew from his grasp and slid off beneath a row of seats.

At once Tyrone was back on his feet. He aimed a savage kick at her. The blow hit her in the ribs, an impact so agonizing she hadn't the breath to cry out. She simply sprawled in the aisle, stunned and utterly helpless to ward off any other blows.

Through the darkness gathering before her eyes, she saw two figures struggling. Victor and Tyrone. Framed against a sea of fire, they grappled for each other's throats. Tyrone threw a punch; Victor staggered back a few paces. Tyrone charged him like a bull. At the last instant Victor sidestepped him and Tyrone met only empty air. He stumbled and sprawled forward, onto the smoldering carpet. Enraged, he rose to his knees, ready to charge again.

The crack of collapsing timber made him glance skyward.

He was still staring up in astonishment as the beam crashed down on his head.

Cathy tried to cry out Victor's name but no sound escaped. The smoke had left her throat too parched and swollen. She struggled to her knees. Polowski was lying beside her, groaning. Flames were everywhere, shooting up from the floor, clambering up the last untouched drapes.

Then she saw him, stumbling toward her through that vision of hellfire. He grabbed her arm and shoved her toward the exit.

Somehow, they managed to tumble out the door, dragging Polowski behind them. Coughing, choking, they pulled him across the street to the far sidewalk. There they collapsed.

The night sky suddenly lit up as an explosion ripped through the theater. The roof collapsed, sending up a whoosh of flames so brilliant they seemed to reach to the very heavens. Victor threw his body over Cathy's as the windows in the building above shattered, raining splinters onto the sidewalk.

For a moment there was only the sound of the flames, crackling across the street. Then, somewhere in the distance, a siren wailed.

Polowski stirred and groaned.

"Sam!" Victor turned his attention to the wounded man. "How you doing, buddy?"

"Got...got one helluva stitch in my side...."

"You'll be fine." Victor flashed him a tense grin. "Listen! Hear those sirens? Help's on the way."

"Yeah." Polowski, eyes narrowed in pain, stared up at the flame-washed sky.

"Thanks, Sam," said Victor softly.

"Had to. You...too damn stupid to listen..."

"We got her back, didn't we?"

Polowski's gaze shifted to Cathy. "We—we did okay."

Victor rubbed a hand across his smudged and weary face. "But we're back to square one. I've lost the evidence—"

"Milo..."

"It's all in there." Victor stared across at the flames now engulfing the old theater.

"Milo has it," whispered Sam.

"What?"

"You weren't looking. Gave it to Milo."

Victor sat back in bewilderment. "You mean you *took* them? You took the vials?"

Polowski nodded.

"You—you stupid son of a—"

"Victor!" said Cathy.

"He stole my bargaining chip!"

"He saved our lives!"

Victor stared down at Polowski.

Polowski returned a pained grin. "Dame's got a head on her shoulders," he murmured. "Listen to her."

The sirens, which had risen to a scream, suddenly cut off. Men's shouts at once sliced through the hiss and roar of the flames. A burly fireman loped over from the truck and knelt beside Polowski.

"What've we got here?"

"Gunshot wound," said Victor. "And a wise-ass patient."

The fireman nodded. "No problem, sir. We can handle both."

By the time they'd loaded Polowski into an ambulance, the Saracen Theater had been reduced to little more than a dying bonfire. Victor and Cathy watched the taillights of the ambulance vanish, heard the fading wail of the siren, the hiss of water on the flames.

He turned to her. Without a word he pulled her into his arms and held her long and hard, two silent figures framed against a sea of smoldering flames and chaos. They were both so weary neither knew which was holding the other up. Yet even through her exhaustion, Cathy felt the magic of that moment. It was eerily beautiful, that last sputtering glow, the reflections dancing off the nearby buildings. Beautiful and frightening and final.

"You came for me," she murmured. "Oh, Victor, I was so afraid you wouldn't...."

"Cathy, you knew I would!"

"I *didn't* know. You had your evidence. You could have left me—"

"No, I couldn't." He buried a kiss in her singed hair. "Thank God I wasn't already on that plane. They'd have had you, and I'd have been two thousand miles away."

Footsteps crunched toward them across the glass-littered pavement. "Excuse me," a voice said. "Are you Victor Holland?"

They turned to see a man in a rumpled parka, a camera slung over his shoulder, watching them.

"Who are you?" asked Victor.

The man held out his hand. "Jay Wallace. *San Francisco Chronicle*. Sam Polowski called me, said there'd be some fireworks in case I wanted to check it out." He gazed at the last remains of the Saracen Theater and shook his head. "Looks like I got here a little too late."

"Wait. *Sam* called you? When?"

"Maybe two hours ago. If he wasn't my ex-brother-in-law, I'd a hung up on him. For days he's been dropping hints he had a story to spill. Never followed through, not once. I almost didn't come tonight. You know, it's a helluva long drive down here from the city."

"He told you about me?"

"He said you had a story to tell."

"Don't we all?"

"Some stories are better than others." The reporter glanced around, searching. "So where is Sam, anyway? Or didn't the Bozo show up?"

"That Bozo," said Victor, his voice tight with anger, "is a goddamn hero. Stick *that* in your article."

More footsteps approached. This time it was two police officers. Cathy felt Victor's muscles go taut as he turned to face them.

The senior officer spoke. "We've just been informed that a gunshot victim was taken to the ER. And that you were found on the scene."

Victor nodded. His look of tension suddenly gave way to one of overwhelming exhaustion. And resignation. He said, quietly, "I was present. And if you search that building, you'll find three more bodies."

"*Three?*" The two cops glanced at each other.

"Musta been some fireworks," muttered the reporter.

The senior officer said, "Maybe you'd better give us your name, sir."

"My name…" Victor looked at Cathy. She read the message in those weary eyes: *We've reached the end. I have to tell them. Now they'll take me away from you, and God knows when we'll see each other again.…*

She felt his hand tighten around hers. She held on, knowing with every second that passed that he would soon be wrenched from her grasp.

His gaze still focused on her face, he said, "My name is Victor Holland."

"Holland… Victor Holland?" said the officer. "Isn't that…"

And still Victor was looking at her. Until they'd clapped on the handcuffs, until he'd been pulled away, toward a waiting squad car, his gaze was locked on her.

She was left anchorless, shivering among the dying embers.

"Ma'am, you'll have to come with us."

She looked up, dazed, at the policeman. "What?"

"Hey, she doesn't have to!" cut in Jay Wallace. "You haven't charged her with anything!"

"Shut up, Wallace."

"I've had the court beat. I know her rights!"

Quietly Cathy said, "It doesn't matter. I'll come with you, officer."

"Wait!" said Wallace. "I wanna talk to you first! I got just a few questions—"

"She can talk to you later," snapped the policeman, taking Cathy by the arm. "*After* she talks to us."

The policemen were polite, even kind. Perhaps it was her docile acceptance of the situation, perhaps they could sense she was operating on her last meager reserves of strength. She answered all their questions. She let them examine the rope burns on her wrists. She told them about Ollie and Sarah and the other Catherine Weavers. And the whole time, as she sat in that room in the Palo Alto police station, she kept hoping she'd catch a glimpse of Victor. She knew he had to be close by. Were they, at that very moment, asking him these same questions?

At dawn, they released her.

Jay Wallace was waiting outside near the front steps. "I have to talk to you," he said as she walked out.

"Please. Not now. I'm tired...."

"Just a few questions."

"I can't. I need to—to—" She stopped. And there, standing on that cold and empty street, she burst into tears. "I don't know what to do," she sobbed. "I don't know how to help him. How to reach him."

"You mean Holland? They've already taken him to San Francisco."

"What?" She raised her startled gaze to Wallace.

"An hour ago. The big boys from the Justice Department came down as an escort. I hear tell they're flying him straight to Washington. First-class treatment all the way."

She shook her head in bewilderment. "Then he's all right—he's not under arrest—"

"Hell, lady," said Wallace, laughing. "The man is now a genuine hero."

A hero. But she didn't care what they called him, as long as he was safe.

She took a deep breath of bitingly chill air. "Do you have a car, Mr. Wallace?" she asked.

"It's parked right around the corner."

"Then you can give me a ride."

"Where to?"

"To…" She paused, wondering where to go, where Victor would look for her. Of course. Milo's. "To a friend's house," she said. "I want to be there when Victor calls."

Wallace pointed the way to the car. "I hope it's a long drive," he said. "I got a lot of gaps to fill in before this story goes to press."

VICTOR DIDN'T CALL.

For four days she sat waiting near the phone, expecting to hear his voice. For four days, Milo and his mother brought her tea and cookies, smiles and sympathy. On the fifth day, when she still hadn't heard from him, those terrible doubts began to haunt her. She remembered that day by the lake bed, when he'd tried to send her away with Ollie. She thought of all the words he could have said, but never had. True, he'd come back for her. He'd knowingly walked straight into a trap at the Saracen Theater. But wouldn't he have done that for any of his friends? That was the kind of man he was. She'd saved his life once. He remembered his debts, and he paid them back. It had to do with honor.

It might have nothing to do with love.

She stopped waiting by the phone. She returned to her flat in San Francisco, cleaned up the glass, had the windows replaced, the walls replastered. She took long walks and paid frequent visits to Ollie and Polowski in the hospital. Anything to stay away from that silent telephone.

She got a call from Jack. "We're shooting next week," he whined. "And the monster's in terrible shape. All this humidity! Its face keeps melting into green goo. Get down here and do something about it, will you?"

She told him she'd think about it.

A week later she decided. Work was what she needed. Gree

goo and cranky actors—it was better than waiting for a call that would never come.

She reserved a one-way flight from San José to Puerto Vallarta. Then she packed, throwing in her entire wardrobe. A long stay, that's what she planned, a long vacation.

But before she left, she would drive down to Palo Alto. She had promised to pay Sam Polowski one last visit.

CHAPTER FOURTEEN

(AP) Washington.

Administration spokesman Richard Jungkuntz repeated today that neither the President nor any of his staff had any knowledge of biological weapons research being conducted at Viratek Industries in California. Viratek's Project Cerberus, which involved development of genetically altered viruses, was clearly in violation of international law. Recent evidence, gathered by reporter Jay Wallace of the *San Francisco Chronicle,* has revealed that the project received funds directly authorized by the late Matthew Tyrone, a senior aide to the Secretary of Defense.

In today's Justice Department hearings, delayed four hours because of heavy snowstorms, Viratek president Archibald Black testified for the first time, promising to reveal, to the best of his knowledge, the direct links between the Administration and Project Cerberus. Yesterday's testimony, by former Viratek employee Dr. Victor Holland, has already outlined a disturbing tale of deception, cover-ups and possibly murder.

The Attorney General's office continues to resist demands by Congressman Leo D. Fanelli that a special prosecutor be appointed...

CATHY PUT DOWN the newspaper and smiled across the hospital solarium at her three friends. "Well, guys. Aren't you lucky to be here in sunny California and not freezing your you-know what's off in Washington."

"Are you kidding?" groused Polowski. "I'd give anything to be in on those hearings right now. Instead of hooked up to all these—these *doohickeys.*" He gave his intravenous line a tug, clanging a bottle against the pole.

"Patience, Sam," said Milo. "You'll get to Washington."

"Ha! Holland's already told 'em the good stuff. By the time they get around to hearing my testimony, it'll be back-page news."

"I don't think so," said Cathy. "I think it'll be front-page news for a long time to come." She turned and looked out the window at the sunshine glistening on the grass. *A long time to come.* That's how long it would be before she'd see Victor again. If ever. Three weeks had already passed since she'd last laid eyes on him. Via Jay Wallace in Washington, she'd heard that it was like a shark-feeding whenever Victor appeared in public, mobs of reporters and federal attorneys and Justice Department officials. No one could get near him.

Not even me, she thought.

It had been a comfort, having these three new friends to talk to. Ollie had bounced back quickly and was discharged—or kicked out, as Milo put it—a mere eight days after being shot. Polowski had had a rougher time of it. Post-operative infections, plus a bad case of smoke inhalation, had prolonged his stay to the point that every day was another trial of frustration for him. He wanted out. He wanted back on the beat.

He wanted a real, honest-to-God cheeseburger and a cigarette.

One more week, the doctors said.

At least there's an end to his waiting in sight, Cathy thought. *I don't know when I'll see or hear from Victor again.*

The silence was to be expected, Polowski had told her. Sequestration of witnesses. Protective custody. The Justice Department wanted an airtight case, and for that it would keep its star witness incommunicado. For the rest of them, depositions had been sufficient. Cathy had given her testimony two weeks before. Afterward, they'd told her she was free to leave town any time she wished.

Now she had a plane ticket to Mexico in her purse.

She was through with waiting for telephone calls, through with wondering whether he loved her or missed her. She'd been through this before with Jack, the doubts, the fears, the slow but inevitable realization that something was wrong. She knew enough not to be hurt again, not this way.

At least, out of all this pain, I've discovered three new friends. Ollie and Polowski and Milo, the most unlikely trio on the face of the earth.

"Look, Sam," said Milo, reaching into his backpack. "We brought ya something."

"No more hula-girl boxer shorts, okay? Caught hell from the nurses for that one."

"Naw. It's something for your lungs. To remind you to breathe deep."

"Cigarettes?" Polowski asked hopefully.

Milo grinned and held up his gift. "A kazoo!"

"I really needed one."

"You really do need it," said Ollie, opening up his clarinet case. "Seeing as we brought our instruments today and we weren't about to leave you out of this particular gig."

"You're not serious."

"What better place to perform?" said Milo, giving his piccolo a quick and loving rubdown. "All these sick, depressed patients lying around, in need of a bit of cheering up. Some good music."

"Some peace and quiet!" Polowski turned pleading eyes to Cathy. "They're not serious."

She looked him in the eye and took out her kazoo. "Dead serious."

"Okay, guys," said Ollie. "Hit it!"

Never before had the world heard such a rendering of "California, Here I Come!" And, if the world was lucky, neve again. By the time they'd played the last note, nurses and pa tients had spilled into the solarium to check on the source o that terrible screeching.

"Mr. Polowski!" said the head nurse. "If your visitors can behave—"

"You'll throw 'em out?" asked Polowski hopefully.

"No need," said Ollie. "We're packing up the pipes. E the way, folks, we're available for private parties, birthda cocktail hours. Just get in touch with our business manager—

at this, Milo smiled and waved ''—to set up your own special performance.''

Polowski groaned, ''I want to go back to bed.''

''Not yet,'' said the nurse. ''You need the extra stimulation.'' Then, with a sly wink at Ollie, she turned and whisked out of the room.

''Well,'' said Cathy. ''I think I've done my part to cheer you up. Now it's time I hit the road.''

Polowski looked at her in astonishment. ''You're leaving me with these lunatics?''

''Have to. I have a plane to catch.''

''Where you going?''

''Mexico. Jack called to say they're shooting already. So I thought I'd get on down there and whip up a few monsters.''

''What about Victor?''

''What about him?''

''I thought—that is—'' Polowski looked at Ollie and Milo. Both men merely shrugged. ''He's going to miss you.''

''I don't think so.'' She turned once again to gaze out the window. Below, in the walkway, an old woman sat in a wheelchair, her wan face turned gratefully to the sun. Soon Cathy would be enjoying that very sunshine, somewhere on a Mexican beach.

By their silence, she knew the three men didn't know what to say. After all, Victor was their friend, as well. They couldn't defend or condemn him. Neither could she. She simply loved him, in ways that made her decision to leave all the more right. She'd been in love before, she knew that the very worst thing a woman can sense in a man is indifference.

She didn't want to be around to see it in Victor's eyes.

Gathering up her purse, she said, ''Guys, I guess this is it.''

Ollie shook his head. ''I really wish you'd hang around. He'll be back any day. Besides, you can't break up our great little quartet.''

''Sam can take my place on the kazoo.''

''No way,'' said Polowski.

She planted a kiss on his balding head. ''Get better. The country needs you.''

Polowski sighed. "I'm glad somebody does."

"I'll write you from Mexico!" She slung her purse over her shoulder and turned. One step was all she managed before she halted in astonishment.

Victor was standing in the doorway, a suitcase in hand. He cocked his head. "What's this about Mexico?"

She couldn't answer. She just kept staring at him, thinking how unfair it was that the man she was trying so hard to escape should look so heartbreakingly wonderful.

"You got back just in time," said Ollie. "She's leaving."

"What?" Victor dropped his suitcase and stared at her in dismay. Only then did she notice his wrinkled clothes, the day-old growth of beard shadowing his face. The toe of a sock poked out from a corner of the closed suitcase.

"You can't be leaving," he said.

She cleared her throat. "It was unexpected. Jack needs me."

"Did something happen? Is there some emergency?"

"No, it's just that they're filming and, oh, things are a royal mess on the set...." She glanced at her watch, a gesture designed to speed her escape. "Look, I'll miss my plane. I promise I'll give you a call when I get to—"

"You're not his only makeup artist."

"No, but—"

"He can do the movie without you."

"Yes, but—"

"Do you *want* to leave? Is that it?"

She didn't answer. She could only look at him mutely, the anguish showing plainly in her eyes.

Gently, firmly, he took her hand. "Excuse us, guys," he said to the others. "The lady and I are going for a walk."

Outside, leaves blew across the brown winter lawn. They walked beneath a row of oak trees, through patches of sun and shadow. Suddenly he stopped and pulled her around to face him.

"Tell me now," he said. "What gave you this crazy idea of leaving?"

She looked down. "I didn't think it made much difference to you."

"Wouldn't make a *difference?* Cathy, I was climbing the walls! Thinking of ways to get out of that hotel room and back to you! You have no idea how I worried. I wondered if you were safe—if this whole crazy mess was really over. The lawyers wouldn't let me call out, not until the hearings were finished. I did manage to sneak out and call Milo's house. No one answered."

"We were probably here, visiting Sam."

"And I was going crazy. They had me answering the same damn questions over and over again. And all I could think of was how much I missed you." He shook his head. "First chance I got, I flew the coop. And got snowed in for hours in Chicago. But I made it. I'm here. Just in time, it seems." Gently he took her by the shoulders. "Now. Tell me. Are you still flying off to Jack?"

"I'm not leaving for Jack. I'm leaving for *myself.* Because I know this won't work."

"Cathy, after what we've been through together, we can make *anything* work."

"Not—not this."

Slowly he let his hands drop, but his gaze remained on her face. "That night we made love," he said softly. "That didn't tell you something?"

"But it wasn't *me* you were making love to! You were thinking of Lily—"

"*Lily?*" He shook his head in bewilderment. "Where does she come in?"

"You loved her so much—"

"And you loved Jack once. Remember?"

"I fell out of love. You never did. No matter how much I try, I'll never measure up to her. I won't be smart enough or kind enough—"

"Cathy, stop."

"I won't be *her.*"

"I don't want you to be her! I want the woman who'll hang off fire escapes with me and—and drag me off the side of the road. I want the woman who saved my life. The woman who calls herself average. The woman who doesn't know just how extraordinary she really is.'' He took her face in his hands and tilted it up to his. ''Yes, Lily was a wonderful woman. She was wise and kind and caring. But she wasn't you. And she and I—we weren't the perfect couple. I used to think it was my fault, that if I were just a better lover—''

''You're a wonderful lover, Victor.''

''No. Don't you see, it's *you*. You bring it out in me. All the want and need.'' He pulled her face close to his and his voice dropped to a whisper. ''When you and I made love that night, it was like the very first time for me. No, it was even better. Because I loved you.''

''And I loved you,'' she whispered.

He pulled her into his arms and kissed her, his fingers burrowing deep into her hair. ''Cathy, Cathy,'' he murmured. ''We've been so busy trying to stay alive we haven't had time to say all the things we should have....''

His arms suddenly stiffened as a startling round of applause erupted above them. They looked up. Three grinning faces peered down at them from a hospital balcony.

''Hit it, boys!'' yelled Ollie.

A clarinet, piccolo and kazoo screeched into concert. The melody was doubtful. Still, Cathy thought she recognized the familiar strains of George Gershwin. ''Someone to Watch Over Me.''

Victor groaned. ''I say we try this again, but with a different band. And no audience.''

She laughed. ''Mexico?''

''Definitely.'' He grabbed her hand and pulled her toward a taxi idling at the curb.

''But, Victor!'' she protested. ''What about our luggage? All my clothes—''

He cut her off with another kiss, one that left her dizzy and breathless and starved for more.

''Forget the luggage,'' she whispered. ''Forget everything. ''Let's just go....''

They climbed into the taxi. That's when the band on the hospital balcony abruptly switched to a new melody, one Cathy didn't at first recognize. Then, out of the muddy strains, the kazoo screeched out a solo that, for a few notes, was perfectly in tune. They were playing *Tannhäuser*. Wedding music!

"What the hell's that terrible noise?" asked the taxi driver.

"Music," said Victor, grinning down at Cathy. "The most beautiful music in the world."

She fell into his arms, and he held her there.

The taxi pulled away from the curb. But even as they drove away, even as they left the hospital far behind them, they thought they could hear it in the distance: the sound of Sam Polowski's kazoo, playing one last fading note of farewell.

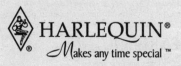